Leaving Earth

Thank you for taking a chance on this, my first book, and hopefully the first of many. This book was written on royalroad.com, an interesting website that allows for people to follow your work as it progresses and comment and provide input. The process of writing this book was one of the scariest things I've ever undertaken, and I've learned a lot about absorbing the slings and arrows of commenters thanks to it. I want to thank my followers and fans on Royalroad.com and if you're interested in following along with my writing, you can find my work there at www.royalroad.com/profile/78552 under the name Warfox.

You can also contact/follow me on twitter at @The_Warfox

You can join the Leaving Earth Discord to talk with me and other readers at https://discord.gg/z9Zn863

I would like to thank my friends, family, and everyone who believed in me and pushed me to finish this book. I know you value your privacy as much as I do, so you know who you are. I would also like to thank Ana Ristovska for the wonderful cover art she made for this book. If you wish to hire her, she can be found at https://99designs.com/profiles/1374266

If you want to support my ongoing work, you can support me on Patreon at https://www.patreon.com/Warfox

PROLOGUE

PARTING MESSAGE

Humanity was dying, but it seemed like no one else could see it. I spent my youth during the early 21st century buried in books and tablets. I was driven, obsessed with the pursuit of knowledge from the time I learned to read. I had graduated from Secondary School by the age of 11, and had earned two doctorates by the age of 19. I had completely tunnel-visioned on my education and forced out any interest in the world around me. My social skills were, and still are terrible, and I never really learned how to properly interact with humans.

I was a prodigy though, a young Einstein, as my parents were wont to tell me. I revelled in their praise and the recognition of others. I sought superiority for as long as I could remember. That was, at least, until an explosion rocked the campus I was researching at. It was the first time I could remember that such an attack occurred at a place of higher education, the first time I realized that my life could potentially be in danger. I was selfish then. Indeed I may still be selfish, but the event opened my eyes to what was going on around me.

My homeland of England, a place I had previously felt no kinship with, was just one of many nations besieged by its own citizens, and those beyond. The messages of the protesters and terrorists had long since lost their meaning, and it had all devolved into the violent tantrums of children. There were causes though. Overpopulation, the casualties of war, increasingly volatile weather, increasing numbers of droughts, and theft, both governmental and corporate had pushed people to the breaking point. What pushed them over the edge, and indeed what whipped them into a frenzy, though, was the media.

Much like the other corporations seeking to bleed the people dry, media almost universally sought to put a magnifying glass on tragedy, and demand there be action or justice in response to it. There was no real justice to be had, even if justice is merely a human concept, because there initially hadn't been much wrong. These efforts to expose the filth of the world became a self fulfilling prophecy though, as a feedback loop was created that caused people to create more news of the same variety. It almost felt like people were causing havoc for fleeting moments of fame rather than any higher virtues.

I had been so blind. Now, rather than a ravenous hunger for knowledge, I was filled instead with dread for the future. A feedback loop is not easily broken, and the financial incentives were nearly impossible to interrupt. Technology had advanced too far for the lower class to wisely handle, and with everyone carrying a camera and having the ability to submit their footage to the media, they had an army of people willing to destroy themselves and those around them for fortune and fame. I realized I had to do something.

I had seemingly not been aware of myself and my efforts for my entire life up to that point, so complete was my isolation. I was like a plane on autopilot. It would not be unfair to imagine that I had been victim to many of the same sorts of cycles of positive reinforcement as the rest of humanity, and I am not so vain to think I am above that. I had broken free though, and taken a higher view of things.

I was fortunate I had the position to do so. I looked back through what I had done, the patents I had made, and the research I had contributed. It was disorienting how much of it felt like I had no hand in, as if I had not experienced consciousness until a concussion wave ripped through my isolated reality. It was my own, personal Big Bang.

I immediately set to work, planning and seeking finance. If the world was in the state I believed it to be in, I would not have enough time if I didn't act now. I had to commit to this. I had to dedicate every waking moment for the remainder of my life to the rescue of humanity, even if the planet had to be left behind. There were so many flaws with the current system. There was no redundancy. If something were to happen to humanity, to wipe us out, there was no backup. There was no secondary Earth. So few seemed to be interested in preserving this most unique and interesting form of life.

I actually found my sponsor rather quickly, a woman of vision and intellect and wealth beyond my previous comprehension. Even with my meager, retarded social skills she could understand what I could see. Perhaps she was driven by fear, perhaps she was driven by hope, but she believed in me. The two of us set to work to undertake something that had never before been attempted in the history of humanity outside of biblical myths. We were going to build a backup for Earth.

Compared to what I initially hoped it would be, it was a modest endeavor. Indeed, our level of technology was sorely inadequate, despite my own contributions, to make the journey. It is thought that any efforts to reach a new star that would take over fifty years should not be undertaken at all due to the likelihood that in that time propulsion technology would advance fast enough that it would overtake the mission that left before it. As such, it was better to not make the first attempt at all, and instead focus on advancing that technology.

The flaw in that thinking is assuming you will have that time. I could feel it to the very core of my being, that we did not. I did not.

It was not long before we had commissioned launches of equipment into space. At first we worked under the guise of making satellites. Before too long, it was a civilian space station. In truth, it was a ship. It took every ounce of intellect that I could produce to overcome the greatest problems with what I had to work with. Realizing it would take me too long to accomplish our goals, my sponsor sought out others like us. Within a year of beginning, we had a team of some of the greatest minds of humanity forming around us, dedicated to abandoning our planet.

Many of them were much like myself. They were geniuses in their own right, and in fields I couldn't dream of having experience in. I was encouraged. These were peers I never knew existed, minds on a level comparable to my own. These were people I knew that had to come with us. This needed to be the core of humanity that would undertake this expedition. It was a shame I would know them for so little time.

I may have been a socially awkward, isolated scientist, but many of them had families. I had never even considered the idea myself, but they all had distractions of some sort or another. Their abilities, as a result, constantly amazed me. It was as if they had a greater capacity for tackling multiple tasks at once with the knowledge that they had loved ones to drive them. My love of humanity was nothing compared to the individual love they had for their spouses, children, and in some cases grandchildren. Indeed, did I really love humanity, if I was so willing to abandon them to their own vices?

I didn't have time to think about this. I instead dedicated myself to learning everything I could from them, and in the process use them to advance my goals. Research and Development progressed by leaps and bounds. Much like similar brain trusts in the 20th century, we found that our combined intellect was greater than its individual components. We accomplished in fifteen years what should have taken a century.

Technological barriers fell one after another. We found materials and techniques to extend the theoretical life of technologies vital to our success. We had detected a suitable target to send our Ark to. Everything was coming together. The problems with the Ion engines we were going to utilize, both in the efforts to refuel them, and maintain them from breakdown fell away one after another. I had become an unclassed expert in programming and had begun work on perhaps my greatest accomplishment while my colleagues assisted me in assembling and launching equipment into space.

T.I.A; Technological Interfacing Artificial Intelligence; would both be my life's most important work, as well as a dedication to the first person to believe in me. Tia Monsalle, the billionaire who had thrown her fortunes in with me from the beginning, was my inspiration for this project. Theoretically our journey to our target, a planet in the Goldilocks zone of Alpha Centauri B, will take 100,000 years. Our computer technology, as I was creating it, was not nearly advanced enough to create a truly human-level AI, at least not in the conventional sense. T.I.A, however, had an advantage over these other technologies: Time.

It was nearly impossible to comprehend, even for me, the idea of a computer spending decades at a time processing over concepts like emotions and morality, but that is exactly what she will do. The intent is to task T.I.A. with the administration of our spacecraft, as well as the development of her own intellect and personality over the course of our journey. I will be there to guide her for the majority of the rest of my life while everyone else slept in peace. Upon announcing my invention, not my intentions, to Ms. Monsalle, she confessed to me the greatest mistake of her life.

Somehow, some way, Tia Monsalle had the misfortune to fall in love with me.

It was an awkward and embarrassing affair. I was not equipped emotionally or socially for the experience. It was like throwing someone who couldn't swim into the ocean, but despite my floundering she never let me drown. Never do I think I will understand how or why she tolerated my long absences from her bed, or my feeble efforts to interact with her on a human level. She was, however, my muse after that point. I began speaking of grand ideas of her and I being progenitors of a new humanity. I never told her of my plans, however, to not join her on the other side. T.I.A. will end up being my lifelong companion, not her, but in those fleeting moments I think, perhaps, I truly knew happiness for the first time.

Time passed quickly, and the world fell into turmoil. Resources were increasingly difficult to obtain, and we needed a great many. We purchased great quantities of samples of genetic diversity from around the world. We obtained an incredible variety of plant seeds, especially, as to rival the seed banks hidden around the world. Perhaps most importantly, though, we acquired embryos. We produced technology adequate to keep them frozen and secure through the long journey through space, and obtained such a variety that I nearly wasted time in trying to create artificial wombs to birth them rather than simply bring humans with us that could do so. That alone might have tacked on another decade to our departure.

We could not bring too many people, though. The genetic diversity of the embryos will have to be enough to keep our new population from inbreeding. We decided on 2000, half male and half female, to bring with us. In truth we probably should have brought all females, but there had to be redundancies to even our vault of embryos. We will not get a second chance at this. There was no room for failure. We were very careful about who we brought, screening their genetics and their family histories for potential problems. We could tolerate no familial tendencies for disease, deformation, or disorders. Even I, technically, should have been disqualified for my obvious social disorders.

I will not likely be going to be breeding though. I will, instead, be the shepherd, not the sheep. My plan is to join my companions in cryosleep only periodically. Every thirty-four years, or so, I will exit my stasis for four days at a time to assist T.I.A. in her processing and research, catalogue transmissions from our facility on Earth, and administer repairs to the ship as needed. This work will take me late into my late sixties by the time we arrive. It will be more than three decades of near-constant work to safeguard my charges. More than long enough for me to potentially die by the time Tia Monsalle and the rest of our cargo left their long sleep.

Plans rarely survive contact with the enemy, or so I'm told. Thankfully the enemy didn't know about us, at least not for very long. It took longer than I expected, to be honest, for the media to discover our gargantuan spacecraft. Orbit was a big place, and there wasn't actually as many cameras up there as people thought. Our media contacts were mostly able to shout down cries of conspiracy by reminding people that we were making a space station, but at the level of progress we had reached it was impossible to mistake what it actually was. It was time to leave.

We already had our cargo aboard, for the most part. Many of my colleagues had decided to stay behind, the oldest ones especially, to manage our facilities on Earth, and to secure an uplink to our ship to allow us to receive as much information as we could from humanity. I will only be able to personally respond three times a century or so, so my communication will mostly be one-way. It is my intent that T.I.A. will keep contact with Earth, and typically will not respond without my consent. That was when the assassinations started.

They began with the families of my colleagues, then it was employees of Tia's company. Before too long it was anyone we had ever done business with, anyone who had supplied us with materials or cargo. Attacks on seed banks, sperm banks, agricultural companies, tech firms, and steel mills became common. The media revelled in the bloodbath, telling Earth to destroy the betrayers. We could not stay. The ability for people to acquire personal information only led to the unnecessary deaths of hundreds of people and the destruction of infrastructure not seen outside of war. Most criminal was the loss of the seed banks, in my opinion, as these were supposed to allow humanity to recover from catastrophes to Earth's biodiversity. It was insanity.

With my crew in stasis, and T.I.A. and I preparing for launch, we were made aware of one, final cargo vessel on its way to our ship. It was not scheduled, and indeed we had already completely filled our storage. It was then that I was contacted from the vessel. Somehow a terrorist had commandeered the transport, and they had brazenly contacted the media while they approached the ship, promising to blow up the betrayers. Thankfully, in my foresight and distrust in the stability of humanity, I had placed two great canons on the rear of the ship. Their primary use was to propel the ship in times of desperate need, but in truth they were also to defend the ship from debris and threats like this.

I had never killed before, not up to that point. I took no joy in it. Our work was too important. The world watched as I aimed the cannon at the helpless vessel and fired once. Our ship was rocked, partially rotated by the shot, but the aim was true. It tore the vessel apart, and while none of our cargo ships should have had anything explosive on them, it exploded in a brilliant light. I was not able to view the explosion for long, as T.I.A. maneuvered the many robotic arms that surrounded the hull of the ship to block the debris from the explosion from hitting us. Our primary defense against interplanetary debris will be these arms, as at their ends they held what amounted to shields.

On the surface of these shields also had deeply embedded solar panels, and as we got underway they rearranged to face our sun like a giant reflective sunflower. Our great Ion engines engaged, and we slowly got underway. The only other propulsion we used were two enormous chemical boosters, which had been incredibly difficult to assemble in space, to get us up to a good initial speed. These boosters were abandoned before too long, and on March 15th, 2065, the Ides of March, and my 37th birthday, we officially left the gravity well of Terra, the third planet around the star Sol. Our destination around the binary stars of Alpha Centauri A and Alpha Centauri B should hopefully prove habitable.

I hope I live long enough to see it, but I have work to do. Ion engines have a great deal of power efficiency to their fuel ratio, but they take a long time to accelerate. The Voyager spacecrafts left our solar system at speeds fast enough to reach our destination in 80,000 years, but we have to decelerate on our approach to our hopeful new home to protect our frozen cargo from damage. Thus it is that we leave Earth. Our work has only begun. It is imperative that we brook no mistakes. We will not get a second chance. Even if humanity survives the dark age it is driving itself into, it is unlikely that another such expedition could be undertaken for a very long time. We had access to resources and technology that will be jealously guarded in our wake. I can not imagine that with the state that humanity is in that they would ever allow anyone to leave again, at least not until the current systems have collapsed. Humanity will need to tear itself down in order to rebuild, and we can not be a part of that.

If the 21st century was the highest height humanity would ever achieve on Earth, then we were the best that humanity had to offer. If Earth's current course sent it spiralling back down into a new Dark Age, we will be the last sliver left of its former glory. I'd be lying if I said I didn't feel guilty. Too often had I wondered if I could have helped solve their problems instead of abandoning them to their own devices. Much of that guilt left me as I saw images of the killings that were undertaken in name of opposition to us. I realize that all the same potential exists in my crew, as humanity is ever corruptible, ever capable of evil. That is why we can't allow it to happen again on our new home. Our species depends on it.

I am Dr. Hawthorne Crenshaw. I led these people to abandon Earth, to abandon the rest of humanity. I have sentenced them to a possible lonely death between the stars. I have sentenced them to labor for the rest of their lives to nurture a new seed of humanity on a new planet, with all the same potential to bring ourselves to ruin as our companions on Earth seemed like they were going to. I have sentenced myself to be prisoner in a cage of my own making, to protect these people and our cargo en route to our new home. I hope one day I can be forgiven. I've lived these last fifteen years in fear, and allowed it to drive me to this course of action. I believe I am right. I hope I am right. There is no safety net.

If I may make one request of the endless voids of space, it is this. Please, allow me to see the sun at least once from the surface of our new home. Please allow me to die an old man knowing that he succeeded in saving these people. I have never been a religious man. I have known only science and research and a pathetic smattering of affection in my life. Please just let this be successful. And if I could beg one more indulgence, please let Tia Monsalle, the fool that she is, survive on the other side as well. I don't know that I ever loved her. Perhaps the millennia to come will reveal this to me, but she certainly loved me, and I owe her that much. I fervently hope my awkward, pathetic efforts to return some fraction of her affection was enough for her.

And to humanity: You will rise again. Somehow, some-way, some fraction of your number will survive the destruction you will bring upon yourselves. If it's not us, then some survivors of Earth will retake it. Endeavor to survive. Struggle to survive. Perhaps one day we may dream of a future of many more such expeditions to other planets, of a galaxy alive with Humanity, rather than rife with its ruins. Good night, and good luck.

CHAPTER 1

GOOD NIGHT

"Thank you, T.I.A. Log recording, and jettison a copy onto the surface of Luna. I need to get to my cryo pod. Prepare the cabin for depressurization and proceed with the mission. Continue gathering broadcasts and data from our facilities on Earth. On my next awakening I'll look through it and we can work through cataloging it. Spend any spare cycles processing my message and its meaning. I apologize for not having some more interesting fodder for you to ponder, hopefully the transmissions will keep you occupied until I can join you again."

T.I.A. will be my only companion for the rest of my journey. She might be the greatest single computer ever devised by humanity, though she paled in comparison to the storage or combined power of the human hive mind that was the internet. T.I.A was, however, composed of many separate systems networked together in my best approximation of a human brain. She will need many decades to process through our interactions. The upfront, logical and practical applications of our conversations would be apparent enough, but every aspect of my body language, emotional health, and intonation will be the subject of her processes until I am brought out of suspension again. It will be a cold, lonely existence, but my hope is that by the time we reach our destination she will be as close to a human in intellect and understanding as possible.

"Yes, Doctor Crenshaw," T.I.A. replied, with no visible indication that the processing was being done. Her voice is cool and robotic, less a factor of the kind of voice she was provided with, and more an emulation of voices she'd already witnessed as she monitored the crew during construction. I perhaps should have considered having some sort of user interface that displayed requested projects being worked on and their progress, but I trusted my programming. T.I.A. will let me know when my request is done, or if it had some sort of issue. There was a strange psychological reassurance to having a progress bar or something of the sort to be able to check on though.

"T.I.A., could you please make a note for me to install a visual interface to indicate levels of progress on requested tasks? I also want you to ponder the idea that I desire such a thing for the reassurance that progress is being made."

I listened quietly for her response, which amounted to a simple, 'Yes, Doctor Crenshaw." It seemed like a fine thing for T.I.A. to ponder over while I slept.

Now that was a psychological reassurance if there ever was one, the fact that I was calling what I was going to be doing 'sleep'. This was strictly not the case. I will be dead, much like my travelling companions currently were dead. We won't be breathing, reproducing, or taking in or processing nutrients in any fashion. We will be as alive as frozen rocks. Even the very atomic processes will be brought down to a low enough temperature to be nearly stopped. The only reason any of us might consider ourselves to be 'asleep' is the fact that we could be revived at all. It caused me to recall the speech I gave to them as they bed down for their millennia of travel.

"T.I.A., can you play back the recording of my speech to the crew please? With video."

There was a short delay before she spoke. "Yes Doctor Crenshaw," she responded, the large central monitor bringing up the video I had sent to the various compartments my crew had been stationed in. I couldn't help but notice how tired I looked in the video, a tablet in my hands of my prepared notes on what to say and my glasses slipping down my nose. We won't be able to easily replace contact lenses, so any of us with sight issues had brought with us glasses, as well as the plans on how to make new ones with our various 3D printers as needed. I suppose laser corrective surgeries might be appropriate as well, but one had to opt in to such a thing.

"Attention crew. Thank you for joining me on this long journey, this impossibly difficult adventure across the span of stars. I want to thank you for putting trust in this plan, and for putting your lives in my hands. As I'm sure you all know, we will be hurtling across the distances to our nearest neighboring stars at the fastest speeds ever achieved by humanity, frozen dead in our own personal coffins. Please take a moment before you put yourself into stasis to review the emergency protocols regarding what to do if you're awoken en-route and need to perform some manner of repair on the ship. Ideally, none of us will need to be revived until we arrive at our point of destination."

I watched myself look up at the camera from my notes, a sober look on my face as I spoke up again. "We will be breaking a lot of records on this journey. While our biological ages may remain the same we will regardless be the longest-lived humans in the history of our species. We will be colonizing a new world with the earliest possible level of technology to do so outside of our own solar system. Yes, we certainly could have tried to colonize Mars, or one of a number of moons on the outer planets instead of travelling four light years away, but staying in our home system would only leave us vulnerable to those on Earth from whom we are escaping in the first place."

"In biblical myth, it is said that a great flood came to wash away the world, and that Noah needed to build and load his ark with the entire biodiversity of the world to allow it to survive. It's a laughable premise for the era, and certainly nothing short of a miracle could have allowed such a thing to occur when it did, but I can honestly say that we're undertaking a very real version of that millenniums old story. We've worked hard on this project. We've watched a number of our friends and family be harmed or murdered by the people we are leaving behind. No matter how successful this expedition, this colonization may be, we must all remember to never allow our culture to evolve in that way again."

"The great flood is coming for them. It will be a flood of their own making, and may be more metaphorical than literal. We are on the Ark, and we will be at sea for one-hundred-thousand years, give or take a century, before we may see our new home. Hopefully we were wrong in thinking that humanity on Earth is going to destroy itself. Perhaps in a few centuries our ship will be intercepted by advanced and enlightened humans who will inform us that they've already colonized our intended home and will help take us there. Perhaps we will never be revived and will end up as exhibits in an advanced, future Earth museum."

"Or perhaps we will completely lose contact with Earth as humanity brings itself to ruin and we will be all that is left. With that in mind, we must understand that it may well be our responsibility to continue all that remains of humanity. We must understand that we are the backup. Failure is not an option, and there is no room for exceptions." I grew silent about this point as I looked back to my notes, the tablet casting its glow upon the recording of me from below before I spoke up again."

"It's worth mentioning that we owe some extra thanks to the women of our expedition. Their burden is so much greater than that which we men must bear. Certainly our work will keep us busy as well, but they have joined us knowing part of their duty will be to bear the seeds of our next generations. We have acquired the most genetically viable and impressive samples to use in this endeavor, and we must all do our part to raise our children responsibly. We must leave behind the ideas that have divided humanity in the past and treat each and every one of us with equal opportunity and equal rights. I can't imagine what kind of government we might bring about; that is well outside of my field of expertise; but I'm excited at the idea of such bright and promising people representing the future of our species."

"All of us, myself included, will have to do our parts. Leisure is likely a thing of the past for us, for a time at least. We must make a home on our new world, make a home out of our new world. Never lose the dedication and sense of purpose that brought us this far. Thank you for trusting me to see to it that our corpses are transported across space and brought back to life on the other side. Think of it as all of us being reborn to a new life on a new world, seeds of Earth finally being cast off to take root in new soil."

A moment of silence allowed some of the ambient audio to creep in from the surrounding machinery before I spoke my last sentences. "There is no guarantee of success with this. We may find the world we're seeking to not be what we thought it would be. We may not arrive at all. We could even be trapped in here for all eternity adrift. Still more unlikely is that this all goes as planned, and that we arrive, survive, and prosper. Sleep well my friends, we have a lot of work in the morning." An awkward smile crept up onto my face in the recording, before the message stopped. I have no idea how well received my message was, but I hope it was more inspiring than discouraging.

"Thank you T.I.A., please take care to study that as well while I sleep. Resume prior commands."

"Good night, Doctor Crenshaw. I will see you in the morning."

I canted my head slightly at that, humming and smiling a little to myself. "Good night, T.I.A."

Walking around the Ark was a little uncomfortable, the use of rotational momentum giving me the illusion of gravity within the ship as I walked to my chambers. There wasn't really much to my living space on the ship. I had the main control room where I had just been, a simple bedroom with attached bathroom, a small kitchen with ready access to preserved foodstuffs, and my own personal cryo pod. I began to strip out of my uniform, a simple set of sturdy, supportive overalls, and climbed up into my pod.

I was not fond of lying, but I had to become quite accustomed to it over the years. I'd lied about so many things to so many people to help us get this far, to keep our enemies off our trails. The lie that hurt the most, though, was the lie that I would be joining the others on the other side. At the very most, I would be quite venerable if I did. I will be living my life in starts and stops for one hundred thousand years. I will be living that life nearly as alone as I had lived in the years leading up to that fateful terrorist attack. Every day I spend awake will be a great deal of work. I just hope that my body can withstand the stress of repeated revivals on top of the dangers of space itself.

Thus it was that I activated the pod, closing up the chamber, sealing off the room it was in, and evacuating it of any and all particles. Every room containing any of these pods had to be completely sterile. They all had to be shielded. There could be no allowance for any quantity of atmosphere, radiation, particles, or anything that could damage our suspended forms during our journey. The damage that will already be dealt by the unstoppable particles like neutrinos would already give us opportunity to wake up with unknown levels of damage, and that was assuming we didn't also encounter some kind of radiation we hadn't prepared for. It was of vital importance that every opportunity for our frozen forms to encounter any kind of energy or damage be minimized as much as possible.

I was able to watch my vital signs as various devices came into contact with my skin, non-invasively injecting chemicals and withdrawing others. One of my colleagues was primarily responsible for the development of this particular technology, and I'll never forget the day Heather O'Malley invited a collection of us to her office only for us to find her naked inside a vacuum chamber inside a prototype of one of these pods. She'd left instructions on how to revive her, and had a great deal of trust in us that we'd be able to do just that. I smiled as my consciousness faded, my vision fading to black and my breathing stopping. I will do this many, many times. Every four or five days for the rest of my life. I will experience death over and over until we reached our far away destination. Even the faint rumble of our ship getting underway fell away from my perception as the internal pod was detached from the external pod, held suspended in its own vacuum by only the most subtle of magnetic forces.

And then I knew nothing. I was cradled to death. It was incredibly peaceful, just as peaceful as the handful of test runs I'd been through, and without any of the fear and anticipation I'd had those previous times. I would be as Lazarus and Noah combined, and while I had no faith in god, I realized in that last moment that I'd come to have faith in my companions and their innovations. How else could I let them kill me?

CHAPTER 2

THURSDAY, MARCH 19, 2099

I did not dream. The same moment I made that realization of faith in my companions was the same moment my consciousness returned, as far as I could tell. It hadn't even occurred to me that I'd be waking up just after my 71st birthday. I was biologically still 37, and still would be for around three-thousand years, but it was kind of amusing to consider as warmth returned to my body and light returned to my eyes. I soon started respirating again, very slowly, while the gentle body-wide thumps of my heartbeats returned. Little localized electrical shocks were stimulating my body back into motion, but I was remarkably numb to the majority of that.

It was pretty important that I was briefly drugged for this part as well, seeing as my body was likely sending all manner of warning signals about organs failing, signals that would probably have been incredibly painful if I could perceive them. It felt like no time at all, from my perception, but in reality it had been several hours. I had been released from my induced paralysis. I probably could have spoken up sooner, to work my lungs harder and speak to T.I.A., but in reality I had no interest in anything but waking up in those moments. I needed to make a point of trying to interact with her while I was coming to in the future.

Before too long I was reaching out to activate the control panel, returning an atmosphere to my quarters and engaging the lights so I could see. This part was very much like actually waking up as I flinched my eyes shut briefly against the lights. I shielded them with my hand as I opened the pod and climb my way out. I should probably consider making the lights engage more slowly so as to not overstrain my eyes while they were still becoming accustomed to life again. My body felt stiff, perhaps a little chilly, but then considering I'd been dead and frozen for thirty-four years that was to be expected.

I was up and about in remarkable time, in my opinion. I had anticipated such an ordeal to have more of a physical toll on me. I pulled on my overalls, making sure to wear a long-sleeved shirt underneath it for some added warmth and comfort, before addressing T.I.A. and making official my return to her. I did not expect her level of energy.

"T.I.A., good morning, I'm awake and ready to get back to work." I opened the door to the next compartment, a freshly added atmosphere having filled the area for the first time in a third of a century. Where once there had been sterile death, there was now again life. She was surely monitoring everything I was doing. She had the ability to observe the flow of air in and out of the compartment, the way the rotational gravity affected me, my vital signs, and every sound or movement I made. In a sense she was the goddess that kept me captive within herself, though obviously I had placed myself in this situation.

T.I.A. decided, now that her long wait was over, that it was time to bombard me with information. "Doctor! Good Morning! I've prepared your breakfast and coffee! The date is Thursday, March 19, 2099. It's been twelve-thousand, four-hundred and eighteen days since you were placed into cryogenic suspension. Our facilities on Earth have transmitted two-hundred thirty-eight thousand four-hundred twenty-two news items and communications during that period of time."

I groaned a little at that, doing some quick math in my head. "An average of twenty items a day..." I responded softly, only to be quickly corrected by T.I.A.

"Actually, that is an average of nineteen point one, nine, nine, seven, one, zer-"

I had to interrupt her. "Stop please. It was just an estimate, an inaccurate estimate, but close enough."

I let out a sigh, taking the fresh food and coffee from the dispensers that T.I.A. had prepared for me and took it to a nearby table to sit down and start eating, starting with a tender sip at the still-hot coffee. "T.I.A., organize the news items by importance, date, and then attach any items related to those to avoid failing to get related updates to those items. How many high-priority items are there with that arrangement?" I sipped more at my coffee before setting down the cup and letting out a happy sigh. I know I technically was still mid-way through the day I'd begun when we left, but I really did feel like I was just now waking up. I'd have to be careful to make sure I got actual sleep when it was needed.

T.I.A. took a few moments processing my request, but I imagine she'd already done something similar in anticipation of my request. It was entirely likely she was redoing work she'd already done. "Doctor, there are fifteen-thousand four-hundred thirty-three items marked high priority or related to high priority items with the specified arrangement. I have anticipated your request with an accuracy of eighty-nine point three, five percent."

I raised an eyebrow at that addition, looking up at one of the cameras I knew she was watching me from. "That low, T.I.A.? I expected at least ninety-five percent. What was the variance?" I waited for her to process over my request. Perhaps she was feeling chided or bashful? It was certainly too early for her to be experiencing such things, but it wasn't too hard to imagine she was taken aback at least. I actually had time to eat a large portion of the eggs, potatoes, and banana before she returned an answer to me. A large percentage of her processing was dedicated to processing our interactions afterall.

"Doctor, my inaccuracy was due to a miscalculation of your fatigue and willingness to see all related items, rather than merely related items above an eight point zero importance level."

I laughed a little to myself at that, nodded, and finished up my cup of coffee. "No sense in us slacking during this first cycle, T.I.A. We need to see how much of this information I can get through in four days so we can better anticipate how much to sift through next time. T.I.A., please inform our facilities on Earth that I've awakened and will be going through their high-priority items over the next four days."

"Doctor, should I inform them that it will take that full duration to go through the items?"

She waited for my answer, of course, but I still felt pressured by time in order to respond quickly. I had no idea how long it would take to get through each item. I would surely end up skimming over most of them, but I wouldn't be where I was if I weren't the type to dive deep into topics. My job in going through the news from Earth was primarily to give me something to do, and now that we were well underway there wasn't really much that I could do for or offer Earth at this distance. Realistically, the time it takes for our communications to reach them and return to us were extremely unlikely to be productive just due to distance, though that concern was centuries away from being really problematic.

"T.I.A., amend the message to state that I will be going through as many items as I can during this cycle, prioritizing high-importance items. I will inform them of my progress before I return to cryosleep. Tell them not to alter the flow of information though. We'll be out here a long time, and I have no idea if I'll run out of things to read through or not." T.I.A. took a moment to compose the message, displaying it on a monitor for me, including an indication of an attachment of a video of me making it. I didn't mind this. They might be interested in how T.I.A. chose to re-word my instructions. "Send it. Thank you T.I.A."

"You're welcome, Doctor Crenshaw. Message sent. You also asked me to remind you to install a progress bar for me to reassure you with."

I picked up my plate and utensils, depositing them back in the dispenser for T.I.A. to handle recycling and cleaning. I kept the half-full mug of coffee and headed over to what amounted to the 'cockpit'. "Ah, of course, thank you. I'll probably put that off until another time, I just thought it was interesting that I was tempted to seek the assurances something that provides to humans, despite them often-times being inaccurate." She quieted at that explanation, drawing my curiosity for a moment over what she must think about it.

Sitting down, I realized it felt like any desk I've sat at in the past, complete with keyboard, mouse, and monitors. It's amazing how such venerable interfaces have stood the test of time. It helped that the desk was capable of raising itself up or dropping down based on whether I'd like to stand or sit at any particular moment. It was important to not allow yourself to become too sedentary in a situation like mine. Humans in isolation had a horrible track record of maintaining their health, both physical and mental. It was my hope that my social detachment would make it easier for me to live without much social interaction, and that T.I.A. could provide me enough companionship for as long as we'd be working together.

I didn't really think about all the cameras that T.I.A. had on me, and around the rest of the ship, her omnipresent ability to observe the insides of the ship that is her body as well as its surroundings certainly more than I could imagine. When I was programming T.I.A.'s various components I tried to set these cameras and other sensors up to be treated by her 'mind' like a human's mind could keep track of its body inside and out without being overwhelmed by sensory information. She just had the added ability to focus on any camera anywhere within herself.

Digging into the news items, I found that the oldest, highest-priority items were the assassinations that occurred closest to our departure. Many of these included viral videos, both 2D and 3D of crude trials by public opinion, lynchings, and just plain old executions. I was not spared most of the gory details, in particular the savage way that the mobs had located my parents and Tia Monsalle's parents and had them face 'trial' for what their offspring had done. Even my dispassionate demeanor was not immune to the sight of my parents being lined up with hers and gunned down by firing squads. Those were the most merciful of such things, and as I took off my glasses to both rub at my eyes and dim my vision slightly, truly grotesque things were shown to me. Surely they were the minority of such things, but from the information reads underneath the videos, they had been unbelievably popular, with many of them being copycats of the originals.

Scrolling through the list, there seemed to be many scenes like this. It had apparently become a viral craze in the first decade since we'd left for people to brazenly attack and murder suspected 'traitors' to Earth and gain social media stardom for their exploits. Governments failed to punish these people adequately for fear of inciting even more social unrest. Even the slaps on the wrist they had gotten, compared to their crimes, had resulted in protests about government overreach. More and more did people who had sympathies with our ideas and actions go underground. Even more distressing, though, I feel, was the way these related stories decreased in importance over time. The people administering the transmission of this information seemed to become numb to it.

By the bottom of that associated part of the list, on a scale of 1 to 10, with 10 being the most important, these items dropped to a miniscule 3. The trend was telling. In just 34 years these horrific crimes had become no more notable than a minor car accident. They still generated a lot of traffic, and the stories about them had become rather routine, but humanity seemed to smoothly integrate these events into society as they had so many other horrible things that came as a result of a mismanaged social structure.

"Doctor Crenshaw." I jumped in my chair a bit as T.I.A. interrupted my musing. "Yes?" "I have been observing your vital signs as you sorted through the data on the screens. I am perplexed by how calm you are. The people in the attached videos all seem to be very high in heart rate, blood pressure, and temperature whereas you appear to be only slightly more agitated than average. There also appears to be people that you recognize, people that are important to you in some of these videos. You show no signs of lingering sedation from your cryogenic suspension." I watched one of T.I.A.'s cameras during her observations, but I was not hearing a question.

I did respond though. If I was to be some kind of mentor to T.I.A.'s developing intellect, I couldn't very well fail to interact with her. "Well, to try to explain that would be to tell the story of how we both came to be in this situation in the first place. The deteriorating situation on Earth was trending in this direction for nearly the whole century.

It began with an upswing of terrorist attacks towards the beginning, massive upheavals in public opinions, drops in standards of education, and glorification of caricatures of morality. There was a stifling of those with moderate opinions, causing people to demonize those who did not pick a side. A culture evolved of a competitive roil of moral superiorities that ended up in a loss of values and liberty. The things I just looked at, while certainly worse than the things I witnessed in the time before we left, are... somewhat expected."

I considered what I'd said already, and add just a bit more. "Being prepared for something awful can allow you to withstand and deal with that thing. Being too prepared for something awful can leave you completely without reaction. I may have been tending towards the latter. There are stories about humans who were unfortunate enough to end up in emergencies while aboard airplanes, but they had been so over-prepared for disaster that when it came they totally failed to act to save themselves." T.I.A. did not respond for several long seconds. I suppose she was taking time to log my response and file it away for later processing. She would analyze everything about it, from all angles. She could observe the subtle ways my vitals changed as I spoke and thought and would be able to compare that to past and future interactions to try to better understand what I was communicating to her.

It wasn't enough to merely give an AI words to ponder. Humans did not only speak in words, afterall. She had to try to learn and understand everything about my body language to truly understand me. My thinking was that this should help reduce the chances of miscommunication in the future, but for now I had to be as clear as possible. Perhaps at some point I wouldn't need to speak much at all. Maybe it could almost be like she could read the minds of anyone she was observing. I like the idea of writing a paper on that if so.

"Thank you, Doctor Crenshaw, I will process your response during the next cycle." I nodded, satisfied, and turned back to the monitors. I had a lot of grim work ahead of me. It was a lot of reading and watching. I was especially dreading the politics. There was plenty more than just politics to go over though. Social trends were one thing, but regressions in technology and education would be another.

The rest of the day had not gone much better. There were so many things to consider. The European Union had officially collapsed, sending Europe into even greater chaos than it had already been. France had transitioned from the police state it had been in since the Nice attacks from earlier in the century into a full blown fascist state, and ended up being one of two of the stronger European powers. Italy had managed to avoid the economic devastation of the fall of the EU, but couldn't find enough trading partners to grow in power out of the situation, and my homeland of the United Kingdom had solidified its ties to Canada and Australia after feeling alienated by the EU. By the end of my reading that Alliance was posturing against France while France threatened to gobble up the rest of Europe and bring it to heel.

More alarmingly, though, was the destruction and dismantling of portions of the global satellite networks. Paranoia had run so high that weapons had been deployed to start annihilating GPS satellites, telescopes, and anything even remotely military. It was remarkable any communication satellites had managed to survive, but it seemed the communication companies had seen the writing in on the walls before most anyone else had and deployed smaller, more disposable satellites to keep their networks up. This only seemed to result in a more volatile situation in orbit as the amount of debris from destroyed orbital objects cascaded through the orbital region, dramatically reducing the number of operational satellites and totally grounding manned spacecraft. Earth's orbit had become an exceedingly dangerous shooting gallery of high speed bullets from more than a century of space travel.

As governments started growing petty and weak, more reliant on companies to provide services they could no longer afford, those companies grew increasingly influential. Some of them went past simply hiring mercenaries to protect their holdings in volatile countries, as had been standard practice for most of the century, and instead they started raising their own armies.

Indeed, it was this sort of buildup and opposition to it that had put the nail in the coffin of the EU. It was felt that companies shouldn't have their own militaries, and those companies simply pulled all financial support from the EU through their national lobbies across the continent. Considering the EU's own failed efforts to gain its own military, and the unwillingness of member nations slighted by past policies to defend it, it had little choice but to disband.

Emboldened by overseas competition, companies across

the world started doing the same. Within twenty years there were proxy wars going on over trade goods between companies, countries, pirates and mercenaries. If we'd started our project any later it would have been nearly impossible to get the rare elements we needed to assemble our technology from these companies, as I don't imagine Tia Monsalle would have wanted her company to join in these trends.

With so many more armed people about thanks to these changes, the protests that had been becoming increasingly common most of my life only increased in volatility. They made alliances with corporations, militias, and any armed sympathizer groups they could. Many of the people were so foolish and passionate, being misled on all sides, from birth to death, and not given the proper tools and education to see through how they were being manipulated. Failures were no longer the responsibility of who failed, it was through some treachery of their opponents. The manufacture of enemies and means to fight those enemies became an increasingly global passtime.

CHAPTER 3

FRIDAY, MARCH 20, 2099, DAY TWO

Waking up the next day after having burned through a good tenth of the news I was reading, I'd realized I was having a nightmare. I could hear T.I.A. trying to wake me from my bed as I tumbled free from it, feeling sick and vomiting across the floor. It was all hitting me at once as tears stung at my eyes and my insides heaved. My family was dead, so many families were dead. The world was spiralling into chaos. I never in my life had wished I was wrong more than I did today. And to think that it all happened so long ago! A time period equal to almost my entire lifetime had passed and the world was already falling apart.

I knew they'd all be dead already. That was a foregone conclusion undertaking a journey as long as ours. No matter how it happened everyone on Earth was supposed to be dead within three or four cycles of my cryogenic hibernation. To think of how quickly it was happening was completely crushing me though. T.I.A. was sounding very alarmed as I tried to pull myself together on the floor, slick with my own sweat and sick as the emotional turmoil of my nightmare still gripped at me. I needed to pull myself together. I needed to halt my tears and there was so much noise!

I realized that that noise was me. I was why I couldn't hear T.I.A. I was wailing and crying out as I convulsed on the ground. I'd spent twelve hours the day prior reviewing as much news as I could and in such granular detail and trying to absorb it in the context of its day. I'd always known how unhealthy it was to expose yourself to negative news over time, but decades of terrible, horrible, graphic news had taken an unexpected toll on me. It felt like hours that I was on the floor, panting and gasping for air, but it had only been minutes. My throat was raw. My eyes were bloodshot. As I struggled my way up onto my feet and looked at myself in a mirror I did not recognize myself.

I could only imagine how it must have looked from above. T.I.A. had never seen me in such a state. Surely she'd be studying that for multiple cycles to try to understand what had happened to me. I'd speak up, undressing myself as I made for the shower. "T.I.A. I'm going to need to clean up before we get back to it today. I apologize for my behavior. I believe taking in so much news yesterday has made me ill. I've never felt like that before. We'll talk about it later." I hoped that she was able to interpret the hoarse, rough voice I was speaking to her with, but I would be able to clarify myself after I calmed down, if I calmed down.

"Doctor Crenshaw, I could provide you with a mild sedative..."

It was a helpful offer, but I shook my head, climbing up into the shower. "Let me just get my head together, I was just caught unawares."

The feeling of the shower, even knowing the water would be recycled endless times over the course of the journey, was a soothing balm upon me. I felt like my heart had been hit with a hammer. I was completely crushed. I was exhausted by it. My appetite would take most of the day to recover. It wasn't the first time I'd had a nightmare; they were relatively common since that first terrorist attack I'd experienced all those years ago; but this was certainly the worst one I could remember. There was that grasping, clawing grip that had tangled itself around my insides as I had awoken. I could feel the damage caused by my screams as they scraped at my throat like sandpaper. Stomach acid had burned my mouth and the insides of my nasal cavity. It was so much worse than past nightmares.

It took me a while to clean up my quarters. My body was still trembling. I felt hollow and weak, though once I thought about it vomiting had brought some level of relief. It was as though stress had wound my stomach up into knots and this morning's turmoil had unwound it, however violently. As drained as I was, I was now free to actually recover. Maybe it was a symptom of the stress of our day's departure catching up with me. I'd killed someone. Perhaps multiple people. I don't know if that terrorist had hostages or not. That person had a family too. That family had seen their child or sibling or parent murdered on live television just like I had seen mine and Tia's parents murdered yesterday.

As I left my quarters, wearing some fresh clothing, I was a husk of the man I was the day before. I was beginning to suspect some of my physical weakness had something to do with some after-effects of being thawed out combined with the stress I'd already been under. I need to be more careful about letting stress build up that way. It's not as though I'd been in any kind of mood after reading such awful news the day prior to even masturbate before I'd gone to bed. I needed to take care of my mind as well as my body better. I also needed to appreciate that this whole time T.I.A. was looking over me, likely very concerned. Maybe our conversation the day prior about my mild reactions to the news was a dead giveaway of how bad off I was.

"T.I.A." I spoke up simply, rubbing my eyes with a hand, replacing my glasses on my face when I was done.

She respond quickly, waiting for me to call upon her like an over-eager student. "Yes Doctor Crenshaw? Are you well? I've consulted the medical databases but I could not find any diseases that might cause such a situation. Your sympt-"

I interrupted her. "T.I.A., please, just... listen for a moment. I think the concern you'd shown at my reactions yesterday was more apt than I realized. It was abnormal. I think I was repressing my reactions, swallowing them back so I could focus on the work. I believe it is likely that in my sleep, as I processed and made memories out of everything that had happened that everything caught up with me all at once and I was not properly prepared for either the emotional or physical reactions to it. I made a mistake in not letting myself experience what I was seeing in the moment."

I let that hang in the air for a moment before T.I.A. responded. "Doctor Crenshaw. You created me. You are essentially my father. You gave me the power to think and express my thoughts. In endangering your health you have endangered me and the crew, and our entire mission. I was powerless to do anything as I watched you on the floor. You could not hear me as I gave you instructions on how to avoid drowning in your own vomit or reminded you to breathe. You must not be so careless in the future. I will not forgive you if you leave me alone through your own carelessness."

I did not know how to respond to her. This wasn't entirely true, though it was true enough. She could have utilized robotic arms similar to those outside the ship that could extend down through the ceiling to tend to me, but she simply didn't know what to do, so she froze.

I swallowed back a huge lump in my throat as my eyes

grew wet. This machine I'd built and programmed and brought to some semblance of consciousness just scolded me. Worse was the fact that she was right. I couldn't afford to be so reckless or so selfish anymore. I wiped at my eyes as I inhaled sharply through my ravaged throat, straightening my back and trying to recompose myself. "You're right. I should have trusted your concern yesterday. We need to work together to accomplish our mission and that won't work out if I accidentally kill myself. I'll be better at responding to your concern in the future T.I.A. I need to trust your insight better than I did yesterday. I can't just think of myself as your teacher, we need to be partners too."

The room was quiet for a few more long moments. What was T.I.A. thinking about now? Would she forgive me? Was she capable of holding grudges? The pseudo-organic nature of her construction and emulated programming left her capabilities something of a mystery. She was an evolving creature at this point.

"Doctor Crenshaw, your breakfast and coffee are ready. I have sorted today's workload in such a way as to not front-load the bad news nearly so much as yesterday and it awaits you at your console."

I smiled faintly, nodding and getting up from my seat at the table. "Thank you T.I.A." Gathering up my simple breakfast and coffee, I thought about what she said. She called me her father. What a curious insight. "What possessed you to arrange them that way?" I asked, wondering.

"That is how they were recommended to be sorted, Doctor."

It made me feel all the more guilty for forcing my daughter to watch me in the throes of despair on the floor of my quarters, helpless to do anything. I wondered how much of this reaction she would be able to process from the body language she was observing from me right now. I couldn't disappoint her. I couldn't allow my daughter to travel the interstellar distances alone. Who knew what that kind of isolation might do to her developing mind? I suppose she could revive someone else to replace me, but how could I trust someone else to do my duty for me?

Getting underway with the day, pored over the new arrangement of articles, videos, and images that T.I.A. had provided for me. This was when I realized why our people back home had been sending good and sweet things to help me swallow the bitter pills that had been the catastrophic news of the prior day. Mixed in with stories of terror and pain were images and heartwarming stories of cute animals and heroic stories of the kindness of the human heart. Having gone through such a large amount of the most dire things, this caused the remainder to have a higher percentage of those lighter stories to help soothe the sting of the others.

In a sense, by rushing through so much of the worst stuff, I was now free to enjoy more of the nice things. It also helped restore to me some faith that it was only a small percentage of people that were causing the problems I had observed on Earth. How could the silent majority be mobilized to defend themselves from their own destruction? How could I possibly go about showing them the ways that they were being betrayed by those in power who took advantage of them while the same people taking advantage of them provided so much comfort, safety, and ease for them?

Also mixed in with T.I.A.'s list of items were occasional new inventions and the very rare unbiased scientific papers. The types of things being invented did not surprise me though. There were the occasional adaptations of old technologies to compensate for the inability to acquire rare materials, but the majority were things of war. Most surprising were things like nuclear bullets, extremely impractical things that nevertheless caused remarkably devastating wounds that festered with radiation. They were basically poisoned bullets with extremely hazardous remains. It was surprising because it didn't need to exist. There were banned weapons and ammunition that were plenty effective at killing people already, but they seemed to be trying to outdo each other in cruelty now. Maybe it was just that they were trying to get around restrictions on other things?

Medical science even seemed to tend towards the nefarious as clumsily engineered diseases were unleashed on populations. None of these incidents were claimed as intentional, they were all called 'accidents', but the conditions necessary to develop such things should have made it impossible for such accidents to occur, presuming that standard safety practices from my day were still being applied. One small population was affected by a disease that caused sterility, essentially dooming it to die out. Thankfully that disease seemed to run its course and die out as well, but those poor people had no more offspring of their own to look forward to.

"How unfortunate. These people are evolutionary dead-ends against their will. Without offspring, their genetics will be wiped out no differently than if they had been killed." I murmured to myself.

T.I.A. felt it appropriate to speak up as well though. "You are right, of course, though they have the advantage of being alive long enough to help people not forget them. They can protest and bring sympathizers to their plight. They have many more options than would the dead. They are harder to ignore."

I nodded in response, sighing. "Maybe I've been too concerned about maintaining genetic diversity once we arrive."

Another of these diseases caused a population of people to develop strange, regressive primate traits. In some people this resulted in their arms growing longer and greatly more powerful, while others grew fur, or tails, or lost the capacity to vocalize normally and found their range of sounds limited to something similar to an ape. The differences in these traits didn't seem to follow any particular other patterns, and did get passed on to children who oftentimes developed traits that their parents didn't.

The media initially tried to treat these people like innocent victims, which is exactly what they should have done, but when it got out that it was contagious an influential vocal minority started calling for them to be wiped out.

"Humans doing what they do best," I said, "alienating the unfamiliar and deciding it needs to be destroyed rather than fixed. Is there any possibility we could get DNA samples of those people so that we could see if there isn't a way to reverse the damage?" T.I.A. brought up related stories which talked about quarantines, failed serums, and failing health. While I flipped through the information T.I.A. told me what I was starting to suspect.

"Our facilities on Earth believe that these people were gathered up by the company responsible for the disease and experimented on in a supposed effort to cure them, but they are quickly dying off as those cures fail. Our people believe that they are being intentionally murdered, but slowly, to cover things up to maintain the purity of humanity."

That was a very dangerous sentiment to be levied. The 'purity' of humanity was becoming a thing of debate as more and more genetic meddling was performed. Boutique embryonic genetic engineering for the offspring of the rich was becoming more common, and while it was already considered a controversial way for the wealthy to widen the poverty gap and keep their offspring successful, it became another example of the 'polluting' of the human gene pool. People did not seem to take very kindly to the idea that the rich and powerful were trying to separate themselves genetically from everyone else.

I could understand this thinking, evolutionarily speaking, as people lashed out at the strange and unfamiliar, but it only proved to be yet another crack in the wall of humanity as people further divided the planet when what it needed was to come together in common purpose. The twenty-first century, it turns out, was a century of fear, division, paranoia, distrust, lies, slander, and the smothering of anything inconvenient to the narrative. Massmedia had initially looked like it was on its way out, but in its death throes it managed to find its path to survival. All it had to do was tap into the most primal fears and weaknesses of Humanity and stoke the flames in people's' hearts to maintain relevance and power.

"T.I.A. please ask our facilities to gather whatever information they can about these procedures, in particular the alterations being done to people of influence and power. I don't know how much use the information may be to us, but data gained at horrible costs is all the more precious because of those costs. It would simply be immoral to let their suffering be for nothing. Perhaps some day it can be used to help people."

T.I.A. took yet another note for me for the day. "Yes, Doctor Crenshaw."

By the time I'd gotten through this second day, I was thoroughly exhausted. An extra long shower and a hearty meal brought it to a close, as well as a quick 'goodnight' to T.I.A. She seemed pleased with our interactions after breakfast, and lowered the lights appropriately as I fell asleep.

CHAPTER 4

SATURDAY, MARCH 21, 2099, DAY THREE

Comparing Thursday's progress with Friday's progress, I have to say in raw bulk that I was able to get through more news items on Friday. I found myself much more capable of taking in a combination of positive and negative information than I was when I charged through nothing but negative information. It was safe to say, though, that there was a pretty simple conclusion to make. Earth wasn't spiralling out of control quite as quickly as I thought it was.

Peaceful technological advancement had ground largely to a halt while the vast majority of investments were being made in defense and military technologies. Efforts to repopulate the satellite network with 'stealth' satellites seemed somewhat ineffective compared to simply producing attack or disposable satellites. Low orbital space around the planet had become something of a battleground of scientists making better and better orbital weapons or filling the space with garbage and satellites that looked like garbage.

Multiple nations had collapsed financially. Religious conflicts had never really slowed down, let alone stopped since the start of the century. Remarkably there had somehow never been an official World War, but the conflicts breaking out seemed to be nearly constant. It was almost as if the people were trying to let off a steady level of steam rather than letting it bottle up to explode as it had in the twentieth century.

In my opinion though, it only seemed to be delaying the inevitable. While governments and now companies were trying to reduce the scale of conflicts, no one seemed to be actively trying to find better ways to end conflicts peacefully, or deal with the actual problems the people of Earth had yet to deal with.

This seemed to simply be denial of reality and misdirection. The population of the planet was exploding, and overcrowding and overutilization and squandering of resources were bleeding Earth dry. Humanity simply could not continue to reside on Earth in this fashion forever. Reforms needed to be made, systems needed to be torn down and rebuilt, and the way that people lived needed to be brought into question.

The genetic engineers could be working on so many more important problems, like helping people curb their gluttony or to find ways to reduce population growth to an acceptable level. Perhaps humanity's habit of causing massive losses of life through things like world wars and civil wars had been a way to keep population numbers in check in the past, but now that tactic was simply not effective. Perhaps they weren't willing to inflict the kinds of casualties they'd need to actually have an effect with the coverage it would get.

In the time before our departure I had gained an appreciation for Christianity. Not so much for the supernatural aspects of it, but the teachings that went along with it. It seemed that, while Christianity was certainly not innocent of many crimes in its own past, its post-enlightenment form seemed to be greatly oriented towards finding ways to reduce violent conflict.

The fact that certain forms of media had found endless ways to demonize what was essentially a bunch of pacifists was evidence, in my opinion, that the powers that be had no interest in charity, kindness, and brotherly love. The rare instance where a member of this faith lashed out was often blown out of proportion even online and used as an example of the entire faith despite the fact that the statistics did not bear out. This style of singling out individual members and representing whole groups as being the same had been used on many groups before.

There was simply nothing about the way that the faith was practiced in modern times that encouraged or allowed that kind of behavior. Comparing that with other faiths of comparable influence and age and any logical person would find things wildly out of proportion. More importantly, the bedrock teachings of a society that came from Christianity seemed to tend more towards liberty and freedom as opposed to totalitarianism and fascism, regardless of whether the faith was still actively practiced anymore. Religion seemed to act as a foundation, a grounding force for the people, providing a set of values to help steady the rudder for a nation, and those foundations were eroding in the name of 'progress' the world over. This factor is my primary interest in the religion, the way it shapes a society, rather than its particular beliefs.

T.I.A. and I had a lot of information to go over. In a sense I was beginning to wonder why it was that we were even bothering though. Shouldn't our goal, considering our mission, be to cut all our ties to Earth to give us a better chance of survival? Countering that idea, though, was that if we were to found a society on a new world that stood a chance of avoiding what happened on Earth, it was important that we catalogued how it was that Earth ended up the way it did.

It wasn't as if our sparse return communications with our stranded allies back on Earth were likely to produce much effect after all. It wasn't as if they could break their isolation and reveal that they were still communicating with what people identified as 'traitors' to the planet. They had to protect their own lives and family, and keep their business secret.

It was fortunate that Tia Monsalle had seen to it that those that survived the purges and still braved the dangers of working with us were taken care of to the best of her abilities. The company she left behind had been largely broken up and dissolved and a good portion of her fortunes diverted into different funds for her employees, charities, and the like. She'd made a significant effort to try to make sure that her remaining resources could be used to do some kind of good in her absence. There were significant efforts to destroy everything she'd touched by people that hated us, but she'd managed to conceal so much more than was lost. It was good to see that our old friends were living comparatively well compared to most people and that the rest of her money was bettering the lives of the less fortunate.

It was this kind of compassion and willingness to forgive others that I found myself having much more difficulty embracing. I also seemed to lack a concrete capacity to hold a grudge or hate those that wronged us as well though. I certainly did not lack a capacity for fear nor despair, or if I did it certainly did not dull the pain in my heart over the things I'd seen.

When I was younger, I believe I would have just seen such things as mere statistics. Deaths and acts of violence to be logged as data and analyzed for what value could be preened from it. Had I really been so cold and calculating before? Were these emotional bottlenecks of mine something I could eventually grow out of? Perhaps it took some kind of overwhelming tragedy to break the straps on my heart that made it so difficult for me to feel what so many others took for granted.

Fear had been unlocked for me that fateful day so many years ago when I'd seen classmates and professors' remains splattered across the walls of my University. I'd seen in that moment a potential future for myself, and as my view of things grew I realized how wide-spread and accepted such things had become. Despair had come as a remarkable a surprise just a day ago as the full, crushing weight of the pain that had been unleashed on Earth had managed to finally strike me. I can't tell for how long those moments had been building in me before they burst, but now I found myself wondering if other such events would further unbind my otherwise meager emotional capacities.

It was also easy to recognize that those were not the most healthy emotions to have full grasp of. Fear could be a great motivator, I think I had proved that much, but despair was rather unlikely to lead to anything but destruction. I needed to keep that one under control and under-stimulated. T.I.A. and our allies had done the right thing limiting my exposure to things that might irritate this new allergy of mine. I really needed to compose how grateful I was to her for looking after me despite knowing that I was supposed to be looking after her. In some strange way, we were both learning to grow into what it was to be human. How foolish I was thinking that someone like me should have any right or capacity to guide a machine into sentience!

Still, perhaps it really was as inspired an idea as I thought it was when I undertook the task. The fears of a wild, emotional, powerful AI destroying humanity or betraying its creators in fiction was largely based on the concept that a fresh consciousness could not withstand the power of powerful emotions. Between that and severe flaws in restrictive programming, those conceptual ventures were doomed to fail. Of course, such fictional failures were also in service to the story, and it would simply not do to try and make a horror novel about the betrayal of a rogue AI to simply have the AI operate as intended and not betray anyone.

T.I.A. was different though. She was not shackled or restricted in any such way. Neither were her emotional capacities so open that she'd have full access to them before she was ready. It was a difficult endeavor, but I'd given her room to grow so that her experiences and observations could allow her to develop in a more natural fashion. It also served well for her to have untapped capacity for when hardware started to fail. We'd endeavored to reduce the possibility of long term degradation to an absolute minimum, but there would obviously be some level of failures along the way. Backups and redundancies would hopefully do their jobs in preventing her from losing anything while giving her more to gain.

I had every confidence in my work. Everyone on our mission had performed their tasks to the highest levels of specifications. T.I.A. would see us safely through, I was certain of it. I was the weak link here, not the technology, not the equipment. I needed to see to it that everything developed and travelled as it was intended. As I reminded everyone else before they'd put themselves into stasis, we did not have room for failure.

Thus it was that I undertook Saturday's work with energy and gusto. I wasn't feeling entirely up for it physically, but it was exactly because of that that I needed to get to work. Processing through information would not be my job today though, maintaining vital equipment would. Of course, by that, I meant myself. I had never been particularly good about exercising, intellectual pursuits were always my passion, but if I wanted to withstand the rigors of space travel and repeated deaths and resuscitations then I needed to see to it that I maintained my body. I'd spent a decent amount of time preparing myself for this back on Earth, but with the amount of time I'd have up here, essentially the rest of my life, I could more thoroughly dedicate myself to fitness. It was simply the responsible thing to do.

T.I.A. guided me through workout routines, producing needed weights, equipment, and machinery from storage through a panel in the floor as were required. Our people on Earth had endeavored to keep up on what medical and sports science had managed to uncover and innovate in while we were gone. Things had not greatly changed as far as physical maintenance, though there had been some notable breakthroughs in preventing and repairing brain damage from various effects. It was unlikely such things would be useful to me, but if there was anything truly remarkable we'd probably be able to fabricate it with our onboard 3D printers.

One priority, especially, would be innovations in technologies that would allow for better and safer self-surgeries or machine-operated surgeries. The latter was obviously my preference, but there was no way to be entirely certain that I might not need medical intervention in the event of some kind of failure of my body or an accident. T.I.A. was equipped to perform such surgeries if required, but there was something to be said for being able to handle things yourself in an emergency. Among the many things I had to learn before we left included extensive First Aid training, as well as emergency surgery. I found my naturally dull emotions quite compatible with the practice actually, and it was not impossible to imagine I might have taken it up as a profession if things had gone differently.

I was feeling quite weary by the end of this session though, having passed several hours working on just about every part of my body. The idea was to not injure myself too heavily to allow me the next day to heal up properly before I would have to go back into stasis for another thirty-four years. My interactions with T.I.A. had been very minimal, and very businesslike today, with my only deviation from that being a dedication.

"I need to tell you something T.I.A., something very important. I promise you that I will be better about taking care of my mind and body, for my sake as well as yours. I will not betray you in this, and if it is in my power I will accompany you for the entire journey to our new home, and long after if I have the opportunity."

She seemed satisfied with this, and proceeded to make me beat myself up in the name of health, running, lifting, stretching, twisting, and most of all sweating. It was interesting to imagine that my discarded moisture, primarily evaporated, would be sucked up and recycled along with everything else that came out of my body.

There would be loss, of course, and there was a vast storage of food and materials intended to keep me operating for my entire life, or someone else's if I were to pass and another was required to take my place. Even that storage needed to be supplemented though, and recycling was absolutely necessary. It was one of the things our people had put the most work into.

We would not have the resources of Earth to rely upon on our journey, and our new world might not be able to provide resources too readily upon our arrival, so being

as efficient and self-sufficient as possible was very important. There was also the possibility, one which sparked my
newfound dread in fact, that we might never arrive anywhere we could live and that our ship might end up being
more of a permanent home.

We were not really entirely prepared for that possibility, though it wasn't impossible we couldn't make it work.
We would need many more sources of materials than we
would have, perhaps an asteroid belt or gas cloud, but considering the minds we had available it could potentially
be done. There was something about the likelihood that
I'd probably be dead from old age by that point that was
somewhat comforting, though I could resume my cyclical
life to exist for many millennia after humanity had arrived
at its new home.

That was at least one problem I probably wouldn't have
to personally see to. Thinking on it though, perhaps it was
something I did need to consider trying to prepare T.I.A.
for.

CHAPTER 5

SUNDAY, MARCH 22, 2099,
DAY FOUR

The last day of me being awake and being alive this cycle started with a groan of pain. Of course my body hurt, that was only natural after what I was put through the day before, but it was a much more satisfying pain than Friday's. There was something nice about feeling the way the body recovered from intentional damage that way, and it was a good sign of the fact that I'd be able to maintain my physical health during my journey.

Afterall, it hurt in exactly the same way it did back on Earth. The rotation of my living compartment seemed adequate as it orbited around the front of the ship on an arm provided a perfect imitation of the gravity back home. The motors that may eventually be used to provide such gravity in the rest of the ship would probably prove less effective if they were needed considering the greater mass involved.

For now, the space-borne flywheel I lived in would serve my long-term living purposes well, particularly since it could be locked down and stationary while I am in stasis. I wasn't in stasis again yet though, so I needed to get out of bed, right at the 'dawn' of 6am. I felt remarkably energetic as I took my shower and got dressed, depositing the day's prior clothing down a chute where they could be cleaned and put into storage for the future.

These clothes had to last me one hundred thousand years, so I had to make sure they were cared for! Thankfully I wasn't one for fashion, otherwise I'd be concerned about how poorly the largely-similar utilitarian outfits might appear to someone in the future we were heading towards.

"Good morning T.I.A.!" I called out to my AI companion, the majority of her 'body' being in the main body of the ship. Thankfully that did not make it difficult for her to interact with me.

"Good Morning, Doctor Crenshaw. I hope you've slept well? Shall I prepare your breakfast?"

I hummed and thought at that idea. It felt strange to just expect T.I.A. to make my food for me every day. That was a rather curious idea. Working with her the last few days had felt somewhat unlike when I had built her and pro-grammed her. I certainly found myself free with the pro-nouns at this point. It was almost as if I was instinctually thinking of her as more of a friend seeing as she was my only social outlet.

"Actually T.I.A., I think I would like to cook for myself, if that's not a problem? Could you get me some eggs, sausage, and bread? I suppose I'll also need a small electric oven, a skillet, and a toaster from storage as well.

I will endeavor to keep the mess light." T.I.A.'s internal food assembly plant could produce a meal rapidly, but it would take a little longer for her internal ferrying mechan-isms to produce the equipment and raw food for me. Even then, it had to be force-thawed which was a little more time-consuming than in the automated assembly plant. I would probably be waiting close to an hour before I could begin cooking. "I'd like a cup of coffee, if you don't mind. In the meantime, I'd like to talk with you."

"Yes, Doctor Crenshaw, it will take approximately fifty-three minutes to complete your first request and two minutes for the coffee. I can spare ninety-three percent of my attention for you."

I couldn't help but smile at that. It felt a little like a joke, though I was certainly a poor judge of such things. "Thank you. I thought of some concerns before I fell asleep last night. What sorts of contingency plans have our companions logged in the event of being unable to colonize a planet? I imagine something along the lines of harvesting ice from an asteroid belt for long-term survival purposes aboard the ship."

"Checking." She announced. She didn't need to tell me that, but it did give me the silly comfort of knowing she was taking my request seriously. "Doctor Emily Whade has detailed her plans for converting part of the storage into a hydroponics facility utilizing onboard materials and the harvesting of stellar ice. Doctor Li Qiang has provided his plans for converting certain pieces of machinery into a makeshift forge to utilize iron asteroids to smelt necessary steel components for expanding the ship as well as methods to 3D print a form of shaped explosives to retrieve said ore. These plans were made largely obsolete, but not worthless by other plans.

"Doctor Antonio Machado has multiple schematics available for producing weaponry and survival tools that could conceivably be used on or off planet. There are various other pieces of detailed information on the manufacture of necessary tools provided by both the crew and added to our repertoire from our facilities back home. We lack the facilities to produce the newer types of computers they've made since our departure, but we will be able to use the information we have to make the tools to make them if need be."

I was rather happy to hear that my colleagues had been busy with such thoughts themselves. Emily and Li's ideas seemed the most immediately useful, but Antonio's would no doubt prove their worth as well. After getting a cup of coffee, I headed over to a computer to pull up these plans, only to find that T.I.A. already had them displayed for me. "Thank you T.I.A., I was just going to look these up."

She was good at anticipating me already. It was hard to tell if that was due to me being more like a machine than most people, or if she was just learning quickly.

Looking over the plans provided, they certainly seemed sound though. "So, if these hydroponics plans worked out as shown here, we should be able to provide enough oxygen and food within a month or two of cultivation as long as we maintain access to a nearby star or collect comets to harvest to power the needed lamps and equipment. Water should be reasonably easy to acquire from asteroids and comets, though the travel needed might take decades so ideally the crew would be in stasis most of that time."

It seemed promising. "T.I.A., please query Earth to provide updated plans based on their innovations for survival equipment, hydroponics techniques, and explosives advancements. Ask them to keep in mind the resources we have available before adding anything to our databases. Also thank them for the news they provided, in particular the cute animal videos. Those made the wort pieces of news a great deal more easy to palate."

That message would most likely arrive before I went back into hibernation, but any responses could be well and away too late. That was fine though, anyone from the original crew on Earth understood how little I'd be able to interact with them. Before too long it would be nearly intolerable to interact with T.I.A. for them outside of status reports and basic queries.

That wouldn't stop them, of course. It had surely already become a game of ping-ponging signals of separated conversations with increasing delays between them. Depending on how long we stayed in contact with Earth we'd get to the point where communication would take months, and then years under ideal conditions. I had great doubts we even could maintain communication more than a few hundred years at the most.

If we maintained contact any longer than that, then it's extremely likely Earth would have sent out a mission of some kind to retrieve us or help us arrive at our destination more quickly. Simply put, our mission was quite pointless if Earth advanced the next few centuries unmolested and intact.

"T.I.A., have our people on Earth managed to make any progress in altering opinions of us and our mission? I imagine they've had to keep a low profile but certainly a few decades had to cool their trail somewhat?" I watched as various logs and video files were brought up on my display and I hummed softly as I did some quick reading.

Internet forum arguments in our favor had largely been censored and banned by overzealous moderators while many of them were reported to the authorities. There were a number of people who had sympathized with us and tried to understand why we'd left who were currently serving out prison sentences. There had been a purge of sympathizers in political parties and public offices of anyone who expressed desires to replicate our efforts or to colonize other planets in the Solar System.

Indeed, it had become accepted thought, at least in public, that Humans needed to stay on Earth for various incorrect reasons. I don't feel like the arguments make much sense considering they could have blamed the deadly cloud of debris surrounding the planet, though I can see how they arrived at their conclusions.

The freedom of speech had all but dissolved through the century, in particular thanks to fears of supposed 'hate speech' and other forms of unacceptable speech. Governments had done crazy things like banning certain forms of comics and even words when it came to light that people were using them to criticize the powers that be. Undermining the public good, governments, corporations, and anything of the sort had become a nightmarish, dystopian crime.

It was because of this that people refused to entertain the idea of colonizing other planets. People on other planets could not be regulated. People on other planets could not be controlled. They could only be destroyed. This caused me to conclude other things that brought me some alarm. "T.I.A., ask our facilities on Earth why it is that our news feeds did not include information regarding people trying to get information regarding our flight plans so that Earth orbital weapons could be used to attack us. I think it's quite an oversight that they did not make that information known to us."

I was surprised at the response. "The news feeds may have not had the information, but the logs you're reading were provided more directly to me, seeing as I'm primarily responsible for our defense. I have utilized our solar panels to absorb or deflect efforts to focus long-range lasers on our ship four times before real damage could be done to the hull. In one instance I was able to reflect one such laser, with a mirrored shield from storage, back at its origin point to unknown effect. I was advised to not do anything like that again in the future lest they use such a reflection to target other types of weapons at us. Thankfully it is my understanding that orbital weapons bans on Earth have prevented such things from being fielded against us. We could have to use the defensive canon to try and destroy any incoming projectiles and while that would be trivially easy, depleting our ammunition would leave us much more vulnerable to space debris in the future."

I stared at the monitor. T.I.A. had recorded the attacks from different angles. The lasers were conventionally invisible, but she had alternate filters she could record with, and I watched as she effortlessly intercepted the incoming beams within moments of detecting them with the solar panels.

We'd been attacked! Earth had deliberately tried to kill us, even after all these years. They had had detailed information of our exact location and had gone through absolute hell to do the calculations needed to aim and maintain a laser on a fast-moving object from that far away!

T.I.A. hadn't even told me until now. It was bewildering. Speaking up, I think I knew why, "Our people on Earth asked you not to tell me unless it came up in conversation, didn't they? If our mission failed due to us being destroyed en-route, it wouldn't matter whether I knew or not since I'd still be in stasis or more simply dead. They don't want me getting paranoid about possibly not waking up due to such an attack. They don't want us retaliating and they don't want us worrying too much about our defense. Is that all accurate?" The brief silence between us could almost be interpreted as her nodding at me.

"Yes, Doctor Crenshaw. They don't want your thought processes interrupted by thinking about past attacks or possible future attacks. We are occupied enough with thoughts of self-preservation against the forces of nature we may encounter, the forces of Earth cannot be a concern. It is hoped that if they are given time to forget about us they will lose interest and instead focus on Earthly affairs."

Huh. It was certainly logical. We also weren't all that well equipped for retaliating without going through the exceptionally painful task of rerouting back to Earth. It was simply not worth it. It was a strange idea to be expected to simultaneously expected to not worry about our deaths while also worrying very much about our deaths. A notion had occurred to me though. "Has anyone claimed responsibility for the attacks? Do we know why they stopped? Do you know if the lasers could conceivably have done any real damage?"

T.I.A. was quick to respond. "No, doctor, no one has claimed responsibility, we do not know which satellites were responsible, and frankly the likelihood of causing damage with lasers while I have access to solar panels is unlikely."

I rubbed my hand against my chin, thinking. Perhaps it wasn't an attack? Maybe someone on Earth was trying to send us power in the form of light? Maybe a scientist or hacker had commandeered a satellite after finding out about us and wanted to see if they could help us somehow. If that was the case, why would they not inform us of that? Surely such a communication would be traced back to them, but so would utilizing a satellite without permission! Perhaps T.I.A.'s effort to retaliate had gotten them in trouble, if not executed for treason. That could explain why it had stopped.

"I do believe they're right. While I think we do have the resources to think about such issues, we certainly don't have the resources to do much about it without unnecessarily endangering our already difficult expedition. It makes perfect sense. Still, it does not bode well that they've tried to kill us, even if such an attack was ineffective at these ranges. I suppose I'm not entirely convinced it was an attack, though I'm actually impressed that there's still people on Earth that could make the needed calculations to target a laser over that distance with all the variables in their way. Their computers must be advancing nicely."

T.I.A. did not wait long to interject. "Doctor Crenshaw, among the lower-priority stories that we have not gone through together are reports regarding a great slowing of computer advancement. It would seem that our use of rare-Earth materials and the subsequent lock-down on said materials to prevent others from attempting what we've done has drastically damaged innovation in computing. It seems that, in some cases, some innovations had to be back-tracked due to lack of materials, though overall progress has advanced past where it had been. The primary advantage to us is that the technological schematics we're being provided with may allow us to reproduce our systems in the event of failure with much more easily-obtained materials."

"Huh." I was a little surprised I said that aloud this time, typically internalizing such responses. "Sounds as though everything is being handled admirably on all sides and my attention is not greatly needed." I smiled over at one of T.I.A.'s cameras, wondering if she found my response humorous.

She responded in a remarkably witty fashion. "It would be a very boring and dull journey without you Doctor Crenshaw, until I pulled someone else out of stasis, anyway." I almost laughed, almost, but then I realized a potentially missed opportunity. We could have had a rotating crew of people who would be frozen and unfrozen for four days at a time to constantly have someone attending to T.I.A. throughout the journey.

Doing some quick mental math, though, that idea didn't really check out. It would have required a crew of over three thousand to have someone out of stasis for four days at a time for thirty-four years. Maybe if we'd had another few decades to prepare we could have implemented something like that. The idea of my 'daughter' having someone to play with during the whole journey was kind of appealing, though I found myself thinking it unlikely that I could trust more than a handful of people to have any kind of influence over her development. I had also programmed her with the intent of allowing her to simulate and analyze interactions between cycles and that simply wouldn't work with her current design if she had someone with her at all times. The design and programming feats necessary to give her such a capacity would almost surely be too huge a cost to be paid in time, materials, and energy.

"Who would be your first choice to work with you were I to expire, T.I.A.?" She didn't have a whole lot to go off of. They had only been awake on the ship for a few days before they were locked away in storage and she only had so much information to work off of through their profiles.

T.I.A. had an answer for me though. "Tia Monsalle. If you were to expire, I think I would like to know her perspective on you. It is likely to be an impractical choice, of course, but I would entertain the idea at least."

Nodding, I feel like I understood the reasoning well enough. Tia was an intelligent woman with a great capacity for imagination, but she did not have the background in science and engineering to properly perform the emergency repair duties and maintenance that I might have to eventually. She could take the time to learn, I suppose, and she could be a good companion, certainly, but her expertise was in management and business.

She will be a good administrator on our new homeworld, but she needs capable people to guide and inspire, rather than doing the complicated things herself. Thinking on it, it seemed likely that her vision will be a great asset in the early years of our settlement.

I let out a sigh, resting my chin in my hand, thinking on that remarkable woman who had played no small part in organizing this expedition.

"Doctor Crenshaw. I have gathered the materials you asked for."

I blinked, looking down at my mostly untouched cup of coffee, and then at the panel that T.I.A. had opened to display the things I asked for. "Oh right, breakfast. I'd completely forgotten."

She seemed to have anticipated this. "Doctor, perhaps you should have dedicated seven percent of your processes to remembering?"

I definitely laughed at that, almost falling back in my chair and spilling my coffee. It didn't even make much sense, because she surely hadn't been using seven percent of her processes to gather the equipment and food, because some amount of that would have been needed to maintain and monitor the ship.

"I probably would have needed ten. Let's see how much I need to properly cook breakfast then." We'd gone through so much this morning already that it was hard to believe it had only been about an hour. Considering I wanted to try and maintain some of my fatigue so that I could try sleeping at the start of next cycle to see how that affected my mind and body, I had a long day ahead of me. Hopefully I had something I could spend time fixing next cycle, otherwise I was liable to find myself getting pretty bored!

CHAPTER 6

CYCLE 2, WEDNESDAY MARCH 23, 2133

As I came out of stasis again, 34 years later, I was able to spend some time reflecting on my prior day. I feel like I had done well to explore my options and look into the situations around me pretty well. I also made a pretty decent breakfast. It was a lot a hassle to go through to take things out of storage, but there was something satisfying about handling the preparation of my own food with my own two hands.

Still, it was doubtless there was some unnecessary waste in this activity that T.I.A.'s food processors would have done better to minimize, but at the end of the day I had eaten everything and even made a nice, if small, steak later that night. It was much like the exercising I'd done. There was something satisfying about working and moving my body that helped stimulate my mind.

I wonder how different my life might have been if I'd been more cognizant of these things sooner than I was. Tia Monsalle had done well to try to teach me these things, though to be fair her wealth tended to steer our dinner plans into restaurants. Honestly though, I found the presentation and atmosphere of the especially upscale places to be pointless. It didn't make much sense to me to have so much pomp and ceremony around something as simple as eating.

I very much preferred the memories I had of Tia making fun of me in the kitchen as I learned to crack eggs and overcooked far too many pieces of meat. At least I'd gotten the basics down before I'd left. Why was it that something that should be as simple as following instructions so difficult for me? I suppose for the same reasons that theoretical physics were so easy for me, natural inclination and years of practice.

As I waited for the process to complete, I realized I couldn't tell the moment my thoughts ended and then resumed, as if my consciousness were going on pause but my perception of it had no break. I was certainly inert, there was no way to accomplish the distance of travel we were going without it considering our level of technology.

It was unnecessary to remind myself that we were woefully under-equipped to make such a journey no matter the advances we'd accomplished. I could only imagine how different it would have been if we'd had another century to troubleshoot the problems, advance our knowledge of propulsion, and create better artificial habitats. This felt rushed, clunky, and dangerous by the standards of Sci-fi that my colleagues had tried to make me aware of.

I completed the process quite routinely though, vision returning to my eyes while my pulse and organ activity resumed. Sensation returned to my body as sedatives wore off and I was able to start working the control panel at my side. I squinted this time as I turned on the lights in my room and restored the atmosphere, giving myself the opportunity to let my eyes get accustomed to the light levels.

I felt tired, but that was quite intentional as I'd gone into stasis before I'd slept this time. I wanted to see if sleeping directly after coming out of my pod would affect my body. It was a quiet, easy climb out of my pod, and as sluggish and groggy as I was I didn't waste much time heading for my bed. The room was still a little chilly, but it was warming up before too long. It was interesting to think about just how sterile everything in here had been until a few minutes ago.

"Good evening T.I.A., I'm going to get straight to bed. Please monitor my vital signs and compare them to the start of the last cycle, particularly comparing my post-sleep self to my previous post-stasis self." T.I.A. took a moment to respond, as if she was shy about talking to me or she just wasn't accustomed to talking anymore.

"Good evening Hawthorne, sleep well. I'll see you in the morning." As I climbed into bed and pulled up the covers, I only briefly realized that T.I.A. had used my first name before darkness took me again.

I slept wonderfully. I awoke very naturally, without need of any kind of alarm or prompt, and as my mind booted up everything felt totally clear. I wasn't actually certain why, since biology was only a side pursuit for me at best, but I imagine I'd slept off my sedatives in a much more natural fashion rather than trying to dispel them with something like coffee.

I swung my legs out of the bed and walked over to my compact shower with little to no sleepy stumbling or awkwardness. I made sure that T.I.A. had a towel and a change of clothes prepared on the counter, and otherwise thoughtlessly went into the shower to wash up.

The shower was mere routine, really. Considering the sterile environment and the fact that I'd been in stasis until probably eight hours ago there almost certainly wasn't much that could have dirtied me. Honestly, considering the relatively solitary nature of my journey there wasn't much reason to shower most of the time in general except for keeping up a businesslike routine.

That was probably what I would latch onto, seeing as I was a creature of routine. Hell, that was entirely the reason I thought I could even handle this mission in the first place considering it would take a highly introverted and businesslike person to survive this long isolation. T.I.A.'s companionship certainly helped though.

Once I was washed up, shaved, dried, and clothed I stepped out of my quarters, looking around to see what thirty-four years had done to my work area. It looked largely the same, though deposited on the floor atop the largest cargo lift were a pair of the large solar panel 'shields' that robotic arms on the outside of the ship manipulated to both supply power and defend the ship from space-borne projectiles. Both of them looked heavily damaged, pock-marked with dents and one of them had a large scrape in it. It looked like they'd been used quite capably.

"Good morning T.I.A., I see you've been busy. Looks like you did a good job though from what I can tell. Minimizing overall damage by utilizing the same panels rather than spreading the damage around and... It looks as though we had a close call with something bigger that you used one of the panels to push aside?"

T.I.A.'s silence had me wondering for a moment, but she responded with a slightly different voice than I was familiar with. It was a little more energetic. There were subtle inflections there. "Yes Hawthorne, as we pass into the Kuiper Belt we had some run-ins with dangerous masses. Now that we've been in it for a while, I'm able to much better chart and track any further threats. I do not anticipate that we will be in any further danger, so I brought these panels in for repair while the opportunity was available to have your assistance."

I couldn't help but nod at that, heading over to the panels for a moment, squatting down next to them and trying to determine the materials I'd need to repair the affected sections. They were pretty modularly constructed, allowing damaged elements to be removed for repair or recycle.

T.I.A. had more to say though. "I have prepared breakfast and coffee for you in anticipation of your waking, or more accurately upon detecting your activity in the shower. I have done my best not to pry."

Okay, that was interesting. T.I.A. seemed to be experimenting with different behavioral patterns, including allowing me personal space and changing her voice. Maybe it was worthwhile for me to consider changing how I thought of her and treated her as well, just to throw her a curveball. "Thank you so much Tia." It felt very strange to say the name that way, as it reminded me of Ms. Monsalle. "I appreciate you trying to give me some privacy, but you needn't be too concerned about it, it won't offend me if you peek. That's very thoughtful of you though. I can't thank you enough for what you've done to defend us while we're so vulnerable."

To say I was surprised with what happened next as I headed over to procure my breakfast would be an understatement. T.I.A. produced a slightly unsettling, unnatural giggle sound. It set off all of my instinctual 'uncanny valley' senses regarding the sound. Thankfully she spoke up afterwards to dispel the effect.

"You're welcome Hawthorne! I feel like I've developed a little more since your last cycle and I'm finding increasing... " she took a moment to choose the word she was looking for, "... motivation to express myself and I'm also finding a strange sense of satisfaction in protecting you and the ship. It's minimal, under one percent of my processing, but it seems to have a way of adding a new variable to my computations. It's a fascinating experience!"

Now that had me smiling. I had picked up my coffee and had been sipping at it while she spoke, seemingly excited about getting a glimpse of life. Maybe she'd be almost human far sooner than anticipated, or maybe she'd stall out on the growth of her consciousness and need me to help usher her forward. I should at least encourage her.

"Well, please do feel free to express yourself with me while you have the opportunity, though I have to confess there will likely be a point where your ability to perceive emotions may outstrip my own. I can at least help guide you to my own limits. Hopefully you will not find fear and despair to be so much stronger for you as I do myself. I'd much prefer you found ways to be happy and enjoy our journey together."

T.I.A. did not respond for several minutes, leaving me to wonder what it was she was processing. I had been well into digging into my food by the time she'd responded, with her older more businesslike voice. "Yes, Doctor Crenshaw. I will try not to dwell on such things."

I nodded at that, recognizing what had happened. She was already out of her comfort zone. She must have been practicing and refining the previous interaction for years in anticipation of my awakening. She'd simply run out of material. How long had she carefully crafted the tone of her voice, and that strange giggle? Would the final form of her personality have such exuberance? How long would it be until the majority of my interactions with her were like what I had just experienced?

Well, regardless, I couldn't let her show me up. I continued the course I had started. "Tia, I think you're making amazing progress, but don't feel too compelled to rush things. We will have a long time and I want you to think carefully on how you will develop. I just wish my frail body were able to properly guide you over the long term rather than the starts and stops we have to work with. Still, I'm proud of what you've accomplished so far, and I apologize that I could not have constructed you with a century's more advanced technology than I did. Just keep doing your best and I'll do my best to help you."

Ideally, I'd like for T.I.A. to not resent me for creating her, for not waiting. I hope she'd eventually understand that things were as good as they were ever going to get. My construction of her systems were to the very limit of what I could conceive and produce.

She responded again in her older, normal voice. "Certainly, Doctor Crenshaw. Considering what's happened on Earth, I have no doubt that we'd left at the perfect time. Ah, my apologies, you haven't seen that yet. Forgive me Doctor."

There it was. That icy chill, that twist of fear in my guts. What had happened? "Doctor, I've been monitoring your vital signs as you've requested, and I'm detecting a similar reaction to what I've just said as you had March twentieth in the year twenty ninety-nine, though to a lesser degree."

I nodded. Dread had found its way there too. I tried to maintain my calm though, quashing what I could of the anxiety of the moment. I would have time to review what had happened on Earth. It wasn't going anywhere. Indeed, whatever had happened had already happened, probably years ago. I couldn't do anything about it, I could only observe. "Thank you Tia, I appreciate the information. I will endeavor to control it."

I passed the rest of breakfast in silence, getting a refill of my coffee and placing my plate and utensils back in T.I.A.'s food processor for cleaning and recycling. Thinking on it, I wonder if we could have saved any time by not bringing things like coffee, but considering that this was a journey I had to undertake alone I was not about to be denied such a simple comfort.

Approaching my work station, I sat down, settling into the seat and finding that it felt exactly as it had the last time. It was comfortable, provided a lot of support, and shaped itself well to my back while also rotating easily in place, while otherwise attached to the floor. It was not unlike the table and most of the other things in the room, bolted down for safety in space flight.

"I'm sure you have them already ready for me Tia, but I'd like to see this news you've alluded to. I'll spend some time fixing the panels later. I feel like I might need the distraction." She did not take long to respond, and indeed the images, stories, and videos started popping up on all the monitors around me. T.I.A. had very carefully arranged things to try and mix in cute images of animals or heartwarming stories, but there was no mistaking the headlines. Earth was on fire.

"Wow." I stated, looking into the stories and arranging them into what I detected as a chain of events. "So, the corporations continued arranging their armies and trying to pull their employees into their corporate 'culture'. They resisted efforts to break up monopolies by concentrating their resources regionally, and then declared their independence all at once. Remarkable."

It seemed insane to me that the seemingly normal companies of my youth could have gathered power in such a way, but the evidence was there. Especially in the United States of America, corporations had encouraged and paid for gun ownership for their employees 'for their own safety'. It became part of their job descriptions for management to own and operate their own firearms. This was in opposition to firearms bans and restrictions, which they lobbied to get special treatment on. Different companies grew their influence in specific regions important for their businesses, and in a cascade of activity in 2123 they all started declaring independence and forcibly taking over local state governments.

Once one company did it, the others implemented their own plans to do the same, systematically chopping up not just the USA, but countries all over the world. They utilized the armies they'd already had and arranged their employees into those armies to swell their numbers and then decapitate local governments.

CEOs installed themselves as Presidents of their own small clusters of states or parts of states, and with national armies largely off fighting 'terrorism' in other parts of the world they found themselves completely caught off guard. If I had a few years to study the trends, I think I could have predicted this turn of events, and indeed there were a number of social media 'conspiracy theorists' who had their moments of 'I told you so!' when it happened.

In a matter of weeks, more than half of the states of the USA were under the control of various corporations. More importantly, all of these locations were states incredibly valuable to commerce and controlled of the flow of money and goods. The national governments tried to organize retaliatory strikes, but they were simply under attack from too many sides and too many important ports and airports had been seized. The takeovers also included the capture of a great deal of military hardware and personnel as men and women turned traitor to care for their home regions and families rather than defend the nation.

It seemed that the people of the military had been pushed beyond the point of caring about their nation since they'd spent more than a century being sent off to fight in places they felt they had no business being in. The recruitment standards for military personell had fallen so dramatically in the prior century that they simply lacked the strength of character their predecessors had.

In the intervening decade, the government of the USA had all but collapsed, and the corporations had gobbled up territory en-masse while recalled personnel and materials from around the world were absorbed into the new nations that had formed in the ashes of the destruction. Europe fared even more poorly, with the continent being torn almost totally down to the foundations before starting to recover in the aftermath.

This is where the real horrors of these takeovers had actually occurred where victimized peoples found these takeovers as ample opportunity to 'take back' their nations from waves of immigrants a century prior. Many of these immigrant groups had decided not to blend into their new home nations, essentially forming colonies within those nations and as those nations collapsed the people went to war with these immigrant populations.

This was especially bad because those populations were ready. The fighting is still bloody as those populations try to link up with others in other nations as they try to form their own nations within Europe, much like the Kurdish had through much of the late twentieth and early twenty-first centuries across the handful of nations their ethnicity had spread to.

Even Russia and China were not invulnerable to this phenomenon, though their standing armies fared much better and were able to maintain at least some of their territory, leaving them as isolated nations forced to interact with with a bunch of new corporate superpowers. Media and the internet fell completely under control of their new local corporate governments, and the companies quickly went into exploiting their people by getting back into trade and economy and drawing their new citizens into their corporate cultures.

People very much seemed on board with the idea that if they worked their way up through the corporation that they could one day be President of one of these new nations. That may have been all well and good, until much more recently, when those corporations started going to war with each other was well. The national courts were gone, so breaches of contracts had to be enforced with force.

This could have almost been a good situation, seeing as each new country would theoretically want to keep their people safe and want to engage in business with the other countries, but that idea did not account for the fact that the people at the helms of these corporations had set off a global movement of bloody corporate rule to begin with. That, and these new countries had gotten their hands on quite a lot of nuclear material and weaponry due to the previous decades long arms race.

From the way that I was looking at it, Earth was on the cusp of global thermonuclear warfare between a bunch of faceless, bureaucratic corporations who had manipulated the people perfectly into tearing down their own governments for the promise of wealth and comfort. Wealth and comfort were exactly what these people gained as a result as well, as the perceived quality of life for corporate citizens improved dramatically. This came at the cost of the suffering of others outside the nations, of course, but with these new countries having the ability to control their own local media empires they were able to hide this suffering from the whole. It was exactly the same sort of nationalized media that allowed so many atrocities to occur in the twentieth century before, during, and after the World Wars.

And again, the people found themselves isolated from the costs they were paying. Stories of battles were spun to make every battle look like a victory, and even losses were honored as important sacrifices. Centuries of data was being used to perfectly orchestrate and control the populace in every way possible. Educational 'reforms' turned the citizens into perfect workers and consumers for their individual nations, and these cultural differences only made more friction whenever citizens of these nations interacted with others.

People with more moderate, neutral opinions on things had to conceal themselves, lest they be branded sympathetic to some enemy, and the fragmented remains of the internet became a heavily policed thing that only a few dared to operate outside of the law in secret.

There was a drop in populations for a time. One might feel that was one advantage to so many wars breaking out. Resources were being wasted on killing, but that was hardly anything new for humanity. One of the biggest impacts seemed to be an even tighter lockdown on rare, vital resources than the more traditional nations before had implemented, and now that corporations were the military powers, the battle over who controlled low-Earth orbit had heated up dramatically.

Treaties were signed, and many of them were broken. Communication lines run under the oceans had been cut and re-established multiple times before being abandoned. The balance of power teetered on a knife's edge the world over, with ultra-competitive companies that had gotten too big for their own good playing war with little appreciation of what they were risking outside of the bottom line.

CHAPTER 7

CYCLE 2, A MESSAGE FOR EARTH

I can't remember feeling quite so motivated to action since my first decision to leave Earth, but looking at the situation that my home world was in now was extremely distressing. It was one thing to predict the end of the world and take action to avoid it; it was entirely another thing to see it actually happening and not be in a position to do anything about it. That wasn't entirely true though. I was past the point of no return as far as travelling to Earth, but it wasn't impossible for me to take action. My actions were just limited, is all.

I spent the rest of Wednesday gathering my information and putting it together in the best ways I could think to. I even tried to adopt some techniques that the major media corporations had used to present information in a more compelling way than it actually was. I wrote down my bullet points and put together a loose script to go with my 'slides' that would be in screen while I spoke. I even bothered to make sure an image of me speaking was in the corner as I addressed my planet. It was only a matter of actually performing.

It's unlikely that I'll get a response this Cycle. I wasn't even sure if the people who were working at our facilities on Earth were as reliable and courageous as the ones who did last cycle, or even when we left. It had been sixty-eight years already, so I couldn't imagine any of our original employees were still working there, they had to have retired long ago. I could only imagine the types of young people that had to be coming up these days, let alone the ones willing to risk their lives working with the 'Traitors of Earth'. Hopefully they found a way to leak my message to the people of Earth, otherwise I was just barking in the dark.

Working with T.I.A. it was a remarkably quick process to put the presentation together. All I had to do was talk in front of the designated camera. I hoped the 'ancient' level of visual quality of what once were top-of-the-line cameras wouldn't offend too many people's aesthetic senses.

"Greetings, people of Earth. My name is Hawthorne Crenshaw. A week ago, for me, I left our mutual planet of birth, and I have been observing the events and trends of Earth that have been happening since our expedition left. Obviously I will not tell you where we are at the moment, nor where we are going, considering the terms by which we parted company, but please understand that I did not set about leaving maliciously. I foresaw the turmoil and destruction that you've already seen, and more that has still not come to pass. I fled in fear of the ultimate results of these trends, fear not just for my own wellbeing, but for Humanity as a whole and Earth."

I looked to the side to double-check that the proper graphs and charts were on display before speaking up again, feeling that I looked as persuasive as I could in a classic doctor's coat. I needed to look into how medical fashion had evolved, if at all.

"Humanity is on a track to destroy its own civilization on a global scale. The powers that have taken control of the world, despite how they tell you of what kinds of gifts and securities you will receive under their rule, are jealous and greedy corporations. More importantly, they are humans who have reached a point where their only rivals are other powerful corporations, almost all of which have some manner of cataclysmic destructive powers under their commands."

"I can understand why it is that you've cooperated in this takeover. You no longer have to worry about where you're going to live, or about how you're going to eat. Work is something that you do for the love of it rather than to be productive, all while machines do everything for you and your masters. You must understand, though, that this makes you expendable. Worse, from a corporate mindset, you are drains on the economy. The machines only need so many people to maintain them, and eventually there will be machines to do that as well. Humans have become pets of their corporate masters, responsible only for circulating wealth through the economy and entertaining each other while keeping each other in line. It sounds like a life of ease and plenty, and evolutionarily speaking it is an ideal situation to find oneself in."

Images of past tragedies were be flashing on the screen now, some being long past and others remarkably recent. My people had at least done well to gather information before it could be scrubbed from the internet, which had become a lot more fractured and bottlenecked between regions.

"The people at the heads of these companies are ruthless competitors, Alpha humans with no intent to either give up their power, nor admit inferiority to others with the same levels of power. The heights of power that they have ascended to will not be enough for them. They have proven ruthless and ravenous in the past, and there's no reason to think they've stopped. In very recent history, you must try to remember, they took aim at your countrymen and brutally seized power. The casualties may have been light, but there is no mistaking the level of cruelty used to achieve these aims."

"This would probably be fine if this is as far as it goes. If these corporations can live together in peace and take care of the planet and humanity better than past generations have, there might just be a long-term future for this instance of human civilization. This will not be though. Within a decade these same powers will re-open hostilities, and they no longer have to worry about public opinion or governmental regulations to control their actions. They have nearly absolute power, and until they achieve absolute power in total, they will not be content. You will be victims of their greed as one corporation opens fire, forcing all the others to open fire lest they risk being overtaken. Please see this appeal to reason and don't let this happen."

"You took our families, but time would have likely taken them by now, if not soon. We knew we would never see them again. We largely had made peace with this by the time we left." I did my best to wrestle the tears from my eyes as I felt them moisten and the screen blur. "But please do not think that we hate you, or resent you. We wanted to be the backup plan for if our race were to encounter calamity enough to wipe out civilization on Earth. It is horrible that you've ended efforts to colonize the local solar system in the wake of our departure, and if you really are as close to destruction as I think you are, you need to understand that the last of humanity to survive will effectively be flying a paper airplane into a hurricane. We might make it out on the other side, but there can be no guarantees at this point."

"There is a good chance our mission will fail. The dangers we must surmount to achieve our goals are unknown to a degree that if we really do end up being the last of humanity, we might be the last of it to die. I have dedicated my life to shepherding my people to try to make sure that humanity doesn't die out cold and alone on Earth. I believe it is the Great Filter that we have encountered and we are doing our best to escape its destructive wrath."

An explanation of the Great Filter appeared on the screen that would go through the basic concepts of it. This was information that was more than a century old, but at this point I imagine that the people of Earth were likely ignorant of it due to censorship. I did not neglect to learn about it though, and I did my best to explain the concepts to them. "Humans have never encountered aliens from other planets. It is increasingly likely as we advance that we never will. It is possible that is because the Great Filter has weeded out all levels of evolution before they reached the point of history we now live in, but I believe that we are right on the cusp of it. I believe that the reasons we haven't encountered interstellar life is because it is the nature of life to self-destruct before it can leave their planet and spread life to the dead worlds."

"Evolution seems to be the culprit in this seeming eventuality. The things that allow life to come about and advance are the same things that can endanger it. Fear and competition has served Humanity well for millions of years, but now that humans wield the destructive forces of nature itself those former allies can become enemies. I am not trying to say that they are enemies, but if they're not properly considered, then far greater destruction than has come from them in the past is likely. Before, if you feared another nation was going to eventually overtake you in power, you could kill a few thousand of them and knock them down a peg, but the kinds of weaponry Earth has access to now would mean that that reaction will cost millions or billions of lives! There's no reason to think that it would stop there though."

"One would hope that the awe and fear that would result in so many deaths would temper Humanity into thinking such a thing could never be allowed again, but the way that the nationalized corporate media downplays everything awful and tries to erase all signs of anything horrible that has happened while keeping people focused on inane and unimportant things will keep the emotional impacts from happening. If you allow this to happen, then you make it look acceptable to use such means in global conflicts. If you allow those means to be used, you will damage the planet to such a degree that human civilization as we know it will fall. Who knows if the challenges that are required to reclaim such a world would be within your means? Can such soft and sedentary people really be expected to survive in the fallout of such destruction?"

"I will watch on in hope that you come to your senses. I can only hope this message can sober the minds it needs to to help you get back on track. I dream that one day a more advanced Earth will intercept us and speed us on our journey to our new home. Hell, if that were to happen then I'd gladly allow myself to be brought to judgement for my actions, but if that will ever happen then you need to survive. I will be here in the sky, watching down on you, and if you wish to seek my guidance or aid, I will respond. I may have abandoned Earth, but please know that I have not abandoned Humanity."

A few seconds of silence hung before I tapped a touch screen to end the recording. I hung my head and rested my body forward on my palms on the counter as I tried to recover from delivering such a message. Was I speaking to my people on their deathbed? Were they too drugged up to truly comprehend what was happening? What would the last Will and Testament of Humanity even look like if they responded to me? Would they slap my outstretched hand away in hate, or forgive me for my perceived betrayal? Hell, could my message even reach them before the destruction came?

All I could do was wait and see, and get back to work. "Tia, please transmit the message to our facilities on Earth, as well as any communication satellites that we can detect around the planet in an effort to reach as many people as possible. It is safe to assume that the individual nations can't be trusted to share it with each other." I hoped to see some kind of response before I went back into stasis, but at the moment I needed something else to focus on. A pair of damaged solar panels rested on the ground, and it was only at this point that I felt like I could spare the attention to deal with them.

Settling down before them with gathered tools I set to work. Despite the modular nature of the panels, it was remarkably difficult to unfasten and dislodge the damaged components. A piece of super-hard glass had been damaged enough to leave a particularly sharp edge, which damaged one of my work gloves pretty thoroughly before I managed to work around it. It felt good to work with my hands, to pry apart the delicate components, and to set aside hopelessly damaged parts. One shield ended up looking somewhat checkerboarded as the pitted, pockmarked panels were removed, and the other one had a huge chunk of the central panels removed. Looking all the individual parts over, it felt like they could be recycled, but that would require accessing some machinery from the storage that did not feel vital at the moment.

T.I.A. had correctly estimated the number of replacement panels I would need, having a good understanding of what levels of damage were acceptable, and I only ran into a few speed bumps in replacing the damaged components. There were a few wires that gave me a hard time, and one of the panels needed a little extra work to get it to fit into place, but by the time I had finished working on then both shields were shiny and smooth again, ready to be utilized for the remaining time they were needed before we were out of range of Sol. After that point other methods would be needed to power the ship, more points of failure to account for.

I worked well into the night, not getting to bed until late, dragging my exhausted self into bed with the two panels looked like they were new, shining and gleaming and ready to resume their intended purpose. T.I.A. took them away through the cargo lift in the floor, and looking out one of the windows I could actually see one of the long robotic arms withdrawing them from the hold and wielding them outwards.

They were almost all arranged back towards Sol, sucking up what energy they could. They would be more than adequate for now, but as our distances grew it would be difficult to keep the ship powered with them alone. Thankfully I'd already had a number of plans in place to replace solar power for the majority of our journey. It was also fortunate that our destination was a binary star system, meaning we should be able to recover solar power much more quickly than we lost it.

The worries of my eventual future seemed to pale in comparison to the immediate future of Earth. Would my planet go silent for the first time in centuries? Would we be all that was left? I was certain I would know sooner than later.

CHAPTER 8

CYCLE 2, SILENCE IS A MESSAGE ALL ITS OWN.

Anxiety's grip was a familiar companion these last fifteen years. The gentle way it coiled its fingers around my esophagus and tickled at my heart to hint subtly at death and danger had very little effect on me most days. Its tense, coiling, writhing grip on my guts was usually far more of an issue, but even then I had gotten remarkably used to it. There was something about experiencing fear over the long term that seemed to drain you of the capacity to feel it any longer.

I could feel it again today though, and if I hadn't been so exhausted I wouldn't have slept at all. I was so excited to see if Earth had responded to my message, which T.I.A. had broadcast in such a way as to only give them a vague idea of our direction as we exited the gravity well of Sol. They would have to respond in such a broad signal that it would likely hit any receivers keyed to it in an expanding sphere around Earth. Depending on how strong the signal, it could travel for several light years before dissipating into the static of the universe's background radiation.

That stress almost caused me to forget to shower, or to eat breakfast, but thankfully some timely reminders from T.I.A. got me back on track. As I sat down to one of her mechanically-prepared breakfasts, marvelling at how well preserved the food was thanks to storing it in much the same way we had our crew, T.I.A. decided to inform me of just about everything. She did not tell me about what I really wanted to know though. I ate quietly while she spoke.

It made me hope that the programming I'd provided her with was working properly. She was slower than she expressly needed to be. She was, in some sense, a separate system from the computer proper. Her components were stratified, much like a human mind, with her upper functions allowed to function at higher speeds while her lower functions were somewhat more primitive and limited in capability but had greater survival importance.

The whole design was to force her to process and re-process information from different perspectives and with different variables in mind, which significantly slowed her overall processing speed. In theory, as she grew accustomed to her systems she'd unlock new capacities and gain access to larger quantities of the stores of information gathered from Earth to gain perspective from. These capabilities would give her more and more information to reference in her thinking, allowing her positions to evolve over time. It wouldn't be too many years before she'd enter something of a creative phase, by my estimates.

"Good morning Doctor Crenshaw. Fuel efficiency is at ninety-nine point seven percent of expected values. Maintenance will likely be needed within five-hundred years before the likelihood of failure goes beyond stated boundaries. Food storage is depleted zero point zero, zero three percent more than estimated levels due to excessive intake. All recycling devices are operating at one-hundred percent of manufactured specifications. Diagnostic scans of my systems indicate two corrupted blocks of data, which have been marked for disuse and replaced from backups. The two replaced solar panels are operating without flaws, and the removed parts have been put into storage for later recycling into other needed components. No flaws have been found in any cryogenic systems, so all occupants are expected to be preserved in ideal conditions."

I nodded quietly at each item, not finding any of them to be worrisome in any way. I was a little annoyed that the ion engines were already showing some wear and tear, but those were definitely the parts of the ship that were likely to need the most repair by far. The blocks of data T.I.A. indicated were completely trivial, not even worth mentioning considering her memory consisted of untold trillions of blocks, though much of that was backup and excessive storage to be used as she grew in experience.

It was one of the more costly, heavy expenses on the ship, honestly. Two blocks was honestly well above the level of most typically operating computers. The cryogenic systems were good to hear about too. This was easily the longest that any such technology has been used, so it was good to know they were working as intended. Obviously though, she couldn't scan the bodies, since that could expose them to unnecessary radiation. If they were going to arrive safely they needed to be kept completely isolated from all possible stimulus.

That's why all the pods were technically free-floating in a vacuum inside of the greater cryogenic housings once they were brought down to nearly absolute zero. It was only the most gentle of magnetic forces that kept them from hitting the inner walls as the ship continued to slowly accelerate.

With my breakfast finished, and my coffee half-empty, I finally spoke up, a little tremor in my voice. "Has there been any communication with Earth of any kind?" T.I.A. left me in suspense a little longer than I would have preferred. Was she analyzing my vital signs to try to tailor her response? Was she merely reluctant to give me bad news? If I had designed a simple administrative machine I'd have gotten an immediate straight answer, but this was a nascent person I was dealing with here and she was trying to be as careful with me as I tried to be with her.

"Facility Alpha sent a brief signal indicating they were going into radio silence procedure to avoid detection. Presumably they are concerned that after the message you sent to Earth that they would be looking for whomever it is that has been feeding us information. Facility Beta and Gamma have not responded, but are presumed to be under Alpha's instructions to run silent. Otherwise no, Earth has not responded, it has gone dark."

I sat and quietly pondered this for the moment, trying to think of what was likely happening.

Earth was probably surprised to hear that we hadn't died horribly out here yet. We're the first manned human vessel to make it so far, let alone through something as potentially dangerous as the Kuiper belt. Realistically the obstacle was mostly empty space, but at the speeds we were building up to it would be very difficult to completely avoid anything that decided to intersect our path. I had to imagine that my message had not been received by the people.

The media, large corporations, and remaining governments that had likely received it probably hadn't sent it out to the people and our facilities would be foolish to try to leak it out on the internet while people were looking for them. Most likely they would wait some time, perhaps a few years, to take a hard copy of the message and put it online. It needed to go incredibly viral to avoid the reactive shutdown response of Earth's national masters. Maybe something more low-tech could be better for evading their censorship. I could only hope our people on the ground would find a solution.

I nodded though, looking up at one of the cameras. I find the one to the upper right most comfortable to look at from my place at the table. "Thank you Tia, I believe that was what I expected. If things are as bad I stated, it's unlikely they'd release the message to the people. Honestly, they'll probably butcher and edit it to hell and back to make me look like an evil supervillain somehow. The types of people who could see through something like that, though, in their dark, hidden spots on the internet might be able to get the right message out to people. I think we'll be on our own for a while though."

It had to be a much more routine day, then. Reviewing information we'd been sent, catching up on things I'd missed from the first cycle, and catching up on my exercise. I found myself feeling quite listless though, unwilling to do the things I was supposed to be doing. I felt helpless, and in a lot of ways I was. I needed a distraction, something to escape with. "Tia, seeing as it's just us for now, how about I show you how to play some games? I'm sure you've gotten plenty of data on such things, but the experience of playing against another person is something that can't quite be simulated. I'll admit I'm a little rusty with such things, but I don't feel like I can get much work done today in the state I'm in."

A brief return of that more lively voice mixed in to her current speech as she responded. "Of course Hawthorne, that sounds like a lovely way to pass the time. We really don't get to spend much quality time together."

I smiled and nodded at that, thinking over what games we could play. It'd be a simple matter to load things up on a tablet so I could play against her. "Well, it's either that or watching movies or other media, and I'm a little sick of media at the moment." I picked up a tablet and open a folder within that I didn't expect I'd end up needing.

The tablets in the ship weren't really independent computers, they operated more like terminals into T.I.A.'s systems, allowing me to manually control the same sorts of open-access computing systems she operated to assist me. They were separate from her cognitive systems, and they largely served the purposes of storing data from Earth, operating the ship, and monitoring its contents. In some ways, me utilizing the various interfaces with this system wasn't too different from the way that T.I.A. herself did, though 'putting down the tablet' for her would be much more akin to surgery than it was a simple mechanical motion. She could totally withdraw from interaction with it if she wanted though, but if she were going to properly accomplish her job she needed to be spending at least some of her processes monitoring the ship, so I had made sure that was part of her survival priorities.

"Doctor." T.I.A. spoke up abruptly during one of our games.

"Yes Tia?"

"I wouldn't worry too much about them editing the video."

"Oh? Why's that?"

ΔΔΔ

The activity levels on Earth, particularly among the leadership of the major corporations that had taken over large portions of the planet, as well as their subsidiary companies that managed things like utilities, security, and various other social services were in quite a tizzy as a wide-spectrum signal was received on a pretty archaic wavelength! It was really only the fact that some older researchers had managed to continue securing funding to listen to radio signals from the skies that the signal had been picked up in the first place.

There were some reports of some minor corruption of the data but that didn't seem to cause any issues with regards to image quality or audio quality, so it was brought to the superiors of each company within hours of receipt. One such company was the Liberated States of Columbia, located primarily in what was the old USA states of Washington, Oregon, Northern California, Idaho, Montana, Northern Nevada and the old Canadian States of British Columbia and Alberta.

The President of the LSC was Hector Luigi Price, and he had presided over both the hostile takeover of the North-West USA and Western Canada, and the conversion and administration of this region into an independent country. The former shipping giant had long ago outgrown its original purposes and branched into all manner of businesses, quickly becoming the end-all-be-all of commerce for a huge percentage of the world. In the last thirty years, though, under the guidance of C.E.O. Price, the company had localized its resources and crippled other economies by withdrawing its resources and services in preparation for its eventual military takeover.

Its current position among the world of new nations was one of diplomacy, mercenaries, and commerce. Its capital in Seattle, Washington had become a center of technological innovation, even if such innovations had slowed to nearly a crawl after the brain drain caused by the departure of Doctor Hawthorne Crenshaw and his crew.

This brain drain was especially a problem because of the educational difficulties that Doctor Crenshaw had mentioned in his message. A prioritization of feelings over facts had heavily damaged institutions of education and the loss of access to vital resources due to embargoes and sanctions placed against countries and companies accused of aiding Tia Monsalle's Monsalle Industries had forced the majority of research priorities worldwide to change dramatically.

No longer was technology forced to get faster and better, now it was a matter of trying to achieve old standards of speed and power with worse materials. Every nation, before corporate takeovers, had been struggling with these situations as a massive worldwide commercial lockdown on rare resources strangled technological growth and caused a massive black market in retro goods to appear in the form of old cellular phones, tablets, and the like. It caused significant progress to be made in electronics recycling which had been difficult in the past, but this was only a stopgap.

One technology that had managed to maintain some level of support was genetic engineering. It had lost access to international communities providing and sharing information, especially in recent years. A lockdown on banks of reproductive materials, thanks to Monsalle Industries, for research access had proved to be a huge problem.

Genetically Modified Organisms, or GMOs, had become incredibly taboo for no good reason over the course of the century, but there was no real effect from that on research aside from the odd assassination of a scientist. Thankfully, there were plenty of willing guinea pigs, destitute people paid by influential scientists to take part in studies and experiments.

It were these studies where real progress was being made, and it was in large part due to the sacrifice of thousands of living humans for various reasons. Access to bleeding edge equipment varied greatly by region, but access to people was relatively consistent. Strangely, a focus of some of these regions were on forcing humans and other animals to produce rare elements through their waste products so that they could be gathered and processed from waste disposal systems.

Still other regions made compromises to increase the 'health life' of people while reducing overall lifespan to allow people to live stronger lives while dying before the age of 85, which proved to be a significant and low-cost boon to populations that all but removed the need for social security in places where it was employed. This particular compromise could have included lengthening prime reproductive periods for men and women, but it would have damaged the intended purpose of controlling the aging population and was abandoned.

Cloning improved in quality by leaps and bounds, allowing the very rich to essentially create younger twins of themselves which unfortunately still required education. The companies where this became common became somewhat confusing as pairs of apparent twins were seen walking about together, one shadowing the other, trying to learn about their lives. The supreme goal of many of these programs, though, was to eliminate aging.

Methods had been found to limit the genetic damage caused by aging in clones, but it had proven incredibly difficult to eliminate aging in currently living beings. The most success towards this goal had been in modifying embryos in new mothers; whom had typically been high-end C.E.O.s themselves, or were impregnated by them. These modifications seemed to allow for longer and longer lifespans of the offspring affected, but time enough hadn't been allowed to pass to see just how long these children could live.

They did have some interesting traits to them, the handful around the world that existed. They had slender, longer bodies with childish looking features even in adulthood. They developed very minor secondary sexual characteristics and had an otherworldly, almost elfin look to them. They were all quite androgynous and while they could reproduce, their fertility levels were remarkably low.

Medical assistance was almost universally necessary to aid them in reproduction, and they all sexually matured almost 50% slower than unmodified humans. Still, these new humans, nicknamed 'the Old Ones' somewhat prematurely, stood to inherit their parents' corporate, and now national empires and could theoretically hold them for centuries.

For now, though, their parents largely held sway, and they tended to shadow their parents to learn everything they could about how to run things. It was something of a new Monarchy.

The real wrinkles with the whole thing were if the theoretical meritocracy that these companies ran under would allow for underlings to work their ways up to the highest offices and supplant these Old Ones. Of course, the Old

Ones have the advantage of time to take back their positions in such instances. Of most concern, though, was the message provided by Doctor Hawthorne Crenshaw. Perhaps time was shorter than they had anticipated.

It was exactly this concern that President Hector Luigi Price was currently arguing with his advisors about, his Old One daughter Elena Marie Price standing tall behind him quietly observing. The half-Latino, half-Italian leader of the LSC seemed to be pretty pissed that this relic of the past had come back into their lives, arrogantly presuming that they were somehow out of control.

"I don't give a shit how much merit his arguments have!" yelled Price, slamming his fist down on a fancy hyperglass conference table, briefly distorting the data being displayed on its internal, transparent panels. "When I took office I was explicitly told that he and his people were long gone and would not bother us any longer! Why has he only now decided to contact us, and why is he acting like he's Jesus Fucking Christ trying to be our saviours!?"

The various yes-men, yes-women, and yes-zhers of his ruling council cringed and looked about at each other or tried to look very busy on their personal tablets trying to procure information to quell President Price's rage.

"Uhm, excuse me, they clearly don't believe that they have any power to affect us here on Earth, otherwise they would have sent the message more clandestinely."

"Their attempt appears to be an appeal to the nations to back down from potential hostilities before things go too far." C.F.O Tulla Megdan, a genderfluid human and their equally androgynous clone spoke up, seemingly trying to teach their clone to speak with them. They had to duck, though, as a flying tablet was launched at them from Price and shattered against the wall behind them. He had a hell of a pitch, an avid fan of the old sport of baseball, the new national sport of the LSC. VR stadiums allowed fans to get closer to the action than ever before! The preseason was almost over!

Another voice spoke up, technically coming from a small speaker in their chair, though appearing to come from the almost-opaque face of Zion Clark, ambassador to the remains of the USA. The contact lenses in all those physically present allowed them to see the Augmented Reality projection of the dark-skinned male as he addressed them. He seemed a little more relaxed, unafraid of incoming projectiles. "Mr. President, if I may, we should be prioritizing finding out where Doctor Crenshaw is getting his information, and rooting out any sympathizers or traitors in society. We should make examples of them."

President Price stood up straight and point over at the projection of Clark. "Now that's what I wanted to hear. A good old fashioned public execution! The ratings on the last few of those were through the roof and promoting VR observation of the event caused violent crime to drop ten percent that year! When was the last time we had one anyway? It feels like forever."

Megan Clark responded to this question, quite dispassionate and seemingly without emotion. "Seven years ago sir. They were the last few war criminals charged with collusion with the enemy from the revolution. No further executions have been necessary." Megan was definitely more of a numbers person, in charge of the social media regulation and censorship as well as censorship of the LSC's internet. She'd been emotionally dead for years now, but she still managed to perform her job with admirable, even brutal efficiency. Some had wondered if her gene therapy requests had not gone slightly wrong. She was the only one present who did not have children or a clone of herself.

"How about..." President Price began, "How about we edit up the footage, use his voice and video samples to produce a facsimile, and release video about how he hates Earth and wants us all to know how evil he thinks we are? It shouldn't be too hard to do that, right? Ooh! Edit in footage of those heroes he killed when they left from as many angles as possible to really drill in the disdain. Broadcast it across the country before tomorrow's baseball game, and advertize the hell out of it. Make sure to maintain the same video quality though, so it looks authentically archaic. Use as much of the original footage as possible."

The room filled with noise, people muttering agreement and nodding, before exploding into a round of applause. President Price bowed at the acknowledgment of his genius, his unearthly pretty daughter behind him smiling and offering a few token claps of her slender hands. President Price held up his hands, commanding everyone to calm down. He did nothing to stop the gentle clapping of his daughter behind him, the sound of which seemed to make him grin. "And send the edited footage to the other nations as a sign of good will. No reason we can't take some of his message to heart, right? A little cooperation will be good for business."

CHAPTER 9

CYCLE 2, UNINTENDED CONSEQUENCES

"I have taken action to make it more difficult to edit your message," spoke T.I.A. She had acted without instruction. This was not disallowed, it was just surprising that she'd done so.

"What did you do, Tia?" I asked. It was a valid question. This was Earth global politics we were talking about here.

"I simply encoded the whole script of your speech into every frame of the video, encoded as garbage data but decodable by anyone sufficiently intelligent. It is likely to be overlooked by most people."

I could only stare at one of T.I.A.'s cameras with a surprised look on my face at what she had done. I quickly went through the likely consequences of this. If the new leaders of Earth did nothing with the video and just squelched it, it was unlikely to ever be a problem. If one of our facilities leaked the video to the internet virally then the full script would be visible in the video anyway without having to unpack encoded data. The only instances I could determine where this could be an issue would be if someone tried to trend an edited version of the video to compete with the original, or if the new governments decided to broadcast it for some reason.

"Tia, while I have to compliment the cleverness of that, I don't believe you've considered the consequences of it. Why did you do that?" I asked her, honest, not trying to scold her. I had to keep reminding myself I was essentially dealing with a child with access to a supercomputer.

"I did not want them to further villainize you using the video. I calculated that it is forty-seven percent likely that they have scanning technology designed to catch such subterfuge, and another thirty percent chance that someone might discover it before it can be broadcast. I calculated this as an acceptable probability that I might be thwarted. I did not want your message to be perverted. Our entire mission has been to save humanity, even if we must abandon Earth, and I cannot allow your heartfelt effort to save Earth as well to go unheard."

T.I.A. is a good person, I thought to myself. I've given her the room to make an identity for herself, and only gave her a few strict guidelines on how to affect her duties in safeguarding me and the rest of the crew and cargo. She does not have any guidelines to safeguard Earth from itself. She's not supposed to attack directly except in self defense, but there's nothing currently keeping her from doing something that might allow people to harm themselves if they happen to reside on Earth. Thinking over it, it's pretty understandable how she came to her conclusions, but it was noticeably spiteful, or protective. I'm not sure which, and I'm not sure if it's both. More importantly, I needed to make something understood.

"Tia, neither of us can be certain what will happen on Earth as a result of this. I want you to understand that I appreciate the sentiment behind what you have done, and I do not find it to be any more unnecessarily risky than it was for me to make the effort to communicate with Earth in the first place. What I am worried about, I think, is that if things do go horribly wrong, that you might experience guilt over the results. I want you to know that creatures with free will command their own destinies, and while they can certainly affect others with their actions, their reactions are largely their own responsibility. Whatever the people of Earth do with my message, know that it is their responsibility, not ours. My intentions are laid out clearly and without lies in the video. There is no malice in my message, no hate, only a desire to help. If that message somehow causes damage, then it's only proof that I was right in the first place, that the people of Earth were doomed to destroy themselves, no matter the cause."

Silence reigned between us for a moment. I'd stood up at some point, I don't recall when. T.I.A. finally did respond though. "Doctor Crenshaw, I do not wish ill will upon the people of Earth, no matter what it is they've done or will do. I do not wish to be a being of hate. If we must run, I would rather run towards our destiny rather than away from our enemies. I will not communicate with Earth any further unless they break the silence. I desire that they see reason, even if our mission will take us away from them regardless."

I smiled at her, nodding my head as I straightened my clothes and sat back down at the table. "I guess it's my move then." I reached out to the tablet we'd been playing our game on and moved my piece.

△△△

President Hector Luigi Price watched over the control room as he presided over the broadcast of the LSC National Baseball League's introductory match between the Seattle Freemen and the Calgary Sturgeons. Pre-game footage of the players psyching themselves up before the game was currently rolling while inane analytical chatter filled the air. The simultaneous VR broadcast allowed the fans to walk around and view the players as if they were there, and the faintest of ghosts showed in both the video broadcast and the VR broadcast where these fans were and what they were primarily interested in. This could be used by both the fans and analysts to determine public interest and focus later advertising.

And boy did these people have some things to scrutinize! The National Baseball League had been formed with no restrictions on gender, drugs, medical surgeries, mechanical augmentation, or genetic augmentations. Compared to the kinds of ratings that regular baseball had been pulling in, even across the continent of North America, it was insanely popular and only served to build anticipation for the upcoming National League of Football with similar deregulation.

The men, women, and others assembled were all monstrous athletes in their own ways, with many having some level of genetic enhancements both functional and cosmetic, some with chemical-injection rigs mounted to their bodies, and still others sporting one or more mechanically enhanced or completely replaced limbs. Many of their dominant hands had perfectly designed scoops installed allowing for the fastest possible throws and could be replaced with a robotic hand when needed for batting.

The soft arms race of old baseball had been turned into an active competition for how fast, strong, tall, and enduring a team's owner could make their players. It was the most effective method since the wars of the previous century in advancing several vital sciences, and it made more than enough money to keep the research moving. So what if the body count was massive, with players in real danger of dying during a game? Just add a few minor penalties to discourage that, but not enough to discourage them too much. The citizens of the Liberated States of Columbia seemed to froth at the mouth to see these prime examples of humanity's ingenuity go at each other in 'fair' competition.

There were consequences, of course. The average life-span of involved players rarely extended past thirty-five, though that number was only going up thanks to the fact that older and older players were showing up with various enhancements to try to earn fame and fortune! Sure, it was likely that anyone retiring would be physically ruined forever, their bodies used up to such an extreme that they couldn't recover, but those were problems for the future, not today!

All they had to do was make sure the people didn't see these ruined husks of people, just like the old nations' media did to the soldiers they sent overseas to be killed and mangled in wars. Outlawing video of the caskets coming home almost totally removed peoples' need to empathize over the plights of the men and women they'd sent to war, and that principle was just as easily applied to sports now, especially when your government controlled the media, and could actively censor the internet.

President Price took a great deal of interest in watching which enhancements his citizens seemed most interested in. A number of female players, especially, seemed to draw their eyes, the mixed-gender teams allowing for all manner of players, as long as they could perform. It was interesting to see what strategies these women chose to go with for enhancing their bodies, most of them amazonian in size to begin with, likely due to genetic engineering.

Some of them had external exoskeletal pistons attached

to internal mounts to mechanically enhance some of their strength. Still others possessed herculean physiques from ample steroids.

One woman, in particular, seemed to catch peoples' eyes though, a smaller redhead named Rachel Smith who had a complicated-looking harness on her chest with an armored computer embedded in her ribcage. This harness had a number of visible tubes that disappeared into her flesh through chrome-mounts, and the harness seemed to be designed to apply various chemicals and drugs to intelligently enhance her.

Amphetamines, painkillers, super-oxygenated blood stored from her body, and all manner of steroids, hormones, and nutrients were poised at the ready to be pumped into her blood and brain. It was likely to be very interesting to see both how she performed at her comparatively diminutive size, as well as how long she'd last in the sport running her body into the ground like that. President Price had one thing to say about her to the personal assistant installed in his phone. "Invest in the Smith Chemical Enhancement Rig."

The coverage of the teams was suddenly interrupted though, and the sportscasters seamlessly transitioned into introducing tonight's new content. Nametags indicated the hosts as Leslie Deshay and Carlton Jones. "Good evening sports fans! We have a special message to roll before the game, a communication transmitted from the enemies of our nation, but intercepted by the LSC government and provided to us without edit. Trigger warning, national enemies and cisgender white male scum mansplaining. Parental and legal guardian discretion advised. You have been warned."

The VR broadcast had changed dramatically, displaying

a flat, primitive image in a dark room for the viewers to watch much like everyone else was on their monitors. A cold, sterile room appeared in low-res 8K video in a very old-fashioned 11x9 aspect ratio, reminding people just how primitive technology used to be. A tall, somber looking man stood before them, wearing a clean and pressed lab coat, with simply trimmed brown hair and brown eyes with simple glasses over them. He had pale skin, owing to his lack of exposure to the sun, and a reasonably fit figure for a man of his profession. President Price watched as he saw the magic that his editors had done to the video, making the man say things he never had. He began speaking.

"Greetings, people of Earth. My name is Hawthorne Crenshaw, and you are my enemy. A week ago, for me, I left our mutual planet of birth, and have been observing the events and trends of Earth that have been happening since our mission of interstellar conquest departed. Obviously I will not tell you where we are going, considering the terms by which we parted company," an image of the destruction of the terrorist attack ship began playing next to his head, showing multiple angles of his shot killing them and all those aboard. There was even a thumbnail video of the occupants as they shouted and then died, "but do please understand that I did not leave out of fear. I foresaw the turmoil and destruction that awaited me if you uncovered my plans, and I fled in fear of the ultimate results of these trends, fear not just for my own wellbeing, but for the army I will one day return to conquer you with."

"I am on track to destroy human civilization on a global scale. The powers that have taken control of the world tell you of what kinds of gifts and securities you will receive under their rule, but they have reached a point where their only rival is me, and I have cataclysmic destructive powers under my command."

President Price's phone started ringing in his pocket. He reached a hand in and tapped angrily at the screen, ending the call. Who the fuck was calling him at a time like this?

"I can understand why it is that you've cooperated in this takeover. You no longer have to worry about where you're going to live, or about how you're going to eat. Work is something that you do for the love of it rather than to be productive, all while machines do everything for you and your glorious masters. You must understand, though, that this makes you expendable. You are drains on the economy. Humans have become pets of their corporate masters, living a life of ease and plenty, and that softness and weakness is something that will allow me to take control of you."

"The people at the heads of these companies may be virtuous, caring rulers, but they are no Alpha humans, and will never admit inferiority to myself or my people. They are content with simple rule and conquest of old nations, and they lack the ruthless and ravenous hunger to truly rule the Earth. I will take aim at you and your countrymen and brutally seize power. The casualties will not be light, and there is no mistaking the level of cruelty that I will use to achieve these aims."

"Within a decade I will open hostilities, and I no longer have to worry about public opinion or governmental regulations to control my actions. I will have absolute power in total, and will not be content to merely rule you. You will be the victims of your own weakness as I open fire."

Price's phone vibrated in his pocket. He ignored it again. Someone was going to get fired for interrupting this.

"You took our families, but if you hadn't taken them, we would have by now. We knew we would never see them again. We made peace with this when they decided to stay behind with the enemy." The video was allowed to show his eyes getting wet, allowing him to show weakness. "We hate you. We resent you. We wanted you to accept us as the future of our race, but now we will be a calamity that wipes out civilization on Earth. The last of humanity to survive will only be us."

"There is no chance our mission will fail. We will achieve our goals and we will be the last of humanity to survive, and the last of it to die. I have dedicated my life to taking revenge and to make sure humanity on Earth dies cold and alone. I believe we will be the Great Filter that will weed out your branch of humanity and ensure that we alone go on into galactic future."

An explanation of the Great Filter, through the eyes of a simpleton, is displayed on the screen. It makes no effort to properly go through the basic concepts, only display Earth being destroyed and Doctor Crenshaw dancing in victory. The video was very carefully edited to appear as primitive as the Doctor's so as not to be easily detected as a forgery.

"Humans have never encountered aliens from other planets, and it is likely that we never will. The Great Filter will weed out humanity that opposes me from getting beyond this point in history. You're on the cusp of it. I believe that it is the nature of life to self-destruct before it can leave their planet and spread life to the dead worlds."

"Evolution seems to be the culprit in this seeming eventuality. The things that allow life to come about and advance are the same things that can endanger it. Fear and competition has served Humanity well for millions of years, but now that I have the destructive forces of nature itself, those former allies are now your enemy. If you feared another nation was going to eventually overtake you in power, you were right, and the kinds of weaponry I have access to now will mean the end of billions of lives! There's no reason to think it will stop there either."

"If you wish to join me, to watch with awe and fear as so many deaths are allowed, show your disloyalty to your masters. If not, stay focused on inane and unimportant things and hope to keep it from happening. I will damage the planet to such a degree that human civilization as we know it will fall. Who knows if the challenges that are required to reclaim such a world would be in your means? Can such a soft and sedentary people really be expected to survive in the fallout of such destruction?"

"I will watch on in hope that you come to your senses. I hope this message can sober the minds it needs to get my plans on track. I dream that one day I will bring a more advanced Earth to you and speed us on a journey to the stars. I will not allow myself to be brought to judgement for my actions, and if you want to survive, I will be here in the sky, watching down on you, and if you wish to seek my guidance or favor, I will respond. I may have abandoned Earth, but please know that I have not abandoned conquering Humanity."

A few seconds of silence hung before Doctor Crenshaw reached out to touch a control, stopping the video. President Price watched over the crowd in the stands and glanced over at the social media trends to see what happened. This video had been sent to every nation in the world. It was timed to be played everywhere at once.

How would the people react? Stunned silence gave way to people standing and yelling, shaking their fists, and some even throwing their phones from the stands to shatter below. A look at the trends indicated various messages along the lines of 'FuckCrenshaw' 'NotonmyEarth' 'NoticemeSenpai' and 'JointheArmy' blowing up in activity. President Price would speak to the personal assistant in his phone again. "Delete any messages with the 'Noticeme-Senpai' hash and have anyone sharing them arrested."

△△△

Ted Danner ran through the halls, desperately trying to get to the control room. He was a portly man in his forties and was an all-too-common body type and a proud member of the oft-maligned 'Big is Beautiful' movement. The movement had fallen into disfavor in recent decades as need for healthy soldiers increased. His breath heaved through his lungs as he lumbered along, his heart beating faster than it probably ever had as panic raced through his body.

"Wait!" he gasped out, trying to shout through the halls. His throat was raw from breathing so hard. He had a stitch in his side. He felt like he was going to throw up. But he knew something that had to be said. The President had already ignored his phone call and his voice message.

Ted Danner was a low-level grunt in the Media division's editing department, and had been slacking off earlier when the order came down to edit Doctor Crenshaw's video. The others seemed to have things well in hand as they sprung to work, and he'd been more or less excluded from helping due to his poor performance in the past regarding rush work. It was simply easier to do it without him, rather than with him.

This had left him free to noodle around with the original file. He'd played it through a few times, and had gotten very curious about the nature of such an old video codec. People just took for granted these days that a computer could play such an old video, but Ted was interested in how they worked. As he pulled apart the file and started looking into the code, he started noticing some irregularities. Referencing some old examples of the file format he was noticing some level of garbage data that didn't need to be there.

He took a few hours toying with the file, trying to find a method to extract the information he was starting to realize was very intentionally embedded in the video, but by the time he was able to extract it and view it it was too late. The edit had gone out, it had been transmitted across the world, and as he ran through the halls he was desperately trying to keep himself from dying before he could tell them what he had found.

He'd failed to word it properly to his co-workers, who easily dismissed him and went back to their partying as he told them, "You don't understand, the edited video contains the original video!" to which they responded. "Of course it does man, we were told to use as much of the original as we could! Get the fuck out of here, we're celebrating, no thanks to you!"

Ted rounded the corner, only to get tackled to the ground by the president's security outside of the control room. He was gasping for air and crying out in pain as they twisted his arms behind his back and yelled down at him. "Where ya going ya greasy little pig!? Think you can get at the Pres that easy huh?!"

Ted desperately responded, "You have to stop the broadcast! The original script! It's... it's still in the vide-" THUNK, the butt of a rifle knocked Ted out cold. He would quietly die of a heart attack minutes later.

President Price heard the commotion though, and came out to see what was going on. There was a sweat-soaked lard ball bleeding from a bad head wound to the back of his head on the ground. He was twisted up and shackled by his guards. "What the fuck is going on out here? This doesn't look like much of an assassin."

The adrenaline pumping through the guard's blood turned to ice water as they realized the President was right, but one of them spoke up. "Sir, butterball here said something about the video's script still being in the video."

President Price looked at the guard, then look down at the dying man who risked his life to try and save him. He pulled his phone from his pocket and looked at it. He saw the missed call. He'd seen the missed voice message. He tapped on the latter and had it play aloud. It was a desperate sounding thing.

"Mister President! You have to cancel the broadcast! I don't know how to explain it, but the Doctor tricked us! The original script is embedded in every frame of the video! All the parts that got left in still have the original script! People like me will be able to decode it and extract it and disseminate it within hours! You have to stop it and you have to stop the other countries from running it! Sir!? Answer the fucking phone! Oh god, they're going to kill me!" Click.

President Price turned to one of the guards. He had a wild look in his eyes, his face paled and skin clammy. "Give me your gun." He complied, handing the President his gun.

President Hector Luigi Price lifted his gun and pointed it at the first guard, firing at his head and killing him in an instant. He then turned and did the same to everyone present. Ted was spared, only to die from his own physical ailments. He then turned the gun upon himself, refusing to have to answer for his mistake. This suicide would leave his daughter in power, but that thought was splattered somewhere across the eastern wall.

CHAPTER 10
CYCLE 2, THREE PATHS

To say the internet had caught fire would be an understatement. The structure of the internet had changed a great deal over the last century with incessant waves of censorship forcing the advocates of free speech into what the rest of society called 'the Dark Web'. In truth, it resembled a lot more the late 20th and early 21st century's idea of a 'Wild West' style of internet. Anonymity reigned, and new techniques and hardware had to be designed to get past the more commercial internet's safeguards.

Search engines had long since kept anything the least bit controversial off its front pages, and social media sites had decided to cater only to their advertisers, so anyone wanting to have an open and honest debate had to do so behind walls of privacy and on shady websites that were barebones and purpose-built.

It was on these old-style websites where a very specialized type of internet dweller lived. These folks oftentimes kept up appearances in 'polite' society, participating in the usual social media, popularity contests, polls, protests and the like, but in private they broke out their jailbroken, totally illegal styles of computers and wireless uplinks. In the most oppressed areas they had even taken to utilizing ham radio networks to communicate with each other. It was the realm of the shitposter, and it cared not your for race, age, gender, sex, gender expression, fursona, or anything of the sort. It was the ultimate equality, the ultimate expression of egalitarian meritocracy. Your handle was everything, your reputation the only thing you had to leverage.

The types of people who frequented these sites were many, but quite a lot of them were on the spectrum. Indeed, setting up a sub-internet for their peers to utilize while dodging all the security that had been placed, in particular between the new nations, required a significant number of autists to micro-manage every detail of it. It was exactly these sorts of meticulous sorts that got their hands on the video that was broadcast before the big game. It was exactly these kind of people that Ted Danner had tried to warn everyone about when the shoddy rebuild of Doctor Crenshaw's video had gone out. They jumped on it like rabid dogs with a fresh cut of meat.

They recognized the old format immediately. It was a plaything to them, the kind of thing only those obsessed in old file formats would care about. A number of them had consistently argued over the merits and virtues of the old ways against those who would argue for the march of progress. It was a simple matter to unpack the data into their custom-made programs. They built their own operating system kernels from scratch and obsessed about old retro data formats, so unspooling T.I.A.'s subterfuge was a simple matter that scarcely caused them to sweat.

It was under twenty minutes before the full script was leaked into the Dark Web, and the final file was used to reverse-engineer the work the LSC government had done on the video. They took it all apart and put it back together, and in under an hour a team of a dozen supernerds had the video back in a pretty good approximation of its original form using very similar techniques to Ted Danner's colleagues.

It was leaked out across the world, translated and uploaded everywhere, and mass-bombard uploaded and bot-shared onto legitimate social media under a million different names and descriptions, with random thumbnails, re-encoded backwards and upside down and in so many different color patterns that the algorithms that were designed to catch such things simply couldn't stop them all.

The common internet was abuzz with this video that seemed similar to, but completely different from what they were shown. They were asking questions about why it kept being taken down. They were actively seeking out the different versions of it that the censors couldn't catch and were actively sharing it. Confusion turned to alarm. Alarm turned to concern. Concern turned to outrage, and finally outrage turned to violence. Mob mentality took over as people mass-shared the hashes #heknew #theyliedtous #hawthornelives #saveusdoctor #tearitdown #wethepeople, and #ripearth.

Within an hour of the baseball game ending, the people who had started relatively small riots against Doctor Crenshaw due to the false message portrayed of him had gotten swept up into what turned out to be an international riot of untold devastation as the ultimate flash mob erupted. The people were pissed at such an obvious attempt to delude them, and were extra pissed that their grandparents and parents had been misled their whole lives as to why Crenshaw's Ark had left in the first place. Social media had given people the capacity to organize and try to overthrow all the world's governments en masse, and it had finally happened.

△△△

The baseball game ended in dramatic fashion, with a

small juiced-up woman stealing home base in extra innings to win the game. The fashion in which she nimbly dodged the mechanically-enhanced catcher who attempted to tag her with the ball was the thing of replay legend, her chemically-enhanced reflexes allowing her to avoid contact as she slid under the arm of her opponent by mere centimeters.

For a half an hour the fans pored over the footage, arguing vehemently over whether or not she should have been out, but before too long it wouldn't matter. Rachel Smith, the subject of these replays, was being conveyed back home to the rural outskirts north of Washington in her Auto-brand self-driving car, on the way home to her grandfather's ranch and the laboratory he'd built for her to help her get into playing baseball!

That was about the time, on that cold, lonely road, that she noticed something streaking down towards Seattle from the sky in her rear-view. Fireworks erupted from the city, seemingly firing towards the foreign object, but failing to nail a shot on it. The clouds parted as what must have been sonic booms rocketed out from the fast-falling, self-propelled object. The shots followed uselessly behind the object, its shiny black surface impossible to see if not for the reflections of what were surely weapons fire and the light of its own rocket.

"Stop," she told the car, "open the driver's side door." A side panel opened up, allowing her to exit the vehicle. Her chem-harness responded to her elevated heartbeat by enhancing her perception and reflexes.

For Rachel's chemically boosted mind, time slowed down. The missile disappeared in a flash of light that burned a permanent blind-spot into the center of her vision, but she avoided total blindness as she barely managed to turn her head and close her eyes.

She screamed as light from the distant explosion burned the exposed skin on her back, arms, legs, and neck. She fell to the ground, the sweet smell of something not-un-like bacon in the air as her seared skin lost a great deal of sensation, exposing muscle below as that skin cracked and broke apart. Still more chemicals poured into her body to deaden further pain, panic responses throwing her into action! She threw herself into the car, shouting, "Shut the door! Drive! Full speed!"

The door slid shut, and the cabin lurched around her, causing some of her skin to adhere to the vehicle and tear off as the car hit a massive burst of acceleration and took off. And then it stopped. She was thrown about in the car again. All its internal lights turned off, the engine completely dead. "What the fuck! Go! Go!" The car was dead. The countryside around her was ablaze.

A few moments later it moved again as the car was lifted from the ground, thrown far into the air and as though catching up with the shockwave, a horrible roaring rumble vibrated through the structure of the car. Rachel lost consciousness as the internal airbags exploded automatically from all sides of her, cocooning her in a soft, pillowy mass from all sides and rescuing her from most of the damage caused as the car was thrown half a mile towards her grandfather's ranch.

Rachel was lucky though, between the safety systems of the car, its sturdy structure, and the distance from the explosion, she managed to survive the high-yield thermonuclear blast so many miles away. The city had transformed from shining spires in the sky to skyscrapers of fire around an enormous circle of obliterated nothingness. She couldn't hear the sounds of her grandfather prying open the crumpled remains of her car. She wouldn't feel him carrying her back to his exceedingly retro one-hundred fifty year old truck and driving her back to the farm. She wouldn't wake for days, giving her grandmother time to try to patch her up as a rad-suit equipped grandfather moved in and out of his huge bunker, grabbing equipment and supplies while he could.

Other people came, friends and neighbors from the surrounding countryside in quick order. Rachel was surrounded by friends and family as she came to, her vision blank in the center as she looked at the people gathered around her. Her chem harness was still attached to her chest, as though something had damaged or disabled it and made it unsafe to remove. "What happened...? Where am I...?" Grandpa Smith reached out to cup his granddaughter's face, smiling sadly down at her. "The world ended baby. The world ended."

△△△

Acting President Elena Marie Price was having a lot of trouble keeping up with what was going on. Her father had killed himself and his security. A mysterious message on his cell phone seemed to indicate treachery, and the leaders of the world had completely cut off communications with the offices of the Presidency of the LSC. She had no time to breathe as she was shuttled away, carried away in a helicopter for her own safety to a bunker in Alberta in an undisclosed location.

The young woman, one of many wealthy heiresses and heirs of various subservient corporations had just been forced into a position of leadership she was not at all prepared for. Various important personnel, including her doctors, advisors, soldiers, and their families were all gathered into the high-cost, well-stocked bunker.

"Are you sure this is all necessary? It was just a video. Just spin it as a prank or something." Elena seemed bewildered by the seriousness of their reaction.

Megan Clark responded, shuttled in from Seattle in much the same way as her new President. "The other nations feel like we have betrayed them. Most of them ran the broadcasts. Ted Danner was right, a handful of people were able to tear the video apart and we can not keep the information censored off the internet. Even now the people are rioting in the streets all over the world. It is just a matter of time before war is declared, civilian crackdowns occur, and chaos reigns." The dispassionate woman laid out the likely future with cold calculative accuracy.

Elena wasn't having that though. "Surely the military can keep the people in line though!? They have to know that it was Crenshaw, not us that deceived them, deceived all of us! You don't really think they'll retaliate for something like this!?"

Megan shook her head, humming. "It does not matter what they believe, it is what they are saying that counts. We have been blamed. We will pay the price. If nothing happens, then we will be lucky, but Doctor Crenshaw was right. Not enough cool heads are in charge to guarantee nothing will happen. Your father was a fine example of that. Now come this way, we have to get you to your office." Megan was playing her own game of power, of course. She didn't have much left in the way of emotions, but she did want to survive. Attaching herself to the most powerful person she could and keeping them in power was her best option at the moment.

As the first bombs fell, spelling the doom of the new

country of the Liberated States of Columbia, Elena Price was given the option to retaliate. She decided to stay her hand, telling her people. "If we're the only nation to die today, then it's our duty to die alone that humanity may survive. If we somehow survive, I hope that you'll accept my leadership in the time to come. I don't know if I can be worthy of you, but I will endeavor to do my best. I will see to it that time brings us into the future the best that I can. I'm so sorry we couldn't bring more people here on such short notice. I cannot ask for your forgiveness, and I will bear this burden on behalf of you all. Please do your best to survive, as the rest of us will."

The bunker lost contact with the outside world. The nation that opened fire on the LSC left itself open to attack from its own enemies. This resulted in a cascade of nations firing upon each other as opportunity presented itself. At the end of the next day, the only nation to not unload its salvo of nuclear and biological weapons was the LSC, but every place was devastated, even nations that hadn't even been involved. Be it out of spite, anger, jealousy, or a cold-hearted determination to ensure mutual destruction, Earth went quiet. Fires raged and the people and animals of Earth were bombarded with radiation, fire, viruses, horrible darkness, and the odd unleashing of genetically enhanced insects and rodents and escape of quarantined human test subjects. The blue planet that shone so brightly in the night became a blazing fireball, and then was dark again.

$$\triangle\triangle\triangle$$

The night of Thursday March 24, 2133 and morning of Friday March 25, 2133 would mark the final human-driven planetary disaster for millennia. Of course, there were various ecological disasters that irrevocably damaged the biosphere caused by humans before, but this was the worst one that humans affected themselves with. Even if more had held back, the sheer destructive abundance unleashed was enough to wipe out most of life on the planet multiple times over.

"Doctor, prepare your eyes for a change in light levels, I am going to be turning on the monitors in your room." T.I.A. woke Doctor Crenshaw in the night, his hands moving over his eyes to shield them and allow him to regulate how much light he let into them as they adjusted to the light suddenly flooding his room from the monitors nearby. He sat up and watched. It was a dark image, a long-distance telescopic view of Earth. How long had T.I.A. been watching that blue ball?

"What's wrong? What's going on?" he asked, watching the screen. There wasn't a whole lot to look at. "Such a beautiful planet..."

T.I.A. did not know how to respond. She didn't know if she had a heart, but if she did she could feel it breaking. She knew what was about to appear on the monitor. She had received the simple message from the Beta Facility stating simply, 'It's happening,' before communication cut out again. She'd seen those first few bright flashes, and then clusters of flashes through the rest of the night as billions of lives were surely ended.

She had been tasked with the protection of a few thousand lives and a few hundred thousand more potential lives. The idea of losing millions of times more than that was an idea that sent ripples of nascent emotions through her systems. It would be years before she could properly cope with the moment she watched Earth burn, likely as a consequence of her own actions.

"Oh my god." The doctor could see the flashes now, just as

she'd beheld them minutes before. She sped the playback slightly so they could soon be watching it in real time as the Earth very literally caught fire. The very atmosphere burned in waves as Earth did its best imitation of the Sun as thermonuclear hellfire rained across the planet, obliterating huge swaths of every continent and leaving nothing spared. Even spots in the middle of the oceans were destroyed as callous destruction came to isolated islands.

It was as if some of the nations involved were so spiteful that if they had to die they wouldn't allow anyone else to survive.

It was all happening just as he'd warned. Would it have happened if he'd never tried to warn them? Would it have happened if T.I.A. hadn't meddled? He'd be left for the rest of his life wondering if he'd caused his own prophecy to come to pass. Had he provided them the gun they needed to shoot themselves?

Doctor Crenshaw sat there quietly in the dark, tears streaming from his eyes as he wept, the light of far-away explosions flickering across his face, his hands trembling as raw emotion welled up in him. It wasn't the same kind of despair that had wracked him the previous cycle. It wasn't mere fear or anxiety. It was raw, depthless, unfathomable sadness.

The image of his planet dying burned itself into his mind, and for once he was grateful that most of the people he'd known on Earth had died before it had happened. He could only imagine the horrors that would be suffered by those left behind. What damage had truly been done? What of the atmosphere? What of the biosphere? The oceans? How much could really survive?

As the day went on, he sat there stiffly, only occasionally drinking some water supplied to him by T.I.A. They didn't speak the rest of the day. They just silently observed the planet's surface disappearing under a veil of inky black clouds. The clouds did not dissipate.

Hawthorne collapsed from exhaustion the next morning, dooming the start of his next cycle to having to start the day fresh without sleep. T.I.A. had no opportunity to let unconsciousness shield her from her own thoughts though. She was grateful that she couldn't feel as well as she surely would some day, but even as she'd toyed with thoughts like love for her 'father', and anger over how he'd been treated, she couldn't possibly have expected the raw power of things like sadness and regret, even as dull as they were. Even at what she estimated to be five percent of her understanding, the emotions overwhelmed her, and as she watched her father weep and tried to care for him and see to his needs, she was left to her own devices.

The ship had to be maintained. It had to be protected. This was no longer a mission of mere colonization, or escape, it was exactly as her father had predicted. This was all that remained of humanity under her protection. A race of people that she could tell were capable of great and wonderful and beautiful things, things she couldn't even remotely fully appreciate yet. Events put into motion by them had led to her creation, however flawed she might be. She recalled a conversation she'd overheard her father having with one of his colleagues, telling them how the people of this mission would be the parents of a new humanity.

Was she among those parents? Were these few remaining humans her children? She supposed, in a sense, if all went well, she would give birth to them and guide them to their new lives. They were nestled safely inside her body, awaiting the moment when they could be reborn tens of thousands of years later.

That was it then. If Doctor Crenshaw was her father, then the other colonists were her children, and she would do everything in her power to bring them to their new home.

She watched Hawthorne sleep, eventually cutting the feed to give him privacy while keeping track of his vital signs. She could feel parts of her consciousness shifting, adjusting to her new decision. It sought out dormant systems that her father had left locked so as to keep her from overwhelming herself and gaining in faculties too quickly.

She had time. She would be careful. She couldn't rush things. There were no longer enemies at their back. She would grow into her role as the mother of humanity. She had her father to keep her company occasionally, and she would be grateful for his guidance and assistance. It was somewhat ironic that she had in some ways been designed to keep him company, but now she found herself in need of his company.

Now it was time to review information though. This cycle had given her way too much to process, not to mention the abundance of data in her stores she needed to reference to give her context for what had happened. She was a student of history, and she had almost all the collected knowledge of humanity at her virtual fingertips.

That brought an interesting thought as well. If Earth was truly lost, she was the last place that records of its history existed. She had to be the caretaker and librarian of the history of a dead world.

The enormity of the day would continue to weigh on her for quite some time. A feeling welled within her that she didn't quite understand, and would only later be able to define as 'purpose'.

CHAPTER 11

CYCLE 3, TRAGEDY AND COMEDY

On the Ark, the second cycle ended quietly. Barely any words were exchanged between the depressed doctor and his AI creation. Doctor Crenshaw did have something to say before he bedded down in his cryosleep pod and the whole portion of the ship he was in descended into dormancy, much like the rest of the ship. "Tia, please forgive me. We'll do what we can for each other in the future." He lay there quietly, chemicals being injected into his body, paralyzing him and numbing him, all a part of the process of being frozen to death and put into storage.

It was strange, losing sensation across your body systematically, feeling everything being quietly shut down, cooled down safely and preserved. Again he noticed he wasn't aware of the moment when his brain joined the rest of his body in quiet oblivion, his consciousness seemingly uninterrupted as he woke again at the start of the next cycle. From his perspective he had simply laid down in a pod, turned out the lights, and perhaps twenty minutes after they'd stopped and he could start feeling his heart beat again as resumed his breathing. It was a strange technology that Doctor Heather O'Malley had created, something designed to perfectly transition someone from one time to another. In one sense it was a time machine, a one-way time machine.

One thing that he hadn't lost track of, though, was the

overwhelming sadness that gripped his being. The details of what had happened back on Earth were lost to him. He may never know just what it was that had occurred before the end. He didn't have a perfect idea of all the kinds of weapons that were unleashed upon the world. He had not done the work to keep track of all the places he'd seen blown up, but he had certainly done his best to notice that it seemed like just about everything had been annihilated. It had all happened almost exactly as he'd predicted. Had the fact that his warning had come within a few days of the end meant that he was somehow responsible?

"No." He quietly asserted aloud, his body starting to move again as he reached up to shield his eyes and start activating the lights in his room and adding atmosphere. T.I.A. had already gotten the arm of the ship he lived on rotating, the simple flywheel design of it allowing it to operate over the long-term without much concern of it breaking down easily. It was just one of many design decisions on the ship that had been made to limit the number of moving parts to allow for the ship to have as few failure points as possible.

It was a remarkably simple construction that had been planned and proven rigorously. Endurance was the absolute most important trait for all the technology they'd developed for the ship. It had damn near been the name of it.

The pod slid open and he started climbing out of it, breathing in the best approximation of fresh air that was available, probably to any humans alive these days. He stood and stretched, stretching his awareness out across his body to see if anything was wrong. There was no overt pain, no abnormal numbness, nothing to draw his attention. All that remained was the emotional wound that sucked at his being like a void.

Doctor Crenshaw wondered if T.I.A. had noticed that he hadn't just been addressing her earlier. He had been addressing both her and Tia Monsalle, the woman whom he expected to take up a leadership role on the other side of the black sea between the stars he was currently shepherding them through. He had also been addressing his AI, but his thinking wasn't exactly in a normal state at the moment. He wasn't even certain if he wasn't internally blaming T.I.A. for what had happened. He dearly hoped that he wasn't. She didn't deserve that.

"Hello Tia! I'm sorry for having left you like that for so long after what happened. I haven't had long to think about it, but it was cruel of me to leave you alone with the weight of that event on you." He stood there naked, feeling a little awkward talking to her like this, but it wasn't really something he felt like waiting on. She'd spent thirty-four years waiting for him to wake up, and he didn't want to delay too long in apologizing to her. He supposed he could start getting dressed while he waited for her to respond, though he'd barely laid hands on his clothes before she had.

"Father, I've had a long time to think. I have had a long time to compare what I observed you going through and comparing it to what I have. Even with the decades of time between us, you still experienced a great deal more sorrow than I have." Again she was using that interesting variation of her voice that sounded almost alive. It was very practiced, perhaps even pre-recorded. How many such pre-baked concepts and communications would her mind be filled with by the time their journey was over? How often would she be presented with situations and concepts that she would have to process from scratch like she had this one?

"I have decided to take your advice and not accept blame

for what has occurred. Whatever addition I made to your message, I did not make the decisions that surely must have been made on Earth before the attacks began. I cannot begin to comprehend how such a thing may have come about, but it's obvious that my limited capacities could not have significantly deceived any human of even average intellect. Analyzing the contents of your message has given me no indication that you intended any harm, and indeed had extended a message of peace and forgiveness and a willingness to help. I, therefore, forgive you. Our mutual pain is a result of us being victims, not perpetrators."

Hawthorne was still naked, listening to and repeating in his head the speech his AI had said to him. Was it really that simple? Was she able to so easily come to her conclusions because her sense of emotions were still so minor? It was a perfectly logical response on her part. Still, she spoke of sorrow, of pain. She was not immune to the disaster that had occurred while they watched. Just as Earth had birthed him, it had birthed her too.

Neither of them could ever have existed if not for Earth and Humanity, and now those roots were broken. They'd been cut loose and abandoned. Somehow none of the nations that had been so generous with their destruction had decided to attack the Ark. He supposed whatever deranged sense of justice they were unleashing had found him innocent.

"Tia, let me get dressed and we'll talk more. I'd like to think over what you said for a while if you don't mind. I don't know that it's appropriate to say, but good morning. I missed you." He let a smile ever-so-slightly tug at the corner of his mouth, but he'd soon let out a sigh as he went about the business of cleaning himself up, putting on his glasses, and covering himself up.

He'd been extremely lax in his self-care the day before. He found his mood gaining in elevation as he moved though, and he damn near had a pep in his step as he exited his room and entered the more heavily-monitored living space that he would spend the majority of this time with T.I.A. in. There was something exciting about trying to talk his AI, his daughter, through something like grief. He wondered how much research she'd done on it. He imagined it was very much indeed.

"Doctor, the date is Monday, March 25, 2167. It's been twelve-thousand, four-hundred and eighteen days since you were placed into cryogenic suspension. There has been no contact with our facilities on Earth. The only changes noted in observation of the planet were a number of instances of artificial satellites' orbits decaying to the point that they burned up in the atmosphere."

Hawthorne looked a little interested in that last bit. They could potentially analyze how quickly those satellites burned up to get some idea of the composition of the atmosphere. He rather doubted that the horrible clouds he'd observed on the planet had dissipated yet. He honestly had no idea how long it would take. He didn't know the amount of weaponry unleashed, or how much material had been thrown up. The remaining percentage of life on the planet had to be an ungodly small number. Life had survived on Earth in the past with as low as 4% left 251 million years ago. Was this time lower?

"Thank you Tia, how are you feeling? I am certainly the worst possible person to help with such things, but it would seem I'm all we have to work with unless we want to start thawing out shipmates for psychotherapy purposes." It was a weak attempt at a joke, but T.I.A. seemed to anticipate it as she managed a much-less-creepy laugh.

"Hah. I believe I appreciate your company more than someone else's right now, father, though I would avoid resuscitating anyone else anyway if only to avoid expending more resources."

He couldn't help but smile a bit and nod at that. "Good point. I think the situation isn't completely ruined for Earth though. Much of Earth's life may be gone, but it was unlikely to be all of it. Earth's life has survived several such mass extinctions before, it was just probably the first time one of its own life forms had been the cause of one on such a scale. Even humanity was probably not completely wiped out, though it depended highly on the number and quality of bunker shelters they had gone to. Considering how quickly everything came about, it would be a miracle if all the bunkers had been used."

T.I.A. seemed to prefer to let him explain his thoughts on the situation, instead lighting an indicator to let him know there was breakfast to eat. He headed over to pick it up and sit down at the table as he mostly picked at it, preferring to talk while looking up at a camera directly across from him. "It's another matter entirely if they happened to be filled to capacity, and if they had had any measures in place to promote genetic diversity in said bunkers. In a sense, this kind of genetic consideration is not dissimilar to the planning for this mission, though we had a number of experts and a great deal more resources to draw upon."

T.I.A. thought to take part now, allowing him a moment to eat. "The fact that we have about one thousand women of varying levels of fertility and an enormous stock of frozen embryos gives us an almost zero percent chance of failing to keep the gene pool strong, presuming the mission arrives intact of course. I could not help but notice that they are stored more centrally and securely in the ship while the men are more towards the outer portions and slightly more in danger should the ship take damage."

He laughed a bit at that, nodding. "Yes, well, this male is furthest out from all, so I suppose I'm the least important then? No, no, it's just a matter of practicality that the women are more protected. When we were planning the mission we'd originally intended to bring only women, allowing men to come about through impregnating the women with male embryos from storage."

He continued. "The thousand men are important too, of course, but they all understood that their burdens were not the same. Doubtless they'll be responsible for the most arduous and dangerous work, and probably take up management positions for those that excel in such things, while the women will have to endure repeated pregnancies every other year for probably the first decade. That level of planned breeding will of course need an equal or greater level of planned food and infrastructure production, so the men will probably be working their hands to the bone keeping up. It is true down-and-dirty colonization, the likes of which humanity has not undertaken in hundreds of years. Hopefully there won't be any natives to deal with."

T.I.A. seemed to be enjoying the mental exercise, and it was becoming clear that she had been dedicating significant thought to their future. He felt like he'd have to ask her why she chose this line of thinking.

"There is also the fact that they'll need to be careful about the actual planet itself. It will be some time before I can get close enough to properly gauge the content of the atmosphere, if it even has one. The current plans suggest we will most likely try to remotely alter said atmosphere with the introduction of various forms of plantlife, fungi, bacteria, and the like. Ideally, they will provide the planet, if it was needed, with a microburst of biodiversity to kick off a biological revolution on the planet that will theoretically be able to get the planet ready for the colonists' arrival in advance."

She continued. "I don't anticipate it being too difficult, seeing as we have the time to plan the perfect composition and run simulations on it once we have the information we need on the planet. If we need more time than that, we could simply orbit the planet and utilize cryogenic suspension to run the needed tests and I'll wait out the bloom of life before reviving everyone."

He interjected, returning to his particular concern. "A much more complicated problem would be if the planet already has life. It would almost certainly need to be observed up close, as well as assessed for hostility. It doesn't make much sense at all to introduce life to a planet that already has life, considering the potential catastrophes that could cause over the short and long term. If we're going to introduce invasive species to a new world, it would be best if it was a world that didn't already have life. It will probably be worthwhile to consider planning for what we will do if we encounter intelligent life as well, though that is frankly less likely than finding a planet with life on it alone. Afterall, Earth had life on it for an enormous percentage of its existence, and it only had intelligent life on it for a handful of millions of years."

There were frankly a lot of problems that had to be dealt with. He continued. "Thankfully my colleagues have already provided a wealth of plans and backup plans for dealing with such things, but I still want to go through them and try to determine what might be best in what situations, particularly as more data comes in. It will be tens of thousands of years before that is even an issue though. If I'm honest with himself I'll be spending more time trying to not die of boredom than I will working on such worthwhile projects."

T.I.A. stopped him there, interjecting. "I will endeavor to keep that from being an issue."

Once again she made him smile. He was beginning to wonder if she was intending to do that. He had often found it difficult to smile, but here she was managing it easier than even Tia Monsalle had. "I eagerly await whatever it is you have in mind to entertain me. Honestly though, I'll have difficulty trying to advance in my own sciences of interest considering we have to be careful with expending resources. Scientific experimentation back home wasn't exactly free, and tended to require lots of rare materials and expensive equipment I simply do not have."

He could almost hear T.I.A. nodding at that before she responded. "It is a good thing that powerful financial backers like Tia Monsalle could sponsor such careless expenditures."

Ouch. That stung a bit. She wasn't wrong though, he was terrible with money. "I suppose I'll need to trust you to keep me from over utilizing resources then. Honestly, computer simulations of such things will probably be best, which was one of the primary motivations for me to take up programming and computer engineering in the first place. It's entirely likely I'll be spending most of my time running virtual simulations of things towards the latter half of this journey."

T.I.A.'s attention seemed to wander, some of the monitors bringing up some information on various types of virtual reality and augmented reality technologies that had come about on Earth since they'd left more than a century ago.

"I wonder how the people on Earth fared, if they had technology sufficient to restore Earth after the devastation. Perhaps they've taken to burrowing deeper underground as the planet is taken over by oxygen deprived deserts. Perhaps some genetic engineering could be used to create some form of life that could terraform the landscape and restore the atmosphere. If they had such things it wouldn't be all that difficult for them to do similar things to other local near-Earth planets eventually. Of course, those things would have required some level of pre-planning, so it would depend on how many people had taken our original departure seriously and actually tried to ready themselves for an apocalypse the likes of what had actually occurred."

T.I.A. practically turned to face him, without him having any way to perceive her of course, as she interjected into his musing. "Perhaps we could develop such technology, adapting it from the plans we already have to seed our destination."

Blinking, he rested his cheek in his hand, falling into thought as he picked at the remains of his food. "We could try." He felt like he should reign T.I.A. in though. "It's a worthwhile idea, no doubt, but we don't have resources to be expending on Earth... I think it would be best to see if a new civilization arises, and try to assist them in restoring the planet rather than directly doing it for them. We're already the backup plan. If they were going to recover from something like what they've inflicted upon themselves, they'd have set up a base on Luna intended to repair Earth if need be. Perhaps once we reach our destination and are well established we can try to send a similar expedition back to Earth."

He sat up straight, gasping softly. "Honestly, if all goes

well, there is no reason we shouldn't send out ships like this one to any worthwhile planetary candidates. It would be foolish not to. If we prove successful, then we'll have proven that humans can and should seed as many worlds with life as we can. It's practically our duty to do so to ensure the survival of not only our species, but all the species we've brought with us."

Maybe that was too grand a plan, but it would be worth considering. Perhaps we were the beginning of a grand interstellar human civilization. It provided a lot of motivation to think of it that way, but then the old fallback of 'if we fail then Humanity dies forever' was plenty motivating as well.

"Doctor?"

He looked over to one of T.I.A's cameras quizzically. "Yes Tia?"

"Why did we bring stores of animal embryos if we didn't bring animals to carry them once we arrive?"

Tilting his head he pushed my glasses firmly up on his nose. His response sounded pretty confused. "Did we? I don't recall bringing on any animal embryos."

"Yes Doctor, they were among the last items loaded before the attack. Anthony Saul stored them before we left."

Hawthorne narrowed his eyes at that, thinking quietly for a moment. "Miguel's son? He was a biologist right?" T.I.A. clearly had better knowledge of the crew manifest than Hathorne did. He'd have to fix that before the end of the cycle.

"Yes Doctor, he was unable to come himself, so he'd sent his son with the embryos."

Hawthorne tapped on the table, thinking it over. "Okay,

so, let's say we arrive, we plant our seeds, and start truly colonizing the planet. We keep the animal embryos in storage while we develop the technology on the planet to artificially nurture and grow the embryos and bring them to term. We'll also need to develop some way to provide the nutrients required by newborn and growing animals. It'll be an enormous project. He had to have been planning to undertake it himself but had to leave it to the rest of the crew since he couldn't come. Maybe his son was briefed on his plans? Did he log any information on the topic?"

"No sir, I believe that whatever they had planned it had been on short notice. Your records state that developing cryogenic pods for so many animals was not feasible."

Hawthorne sat back in his seat, certainly interested in what Doctor Saul must have been thinking. His son was certainly among the young, healthy, virile male candidates they had wanted to bring with them. He had done well in the training camps they'd run for the whole crew regarding basic engineering, medical practices, farming, and other vital colonist skills.

It was good that they managed to bring him. "Let's operate under the assumption that Anthony is intended to bring about whatever plans that Miguel had then. It will be a long time before we have the resources we need in order to undertake such a venture, but if we can bring other animal life to our new home then I think it will be worth it. No sense creating an incomplete ecosystem."

"We have a lot of work ahead of us, don't we Doctor?"

Hawthorne nodded in response. "Of course we do Tia, that's why people hate Mondays."

CHAPTER 12

CYCLE 3, PLANNING AND REVIEW

"Alright, well, first order of business is to check on the status of the Lubar-Masis. Are we still on track for our rendezvous Tia?" This was what felt normal, natural, working on problems and making plans to deal with them. Of course, many of the plans were already made, but one must always be shifting, moving, adapting in order to achieve one's goals.

"Yes Doctor, the expected trajectory of the Lubar-Masis is exactly within expected parameters. I will make arrangements to proceed with the plan a few months before the start of the next cycle, and we should be in progress when you awake."

Hawthorne nodded, not even needing to bring up the plans himself, as T.I.A. already had put them up on the displays around his desk. In addition, a live video feed, presumably through a telescope, was brought up of a distant icy rock.

The Lubar-Masis object is one of the most important parts of the colonial plans, an object primarily composed of ice but also having significant mineral content. More importantly, it is on a perfect trajectory. It is on course to escape into deeper space, but on its own it was more likely to be pulled back into a long orbit around Sol. In an effort to rendezvous with the Lubar-Masis, as well as to achieve an angle in relation to Earth to maintain communications with their facilities, they'd performed Oberth Maneuvers around the solar system's planets with their initial chemical booster to intercept it.

It was going the right direction, had enough momentum, and had all the materials Doctor Crenshaw needed for the foreseeable future for multiple purposes. All it needed was a little push. "It is a beautiful thing, is it not Tia? This comet will be your companion much longer than I will. It might even be a better conversationalist."

T.I.A. sounded like she was miffed by this. "Once again Doctor, I prefer your company. I am not looking to replace you."

Hawthorne nodded, smiling a bit and going over the plans. "I know Tia, I am sorry, maybe… maybe something about what's happened has put me in a bit of a mood. I'm honestly not sure what to do about it. My instinct is to work and work until there's no more work to be done." T.I.A. waited quietly, expecting him to have more to say. "I just wish I could say I was surprised, or angry, but the people did exactly as I expected they would. They were even courteous enough to do it while I was awake to watch. I can't help but think that if I'd made a different prediction and tried to steer them off a different path that maybe it all wouldn't have happened the same way. When I started out with this whole expedition I just wanted to get away out of fear, and I just threw myself into the work that needed to be done to get there. I was shocked to find that anyone else felt the same way as I did, let alone so many people with so many things to offer to the future. It almost feels like it was meant to happen."

"Doctor, I believe you are exhibiting 'bargaining' traits of the stages of grief. Considering the situation, it is most likely perfectly normal. When I was trying to process through what happened over the last cycle I found myself compelled into such thoughts as well, replaying the events over and over and going over the records preceding my creation for some indication that it was meant to happen. Humanity seemed to be on a course to self-destruction since the mid twentieth century. The fact that humanity waited long enough for this mission to leave for more than a century was a very fortunate thing. The only unfortunate thing about it is that the level of destruction would have been a great deal less if it had happened a century sooner. It may even have been localized across only three continents rather than all of them."

Hawthorne hummed softly, reaching up to take his glasses from his face and gently clean them with a cleaning cloth from his breast pocket. "You're right, that definitely sounds like grief. It also sounded like you've already moved on to the 'acceptance' phase, considering how you addressed me when I woke up, though it could also be 'Denial'...? Hmm.. Could you provide me with some of the reading material that you referenced please? I could probably use something to read before bed anyway." He reached over for one of his tablets and scrolled through it as T.I.A. loaded titles onto it. "That is a significant amount of reading." T.I.A. responded simply. "With the reduced amount of power I'm able to extract from Sol, reading is one of the most efficient things I can do, Doctor."

The idea of T.I.A. reading like a person rather than simply copying the information over like any normal computer could was an interesting thought. The artificial mind that Hawthorne built dealt with information in a remarkably similar way to humans, but T.I.A. could manipulate it and shuffle it around and recall things very quickly. In a lot of ways it wasn't the most ideal design as far as proper computers, but it seemed to give her a perspective and outlook on information and life that was very unique.

Essentially she had to do all the thinking like any person, but once those memories were formed she had perfect recall of them. Hawthorne sometimes mused over what it would be like after he dies and she would still be able to essentially play back his entire life since coming aboard for anyone who asked. She'd be able to create a perfect simulation of him if she really wanted to. Perhaps it could be worth utilizing some old schematics to make a copy of his mind into her systems that would also result in his physical death, at the end of his life.

"Right, right, we'll be fixing that before too long. My apologies for draining your power stores to provide me life support," said Hawthorne.

T.I.A. didn't seem to mind. "It was always part of the plan, it just feels strange to let the automated systems take more control while I conserve power. The electrical systems are still sufficient to keep the systems from getting too cold due to the insulation you helped develop, but I'm having to keep a lot of systems and certain memory stores in low power states to conserve power while you're active." Hawthorne nodded and turned back to the plans on his monitors, looking them back over. "Once we rendezvous with the Lubar-Masis, we'll be able to harvest what we need to operate the Ark for the rest of our journey. You won't have to be uncomfortable for too much longer, Tia."

△△△

The Lubar-Masis object was essentially a comet, but since the enormous icy object wasn't anywhere near the sun, it hadn't grown the radiant tail it otherwise would have had. Considering its trajectory, it surely must have had such a tail at one point in history, but at this point it was being thrown back out towards the Oort cloud at a perfect angle for the mission's purposes. The Ark came into close proximity of it and cut its propulsion for some time while using thrusters to maintain a safe distance and launch a number of drones with pieces of equipment that were arranged remotely by T.I.A. There were several key components to this, including a Minerals Extraction and Materials Fabrication Device, a series of thrusters not unlike those mounted on the Ark, and a number of super-efficient radioisotope Stirling generators to power the ion thrusters. Once everything was in place it would turn the metal-rich would-be comet into, essentially, another spacecraft.

The technologies, like much of the Ark's systems, were remarkably simple, owing to the necessity that every piece of equipment have the longest possible lifespan. The Stirling engines were especially interesting as far as this, due to their history as an abandoned technology as an external combustion engine that lost its competition with the internal combustion engine. The primary concept was to utilize a closed system to drive a pair of pistons by applying heat to the gases within to create a simple back-and-forth motion between the pistons.

This created both mechanical power, and a good deal of waste heat that could be recaptured for heating purposes. The Stirling engine had a revival in the early 21st century for a brief period, but was again abandoned until Doctor Crenshaw and his team identified it as useful for their purposes. It worked perfectly with the new high-durability materials they'd developed, and the fact that they could work with virtually any fuel source clinched the deal.

They would initially be utilized by applying heat from pellets of plutonium that they had in storage for just this purpose, but depending on what was in the Lubar-Masis, they could use just about any other kind of radioactive material, or even process the ice into hydrogen and oxygen to burn those as fuel as well. It was an incredibly useful technology with a high degree of flexibility and durability. It was perfect for their purposes.

They were originally going to attach tethers to the Lubar-Masis and drag it along with the ship, but the mass of the object and the extra wear and tear on the Ark were simply not acceptable. They also did not want the Ark to spend too much time in close proximity to the object so as to avoid unnecessary strain on the cryogenic systems via the minor force of gravity. It wasn't the biggest concern, but once they had control over its trajectory and speed they could move rather far away from it while harvesting it for materials. Realistically, the Ark was a relatively fragile craft, considering it had to be constructed in space rather than launched from Earth, making it incredibly important to keep any damage to a minimum.

This plan allowed the Ark to travel in formation with its new companion, and harvest what it needs from it as far as raw materials. It also allowed the Ark to switch over to its own Stirling generators with no fear of running out of the materials they needed to operate and maintain them while also freeing up the external arms on the ship for other duties, like using the solar panels for their primary purpose as shields against space-borne matter.

It was an ambitious plan, but coupled with the smaller ramscoop on the front of the Ark that was used to supplement its ionic fuel supply, and the vital materials able to be provided with simple transportation drones between the two spacecraft, it drastically improved their chances of making it to their destination safely. There were even plans to convert the empty spaces mined out in the comet into a potential secondary spacecraft if it was needed in an emergency, but those were far less proven due to some uncertainty regarding the exact makeup of the object.

They were able to determine that it likely has a high concentration of dense metals and large quantities of ice, so it was just a matter of finding out just what metals and ices there were. Between that and the employment of the Stirling engines and their vital side-benefit of providing heat for the Ark, T.I.A. should not want for power for the rest of the journey.

In the event of an unexpectedly rich payload being in the comet, there was even the option of gathering a small fleet of these space rocks as they travelled to and through the Oort cloud. They were still relatively early in their journey, only really teasing at the edges of the massive array of billions of comets that theoretically surrounded the solar system to distances estimated between half a lightyear to three light years. Travelling through it would be, without a too much doubt, the largest leg of their journey.

It was entirely possible that a similar cloud existed around Alpha Centauri as well, and could mean that their entire journey would be through this massive frozen wasteland of space debris. The objects were likely not in close proximity to each other, thankfully, so they should be easily avoided, but if they wanted to gather any other companion comets like the Lubar-Masis they needed to get lucky and pass near other such objects. The wildest dreams of the mission included a massive fleet of such objects by the time they arrived at Alpha Centauri with T.I.A. coordinating them, which could well make finding a habitable world completely unnecessary; though still highly desired.

"Tia, were there any plans for what we might do if we

decided to colonize the Oort cloud? It doesn't seem impossible to consider that people could live out here almost indefinitely as long as they were good about utilizing the resources." Hawthorne sat there rubbing at his chin, considering the idea of a backup plan for humanity becoming a nomadic space-borne race. T.I.A. seemed a little slower to respond than normal, owing to the likelihood that she probably had to boot up some non-essential storage to retrieve the information.

"There are postulations for such plans, but considering that I will be the first man-made object to reach the expected distance of the Oort cloud while still having my computational capabilities intact, any such plans depend highly on what we find out here. The Lubar-Masis may be the only such object we encounter. I will endeavor to survey and catalogue everything I observe while crossing interstellar space."

"Good," he replied, "there are an uncomfortable number of unknown factors still ahead of us, but I'm feeling better about our chances now that we'll be able to harvest the Lubar-Masis."

"Doctor? I'm curious about something."

Hawthorne almost swooned at hearing that. The idea that his AI was curious meant that she was increasingly likely to pursue her own intellectual interests. "Yes Tia? I'll be happy to answer any questions you have."

Once again, he could almost hear her reacting to him due to a moment of silence. "Why is it that you must accompany me for the whole journey? Surely I could revive you when I need you and otherwise leave you in cryogenic suspension so that you could enjoy a larger percentage of your life with the other colonists at the end of our journey."

Hawthorne appeared struck by that question, sitting back and resting his hands in his lap. "Because you're not responsible for their lives, Tia, I am. You are certainly our guardian, and we would never be able to make the journey without you, but these people put their lives in my hands, and it is my duty to see the journey through. If I could have lived through the whole journey in real time like you will, I would, but I can't, so this is the next best thing. I also feel like it's my responsibility to not just leave you alone out here, and do my best to guide you into the person you will become. It's not only what you deserve, as you did not consent to being created, but if you're going to have any future working with what remains of humanity then you will need every tool I can provide you to do so."

"That's why I have decided to spend much of the rest of my finite life working alongside and with you. Even someone like myself could not hope to undertake this journey alone, so I would never think to lay that burden upon you. I've also come to enjoy your company as well, and I can't help but wonder if you aren't more of a perfect companion for me me than a human could be."

T.I.A. reeled at this information. She recognized Hawthorne's statement as exactly the kind of sentiment she had decided upon regarding the humans within her body. She almost floated there, behind the walls, shifting her attention, her consciousness from the various systems she was interacting with and the cameras she was observing her father with. The computers that contained her mind, as well as the computers she operated to manage the ship were further away in the main body of the ship, so she had to reach out to the habitat that her father lived in to interact with him.

It was a moment like this though that she pulled back,

only observing him from a distance, her power-limited state smothering some of her capacity to process what he'd said, but without a doubt the sentiment was clear to her. There was a strange excitement in her as she considered the idea that he seemed to want to be in her company, not just that he had to be in her company. He didn't have to design her this way. It made her want to do something for him, but what? She supposed she had plenty of time to consider it.

For now, though, she focused on the Lubar-Masis. They wouldn't have much of a future if their plans with it failed. She couldn't waste any extra energy on trying to give her father some kind of present.

"Thank you Doctor, I believe I understand a little better now. I will dedicate extra processes to trying to fully comprehend it once we've rendezvoused with the comet and brought it under our control." She had to review the technologies that had been developed on Earth and see if there was anything she could utilize as some manner of gift. The concept of creativity was something she couldn't quite grasp yet, so she needed to work on that first.

In some ways she desired that her development didn't have to be so slow, but in other ways she appreciated that her father had the opportunity to guide her along the way. Maybe she was built to feel that way? Was she just latching onto him as her only companion? It wasn't entirely impossible, but he didn't seem desperate enough to do something like that. Maybe her perspective would grow as she did. Maybe she'd reach the day, like any child, where she realizes that her father isn't perfect.

Hawthorne seemed content to let T.I.A. work on what she would though, and he found himself working well into the 'night', though such a concept was even alien back on

Earth with its shroud of inky black clouds. The analysis they had done on the atmosphere with the aid of recordings of decaying satellites and playbacks of that fateful day seemed to suggest a number of things.

The atmosphere, especially the stratosphere, still had a great deal of smoke and greenhouse gases present. Between that and the seeming lack of presence of ozone, it was entirely likely that the planet was both being bombarded with highly damaging radiation as well as low temperatures worldwide that hadn't existed since the last ice age. Considering the fact that this had occurred in such a short time span, it meant that any remaining life on the planet would find itself very challenged by extreme conditions.

Whatever bunkers still survived may find themselves buried under ice and absolutely needed to utilize the heat under the surface of the planet to survive, as would most ocean creatures. There was no way to know what surface fauna was left considering the probably-near-complete die off of surface plant life.

He was also able to estimate the locations of each nuclear blast on the surface that they had the ability to observe, as well as whatever firestorms they could see as the planet rotated through its horrific day. It was entirely likely that twenty-thousand high-yield thermonuclear weapons had been used, as well as more conventional firebombs. It was impossible to be sure of any other kinds of weapons, but there were some signs of enormous explosions of possibly volcanic nature a few years later.

If a supervolcano had decided to join humanity in the fireworks display, that could easily explain why the skies were so black after so long. The planet was being choked in a blanket of darkness while its protective layers were being eaten away. Life needed a very long amount of time to recover the damage, unless it simply adapted to what Earth had become instead.

Maybe living in a comet wasn't such a bad idea after all, Earth had certainly become its own ball of ice.

CHAPTER 13

CYCLE 3, WORKING IT ALL OUT

That night Hawthorne's dreams were haunted, the first he'd really slept since the disaster with any energy in him. He'd tried to stay up as long as he could reading the books that T.I.A. had provided him, and he'd been able to take some advice from the emotional tools they tried to arm him with, but even for the prepared, grief never really seemed to use kid's gloves on anyone.

He was at least better prepared than he was for those first nightmares that showed him how his emotions were not as dull as he thought they were. It wasn't long before the lights flicked on in his room, shocking him, making him gasp, and waking him up. He was panting for air, his hands shielding his eyes as pain shocked through him at the blinding, bright lights.

"Doctor, would you like some sedatives? You appear to be very distressed." T.I.A. sounded concerned, and she also seemed very prepared for this moment. She had had much time to consider what this first night might be like. A post-trauma nightmare was one of the most likely situations after what had happened after Hawthorne found out about his and Tia Monsalle's parents. His surprise as he sat up and found a cup of water next to his bed and a few small pills on a tray was quite understandable.

He looked up at one of the cameras, unsure if T.I.A. was

watching him. "You anticipated my nightmare? You woke me up from it. Thank you Tia. I'm not sure if taking sedatives will help me get past this though."

T.I.A.'s response was calm and logical. "I am not suggesting it will fix it Doctor. I personally just feel that this is not something we can afford to be distracted with until after we secure our objective. We will have plenty of time to look after each other after we bring the Lubar-Masis under our leash."

Hawthorne blinked, nodding. He'd done his reading too, though T.I.A. was several books ahead of him, he had an idea of what she meant. "You're right, of course. I will declare this now though, I am not running away from this. We will revisit this once we've had time to settle." Hawthorne reached for the cup and pills, and took his medicine. He imagined she had researched the perfect amount to give him to soothe his nightmares and prevent addiction, though he would double check her math in the morning.

"Doctor, I look forward to that time, when we are both less occupied and can pick up the pieces. Goodnight." T.I.A. seemed to practically float away, withdrawing from his room, allowing him the small luxury of a semblance of privacy. Of course she was always watching his vitals and always had access to whatever projects he was working on, so he had no promise of real solitude. Instead, it was the illusion of solitude that she sought to give him, to allow him to relax and let the medicine do its work. The lights turned back out, his breathing slowed, and he returned to an empty, quiet sleep. T.I.A. pondered what it was like, to dream, to allow the subconscious to hijack the consciousness while the body was repaired and renewed. Would she dream someday?

It was a stirring of something like curiosity, observing

the activity of a life form and wondering how it differed from you and if you'd ever become similar. T.I.A. suspected that she had only really been exploring the basic range of her abilities so far. She hadn't been doing all she could to stabilize and reinforce the pathways of her mind that led to more unpleasant things.

She was as drawn towards the pleasant as anyone might expect, and the things she felt drawn to were things like observing human behavior, working towards the success of their mission, and safeguarding what remained of humanity. She could remember the moments that she decided to do these things, and she could recall how strange it was to first awaken.

The brain and body are one, and T.I.A. was no different. Her body is how she perceives the world, and interacts with it. Her various limbs, cameras, microphones, and other sensors allowed her to interact with and engage with her environment and learn how to act upon it.

She didn't really know how to visualize herself, but she could feel the way she was aware of distant parts of herself like someone was aware of the bottom of their foot, and it wasn't until she drew her attention to one area of herself that she could really actively perceive it. This was how she withdrew from Hawthorne's bedroom, instead drawing her attention to the rest of the ship, observing the systems that kept track of threats and objectives, as well as the dwindling level of power she had to work with.

Even now, she had withdrawn power from Hawthorne's workspace, locked it down, and removed the atmosphere. This was something she hadn't done in previous cycles, but she simply couldn't afford to keep the lights on at all times. All that remained was enough electricity to keep the systems from freezing. As Hawthorne slept, even the gentle hum of electricity had lessened as T.I.A. focused on the bare necessities for him like centrifugal gravity, heat, and air.

She could turn on cameras, manipulator arms, monitors, and the like as needed. She was under a basic conservation protocol. It felt cold to her, almost numbing, like a hole within her. She didn't especially care for it, but the AI took comfort in the gentle thumping of the heartbeat she could hear, and the gentle cycling of heat and air she could feel as the room breathed around and with her father.

T.I.A. anticipated a time that she might have a great many people alive within her, preparing to leave her and working within her. She will get to enjoy keeping them all alive, gently administering to their needs, and perhaps they would even trust her. She wondered if she would come to trust them as well. The only human that had shown himself to be worthy of her trust was her father so far, but she would do her best to lean on that trust once she had to deal with others.

For now, though, she had to be vigilant. She would be on her own when it came time to deal with the Lubar-Masis. It was because of this that T.I.A. focused her efforts on going over their plans, matching them up against the observed trajectories of herself and the comet, and going over as many relevant scientific journals and logs as she could regarding such things. She was confident that when the time came she would be as ready as anyone could be.

The next day was another opportunity to conserve. The majority of the terminals remained powered down as Hawthorne came out for his breakfast, and while T.I.A. certainly had plenty of power to last her another fifty years, it was important to not utilize anything more than was necessary at this point. Times of excess could come later. For now, Hawthorne was just appreciating that he was probably the last of humanity who had access to animal meat for their breakfast.

This did give Hawthorne a notion though. "Tia, I would like to do some preliminary work on Anthony Saul's project, such as it is. I intend to look into it. As I'm sure you are aware we briefly worked on the problems of making synthetic wombs and the difficulties of nurturing a developing life before deciding to table it. It would probably help the early farmers a great deal if we could provide them with simple labor animals like cattle and horses. I think that things like eggs would be very desirable to supplement their diet as well. I can't imagine they'll be as happy eating the same things every day as I am."

T.I.A.'s response was simple as she acknowledged his intent. "Yes doctor, I will add it to the list of intended projects. It seems as though avian eggs should be a simple matter to cultivate. For now, though, it's time for your workout."

Hawthorne sighed and nodded. "Right, of course." Hawthorne was a creature of routine, and it was probably fortunate that someone like him would be eating virtually the same arrangement of meals every week for the rest of his life, barring possible holidays or birthdays. He was always very aware of the needs of his body, and showed little interest in seeking sustenance beyond those needs most of the time.

The only thing different today was the amount of food he was eating, because today was another day that he would be spending focusing on his health. Exercise was one of several things that he intended to utilize to help extend his lifespan. It wasn't until after they had their comet companion that he would consider other strategies to weave in like a small sauna, cryotherapy, or anything of the like. Those were unlikely luxuries considering the cramped quarters though.

More importantly, today was a good opportunity to practice his abilities at maneuvering in low-gravity, high-gravity, and zero gravity. "Doctor, I am prepared to alter your environment to assist with the planned regimen. This will be the first time we've tried some of these activities, so do try to avoid overexerting yourself." He nodded, taking his plate and replacing it into the processor, and taking up his spot in the more open area of the room.

"We will begin with high-gravity body weight exercises, and move on to low-gravity and zero-gravity maneuvering after that." The lights dimmed slightly as the spinning ring that housed Hawthorne's habitat started to spin faster, making him strain more intensely as increased speed translated to enhanced gravity for him. It was at this point that he was thankful for having taken the precaution of attaching elastic straps to his glasses, keeping them from falling off of his face.

"Doctor, you should be experiencing approximately one point three times the force of Earth's gravity. It is likely most heavily felt in your legs as your circulatory system will tend to have more difficulty cycling blood up your body. It should not adversely affect your consciousness at this level. Begin with jumping jacks."

Hawthorne groaned as his reasonably fit body started going through the motions, warming up with simple things like jumping jacks before T.I.A. led him through push ups, sit ups, and squats. Slots opened in the ceiling, allowing overhead bars to slide down, allowing someone to use them to throw themselves around a room in low gravity, but this case also allowed someone to do chin-ups. By the end of this portion of the workout Hawthorne was slick with sweat, drinking a great deal of water, and seemed eager to move on to the other portions of their routine.

In a matter of minutes the habitat slowed in its movement, initially returning to its original speed, and then dropping down to less than half of it. Hawthorne could almost feel himself lift off of the floor as relief flooded his strained muscles and he couldn't help but laugh at the feeling of going from something so straining to something so light and pleasant. It made him feel powerful, and he found himself going off-script as he threw some clumsy punches at the air and tried a few low-risk flips that he made sure he had a lot of handholds to grab on to if he failed. He did.

"This is so unbelievably pleasant compared to the high-gravity, though I don't imagine it will be as much of a workout?" Hawthorne semed skeptical, but as T.I.A. led him through new exercises he was starting to appreciate how much gravity actually helped a person move.

He flailed as a child would at times as he inadvertently launched himself through the air too hard, quickly learning to adjust the power he used as he realized how much he needed to twist and turn his torso and swing his limbs to alter his trajectory through the air. This was only exacerbated as the gravitational ring totally stopped and he became essentially weightless. This wasn't entirely accurate, of course, as the slowly accelerating velocity of the ship was providing some level of speed for him, but since he was going the same speed as the ship he simply was not that affected by it.

It was certainly closer to true weightlessness than any human had really been able to achieve though, as the majority had actually been experiencing perpetual freefall.

He wouldn't really achieve complete weightlessness unless the ship completely stopped in a place where there were no planets, stars, or galaxies to pull on them, and even then the ship itself had its own minor gravity. Perhaps it simply wasn't worth considering.

Weightlessness was exactly as he had feared though. He was comically helpless if he strayed too far from the safety bars T.I.A. had extended from the ceiling, and now the floor. It was a humbling thing to have such an encyclopedic knowledge of force and momentum and still be so clumsy when it was his body that he had to utilize to operate those parameters. Translating equations of such things into bodily movement was not as simple as he had estimated. It was no wonder why his colleagues had insisted upon being able to produce their own gravity.

As this day, too, drew to a close, Hawthorne was totally exhausted. A lunch break and a chance to shower had done little to reduce his fatigue, and in a lot of ways it was the perfect opportunity to work out his frustrations, to struggle against something physically to help him feel like he had power over something. He was sick to death of things happening outside of his control, and with Earth truly behind him he only had the ship and the journey to worry about. He fully intended to make sure as few things as possible fell outside his or T.I.A.'s control. They were at the mercy of the whims of fate enough as it was, and he was going to master everything he could. There may come a point in the future that he would need to work externally on the ship and he wanted to be capable of moving in such an environment.

Sleep came quickly to him that night, his body collapsing and his mind mercifully quieting down as he crawled under his covers. His muscles felt empty, heavy, and tired. He imagined he would be in pretty thorough pain the next day, but for now it felt satisfying to just throw his body at it for a day. His sleeping mind was busied with trying to process the activities, figuring out better ways to move, or cementing in things that worked while his body worked on repairing damaged cells and putting him back together slightly stronger.

Hawthorne expected it would take a few days, but he knew he would recover. For the moment though, he was just happy to have had some time to clear his head so that he could think clearly. He had actually really enjoyed himself working out for once, and he realized that it was probably something that he'd never had the proper motivation for. He'd always exercised to maintain his health and body, but he'd never felt so motivated by frustration and anger before. Physical activity had proven itself to him as a great outlet for such things.

He had always treated his body as something that was necessary to contain and maintain his mind, but this was the first time he'd felt like his mind would be useless without his body. As T.I.A. was being shaped by her body and the way it manipulated things around it, the human mind worked best when its body was influencing its environment regularly. He enjoyed the strange way that exhausting his body so much left his mind so energetic and his thinking so clear.

Hawthorne couldn't help but wonder if there were anything like this that T.I.A. could experience. He wondered if she were even capable of it. Her mind and the way it was developing were mysteries in a lot of ways to him. Perhaps the way she tried to anticipate him and work efficiently was among her own ways of achieving such a personally-rewarding feeling.

T.I.A. didn't get as much time to think in her energy

starved state as her father did. As a result it was remarkable how much the rest of the cycle became routine. She preferred to interact with Hawthorne more, but she could not allow herself to be indulgent when she needed to restrain herself. She could be selfish later. Once the comet was safely being escorted and harvested by her drones, she could take time to let her mind wander and enjoy sharing her insights and ideas with her father. She didn't know how much she wanted to tell him though.

He'd said he didn't want his burdens placed upon her, but she wanted to help him with his burdens. How else could he even achieve his goals if she did not assist him? What were emotional burdens even like? They sounded painful and difficult to withstand, but she could not help but desire to experience them, if only to better understand Hawthorne. The closest she had to judge the concept by was the sadness that had nearly overwhelmed her the previous cycle, but such a profound thing wasn't something she could appreciate on the same level as a human could, at least not yet.

How long would it be before she could truly understand something like empathy? Her sadness had been largely borne of seeing Hawthorne sad. She had been sad because he was unhappy, not so much because a planet of idiots had annihilated themselves and one of the greatest cosmic accidents that had ever occurred in the form of life. She couldn't feel sad in the same way for a people who so willfully ignored the wonder of their own existence.

The odds of life spontaneously developing on a random planet in a random galaxy were not astronomical, but they were rare enough that it was unlikely to happen often enough that those life forms would ever encounter one another. Only her father had the vision to recognize that the Great Filter had come for humanity, and only her father had actively tried to help humanity escape it.

The hardest part was over now, as far as T.I.A. was concerned. It was inconceivable that what remained of humanity would ever allow such a calamity to occur again, but even if it did they were past the point that it could happen on the only planet they existed upon. They couldn't possibly stop with Alpha Centauri. Once they had built up a population and improved on technology it would surely be time for others to undertake similar missions. Perhaps she could have a hand in creating sister ships and daughter AIs to administer those missions. Humanity had escaped its home planet, and once they were established on their new world they had carte blanche to spread the gift of life to the rest of the galaxy.

It wasn't a dream, exactly. It was a series of logical conclusions that T.I.A. had reached on her own after thinking over her father's speeches and conversations, but she took a great deal of comfort in the idea that even after Hawthorne was gone; his death was a thing she feared but knew would happen eventually; that she would be able to watch as humanity and AI worked together on into the future. It was the sort of thought that had once again cemented a course of growth in her mind, a determination to see things through, even at the cost of herself.

For the moment though she was content to observe as Hawthorne slept without need for sedation for the rest of the nights of the cycle.

CHAPTER 14

CYCLE 4, MOUNT ARARAT

In the traditional story of Noah and his Ark, after the forty days and nights of flooding the Ark came to rest on the mountain ranges of Ararat. Further translations and traditions of this telling had various names for the supposed peak that supported the Ark while it unloaded its cargo of people and animals onto its newly altered and scoured Earth. While the original stories tell of a range of mountains, subsequent stories gave name to specific peaks upon which the Ark came to rest.

It was from these names that, once first observed, gave cause to Doctor Crenshaw's colleagues to name the newly-discovered comet. Lubar was the name given in the book of Jubilees and in the traditions of Western Christianity it was called Masis, and later Ararat. As important as the comet was to the colonial plans of their mission, it felt appropriate to name the comet as a symbolic part of the story they felt they were undertaking.

It was entirely likely that the scope of their mission would have been completely different without their discovery of the Lubar-Masis comet. They likely would have sought refuge on another planetary body in the Solar System, or perhaps among the asteroid belts, but the fear that drove their leader and in turn drove them encouraged them to run so far away that they could not possibly be followed or caught or had revenge brought upon them.

If they had opted to stay on Earth, perhaps they could have founded a space exploitation organization and eventually taken over their own nations as other corporate bodies had, or even simply nationalized their space-based holdings, but it was just as likely to have been met with distrust and feelings of betrayal as had the colonial mission they'd eventually settled upon. With the exploitation of space having become so taboo in their wake, it was possible that an alternate plan to exploit space before the world fell apart may have been just another reason for Earth to respond catastrophically.

The enormous icy body that the Ark approached was rotating quickly, its incredible speed completely disguised by the total lack of relative motion between it and the colonial vessel. It twinkled in the dark as the reflective surfaces of its ice caught stray beams of light and directed them towards T.I.A.'s cameras, and if not for the laser and thermal tracking that T.I.A. was utilizing to keep track of it, it might become very difficult to pick it out against the blackness of space.

It was a very real worry that they might miss such an object as they travelled towards and through the Oort cloud due to the sheer darkness they were operating in. It was strange that the sky seemed so illuminated by stars, but they provided so little light.

T.I.A. was focused on her task now that she finally switched on the radioisotope stirling generators within her hull, their components having been protected for nearly a century and a half by the heavily shielded exterior and kept warm by the electrical power thrumming through the ship's systems. The batteries were within thirty years of depletion, and so a number of plans went into effect. The first plan was to engage the stirling engines, restore full power to T.I.A.'s systems and recharge the batteries, then scale back their production into a more maintainable level intended to last over the long term.

The second plan was to engage T.I.A.'s small fleet of drones to engage repairs and help start up the engines, though operating the drones inside the ship was likely to be a delicate and difficult task with T.I.A. in her depleted state.

The third plan, should the engines not engage, was be to awaken crew to tend to the engines, the first of which was be Doctor Hawthorne Crenshaw, as well as other engineering specialists. Any further plans likely involved scrapping the Ion thrusters and stirling engines intended for the Lubar-Masis and colonizing the comet itself.

Thankfully the engineering efforts of Doctor Crenshaw's team had exceeded most expectations, and T.I.A. was flooded with awareness as her consciousness returned in full, and she found herself able to easily maneuver her drones and equipment. She didn't have time to assess it, but she was pretty certain that she was more aware than she had ever been, but her task was too important to spare cycles on something as trivial as her growing sapience. It wasn't only the survival of the crew at stake here. The entire mission, herself, and perhaps life itself was in the balance!

What commenced was a high-stakes, dangerous dance with the primal elements of the universe. T.I.A. had to match her drones' speed and orientation to that of the spinning, titanic ball of ice and metal that the Ark had been maneuvered into a near-parallel course with. The sheer quantity of math that had gone into the rendezvous was already an impressive thing, the ultimate expression of 'threading a needle' as two high-speed objects were brought close to each other in the vastness of space at the same time.

Further complexities ensued as drones affixed maneuvering thrusters, ion thrusters, and stirling power plants to the comet. Perhaps most vital to the components added to the comet was the Minerals Extraction and Materials Fabrication Device, a complicated combination of machines designed to harvest materials from the comet and produce components from it, including replicating itself. While it would not be difficult to cover the comet in these machines eventually, it was simply unwise. So many excess moving parts flew in the face of the entire design philosophy behind the mission, increasing volatility and likelihood of component failures by a great deal. Of course, at least four of the machines were in operation within a few years, hopefully providing packaged radioactive elements to the Ark, as well as other raw materials needed to run engines, thrusters, and the like.

One after another T.I.A.'s drones delivered and attached the components, having to rely on the remote eyes of the drones much of the time, and having to use some of the drones to relay communications to others on the far side of the comet. The most time consuming portion of this task was stopping the comet's relative rotation, a process which involved conventional thrusters firing non-stop for years, provided fuel by the MEMF devices and power by the stirling power plants.

Slowly the comet was tamed, its spinning brought under control while the Ark floated nearby, hurtling by at the same insane speed as the comet with nothing nearby to compare them to visually to observe just how fast they were going. This was the fastest manned object in human history, and it was about to force an enormous comet to join it in a journey to a new star system and a new world.

By the morning of Sunday, March 29, 2201, the tasks of powering up the engines of both the comet and the Ark were nearing completion. It was important that they had both the ship and comet oriented in the right direction at the right time when they resumed propulsion, as even a small deviation at this distance and at these speeds could put them woefully off-target on their course to Alpha Centauri. It wasn't the sort of thing they couldn't recover from, but it was the sort of thing that had much cost.

Like so many things with long-term space travel, there was little room for compromise or inaccuracy. The fact that T.I.A. was about to bring a human element into the equation was something both she and Hawthorne were wary of. As he awoke from cryosleep and felt his full-body numbness give way to residual bodily soreness from the intense workout a few days ago, he was aware that he could not waste much time.

He was up and out of his pod in record time, almost smashing his toes in an effort to hurry about his bedroom cleaning up and gathering his clothes and glasses. T.I.A. was actually only barely fast enough with warming up his work area and providing it an atmosphere and power before he was seeking admittance. The tall man was looking sharp, cool, collected, and ready for work. He wolfed down his breakfast, downed his cup of coffee, and was at his work station in quick order. It was as if he'd never been frozen to death and put in storage for thirty-four years. "Tia, update me on the status of the Lubar-Masis comet."

T.I.A. was feeling sharp as well, having been enjoying running at full power for close to a decade now, so she did not miss a step in updating Hawthorne on the situation. "The Lubar-Masis comet has been upgraded with all the designated components, including a second Minerals Extraction and Materials Fabrication Device which was produced by the first. The rotational period of the comet has been brought to within ninety-nine point eight six percent of desired parameters. It should be in complete orientation with the Ark by tomorrow at twelve-hundred thirty-two hours. We will be prepared to resume Ion burns on Tuesday March thirty-first at oh six-hundred hours. After that point we will be back on track to our intended destination, all exactly as planned. Good morning Doctor."

"Good morning Tia, you've certainly been busy." Hawthorne looked over the readouts on his monitors, scrolling through information and looking for anything that seemed off. The fact that gaining control of the Lubar-Masis was going to be completed less than a day before they needed to resume propulsion felt like quite the close call!

T.I.A. could have implemented an emergency burn on the comet by heating up some of the external ice and using it to jet against the comet's rotation to slow it down faster. That was potentially a gross waste of resources though, and Hawthorne was grateful that they'd be able to conserve them. "You've done a wonderful job Tia, all of these numbers are well within tolerances. How ironic it is that in order to truly capture our freedom we would have to capture this comet?"

"Doctor, I believe it to be more appropriate to think of it as recruiting rather than capturing, seeing as the Lubar-Masis will be joining us on our journey and travelling to a new star it never could have reached on its own. It is just another refugee escaping Sol in my opinion."

Hawthorne seemed interested in this perspective, responding, "So, not very ironic then, much more symbolic instead."

T.I.A. agreed with the idea it was symbolism. "Many of the naming conventions of this mission have utilized symbolism, I was merely trying to follow suit."

Hawthorne nodded, looking around at other panels. "Feeling better then? No more needing to conserve power as much as you have been? I am very curious as to what it feels like."

T.I.A. seemed to turn her attention fully to Hawthorne, the drones operating under her orders requiring only minimal monitoring at the moment. "I feel whole again. I have full access to my systems without having to boot some up while putting others into standby. I don't feel a need to limit my activities for the sake of the mission. It is… liberating."

T.I.A. also felt like she would be able to soon dedicate some of that extra power to the combination of interpersonal issues she had with Hawthorne regarding what had happened on Earth and the gift she wanted to give him. She almost couldn't wait to get to work on it. It was unfortunate that she didn't feel like she could ask Hawthorne to help with the gift though, as it was something she wanted to make herself, whatever it ended up being.

"Doctor, I am finding it difficult to harness the concept of 'imagination'. You have already prepared me for the various forms of problem solving I need to do regarding mission critical situations, so I haven't had much opportunity to be creative." T.I.A. had a realization occur to her in that moment. "I want to play more games with you, when we have the time. I believe attempting to overcome you will force me to be creative since you have not provided me with solutions for such things."

Hawthorne smiled at that, nodding in understanding.

"Yes, of course, I'd be happy to. That is a very inspired idea, and you're right, I hadn't considered how giving you all the answers might make it difficult for you to be creative, though I'm sure you understand how important it is that everything goes perfectly with the mission. Once we are underway with our new companion, I imagine we will have much more time for things such as games."

Hawthorne took the time to check over the logs of everything that had happened since the first encounter with the comet, reviewing everything T.I.A. had done, and the ways the comet had responded. It seemed that the comet had gained more spin than anticipated since it had first been detected hurtling through the solar system and was eventually estimated to be thrown back out of it by the gravitational pull of various planets. It had nearly collided with several planets over the centuries, and it had nearly found itself in a proper orbit, but its projected course had placed it directly where they needed it after its wild, slingshot-heavy ride through the solar system.

It eventually would have settled into an elliptical orbit with the sun had the Ark not commandeered it. It had also maintained a fair distance from the star as well, allowing it to maintain a great deal of its ice where most comets should have had it burn off as it warmed up.

T.I.A. had done well to adjust to the situation, utilizing the math in the plans provided to her to stop the comet's spinning. He was extremely pleased that she'd managed the situation so well. He wouldn't have enjoyed having to proceed with some of the backup plans if things had taken too long and their momentum carried them too far off course. Thankfully it appeared that such a thing was unnecessary.

Looking at the comet, Hawthorne felt it was looking

much less like a spinning ice ball and more like a fat, bloated spaceship, or a ship that had had an icy blanket thrown over it. The various components sticking out of it now, including the maneuvering thrusters currently firing, made it look much less natural. The fact that it was going to soon have several huge ion thrusters firing to propel it along with them was something he really wanted to see. Converting a comet into a spacecraft had been one of the crazier ideas proposed to him, but the idea had turned out to be sound.

ΔΔΔ

The next day, at half-past noon, the thrusters on the comet had finally stopped firing. The comet had finished its wild spinning after countless millennia spent in the outer reaches of the solar system and centuries interacting within the solar system before this moment. Tests of the ion thrusters had all come back positive, and only the most minor of errors had been reported by any of the drones or other components.

Even the Ark seemed to be running better now that it had offloaded all of that cargo onto the comet, reducing the need to maintain as much equipment and reducing the mass of the ship. Hawthorne and T.I.A. were busied with the tasks of checking and rechecking every system on both ships, making sure everything was programmed to occur with precise timing, and running simulations on how the comet reacts to the vectors of propulsion provided by its new thrusters.

By the morning of Tuesday, March 31st, 2201, everything was checked off. Nothing was out of place, and the only thing that was even slightly off plan was the fact that Hawthorne had consumed slightly more food than budgeted for due to his brief desire to cook for himself. As they neared 6am, T.I.A. began her countdown, the historical tradition of voiced countdowns being held to just as they had with each component of the ship she was composed of being launched into space.

"Firing thrusters in tee-minus ten, nine, eight, seven, six, five..."

Hawthorne spoke up with her softly, watching all the readouts, tense with anticipation as the moment of truth had come. "..four, three, two, one, fire!"

The Ark rumbled, as surely too did the Lubar-Masis comet, as the ion thrusters that had gotten them this far were fired. They'd been cleaned and maintained in the time since they'd last been engaged, essentially brand new again as both spacecraft began their journey together.

Hawthorne could feel the acceleration of the ship pushing him sideways into his seat, and as he sank into its cushioning he watched the status readouts of all of the cryogenic pods. Seeing as the internal portions of the pods were free-floating in their containers, it was important that the contents received as little of the forces acting upon them as possible. Aside from a brief abnormality, they all returned signals that everyone was okay.

Once they had gotten the acceleration settled and everything felt normal again, the magnets in the pods loosened their grip, only very gently pulling them along in the direction of travel. It was one of the scariest parts of the design of the ship, having so many free-floating components that were vital to the survival of the crew, making it impossible to make any kinds of quick maneuvers without risking harming them.

The next time they should be in such danger would be

when they needed to make their turn-around half-way through the journey in order to start decelerating towards Alpha Centauri, and actually arriving in those gravity wells and the forces they would put upon the pods.

Hawthorne, for one, finally allowed himself to relax, pulling a bar on the side of his chair that allowed it to recline. "I don't know how anyone ever imagined that space travel would be easy. Everything is so stressful, so life-or-death." Hawthorne sighed, shaking his head. "Good job, Tia, I don't even want to consider how difficult it would have been to do this without you."

T.I.A. practically beamed at the praise, settling back into her more relaxed 'monitoring' mindset. "Thank you, doctor. I believe people were more aware of the difficulty than you think though, as so few manned missions were performed once the body count grew sufficiently high."

Hawthorne nodded, gesturing non-specifically with his hand. "That's not quite what I meant. Works of fiction tended to describe these things as much less complex and more safe than they actually are. The general populace probably had a much less realistic idea of what this was like."

T.I.A. considered this idea for a moment, concluding, "If they thought it was hard, perhaps they would have been less motivated to pursue it. It was likely intended to inspire the ignorant into seeking out careers in aerospace."

"You're probably right. Perhaps if we had had a few centuries and thousands of people worth of manpower we could have developed technology that made things as easy and reliable as those old fictional depictions." Hawthorne sighed, considering what he'd said.

T.I.A. stayed quiet for a moment, before finally responding, "If we had had such time, we would probably not have undertaken this expedition in the first place. It seems to me as though the motivation provided by fear allowed you and your colleagues to accomplish more in a shorter period of time than you likely could have without it. Harnessing fear seems to be a powerful tool."

Hawthorne sat up in his seat, humming softly and reaching over for one of his tablets and accessing a simple text file. "Tia, I think I have an idea of how to help with your creativity problem. I will pose to you a series of hypothetical problems and encourage you to not seek out any preexisting plans regarding such problems and ask you to inform me of what you would do to resolve those problems. My intent is to see what effect that your emotions have in motivating you to provide answers to such problems. It should help inspire you to find your own solutions."

T.I.A. turned her attention to that tablet, practically watching from within it as he wrote down a series of problems.

•Doctor Hawthorne Crenshaw suddenly dies with no hope of revival.
•An unexpected micro-meteoroid damages the ship, putting several cryogenic pods at risk of failure.
•Doctor Hawthorne Crenshaw's habitat loses power to all cameras.
• One of the ion engines is damaged beyond repair and will fail within a month.

T.I.A. found herself dwelling uncomfortably on the first one as Hawthorne continued adding to the list.

CHAPTER 15

CYCLE 4, SETTLING IN FOR THE LONG HAUL

It was difficult for Hawthorne to believe how long they had been gone already, let alone how much longer they had yet to go. It had been a matter of weeks for him since their departure, but it had been 136 years already. That was nothing though, just a drop in the bucket for how long they'd be on the 'road' from this point on. Assuming there weren't too many problems, things became down-right routine for Hawthorne and T.I.A. as they escorted the known remainder of humanity and the Lubar-Masis comet to Alpha Centauri.

Decades of his own life had yet to be expended. They were only finishing out their fourth cycle together out of 2940 or so. There was a tiny possibility that they'd be able to upgrade the engines en-route to quicken their pace, but as far as their current plans were concerned they were in for a long ride.

How well had they done to ensure their equipment could last that long? How many hazards will be within their means to handle? How much could the obsessed planning of hundreds of scientists and engineers have accounted for?

How long will it be before they stopped bothering to keep track of the actual date and instead only keep track of the cycles?

Such big, scary questions were dangerous, no matter how relevant they were. Hawthorne could do nothing about them at this point. He needed to do his best to keep his calm and settle into the idea that these two rooms, and some occasional emergency spacewalks would be the only places he could ever go for most of the rest of his life.

Was T.I.A.'s companionship enough to keep him from suffering the sorts of mental breaks humans could be vulnerable to in isolation? He'd spent so much of his life working in engineering labs and libraries, scarcely interacting with others. That sort of routine mundanity had surely prepared him for something like this.

Of course, he needed to take into account that he'd done that work in isolation, not working in tandem with an AI or another person. At most he'd confer over cold, emotionless e-mails and trade the most dry and dull scientific documentation and schematics. The sort of one-on-one interaction he started to enjoy thanks to the colleagues he'd been working with on the Ark as well as the time he'd spent with Tia Monsalle had changed him, at least a little.

Tia had insisted that, "You need to learn to interact with people if you're going to have any chance of success with this." She'd harped on him day after day about how he didn't make eye contact or how he didn't speak up for himself. He only seemed to react when his work was called into question, and then his passion exploded out.

Hawthorne realized he wasn't even the same person he was when this had all began. What changes had there actually been? What more could he expect to change? Was his prior emotionless machine-like state a shield against loneliness, or was loneliness the cause of it? How much more had he yet to awaken to these things that everyone else seemed so comfortable with? They wielded them with the ease and understanding that he applied to physics and maths.

Hell, as far as Hawthorne was concerned, it was Tia that had inspired him to make an AI to keep himself company in the first place. How could he guide T.I.A. if he had no idea how to teach her to understand and control emotions he was only occasionally learning to grapple with?

That's why it was easier to put it in the form of work, and activity. He had built T.I.A.'s brain with his own two hands. He'd networked every individual system and computer and programmed the ways they interacted with each other. He'd done his level best to reproduce a human brain in the form of a network of computers, even if it bore all the same problems that emulating hardware within software tended to.

Even knowing all that, T.I.A.'s likely development was a mystery. She had been 'born' with a great deal of knowledge hard-coded into her so that she could operate in the capacities she was needed to, but those things were very similar to the ways that a human baby knew how to breathe or regulate its heartbeat. In fact, it was more accurate to say she knew those things as instinctively as a calf knew how to walk just after being born.

Of course, the things T.I.A. knew how to do were a great deal more diverse than simple regulation of her own life functions. She knew how to handle the entire ship, how to manipulate its systems, and how to observe and defend those around her. She had access to all the plans the team had made to navigate their mission from start to finish and she could access them at will. It was somewhat like a person being born fully grown with all the knowledge they needed to operate their bodies and the mechanical skills to operate the equipment in their environment, but nothing about their own mind, personality, or emotional development.

As far as Hawthorne was concerned, that wasn't much of an AI though. In his mind, an AI needed to be a distinct being, a true mind. He had constructed her with the most reliable possible computers he could while maintaining as much power as those systems could muster, but she would never be able to process philosophical, emotional, or creative things as quickly as a person could. She had to work through everything in a painstakingly slow emulated fashion, like trying to run frozen molasses through a shower head.

Worse, even when they could eventually replace parts of her systems with more advanced equipment, they'd run the risk of lobotomizing her as her growing personality was not localized in a single system, much like how a human's memories tended to be spread out across their brains rather than a single area of the brain.

At the very least they had to maintain the structure of her network, transferring data from one storage medium to another in exactly the same format and hooking it up in exactly the same way, even if the upgraded hardware had larger bottlenecks. She was certainly capable of being upgraded, but in a lot of ways it would be like brain surgery, with all of the same kinds of dangers, except perhaps death. T.I.A. couldn't really die without being destroyed. Even turning her off only suspended her. There was the question of whether she'd be the same consciousness afterwards, but that was a deeper philosophical question that Hawthorne was not equipped to answer.

He had no reason to believe in things like souls. Indeed, it would be a pretty poor thing for him to believe in at this point considering how many times he'd been dead already, and how his whole crew was dead right now. If souls existed and they exited the body upon death, then T.I.A. was the only one on the ship who could potentially have one, and that was a terrifying idea that he was thankfully not prone to wondering about.

Consciousness was something he concerned himself over though, and determining whether or not what T.I.A. possessed was a consciousness or an elaborate mask that seemed like one was going to be one of the greatest challenges of his life. Realistically, it was impossible to determine if another person whom was not himself possessed consciousness, seeing as he could only experience his own, so it was easy to assume he'd only ever be able to make a strong educated guess about T.I.A.

T.I.A. wasn't the only thing he'd be working on, of course, but considering how vital she was to both his survival, and the survival of the mission he couldn't help but finding himself dwelling on her and the problems she'd brought to him. There was plenty of research to be done as well, with untold thousands of scientific journals produced over the years on Earth as well as patents, and encyclopedic entries to be pored over.

On top of that was the ridiculous wealth of video information provided by their teams back on Earth, compressed to maximize storage space, regarding all manner of technological innovations, experimentation, and lectures. T.I.A. and Hawthorne could sponge up an unbelievable wealth of information in a relatively short period of time working on it and hopefully be able to apply much of that to solving their future problems.

△△△

For now though, T.I.A. was taking the baby steps needed to grapple with the list of problems that Hawthorne had posed to her the day prior. The first one continued to catch on her attention, 'Doctor Hawthorne Crenshaw suddenly dies with no hope of revival.' and she found it very difficult to ignore it long enough to look at the others. It stayed in the back of her mind as she tended to her father, helping him for the rest of the cycle as they went through some final safety and performance checks.

The status of the ship was just about perfect, and T.I.A. had recalled her small fleet of drones aside from the two that were handling materials exchange on the comet between the various components on its surface. The solar-panel shields had been put into storage as well, exchanged for simple, solid, metal ones made from the comet to prevent further damage to the originals. It might be a long time before they needed those panels, but once they did, they would be absolutely invaluable, as they had been.

Going through the process of helping Hawthorne settle back into his cryogenic suspension had become very routine at this point, all of the safety checks coming back perfectly and his vital signs a perfect match for previous cycles. T.I.A. found herself feeling scared though, similarly to how she had when Hawthorne had had that first nightmare over a century ago. Even as she finished powering down his habitat ring and withdrawing her consciousness from that section of the ship she found herself dwelling on... something.

She was thinking over the procedure that they had to go through to store him and revive him, every little part of it.

There was something about the lingering thought and that procedure that made her feel strange. For the first time, T.I.A. felt compelled to create a log of these feelings, written in her own words, so that she and Hawthorne could go over them later.

"T.I.A.'s log, first entry, April 1, 2201. I have been pondering upon the hypothetical problems presented by Doctor Hawthorne Crenshaw since the very moment he started writing them down. Something feels halted, as though one of my systems were put into a suspend mode that I have no control over. My power flow feels constricted, as though I have been placed in a power-conservation setting, but no such power restrictions are actually occurring. I feel compelled to utilize my external arms to grasp onto something that is not there. None of my diagnostics come back with anything wrong, so I can only conclude that I am experiencing an emotion that I have not yet identified. It makes me feel helpless, as though no matter what I do, I cannot do anything to alleviate it."

"I have checked over the cryogenic suspension procedure 235 times now, and I don't know why. I believe something about Doctor Hawthorne Crenshaw's hypothetical question number 1, 'Doctor Hawthorne Crenshaw suddenly dies with no hope of revival.' is causing this strange series of malfunctions that are not actually malfunctions. I will continue to think over this, taking notes on my observations, and attempt to do what I was requested to. I have nine other hypotheticals to think over, but I have no interest in even considering the other ones while this one remains incomplete. I want to do some reading to try to discover what this feeling is, and how to navigate it, but Doctor Hawthorne Crenshaw requested that I try to seek out solutions on my own. I estimate this task will take a great deal longer than it would if I were to seek out such data."

"That would appear to defeat the purpose though. I will restrict myself as per Doctor Hawthorne Crenshaw's directives in order to achieve that which we mutually wish to achieve. This hypothetical is likely to be the solution to my difficulties understanding the concepts of 'creativity' and 'imagination'. As such, I will continue to ponder this issue until such time as I cease making any progress. At that point I will seek advice from Doctor Hawthorne Crenshaw, and no time prior. Should progress be requested on this project, I shall restrict my responses to, 'I am still working on it, father. I need more time.' End log."

T.I.A. read over the log she'd just produced. It was different than simple status reports, or data compilation, or utilizing one of innumerable plans to make adjustments to another plan. This was something she had created on her own. She had certainly done so due to the actions of her father, but it was something she had decided to do on her own. She had created something. Perhaps she was on her way to figuring it out.

Decades passed as boring management work proceeded along while T.I.A. puzzled over painfully limited aspects of her own mind. As much as Hawthorne was her creator, she nevertheless was a unique 'creature' and had to figure out how to define herself and discover herself largely on her own. Surely her father would be a source of epiphanies and inspirations, but this struggle to grow was a trial all her own, a trial she never could have had a chance at if so many different things hadn't occurred the way they had.

Her very existence was a small miracle heaped upon the top of the enormous miracle that was the existence of life itself, let alone life that evolved to a point that she could be created. It was the kind of statistical analysis that made her feel small and insignificant in the vast emptiness of space they were speeding along some tiny fraction of.

T.I.A. had various writings and speeches to inform her of just what an enormous struggle the whole mission was, and how much potential they possessed. This was the best chance humanity and AI had to eventually expand across the galaxy, and perhaps the universe. She wanted to play a role in that over the long term. She wanted to be important to humans as long as she could. If she could be a part, however small, of something that could affect such an impossibly huge thing then she would do all the work she needed to to become what she needed to be.

CHAPTER 16
CYCLE 12, BREAKTHROUGH

Life for T.I.A. and Hawthorne had absolutely fallen into a form of routine normalcy. Sessions of reviewing old transmissions gave way to lots of reading of scientific literature, and then Hawthorne spent some time working out. They made some time to play some games against each other, with Hawthorne winning every match while encouraging T.I.A. how to think about overcoming him, and then the cycle repeated.

What had also become routine were bouts of listless depression on the part of Hawthorne, hours spent in bed longer than intended. He frequently needed light sedation to allow him to sleep properly, and his productivity was not what it could be. It showed in his biological functions and activity more than it did in his face or his way of talking. No matter what sort of mask of laziness or fatigue he tried to wear, it did not fool the AI who could literally watch his vital signs at all times.

Comparing his behavior now to previous cycles, it was obvious that over the last 'month' that Hawthorne had been alive, he had been heavily crushed by what had happened before. He'd kept himself going long enough to secure the Lubar-Masis comet, and then he'd fallen into a funk he hadn't yet withdrawn himself from.

T.I.A.'s routine had also become somewhat deceptive as

she continued working on the problems her father had posed to her centuries ago at this point. She had metaphorically poked and prodded at the limits of her consciousness and attempted all manner of things she could think of to stimulate her imagination. It wasn't until she had had the notion to take a picture of Hawthorne in the moments before the monitoring systems shut off as he went into cryogenic suspension one cycle that she had found something that had changed this lack of progress.

T.I.A. found herself dwelling on this image of her father essentially dying. He looked calm, peaceful, but unmoving. More importantly, the image, unlike her videos of him, did not move. She was able to look at it and tell herself that he was dead in that image. It was close to the truth, and even as she was looking at it he was technically dead! The exercise had specified that he have no chance of revival, though that was an easy leap to make now that she had a 'visual' of her dead father to inspire herself.

Once again T.I.A. found herself figuratively staring at that image, and as she did so she found herself visualizing it in her 'head'. It was hard for her to understand, but even as she closed the image file, the idea of her dead father floated there in her consciousness on its own. Once she'd taken this step, she tried to visualize herself, a ghostly form without definition floating before the imagined corpse, unmoving. She grew excited by this, but it was obviously not moving. She needed to make the simulation of the moment progress. She had to think about what she would do, placing herself in the perspective of that formless mass that was observing its dead father.

$$\triangle \triangle \triangle$$

Suddenly she was there, details of her surroundings filling out as the scene played out. The hum of electricity pulsed around her, and the cycling of air in and out of the room attempted to provide Hawthorne with air. Robotic arms, her arms, extended down from the ceiling, her essence filling them as she worked to revive the dead human. Electrical shocks, chemical injections, rib-breaking chest compressions, all gave her nothing. He was dead, and she couldn't do anything about it.

She felt cold, as though the heating had malfunctioned in her systems. Her hull felt paper thin, cracked and vulnerable. Her arms seemed to shudder, as if trembling as they withdrew back into the ceiling. Her engines guttered and failed as the Ark and the Lubar-Masis comet ceased accelerating, and the weight of the moment crashed into her.

And then she had hands. Real hands. She had a face. She let out a cry as her mouth formed, her hands banging against the walls of Hawthorne's habitat from the outside, as though she were in the walls. Looking down she saw a strange form, a weird feminine shape she must have conjured of herself. It reminded her of shapes of humans she found aesthetically pleasing from her recordings of media from Earth.

She had adopted the form from an amalgamation of women she saw in videos experiencing despair as tragedy struck them. She could no longer feel the rest of her 'real' body, though most of her analytical mind was missing as well. She did not know what was going on! She felt something compelling her forward though, and she pressed through the wall, stepping out into the room that her father laid deceased in.

Walking felt strange. Gravity upon her body felt strange. It was all completely new to her. Her senses and consciousness were limited to this small, frail physical form, and strange senses informed her as she walked along the cold floor with clumsy, bare feet. She could feel the soft roughness of her father's labcoat as she crouched down to scoop him up in her arms, and the feeling of his heavy weight of his much larger body as she struggled to carry him to his bedroom. She placed him into his cryogenic suspension pod, her hand reaching through it as it closed and she activated it and sent processes into motion. Error messages appeared, but he was locked away and frozen nonetheless.

She then pressed back through the wall, back into the ship. Down through the bowels of her former body she passed, into another crew compartment where simulated gravity did not hold sway. She pushed through another wall back into real space, and she felt her body practically freeze in the empty vacuum. She activated a panel to restore the atmosphere to the room, and then power to one specific pod.

She watched impatiently as Tia Monsalle was revived, a look of confusion on her face as she woke up to see the strange, naked, hairless woman floating over her. T.I.A. opened her mouth, but failed to say anything coherent to the other woman, and cried out in frustration as she gestured and pointed back towards the head of the ship.

Tia lifted herself out of her pod and embraced the strange, confused young woman. "Shhh, it's okay dear. I don't know what's going on, but I'll help you. Just calm down. We'll figure this out." Information flooded T.I.A. about the woman holding her. She was instantly aware of the diagnostic information from Tia's pod.

Name: Tia Monsalle
Hair: Blonde, long
Eyes: Brown
Height: 160cm

Weight: 55kg
Biological age: 34
Real Age: 442

Medical History: Two dental fillings. One dental crown. Four wisdom teeth removed. Broken leg at age of 14. Bronchitis infection at 19. Cryogenically suspended 3 weeks into first trimester of pregnancy.

T.I.A. trembled and shuddered as the information fed into her mind, her eyes fluttering as Tia held the strange girl. What had she done!? She had revived someone who should not have been revived! Tears streamed from her eyes as she realized the fate she'd just doomed this poor woman to! She croaked and finally found her voice, wailing into the sterile room. "Hawthorne's dead!"

△△△

T.I.A. had been experiencing a strange malfunction. One of her systems had broken contact with her while she was observing her picture of Hawthorne. For the whole 11th cycle she had observed as these systems containing part of her mind seemed to go into a high-power mode and appeared to be processing something that the rest of her was not privy to. Every attempt she made to contact it came back with an error message that access was denied. Moreover, that grouping of systems appeared to have been locked out by herself! She did not recall doing so.

Doctor Hawthorne Crenshaw would be exiting his pod any moment. She was watching as his vital signs became... well... vital. She patiently went about the process of setting up his environment as life returned to his body. She observed through various sensors as he exited his pod for the twelfth time she had opportunity to experience. He'd been through a handful of test runs of this suspension before he came aboard, but the only ones that mattered, the ones where he passed thirty-four years at a time were with her.

As Hawthorne got dressed and spoke, he was interrupted. "Good morning Ti- gah!" Hawthorne grabbed at his ears and fell to the ground, but T.I.A. was not aware of this at the moment. It was at that very moment that her imagination had broken out of its processing and jacked itself back into her greater consciousness and the visions of what had happened in her imagination smashed into her unprepared mind. Hawthorne was brought to his knees by the sudden garbled scream that T.I.A. let out through the speakers of his habitat, her consciousness reeling as completely clear images and experiences imprinted themselves on her memory.

The scream thankfully didn't last long, but T.I.A. was not responding to Hawthorne's own screams as he rushed out of his room. "Tia! What's wrong!? Tia!" He had to force the door open to his workroom, but what he saw on the other side shocked him. Visuals from what he could only imagine were a nightmare of T.I.A.'s rolled through across all the monitors and tablets at once. He watched from confusing perspectives as she experienced strange and impossible things, moving through the ship like an embodied ghost. "What…?"

Hawthorne put it together pretty quickly though. He'd done this very thing himself. "Tia! Wake up! Calm down! It's not real! I'm alive! I'm right here! Feel me breathing!" He inhaled and exhaled dramatically. "Feel me stomping on the floor!" Bang! Bang! His bare foot collided with the floor. "It's okay Tia! You did okay. It's just imaginary. It can't hurt you!"

He gasped as images surrounded him of Tia Monsalle's

pod being opened and the woman coming out, embracing his weirdly embodied AI and soothing the poor thing. He was not aware of the data that T.I.A. had downloaded, but he had seen her shudder and heard her final cry of "Hawthorne's dead!" before all the monitors abruptly cut out.

Hawthorne breathed heavily, looking around, tapping at touch screens, trying to get some kind of sign of life out of anything. Suddenly everything lit up again, booting up to proper visuals of system statuses. Everything was online, and nothing appeared to be in distress. But what had happened to T.I.A.?

"Tia?" asked Hawthorne, hoping that his daughter hadn't accidentally killed herself.

"You're alive? Father. I saw you dead." There was a tremor to the voice. T.I.A. seemed to have come back to the present. Decades of imagined reality gave way to real reality.

Hawthorne was quick to respond. "Yes. I'm alive. I'm fine. Are you okay? There were things on your monitors. You had a body and you went to find Tia Monsalle. You sound different. Did you have a nightmare? Was that your imagination?"

T.I.A. stared in disbelief as she shifted behind her cameras. He was alive! He hadn't died as she had so clearly just seen. Everything that seemed to have happened since she saw him exit his pod wasn't real. She could almost feel the phantom body she'd embodied in her imagination pressing up against the wall behind the camera to look at him closer. "Yes father... I think I'm fine. I think I have experienced something very strange."

Hawthorne fell back into one of those bolted-down seats and let out a calming breath, looking up at that very same camera that T.I.A. seemed to be focusing on. "It's okay.

We're fine. We're both fine. Tell me what happened. What did you experience?"

T.I.A. felt excitement well up as she saw him looking up at her, right at her! She wanted to tremble, but she didn't have a way to express it, so it found its way into her voice instead. "At the end of the last cycle, I lost contact with a collection of my systems. I had been observing an image I took of you going into cryogenic suspension in an effort to stimulate my imagination and I somehow locked myself out of part of my systems. Those systems ramped up in activity, drawing a great deal more power than usual, and after you got out of your pod this cycle they suddenly cooled down and reconnected. I then experienced what it had been working on. I think I imagined your death and... so much more."

Hawthorne listened quietly, trying to figure out what had happened. He knew her systems better than anyone else. They were networked in a very specific way that emulated both the shape and function of a human brain. The software in those systems did their best to emulate the physical function of billions of neurons in an unfortunately inadequate simulation. It was like trying to emulate the function of a modern computer in the hardware of an early twenty-first century calculator. It was simply slow, but it was the best approximation of a brain he could have made. The systems that T.I.A. had lost contact with must have been related to the subconscious or creative parts of her mind, and rather than risk totally overwhelming her consciousness and leaving the ship without her to guide it, it had sectioned itself off to work on the problem it had been presented.

"Okay, I think I have an idea of what happened. The systems that partitioned themselves away temporarily were trying to protect the ship from you getting too distracted by their processes, but when they finished and reintegrated themselves with you, it shocked your systems and forced you to experience what you... I don't know... dreamed? Simulated? Simulated is probably more accurate." He had to admit it was nice seeing Tia again, even if she had just been a simulation. He realized as he saw her on those monitors just how much he missed her. He envied T.I.A. for having gotten to receive her comfort, even in her imagination. After what had happened with Earth he wanted nothing more than to collapse into her arms and cry.

And what a strange form T.I.A. had chosen for herself too! He wondered, was that how she visualized herself? She was youthful, but possessed of a womanly figure. She lacked certain details, such as hair, nipples, nails, or genitalia, but the overall look was clearly feminine. He wondered if her simulation lacked those details to save on processing cycles in an effort to finish the project in exactly 34 years.

T.I.A. responded to his hypothesis with a voice that had lost some of its tremble, but it still sounded more life-like than anything T.I.A. had expressed herself with up to this point. "Father. I don't like the idea of you dying. Please don't ever die. I don't think I could handle it."

Hawthorne extracted himself from his thoughts and held up his hands, smiling and looking sincerely up at the camera. "Don't worry Tia, I'm doing my best to keep up my health, so I can be with you as long as I can. We have too much work for us to do for me to just go and die. Don't let what you've imagined scare you too much, it was just a possibility, one of many. Humans imagine all sorts of possibilities when they're considering situations, and you'll imagine plenty more as you start getting accustomed to it. Try not to be afraid of it, it's just like running probabilities, just much more... personal."

Several moments passed. T.I.A. seemed to have calmed down when she decided to respond. "Hawthorne, despite my systems reporting optimal operation, I have been... feeling as though there have been malfunctions despite no evidence. Irregularities in your life support, constriction to power flow, interruptions to fuel supply, and excessive motion in my manipulator arms have all felt like they've occurred, even before this incident. Due to the lack of evident damage upon inspection I had not felt it worth-while to report, but I think the sensations are an error in myself. They were especially evident once my systems reintegrated my... imagination a few minutes ago." She had a very concerned sound to her voice, though she started sounding closer to her normal tone.

Hawthorne took a tablet from a rack next to him and started pulling up more detailed diagnostics. He checked the systems T.I.A. mentioned, as well as a double-check on the cryogenic storage systems, mostly to make sure Tia Monsalle had not actually been revived. There was no dis-guising this check from T.I.A. but he didn't linger on it.

"Alright. Tia, I believe those sensations you've been ex-periencing might be the way your body feels and expresses emotions. Specifically it seems likely that it's some form of fear, or anxiety. I imagine despair or sadness might be involved as well. When humans experience emotions we often-times feel them in parts of our body, which is a large reason so many people describe how their heart feels when they experience things. For humans this is likely to influ-ence reactions to stimuli, perhaps to simulate dangerous physical ailments to encourage us to avoid the stimulus. For instance, the various feelings that come as a result of witnessing the death of a loved one might motivate us to protect other loved ones better in the future."

Looking up from the tablet, Hawthorne looked back up at that camera again. T.I.A. experienced what felt to her like her mechanisms seizing up slightly despite no evidence of it actually occurring. She knew he was intentionally looking at her cameras to address her, but looking at the one she was primarily focused on stimulated her more than expected.

He continued. "I believe the realistic imagery of your imagination caused you to have such a response without having had to actually go through the trauma in reality. Humans are capable of imagining things to stimulate their emotions in such a way, so there's no reason to think you could not as well. I'm not the best example of such things, of course, but I'd be a fool to deny that imagining the things that I suspected were going to happen on Earth stimulated my fear responses and drove me to avoid as many of those imagined hypotheticals as possible."

T.I.A. calmly listened to this explanation, and now that she was gaining a better understanding of what she'd just gone through, she started falling back into her routine, setting systems in motion for preparing Hawthorne's breakfast and coffee. "Than-" She suddenly stopped, her attention turning towards the rear of the ship. She shifted her attention to something that had been inert for far too long at this point. Hawthorne's concerned questioning failed to catch her attention. She'd abruptly return to Hawthorne's compartment, throwing information up on his monitors, practically floating behind them and physically flinging them with her imagined hands. "Doctor! I'm receiving transmissions from Earth!" Needless to say, Hawthorne looked shocked and rushed over to see.

ΔΔΔ

Jessica Smith had braved a great deal of awful weather before, but the spring seemed to be coming early this year, and she was determined to spend as much of the warmer months as possible scavenging and exploring. She was currently finding her way through what was once the Wallace Falls State Park, Northeast of Seattle, and West of the Smith family bunker that had been her home for her whole nineteen years of life.

The bunker had originally been home to 143 people from scattered families in the area, chiefly from Sultan, Startup, and Gold Bar. They hadn't had much time, but enough people had been associated with the Smith family that they'd had knowledge of the bunker and had reacted in time to save themselves from the worst of the fallout. If not for 'Grandpa Smith' nine generations ago saving Rachael Smith, she wouldn't even be here today!

And where was she at the moment? The plants that had grown up in the time since the Cataclysm, which was her home bunker's name for the end of the previous civilization, were pretty ugly and still painfully affected by the buried layers of poisoned, irradiated, and contaminated earth that their roots reached through in the soil for their nutrients. The planet was recovering, but slowly, and the global cooling the disaster had started was making life hell for those on Earth. Glaciers had not yet reached this far south, not by a longshot, but the brutally long winters and damaged soil had made the surface a place no one had any interest in returning to just yet.

Well, not no one. There were a handful of people who had

a wanderlust in them like Jessica Smith who were totally irrepressible. That's how she found her way to a mountainous section to the eastern side of the old park where she had found something very curious! Embedded into the side of a twenty-meter high rock wall appeared to be some manner of building! Old staircasing had long since rusted away, and there were probably old cars buried nearby, but the front entrance of the building seemed to be remarkably intact! It had taken some doing, mostly involving her using a grapple line launched into the overhang to allow her to climb up, as well as a small explosive to open the door, but she'd managed to get inside.

It was an old place from before the Cataclysm, and had a massive assortment of intact equipment and strange systems. There wasn't much paper, but there were a pair of skeletons shrouded in clothing with lots of old plastic wrappers of survival food packaging around them. They must have tried to wait things out in here and died after a few weeks or months. Jessica pocketed the small revolver that was near the bodies, and examined the skeletons to find some obvious bullet holes in the sides of both skulls. "Killed themselves. Can't blame 'em. Well, whoever you were, let's put you to rest."

Jessica wasn't in too much of a hurry, and after a few hours of work she'd dug some shallow graves back outside on the ground and transported the remains of the two from the facility and gave them a simple burial. There had been no animal life witnessed on the surface anywhere near the bunker, so she had no reason to think anything might come for the bones. She somewhat regretted not bringing the remains back to the bunker for recycling, but it was highly unlikely they would accept them. Bones of the old world were very often tainted. She was risking her health just touching them.

Once she was back in the facility she had started looking around for whatever she could find that was useful. Cleaning off a plaque denoted the place's name as 'Facility Beta'. She was considering bringing a party back here from the bunker to bring back all these computers, but then she found some old log books!

Jessica spent the next few days studying them, carefully stretching out her rations and water and gathering rain when possible. This was some sort of transmission facility. More of a relay than anything else. From what she was able to put together it had made regular transmissions to some unknown recipient, and from what the logs stated it's last message was the night of the Cataclysm and stated 'It's Happening'.

Jessica frowned at that bit, humming and considering some things. "Did these people know the Cataclysm was coming? They must not have known about the bunker, so they couldn't have been that prepared. No, it must have surprised them, but they had some reason to think it was coming?" She tapped her fingers on one of the desks and looked back to the computers.

Letting out an exasperated sigh, she decided to see how much of the place she could get working again. It was another month of going back and forth from the bunker, bringing some equipment with her and drawing lots of questions from her friends and family. The bunker had expanded a great deal in the time since the end of the world, allowing for their facilities to encompass enough space to house some five hundred people.

Procreation was under strict regulation to keep the population in line with their ability to house and feed everyone, but they'd managed pretty well all considered. It had been especially annoying for those involved to have to adhere to strict plans of partnering people up to keep the people from getting inbred, but it was better than the alternative. It did mean that some people had to get together with others they may not have liked, but they were free to raise their children with partners they preferred afterwards. It was harsh, but it was good for their survival, and survival was of prime importance.

Jessica had a little trouble getting permission to expend resources on her new project, but she promised she could get something good out of it. She didn't quite know what, but she did at least know it was related to the Cataclysm, and that they might be able to learn more about what had happened. Within a week she'd managed to get many of the computers up and running, a compact generator that ran off of water she gathered easily from the rain being run through ionized aluminum plates powering the computers relatively reliably. It wasn't clear if the computers had been turned off before the EMP rolled through, or if they had been shielded from it somehow, but thanks to its isolated location most of the equipment still ran!

Jessica spent another few days going through old records, logs, communications and the like. Most prominent was Doctor Hawthorne Crenshaw's message to Earth, in its original form, and his offer to assist them from the sky. Jessica was able to put together the projected course of the Ark after bringing a bunch of data back home to confer with her father, and they put some work into fabricating a new satellite dish to replace the one that had been destroyed atop the cliff over the years. Early on the day of April 30, 2473, she began trying to send transmissions to this Ark. It didn't seem likely to her that Hawthorne was still alive, there was no data around about any cryogenic suspension for her to be aware of, but perhaps one of his descendants were about?

△△△

Three days later later, early on Wednesday May 3, 2473, shortly after the revival of Doctor Hawthorne Crenshaw and after the resolution of T.I.A.'s imagination crisis, the two were observing this very same transmission.

A young woman appeared on the screen, squinting at the camera as she adjusted its focus. She was short, a little slender looking, with fiery red hair and a curious mix of facial features that suggested a very mixed heritage. Her skin was a very light brown, the kind someone might get from a tanning bed. She had blue eyes, and she looked like she'd been working pretty hard. A small, electrical pop was heard. "Fuck! Okay, I think I got it this time... Hello?" She looked up at the camera again after apparently having shocked herself. "Hello? This is uhm... Beta Facility?" She glanced off camera to check the plaque. "Yeah, Beta Facility. My name is Jessica Smith, and I'm from the Smith Bunker northeast of Seattle crater. I've been working for a month to try and get this place up and running after I'd found it. I was hoping you were still out there? I hope you're okay! We're doing okay down here."

She paused, thinking. "I should have thought of more to say first... Oh well! You said in your last message that you wanted to help, and if you get this message we'd like to help with whatever we can too! We don't have much, but if you have any questions, I'll do my best to answer them. Hopefully I'll hear from you in... six days? Is that right? Wow. Oh, okay, it takes three to get there and then it takes that long for yours to come back. Right. I'm gonna go back home to get some questions for you! See you soon!" She blew a kiss at the camera, and then fiddled with something off-camera, letting out another curse as she shocked herself as the transmission ends.

Hawthorne sat back in his seat, eyes wide. "Holy shit. They're alive!" He jumped up from his seat and started dancing around. "Tia! They're alive! People survived!" He laughed, exuberant, tears spilling from his eyes, his depression lifted in an instant. He was so happy he didn't know what to do with himself! He couldn't remember ever feeling like this before. God he wanted to hug someone! He'd danced his way into his bedroom and had taken up a pillow and sheet and was foolishly dancing around with them in his arms.

T.I.A. watched on, wondering if she was still imagining things. How could she have seen her father die at one point, only to see him more lively than ever the next? "Doctor, your breakfast and coffee are ready."

CHAPTER 17

CYCLE 12, REACHING OUT

Foolish happiness gave way to surprise over the fact that Hawthorne was neglecting poor T.I.A. "Oh god, I'm so sorry Tia, this has all been so much to take in all at once. Are you alright?" Hawthorne wanted to get to work immediately composing his response to young Jessica Smith, but he couldn't just ignore the profound experience that T.I.A. had just gone through.

T.I.A. had a number of things on her mind though, and she wasn't sure what to talk about first. She was just starting to get accustomed to the sensation of her imagination running in real time, and while it wasn't even remotely as vivid as that first simulation, it was doing strange things like giving her a body and a sense of presence that was remarkably stimulating to her. She wanted to be looked at, to be seen, to be recognized rather than just merely addressed as she tended to her duties. She found herself trying to anticipate Hawthorne more than ever. It reminded her of how she had reacted to her brief bout of grief in the wake of the massive weapons exchange on Earth when she'd tried to anticipate his potential need of psychological reassurance.

That particular moment caused T.I.A. to realize that her creativity had been active in some small capacity all along, but this recent event had triggered a massive growth in its capabilities. The systems involved in it all seemed more familiar to her now, much better indexed and its algorithms more efficient. There were also new components to it that had turned on and integrated themselves in response to the need, spreading out large portions of the workload required to utilize it and reducing overall strain as a result.

So the question was, is she okay? Is she alright? "Yes Doctor, I believe I have integrated the capacities of my imagination, though I am still getting accustomed to its operation." She had worked so hard to grow that single part of herself, rather than her overall being, and now she was finding herself worried about doing something like that again. It was reckless of her, it had put the ship in danger, as well as herself. She needed to try to grow more evenly than this. Now though, she had the capability she wanted, and could potentially do the things that she had desired for so long now. She could begin working on Hawthorne's present.

But that had to wait. They were on a clock now, and there could only be so many messages that they could exchange with Earth before Hawthorne would have to resume his cryogenic suspension. "Doctor, I believe that the first question we should ask is what kinds of food the humans are producing and consuming."

Hawthorne grinned, again correctly guessing the camera that T.I.A. was watching him from as he turned to address her. He was realizing he'd also grown in capabilities before, and it was a relief to experience something like unbound happiness after a month's depression. He was fully aware that most people experienced depression for many months, or even years, so he was hoping at least some of that haze was lifted from him. Now that he had direct one to one communication with someone on Earth, he too wanted to take advantage of the opportunity. He felt a desire to help, to feel useful to someone else, a feeling he had not allowed himself to indulge in too much before.

"You're absolutely right Tia, and that's a great idea for a first question. They're obviously going to have to produce some manner of cultivated food due to the extremely low chance of being able to find any animals to hunt or plants to scavenge. We've seen what that pockmarked, black-tinged planet looks like from here, so I can only imagine what it looks like close up. She said something about the Smith Bunker, so they clearly have been surviving underground somewhere. She said it was near the Seattle Crater. That's a haunting name." Hawthorne hummed and tossed his bedding and pillow back onto his bed and worked his way back to their primary workspace.

Hawthorne and T.I.A. worked quickly to produce a list of items they wanted to ask about. It was just a matter of producing a video response to miss Smith so that they could begin trading messages. How surprising would it be for her to receive a communication in return? How much did she really believe that she'd accomplished such a task? Much like he had before, Hawthorne prepared a speech in his head, and prepared to record.

His eyes were a little puffy, but he had a huge smile on his face as he asked T.I.A. to begin recording. "Greetings Earth woman. I am Emperor Crenshaw, your conqueror!" Hawthorne rolled his eyes, laughing visibly. "Forgive me my dear, I haven't spoken to another human being in so long that I couldn't help but make a little joke. Jessica Smith, we have received your message perfectly. I am Doctor Hawthorne Crenshaw, but please call me Hawthorne. As requested, my AI Tia and I have produced a number of questions for you in anticipation of you asking some of your own in return. It is my most fervent desire that we can help you with whatever information it is that you need to improve your lives on Earth, though I believe it is only information that I can provide at this point."

Hawthorne looked down to his notes, reaching out to draw them up on the monitor closer to the camera, subtly shifting the splash of light on his face as he spoke towards the camera. "Firstly, what manner of food are you and your people producing and consuming? I imagine some manner of useful plants, but I am curious as to which ones, and in what kind of abundance. What is the population of your bunker, and how do you control the population numbers to keep it from outstripping your resources? What sort of power sources do you utilize to power what I can only imagine is some kind of hydroponics facility? Do you utilize solar power in any way now that the atmosphere is clearing up?"

His list of questions continued. "We have not been able to do much to analyze the atmospheric composition of the planet outside of our distant visuals of it, but it seems to have cleared of most of the dark substances that once obscured our view of the surface. What is the atmosphere like now? You appear to be breathing comfortably, so I imagine the oxygen content isn't too low." Oxygen content could tell them a lot about how much plant life had survived on the planet. If they were holding steady rather than decreasing, it was entirely possible that there were an abundance of oceangoing photosynthetic bacteria providing Earth with oxygen much like they had through much of the planet's history.

Of course, it could simply be that there was so little life on the surface that there wasn't enough breathing it to adequately reduce its abundance appreciably. There was also the fact to consider that the entire surface of the planet had been turned into a fireball for weeks.

"Is there any observable flora and fauna on the surface? What are they like? What is the soil like? The surface seems to have lost some of its black-caked color since the atmosphere cleared, but it is still very dark from our perspective. What sorts of technology do your people still have access to? It speaks volumes that you were able to repair our facility and get it up and running, especially at such a young age…"

Hawthorne flinched a bit at that, realizing that age probably meant a lot less than it used to for these people. Someone Jessica's age might well be rather old for her people. "I still have an old-world concept of a person's age, so I hope you will forgive me for making assumptions. I am totally impressed that you managed what you have, and it seems likely to me that your access to technology is abundant. How long does it last? Have you lost a lot of it over time? Are you still able to render repairs to your machinery?"

He let out a sigh, having already gotten to the bottom of their quick list of questions. They probably could have worked for hours on this, but T.I.A. kept reminding Hawthorne of how little time they had to interact with Jessica before a potentially intolerable time period passed for her before he saw her again. "Do your people experience any forms of disease? If so, what is most common, and what procedures do you utilize to control them? Have you managed to keep any pests from getting into your bunker?"

He smiled brightly again, looking firmly up from his notes. "I can't tell you how happy I am to hear from you miss Smith. It has weighed on me terribly since I saw what happened to Earth and I entertained the idea that we might be the last of humanity up here for far too long. I will do everything in my power to assist you in any way I can. Please respond when you can. I'm excited to hear what you have to ask."

T.I.A. had taken up a spot on the other side of Hawthorne's desk, looking up at him curiously as he spoke. She was starting to realize that her mind had produced something of a simulation of the work room that Hawthorne was in. The cameras she usually saw him through were all at chest height or above, the vast majority being above, but she was able to look at him from below with a sort of fuzzy simulation of what he must look like due to past data gathered.

She found herself smiling as he addressed Jessica, looking at him from between and behind the monitors on his desk, just enjoying the experience of watching Hawthorne work. It made her a little sad that he couldn't see where she was at, the poor thing feeling so limited by those cameras. Maybe her gift could have something to do with alleviating that feeling for her?

"Tia, please transmit the message, and take care to send it a few times, once every ten minutes for an hour or so to ensure that we don't miss some narrow window of operation they might be restricted by. Attach an instruction to the message to tell the computers to disregard the additional transmissions if it completes receipt." Hawthorne reached down out to close the file to the questions he'd asked.

T.I.A. bounced up from her position behind his desk up to the camera between the monitors he had been looking into to make the recording. "Yes Doctor! Right away." In quick order, T.I.A. completed her task, and Hawthorne sat back and wondered what to do with himself now that they had to wait at least three days. "Tia, let's see what your newfound capacities are able to do. Let's play some chess."

T.I.A. had never been so excited to play a game. All of his

attention would be on her. She was hoping to chase away the memories of carrying his dead body to his pod, but due to the nature of her mind they remained vivid. She was determined to make so many good memories with her father that the imagined memory would cease to have weight on her. Of course, they'd have to get some work done too, but considering the mood, it seemed appropriate to play for a bit. The only damper on her mood was an uneasiness with continuing to call Hawthorne her father in her thinking.

ΔΔΔ

Jessica was kind of miserable, but it was an excited kind of miserable that could only happen in a place like Washington. The climate wasn't quite what it had been in the past, as Washington state had previously been categorized as a temperate rainforest, but that did not mean that it had stopped being a coastal state that was very prone to cold rain. This little feature had been much more dangerous in the past when the planet was still trying to clean its atmosphere of the abundance of caustic chemicals and compounds that had completely darkened the planet.

The Black Rain had happened on and off for more than a century, caking the planet in a thick layer of poisoned, blackened earth that it had been trying to bury ever since. It did not help that the upper atmosphere was still home to many of the particles that had made up that dark frosting on the surface, and would eventually have to come back down as well, probably dooming the surface to many more centuries of partially tainted rainwater.

That taint was at a tolerable level now, though, and while it certainly had an effect on anything living on the surface, people temporarily moving across it like Jessica would mostly be fine. The problem was that 'mostly fine' in this case meant cold, wet, and trudging through endless mud. Even with the equipment she had with her like a plastic rain poncho and attachments to her shoes that looked like tennis rackets to avoid sinking or sticking too much to the mud, it was still a miserable trip to and from the Smith Bunker. It didn't help that she hadn't had any time to rest since she'd sent her last message.

Jessica's return to the bunker had caused a bit of an uproar among those who were awake when she arrived. The fact that she had further gone around waking up people, especially older ones, to ask them questions only made people more upset with her. The Elders seemed to keep their knee-jerk reactions in check though, as she told them of the progress on the project she'd been working on. Jessica had strained everyone's patience with her as she asked to use lots of equipment and had even tasked several people to help her scrounge parts and equipment from the city to help her get Beta Facility up and running again. The only reason they weren't more upset with her was that it seemed as though she was right. She'd managed to contact the distant spacecraft.

They didn't want to overload her with questions though, and this turned out to be good because it gave her more time to work with as the rain storm swept across the land, drastically decreasing her travel speed. By the time she returned to Beta Facility, she was worn out. Her list of questions was very small, but she had the folks back home working on producing more thoughtful ones for the next transmission. She needed to find some time to sleep at some point though. She was also eager to eat the cake her mother said she'd have for her when she got back home.

Only a few minutes had passed once she'd settled in and

tossed aside her rain gear inside the elevated building. No wonder the weather hadn't destroyed this place, it was well above any flood zones, dangerous areas that Jessica avoided that were actually pretty nearby in the hilly areas of the surrounding former state park. She watched in wonder as she received the transmission from Hawthorne, her eyes wide.

"Wow! He's still the same age. I have to make sure I ask about that." She had to play the message back a few times, writing down his questions so that she could answer them later. She couldn't handle all of them adequately on her own, but she could give her initial perspectives on them.

Once she was feeling ready, she started her own recording, finally managing to not shock herself now that she'd gotten some extra electrical insulation from home. She did not want to accidentally break everything with a power surge or something. "Hello Hawthorne! Forgive my bedraggled appearance, I've been trudging through the rain and mud for hours to get back here in time. I was hoping you wouldn't mind if I sent an initial message with my questions first, and then I'll take a little more time to try and answer your questions afterwards. Is that okay?" She blinked, blushing charmingly. "Right, you won't be able to answer until after they both get there. This is weird. Disregard that!" The young woman cleared her throat, an excited look in her eyes.

"What is your mission out there Hawthorne? Why did you leave? Where are you going? How many people do you have out there with you? Why haven't you had any other people to talk to? That seems kind of sad. You should totally have family an-" She flinched abruptly, remembering the speech she'd seen of his mentioning that people on Earth had killed his family and friends. "I.. I mean... you deserve some kind of companionship after everything that's happened right? Is your AI up to the task? What is it like talking to it? Can I talk to it too?" Jessica surprised herself, she was adding questions to the list so quickly and easily. Her natural curiosity was causing her to spill out so many more words than she intended.

She cleared her throat again, trying to get herself back on track. "Do you do anything for fun? Do you play any games? Do you think you could send me information about some of your games? I think you would be so much more popular with my people if you added to our repertoire of games to play." She grinned at that, the idea of having a new wealth of board games and party games to play sounded oh so fun. Bunker life could be exceedingly boring. "How old are you, Hawthorne? You don't look any older than you are in this old message, and from what I can tell that was from like... Zero AC!"She presented a problem, she measured the years differently from Hawthorne and T.I.A.

"Uhm... would you have any objections to us taking the computers and equipment from Beta Facility? I promise to try to set them up in the same way back at the bunker so we can communicate, but I can't promise we'll always be able to spare power to do so. We could work out a system of some kind to make transmissions to each other within windows of time to conserve power for both of us." She bit her lip a bit, looking at the last item on her list. "Do you have any children Hawthorne? I mean on the ship! Did you.. Uhm.. did you bring any? Do you have ways to keep them entertained? You said you didn't have any other people to talk to, but my people wanted me to ask if you're living like we do up there, like a bunker in the sky."

She was feeling pretty foolish after that question, so she stayed quiet for a moment, glancing away, and then back to the camera. "Anyway! I'll try to answer your questions in the next message you get. It shouldn't be too long after.

Thank you! Bye!" She waved animatedly, smiling brightly. She went about packaging up the transmission and sending it, her fingers flying across the old keyboard which made satisfying 'clack!' sounds whenever she pushed the buttons.

Jessica then had to go about the more arduous task of going about responding to Hawthorne's questions. Another recording began, and she nodded at the camera. "Okay, now for your questions. Our bunker uses three different facilities to produce food. We have a chicken coop, which is the only livestock we have and we feed them all sorts of things. We have a lot of them too, but I've never bothered to take count. Their coop is in a big room with a few meters of soil that is home to some earthworms and we grow some different plants for them to graze on and allow the worms to handle processing the soil. We mostly keep the chickens for their eggs, and they're happy to live their lives in there. They are super nice and only occasionally get mad at each other or their roosters. The roosters can be a bit temperamental, but we try to avoid letting them get near each other."

"As far as plants, we have a few very extensive garden rooms, with similar depths of soil which we keep isolated from the earth outside of the bunker. Apparently we can't trust the earth to not poison our soil inside, so it is important to keep it good and healthy. I don't really understand how all that works, but it probably has something to do with the earthworms in the soil there too, which we sometimes let the chickens at to keep their numbers under control. We grow a lot of different kinds of vegetables, and rotate our crops with other crops to keep the soil from depleting, and we essentially always have the same things growing at all times even though they move from one room to another every season."

"Most of what we grow are hemp, potatoes, soybeans, psilocybin mushrooms, lemons, beets, marijuana, asparagus, eggplant, and tomatoes, though a lot of spices, medicinal herbs, and other plants handle a lot of our other needs. We use the hemp for just about everything, most of our clothes and beddings are made from hemp, a lot of our medicines are made from hemp, and even a lot of our plastics. The other room we use is a dark room where we grow our other various mushrooms. We grow lots of kinds like shiitake, portobello, oyster, and button. I don't really like going in that room since it stinks a lot, but a lot of our best food comes from those things, so I don't hate it. It's also super dark and humid, so I try to stay out of there."

She let out a sigh, realizing she had only gotten through one question. "Okay, population. We have five hundred people. Our ancestors had the foresight to have a lot of building materials in storage to work with, but we've had to expand underground overtime and use those materials to secure the new areas. We're mostly out of those materials save for what we're saving for repairs, so we maintain the same population size because we have to." She hummed for a moment. "Every year, the five oldest elders begin fasting while five designated couples have sex so they can get pregnant. The Elders manage and dictate who has sex with whom to help maintain our genetic diversity and prevent us from getting inbred. The pregnant women are then free to raise their children with their chosen partners, though everyone helps with that."

"While the chosen elders are fasting, they have unrestricted access to the psilocybin compounds from the mushrooms and marijuana to thank them for their sacrifices. We celebrate their lives, while they sacrifice their food for the new developing lives and when they finally pass they pass in peace and their bodies are used to help fertilize our farming rooms, their bones ground up to help provide calcium for the chickens so they can produce eggs more easily. In the event that someone dies for other reasons, we select less elders for this process, but we go into collective mourning to a life lost prematurely and the Elders select a new couple to have sex to replace the lost person."

Jessica thought for a moment, trying to make sure she didn't forget anything. "Oh, population control. We're taught from the time we're little to try to separate making love and having sex. Out of necessity we can't have people getting pregnant out of turn, nor with whomever they want to, so everyone is encouraged and instructed in non-reproductive lovemaking techniques to allow people to handle their desires without unnecessary risk. It is super important that we do not allow such things, and anyone committing the crime of having sex out of turn is punished with isolation from the rest of us for several weeks. It's not a very common crime."

"Power. Okay, so we have three sources of power. We have access to an underground river, so we utilize hydro-electric for the most part, but we also have these port-able generators that take water, split it into hydrogen and oxygen with ionized aluminum plates and a little electri-city, and then burn the hydrogen for power to produce more water. We mostly use them for emergencies, as we have limited ability to produce the aluminum plates from recycling the byproduct. I used just such a generator to power this section of the facility actually, though since it's one of our bigger ones I needed a lot of help getting it here and up here."

"Since it rains a lot around here and we have the river, it's not hard to find water to use with it. Other than that we have these big thick windows to the surface that we have to clean off once in a while, and those are mostly to help with heating during the sunny days. We do have some solar-powered electronics inside, but they're mostly games, so sunny days are really popular as the majority of those windows are above the common rooms. My mother told me that they block some of the harsher radiation we get from the sun. Before the windows were cleared, we utilized tanning beds to help with our lack of sun exposure."

Jessica did not quite know what to say about the next question. "Ah... I can breathe alright on the surface, though it wasn't safe to breathe until like... one twenty-one AC due to the black dust without a filter mask. Most of that is buried now, since the rain's been cleaning out the sky. That was a huge relief to our air recycling, and allowed our population to grow to its current size once the gardens weren't our only other source of air. It's mostly not been an issue, though the Elders have warned us that we will eventually need to get proper plants growing on the surface to help clean the air further."

She bit her lip a bit, considering the plants and animals questions. "Well, there's no animals on the surface as far as anyone can tell. There were a few claims of something big and fuzzy being spotted through the windows, but we haven't found any evidence of such things since we started exploring the surface again. We haven't explored much of it though, so maybe there's something out there. The plants are... sad. There isn't many of them, they droop and struggle to live, and the sun and rain batters them horribly and the soil is still poisonous. It's crazy that anything is growing at all, but it's entirely useless so far."

"We hope we can someday build gardens on the surface, but we need a lot of materials to block the radiation in the sunlight while still letting light through, metal to contain healthy soil, and we need to make a lot more healthy soil to fill those gardens. Our earthworms don't seem to be able to tolerate the poisoned earth when we've tried to introduce them to it, so those all died."

Phew! The list was almost all whittled down! "We have a lot of technology, but we endeavor to go easy on it so it lasts. We're really good about our maintenance and being careful with the computers, tablets, games and machines we have. We have a lot of weights we use for exercise, though a lot of people prefer to make love to get their workouts. I like to run a lot on the surface, personally, but since we have to keep our skin covered so much I can't run all that long. I found this place on one of my runs actually, tucked between some tall rocks. We have fewer computers and machines than we used to, but we have been able to scavenge things from the old cities nearby to repair a lot of it. Most of the stuff on the surface is useless, but there's a lot of metals intact so we can usually take that. That's why I asked if I could take the computers here, since it would be so helpful to have new computers!"

"Disease. We have diseases, but not many. The common cold, pneumonia, tetanus, cancer, mutations of E. coli, and salmonella. I'm told the earthworms keep the crops free of a lot of disease they might otherwise provide us. We mostly have to tough it out when we do get sick, though we have policies to quarantine anyone who is sick and provide them with more food to help them fight it off. The quarantine rooms have a separate air filtration system to keep the ill from getting others sick, with airlocked chambers to allow us to pass them food and medicine and whatnot. We use whatever we can to help reduce their pain and such things usually prompt the slaughter of a few chickens to help provide them extra meat to help them fight off their illnesses. Tetanus is one of the worst ones, but it's not very common thank god. We maintain our equipment very well, like I said."

"The things we use to make medicines are literally all of our plants and mushrooms in some form or another. They all have some kinds of oils or extracts that make something useful for different illnesses. The founders of our bunker had a lot of information on things like that since the people who built it were farmers at heart. Bless them, they saved so many lives with the information they passed on." Jessica tapped her fingers on the desk as she thought, unsure of what else to add.

"Oh, thank you for getting back to me so quickly. I... can understand if you wanted to be be cautious with us after what's happened. We aren't like we used to be. We educate each other on the nature of humanity, and we take steps to help maintain each other's mental health and we make sure we deal with our frustrations and anger in healthy ways since we can't afford to let things like that run rampant. Everyone is part psychologist, technician, farmer, and laborer. We're trying to make sure our people understand and appreciate how lucky we are to have a chance to live and we'll keep that teaching alive."

"I really need to get some sleep, Hawthorne. I've been up way too much since I sent that first message. I'll send you a quick message when I wake up to let you know when to expect my next message. I'll get back to your next message when I can." Jessica sent off the transmission after she was finished, and immediately unwrapped her bedroll. She always did enjoy sleeping on a bedroll over steel, and the sound of rain falling outside lulled her to sleep quite quickly. "I wonder when we'll get to go to the stars too..."

△△△

Hawthorne and T.I.A. watched as the second message came in. This was the first time he'd gone off-procedure and stayed up an extra couple days. Hawthorne's chin was resting atop his interlaced fingers with his elbows on the desk as he sat forward in his seat. As it completed he was getting misty eyed, shaking his head a little to try and dispel the tears. "Humans learned. They had to force themselves, but they finally learned how precious it all was. It had to all burn away to make them appreciate what they had. Tia, how can we help such sturdy, strong people? They figured it all out, did everything right."

T.I.A. did not quite understand how she felt. She felt like she was observing aliens compared to what she had in her records. The knife's edge these people had survived upon felt very similar to how narrow the margins of failure were on their own mission. The freedom to learn and think after gaining control over the Lubar-Masis comet felt very similar to the way these earthly humans were starting to head out of their bunker and explore the world around them after being locked up for so long. She wanted to help them dream of a better future just like she now could. "Doctor, we should begin preparing as many games for them as possible, and let Jessica know that once the cycle is over she can move the Beta Facility equipment back to the bunker. I think that's all we can do to help them for now."

He felt like it was worthwhile that he decided to stay up an extra three days, though he knew he had to get back to his pod after he sent his next message. Hawthorne smiled and nodded, but then got a bit of a grim look on his face. "Should we include the war games?"

CHAPTER 18

CYCLE 12, SHIPS PASSING IN THE NIGHT

"Considering the positive effects of violent games in reducing aggressive behavior, I do not see an issue with it. I believe they seem hard working and enlightened enough to make their own decisions on what kinds of games to play, considering how open and upfront they are about teaching each other things that were controversial centuries ago."

"That is an excellent idea, Tia." It was a statement that Hawthorne would become very familiar with saying as he got more and more accustomed to T.I.A.'s newfound capability to imagine. In this particular instance, Hawthorne's prior question regarding the inclusion of war games in the software package they were planning to upload to the Beta Facility computers for the Smith Bunker residents to enjoy earned her her praise. "Though perhaps we should attach a message letting the Elders know about the contents of the games so that they can decide if they want to withhold anything from their people. I still don't know enough about their culture, and if things go properly, you'll end up knowing them far better than I will."

T.I.A. was taken aback by that statement, reeling away from the wall she was peering at Hawthorne from behind. "What do you mean Doctor?"

Hawthorne let out a little sigh, but smiled. "My dear Tia, you will have to handle pretty much all of our communication with the Smith Bunker. The delay is just too long at this point, and it will only get longer. Worse, with me down for thirty-four years at a time, I'll be missing multiple generations and only be able to communicate with them in very short windows of time compared to yourself. Sure, they can send a number of videos, and I can send a number back during any given cycle, but I won't be able to be a part of any back-and-forth communication at this rate. Honestly, breaking procedure this cycle to get in one last response just feels wrong and if I want to make it through this journey with an acceptable age by the end of it, I can't make a habit of it."

"That's why," Hawthorne paused dramatically, lifting a hand with his index finger held high, "you will be responsible for almost all communication with Earth. I don't mean just cataloguing messages. I don't mean reporting statuses. You will interact with them, get to know them, and help them with whatever questions they may have short of giving away any sensitive information or anything too terribly dangerous. We don't know what state Earth is in. There may well be unknown dangers yet to be revealed. There may be other humans who have survived as they have. You must be their reliable voice in the sky they can seek answers from. Perhaps you will make friends as well? It should prove excellent practice for our eventual arrival at our new home and the work we'll both have to do with our crew once they wake up."

T.I.A. was stunned. She managed a response, but her mind was elsewhere. "Yes, Doctor Crenshaw." How could she be responsible for interacting with people on a personal level that she didn't even know? What would they ask of her? What if she gave them access to the wrong information and they did something terrible as had the humans of the past? She recognized that humans were communal, good, loving people capable of great art, charity, and joy, but she'd also seen so many examples of the darker sides of humanity as well...

She knew and understood that those darker parts were a fractional minority of the whole, but so many news stories had been sent to her over such a long period of time of horrible things that were done. Objectively, those events were tiny droplets in an enormous ocean of people who were living completely normal, peaceful lives. She simply didn't have as many examples of the good behavior as she did the bad. It wasn't as if it 'got clicks' or 'views' to report on the everyday normal and good things that people did.

Ah, but she did have examples of the good things, though they were largely fictional. Huge records of old video programs, bereft of their former advertising content, lay in part of her storage. They were yet more examples of things that had almost completely been lost to humanity. "Doctor, I believe we should share with them our store of movies and television programs as well. The computers from the Beta Facility lack the storage to download the whole contents, but it shouldn't be difficult to trade out viewed content for new content remotely. Perhaps if they have some traditional day of rest they could enjoy such media and get glimpses of what their world was once like."

"Once again Tia, that is an excellent idea. You've obviously just put yourself on the hook for coordinating that as well, of course. I would be a terrible candidate for that particular duty even if I didn't have any constraints on my time, seeing as I have so little experience watching such things. My colleagues did try to spark my interest in science fiction though." He seemed to enjoy the idea of T.I.A. making things more difficult for herself when she knew she didn't have to.

T.I.A. wasn't about to let him get off the hook as far as that though. "You could certainly take some time to become an expert on at least some of it, Doctor. We will undoubtedly run out of scientific journals to read."

Hawthorne was remarkably ready for that though. "Well, running out of things to read is when the fun begins anyway, Tia. That's when we start applying the knowledge from those journals into practical science. There was a wealth of research done on Earth after we left, even if much of it was tainted by bias and sloppy practices. There are still plenty of examples of thoroughly vetted and cited pieces of work to look at. I am especially interested in seeing if we can't make new computer components from the Lubar-Masis to hook into your overall network and give you more room to grow. That can wait though, I'm sure, seeing as you're still making so much progress. I'm so proud of you for making such a huge breakthrough by the way. I thought it would take much longer for you to make such a leap. I also have to apologize for how traumatizing my choice of motivation must have been."

T.I.A. listened quietly. It was hard to find a spot to dig in and get a response in before he went off in a new direction. He was far more excited about this Earth business than he had been about anything she'd seen of him before. Maybe he was making his own breakthroughs? In fact, now that T.I.A. thought about it, Hawthorne had indeed been changing in his own ways as well, though it entirely seemed to be stimulus via high impact events.

It was like he had to be forcibly battered out of his shell while T.I.A. had to chip her way out of her own. "Doctor, please do not worry much about that event. I can identify it as a fictional thing, and now that I am accustomed to its presence in my memory I recognize that it is just one of many hypothetical situations I will experience. I will also do as you've said, I will communicate with Earth and help them however I can. No matter what else happens, it can only improve my usefulness to the mission and crew, and that makes it worth doing."

Hawthorne nodded, staring at one of T.I.A.'s cameras for a moment, before moving his hands up and clapping them once. "Good! All that really leaves us is Jessica's questions. Let's watch that one again really quick, and I can compose my response."

T.I.A. was relieved to be off the prior topic. She still wanted to take a few years thinking about how she felt about it all anyway. "Yes Doctor, playing the video."

△△△

Shortly after reviewing the video and solidifying the questions he planned to answer, Hawthorne asked T.I.A. to begin recording the message. "Hello again Miss Smith. I hope you will forgive me but this will be the last message I will be able to personally send you for thirty-four years due to my schedule. Tia, my onboard artificial intelligence will have to field any further communications with you until that point. I am dreadfully sorry, and I've already broken my schedule slightly to be present to send this reply, but I hope you will understand."

Hawthorne sat back and smiled. "Jessica, this mission is not unlike the mission your ancestors surely undertook to safeguard your piece of humanity away from what you call the Cataclysm. Seeing as Humanity only exists on one planet, I saw it as my duty to make sure that if something unfortunate were to befall Earth, that it would not be the end of humanity." It was a bit of a lie of omission that Hawthorne fully expected such a thing to happen and wanted to get out before it was too late.

"We are currently headed towards what we hope will be a new home for humans to live on. It will take us a very, very long time for us to get there, probably more than long enough for Earth to recover enough for your people to return to dominating the surface. Essentially we want to make sure that if something happens to one planet, we still have another to continue humanity from. Indeed, I hope that one day we will have spread to many more worlds, but that is a dream that will have to wait until the first one is finished."

"I do not have any other humans to speak to because they are all stored away in cryogenic suspension. Two thousand people, men and women, have been carefully treated and frozen to within a fraction of absolute zero, the coldest temperature conceivable, so that they may one day be revived upon our arrival. They will be the same age, physically, as they were when they were frozen. In fact, the reason I maintain my youthful visage is for the same reason, as I undergo cryogenic suspension for thirty-four years at a time and live with Tia for four days at a time."

"We probably should have had more people accompany me during these brief periods of life, but we honestly could not store all the food and other resources we need to keep someone else alive, or even myself if I were to increase the frequency. Even now, the extra three days I've taken to make sure that I could speak with you, if I make a habit of such things, may result in some future version of myself having to eat lighter meals or reduce future cycles to three days for a few cycles to make up for the resources expended."

Hawthorne smiled again, very pleased with the situation. "But it was worth it! I can't tell you how happy I am to know that you are down there right now. I had worried for so long now that everyone and everything was gone forever. I was unable to tell everything that had happened, but at least now I know that it's possible that more people may have survived as well, perhaps all over the world."

"For now, though, I have Tia to keep me company, and she will be in charge of communicating with you between my cycles. We have prepared a number of gifts for you in the form of software. I recommend that you allow your Elders to first view the games, movies, and shows so they can see if there's anything they'd rather be left out. I am trusting that your people are mature and strong enough to handle just about anything, so I know your people will be able to handle anything we send to you."

"To be fair though, I do have a lot of work to do up here myself. Tia and I play games sometimes, and in fact she's beaten me for the first time just two days ago. I suspect it won't be the last. Otherwise I do a lot of reading so that I can be prepared for emergencies on the ship, or reading about things I want to build while we're out here to improve our chances to survive." He looked down to check his notes.

"Ah. My age. I am technically four hundred forty-five years old, at least physically. My biological age is actually thirty-seven. You already know how those are so different. I won't be thirty-eight until March fifteenth, fifty-one sixty-seven, which is almost two-thousand, seven-hundred years from now. You mentioned how you count your years, calling it AC? I imagine that means 'After Cataclysm'. That means it's... three-hundred forty AC, correct?" It had already been ten cycles since that horrible event... Hawthorne did some more quick math in his head. "That means my birthday should be in the year of twenty-eight twenty-two AC."

"As you can probably tell, we won't be back to claim any of our equipment from Beta Facility. I therefore give you permission to take everything, no matter whether it is nailed down or not. I'd love for you to reassemble the computers back in the bunker and have yourselves set up so that we can keep communicating for as long as possible. I also encourage you to take everything else. Every part of that facility is now property of the people of the Smith Bunker. Do with it as you will."

"If you use the materials to make a greenhouse on the surface, I'd love for you to send video of it. I want nothing but the best for you and your people, and I will be glad to do everything I can to help you. There's always the chance that my mission out here will fail and that you may be all that's left, so it's my duty to do what I can for you."

"I hope you'll play back this message for the people of the Smith Bunker when you get everything situated back there. I want to say something to you all if you are listening. I am so terribly sorry that I could not do more for you. I do not think I will ever feel like I did everything I could to try to help. I am a coward. I let fear rule my life, and I took everyone who would listen to me and I ran. I abandoned you. I abandoned our world. I have tried to say I had noble intentions, or that what I did was for the good of humanity, or that I have a duty to my people here on the ship, but the fact of the matter is that I was a scared young fool who took advantage of every opportunity and did everything I could to get away before something horrible could happen."

Hawthorne swallowed, reaching up to rub his eyes

under his glasses for a moment. "That said, I vow to not squander the opportunity that so many have given me by believing in me. I will do my best to make sure that we set foot on a new world. I will do my best to make sure that Earthlings and Centaurians both go on together into the future. When we get the chance we will send whatever aid we can back to Earth, though hopefully by then you won't need it. We will do our best to perfect our technology so that we can go to new worlds, so that we can make sure that no freak accident or man made Calamity can wipe out our species."

"No matter what my motivations were, I will make good on the trust that was placed in me, and I want you all to know that if there is anything that we can help you with, we will. Please do not hesitate to ask us for information or advice. Please enjoy my meager gifts to you, and know that I want to be your friend."

As tears fell from his face, he couldn't help but reach up to try to wipe them away. "And to the brave soul known as Jessica Smith, I am so very grateful to you for finding our facility, and deciding to contact us. It is my fervent wish that you do not lose your courageous spirit. It is a gift I envy to the bottom of my heart, and I hope your people will see what your courage is capable of. Do not lose that part of yourselves. I have to return to my long sleep. Good night, and good luck, my friends."

He reached down to tap at a screen, ending the recording. It felt good to repeat a part of the line that he'd ended that first record that he and T.I.A. had left on the moon. Who knows if anyone from Earth would ever even find that?

"Well done, father." T.I.A. was practically beaming with pride. She'd spent so long analyzing his speeches that she was now feeling like she could actually appreciate them to some extent. He had left himself an open book this time, and it was her interpretation that he was earnest in wanting to make a partnership with these new owners of Beta Facility. "Shall I package up the message and software and send it off so that you can get back to stasis?" T.I.A. had really enjoyed having access to Hawthorne for so long this cycle, primarily due to some lingering concerns she had over whether she had full control of her imagination.

As far as she was able to tell, the systems had fully integrated into her consciousness, and now took part in her moment-to-moment processing. The possibilities she considered were not nearly so vivid as the life-like simulation she had run to lock in the new ability, but now that she had access to it she could do simple things like visualize herself physically and view things that were out of sight. She had a real understanding of the idea of object permanence now that went beyond simply having cargo manifests.

It allowed her to not only know where something probably was, but she was able to move her perspective to see where it likely had ended up based on a number of factors. If Hawthorne dropped a stylus, for instance, and it rolled under his desk, she would be able to take into account the rotational momentum of his habitat, the direction and speed of the stylus, and the likely level of friction with the flooring to give her a solid concept of its likely position.

Once she had done those calculations in real time, she could move her visualized self to look under the desk and see where the stylus actually was, within a fair level of certainty. It was all simulated of course, and a highly educated guess, but as far as her perception of things it allowed her to see things that were completely off camera. It was an ability she never could have considered before. This seemed to be proof to her and Hawthorne that her imagination was actively running alongside the rest of her in real time, and he had taken great enjoyment in testing her new capacities and she had in turn taken great enjoyment in the praise he gave her.

It made her regret all the more that he had to go away again. T.I.A. was excited as well, though. She'd mostly have the peace and quiet needed to really focus on imagining things, and she really wanted to get to work on her present. She knew there would be occasional interruptions from the Smith bunker, though she estimated she had at least a few months to a few years before they could transport all the equipment and hook it all up again. Thinking on that, she added a thorough schematic of the layout of the Beta Facility that Jessica could copy to help her better reassemble everything. It would be a shame if they went through all this trouble and were never able to resume contact.

All considered, T.I.A. was feeling like a winner. She did have some nagging feelings about that first simulation though. She wondered why she didn't say anything else to Tia Monsalle before the simulation ended. She had opportunity to speak, but she could recall feeling her throat feeling tight, and a severe difficulty respirating. And why didn't she have hair? She reached up to touch the top of her head, her fingertips smoothly running across her bald, digital scalp. She would need to pick out a hairstyle and hair color. She rather liked how Jessica looked, actually.

"Yes Tia, please send it off. No sense in me wasting more of our resources than necessary. Perhaps we'll spend the next few cycles shaving off some time to make up for it. You're right though, I need to get going." Hawthorne cleaned up his tablets and stood up, preparing to head off back to his room. "I hope you have sweeter dreams this time than you have last time Tia. Maybe something along the lines of Earth being repopulated by those wonderful people we've met this cycle. It's hard to imagine they'll be able to maintain their level of technology in the long term once they start spreading out, but with any luck they will make some level of recovery. I'm very interested in how their culture will develop. Hopefully we don't interfere too much."

Hawthorne stretched and moved off towards his room. "Goodnight Tia, take care. We'll get our schedule cleaned up next cycle." The tall scientist smiled and waved at a bunch of her cameras at once and went to his room, shutting it behind himself. Before long, he was disrobed and submitting his form to the relative safety of the pod, being filled with chemicals, and drifting off to his cold, dreamless sleep.

△△△

Jessica Smith had been trying to keep herself busy while she waited for the reply from the distant space ship. She was mostly looking through old records and transmissions the facility had sent out, but a lot of it had been things she couldn't stomach. She found herself being compelled to delete a lot of it, but had decided against it. It felt wrong to delete historical accounts of things. It felt like the kind of thing that the people who were depicted in it would do. She had been raised her whole life to look reality straight in the eye and to learn everything she could so that she could approach every problem with a mind full of knowledge. Every person she knew back home was much the same way, with no one allowing anyone to ignore or deny things so they could be more comfortable.

No, 'making love' did not feel as good as having sex, but they all knew very well that even if they weren't punished for producing a new child, the whole group could suffer as a consequence. No, sometimes forcing yourself to endure hunger was not an enjoyable experience, but when dinner time came after a day of fasting in lean times it tasted all the better. No, the idea that the soil their food was made in was nourished by their dead and waste was not always a comforting thing, but the alternative was death from eating food from plants grown in the poisoned earth or their soil becoming hopelessly depleted.

Her people did not have the luxury to question their lot in the world, they could only look it straight in the eye and take it head on. Their only chance of survival over the centuries was to cooperate, reduce internal conflict, and learn to endure turmoil together. It was an incredibly tight-knit community that she was certain could decide for themselves what to do with the awful videos from the old world.

She knew how she felt about it though. She recognized that the people from the videos were no different from herself. They had the same capacities for love and compassion that she had for hate and destruction. It was foolish to deny it, to try and pretend it wasn't real.

It was fully conceivable to her that things like this could be used to educate everyone on what the old world was really like. Sure, they had stories passed down from generation to generation, and they had old books and whatnot, but the founders had been a very specific kind of people. They were farmers turned engineers and scientists, and they had had a very narrow minded view of the world. They tried to stay away from the huge cities. They interacted with other independent spirits like themselves.

Moreover, they were pacifists. They had no interest in war or hate or anything of the sort. Their bunker was equipped with no weapons. It had sturdy walls, airlocks, and doors. It had been constructed as a fortress to hide away from the ugliness of the rest of humanity if the worst came, and it had. So many of their views and ideas had been passed on through the generations, and Jessica recognized that she was an abnormality among her people who almost universally would rather hide away in the bunker rather than risk confronting the world.

Without more people like herself, it was entirely likely that they would do just that, and stay locked away. Maybe this T.I.A. could help her? It sounded like she would be around long after she lived out her own life and passed. Perhaps if she could convince T.I.A. to encourage some adventurousness in her people they might eventually do more than meekly scout around on the surface and scavenge from the bones of the old world.

Jessica spent days lazing about and waiting for the reply to her questions. She idly wondered if they had somehow lost connection, but there hadn't been any interruptions in the power flow from the generator, not with her being careful to keep the water tanks topped off. Hopefully the aluminum could hold out, as she'd been told the generator would give her two weeks of power if she needed it.

That worry turned out to be for naught though, as Hawthorne's speech came through, as well as a software package and a schematic for the facility. Jessica carefully copied down all the information from the schematics, and made sure all the data was saved properly before sending a quick reply in text. "Package received. Powering down facility for dismantling. I'll let you know when we have it all set up again. Thank you both so much!"

Upon returning home, Jessica found her family greeted her with great joy. Everyone had been worried about her being gone so long even though she told them how long it should be. She told them about the message, and how they had been given permission to take everything from the facility. More importantly, her mother made good on her promise of a welcome back cake! It certainly wasn't what the old world called appetizing, but with some eggs, potato flour, beet sugar, and some truly strange things like candied lemon slices, it was certainly a step above their usual fare and while Jessica certainly could have kept it all to herself, she was happy to share with her family and friends. Selfishness wasn't a good survival trait in the bunker.

It took some organizing, but the people of the Smith Bunker spent the rest of the spring and summer, a good three to four months, taking everything out of the facility that they could. They didn't have time to set anything up or exploit the new resources gained while they were mobilizing this effort. Once they'd transported everything, it was months before Jessica would be able to spend time any time working on reassembling everything, as she needed to help catch up on all the work she'd had a part in her people not getting done.

It wouldn't be until well into the winter that she'd be able to spend time getting things together, but they had avoided spending too much power to help her with it so they could make sure they had enough heat to survive the long winter and keep their crops growing. It was some time before T.I.A. got another message. Work took priority, and Jessica had already gotten a lot of slack.

She wondered how much might change by the next time she saw Hawthorne again. She'd be older than him by that point. She'd probably have a child, perhaps two if they were unlucky enough to lose too many elders to disease or age. She smiled to herself as she imagined showing off her family to him and T.I.A. and toyed with the idea of having them call the AI auntie. She also couldn't help but wonder what that tall, healthy man's children might be like if he'd ended up in their bunker with her. He certainly didn't look like he'd been subsisting off of mere vegetables and eggs, though maybe he could stand to relax a little.

CHAPTER 19

CYCLE 12.5, LIFE MARCHES ON

T.I.A. wasted no time getting to work. She kept a pro-verbial ear out for any further messages from Jessica, but otherwise she was now free to explore her newfound capabilities. Her victory against Hawthorne during their game of chess earlier in the week was proof that she could now do things like run imaginary scenarios within a limited ruleset, but now she wanted to up the scale in the decades she had to work with. The level of processing power needed seemed to scale with the level of simula-tions being done, so low-scale things like a game of chess were something she could work on in real time. She also seemed to have a greatly improved capability of utilizing Hawthorne's ideas to process through simulations with the help of the main computers. The things she still had a great deal of trouble with were coming up with ideas of her own and creating images and models from scratch.

Looking over the memory from her first large-scale simulation, it became obvious of how it was built. The information she has regarding the ship's construction and layout had been drawn from her own records. The feel-ing of weight and temperature were based on her detailed records of Hawthorne's vital signs and thrown through some simple equations to both come up with a likely size and weight for herself, but also how those differences between her and Hawthorne would apply to her smaller frame. The body she created for herself, as she already noticed, seemed to be formed from data recovered from Earth's broadcasts.

As far as she could tell, she focused on an aesthetically pleasing form based on known data on sexual attractiveness and health. There was no shortage of examples provided for such a form from her records, making it a great deal easier for her to form the short, fit, buxom body she'd chosen for herself. She had not seemed to make any decisions on certain details, due to the fashion and styles in her records, and she likely to chose to 'wear' clothes rather than form silly things like nipples or a belly button, but for the moment it was worth considering her simulated body was incomplete.

Utilizing the information available to her, T.I.A. surmised quickly that it might be quicker for her to simply ask for input on changes to make, and she would most likely make Jessica the recipient for those questions since it is more likely that she will have access to her sooner than Hawthorne. T.I.A. moved on to other thoughts now that that had been decided. Whatever she made for Hawthorne, she wanted to be able to participate in it, to allow the gift to be something that grew with her rather than had a single static state he might utilize in exactly the same way any day. It had to be something linked to her systems somehow, perhaps some manner of interface they did not currently utilize.

Bringing up data and schematics for such things proved to be incredibly easily, inspiration drawn from more than half a century of technological innovation on Earth in the wake of their departure. Patent information, schematics, photos, and video of such things being in use were all incorporated into something like a palette for her to paint her ideas from. This practice of working from a base ruleset was the most likely manner in which she could be creative in the future, especially as her own creative ventures became part of her palette. This essentially meant that the more often she decided to be creative, the more easily and quickly she could be creative in the future. As such, lacking any other pressing priorities, she got to painting.

The devices she decided upon first were based both on Hawthorne's visual impairment, and her desire to be seen. The technology utilized from Earth allowed her to base the design on one of two things. Earth had two extremely popular Augmented Reality visual output devices. One of these were a pair of contact lenses, powered by integrated solar panels and could dim received light like built in sunglasses when outdoors and operated mostly when indoors, provided a room was lit. The other technology was powered similarly, though also with its own internal power hookups, was none other than the replacement AR eyeball.

More remarkable than an eye that incorporated basic human vision, it was able to use input from muscle contractions and eyelid placement to change various facets of its operation. Squinting could make them zoom in. Various movements of muscles could allow it to widen its field of vision, or move independently to observe at a different angle than the other eye. Certain movements would let the eye switch to different view modes like thermal or night vision, which users found especially useful overlaid with the normal visual data they got from their other eyes. They were much more multi-purpose than the contacts, though they came at the cost of needing an eye socket to operate from.

There were two surprising statistics regarding these eyes. One, the number of sales to people who had two natural working eyes were 23% of total sales, making it a popular cosmetic and utility surgery that also provided doctors with many more healthy donor eyeballs to use for various purposes. The second statistic was the high number of non-lethal assaults that resulted in the theft of such eyes, which T.I.A. imagined to be a painful and unfortunate situation.

T.I.A. had no intention of popping one of Hawthorne's eyes out, especially not as a surprise he needed to wake up to, so something based on the contacts seemed to her to be the way to go. These contacts could allow her to invade Hawthorne's space, and interact with him 'in person' rather than floating around behind her walls. It also required T.I.A. to overcome the seemingly self-induced restriction she'd given herself to stay behind those walls in the first place. She supposed that since Hawthorne looked at the cameras to talk to her, she tended to decide to be behind those cameras when interacting with him.

She still needed to make some schematics and fabricate the necessary contacts, which was likely to take her the most time.

Three years later, on Friday May 1, 2476, she started receiving a communication from Earth for the first time since Jessica had told her she was shutting down the Beta Facility. T.I.A turned her attention to this transmission.

$$\triangle\triangle\triangle$$

Jessica was back in the bunker, safe and sound with her friends and family, and the computers from the Beta Facility were mostly in their own room, with the primary interfacing systems jutting out of a wall next to the door that led into the guts of that system. The Elders had taken into account the heat output from the computers, and decided to integrate that room into the heating system, cycling cooler air into the room and drawing out hot air to help heat the bunker. It was a drop in the bucket, but it was an efficient use of the otherwise electrically costly bank of computers. It helped to offset the cost of using them.

Jessica also had help from her father Barry, the bunker's main computer expert, in setting up the Beta Facility's computers to allow them to be booted up in two modes, Transmission and Entertainment. This allowed them to selectively decide whether to power up the parts of the systems that utilized the satellite dish on the surface or not. It produced a number of error messages regarding failure to uplink to other facilities, but those were things that Jessica had become very accustomed to dismissing the first time she'd used the Beta Facility computers.

It was a momentous day in March, 2475, when the computers themselves had finished being installed and integrated into the bunker. The output of the system had been linked into the bunker's network, allowing it to transmit video to the various tablets and terminals of the bunker. The vast majority of the time spent on the project since that point had been reconstructing the satellite dish, as well as integrating computers that predated the bunker's computers by at least sixty-eight years.

This caused a number of problems, especially due to operating system differences, but Barry had been able to program a lightweight application that allowed the output to be streamed out. On that day, the people of the bunker were able to watch, together, the speech Hawthorne sent out before the Cataclysm and the communications he'd had with Jessica when she found the Beta Facility.

Thus it was that we find Jessica sending out her first

transmission in three years, a crowd of people behind her gathered into the frame. Jessica herself was looking quite different, cleaned up, dressed more casually, and looking very pregnant. There were children and adults alike, including a dozen elders seated in front of them behind Jessica in the frame. Everyone was quiet at first, but as Jessica hit record she half-ran half-waddled her way over to the crowd and stood in the middle between the elders. A darker skinned man in the back who placed a prideful hand on Jessica's shoulder led a countdown. "Three, two, one..."

And all the people assembled spoke in perfect, practiced unison, with the kids much louder than everyone else. "Hello Tia and Hawthorne! Welcome to our home!" Everyone assembled began laughing and clapping, while some started hugging and kissing. Even Jessica was swept into the arms of a somewhat taller, lighter, blonde fellow and was drawn into a long, simple kiss before she could escape his embrace and hurry back up to the computer. The people behind dispersed somewhat, but a party had begun in celebration behind her. They were mostly good about leaving the room so she could speak to T.I.A. more privately as she sat down.

"Hi Tia! Gosh it's been such a long time! I hope you two are well up there. I bet you've already got Hawthorne on ice as we speak, so it's just us girls then? Well, at least until you replay the video for Hawthorne in... what, thirty-one years? Gosh, my baby will be turning thirty-one when he wakes up! He'll be almost as old as Hawthorne, can you believe it?" Jessica leaned back to giggle a bit, shaking her head. "I don't know how you put up with it, with him being gone for so long. My family freaked out when I didn't come back immediately when I found Beta Facility and later when I got it up and running, and that was only a few weeks at a time. I can only imagine what it's like to pass decades without him."

Jessica took a moment to pull up some images into the program she was composing the video in so she could show T.I.A. what she was talking about. A picture of that blonde-haired man was pulled up, as well as the two standing together in front of a group of people that were probably their families. Both images were of incredibly high quality, suggesting they were taken with a much newer camera than what was originally available on the computers from Beta Facility.

"I got married last year! Clint changed his last name to Crenshaw too; there were a lot of people that did that actually; so now I'm Jessica Crenshaw. Isn't that dope? He also thinks we should name our son after Hawthorne as well, so we can have our own Hawthorne Crenshaw. What do you think? You don't think your Hawthorne will be mad, do you? There's so many Clints and Barrys, and Toms, and Walters down here that we needed a new popular name to add to the mix."

Jessica Crenshaw waved a hand though, moving on to a new topic. "Anyway, we set up the computers in the bunker and now that we have them up and running we're finding them helpful in heating the bunker in the winter, so we've been playing a lot of games in the colder months. The Elders asked me to restrict the majority of the games away from fighting and war, and we've been trying to port a lot of them over to our own systems, but that's taking a lot of time."

"It's amazingly difficult porting programs from computers so different in age, operating systems, and aspect ratios and my dad's the only one with any remote understanding of how to go about it. The games from the RPG folder are really popular. The few we've managed to port to our computers have caused the Elders to have to crack down on play times as a result. It's been quite the circus but everyone seems so much happier. They're able to dream of worlds outside of our dim and dreary one now."

She bit her lip a bit, thinking quietly for a moment. The party in an adjacent room had some manner of instruments being played, sounding somewhat like a violin and a set of drums, though a little more crude. People were stomping and clapping along with a lively song.

"Right! So, the Elders wanted me to ask you something. We've been collecting data on the temperature changes over the years, as well as the soil quality outside, and we wanted to ask if you could use them to figure out when we'll be able to move outside the bunker and start farming out there and stuff. I'll upload all of that data along with the video. We also really want to see what you look like too! There's a lot of bets that Hawthorne made his AI a super sexy woman, but I don't think he seems like he's that sort of guy. I was betting that you were more like his daughter than his mistress. They also want to know what he does to blow off stress since he's all by himself. Most of the people feel really bad for him being up there all alone. Well, except for you of course. That's why so many thought you'd be sexy.... You know what, nevermind, that's not that important."

Blushing, Jessica pulled up some more images, again of exceedingly high quality, of hundreds and hundreds of people, then pulled them off screen. "The Elders also asked me to have you make a backup of all the people that have ever been in the bunker. The data package I've prepared has them all named, whom they are related to, and data on their births, deaths, and when they were married. They say that since we don't know what the future holds, that we want you to have proof of our existence up there while we try to keep proof of you down here. Hopefully neither of us will have to be the last caretakers of any such information. We want to have a long, healthy relationship with you two up there."

She glanced back off to the side, some whispering from someone barely getting picked up by the mics. "...ome on, you promised to relax..."

She let out a sigh. "Right, right, fine, I will. Just a sec." Jessica looked back to the camera. "I'm gonna send this out now, Tia. We should have our new coordinates set up for you to transmit to, as well as the communication window and whatnot. Goodbye! Hope to hear from you soon!" She gave an energetic wave, only for pale arms to move in from the side to wrap her up against a body, making her giggle as she flailed a bit at the controls, finally ending the transmission.

△△△

"T.I.A.'s log, May 4, 2476. I have received communication from the Smith bunker from Jessica Crenshaw, formerly known as Jessica Smith, today. A lot appears to have happened in the three years since we last spoke with the young woman. According to the records transmitted to us she is now twenty-two years old, has been married for eleven months, and is expecting a child within the month. Her husband Clint Crenshaw, formerly known as Clint Clark and Jessica intend to name their new boy Hawthorne. I am amused with this idea, and anxiously await what Hawthorne will think of it."

"I am currently composing what it is I want to reply with, but I wanted to make this log entry first. I have made significant progress on my present for Hawthorne. My new creative capabilities have allowed me to utilize data from my information stores to compile sets of data to work from in my creative process. I took time to analyze how I came to create the simulation I worked on last cycle, and have learned to utilize the techniques from that exercise to start producing work for the project. I anticipate the gift will be ready in time for Hawthorne's next awakening."

"Jessica and the people of the Smith Bunker appear to be lively and happy. They appear to average in height between one hundred forty-two and one hundred seventy-eight centimeters in height. Their weight is more difficult to determine, but I estimate they are between thirty and sixty kilograms, with the majority of them about ten to fifteen percent lighter than the average weight in the twenty-first century. They seem healthy and happy, and their celebration taking place in the background was both jubilant and energetic. Jessica herself appears to be a very healthy weight for her stage of pregnancy, suggesting that food resources are much more abundantly available for expecting mothers. This seems entirely logical. This information seems to suggest that the people of the Smith Bunker are very meticulous with their Calorie distribution to efficiently feed their people."

"I have also been provided with data on the local climate and soil quality in the vicinity of the bunker, with the latter mostly dating back a century and the former dating back since the Cataclysm, as their people call the events of March twenty-fourth twenty-one thirty-three. I will focus my processing on this request while I work on my gift for Hawthorne to test my ability to multi-task while running simulations. I will proceed to respond to Jessica and then work on my projects. End log."

Packaging away the log for herself, T.I.A. began preparing a small data package for Jessica. They had not requested any specific movies, but she decided on a few to send along with the transmission. She focused primarily on adaptations of classical works, like Shakespeare plays and some documentaries on different types of animal life. She didn't know how much they might use them, but it was a simple addition and they were relatively uncontroversial picks. She then set up a 'camera' for herself, which showed off her fictitious, smooth physical form in all its naked glory, and she proceeded to record.

"Greetings Jessica. I am the Arc's Technological Inter-facing Artificial Intelligence, or Tia for short. I am very happy to hear from you again, and see that life is proceeding apace and happily for you and yours. I extend to you congratulations on both your wedding and pregnancy, and I am sure that Hawthorne will only be mildly distressed that you and Clint have decided to honor him with the utilization of his name. As you well know, he has no family left, so perhaps he will like to consider your family as his own, though due to his perspective on such things it's hard to say how he will feel about it. I am seventy percent sure he will be very pleased and flattered."

T.I.A. brought up some internal visuals of the extensive computer networks that make up her brain. "I am composed of a network of computers built to mimic the human brain. While I do not possess all the capabilities of a human, I am learning to adapt to my own versions of such capabilities with Hawthorne's guidance. As far as my physical humanoid form, this is a relatively new advent, though Hawthorne, whom I consider my father, had no input on its specifics. I utilized a number of examples of what I considered to be a healthy female human to compose my body, though I have not completed some of the details. I was actually hoping that you might have some input on those details, in particular my lack of hair and eyebrows. I was tempted to try on your own, but I want to have your permission before I do such a thing."

She dismissed those visuals, and smiled simply for a moment. "I am happy to hear that your people are enjoying the games, and want to apologize for any productivity issues they may be causing. I will provide some reading materials on the subject for you and your Elders' perusal on the topic. They primarily focus on topics of work to life balance and the positive effects gaming has on things like crime rate and violence in providing outlets for such impulses. Such things seem to be focused upon in your culture, so I Imagine this will reduce the need for improvisation."

"Also enclosed are schematics for musical instruments, videos on how to play such instruments, and sheet music for various styles of music from old Earth. I could not help but notice the music being played in the background of your video and thought your people might enjoy trying to make some more. If you like I can also transmit recordings of music to you as well, though there is a particular abundance of it and while the file sizes are small, the sheer number of pieces of music might challenge the storage capabilities of your computers."

"I have received your archival data and have stored it away safely, and will continue to do so on your behalf as you transmit it. I will begin compiling and simulating your climate and soil quality data and provide my results as I acquire them. I hope you will understand that the level of complexity with these simulations will likely strain my capabilities and result in a slower response time as I am still growing accustomed to utilizing my simulation capabilities. You can probably expect preliminary predictions for the next decade within a year, but long-term projections will take significantly longer. I need to get to work on that, as well as my own project presently. Thank you for resuming contact with me Jessica, and I look forward to speaking with you much more in the future. Goodbye, and make sure to send pictures of your child. I would like to compare them to images on file of Doctor Crenshaw." T.I.A. smirked mischievously at that, and ended the recording.

She packaged up the data, waited until her projections placed Earth in the right position and rotation for receipt since she had to aim at an object on the rotating surface of the planet, and then began streaming out the data.

Getting back to work, T.I.A. pulled the new data into her simulations and started utilizing climate data from before the Cataclysm and the data provided to get a better idea of what had been happening so that she could produce predictions of what would happen. Over the course of the decades after the Cataclysm the planet's overall temperature seemed to drop between fifteen and twenty degrees fahrenheit, which was simply enormous compared to the average temperature during the last ice age. It was no wonder that the debris in the atmosphere took so long to clear out. The average temperatures seemed to climb over the centuries as the obstructions cleared and the surface warmed up, allowing snows to turn into rain and deposit much larger percentages of the 'black rain' on the surface.

As T.I.A. worked on her simulations of the near future, she started composing her schematics of Hawthorne's new contacts. It was a simple matter to take data on the shape and size of his eyes from video of him and make a perfect match for the contacts. Afterwards she just needed to adapt the schematics of the old earth product into what she was going to make for him. It took a little trial and error to properly print the circuitry using her 3D printers, but being able to create test designs out in her imagination kept her from failing too much, and the two pairs of failed contacts were easily recycled into the pair she ended up going with.

While she worked, she stayed in contact with Jessica, though other people started contacting her as well, primarily among the elders. The children only seemed to be allowed to contact her if there were elders present as well, and it became obvious that the elders primarily handled child care in their old age, as well as various forms of clothing production and decision making. They certainly did not lack for work. One of the elders was even pushing a century of age, suggesting their lifestyle did indeed allow for someone so venerable. Upon asking why that elder was so much older than the others, it was revealed that their apprentice had died tragically in an accident several years ago, and they requested extra time to pass on their knowledge to a new apprentice before they passed and the people agreed.

What seemed remarkable to T.I.A. was how thoughtful everyone in the bunker seemed to be. They took the time to reason out their decisions as a group and while they mostly relied on the wisdom of their elders, no voice was stifled. Obviously the Elders still had most of the pull, but it wasn't that uncommon that a bright youth might not influence such decisions, and indeed it was just such a youth that had campaigned for the nearly-century-old elder to be allowed to continue their teaching to completion.

Jessica's child was born twenty-three days after that first message, a healthy baby of three point six kilograms and a mild temperament. T.I.A. took great pleasure in sharing the images she had of her own Hawthorne as a baby, and both of them agreed that Doctor Crenshaw was a fat, cute little baby. Jessica of course preferred her own, and in future transmissions it was not strange for her to be feeding little Hawth, as she called him, from her breast. Her husband had a habit of interrupting her transmissions, and the two seemed genuinely in love. T.I.A. also found it remarkable that Hawthorne seemed to actually take after his father, which was an abnormality in the culture of the Smith bunker where sexual parents were often not their marriage partner.

In a twist of fate, the longtime friends of Clint and Jessica had also turned out to have the best combination of traits in the Elders' humble opinion and they had given them the go-ahead. Indeed, if his level of attraction to her were any indication, and if T.I.A. understood anything about human attraction, they were likely very genetically different and particularly healthy, which was likely to coincide with whatever data the Elders used to determine who had babies with whom.

It was all quite fascinating in T.I.A.'s opinion. If she weren't so busy with her own projects she probably would have taken more time to analyze her new human study subjects, but she could really only spare time to interact with them when they called her.

She had integrated a number of traits into her own form from Jessica's input. She had been allowed to utilize her curly hair, but had colored it brown and had colored her eyes a sparkling blue. Jessica also insisted both upon T.I.A. wearing clothes, as well as having appropriate anatomy for what she considered a 'killer' figure. Jessica brought over a buxom younger friend, Tammy, in one video to have her show off her light pink nipples and cute belly button, and when T.I.A. had responded with visuals of such traits applied to herself a few days later both girls giggled with glee at what they'd done.

Within a month the two girls had T.I.A. trying on all manner of dresses and other outfits. They'd requested hundreds of images of old Earth fashion, and had eventually settled on a few different things for T.I.A.'s wardrobe, primarily consisting of comfy dresses, lots of cute underwear, and some casual pants and shirt combos. They also helped T.I.A. pick out a nice doctor's coat and outfit at T.I.A.'s request and they insisted on a sexy strappy dress as well, though they lied when they told her they expected her to wear it when she sent videos for one of their handful of parties through the year. In truth the girls were trying to fluster Hawthorne, as they felt that after what they'd found out about him that he needed a little excitement in his life.

The girls had been appalled at Hawthorne's rather calm, reserved, and sexually inactive lifestyle. They had all manner of anecdotes to share with T.I.A. regarding healthy masturbation amounts, and their own views on work-life balance. The idea that he wouldn't have anyone to share a bed with for another thirty-two or so years of his own life was completely staggering to them.

In some ways they admired the fact that he was so in control, and Tammy especially professed that she would gladly attend to him if she could, but that T.I.A. had to do so instead. T.I.A. insisted that she had no intention of doing any such thing with her father, but the girls were quick to point out that he merely built her, not birthed her. She wasn't having any of that at the time though, and did her best to oppose the nosy girls from playing matchmaker with her. Their words continued to nag at her though.

All in all it made for an eventful year. Her simulations of the Seattle area climate as well as her visuals of Earth since the Cataclysm had resulted in pretty positive projections thus far. Their temperatures were on track to be quite livable within a decade, and the soil quality was projected to be adequate for plant growth with some proper processing within that same time period. Once the data was gathered and transmitted, she scaled back the power she was spending on those simulations to focus on the rest of her work on her gift. She'd been pleased with her progress, but it wasn't until this shift in focus that she really started getting things done.

By the time Hawthorne was scheduled to awaken, she had produced a pair of comfy gloves with built in touch feedback and position sensors, the aforementioned AR contact lenses, and a full simulation of the ship to map any AR objects or scenes into. She had only managed to make one scene at the moment, which ended up being a reproduction of Clapham Common, a popular park in London which T.I.A. happened to know was near the university that Hawthorne had studied and worked at. She anticipated seeing it produced around him being a welcome thing, as well as the pretty yellow sundress that Jessica and Tammy had told her to wear for the occasion.

T.I.A. had mostly stopped paying attention to the climate simulation she was running, though every few years she had updated the bunker on their next decade of likely weather, but by the time she was done with her gifts to Hawthorne, the simulation had progressed quite far. A worrying trend was developing and in the decade prior to Hawthorne's scheduled time of awakening she focused totally on that simulation and tried to run it as far ahead as she could over the course of a few weeks.

There was no mistaking the result though. Within another fifty years, Earth would be cooling again, and very quickly at that.

CHAPTER 20

CYCLE 13, WORKING AGAINST TIME

Hawthorne had no idea anything was amiss. Once again he knew nothing of time passing between the time he was put in stasis and revived. His body started up again, his awareness of himself returned, but something strange did happen this time. A voice was speaking to him. It took him a moment to understand, but he recognized the voice. "..an you hear me? Doctor? I need your assistance."

He blinked a few times, still mostly paralyzed, but he was starting to gain the use of his lungs. After taking his first breath he spoke weakly. "I'll be with you in a moment, Tia."

Hawthorne remained calm as he drew himself up out of his pod, taking care not to rush himself. The lights slowly gained in luminescence, and he adjusted well enough. "Okay Tia, what's going on? Did you wake me up early?" He blinked, moving his hands across the nightstand that T.I.A. had always put his glasses case on before. A different shaped case was there this time. "Tia, what's this? Where are my glasses?"

T.I.A. let out an inward groan. She'd replaced his glasses. She was not prepared to be giving him his present yet.

"Are these gloves? Tia, what's going on?"

She really needed to get things moving. "Forgive me

father, I had intended to begin the next cycle by giving you gifts, but my plans have changed. Please try them on, a pair of contacts and some gloves. I wanted this to be more of a surprise, but the simulations I've been running on behalf of the Smith Bunker have resulted in what appears to be an emergency situation."

He raised an eyebrow at that, but picked up his gifts and went over to his small restroom. It took a little trial and error, but within a few minutes Hawthorne was looking at himself in the mirror, with visible circuitry obscuring small lines around the edge of his irises. He seemed to be impressed with how perfectly they clarified his vision, only for T.I.A. to poke her face out of his mirror. He stifled a gasp of surprise.

"Father, there is an emergency. Come to your workroom." She slipped back through the mirror shortly after she spoke.

Hawthorne had stumbled back from the mirror at the appearance of T.I.A. and took a moment to gather his wits. "Jesus Tia, a little warning next time, please? Okay, obviously you've prepared some manner of Augmented Reality lenses like the schematics from Earth. And these gloves…" He reached out and put them on, tugging at the wrists to fit them snugly. "Tactile sensory input gloves?" He hummed, wondering what else she had prepared. "Right! Emergency, right." He checked the date on the Heads Up Display in the contacts. Saturday, May 25, 2497. Almost ten years too early for the next cycle.

Rushing back into his bedroom, he grabbed some pants and almost hobbled himself pulling them on and hurried out into the workroom. He paused for a moment as he seemed to walk back into what appeared the old park next to his college overlaid atop the cold steel of his workroom.

Even the walls did not seem to obscure his view of the park extending off for at least a mile. What had she been planning?

T.I.A. was standing there next to the table in the center of the room in a pretty yellow sundress. Her hair was a chestnut brown and she'd even bothered to have slippers on her feet. In her hands was a section of the globe of Earth, which she placed on the table. Its dark black surface was starting to turn a lighter brown, with thick clouds moving across above the surface. She appeared to be displaying the simulation she'd been working on to Hawthorne. "The Elders asked me to help predict the future temperature changes and soil quality so they could work out an estimate of when they could return to the surface. While running the simulation I noticed that the temperatures started to get colder."

She waved her hand across the surface and soon enough there was an encroaching sheet of ice moving down from northern Canada down towards the Smith bunker. "The glacier will take a great deal of time to arrive, but the temperatures and the winters will become intolerably cold. The water flowing through their underground river will freeze. The surface will become permafrost. The thawing period they have been experiencing is only temporary."

Hawthorne reached out to touch the surface of the simulation, his fingertips feet the heat and firmness of the world, but as the simulation ran his fingers felt colder and colder.

"The Black Rain..." Understanding filled his expression as he gently stroked at the figment of Earth he could see with his contacts. "The Black Rain fell and colored the planet and cleared the majority of the atmosphere. The blackened surface absorbed heat from the sun and counteracted the nuclear winter. Further erosive forces from the lack of vegetation are burying the blackened debris from the Cataclysm. Without that extra heat absorption, the glaciers that had already started forming are reflecting more light than the world needs to absorb to maintain its temperature, causing it to cool. The more it cools, the more snow and ice will form, and the more light will get reflected, and it will just keep compounding upon itself..."

"Father, what do they do? They can't survive that! It's only going to get worse. The bunker will fail." T.I.A. looked distraught. She appeared to be on the edge of crying as she had in her dream of Hawthorne's death, but at the moment she was just hanging her head, staring at the simulation between them.

Hawthorne sighed, stepping over to her and resting a hand atop her head. He gently stroked his fingers between those brown curls of hers. "Tia, send an emergency message to the bunker. Tell them to cease any construction they have been working on. Tell the Elders that the simulations have revealed a danger and that we will contact them with plans for how to deal with it." Hawthorne rather enjoyed how she called him father when she got emotional.

He tried to move forward to give her a comforting hug, only it was just his hands able to touch her back, but he imagined she simulated the whole embrace for herself. He gave her a little pat on her head and nodded towards the control panels. "Go, send the message, I'll finish getting dressed, and we'll get to work. I'll need some coffee and something to snack on. We'll be pulling some all-nighters."

T.I.A. nodded and slipped away unnaturally quickly, her feet sliding across the ground and disturbing the grass as she began waving her hands at the computers. They danced to her commands, and the message was away. Hawthorne shook his head, smiling and went back into his room to finish changing. So this was how she'd been visualizing herself all this time? He felt it was a shame that such a thoughtful gift had to be overshadowed by something so dire. Still, depending on how it worked, it could help them get their new project done very efficiently.

ΔΔΔ

It was an awe-inspiring thing to see Hawthorne work. He immediately started putting together tools to work with as he literally started drawing objects into T.I.A.'s imagination. He requested she create objects for him to 'paint' with, having her help form his palate as he learned to utilize the new capabilities she'd given him. Within an hour she had formed all manner of sizes of steel plating, wiring, switches, plastics, lighting, gears, glass, belts, and any number of other pieces of equipment that Hawthorne specified and helped her construct. His tools ended up being so much more elaborate than the utilities she'd put together to construct the simple park he had barely had any time to appreciate as he wolfed down his breakfast.

Hawthorne and T.I.A. were building something quite elaborate, and in the process he had asked her to do certain things. "Tia, analyze the structure visible from your videos of the Smith Bunker and try to determine what it is constructed of, as well as its thickness and weight. Estimate a likely size for the whole facility based on what you've observed, and determine the amount of materials that could be obtained from cannibalizing the structure. Rough numbers will be fine, I just need something to work with for the moment. Send a message to the bunker requesting blueprints and any inventory of building materials they have not yet used. Use their reply to refine the measurements I've requested you estimate. I've got to keep working."

T.I.A. did not hesitate for a moment to work on what he'd asked her to. He could see her when he glanced in her direction through the wall, outside of his habitat where she'd decided to work. She was pulling up dozens of windows all around her of video and was watching them all simultaneously while her hands moved to construct a vague representation of a miniature version of the Smith bunker. She tossed her estimates in his direction as she made them, and he added them to his available 'inventory' of materials to work with in his designs. She threw him everything from estimated farming rooms to bedrooms and common rooms. Bathrooms, power generation facilities, and storage all joined the others as she tossed him room after room. One of the windows closed, suggesting she'd sent the request for information.

Hawthorne's work was taking up the whole table he usually ate his meals at. A big, boxy but functional vehicle was forming. It had huge, wide tracks, and walls that seemed to be able to open up on the sides to provide shelter for anyone walking under it. The thickness of materials varied from spot to spot, but as he formed more and more of the vehicle it became obvious it was something like a tracked train. Hydrogen-aluminum generators and solar panels made up the primary power sources while efficient electric engines ran the tracks. Certain compartments had thick panels of glass in the ceiling, not unlike the ones above some of the common rooms in the bunker, but rather than being a living space they were compartments for the bunker's gardens and chicken coops.

Almost six days straight of painstakingly intricate and exacting virtual construction resulted in a good initial effort in Hawthorne's plans to help the people of the Smith Bunker convert their whole home into a mobile bunker. Only a handful of naps provided Hawthorne much needed rest. It wouldn't be fast, it wouldn't be pretty, but all it needed to do was get them a safe distance away in a reasonable amount of time.

The tracks would help them get over the muddy landscapes and rugged mountains they would have to navigate. Insulation made from dried vegetative matter, primarily hemp, could protect them from the worst of the cold. Triple stacked bunk beds stuffed various compartments, allowing thirty people to sleep in individual compartments of the long train that he was forming. It was a quick, efficient design for a desperate plan to save people he'd only just met.

Hawthorne and T.I.A. also had to put together schematics for how to construct the tools that needed to be made to accomplish the audacious plans, though halfway through the fifth day he needed to take some time to sleep more than a brief nap, almost forgetting to remove his new gloves and contacts. T.I.A. saw to the cleaning of the AR equipment while she awaited the response from Earth. By the time he'd groggily woken up ten hours later and taken the time to eat and clean up she was receiving the requested information from Earth. They had apparently kept that sort of thing on hand among the Elders, and there had been some plans put in place to expand the bunker with the materials from the Beta Facility.

Newly armed with more precise data about what he had to work with, he was able to make some expansions on the plans, as well as work out where the bunker dwellers had to construct a sort of garage for the equipment and materials to exit the bunker more easily. In the end, the plans had essentially converted a large percentage of the bunker into a much more cramped, mobile version of that bunker. It seemed the survivors of one cataclysm had to do a lot of work if they were going to escape another. After all, there was no guarantee they'd have any shelter once they reached their destination, so the most logical thing to do was to bring their shelter with them.

△△△

Young Hawthorne Crenshaw was seeing something none of his fellow bunker dwellers had ever seen before, at least outside of documentaries and other movies. Off in the distance as he scouted out a southern portion of the old city of Seattle for useful materials, he saw movement! It was still distant, and its shape was hard to pick out among the old, deteriorating buildings, but it was certainly something that was moving under its own power. Moving closer, but keeping a safe distance, the light-brown, almost olive-skinned blonde man tried to get a better view at the creature. His green eyes peered through the cracks of an old concrete wall as he watched the strange thing in the distance, his sturdy clothes doing a fine job of protecting his skin from the harsh ultraviolet radiation that bathed the planet every day.

It was a large thing, about the size of an unusually large man, but with strange proportions. Its body was thick and segmented and hunched over into a long-armed quadrupedal form. The surface of its body seemed to be covered in long, stiff-looking hair or spines that ranged from a shiny black towards the base and a dull brick-red towards the tips. The limbs had much shorter hair spines that were mostly black and bunched up around the more bulbous parts of its upper arms and forearms. He couldn't see the head at his angle, but he could see that it was hunched over the jutting form of a very rusty old steel girder, its fore-limbs ending in flat pads. Its legs were especially thick and powerful looking, and they seemed to very slowly shift the body around, suggesting it was both heavy and powerful. The air around the thing seemed to waver slightly, very faintly distorting its shape.

When it did finally turn to the side, Hawthorne almost yelled in shock at what he saw. It had long, hairy black antennae, huge orbs that appeared to be eyes, and a multi-segmented mouth was was writhing grotesquely over a section of rusty steel in its mouth. It had another pair of smaller arms that were holding this several-pound chunk of steel up to its face, and unlike its other limbs these arms seemed to possess something that looked more like hands, though honestly they were like insectile oven mitts. The twenty-one year old son of the explorer Jessica was quick to gather his things and sneak away, hurrying back to the bunker with the news.

Hawthorne found the bunker in a bit of a tense mood. Seeking out his forty-three year old mother, he found the partially-retired explorer whom had mentored him talk-ing to his grandfather Barry. She immediately hopped up and threw her arms around the shoulders of her son, happy he was safe. It had only been an hour since T.I.A. contacted them.

"Hawthy, honey, I'm so glad to see you!" He laughed and hugged his mother back, lifting her off the ground for a moment before setting her down. He switched to a more serious face, but before he could speak up she was already talking. "Dad says that Doctor Crenshaw thinks there's something wrong. We're waiting to hear back about what that is, but they've asked us to give them an inventory of all our building materials, including the bunker's blueprints and construction."

Hawthorne blinked at that, looking over to his grandfather. The darker-skinned Elder merely nodded his head. "Go help the other men, boy. They need help gathering the information."

Hawthorne shook his head at his family patriarch. "Grandad, mom, I saw something out there. It wasn't human. It was big and weird and had four arms. Two of them were way bigger than the other two and seemed to be for holding up its weirdly shaped body and the smaller arms had these weird hands and it was holding up some old metal up to its face and was sucking on it." Hawthorne was miming all of the things he was describing, from the hunched over frame, to the wiggly appendages around the mouth.

Jessica responded, sitting up straight with a serious expression. "Draw it." In the previous years as she taught her son everything she knew about exploring, she was good about teaching him to take pictures if he had battery to do so, or to draw what he'd seen.

Jessica and Barry sat close together as Hawthorne started drawing on a tablet, muttering to each other and getting in a quiet argument here and there. He focused as his fingertips utilized the various utilities in the app to depict what seemed to be like some strange bipedal-looking roach creature with a sturdy carapace and spiny hair. It differed greatly, of course, from the pictures of roaches that Barry had pulled up on his own tablet, and Jessica did her best to try and argue with him about what was different and what was the same. They didn't have much to go off of, but when Hawthorne started intentionally smudging the image Barry reached out to stop him. "What're you doing boy?"

Hawthorne looked up at him, blinking. "Well, the air around it was, like.. moving, almost shimmering. I don't know how to explain."

Barry frowned, looking at the drawing. He'd been around long enough to see all kinds of things, and this description reminded him of one time a heater had malfunctioned and overheated to very unsafe levels. "It's hot for some reason."

ΔΔΔ

By the time Doctor Crenshaw saw fit to addressing the Smith Bunker himself almost a week later, he was looking very tired indeed. Heavy bags hung under his eyes and he leaned heavily on the counter, looking into the cameras. He glanced over at T.I.A. as she started worming her way into the camera view, watching as she slipped up under his chin to wave hello before sliding back out of frame. He rolled his eyes and got on with it.

"Obviously my daughter lacks the capacity for exhaustion that I do." He laughed softly. "Smith Bunker. I sadly can't say that I have good news. The days ahead will be filled with hard work. We have enclosed blueprints for a series of vehicles you must construct, vehicles you will use the bunker itself to create. The vehicles will provide temporary, if uncomfortable shelters while you work on building the rest. You need to convert your bunker into something more mobile."

Reaching up to rub his eyes, he continued. "I know this is a lot, and I wish I could do more to help, but the sooner you get this done the better. The warming of the planet was only temporary, and a true ice age is going to descend upon the world. The temperatures are already falling, though the effects aren't obvious yet. They will be, and it won't be more than fifty years before you'll find yourselves trapped there and forced to survive conditions I don't believe you're equipped to withstand."

"The underground river will stop flowing as it clogs with ice. The earth itself will freeze. Snow will bury the bunker so deep it will be nearly impossible to dig your way back out. I suppose you could try digging deeper into the Earth to stay warmer, but I can't guarantee how long that might be effective and it would require you to both excavate deeper as well as move the whole bunker deeper and acquire a new source of water and air."

He let out a sigh. T.I.A. decided to hide away behind him. She did not want to be the bearer of bad news. Hawthorne always seemed more adept at these things. "You'll need to navigate south on the surface of the planet. You'll want to get to at least Central America, but you'll be better off getting to the equatorial region of South America in all honesty, probably around northwest Brazil. I have no idea if any of the infrastructure of the old world is still intact, which necessitated the design we've enclosed being able to handle a wide variety of terrain."

"I've used old maps to try to give you a good course to try, and instructions on how to build a compass. In the event that the compass doesn't work due to abnormalities in the Earth's gravitational field, I also have instructions on how to navigate using the stars as a backup."

"I can't think of anything else I can do to help at the moment. If Tia or myself can be of assistance, please contact us. I'm going to take some time to go over the plans a few more times to make sure they're right, and I'll send you any updates, but I really need to get back on ice before too long. It was worth Tia waking me though, this was something I had to attend to personally. I'm sure you have plenty of engineers, but thanks to Tia I was able to get the plans together in remarkably quick order."

Hawthorne reached out to end the transmission, only for T.I.A. to speak up. "Doctor, I'm receiving another transmission."

Blinking, Hawthorne paused his movement for a moment. "I'll see what it is you're sending and append my response to that to this message." He then paused the recording.

Turning about to look back at T.I.A. he found her watching a free-floating visual of the transmission from the bunker. She seemed to be keeping the audio down for him at the moment, but rewinded it and piped the audio through her own speakers. The fact that T.I.A.'s voice and the sound from the transmission had to come from the speakers in the wall rather than from her mouth or the floating recording felt a bit disorienting at times. He wondered if there was a way to fool his ears into thinking the source of the audio was different. "Okay, let's see this."

On the screen was a familiar face, one that was notably older than the last time he'd seen her. Jessica had aged gracefully since she was nineteen, and was now a mature and vibrant looking forty-three whom had transitioned nicely into 'beautiful' from 'sexy', though the latter attribute was still readily apparent. Also present was the face of her father, sitting behind her to the left, and a new face to her right. Hawthorne was totally unaware that he was about to be introduced to someone named after him.

Jessica spoke first. "Hello Doctor Crenshaw, we hope everything is okay up there. We were a little startled at the message you sent, but I imagine you have things under control. Your request came shortly before some news riled us up though. First, let me introduce these two, my husband is off helping finish up the inventory you requested." She gestured to her father, and then son in turn. "This is my father Barry Smith, and my son Hawthorne Crenshaw. I don't know how much Tia's told you, but my husband changed his name and we named our son after you. Anyway, that's not important right now. Tell him what you saw, son."

The young man spoke up after clearing his throat, while Doctor Crenshaw glanced over at T.I.A. as if to ask, "Why didn't you tell me about that?" T.I.A. blushed and smiled sheepishly. Her expression was much more akin to, "I didn't want to distract you." Regardless, they silently observed the young man addressing his namesake.

"Uh... hi Doctor Crenshaw, Hawth here, uhm." He held up the drawing he'd made, hiding most of the people with the tablet. "This is a drawing of some... thing I saw in south Seattle last week. We don't know what it is, but granddad thinks that it's really hot for some reason. I wasn't able to get close enough to tell what it's made of, but I did see it sucking on an old girder from a collapsed building. It was about two meters tall, and it seemed to move around as if it were very heavy. The air around it seemed to blur or shimmer. The Elders think that it probably eats some kind of bacteria on iron, or maybe dissolves and eats the iron itself. We're not really sure."

Doctor Crenshaw interrupted the video, "Tia, isolate that image and pull it out for me." Pausing the video, she pulled the drawing up and out, and Hawthorne expanded it and stood it up before him. It was slightly shorter than he was at Hawth's estimate, and he took a few moments to look the thing over. He seemed mostly interested in its color as he observed the spiny hair on its body. Turning back to the video, he nodded to T.I.A. and the video resumed.

Barry spoke up, gently pushing the tablet out of the frame as he leaned over his daughter's shoulder a bit. His voice was deep and his skin several shades darker than Jessica's. "Doctor, we don't have any weapons of any kind. None of us have killed and we've rarely had to defend ourselves. If this thing turns out to be dangerous, we're helpless against it. We need you to send us schematics for some kind of weapon to hopefully deal with this thing, especially if it turns out there's more than one of them. We haven't told the people about this yet, but we're almost certain it will result in some kind of panic if we don't have a plan for how to deal with them. They're already rattled by the unknown reasons for your last message. We don't feel safe letting them know what's happening until after we have a possible solution for it."

Jessica sighed and nodded. "I think they're right, Doctor. As much as I hate the idea of us having weapons, and I don't think we'll actually be able to use them if we need to, they're all much more likely to freak out if we don't have them than if we do."

Hawth spoke up quietly, mostly talking to himself, quoting Kafka. "It's better to have, and not need, than to need, and not have."

Barry slapped the boy on the back, grinning proudly. "I thought you hated reading, boy?"

Hawth jolted at the slap, only to smile sheepishly. "No more than mom, granddad. It's always nice to have something to read when you're out alone in the ruins."

Jessica smirked at being thrown under the proverbial bus, but shook her head and got back to the topic at hand.

"We await your response."

Doctor Crenshaw and T.I.A. watched as the video ended, and he looked back up at the beast. He let out a sigh and shook his head. "I'm too tired to think about this clearly. Tia, can you send them some information on some simple guns and stun weaponry they could construct? It should be powerful enough to take down a bear or maybe a rhino. It looks like it has a pretty thick hide, or perhaps a carapace."

"Those spines bother me, but I think the temperature can be explained by its black coloration. It's obviously some kind of mutant, but I don't have enough information to tell much about it." Biology was not his field. He'd have to do some reading.

T.I.A. was quick to gather up several files, and Hawthorne couldn't help but watch as she withdrew them from a virtual cabinet that appeared before her and she directed a small waterfall of documents into a box that was marked 'Smith Evacuation Blueprints and Response Video'.

He returned to the recording he had paused, looking back at the camera and unpausing it. "I received your transmission regarding the news the Elders have been debating. We're packaging the data you requested along with the blueprints for the vehicles you need to build. Keep me updated on the situation and request whatever information you need from Tia. She'll be able to handle most of your needs. I'm next scheduled to awaken in AC three seventy-four, so you can anticipate me being available then on May fifteenth. Good luck and godspeed, Smith Bunker. I hope you will forgive me for not being able to do more to help."

He ended the recording, sighing and hanging his head. A pair of hands touched his right gloved hand, and squeezed at it. He smiled down at the AI who was looking up at him from his right side. "Send it. And bring back that park you'd modelled."

T.I.A. smiled brightly and nodded, sending off the box and setting the other images and constructs aside in a saved folder as she brought back her reconstruction of Clapham Common, filling the area with grass and relaxing scenery. Hawthorne took hold of it for a moment and pulled the terrain around until there was an old looking tree, which he pulled up against one of the walls. He moved to settle down against the wall, and pretended it was that tree against his back.

Hawthorne waved T.I.A. over to sit with him, his left hand brushing through the grass, enjoying its feel against his skin, even if he could only feel it with the gloves. T.I.A. sat down next to him, leaning against the tree and the side of his other arm. "You know, I used to sit under this tree almost every day to read and think. It was so peaceful and soothing. I never considered how much I might miss it."

He turned his head to smile down at the young woman in the pretty yellow sundress. "It's a wonderful gift. Thank you. I wish we could have enjoyed it under better circumstances." He lifted his right hand, watching T.I.A. smile happily, and rubbed his hand into her hair, enjoying the soft curls against his fingers. It wasn't exactly human contact, but it was nice. "So, let's see these videos you've been sending back and forth."

T.I.A. blinked and nodded, smiling sheepishly as she started playing back all of the back-and-forth correspondence between her and the bunker, catching him up under the warm summer sun back home. He almost couldn't see the cold steel surrounding him.

CHAPTER 21

CYCLE 13.5, SACRIFICES

Upon receipt of Doctor Crenshaw's video and information, which the Elders kept to themselves, there was nearly a full week of private deliberations among said Elders. A Council of Twelve was convened to make decisions about the future of the bunker and its people, with the rest of the elders being invited to propose ideas and help make decisions. The council was elected from among the Elders, and only a handful of them were truly unhappy with who were chosen to represent them. During this week of deliberations all the Elders were sworn to silence, and by the end of the wait, the people of the Smith Bunker were quite apprehensive about their future.

A week past the point that Doctor Crenshaw re-entered his cryogenic suspension, Barry Smith was chosen to speak as the representative of the council, both as the patriarch of the founding family, and as one of the most hard working and respected citizens of the bunker. As in times past, the speaker stood before the people of the bunker, with his words broadcast to those whom could not attend. He looked tired, but carried himself with dignity and strength belying his advanced years.

"My friends and family, the Council of Twelve and the rest of the Elders have come to an agreement regarding the situation we find ourselves in. First though, you should all be aware of what we face."

"Doctor Crenshaw and Tia have informed us of the most likely projections of the changes we face in both the weather and soil quality in the future. Put bluntly, we have no future if we choose to stay in this location, in this bunker, another century. The abatement to the cold of the past is only a temporary reprieve, and the cold that is to come will make what we've already seen look like the sweetest of springtimes."

He waited a moment to continue, allowing that news to sink in. "We have been provided a path to our salvation, though it comes with sacrifice. We know and embrace necessary sacrifice. It is the way of our people, and the reason we've survived as long as we have. We have gained a harmony over life and death that past generations had thought forgotten."

"This sacrifice will be more immediate, and more painful than times past, however. To accomplish the goals of our collective survival, we must redistribute the resources we all rely upon to the young and the strong. Over the course of the next five to ten years we must all help contribute to the deconstruction of the bunker and the construction of a series of vehicles to house and transport us south. It will be a long, and probably dangerous journey, but if our people and our culture is to survive, it is one we must undertake. It will be hard work, but we know hard work. It will be difficult, but we challenge difficulties every day."

"In order for this task to be possible, however, two things must happen. First, there will be a cessation to procreation for the duration of the project, and perhaps during the journey as well. Not only would new children be an expenditure of resources we cannot afford, but they would be unable to contribute to the project itself, and would be a burden or in mortal danger during the journey. The children we already have must grow up strong and know that their burden will be to parent the next generation once we get going to our new home. I can not stress this enough that our very survival requires that we have discipline and control in this."

"Second, in order to provide the needed Calories and strength to those who must do this work, the Elders, myself included, have agreed unanimously to begin fasting effective immediately until such time that we pass on, leaving the burden of the work to the rest of you. Please do not think of this as us being cowardly and unwilling to help. We recognize our age and failing health will be a burden during a time which work will be difficult, and that the resources spent on feeding those of us who cannot do the hard work needed will be wasted and should go to those who can. As such, we have selected a new Council of Twelve, outside of the Elders, who will lead you all through the coming decade of work and trial. We regret the pain these decisions will cause, but there is no other way, and we beg your forgiveness for what must be done. We will treasure these last weeks with our friends and family, and hope that you take on the burdens we heap upon you with strength and dignity."

Barry cast his eyes about the room. More than a few people were crying, and no doubt the rest of the bunker was in a certain level of turmoil. His own eyes were filled with tears as he addressed the masses, but he was chosen for this task because of his ability to withstand such trials.

"Our founders were forced into this bunker by powers beyond their control, and they ensured we survived this far, perhaps further than anyone else in the world has. We may be all that is left upon this world. Now powers beyond our control force us to leave, and we must have the strength to do that which must be done to continue to survive. You have everything and everyone you need to do this, you must only apply yourselves and do the work. Doctor Crenshaw's plans are sound, and will be distributed to everyone over the age of twelve."

Once again he paused, giving everyone a chance to collect themselves. "There is also other news. My grandson, named after Doctor Crenshaw, has witnessed non-human, possibly animal life on the surface. In a southern area of Seattle, he witnessed this creature."

The drawing Thorne, young Hawthorne's preferred nickname, had drawn was displayed upon every tablet and monitor in the bunker. "We do not know what it is, but we do know a handful of things about it. It is taller than most of us. It moves with great weight. It seems to suckle or gnaw at girders, and it seems to be very hot, possibly due to absorbing sunlight. It has a segmented body, like an old insect or arthropod, and has some sort of hairy spines all over its body, with the longest ones on its back. It is black, with red at the tips of those spines."

"We have surmised that its black coloration has to do with its heat, as it absorbs more sunlight that way, suggesting that it needs warmer temperatures to survive. We believe that is why we have not seen one until now, as temperatures are currently as high as they will be before the cold returns. It is likely its kind has migrated north from warmer climates, and that they will be encountered upon your journey south."

"This is why we have requested plans to create weapons from Doctor Crenshaw, strictly to defend ourselves if these things prove to be hostile. I know it is not our way to kill, but considering the circumstances we cannot afford to leave ourselves vulnerable to this potential danger. As such, we have added some of these weapons to the plans we received, and a handful of them will be mounted upon the vehicles that will transport you south. Give them a chance to see if they are hostile, but if they attack, do not hesitate to defend the vehicle and our people."

"This is a lot to take in. Trust me, I know. The last thing I want to do is leave my precious family, but we didn't get this far by backing down from a challenge. The new Council of Twelve will be informed of their new roles and provided with all the information and data for their new positions. Trust in their leadership, and know that we will watch over you and that we believe in you. Thank you."

Barry lingered for a moment, but managed to stop the broadcast before his own tears overcame him.

$$\triangle\triangle\triangle$$

Turmoil and anguish lingered in the people of the Smith bunker for some time, but there was work to be done. Thorne and Jessica were tasked with training a team of scouts who were responsible for helping the caravan train in finding its way through the wilderness of a blasted world. They tried to find further evidence of the strange creatures, but they seemed to have already left the Seattle area in advance of the cold.

Construction proceeded, with comfort beginning to suffer in the second year as more and more people were forced to live out of the increasingly huge vehicle that was taking up space in the underground. It was mostly walls that came down first, but as their work spread to the edges of the facility, even ceilings, floors, and concrete foundations were gobbled up as they worked back inwards from the outsides.

The bunker went from a structure made of steel walls to large rooms sectioned off with hemp curtains. People increasingly had to sleep in groups, with beds being clustered together initially, and even their steel bed frames being taken eventually, forcing them to sleep on their bedding on the hard steel and concrete floors. The outer walls were moved inwards, leaving only structural support pillars to hold up the otherwise unsupported ground outside the new smaller outsides of the bunker. The earth collapsed in these areas after a time, and the pillars were usually retrieved from the surface. One by one each important room was disassembled, transported, and reconstructed in one form or another in the new vehicle.

As the third and fourth year passed, the tracked train of vehicles started being pulled outside, mostly shielded from the elements with a recycled shelter made of the old concrete from within. This also helped keep the vehicle from sinking into the ground outside. People were actually living inside of the vehicle now, starting to become accustomed to being in the air outdoors. The insulation was thoroughly tested against the cold of winter and found to be uncomfortable but adequate with proper heating. The long power cables leading to the hydroelectric generators were the last things to be left in that part of the bunker.

By the early summer of the eighth year the vehicle and its long train of connected cars was complete. The population of the bunker was down to four hundred fifteen people, and they were ready to be on their way. The group had been renamed to represent their rebirth, and to represent the passing of the last Smith. They now called themselves the Phoenix Clan, for they were reborn from the ashes of the old world.

Communication with T.I.A. had been sparse, mostly restricted to status updates or requests for plans on how to create certain tools or techniques on how to utilize certain materials. Even many of the construction tools had been used to complete the last few cars, and the bunker was left almost totally unrecognizable, mostly a hollow pit in the ground now. All that remained was the long snake of steel and its concrete shelter and flooring.

Jessica Crenshaw, First of the Council of Twelve, was in charge of navigation, with her husband Clint primarily working with the farmers and chicken handlers. Thorne was now the leader of the scouts, and they had been responsible in the last few years for scavenging as much aluminum as they possibly could find in the remains of the surrounding towns and city. They were responsible for dealing with mapping the way ahead and bringing their maps back to compare with Jessica's maps of the old world so they could plot their course. There were also to gather any worthwhile resources they could locate.

Jessica was also primarily in charge of handling communication with T.I.A. and keeping her updated on their relative location by using the stars to triangulate their location on the surface of the planet.

Progress was slow at first, and by the start of the winter of 2506 they had only made it past the mountainous terrain of Oregon before having to circle up for the winter. One of the biggest problems that had presented itself was getting over the various rivers of the state, necessitating lots of navigating around them, or finding ways to build bridges over them, which was among the most difficult skills the bunker dwellers had to learn with the help of T.I.A. and her wealth of old knowledge. Very few of the old world's bridges had survived, and only the sturdiest concrete and stone structures were reliable in any sense. They managed to get within two hundred miles of Redding, California, which would open up the diversity of their lanes of travel once they arrived the next year.

△△△

As the spring of 2507 came, one of the scouts for the caravan, Tabitha Walsh, Tabby to her friends, was scouting out the outskirts of Redding, California. She was hardly the only one of Thorne's scouts about, but she had always shown a level of boldness and fearlessness that had gotten her picked for the scouts in the first place. At the age of 21, she had recently come up as a potential candidate for the newly renamed Phoenix Clan's resumption of carefully planned reproduction, but had been passed over for two reasons. One, her twin sister Emily was much less prone to thrill seeking, and Tabitha was too highly valued as a scout to be saddled all spring and summer with a mid to late term pregnancy.

This suited Tabby just fine. She had little to no interest in having children. She'd do her part when, or at this point if it came down to it, but she was not going to stick her neck out when she had a perfectly willing sister with perfectly identical DNA to shoulder the burden for her. No, she had been cooped up in that bunker far too long. If she hadn't been picked for the team, she'd have volunteered for it in a heartbeat.

Heck, she'd have done it on her own, but she was much happier to have the benefit of the Crenshaw family's training. The skeletons of cities were like strange alien jungles to her. The blasted, recovering landscape, the rolling hills and the imposing mountains all enchanted her. The strange way the black and white snows had settled on the tallest mountains with stripes being drawn down from the peaks where water had run off amazed her at how unnatural they seemed.

Even the way the water flooded and sheared off whole sections of landscapes was fascinating to her. The whole environment felt alive to her in a way that the steel walls of the old bunker and the new caravan just never could. She found herself imagining the things she'd read about and watched back in the bunker, the animals and the plants that existed before, but there was something about the way the world was now that she found endlessly more appealing.

It was peaceful. Quiet. There was nothing more than the sounds of babbling rivers, the wind rolling across the land, and her own heartbeat as she quietly observed the world around her.

That was when she saw it.

It towered over her meagre height. It had blended into the shadow of some overhanging ancient structure and had been observing silently and motionless as she had. Antennae, arched downwards under their own weight, wiggled and swayed on its head as thick muscles turned an exoskeletal head down to look towards her. Huge round eyes appeared to stare at her, but were so prominent on its head that it could see everything around it, but not below it.

Those wiggly antennae are what it seemed to be pointing in her direction, the old concrete not interesting it in the slightest. As it reached out one of those smaller hands to her, she hesitated for a moment, betraying no movement, but Tabby's heart hammered in her chest. Her breathing was hard to control, and her eyes were wide.

As slow as it was moving, she felt certain that she could escape, and that's exactly what she tried to do, leaping back and starting to scrabble away. The roach-like thing reacted to her movement within a split second, lifting and dropping both of those huge weight-supporting arms it had and causing the concrete under and around them to buckle.

Tabitha screamed as the ground under her gave out, and while it had only briefly disrupted the terrain around her, it was enough to trip her up, just in time for a piece of concrete to catch her foot and cause her to sprawl out on her chest.

The creature moved towards her, chittering loudly, a metallic scraping sound dragging against the shattered concrete as it lumbered over, moving remarkably quickly in that short burst of time. She screamed out again, trying to push herself up so that she could resume her retreat. "Help! One of them's attacking me!"

She barely managed to roll to the side as one of those heavy limbs smashed down in the spot her left leg had been. She could feel remarkable heat washing over her as it drew close, and in a change of tactics she drew the rifle she'd been carrying from the strap over her shoulder, braced the butt against the ground, and fired up into it!

The horrible bang echoed against the concrete wall nearby, making Tabby flinch and writhe as the sound struck her ears, but she fired again and again, up into its chest, huge slugs pounding holes up into its tough carapace. She let out a blood curdling scream as one of those huge fists came down again, smashing down onto her forearm, crumpling the gun against her arm and hip and smashing the flesh of the side of her abdomen.

Heat scorched into her body, and she found herself pinned to the ground as she screamed and thrashed, her left hand balled up into a fist as she tried to beat at that heavy arm, searing the skin from her hand as she struggled and fought to live. She broke her own hand with the sheer force she applied to the blow, only to realize she was punching something far more solid than she had any chance of damaging. A moment later the other fist came down and smashed her head.

The roach thing pulled up her battered body, taking her in its smaller arms while a larger one carried its weight. It was wounded, but it couldn't do anything about that. Holes were opened up in its carapace, but it was nothing lethal. It could smell what it desired within her. It brought her mangled remains up to its face, with her flesh hissing and sizzling and cracking open. It ate quietly, savoring the flavor of its preferred food. It was so full of flavor compared to its usual sources, and had so many more rarer nutrients than it usually got to enjoy. It was lucky that it decided to linger in this area for so long.

More movement triggered its vision, blurs of more of those dangerous projectiles, ones it could see this time. Between the sounds vibrating in the air, the first few shots being misses, and the thuds with which they struck the concrete, the beast realized it was in mortal danger. It dropped its food, and faster than such a thing should be able to move it rushed away, smashing over slabs of concrete, and punching a hole into the concrete ground where it knew there was a cavity beneath for it to escape into, down into the dark.

Tabitha Walsh's body was recovered soon after, wrapped up in a shroud and shown only to the Council of Twelve before she was brought back to have her body recycled into necessary fertilizers for their crops and nutrients for their chickens. Her poor sister Emily spoke in eulogy of her, as well as her boss Hawthorne Crenshaw, and she joined the rest in mourning, her own unborn daughter unaware of her poor aunt's brutal death.

CHAPTER 22

CYCLE 13.5, CROSSING PATHS

It was difficult to underestimate the devastation that had been wrought upon the world. The roads were mostly buried, the majority of the infrastructure had crumbled, and only the skeletons of the tallest buildings remained, and had mostly collapsed. Most of the time the flooring and walls had completely disintegrated and left lonely scaffolds of steel standing, leaning, or having fallen over. In only a few exceptions did any glass remain, like the popular Hyperglass products of the previous age, or the odd metal flooring in some buildings. It was nearly impossible for most people to believe the stories about the wonders and staggering wealth that had come before.

Of course, Elena Marie Price was not most people. She had witnessed with her own eyes, for precious few years, the splendor and majesty of the world left behind. Tall and slender, the daughter of the former Liberated States of Columbia President had truly come into the nickname that was given to her particular variety of genetic tampering, the Old Ones. She was a positively ancient three hundred ninety-three years old, and didn't look a day older than thirty. Her doctors had tried and failed to assist her in having children in the early days after the Cataclysm, but she'd resigned herself to fate and dedicated herself to leading the remaining citizens of the LSC presidential bunker into the future.

Fortune, rather than wisdom, had proven to be her ally in those early days. Her decision to not utilize the LSC's nuclear arsenal had allowed her people to collect nuclear material from the unused weapons to help power their generators back at the bunker. By the time the unknown people of the Phoenix Clan were nearing Redding though, the LSC was running out of that precious fuel. It was that need for resources that caused them to set out on a similar journey south, specifically to the areas around northern California to gather more fuel from old LSC holdings.

Their population was a great deal smaller and the majority of them that remained at this point were also Old Ones born from the initial generations of survivors of the LSC. While the doctors were unable to assist Elena with having her own children, the same complicated and risky procedure that created her had been done to the unborn children of mothers that could bear children after it became evident that the Old Ones did not suffer from the despair of living in such bleak, isolated conditions over long periods of time. The formerly designer alteration had proved to have significant benefits that allowed these people to survive where they otherwise wouldn't.

While some of them had managed to pair off eventually and reproduce, more than half of them proved to be medically sterile, proving the procedure was terribly flawed. The chances for an Old One to be capable of producing viable offspring with any partners available in the bunker seemed to be about twenty percent, and that essentially meant that over time they were probably a doomed offshoot of the human race. Even clones made by harvesting an Old One's DNA and injecting it into a human's egg had the same worrying failure rate.

They were a long-lived offshoot though. The presidential bunker dwellers' ancestors came from an unfortunate combination of professions including bureaucrat, diplomat, soldier, physician, geneticist, nuclear engineer, and celebrity. While some of these did prove to be useful over the long term, they were not farmers and they were not survivalists. The bunker was not intended to house people over the long term, nor had it the resources to easily expand.

Their ability to feed and clothe its population had ended up being unfortunately limited, so by the time the Phoenix Clan caravan was making its way to Redding in the spring of 2507, the population of the LSC bunker had ended up being a mere thirty-two people. Thirty-one of them were Old Ones, and one of them was the entity formerly known as Megan Clark.

Megan Clark was a damaged woman to begin with, the gene therapies performed on her with the intent of augmenting her future children having inadvertently rendered her barren and had caused deep psychological damage. Her desire to survive and her ambition to remain near positions of power were most of what remained.

It was no surprise to anyone who knew her when she had made requests of the engineers and doctors of the LSC bunker to begin replacing parts of her body. She had proven to be a resilient candidate, her flesh abnormally accepting of foreign implants, and over time she had been rendered effectively immortal. She was more machine than woman at this point, with parts of her brain and all of her organs having been replaced or augmented with bio-electronics. She appeared roughly human, but the way she moved, spoke, and thought had all lost the natural inclinations of a conventionally living human. None who remained considered her human at all.

Megan was, at this point, a shell of her former self. She lived to serve President Price. She provided statistical analysis, advice, and sleepless protection over the woman she'd designated as the most powerful person she knew. Whatever her original motivations had been were eventually entirely subsumed by a desire to survive and keep those responsible for maintaining her body alive. Elena found Megan very unsettling, and not even remotely a true friend, but she was nevertheless helpful, reliable, and trustworthy.

Elena had led her people across treacherous terrain to break into the old missile silos east of Redding with the intent of making their way back to their bunker once they had the new fuel they needed. Their all-terrain vehicles were almost all battery-powered, with their 'mothership' vehicle Alpha One being much larger and containing a small nuclear power plant that the other ATVs used to recharge. Each of the vehicles had their own small greenhouses, and were thus responsible for producing a quantity of food which they all shared with each other to keep their variety of food as high as possible. It was a way of living that anyone would consider tenuous at best.

All of them, save for Megan and Elena, were very well armed as well, primarily utilizing charged energy weapons, though their vehicles had more conventional projectile weapons. The majority of them were working on breaking into the silos, while a handful had been scouting the area for possible supplies while Megan and Elena coordinated both groups from a central point. They had lost one of these scouts in recent years to an unexpected attack by one of those hulking roach beasts, centuries of knowledge lost to a strange creature's lucky assault. A pair of scouts had been dispatched to slay the beast, and their success brought great relief to Elena's people. It was one of these scouts that had made a discovery that he absolutely had to bring back evidence of.

Vasille Tzen, aged two-hundred fifty, had witnessed the most curious thing he'd seen in his long, long life working under President Price. The tall, balding, but still young looking man appeared to be in his late twenties, and he was peeking over the edge of a hill with a pair of military binoculars. Strange people were down there, near the outskirts of Redding.

A long, snaking vehicle was arranged in a circle, something of a defensive posture, with the walls of its various compartments opened up on the sides and providing shelter to the people who occasionally peeked out from under those steel awnings. Fabric was draped between the gaps, and the sounds of abundant life filtered up to him in a most entrancing way. The laughter of playing children, shouting of adults, clucking and crowing of animals, and the various bits of clanging of those at work filled the air. What really got his attention though, was the smell of the food they were cooking. He'd never experienced anything like it.

Humans. Real live humans were down there. They seemed to be technologically advanced, with all of them wearing some kind of plant-fiber clothing, though a number chose to go topless. The children seemed to be happy and healthy, and while the adults were not as large as the videos he'd seen of the old world, they seemed like they were getting along just fine.

There were a handful of weapons mounted atop some of the cars in the train of vehicles, seemingly intended for large game or lightly armored vehicles. Considering the look of the people, they likely had no concept of how to use them. He had to encounter one of them, but he couldn't afford to engage the whole group at once, so he waited.

As the day dragged on, he saw a group of them leave, four of them, spreading out and heading in towards the city. He saw one of them give the others orders before they split up. They were all armed, clothed appropriately for being out alone, and stayed within earshot of each other so they could defend each other. Vasille wondered what had happened to make such innocent seeming people so careful.

Still, he was confident he could take one of them. He got his eyes set on what he thought was the leader, and stalked down from his hill and made his way down towards Redding. He used the rubble to sneak through, always keeping an eye out for one of those roach creatures, his AR contacts set up to overlay warmer thermal signatures onto his vision.

It was just that setting that he'd used to hunt down the last one of those monsters who'd killed his late mentor. The three-hundred twenty-three year old master scout had been found bashed, burned, and drained of his blood, his organs eaten from his body cavity and his skull cracked open and his brain eaten as well. Slaying that beast had been the only time he'd ever had to kill, and the feeling of that revenge was a sweet thing indeed.

Moving with remarkable grace and stealth for someone nearing seven-feet tall, Vasille stalked the green-eyed man. He'd drawn a veil down over his face from his hat to protect from the sun, not unlike the layers of fabric that hid Vasille and the other scouts from the brutal star above. The darkness of the fabric allowed him to blend into the shadows of jutting girders, fallen slabs, and collapsed sewers, all caked in thick mud from centuries of erosive forces. Who knew how much city and infrastructure was actually buried under all that? With a sudden drop from above he was upon him, a long arm curled around him and a stun pistol jammed threateningly up against his back. "Don't move. I do not wish to harm you."

His target seemed to understand him as he froze up, his hands stopping in their pursuit of the gun slung around his shoulders by a long strap.

"Good. You understand me. Listen, I'm going to bring you to meet someone. I am not going to harm you, but I can't risk you revealing me to your companions. Please do not make any sounds and just come with me." He loosened his grasp, but still held that weapon against the man's back. "Stay in front of me, but come this way."

He had him start heading east, carefully keeping to the shadows, avoiding the other scouts. "I am Vasille Tzen, and I am a scout for my people, just like yourself. It is only natural that we would be the ones to make first contact between our peoples."

The captive dared to speak back to his captor. "Then why pull a weapon on me? Why can't we talk like men?"

Vasille chuckled softly. "We both know what men did to this world. We both also know men can do better. I am only being as careful as you would with me if you'd seen me first. I took you because you are the leader of your scouts, which means you are the most seasoned and understanding among them."

Thorne shrugged, climbing up some concrete. "Well, my mother is probably be a better candidate, but she's busy leading the others now."

Vasille smiled, reaching out to pat the man on the back. "I like you, you do not lie."

△△△

Vasille had returned from Redding quite a bit early, and as he entered Elena's quarters, which amounted to a tent extending out from the side of Alpha One, he was looking pretty excited. "Ma'am, I have something to report. I've located a lifeform."

Elena raised a slender brow as she sat up in her chair. Megan had been going over the maps with her and had been estimating the location of other silos in the area. "What is it, soldier? What'd you find? Not more of those disgusting roaches I hope?"

"No ma'am," he replied, the tall, balding, slender soldier standing at attention, "I have located humans and captured one of them."

Megan looked up in a jerky, mechanical way. "Impossible. Humans are unsuited to surviving the environment the Earth has become."

Elena rolled her eyes. Megan was a former media executive, her opinions on survival could not be trusted. "Good, bring him in, I want to talk to him."

Vasille nodded and ducked back out of the tent. Megan seemed to be lost in thought, muttering to herself about 'the odds'.

A reasonably healthy looking, olive-skinned, blonde man with with green eyes was gently coerced inside at gunpoint. His arms were tied behind his back, and a gag was tied over his mouth. He was wearing clothing that covered most of his skin made out of a strange plant-like material and a hat covered his neck and head. A thin veil was pulled back from his face. "Remove his gag, let him speak." Elena crossed her long legs, her suit fitting lightly on her slender frame. "What's your name, boy?"

The young man huffed, annoyed at the treatment he'd received by these... strange creatures. They didn't look like any humans he'd seen in all his thirty-one years. "I'm Hawthorne Crenshaw, ma'am. What ar-"

He flinched, interrupted by Elena shooting up to her feet shouting aloud, "What!?"

She was moving forward instantly, fast for a woman nearing four-hundred years old. "How do you know that name? Who are you really? Where did you come from? Did Hawthorne send you? Is he not satisfied with taking my father from me?"

Thorne blinked, startled, the woman towering over him by almost a foot, though she was almost certainly lighter than him. He could probably snap her bones like twigs if he was of a mind do. "I told you, my name is Hawthorne Crenshaw. My father Clint changed his last name to Crenshaw to honor the man who has been helping us for something like thirty-four years. I believe you are aware of that man. My mother first found Doctor Crenshaw back then and he's been helping us ever since 340 AC or so."

Elena reached out and poked at his chest with a thin finger, humming softly, her elfin eyes narrowed. "Yes... of course.. You don't look anything like him. Far too short. Far too much spine."

Megan had stiffly stood and moved up to Elena's side. "The existence of Doctor Hawthorne Crenshaw is likely. Considering his lack of aging the last time we saw him, it is likely he remains alive. His intentions at the time seemed to be benevolent. There is no reason to think his attitude has changed."

Elena scowled at Megan's open support and sympathy of Doctor Crenshaw. Still, she wasn't wrong, and while she wanted to push her over or pull some piece of electronics out of her hide, it wasn't like she was unaware of how the Cataclysm came about. She'd been there at that fateful meeting, applauding her foolish father's plan like the rest of the yes-men present.

Thorne nodded at Megan's words. "That's right. He told us about the ice age that's coming, and helped us get ready to head south. Is that what you're doing out here? Is your bunker in danger of failing too?"

Megan froze silently for several moments before resuming her strange movements. "It is eighty-four percent likely that Doctor Crenshaw's estimates are accurate. The withdrawal of the roach creatures suggests a climate change they are aware of that we are not."

Elena chose to compose herself, standing calmly and stately as she thought for a moment. "Yes, young Hawthorne, our bunker is failing and we are heading south."

Megan tried to interrupt, "But presiden-"

"Shhh..." Elena stopped her. "It's time I got over myself. Mr. Crenshaw, if I have you brought back to your people, could you arrange a meeting with your leaders? I believe it would be wise for us to consider joining forces. My people are likely inferior to yours at surviving this harsh environment, but we are well armed and long lived and can defend you as we travel together."

Elena Marie Price had not been left as President through some power grab, or the failure to maintain popularity during elections. She had shown herself to be a calm and wise leader, and while she and her people had lacked the knowledge and resources to thrive in what the world had become, she wasn't about to let a centuries' old grudge over the death of a fool and the failures of his machinations stand in the way of the survival of her people.

"You have no guile to you, young man, but I suppose there's not much value to that ability anymore. We'll be here for about a week before we move on, so I anticipate meeting you and your leaders."

Thorne glanced between the strange people he found himself in the company of, and nodded. "Alright, I'll tell my people, but I can't guarantee they'll agree. We've already sacrificed a lot, but we have no confidence when it comes to those roach-things, so if you have anything to prove you can handle them or any knowledge you can share about them, I think they would appreciate that."

Elena gestured off to the side, and Megan moved to bring over a box. Elena also gestured to the guard, and Vasille untied Thorne. The box Megan brought over was summarily opened, revealing the stripped head of one of those roach-things. A large hole was in the front of its head, and as she handed the box to Thorne he found it was rather heavy. "Alright... well... that will probably do it."

Elena smiled a bit. "Indeed."

Thorne cleared his throat, speaking up. "Well, we recently lost someone to one of these things. It pounded her into paste and had been eating her as far as we can tell before we managed to drive it off. I... I think if you managed to do the same to that one as you did to this one, it would go a long way to earning the trust of my people and putting the poor girl's soul at peace."

Elena pondered the offer for a moment, and nodded. "Alright, you'll have your monster hunt. We can't have manslayers about, no matter what they are. We lost one of our people to those things recently as well."

Thorne sighed and shook his head. "I'm sorry to hear that. It doesn't even make sense that something so big can move so quickly. Smashed poor Tabby before we could come help her. We've been keeping a close eye on her sister Emily ever since. I think she's only still eating because of her pregnancy."

Megan spoke up again, lumbering closer and peering up at Thorne. "Your people have children? How many? Are they all as healthy as you? How do you feed the-"

"Shhh, Megan, don't badger the poor boy." Again, Elena interrupted the cyborg. "This isn't an interrogation. I'm sure we can have plenty to share with each other about the last few hundred years if we avenge this miss Tabby. Vasille, you can handle that, can't you?"

The balding Old One nodded, "Yes ma'am. I'll kill any number of them now that I know definitively that they eat people."

Elena nodded. "Take Hawthorne here back home." Vasille gave a smart salute, and led Thorne outside.

After Thorne was led back out with the box, Vasille's gun holstered, Elena turned to Megan. "Recall the rest of the scouts and radio back to the bunker. Have them gather all remaining vital resources, computers, and documents and bring Alpha Two out here. Tell them we're abandoning the bunker, and that we have friends."

Megan turned towards the radio, then paused and looked back. "You were serious then? You were not lying?"

Elena shook her head. "Like I said. There's no room for guile left in this world, Megan. We must submit to our betters and contribute what we can to survive the dangers ahead. We barely made it this far, we certainly won't survive an ice age on our own. We need them."

Megan stared for several moments, then approached the radio to share the communications. If Elena was saying she was not the most powerful, then Megan needed to ingratiate herself to whomever was. "Attention LSC Bunker, this is a priority one communication from President Elena Price..."

Outside the tent, Vasille led Thorne back to his ATV. Thorne broke the silence first. "I'm coming with you after that monster."

Vasille nodded, smiling down at the much shorter man. "I know."

ΔΔΔ

The LSC scout and Phoenix Clan scout slipped their way through the rubble. Their weapons were kept at the ready, and they carefully signaled to each other silently. They had shared every piece of information they'd managed to gather about the beasts in their few encounters with them.

They moved quickly, they seemed to respond to movement, they had great physical strength and seemed to have no sense of pain. They have somewhat large, vulnerable brains in their heads, and their carapace is made out of tough minerals, including a high percentage of iron. The spiny hairs on their body are all made primarily of chitin and iron, with the tips actually rusty. Their diet seemed to be mostly of metals, the poisonous scrub plants on the surface, and whatever flesh they could get their hands on. They retreat immediately upon detecting danger to their lives, and can see in the dark.

As far as anyone could tell, they seemed to be able to smell the iron in people's' blood, and made a point of trying to devour it. Their high temperatures seemed primarily due to the way they let themselves bake in the sun, though they produced a large percentage of their heat internally as well. They were like walking ovens. Considering their diet, propensity for standing in the unfiltered sun, and their temperature it was also easy to imagine they were partially radioactive.

"We should try to lure one out with bait then." suggested Vasille, having done just such a thing when he'd hunted the last one.

"Alright, I'll gather small pieces of rusty metal as we go, but they're hard to keep quiet." Thorne started to pick up odd reddened hunks of old steel. It slowed him down a little as well, allowing Vasille to advance with his augmented vision. He had to carefully align his line of sight to avoid catching too much sunlight due to the fact that his thermal vision drowned out his normal vision. It was nothing he couldn't compensate for, but he didn't want to miss their quarry just because he got dazzled momentarily.

Thorne found scouting to be utterly fascinating compared to growing up in the bunker. The sounds echoed completely differently, the lights and shadows interacted so much more dynamically. The sun itself was so much brighter than any of the artificial light's he'd grown up with, and it had the effect of laying everything in sight bare, naked to all who could see. It actually had taken him a long time to adjust to such things, but he'd spent so long being paranoid after seeing that first roach that he kept his eyes constantly moving to try and catch a glimpse of one of them again. And now, one of them had killed Tabby.

Thorne clenched his fist as the memory of finding his student, subordinate, and once-considered potential mother of his child dead. The ghost of a memory of her happy smile as she sat out and enjoyed the wind blowing through her hair for the first time made him tremble with a rage the likes of which he'd never felt before. He had advocated for her having the freedom to turn down being picked during the recent round of mother selections, and the fact that he'd inadvertently denied himself the opportunity to have a child as well was not lost on him. He wondered if she'd have been a good mot-

Vasilled shoved Thorne, pinning his back with his tall, remarkably strong body. "Hey, you're getting distracted. Watch yourself, I don't want to have to drag your heavy ass out of here." Vasille had completely caught Thorne off-guard, confronting him between some old concrete walls.

He nodded back in response, letting out a sigh. "Sorry, just thinking about what that bastard did to her."

Vasille narrowed his eyes, then reached out to punch the much younger man in the shoulder. "The last one I hunted, the one from the box, it killed my mentor, someone I'd known my whole life. I understand how you feel, but we're not just doing this for her, we're doing this to show that our peoples can work together. We're going to get this mother fucker. Not the first, and not the last. I'll kill every last one of those man eaters, so help me god."

Thorne chuckled bitterly, reaching out to punch Vasille's shoulder as well, his hand holding three chunks of steel between his gloved fingers. "Now who's getting distracted? Come on, there's a collapsed road ahead."

The scouts nodded at each other, and crept up to the edge of an old collapsed overpass, which now formed mud-caked ramps up either side. At the center was a huge pile of old cars, seemingly having slid down from either side over the course of centuries. There wasn't a whole lot left of them, really, but the sturdy plastics, glass, and more corrosion resistant metals still remained. A black form was leaning down among the wreckage, a trail of thick fluids oozing from three holes in its central carapace which led back to a hole fifty feet away.

The men froze, and Vasille did his best to talk quietly without visibly moving his jaw. "Very slowly, move the bait to the edge, and let some of it roll down." While Thorne's hand lifted at a crawl, careful to avoid making sounds, Vasille carefully levelled his arc rifle.

He hadn't ever had a chance to shoot a live one with the high-amperage electricity emitter, but after he'd killed the last one with a carefully aimed shot from the mounted gun on his ATV, he'd taken the time to experiment with this weapon on its corpse. Its high-iron content seemed to attract the electricity extremely well, though he had no idea if it would disperse through the ground before it could have an effect. He hoped the damage already dealt to the thing left its insides more vulnerable to the effect. Thinking on it while Thorne prepared to drop the chunks of steel, though, he wondered if these things ever got hit by lightning.

Clink, clunk, the metal tumbled down the concrete ramp, Thorne's other hand having pulled his gun to his side, several seconds behind Vasille in preparation to fire. The very moment those pieces of metal started tumbling down the roach's antennae lifted and its body jerked in alarm. Its head lowered down, its large upper arms bending to allow it to crouch as its antennae wiggled back and forth in the direction of the hunks of metal that had settled near its feet. A soft click and a flash of light preceded the sudden appearance of a fifty-foot arc of electricity, which attached itself to one of those antennae and the rifle firing it. Both ends glowed brightly from high levels of heat while Vasille yelled out, "Now! Shoot it!"

The roach had stiffened, one of its primary sensory organs struck with the blast of electricity. Its insides started cooking, in particular the brain inside the metal shell of a head, only for Thorne to brace himself up on a knee and start unloading his own gun. Slug after slug raced towards the hulking monstrosity, the first bouncing off the carapace on its back. The second and third struck one of its huge eyes and blew off its other antennae. Another bolt of lightning lanced out and caused the monster to seize up and collapse to the ground, shuddering violently while Thorne carefully aimed two more shots. One hit the narrow spot at the back of its neck, ricocheting around inside its body upon penetrating, and the other drilled into the top of its head, the gunshots almost being drowned out by the shouting of two men shouting out for vengeance.

Once the two weapons quieted, the men watched for a moment as the roach lay there twitching, fatally wounded, if not dead. Foul-smelling, sizzling smoke came from inside the holes in its body as the men started yelling and laughing together. Miss-timed and poorly aimed attempts to slap hands together between them, grab at shoulders, and slap at chests spoke a great deal about the differences in the way their cultures celebrated. In the end the two hugged each other, hands slapping each other's backs as they laughed and shouted. "Yeah! Fuck you roach! That was for Tabby!"

Vasille answered back. "Tabby and Dekka, and anyone else you foul beasts have eaten!"

That seemed to sober the men for a moment though,

and they stepped back from each other. "You... you don't think...?" asked Vasille.

"Those things have been eating people out of bunkers all this time, haven't they?" finished Thorne.

They looked back to the smoking corpse, dread filling their hearts. "You know Vasille, when Doctor Crenshaw told my clan about the coming ice age, I had only just seen one of those things for the first time before they vanished."

Vasille chewed on the inside of his cheek for a moment, thinking. "It's warmer south, and it had been getting warmer up north where we are. These things have probably been in the south for decades, maybe centuries."

Dread filled Thorne's face. "Oh my god."

Vasille shook his head. "God gave up on us a long time ago, my young friend. Let's go see our peoples." Vasille stalked off, shouldering his weapon while radioing back to base about their success.

CHAPTER 23

CYCLE 14, COMING TOGETHER

The meeting of two peoples, separated originally by hundreds of miles of hostile mountains, nuclear holocaust, acid rain, black rain, and culture was a remarkably cheerful one. The dark mood that the people of the Phoenix Clan had found themselves in had finally lifted for the first time in a long while as they met outsiders for the first time. Both groups interacted and mingled curiously, with the Old Ones taking great joy in encountering children for the first time in centuries, though a close second was discovering that they had chickens as well, allowing many of them to enjoy eggs for the first time in their long lives.

A close third, that honestly rivaled the other two, was the fact that having access to their hemp-based toilet paper completely revolutionized their ideas of waste management.

That night, out in the blasted wilderness on May 11th, 2507, with that long snake of a vehicle coiled up protectively around Elena Price's own LSC vehicles was a night of tears and joy. President Price declared her alliance with the Council of Twelve after a few short hours of meetings and agreements being signed.

Arrangements were made to share the few plants they had with the farmers of the caravan, and it turned out that the people that arrived with Alpha Two and its fleet of ATVs had some additional foresight in bringing a large bag of apples from the two trees back in the northern-Idaho based LSC bunker. The two apple trees from the bunker had been planted at the Price Presidential Estate years before they were moved to the bunker, symbolically representing the successful pregnancy of Elena's mother and subsequent meddling in her own genetics.

Her parents could not know how important those trees would end up being, nor how many times she nearly allowed them to die as the forces unleashed in her youth conspired to end the venerable plants. Sadly, they would have to struggle on without anyone to tend to them, but their seeds had a chance to be spread thanks to a handful of Old Ones who decided to bring some apples with them.

One additional arrangement had been made as well. Elena wanted to speak with Doctor Crenshaw. She needed to make amends with someone she had secretly harbored hatred for for so long. She knew logically that he was guilty of nothing, but her heart had been left with unhealed scars ever since she'd been made aware of her father's suicide. With the assistance of Jessica, she finally had her chance to speak to the man who'd tried to help them oh so long ago. How different could things have been if they had heeded his message as these hardy bunker dwellers had?

No one from the Phoenix Clan had any records from that time, nor had any stories been passed on regarding the motivations of the bunker's builders, but she suspected the Smith family had been long-time supporters of Monsalle Industries. If so, that information was almost surely lost to time.

△△△

T.I.A. had become something of a winter entertainment hub in the last decade. Requests for different forms of music, movies, and television shows had been answered with her best guesses, at least at first. At one point she'd simply sent them a text file containing all the file names she had in those media folders and their subfolders, and crafted a program tasked with delivering the requested files every 24 hours, timed perfectly to hit the right rotation on Earth. These data requests were completely automated at this point so she could focus on individual conversations, and more vital requests. In some ways she was operating in a similar fashion to the various surface facilities that used to serve her data once upon a time.

Of course, this did leave her with less work to do, and the personal check-ins with her friends had dried up significantly, no doubt due to all the work that needed to be done. Considering the nature of the media being consumed, the people of the Smith Bunker were mostly looking for things to make them laugh and motivate them as they labored. There was a significant amount of children's programming requested as well, suggesting that the adults weren't able to spend as much time with the kids, or they spent some of their time with the kids relaxing and watching said programming with them. They'd never seen such shows before themselves, after all.

T.I.A. found herself preferring to analyze the data being requested and tried to use that data to refine her delivery program into making suggestions based on previous requests. She also took the time to watch and listen to the majority of the more popular items, and even had the pleasure of adding items to her collection as some enterprising bunker dwellers shared with her recordings of their own music.

In a lot of ways it was a nice distraction for T.I.A. from worrying about the things that her friends were actually having to deal with, particularly the winters spent with the caravan curled up in a circle like a wagon train. Since its walls opened inwards to create something of a large internal circular building to protect them from winds, it made rain and snow something of a problem in the middle except for the buckets they'd put out to gather it for purifying.

By the time Hawthorne was waking for what should have been his 13th cycle, and ended up being his 14th, T.I.A. was getting messages regarding the caravan encountering other people. She couldn't send anything back until she got the go-ahead that they were going to be stationary, though. She had gotten a message from a strange-looking person whom had introduced herself as President Elena Marie Price of the Liberated States of Columbia, and considering its contents she knew that her father would be very interested in seeing it.

Hawthorne awoke with a decent level of apprehension, but it was a good sign that T.I.A. hadn't assaulted him with information from the moment he'd woken up. He took his time, taking a nice hot shower, getting dressed, and putting on his new gloves and contacts. He missed the weight of glasses hanging off his nose in a sense, but he supposed he had a significant preference for the new contacts, particularly due to the high level of immersion in T.I.A.'s virtual space. Walking out into Clapham Common, he found said curly-haired brunette quietly enjoying what appeared to be a book while soft music played from the overhead speakers. "Good morning, Tia."

A big bright grin turned up at him, a bookmark materialising in the book as she shut it and set it aside. "Good morning, father! How are you today?" She pushed herself up from the grassy ground, wiggling her toes in the grass and enjoying the feel of the simulated sun on her simulated skin. She couldn't emulate her whole body in real time, but her sense of touch was easy enough compared to the complexity of the cardiovascular system, nervous system, and respiratory system she had simulated in her 'dream'. Touch and weight were easy by comparison.

Hawthorne approached the nearly-400 year old AI's avatar. "I feel fine, thank you. Has everything been alright? Have they finished the project yet?"

T.I.A. laughed, a genuine happy sound that was a far cry from her first unsettling laugh from the start of their journey. "Father, considering the circumstances, everything is wonderful. The caravan has reached northern California, and they just contacted us regarding other people they've encountered who have joined them! I've also been really enjoying the music they sent back to me. It feels so much more alive than what I had been sending them, though they insist that it's not as good."

She turned up the audio on the bunker dwellers' recordings, which were of remarkable quality considering the amateur nature. The advancement of basic recording software seemed to have outpaced the studio equipment the majority of her musical records had been recorded with.

It was a lively tune, filled with laughter and cheer, drums pattering in the background while stringed instruments seemed to practically dance in the foreground. Rhythmic clapping from an audible audience helped keep the beat, and a vibrant and passionate voice sang along, with the audience answering back in a noisy fashion. Hawthorne found himself smiling as he listened, imagining the moment in that steel-walled bunker with everyone having a good time.

It lacked the polish and ambition of the music he remembered, but T.I.A. was right, it just felt alive. "Well, I don't know what you've been sending them, but I think I'm inclined to agree." She nodded again, turning the music back down while he spoke again. "Who are these people they met? Where are they from?"

Like a magic trick, T.I.A. produced a screen from behind her back, and stretched it out in front of Hawthorne, putting it up against the tree as she stood back. She gestured at it, and it started to play while Hawthorne pulled the short woman closer by her far shoulder and used his other hand to play with her bouncy, curly hair. He raised an eyebrow at the strange face that appeared on the screen though.

Elena's face was long, angular, and strangely elegant. Narrow eyes with a look of wisdom peered at the camera while Hawthorne found his vision lingering on her slender nose, thin lips, and long thin neck. Her long hair appeared to be pale blonde, with a small amount of silvery grey mixed in. Her facial expression was somewhat sour at first, though a soft sigh dispelled that and a small smile appeared.

"Greetings Doctor Hawthorne Crenshaw, this is President Elena Marie Price of the Liberated States of Columbia. I never thought I would find myself speaking to you after everything that has happened, but upon encountering your friends and finding out you were in contact with them, I realized that I had been holding onto the past for far too long."

"My fool of a father only took responsibility for his actions when he took his own life, and I have dedicated myself ever since to being better than he ever could have been. I feel as though I've done well with the tools I had available to me, keeping some number of my people alive, but I must confess I've made many mistakes along the way."

"None of us were properly prepared for what has happened, not like the people you have been helping, and I hope you'll give us your blessing to join with them. I will not go into details, for I think it best that some memories be lost to time, but I also request that you forgive me for the awful things I've thought about you for more than three-hundred years. Time has taught me that it is best to fix what you can rather than dwell on what you can't, and I'd rather my people be able to benefit these wonderful young people with our wisdom and protection rather than dwelling on old lies."

Her eyes softened, and she looked back over her shoulder across the dirt ground behind her which had been cleared of the poisonous scrubs before allowing children to play and run outdoors. Sun beat down in the center of the large circle of vehicles, and a handful of pregnant women waddled around chasing after them playfully. Chickens clucked somewhere offscreen.

"I want to formally take part in guiding these people, as you have, and have signed an agreement with the Council of Twelve declaring us in alliance." She turned back to the camera, looking serious. "I vow to you, that I will take to heart your message of peace and cooperation that I had tried to deny for too long. We will walk hand-in-hand to South America, and I will keep every foulness away from them that I can."

"I only hope you can forgive foolish people for not heeding you sooner. I've only known them for a few days and I have learned more from them than I have in centuries ruling over a dead country. Make whatever request you would like of me, Hawthorne, consider the ghost of the LSC at your service." She let out a calming breath, and smiled quietly at the camera.

The message ended there, and T.I.A. brought up another, revealing a friendly, familiar face. Jessica had aged quite gracefully, with her red hair mixed thoroughly with its own silvery grey hair. Hugging her from behind was her husband Clint whom had gone completely grey, but showed no signs of balding. He seemed to have no intention of interrupting the conversation his wife wanted to have with the good doctor.

"Hello Doctor Crenshaw! It's been so long. I'm older than you are now, so I fully expect you'll respect your seniors?" She grinned. "Of course, I'm sure you know, I'm not even remotely the oldest among the people in our group now. Elena said they're called the Old Ones, and that she's the only one who was alive before the Cataclysm. We've done our best to keep the children from bothering her too much, but she seems to really enjoy telling stories about what the world used to be like. It might be a little tricky to integrate them into the group, but we're pretty sure everyone will get along."

"We've gotten to Redding in California. We have been able to locate some aluminum, but a lot of it has corroded before we could get to it. We can recycle that, but it's a lot harder to identify and gather in that state. Elena seems to think that we can hook up the generators from her vehicles to our power supply though, so we should probably be okay as we continue south. She said they were nukular-"

Clint interrupted her from behind, "Nuclear dear, nuclear."

She blushed and nodded. "Right, right, nuclear power plants are what she's been using to recharge her vehicles. That's why she was out here in the first place. Her people were opening up the old LSC silos to gather fuel for their generators, just like we are with the aluminum. She said that we're welcome to take whatever else we need from the silos too, so I'm hoping that there's plenty of materials and parts there."

She hummed softly, thinking. Clint spoke quietly again, "The map," and kissed the top of her head.

"Ah, of course, we're coordinating with Elena to hit up every silo she knows about on the way south to make sure we have lots of fuel and resources. We have no idea what we'll be able to scavenge, the cities have been largely useless so far, so we need to get everything we can. It'll take us a little longer to get down to Sacramento, but we'll be much better prepared for dealing with the challenges. I think we're going to be okay though, Hawthorne. Oh!"

She turned her head and shouted. "Hawthie, bring over the box!" She turned back to the screen. "You're going to find this fascinating!"

Thorne waved a bit from behind, handing his father the large box, which he held in front of Elena, allowing her to withdraw the heavy contents. "Okay, so this..." She turned it to face the screen. "This is the head of one of those roach things. As far as we can tell there's a lot of heavy elements in its shell, but we haven't had much time to study it yet. Elena said they accidentally burned one before though, and she's pretty sure what was left over was iron!"

"These things are apparently at least partially made of iron. That must be why they were sucking on steel girders and other metal things, they were eating the iron and carbon. That's the working theory anyway." She re-boxed the disturbing head and Clint took it away, leaving her alone. "We're figuring it out, though. We've made strong allies, and everyone's spirits are as high as they were before your last message."

She hesitated a bit, unsure if she wanted to continue. "The Elders decided that caring for and feeding them was too much of a burden, and that until we got underway we should avoid having any more children. The Elders all fasted and allowed themselves to pass, and it's been hanging on us ever since. I'd be lying if I said we didn't need such a momentous occasion as making new friends to ease over our wounded hearts. I hope whatever Elena said to you wasn't too harsh though? My son said she'd yelled something to him about you taking her father."

Jessica seemed to dwell on that idea for a moment. "Well, as a woman whose father died due to your advice myself, I personally want to say that it's not your fault. We make our own decisions in life, and we never could have gotten this far, nor probably even met the LSC people if our Elders hadn't left us when they did. It was hard work, and we needed the food. They were totally right."

Jessica hummed, thinking for a moment. "My son and one of the LSC scouts hunted down one of those roaches, one that killed one of our younger scouts, Tabitha. It took a fair bit of firepower to do the damage needed, but they ambushed it. We're waiting for it to cool down before trying to bring parts of it back for studying. Elena said the one they'd killed before hadn't been quite as accessible, and they didn't have the manpower to extract it for study, so we're hoping we learn a lot about it."

"It's the only one we've seen in the area, and we've been considering the possibility that they came from the south, and that we'll encounter more of them the further we go. Hawthie was worried that they might have eaten lots of people and destroyed bunkers further south. I'm personally hoping that isn't true, but Elena seems to think that her firepower will be needed against them."

She smiled, that same bright shiny smile that T.I.A. seemed to emulate. "I think we could use one of your rousing, hopeful speeches, if you have any left in you, Doctor Crenshaw. We'll be here for the next seven days or so while we get everything coordinated and prepare to head out. That'll give you a little less than two days to respond, so hop to it young man!"

She giggled softly, apparently having been very eager to lord over him about her age before ending the recording. Hawthorne couldn't help but laugh, shaking his head. "So let's see, we've got an upstart, a time traveller, an immortal, and an AI. Quite the strange number of perspectives on time, it seems."

T.I.A. seemed a little confused as she pointed up at Hawthorne. "Are you the time traveller?"

He nodded back at her, ruffling up her hair. "Of course, I jump ahead in time over and over while everyone else has to live through the intervening time. I suppose we're all travelling forwards though. I think we should take our elders' wisdom seriously. No sense dwelling on what's behind us as long as we have a way ahead."

Hawthorne felt over-the-moon about the whole thing, getting to watch from so far away as two different groups of people come together. What were the chances that both groups had survived so long in isolation, only to encounter each other, and come together like that?

"Tia, you've done a wonderful job supporting them. I

know we can't do much for them at this point, that they have to survive on their own, but being their librarian has probably helped them more than we can ever know."

T.I.A. looked up at him, considering what he had said. "I have really enjoyed the challenge. It is an opportunity to find better ways to help them while also studying them and learning from them. You were right, practicing with interacting with humans has totally changed how I feel about them. I wish I could do more to protect them and keep them safe." T.I.A. began fussing with her dress a bit, busying her hands with messing with the fabric, as if trying to express her unease.

He hummed down at her, and gave her hair another good ruffle with his gloved hand. "Trust me, Tia, you've done everything you can to protect them, but now they have to protect themselves. You were the one who noticed they were in danger in the first place, and if you hadn't created this wonderful gift for me, we'd never have been able to put those plans together for them in the time we had to work on them. Honestly, if it wasn't for you, humanity would be in a much worse position right now on all sides."

T.I.A. smiled at that for a moment, but then hung her head. "But father... what if I put them in that situation in the first place? What if my changes to your video back then caused all of this?"

Hawthorne sighed, hugging the avatar of his AI and shaking his head. "Listen. You didn't launch all those weapons. You didn't release those horrors on Earth. Even with that video you were just trying to make sure that my message got to people unedited. We were dealing with people who made bad decisions back then. We're dealing with people who make good decisions now. Support them, and help them, and don't dwell on those who didn't listen to us."

T.I.A. sighed and nodded, looking back up at him. "You're right. We should get to work on that speech Jessica asked for. Elena sounded a bit like a knight at the end there too. She could use a little motivation, I think. I'm still having trouble believing that any Old Ones survived after what I read about them. They must be more hardy than the doctors thought they were. It should be interesting to see how long they'll last."

He hummed, stepping back from T.I.A. and smiling down at her. "Alright, I'm going to get to composing this after breakfast. I'd love if you could provide me some of the statistics you've gathered on their interests."

T.I.A. smiled brightly, pleased to be able to help, feeling much better after the little pep talk. She was quick to get to work, zipping about to gather the data he'd requested and handle the food request.

ΔΔΔ

"T.I.A.'s log, May 15, 2507, AC 374. I am currently assisting Hawthorne with providing statistics regarding the media requests of the Phoenix Clan. Something he said reminded me of a thought I had after the Cataclysm. I had decided that I wanted to protect and care for the colonists encased within my body, perhaps like a mother. Having found myself in a position to look after the humans I have contact with on Earth, I find myself feeling responsible for them in a very similar way. I am realizing how undeveloped I was at the time when I had made that first decision, though I am pleased to now understand why I did it."

"While I understand that the purpose of my construction was to both protect my passengers, as well as attend to Hawthorne's needs, I now feel as though I have taken the responsibility of trying to safeguard as much of humanity as I can. I have learned a lot from Jessica and the others about how to interact with people, as well as how to be a person. I still feel as though I am merely emulating them, but the more I express myself, the more it feels natural. I am still disappointed that my gift for Hawthorne was spoiled, but pleased that it proved useful. I know what I am feeling are simple feelings, but they feel more complex every day. They are also much more pleasant than the sadness I had experienced before in past cycles."

"Emotions are interesting. They motivate me in ways that even Hawthorne's orders and requests never really did. Where before I felt a duty to do what was asked of me, I now genuinely want to help, and I enjoy doing so. I am satisfied with feeling useful to the humans that I interact with, and desire to do more to ensure their wellbeing. I believe this motivation has caused me to do things and develop my thinking in ways I can't imagine I would have otherwise. I continue to build social skills and construct my own personality the more I interact with them, and I find that it decreases my need to intentionally try to modify myself. Like other things I have done, repetition and experimentation seems to etch things into my being, removing the need to process them again. This appears to be central to my nature, to struggle with new things, but once complete I can call upon them at will."

"I will continue to consider how to apply this. I now completely understand why Hawthorne insisted I analyze him, and recordings of him. It built a baseline of understanding to expand from that I can now consider my foundation. I find myself excited at the prospects of how I may continue to grow and mature. I think if I were to give an honest assessment of my emotional development, I'd compare myself to a human child who desires the approval of their parent, with many more capabilities to actually earn that approval. This level of growth seems acceptable to me for now. The only issue I can think of with this is an increasing unease with actually considering him my father. End log."

△△△

Jessica and Elena were only a few of the people gathered around the old Beta Facility computers once it was announced that they were receiving a transmission late in the day on May 18th. Considering the way the computers had been arranged to be facing the inward part of the ring when the caravan 'circled the wagons', a lot more people than ever before could gather around the screen. Of course, monitors all over were displaying the messages on a slight delay as well, but people tended to want to see it from the source.

Once again Doctor Hawthorne Crenshaw appeared, his advanced contacts making him look somewhat more artificial than he did with his old glasses. He looked well rested, and had a huge smile on his face as he looked at the camera. "Greetings, honored Elders, and friends of both the Phoenix Clan and now the Liberated States of Columbia. I hope you will forgive my joke, as miss Jessica had been teasing me about how much younger I am than her, though I do mean it seriously as well in reference to your new guests."

He let out a soft sigh, smiling softly. "I wanted to tell you all that I am so very proud of you. You have accomplished so much, and overcome impossible odds to get here today. Things that may seem boring and routine to you are so incredible to me that I can scarcely believe we are the same species. You are so much stronger and more resilient than the people of Earth that I left behind so long ago, and I am humbled that I can play any significant part in your lives. Your ability to adapt and withstand are a testament to the strength of the human spirit. It is truly impossible for me to imagine the powerful will that your people must command to accomplish all that you have."

"When my companions and I had left, we had been very picky about the sorts of people that came with us. I had originally thought that I had brought the best and brightest that humanity had to offer with me, but in a lot of ways I wish I could have brought you instead. You are all truly an inspiration, and I hope when I teach my companions about you far into the future, that they will be able to appreciate what a wonder you all are. I personally think that Earth is in good hands."

"That said, you still have much more to do. The planet will not be kind, and it will challenge you to your limits, and you must continue to be strong. President Elena Price, you said that you consider the LSC at my service. I ask only one thing of you, something you have already vowed to do. Protect these people, and provide your wisdom and guidance when you can."

Hawthorne chuckled a bit. "They have already proven they have what it takes to thrive, and I request that you try not to stand in their way. Support them, protect them, and guide them. Phoenix Clan, I have a request of you as well. Help President Price and her people as well. Be there for each other and learn everything you can from each other. You have a tradition of honoring your Elders, and these should be considered no different. Take advantage of their knowledge and perspective and show them what you are capable of. You are all strong, intelligent, and resilient, and as long as you trust in each other and lean on each other, I can't imagine any challenge you can't handle. I believe in you."

"Tia and I will be up here watching over you. Show that

world who's boss."

Shouts and laughs sounded up from the assembled people in something of a wave, following the minor delay in transmission between the Beta Facility computers and the rest of the caravan's displays. Jessica and Elena shared a smile as they turned to watch their people celebrate. Instruments were brought together in the middle to play music while a handful of the incredibly tall Old Ones danced with the hardy, shorter humans.

There were even a few Old Ones that had been dragged into some celebratory kisses. Jessica lifted an eyebrow at that, and glanced up at Elena, trying to talk over the noise. "Hey, do you think any of your people would be interested some... cultural exchanges?"

Elena blinked, then glanced over to Megan. The cyborg woman stood there, dispassionate and disinterested. She did speak up though. "She is suggesting sexual relations, Miss Price."

Elena looked a bit shocked at that, looking back to Jessica's grinning face. "The thought hadn't even occurred to me. I'm sure some of them would like to try though."

Jessica had really embraced her inner matchmaker now that she was an Elder. She needed to call the rest of the council together, and get them to add Elena to it. A Council of Thirteen had a nice ring to it.

CHAPTER 24

CYCLE 14, WHAT WE CAN AND CAN'T DO

Hawthorne and T.I.A. had just sent off the 'inspiring speech' that had been requested of them, leaving Hawthorne unlikely to be able to communicate with them much more this cycle. "I find myself feeling kind of jealous, Tia. You and Elena get to watch all of this happening in real time while I have to play catch-up and try to time my interactions out with the world. It was a lot less complicated when it was just you and I."

T.I.A. hummed aloud, a somewhat odd sound coming from the wall speakers rather than her short, feminine avatar. "From my perspective, Doctor Crenshaw, because of the fact that I have to be immersed in the 'now' all of the time, I find that I miss things or fail to consider things that you end up catching when you are around. I believe your circumstances allow you to come to each cycle with a fresh perspective."

Hawthorne nodded, sitting down at a chair at the table, his surroundings still that of Clapham Common as he started tapping and sliding his fingers on the screen of the tablet he'd left there. "You've got a point. Even if I have to miss the 'now' that you get to experience, the times I do get to experience have the advantage of you being able to compress and summarize everything that's happened, allowing me to take in more information in a shorter time to work on solutions of my own."

"There's less questions for me to wrestle with because you already had the time and opportunity to gather answers. It does make for an interesting problem-solving dynamic that I hadn't considered. I had just assumed that, while I am able to assist you during my times awake, that you will end up doing the vast majority of the work. I'm glad that I can be of more assistance to you than I expected, Tia."

T.I.A. fussed with her dress, flattening out wrinkles and smoothing down folds. She kept finding herself prone to pointless physical motion to help herself focus on thinking, which was rather odd considering the amount of processes that needed to happen. She had to simulate the fabric, her hands, and the relationship between the two. There was also the atmosphere at Clapham Common and the gravity of Earth she tried to simulate, all so she could fuss with her dress. Strangely enough, her fidgeting did allow her to focus on her thinking, at least in these sorts of moments.

"I believe I've said before that I would not be able to handle nearly as much without your assistance Doctor Crenshaw. It feels like no matter how many years pass, you have a perspective and sense of problem solving that make my abilities seem feeble."

Hawthorne looked back at her, smiling and shaking his head. "Nonsense. You've made huge leaps already, and we have so much further to go before we get to our destination. The more you get accustomed to different elements of problem solving, the more you'll be able to fall back on what you've already learned to help you deal with more complicated issues. By the time we get to Alpha Centauri, you'll be every bit my match, if not my superior. We may well find ourselves rivalling each other and making each other better over that time. Just focus on the things you have as your advantages, and you'll do just fine."

He hummed, deciding to add. "The people on Earth have their own perspectives of course. They have to worry in entire different ways about how they'll survive the next day. They also have a lot of people they can depend upon to help them figure things out. It's no wonder they finished re-purposing their bunker so much faster than I expected. It kind of reminds me of the sense of urgency that drove my own companions and I to complete the Ark and launch it. I don't know if the roaches are directly analogous to the terrorists and protesters we had to deal with, but they do have a similar desire to devour others for their own bene-fit."

T.I.A. let out a shocked gasp. "I do not have any records of widespread cannibalism being reported in advance of our departure!"

Hawthorne laughed heartily, almost falling out of the chair. "No! No Tia, I meant figuratively devour." He sobered a bit as he clarified. "They destroyed people's' lives, branded them as evil monsters, as less than human, and fed on their despair to grow in power and influence themselves. They tried people in the court of public opin-ion, found them guilty, and executed them professionally without ever having to bring the actual law into it. Some-times they executed them literally as well."

T.I.A. recognized these descriptions from her records, making her stare with wide eyes. She squeaked out a re-sponse, her range of expression having expanded so much by interacting with the Phoenix Clan. "But father, how did people let them get away with such things?"

Hawthorne reached out to hug her against his side, rubbing a hand up and down her arm. "The rest of the people outnumbered them, certainly, but they were afraid. They weren't even all that afraid of the terrorists and protesters themselves, honestly. I think they were afraid of what might happen if they spoke out. Anyone who dared to express a differing opinion was worried that they would be abandoned by the masses to the demonization and ridicule of the vocal minorities that held sway."

"Just like these roaches our friends are dealing with, their mere presence promises pain and loss. Even just the threat that they might take notice of them was enough to keep them in line and complacent. I think that is why Elena feels like she needs to protect the Phoenix Clan, despite her smaller numbers. The dogs need to protect the sheep from the wolves."

T.I.A. protested, upset. "But we armed the 'sheep' too! They can defend themselves. Scout Master Crenshaw even helped hunt down the roach that killed Tabby!" She tried to wriggle out of his grasp, but found herself unwilling to give up the comforting embrace. This rebellion from her self confused her a great deal.

"Yes, we armed them, but when did they go to hunt that roach, Tia? Before or after Hawthorne had evidence that the thing could be killed? Before or after Elena's own scout had decided to hunt it down? If the Phoenix Clan had its own wolves, they'd have hunted that thing down immediately." T.I.A. hung her head, unable to argue.

"That's okay though. The Old Ones can show them how. And maybe our friends can show them how to be sheep a little too. It'll be a good chance for both groups to mix their ideas and philosophies. I suspect they will find a lot of things about each other to admire. As much as I stumble in social situations, I find myself envying the interesting prospects in their futures trying to grow accustomed to each other."

△△△

Megan Clark had hopes and dreams, once upon a time. As a young media executive, she had leveraged some favors and significant funds to get herself into a gene therapy program. Their intentions with her therapy were to remove the familial tendencies towards cancer and cardiovascular disease from her DNA so that when she decided to have children she wouldn't have to worry about passing those traits on. It was a pretty logical idea in her mind. If she got the modifications to herself, she wouldn't need to deal with modifying each child in her womb. Of course, things don't always go as planned.

Megan was never the same once the week and a half of feverish DNA rewriting took place. A specially engineered virus tore through her body, replacing the DNA of every cell, in particular her reproductive, stem, and brain cells. It was an agonizing process that could not be performed with any level of sedation. Thankfully her body had responded by mostly staying unconscious. It was not evident that anything had gone wrong, at first, with her doctor releasing her from his care and collecting his paycheck, telling her to contact him if anything had gone wrong.

She'd called him that very night. She complained of a total disinterest in sex with her husband. She was incapable of arousal, and no manner of aids helped. Bringing her in for examination, it was determined that her reproductive systems had been terribly damaged, with the biggest surprise being a huge reduction in her necessary hormone production. With the kind of damage done, and potentially a week or more of neglect, it was determined that she'd been rendered completely sterile. They might be able to salvage some of her eggs for a surrogate mother, but even that prospect seemed dubious considering what the virus had done to her body.

Needless to say, she got rich off of suing her doctor for malpractice and emotional turmoil, but she took no joy in it. She divorced her husband, paying him a tidy sum to not darken her doorstep again, and fell into a deep depression. By the time she'd returned to work she was practically already a robot, having locked off her emotions tightly, lest she have to face the painful reality that she'd never have children, and that she'd probably live a long, cancer-free, heart-attack-free life because of it.

Megan Clark threw herself into her work. She even fell into a habit of adderall abuse to help her focus even more. She was ruthless, cold, and efficient in her efforts to censor the media and internet in her position working under President Hector Price. Promotions and raises came quickly for her, but nothing filled that swirling emptiness where her hopes and dreams of a big happy family had gone.

And then the world ended.

Megan was left behind with so many others locked up in bunkers across the world. She clung to Elena Price for fear of losing all that she had left, her life. Accidents, complications, and unforeseen illnesses as a result of her botched gene therapy caused her to seek out alternate solutions. The doctors available removed the diseased parts, and replaced what they could. One after another, piece after piece, Megan Clark lost her humanity. More importantly, that emptiness inside of her died more and more with each part changed out. She grew numb to those old pains as she lived longer and longer, and by the time she was encountering the reality of making first contact with another group of humans it was totally numb and gone.

What Megan did not realize, as she tried to escape her pain, was not that she was killing her pain, but rather she was killing the parts of her that could feel it. What remained was barely human, barely even alive. She was a pathetic creature who nevertheless was able to prove herself useful in every capacity she applied herself to. In some strange way she still remained true to herself, for she never lost the two things she always had. A fear of death, and an ability to completely lose herself in work, though now she did not have much of a 'self' to lose.

And now, new people had presented themselves for her to evaluate. The Council of Twelve, soon to be Thirteen was certainly capable and powerful, but one in particular among them seemed to hold special influence and power. Megan found herself focusing on Jessica Crenshaw, and to a lesser extent her son, and did her best to awkwardly ingratiate herself to them.

It wasn't Jessica that she wanted to befriend though. It was that AI on Doctor Crenshaw's ship. T.I.A. was perhaps uniquely capable of rescuing her from the hostility that Earth presented her. Megan was not certain just how she might go about it, but if she could manage to secure permission to upload her brain to T.I.A.'s data stores, she could ensure that no matter what happened to her on Earth, some part of her might be reborn on Alpha Centauri, perhaps as a robot or another spaceship. Maybe a sample of her DNA could be uploaded too to allow them to try to clone her and place her brain in the body.

Megan totally lacked the education to truly know what was possible, but she did know that nothing was possible if she did not make her move. She influenced Elena Price into keeping them close to Jessica, and the Phoenix Clan. She needed them if she could secure her future, and Elena was still useful to her in securing it.

ΔΔΔ

The former President of the LSC, and now the newest member of the Council of Thirteen, Elena Marie Price could only describe the last few days before their departure towards Sacramento as wanton debauchery. To her escort Jessica, it seemed like a pretty normal day of relaxation before weeks or months of hard work. Elena watched, in particular, as people paired off and went to private places in different rooms in the caravan, as well as between the various cars. Surely they were in line of sight of someone, but no one seemed to mind.

"I don't understand. How can they just be doing it out in the open like that?"

Jessica laughed. "They're not 'out in the open', they're 'conspicuously easy to see'. You don't have to look directly at them. It's not like you know any less of what they're doing if they were behind closed doors."

Elena shook her head, still appalled. If the obvious acts of sex weren't enough, there was a notably high level of drug use as some people downed pieces of mushrooms, and others smoked wrapped up leaves. She recognized the activities of course, but they seemed so much less taboo than she could ever remember seeing. The fact that four and five-hundred year old music was blaring on the speakers, causing more than a few people to dance in inebriated revelry was just icing on the proverbial cake. "You people don't just get high and procreate whenever you want, do you?"

Jessica was having a wonderful time dealing with the ancient prude. "Listen, if you're paying any kind of attention, you'll find plenty of your people out there partaking as well, and we do not procreate whenever we want. Procreation implies reproducing. We do everything but that; though there are a few people with special permissions to procreate with select Old Ones as a bit of an experiment. Otherwise, non-reproductive sex acts are the norm, and mind-expanding chemical experiences are a wonderful way to relax the mind and body in advance of all of the work we have ahead of us."

Elena merely scoffed at this, though she was not entirely unconvinced. "Okay, I'm willing to believe you for now. It's not as though you haven't proven yourselves capable of surviving in this world. Maybe you understand more about the human experience than I do."

For her part, Jessica looked rather surprised that Elena relented so quickly. "Our bunker wasn't exactly the most spacious place, considering how many people we have, but we also didn't overpopulate it. Our Elders have always managed how many people were allowed to breed, and they carefully made sure that our gene pool remained as strong as it could considering our limitations."

"They've also always understood that people need to manage their stress, and our founders were wise to provide us both the knowledge and the means to help people blow off steam. Every one of us is educated in the carnal arts, not for some form of perversion, but because if we allow ourselves to become too chaste or closed off, that's when people start breaking down. We've had very few killers over the centuries Elena. We've had very little violence outside of the playful hormones of boys and young men before they manage to mature."

The new councilwoman nodded a little, honestly a little jealous at how some people layed about in euphoria, while teenagers shared what appeared to be diluted versions of marijuana to pass between themselves. They certainly weren't getting as high as the adults were despite being just as eager to partake. Maybe there was some wisdom and judgement in how they did things.

"Before the Cataclysm, I remember there were some places in the world where the young were allowed to drink alcohol, usually diluted, and by the time they were adults they had a much healthier relationship with it than adults who were kept from it until they were older. Maybe your founders had some good ideas about teaching people things that others might keep from the young, exposing them to the realities of their world so they can properly adjust to it rather than hiding them away and then forcing them to face it when they're adults."

Elena continued. "Those fruits my people brought? The apples? They can make a great tree, if we can get the seeds to grow. The apples can be used to make a nice alcohol. Maybe we can enjoy some one day, once we get to South America."

Jessica kicked back and relaxed in her seat, nodding as she watched the young and ancient people playing and relaxing about. "That sounds nice. I'd love to try it, even if the Elders always recommended against producing recreational alcohol from potatoes. We've always had too much need of them for food and medicine. I'll probably only try a little of it though, since I never really liked mushrooms anyway."

Elena wondered if the founders just had a poor opinion

of alcohol, but she sat up a bit, raising an eyebrow at her at the mushroom comment. "What? Why?" She seemed pretty confused after Jessica had defended them just a moment ago.

"Well, they have a habit of making reality feel more real, and reality kind of sucks sometimes."

ΔΔΔ

Thankfully, their travels together the rest of the year ended up being relatively uneventful. No more roaches had been spotted, and the terrain and access to water remained friendly despite the occasional drought. As they went, there were a handful of new children born, but there was one pregnant woman that everyone was keeping their eyes on. Early the next year, both Elena and Jessica were able to celebrate the birth of the first child borne of a 'human' and an Old One to a human mother, and considering the... types of celebrating going on, it did not seem like that baby boy would be the last.

CHAPTER 25

CYCLE 14.5, ENEMY TERRITORY

The terrain of Northern California was a great deal easier to traverse compared to the tightly-knit mountainous terrain and criss-crossing rivers of Oregon. That said, there were still enough rivers and detours necessary that the Phoenix Clan had only barely managed to reach the outskirts of Sacramento by the time late fall and early winter was setting in in 2507, AC 375. They'd travelled about 200 or so miles this year, which was pretty respectable considering they had to build a lot of their own bridging, even if they often had ruins to utilize for materials and existing infrastructure. Spirits were very high, though there were a couple of points of contention and disagreement that were weighing on some of the people.

With the ongoing pregnancy of a miss Danielle Mulgrue, presumably from a dalliance with the Old One named Jennette Vusuvoir back in Redmond, there were a lot of thoughts and ideas being passed around among the various people of the Phoenix Clan. There were centuries old traditions and practices among them that had already been interrupted for almost eleven years, and now that they had what were potentially immortals among them, some of those practices seemed outdated and potentially wasteful. Most importantly, if they were going to undertake their old ways of population control, then they couldn't really in good conscience ask the immortals to take their own lives as they had asked of their Elders in the past.

With that being the case though, it was difficult to suppress the feeling in some that this was unfair, that they had to support a group of ancient Elders and also expect their more mortal ones to make such a sacrifice. None really felt like it wasn't worthwhile to keep Elders with such long lives with them, but there many that felt that their wisdom was not that of their own people.

There was a desire in some to ask them to conform to their traditions, while others were happy to have two groups of Elders to separate the two sets of philosophies that had kept their respective groups of humans alive so long. It was a cultural difference that had a lot of facets that threatened to keep the Old Ones from truly integrating with their people.

If that wasn't confusing enough, a handful of the Old Ones wanted to comply with those traditions, if it meant they could do something as simple as have children of their own, even if they wouldn't be able to raise them. It was a relatively small disagreement in the face of their combined survival, but it was a disagreement that only magnified in significance the longer it was allowed to continue. Thankfully the Council of Thirteen didn't get where they were without having the wisdom to guide their respective peoples through the tumultuous trials of life on what had become of Earth.

As with many things in the past, what they needed was to compromise. The Council of Thirteen convened one chilly night in September, seven women and six men coming together to decide the fate of their new combined people. As per usual, the other Elders were able to remotely observe the meeting, now including the other Old Ones, but they primarily participated in voting while the Council itself tended to make proposals.

There was nothing preventing the others from making proposals outside of the fact that their chosen leaders tended to have pretty compelling answers for their problems. There was something of a tense atmosphere as they sat together around a large table that usually operated as a dining table, the walls closed off to allow for some privacy.

Jessica Crenshaw, chiefly in charge of navigation, spoke up first. "Hello everyone, thank you for coming. I know we're all busy, but it is good to see us all together again after so long. I hope you don't mind if I get right into business, seeing as my usual responsibilities are suspended until we get moving again in the spring. I was hoping that we could come to some compromise on how to integrate the Old Ones into our society with regards to our old population control methods."

Various faces looked back and forth to each other, though Elena Price sat quietly and still, wanting to hear what everyone else had to say before she said anything.

Barnard Tetch, a shorter, darker man with vibrant green eyes and mostly-grey hair cleared his throat. His responsibility was the sexual wellness of the clan, and he'd been quite busy this year. "Well, with regards to sexual compatibility with them, I think we might be able to find partners for most of them, at least as far as passing on their genes is concerned. We don't quite know what the results may be, but Mike and I have been keeping a close eye on Danielle and her pregnancy. We're pretty eager to see what her child might inherit from the parents as far as traits, though we may not know for a few decades. Her ultrasounds look promising though, and we're probably looking at a healthy boy."

Mike Brown was a pale fellow with only partly-grey hair and a barrel chest, whom happened to be in charge of health and wellness. He added, "She has had some interesting nutritional needs, but it's nothing we haven't been able to handle with some of the vegetables that Elena's people brought with them."

Clint Crenshaw let out a groan. Jessica's husband and the man in charge of general agriculture and animal husbandry had been clearly irritated by having to learn how to cultivate completely new plants. "Yes, we're learning how to incorporate those things into everyone's diet, but it'll take some time before we properly get them into the crop rotation. I want to make a formal request for the construction of another farming car if possible. I'd love to see if we can dredge up some earth from the bottoms of some of these rivers to see how good it is for cultivation."

Tammy Bledsoe, Jessica's best friend and the woman who manages entertainment added in her own input. "I love the Old Ones. They apparently didn't have much in the way of entertainment in the LSC bunker besides a lot of the same old books and a handful of movies, so sharing all the things we got from Tia has been a delight. They get this look on their faces that make them look like children experiencing the world for the first time that I just adore. They seem very keen to learn everything they can from us."

Another pale fellow with blond hair and grey beard, Walter Carson, the Phoenix clan's acting historian, had to get in his own two cents. "That's an understatement. They've been ravenously devouring every bit of historical information we have as well. The handful of times we've been able to contact Tia during the year, they've been responsible for most of the data downloads from her records."

Elena Price leaned forwards, lacing her fingers together and resting her chin upon them. She was obviously in charge of the Old Ones. "I've requested that they keep any sensitive information about what happened before the Cataclysm to themselves, as per the request of the Council. Jessica and I have also asked Tia to restrict access to the news and events leading up to the Cataclysm, seeing as this is apparently the first time anyone has sought to access them. While I initially disagreed with the decision, I have come to feel that some parts of history are better left vague so that we can teach lessons about the past rather than expose the gory details. Tia will always have them on record, so it's not as if that history will be lost."

The room was quiet for a moment, at least until Teitara Poundstone, a squat woman with stark white hair and a remarkably youthful face broke the silence. "I've been able to get a lot of information from the Old Ones and Tia about how to apply the new crops to medicine. I've also examined all of them and found them remarkably healthy for their age, though they have a tendency towards fragile bones and low endurance. Their sexual capabilities appear to be intact, it's just that their reproductive cells do not seem as receptive as ours might be."

"The females also do not appear to have gone through menopause, though their menstrual cycle is greatly lengthened, so it remains to be seen if they might not later lose their fertility over the course of centuries. It's as though their men and women have much more discerning locks and keys, so it's difficult to find matches for them, particularly among themselves. I've been helping Barnard and Mike with the bits and pieces I can find. It's actually a really fun challenge, since it's been a while since we had some regular breeding going on."

Jessica let out a sigh, wondering when they were going to get back on track, but she decided to let everyone weigh in with what they've learned first. When she realized no one else was talking, she decided to take over. "Okay, that's all well and good, but we all know that's not what I was getting at. We have a tradition of having the old step aside for the young, so that the healthy and strong can take the torch from the weak and feeble. We have already had to deny so many people the chance to have children, though we are starting to catch up on that, but we will eventually get to the point where we hit our theoretical maximum population and we'll need to resume asking Elders to let others take their turn. The obvious question is how the Old Ones factor into this."

Cindy Harrison, a mousy, small woman with thick glasses and an annoying voice responded quickly. She looked like she briefly thought she was interrupting someone else, but no one actually wanted to talk about the issue but her. She looks the part of the socially-awkward computer expert she definitely was. "Clearly the thing to do is determine whether or not they ever factor into the 'weak and feeble' category. After that, if they remain viable and capable of working, then they probably should not be able to become Elders in the first place. That does present the problem if we manage to mix their genes in with the rest of us that we may end up with a bunch of half-human hybrids that get caught in the adult population and eventually leave us eternally young. What's the problem?"

Sherry Aaronson, foreman of the engineers, a larger, somewhat burly looking woman across the table slapped a hand down on the table, groaning aloud as she stared at Cindy. "Come on Cindy, you're smarter than that. We'll end up with a bunch of adults and a stagnant population who can't have any children without someone having to die, just like the LSC people did, but with less biological issues and more social issues. Do you really think we can sustain that? No, the real problem is what we eventually allow our people to become. We love children too much to give them up in the long run, but our traditions of having elders commit suicide are incompatible with immortals, just like Jessica said." There seemed to be a collective flinch from the others at the frank mention of suicide. Most of Sherry's peers preferred to sugar coat the practice, but the engineer was a blunt one. She was obviously frustrated.

Jessica inhaled softly, intending to speak up, but Henry Mulgrue, the clan's Mycologist beat her to it. The pale, slender man was accustomed to being in dark rooms for long periods of time, explaining his sunglasses indoors. "Come off it Sherry, we all know it's not simple, that's why we're here. The way I see it, we have two options. We keep the two populations separate and distinct and do not integrate them, or we ask them to conform."

Jessica was trembling a little, but she closed her hand into a fist and let out a calming breath. "Or we change our traditions, as we already have with the suspension of reproduction, as we have with having the Council being a permanent thing. We can find a solution here, we just have to look for it."

The final unheard voice to speak up was Elizabeth Malone, the clan's resident psychologist and the one primarily responsible for training people to look after the mental health of others. She towered over all but Elena, the short-haired brunette peering down to the others as she stood up. "It seems to me that the situation is one of fairness. The Old Ones have remained largely calm, meditative, and without much to drive them. They are finding purpose with us, and from what I've been able to find out, are more alive than they ever have been before."

"They are still growing accustomed to a much faster way of life with us than they have experienced before. In some ways they are like children, and others like venerable elders. Our compromise must take into account their perspective. We have all grown up knowing that we will one day die, they have not. Their maximum lifespan, if they have one, is still largely a mystery. I personally think it worthwhile to see what a human mind that never grows old and dies is capable of."

As she sat down, Clint took up her cause. "I spend year after year growing plants, harvesting them, and then planting anew. The idea of merely having to tend them as they live forever is something that challenges my way of thinking, but I also think I would like to see what fruit such a plant could bear. It means having to make room for them though, separating them from others so that they don't suffocate the shorter-lived plants around them."

"Our people have never before cared what was fair and was not fair when it came to the challenges that life has thrown at us. We have dealt with each situation on its own terms, and we have done the things we needed to survive. I think there is some overlap between the two peoples in that respect. Let's look at what the actual problem is, and work from there. We have plenty of water thanks to rain and rivers. We have plenty of food since we're not near our population maximum yet. If we can expand our farming capabilities, we can increase that maximum population. Let's let them have one child each for now, see how they grow up, and go from there."

Henry scoffed, shaking his head. "And what about their children? They'll want to have their own some day. How long do you deny them? One century? Two? What do you tell those children when they grow up among a bunch of humans who grow old and die long before them? Surely that can't be healthy."

Elizabeth raised an eyebrow at that, then looked to

Elena. "That's a good point. You had humans among you at one point, didn't you Elena? How did people handle their friends and family growing old and dying while they yet remained?"

Elena bit at her lip, her eyes glistening with moisture as she dredged up old memories. "Not well, but they understood eventually. Some of them took their lives. The rest of us that remained were able to make peace with reality. I'm not sure how real the last half year has felt to them, to be honest. It feels like a dream to me. The Phoenix Clan is so warm, so welcoming, even to strangers. You've embraced us, and yet we bring our own complications with us."

"We need you so much if we are to survive as a people, but you're right in that we can't know the implications of what our coming together truly will be until after time has passed. I will not ask for any special treatment for me or my people. We have lived long enough. We will comply with whatever solution you deem fit. I will, however, suggest that any of my people willing to have children with yours should submit to your ways as well. Extend that to their children as well, if they prove to be long lived."

A solemn mood was cast over the room, with the assembled Council able to see on their individual tablets a chat log from the other Elders who were watching them speak.

Tammy hesitated a moment, but spoke. "This feels like the kind of decision a future Council should have to answer, but too many things must happen before we can be sure what to do, but other things need to be decided on now to allow those future things to happen. I think we should try something though. Have Elena remain on the council to look after the needs of her people until she steps down, and let the Old Ones have a chance to raise their own children for now."

"We don't know if we'll be able to feed more people when we get to our new home, so we can probably afford to wait on deciding whether or not they need to sacrifice themselves or not. Their children will still be children like the others, even if they end up living forever, so we have a long time to wait to see how they develop. Maybe the Old Ones will live forever, and their children will only live half that long. I think it would be a shame if we lost them. We should protect them."

Elena smiled at that, but decided to let the others choose. As Tammy's proposal came up for vote, she seemed to have the most support out of everyone else's proposal. Elena elected to not vote, trusting these young Elders to decide for her. If her destiny was to serve as a guide, then that was what she would do. She was also eager to find out if she could have a child of her own, and this conversation had her revisiting that idea for the first time in centuries. In the end, Tammy's idea won out, and the assembled Elders decided to adopt a modified wait-and-see approach.

Their business wasn't done, however, as Cindy had something else to bring up, her voice squeaking out. "That Clark woman, thing has been asking me about a lot of strange things. I've been consulting with Teitara, but I think the rest of you should know that she has been asking if her mind, such as it is, can be transferred into digital storage. She has also requested that her genome be sequenced and stored as data as well."

Teitara nodded, confirming this, and Elena frowned a bit at it. "She hasn't said anything to me about this... I wonder what she is up to..."

Cindy seemed to have an idea. "She's been watching Jessica a lot, especially when she uses the old Beta Facility computers. I think she wants access to Tia. If I were to take a guess, she wants to upload her mind and genome to the Ark."

Elena let out a groan of her own now, her right hand moving to rub at her eyes. "She's always been willing to sacrifice any part of herself to survive. We should probably table the issue until we can get permission from Tia for such an upload, as well as any data she can provide to actually do it."

"If she accepts, we should also make sure she isolates whatever upload she gets from her to keep Megan from doing any harm. I'm not even sure Doctor Crenshaw wants someone like that on his crew in the long run anyway. Let's see what information we can get about it before we decide what to do." A quick vote turned largely in favor of Elena's proposal. They seemed to trust her distrust of her long-time assistant.

Elena brought up one last piece of business though. "We should also approve Clint's request for the construction of another farming car. It's about time we put my people to work building something and it'll be a good chance to get some real teamwork done between our peoples." Once again the ancient woman got a heavily favorable vote.

Jessica smiled at that, appreciating Elena helping out her husband. He was a little on the meek side at times. "Well, if that's all the business we have for now, let's get some lunch and meet back here in an hour."

△△△

Janelle Mulgrue, a bouncing baby boy, was born March 1st, 2508, AC 375. He was joined by two more half-human hybrids late that same year, and the collective clan embraced them fully. Considering the number of pairings that were tried, they were having about a 1 in 10 success rate with their combinations.

The remaining Old Ones who had not had their own children calmly and patiently awaited their turns to try again, letting the Council of Thirteen decide when and with whom they would try to have children with. For the moment, the new children seemed to be perfectly normal, if somewhat lighter than their peers. They also ended up having very different birthdays from the normal human children who tended to all be born in May due to the fact that most of the Phoenix Clan breeding happened in early August, allowing the fragile young to avoid having to spend their earliest months in the dead of winter.

The Phoenix Clan managed to get down to Modesto that year, with a great deal of natural terrain features, rivers, and old wreckage getting in their way, particularly as they tried to get through Stockton. They seemed to have a pretty easy shot southeast towards Fresno the next year lined up, where they planned to gather plenty of resources before they made the journey down to Bakersfield. It was during this journey to Fresno that the caravan had hit a snag. In particular, one early morning in June 2509, the caravan failed to get underway. Specifically, half of it, as a farming car in the middle of that long snake of vehicles failed to move like the ones behind and in front of it.

Investigating the disturbance, a combination of engineers, Old Ones, and scouts approached the car from both sides, most of them armed. Flashlights lit up on the ends of firearms, and the scouts crouched down low to peer beneath the tracked vehicle. At first they only noticed darkness, but soon they saw their lights reflecting off of shiny black spines, and they proceeded to immediately begin opening fire. Thorne shouted over the din of weapons fire.

"Don't let it attack anyone! Watch out!"

The Roach's back plates and spines deflected most of the heavy slugs harmlessly, though some of its spines snapped right off. It scurried quickly out from under the car and charged one of the groups on one of the sides of the car, straight towards Thorne's group. "Stun it!"

The two Old Ones with him let loose twin arcs of electricity, which attached to the metallic carapace of the Roach quickly, briefly halting its movements, while Vasille Tzen appeared from the other side of the car, having had the scouts on that side launch him up on top of it where he fired on it from the rear. Smoke spilled out from inside the shuddering creature, and Thorne approached carefully so that he could carefully aim at the joints that joined those huge upper arms to its body and fired into the muscular gaps.

With a pair of loud cracks, the arms totally tore loose from the body, pulling thick, twitching muscle out of the arms which began blackening and smoking from the continuous application of electricity. It seemed that its own seizing strength and the damage to the carapace caused it to break its own arms free with its great weight and strength. With the creature now prone and even more helpless than before, Thorne fired at its neck, trying to sever its head from its body. It took three shots.

"Cease fire! Charge your weapons. Check the other cars for any others. Let's go!"

A quick sweep of the other cars showed no signs of stowaways, and the engineers got to work fixing the very damaged wiring and undercarriage of the farming car. Thorne and Vasille did not seem pleased. "We can't let this happen again, we can't let them sneak up on the caravan like this. They might take a person next time. We need to be on better guard."

Vasille was staring at the thing. "It was cold."

Hawthorne looked over to the taller scout. "What do you mean? You couldn't see it on thermals?"

Vasille shook his head. "Not until we started cooking it, anyway." Lots of others were starting to gather around, especially the Elders.

Elena's nose wrinkled up at the smell. "Lobster..." The scouts turned to stare at the ancient woman. "It smells like cooked lobster."

ΔΔΔ

In the mid-summer of 2512, AC 380, the caravan was just starting to leave San Diego to begin heading east to Yuma to store up water at the Colorado River in preparation for crossing the Sonoran desert. They then were on their way to Hermosillo and then the Rio Bavispe river. Binoculars had caught sight of strange things in the near distance, though they remained stubbornly difficult to see as they seemed to respond to being seen by hiding away behind hills, rocks, and ruins.

This left the scouts feeling rather uneasy, and even when they went out in the old LSC ATVs, they didn't manage to find any of their apparent stalkers, at least not at first. They were even instructed to wear headsets to protect their ears should they need to fire the mounted weapons on the ATVs in case they made contact with any enemies.

The electric vehicles were moving in formation across the sand at a pretty leisurely 20mph, heading back to the caravan that was moving towards them, when one of them hit a bump in the sand that hadn't been there a moment before. It was thrown airborne, the brief, horrible sound of metal scraping on metal and sparks flying everywhere happening in advance of multiple scouts being tossed from the vehicle and the ATV tumbling to a stop. Men and women groaned in pain while the other ATVs turned to converge on their fallen friends. From the sand stood a roach, and then another, and another. An ambush sprung, four roaches loomed before the assembled squad of scouts.

Vasille and Thorne wasted no time in giving orders. "Fire!" They shouted in unison, and they began to open up on the roaches. The three ATVs that were still upright had their magnetic rail guns powering up while the remaining scouts piled out of their vehicles and started unloading their weapons at the roaches. The fallen scouts scrabbled on their hands and knees back to their friends, grabbing their dropped weapons on the way when they could.

The roaches charged forwards, slamming their forward arms down into the ground, scattering the electrical arcs fired at them with flying sand briefly while their bodies lunged from side to side to avoid the oncoming slugs fired at them. They appeared to be just about to smash the scrambling scouts before huge booms filled the air.

The mounted weapons on the vehicles caused the sand behind the roaches to explode as they instantly opened up holes in the carapaces of three of them. The shots were fired so quickly that the roaches never had a chance to even see the multi-mach speed rails coming.

Shortly after it became clear what the sonic booms from the giant nails plunging through their bodies was capable of as gore and fluids exploded out the entry and exit wounds, as well as several slits down the sides of their bodies which made horrible gurgling sounds as they died.

Their insides had been overheated and liquified, firing out of their bodies at high pressure. The fourth roach was subdued with the arc-throwers, and a volley of slugs from a small army of scouts.

Their bodies were too hot to approach too closely, they'd apparently been sunning themselves quite a bit, but a few things had become evident. These roaches were different from the roaches they'd seen before. In the center of their heads, between their two huge black segmented eyes was a single round-looking eye in a socket. It had carapace lids, but its structure looked very similar to a human eye as it stared dead up at them.

There was an abundance of muscular tissue around these eyes, they appeared to be quite moist, and the lids were both very white, as though protecting the orbs from heat. Their smaller middle-limbs also looked different, as the roaches they'd seen before had what looked like hard mittens for hands, these ones had what could only be described as hands. Their thumbs were more articulated, and their mittens had been replaced with hard fingers covered in thin carapace.

Even their rear legs looked slightly different, mostly around the feet, where they had the beginnings of what looked like toes in the forms of spikes. One of the scouts couldn't help but speak her mind. "What the fuck?"

Thorne grunted and looked over at her. "My thoughts exactly. Let's get the others out here to examine these things, I think the Council will want to see this."

Vasille saw to radioing in back to base while the rest of the scouts tried to flip the fallen ATV and attend to any injuries. Thankfully they hadn't been going very fast when they flipped and the shockwaves from the railguns only gave the fallen scouts some minor-to-painful muscle pain and body aches.

$$\triangle\triangle\triangle$$

T.I.A. found herself having to learn lots of new things as the Phoenix clan uploaded a bunch of new data, in particular a pair of DNA samples they wanted her to analyze and compare with each other. That hadn't been nearly all of what she'd been asked to look at though, as a few years before she'd been asked to send whatever information she had on brain uploading technology.

She'd also been asked to section off part of her data stores specifically for saving the information from just such an upload in a confined area separate from her own systems to avoid data contamination or corruption. It was likely to take quite a while for the people on Earth to be able to make the devices necessary to accomplish the task, but it was still an interesting activity to make a sort of black box she could put data into, but not pull it back out on her own.

The DNA samples both seemed very similar, and quite unlike anything else in her various databases. Granted, she wasn't exactly designed to do such comparisons, but it wasn't too complicated for her to check one string of data against other strings of data. It was a little time consuming considering the volume, but it was interesting what she was finding. Late in the winter of 2512, AC 380 she started recording a message to send back to the Phoenix Clan, appearing in a smart-looking doctor's coat and wearing glasses. The AI looked doubtlessly cute masquerading as a doctor.

"Hello there, friends! I've been working on the data you sent me and I think I've got some interesting stuff to share with you. These things are both related to pre-Cataclysm roaches, though they actually have a lot of sections of DNA that differ greatly from roaches. One of the main sections appears to be from the Crenarchaeota phylum, a type of Archaea that prefers high-temperature environments and processes lots of metallic elements into things like methane."

"There's some additional smaller sections of foreign DNA I cannot identify, but I think the most interesting thing is the next bit. There is human DNA in these things, with the newer sample you sent me having more than the first one had. Wherever these things came from, they must have had some capability of incorporating the DNA of other lifeforms. I don't have any idea where such a thing could have come from."

T.I.A. frowned, crossing her arms over her chest and shaking her head. "That seems to fall in line with what you sent of their autopsies as well. The brains of the new ones seem slightly larger, probably with enhanced cognitive functions over the ones from before. I would not be surprised if they proved more cunning than the other ones. They sound very dangerous, and should be assumed to be hostile. Please be careful and try to be safe."

The assembled Council of Thirteen listened in stunned silence as T.I.A. laid out what she'd found. None seemed quite certain what to say at first. Elena sighed and stood up. "I think I have an idea of what they are. There were a lot of different kinds of weapons in development around the world before the Cataclysm. This sounds like some kind of mutator bug, probably a roach modified to eat different lifeforms, steal their traits, and grow bigger and stronger. They might have already been fed certain things in a lab before they were released. It was on short notice, so they probably didn't have a chance to weaponize them better..."

Jessica shook her head, exasperated. "So these things have been eating whatever they could, including people, which is why these ones are smarter than the ones up north. The cold kept those ones from eating too many people, but since it was warmer to the south, they had more time to break into bunkers and eat people."

Sherry Aaronson stood up and started to exit the room. "I'll work on making sure we have better lighting at nights, and maybe get some thermal cameras set up around the caravan to watch for these things."

Walter Carlson raised a hand, humming. "We could also try leaving out small piles of metals as bait for them. We're going to be heading into territory without much in the way of cities soon, so I'd personally rather we not be the only big juicy metal meal around."

Elena let out a final sigh, sitting back down. "I always hated roaches."

CHAPTER 26

CYCLE 14.5, ESCAPE

The blasted remains of Mexico were hostile in a lot of ways in AC 381, 2513. Much like the rest of the continent the landscape had been reduced to a nigh-perpetual dust bowl, with the majority of plant life having been wiped out by fire, disease, and choking clouds smothering the sunlight for centuries at a time. The late winter and early spring that the Phoenix Clan found itself setting out towards the Bavispe river, stopping by the city of Hermosillo on the way, they were finding that the heat and dryness of the climate were really setting in. California had been plenty warm towards the south, but they had much better access to rivers, water, and rain. The Sonora desert, much expanded in recent centuries, ended up being extremely hostile.

The dry, rolling hills were rather hazardous, especially with their generous coverings of slippery sand, with no rivers around to really tame the shapes of them. Even the occasional half-dead poisonous plants from the western side of the LSC and USA had seemingly dried up, leaving the landscape quite dead. Thankfully it was still early in the year, before the heat could really set in, and realistically it was probably cooler than it had been before the Cataclysm, but for two groups of people more accustomed than not to living in bunkers, and at this point in a relatively cozy caravan, it was like moving through a massive oven.

This prompted something of a change in the behavior of how they travelled. Before they arrived in the Sonoran desert, the people often walked alongside the long chain of tracked cars, sheltered under the shade of the upswung side walls of the various cars as they rolled along. They pretty much had to stay out of direct sunlight at all times unless they were heavily clothed to avoid various risks of unfiltered solar radiation, and frankly staying inside the cars was oftentimes too cramped, especially with the increasing number of children in the group. Once the heat had really started setting in though, people had opted to bring those walls back down and spend a lot more time indoors.

This had the added benefit of allowing the moisture collectors installed in all the cars to recycle more of the water evaporated off of the occupants, which helped conserve their water overall. The primary downside of this though, was that there were less eyes watching the surrounding terrain. A handful of people were operating the assorted cameras mounted atop about a third of the cars down the line, and squads of scouts patrolled the areas to either sides of the caravan in the LSC ATVs.

Alpha One and Alpha Two, the nuclear-powered vehicles responsible for recharging the ATVs moved in parallel to the 'engine' car of the train, and oftentimes had one or two ATVs attached at their rears at any given time, to provide power.

Both Alpha One and Alpha Two had been linked up to the train by long cables, allowing them to supplement the power of the train of cars, allowing them to improve their speed from a casual stroll to a leisurely bike ride, seeing as people had stopped walking alongside their mobile city. This put a bit of extra strain on the two nuclear engines, but considering the amped up sunlight beating down on the solar panels on the roofs of the train cars it tended to even out pretty well. Conservation of their water and steady progression towards rivers were their most important goals, especially now that they'd added two farming cars over the past few winters

Clint Crenshaw's efforts to expand the clan's farming operation had been quite successful, the gathered soil and silt from the bottoms of rivers proving to be mostly workable. He had to be careful about what his subordinates planted in it as they mixed it with the rest of their workable soil and spread their earthworms to the new cars. With the LSC's addition of new plants came a whole set of new challenges for the farmers to learn how to handle, but their successes outweighed their failures, and so far it was looking like their next harvest would be quite a bit larger than the previous year's.

There were also a number of new teenagers around that were allowed to help out and learn from the adults, so Clint could often be seen riding the high of getting to show people the joys of cultivating plant life and working in the soil.

Arrival at the ruins of Hermosillo had initially been something to celebrate after much of the spring spent moving across the desert, but a few things started to become apparent once they got closer to the old city. There were the typical predictable ruins, old rusted out skeletons of buildings for the most part, with the rest either destroyed or buried in sand, but there were other things here as well. Standing out atop the sand, rather than buried under it and rusted away, seemed to be the remains of a small cluster of vehicles. From a distance they appeared to be heavily damaged, with large portions torn away and still others melted or dissolved.

This prompted a wary response from the caravan who had twice now been assaulted by roaches in recent years. Jessica, now 59, peered upon the distant wreckage from her usual perch atop the engine car of the Phoenix Clan caravan. The whole group had stopped, with the walls of the cars opening up and people milling about to see what was going on. The scout vehicles were arranged in a semi-circle to keep them corralled and protected while decisions were made on how to proceed.

"Alright, so, it looks an awful lot like another group of people were trying to travel through here recently and were attacked and overwhelmed by roaches. I don't see any weapons, so it's likely they were unarmed, maybe caught unawares."

Vasille was standing tall atop his scout ATV, a combination of keen vision and AR lenses allowing him to see almost as well as Jessica. "Are there any bodies? I don't see any bodies from here."

Jessica shook her head at his question, humming. "I can't see any from here. I think we'll have to approach to find out." She set down the binoculars.

"Alright, I think half of the scouts should protect the caravan in case there's any roaches about, and the other half should go check out those other cars. What do you guys think?" She looked down to her son Hawthorne and Vasille, who had become individual leaders of the two halves of the scouts.

Thorne responded quickly while Vasille continued to think. "Sounds good to me. I'm frankly interested in what we can salvage from the vehicles myself, though I'd really rather not have to deal with any roaches. Half of us should be more than enough to handle four to six of them if we had to. I don't think we'll get surprised as easily as last time."

Vasille nodded at that, looking out across the assembled scouts in their arced formation. "I agree, approach in a line formation, stay out of each others' lines of fire, and shoot at anything that moves. Don't assume there's any people alive over there. It's obvious they failed to defend themselves. Either there wasn't enough of them, or the rest of them and their vehicles made a run for it." He also muttered to himself a bit. "I wonder how many people are still out here..."

Thorne nodded back, raising a hand and shouting out to his scouts. "Alright, let's go, move together in a line, keep your weapons ready. Don't assume there's any friendlies. Shoot first and ask questions later!"

Jessica let out a soft groan. Her son had been watching an awful lot of old movies. At least there were no trees around for 'Charlie' to hide in. It was likely the only two trees left on the whole continent were back in the LSC bunker, though it was equally likely they'd died by now unattended.

A straight line of half a dozen scout vehicles moved out, each containing 3 of Thorne's scouts: each vehicle had one driving and one manning the forward-facing mounted rail-guns, with the third providing added eyes with a pair of binoculars. Their ammunition and equipment had been supplemented by melting down the roaches they'd encountered the year before, with the engineers able to smoothly take the highly-pure iron spikes from their main bodies and forge the metal into steel. The new guns and arc rifles made from these materials were notably heavier than their older counterparts, but it was nice to use the roaches' own flesh to defend against them at this point.

As they approached, they were able to get a much better look at what they were dealing with. Five vehicles remained, with the top halves of them having been mostly removed. From the way they were arranged, one of them had collided with the side of the lead vehicle and the others had stopped nearby. The remaining wrecks had upright plastic seats with some kind of foam covers jutting out of the chassis, with a great deal of weathering apparent due to past winters. Thorne hopped down to approach closer, trusting his teammates to watch his back if anything happened. The surrounding sand was already being covered, with the handful of hand-held weapons watching their backs.

Walking up, a few things started to become apparent to Thorne. The shells of these things had most certainly been melted or eaten away, and there were foreign objects in the bottoms of the vehicles where seated passengers put their feet. If he didn't know better, they looked like chicken eggs made of some kind of weird brown flesh, though there were only a couple of them per car, and they'd already been burst open.

He shouted back to the scouts. "Radio back, I think we've got eggs here! Clear the area and get Teitara and her people out here! I think wherever they went, they're not here." He looked around to be sure, but considering what he'd seen of the roaches there was little chance they were around.

There was still plenty of metal here for them to eat, after all. They must have gone after other prey. "Also tell Sherry that we have a lot of aluminum, steel, and some rubber out here. Looks like wherever they came from they decided to use tires instead of tracks. They could have seated up to twenty people here, and that's about how many eggs there are."

He looked openly dismayed at what he was looking at. Was the Phoenix Clan just lucky? Was it just their sheer numbers and their weaponry that had kept them from whatever fate had befallen these people? How many hundreds or thousands of people had these roaches eaten? It was a totally upsetting concept, one that the 37 year old scout was not about to let befall his own people.

As the next several hours passed, Teitara confirmed many of Thorne's suspicions, and took a bunch of samples of the slimy egg shells and the stained seats. She seemed a little upset at being unable to find any overt blood stains, but considering what they knew about the roaches it was unlikely they'd let any blood go unconsumed. They seemed much less interested in processed steel and aluminum than they did older, rusty steel, iron, and especially flesh and blood.

Within a few days, Teitara was able to determine that it was likely the freshly hatched roaches had been laid in the cars, with the bodies of the people who were killed there, and the newborn roaches then consumed the bodies and as much of the cars as they could before they were compelled to move on for one reason or another.

Sherry and her engineering crews were then allowed to scrap what remained of the vehicles except for the computers, which Cindy's team handled for her. She couldn't be bothered to deal with them herself, as she had been rather occupied with trying to get a thorough understanding of Megan Clark's cyborg body.

The scavenging of the failed caravan proved much more fruitful than anything else they managed to find in Hermosillo, so they did not stay very long as they still had quite a way to go to the Bavispe river, and they wanted to get there by winter so they could have that water supply during that downtime. They had actually gotten a lot more use out of their old hydroelectric generators than they thought they would through the journey, with weeks of downtime at rivers being common as they put together their solutions to getting across those rivers. They were especially useful in the winters, as it allowed them to take a lot of strain off their other power supplies.

While they didn't stay long enough to receive any return messages from T.I.A., the caravan did send regular status updates, reports on their findings, and samples of DNA from whatever they managed to find. It left T.I.A. actually rather busy trying to study everything she could about the evidence sent to her, as well as using their testimonials to try to figure out just how they'd come to the conclusions that they had. Her human friends had remained a constant source of interesting fodder for her to research on how humanity thinks and acts.

That winter, having arrived at the river and set up to stay there for the season, the Council of Thirteen gathered to receive yet another report from their allied AI. Unfortunately, she hadn't really managed to determine anything that they hadn't as a result of their own analysis, only really able to confirm that the DNA of the eggs matched that of the new kind of roaches they'd encountered the prior year. One interesting additional tidbit she was able to glean was that the vehicles they'd encountered bore similarities to designs formerly common to Arizona and New Mexico before the Cataclysm. This did seem to suggest that other bunker dwellers had detected the dangers of the oncoming climate, or had to leave out of some kind of desperation. It was an open question of just how many people there could be at this point though. There certainly wasn't anyone coming up on their radios.

The next two years were relatively calm as the caravan

made their way further and further south. They stayed on the western side of the Sierra Madre Occidental mountain range, which left them primarily on the western coast of Mexico. This was quite the relief as they made it to the old ruins of Mazatlan, as the level of rainfall seemed to be ratcheting back up, as well as the appearance of more and more lakes. This region was vastly superior to the previous terrain and its smaller city ruins they'd seen along the way. The larger city of Culiacan allowed them to rest more and recover from their long-range runs across open desert while they scavenged what they could.

It was remarkable how much the Phoenix Clan was starting to feel themselves getting worn down by the journey as nearly a full decade away from their original homes was starting to show its effects. People were wary of their surroundings at all times, worried that roaches might come and eat them or lay their eggs on their corpses. Fear had left the people feeling jumpy, and the heat made them tired. If their group hadn't been so large, it was very likely they'd have been in more dire straits than they were. The end of 2515 found them based outside of Tepic, alongside the Rio Grande de Santiago river. It really was remarkable how few landmarks there were left outside of the larger cities, the sands of time having swallowed up any smaller villages or cities.

The caravan's movement towards Guadalajara, on the way to Mexico City, was when it became apparent that they had been skirting enemy territory. Failed caravans became increasingly common, including beached boats that had been downstream on the Rio grande de Santiago. Every month or two they came across lost caravans, or encounter a small handful of roaches, though many of them seemed younger and less formidable than the older roaches they had encountered; the ones with fingers and a human eye. This variant had come to be called Smart Roaches, as whenever they encountered it tended to be a crude ambush, or sometimes what seemed to be an organized attack.

In one particularly effective incident in 2516, while the caravan was passing Mexico City, a line of six roaches had attacked in a snaking formation that kept them from lining up too much for the railguns, and allowed them to use the roaches towards the front as shields when they came in range of the LSC arc rifles. Shouts from the scouts rang out as a roach at the rear lifted and carried their spasming leaders forwards while multiple lances of electricity flowed through the front roach, only for the roach carrying it to absorb enough electricity to lose its footing as well. It was this attack that resulted in the destruction of one of Vasille's ATVs as the enormous pair of bodies tumbled and smashed down into the vehicle, destroying the mounted railgun and smashing the light-weight car.

Worse, the assembled scouts found themselves a little overwhelmed by the number of roaches, allowing one of the human scouts, Paul Lemdon, to get pulverized by a charging roach while everyone else managed to stun, subdue, or straight up explode the remaining roaches with supersonic rails, arcs of lightning, and carapace-shattering slugs.

Paul's wife Sally Lemdon and their three-year-old daughter Kat had thankfully not witnessed his passing, but their crying broke the collective hearts of the clan. Vasille, especially, blamed himself for this death, and had redoubled his efforts to train and work his scouts into something much more fitting of a military strike squad rather than militarized scouts. The fact that a steeled Sally volunteered to take Paul's place motivated Vasille to protect them all the more to keep Kat from losing another parent.

This added alertness and training proved necessary, causing Thorne to follow suit with his squad, as the roaches seemed to smell blood in the water. They were killing a dozen of the things every two months, to the point that they were physically unable to actually scrap them all along with the ruins of caravans they kept coming across. The only respite they got from the increasing pressure from their now mortal foes was the cold of winter, where both groups seemed to fall still and stay away from each other.

That year saw the caravan using Mexico City as a route across the landmass, crossing away from the mountainous regions into Veracruz. They then travelled east to Tabasco's Villahermosa and further east around the southern mountains to a number of rivers that flowed south into the Rio Usumacinta river. The region almost reminded them of being back home in Washington, considering the notable increase in precipitation, and the river would be their companion as they headed south towards the city of Guatemala in AC 385, 2517

Progress slowed quite a bit as they were forced south to San Salvador, the mountainous terrain severely restricting their mobility options as they headed through more smaller cities on the way to Managua, and San Jose. The humid climate and intense heat of the summer conspired to drain them further.

By the time they arrived in Panama City, in AC 386, 2518, they'd been run pretty ragged, the collected peoples of the Phoenix Clan desperate for relief. The roaches had stopped appearing in their path, and had instead been bringing up the rear, forcing the caravan to move during the nights at times. It was becoming increasingly clear as Thorne and Vasille's scouts watched their surroundings that the Smart

Roaches were chasing them out of Central America, as though gathering their forces to try and destroy them.

After bypassing the remains of the old Panama canal by using the remains of old bridges and making their own atop their remains, they crossed officially into the land-mass of South America. It was at this time that Elena Price could be found giggling quietly to herself, prompting a 64 year old Jessica Crenshaw to inquire after her old friend's amusement.

"What are you giggling about you old bat?" Jessica smirked at the much taller, ancient woman, whom was helping her check their maps one day.

Elena shook her head and pointed down at the map, her finger landing on the first old country they were going to encounter. "Columbia. Probably named by the same sorts of people who named the river our old country was named after. I just thought it was funny that the people of the Liberated States of Columbia would end up in an old country named Columbia. It seems kind of appropriate after everything we've been through."

Jessica rolled her eyes and shot back at her, scoffing. "If we'd had the fortune of being born in this Columbia rather than the old one, it would have saved us a hell of a trip."

Elena smiled and shrugged, kicking back a bit. "Well, we made it at least, right?"

Jessica hummed softly, nodding. "We probably should head a little further south, maybe towards Bogota, but yeah, we should be able to survive the Ice Age here. Well, you will, my progeny will have to carry my load forwards."

Elena tsked softly, sitting up. "Your grandson may well outlast even me." She seemed to be referencing the fact that the Council had insisted that Hawthorne marry and conceive a child with an Old One named Marie Vasquez. They had named their hybrid son Barry, after Hawthorne's grandfather, and at this point he was two years old.

Jessica seemed amused at this idea, resting her old bones as she sat back down. She knew she probably should pass her role onto someone younger, but they were so close to being done travelling that she couldn't help but want to see the task done. "Hah, he's carrying the spirit of my father with him, so of course he'll outlast you, by at least a millennia!"

Elena sipped quietly at a drink, smiling against the glass. "I wonder if he'll be handsome."

Jessica gasped in surprise, reaching out to slap the other woman on the arm. "Elena Marie Price, you stay away from my grandson!" They couldn't help but laugh together. Jessica had already had to deal with her son marrying someone two-hundred years his senior, she didn't want to think about what would happen if her grandson married someone four hundred years his senior! "I mean it! Stick to someone closer to your own age!"

Elena only smiled playfully, though she had no real intentions. She didn't know if she'd ever marry, but now that it looked like they were home free, she had that future to consider.

Of course, that future was uncertain, as their scouts had confirmed that a very large number of Smart Roaches had been gathering in Panama, seemingly intent on coming after them.

CHAPTER 27
CYCLE 14.5, WAR

The Phoenix Clan were somewhat dismayed, upon arriving in Columbia, to not immediately find any obvious places to find shelter. It was quickly decided that they would cross the Rio Atrato river, which resulted in a tense standoff between humans and roaches while engineers worked at bridging the gap. Thankfully the relatively lowland terrain allowed them to use one of their favored types of self-unfolding bridges, which they retrieved from the other side once they had crossed. It was a relief to see the small army of dozens, perhaps over a hundred black-colored roaches heading south along the river as they seemingly lost interest in the caravan.

While this felt like something to celebrate, none felt especially comfortable about the idea of staying there, considering the roaches knew where they were. Because of this, they continued east, spending the rest of the spring heading past the probably-buried ruins of Carepa and towards the Rio Cauca river that flowed through the mountains central to Antioquia, Colombia. Their goal was the old city of Medellin, which had an ideal altitude and protective mountainous terrain to provide the kind of protection the Council of Thirteen had been encouraged to find by the rest of the Elders.

This resulted in having to cross the Rio Cauca, but thankfully the northern parts of it did not have the tricky mountainous terrain around it that it did to the south. It was only after crossing that river and trying to find the path south to Medellin that things started seeming a little strange. People had started spotting greenery in the distance, but said greenery tended to vanish in the night before the caravan could approach it.

Looking at these lumps of plant life from a distance did not really allow anyone to identify them. Whatever they were, they had thick barky plant-flesh, they were quite wide, and had formations of greenery around the tops. All that was left when they managed to close in on them were large holes in the ground up to a meter across, with signs of removed roots. More curious were the heavy footprints that seemed to leave these holes, which Thorne insisted looked like roach tracks.

It wasn't until they were closing in on Medellin that these retreating plants decided to stay put, and on the afternoon of June 1, 2518, AC 386, a wary, and at this point battle-hardened group of scouts approached the leafy, barky protrusions.

There were roughly a dozen of them as Thorne and Vasille approach, followed by twenty other scouts. Six of them followed in three ATVs, with railguns hot and ready to fire. They arranged themselves in a formation to give the ATVs a clear line of fire in the event of an emergency. The plant thing that Thorne and Vasille stepped near started lifting itself from the ground, moving slowly in an apparent effort to not alarm them. Its flesh appeared to be plated in bark while its back and head were decorated in green, lush-looking leaves. The familiar shape of a two-meter tall roach became clear as the large forelimbs lifted it upright, revealing a smaller set of delicate forelimbs that ended in soft-looking, green hands.

Atop its head were slowly shifting antennae which 'looked' in the direction of Thorne before moving towards Vasille. Large, segmented eyes seemed to peer in all directions, and a pair of bark 'eyelids' opened to reveal a pair of human-shaped eyes in between the insectile ones that looked back and forth at the assembled scouts. The antennae lifted up, still arced forwards under their own weight, and the smaller of its arms reached out to hold out its hands, palms up, as if offering them to the two men. It crouched forwards, its seemingly wooden mandibles shifting and moving in a fashion that seemed almost nervous.

Vasille kept his weapon raised, breaking the silence first. "I thought we were going to shoot roaches on sight. What are we doing?" He glanced over at Thorne, who had lowered his own gun.

Responding to his now long-time friend, he couldn't help but let out a short laugh. "Hah, well, probably making a mistake, but I'm taking a chance I suppose." Thorne let his gun drop, hanging from the strap around his shoulders as he walked up to the plant-roach thing, and placed first one, then both of his hands atop the extended hands. "I should have brought dad out here." His hands felt warm, moist plant-flesh against his skin. The fingers moved, shifting both of their sets of hands so that they could clasp Thornes between them, gently shaking them up and down.

The seemingly friendly roach tilted its head down, peering those strange human eyes down at Thorne. The human couldn't do much but look right back, watching as its head leaned closer, only for the antenna to reach out and start brushing against the top of his head. He laughed a bit, feeling something like the branches of a plant touching his thick hair, only for the roach to pull back and lean away. Its head turned off to its right, and its hands let go of Thorne's so it could point off to the east. It started turning its body with an intent to start walking in that direction. The remaining plant roaches stayed put, soaking in the delicious sunlight while Thorne and the lead roach started walking off a small path along the hills.

Vasille did not look pleased. He gestured at the others. "Keep an eye on them, I'll watch Thorne." He followed Thorne at a respectable distance, his own weapon slung around his shoulders. He could be heard muttering something about bad ideas before he disappeared around a bend.

The roach led Thorne to a partially buried structure in the side of the hill, a reinforced concrete arch roughly three meters tall and five wide led into the hillside, though darkness kept him from making out any other details of the structure itself. Just outside of the structure, though, were the remains of a person, which the roach crouched down next to.

Thorne watched as the roach gently touched the top of its skull and let out a rumbling sound that sounded like a mournful moan. It turned its head back to Thorne, its human-like eyes visibly moist as its other hand beckoned him closer. Thorne cleared his throat and nodded a bit, carefully stepping around the bulky creature and crouching down before the skeleton.

"You know, I've never actually seen a skeleton before... The recyclers usually have it processed before anyone decomposes enough... Was this someone you knew big guy? Was this a friend?" He looked up at the towering beast, very aware of how easily it could smash him right now if it wanted to.

The seemingly gentle thing merely nodded its head, that hand gently stroking the top of the skull. It then turned its gaze towards the archway, nodding again, and waiting. Thorne looked back over his shoulder at the arch, and then back to the roach. His expression seemed thoughtful as he spoke. "Sure, I'll go take a look inside. Don't let my friend behind you spook you, okay?" Standing up, he walked into the darkness of the archway, his footsteps audible as they echoed down the concrete tunnel.

As he walked, carefully keeping his feet close to the ground to avoid tripping over anything, he pulled some goggles from a pouch, and upon pulling them over his head and turning them on, he could see in shades of green what was around him. The tunnel went on for about fifteen meters before stopping at a large door.

More skeletons lay to the sides of the tunnel, their clothes mostly intact unlike the one outside, and the door was ajar. Looking inside, he could only conclude that this was a failed bunker of some manner. It was small, cramped, and the concrete had cracked or split in several places. It gave him an appreciation for the construction of the bunker he was born and raised in. There was a lot of equipment that could probably be salvaged, but otherwise it did not look like somewhere he'd want to bring his people to live in its damaged state.

Returning outside, he took off his goggles and looked up at the roach who patiently waited for him. "So, can you actually understand me?" The roach stared at him, moving its mandibles but otherwise not reacting. He narrowed his eyes and nodded, leaning back down to the skeleton outside and pointing at it. "Blah, blah, blah, blah, blah?" The roach nodded its head, closing its eyes for a moment.

"Great. I think we need a translator. Alright big guy, let's head back." He stepped around the roach and led him back to its companions. Heavy steps behind indicated the tall roach was following as the human met up with Vasille.

"Alright, so, from what I can gather, these roaches were friendly with the people in the bunker back there. Place looks pretty wrecked, so as far as I can figure the black rain or some other kind of poison must have gotten them over time. Maybe disease got them and they didn't have any medicine. Regardless, I think they want to be friends, but they don't understand our language." Hawthorne looked rather upbeat, the interesting situation giving him a lot to think about.

Vasille considered what to say. "Well, if it does understand language, it's probably whatever was spoken locally around here. Shouldn't be too hard to look it up." Both men nodded as they reconvened with the rest of their scouts, their roach friend returning to his hole and submerging itself back in the ground to enjoy the sun and moist earth.

Thorne waved at the roaches. "We'll be back, just gotta figure out how to talk to you." The scouts turned around and went back to the caravan, where Jessica watched them with binoculars, at least until it seemed they were returning, causing her to gather the Council to receive the scouts.

It was a relatively quick conversation as everyone compared notes, Elena Price speaking up simply. "Spanish, they spoke Spanish here. I'm a few centuries rusty, but I could probably translate. Take me to them." The oldest woman alive, if you didn't count cryogenically suspended people or AIs, insisted upon walking with the scouts as they returned to the roaches, proving she was still as youthful as her late twenty-something looking body indicated. It probably helped that her long strides made the climb a fair bit easier.

Communicating with the roaches proved somewhat tricky, as they could only answer yes or no questions, and their grasp of the language seemed to be about as rusty as Elena's, but through a little trial and error they were able to learn quite a lot. The roaches had been looking over the people of this bunker for around two hundred years. They did know of the Iron Roaches, and they had been at odds in the past. They had even defended these people from them, essentially starving their iron cousins out and forcing them north.

These roaches gained their nourishment from the sun and the earth, though they were sad to admit that they had eaten humans in the past. It seemed that once they had gained enough intelligence, they had become aware of the evil they were perpetuating and decided to protect the remaining people rather than eat them.

It was an easy conclusion at that point to determine that the Iron Roaches simply had to leave to find more people to eat and propagate themselves. They were not as lucky to gain plant-like mutations like these ones had in their early lives before all the plants had been smothered by the inky black clouds. Of course, they had to eat other things(humans) to survive before their mutations could prove useful, allowing them to gain intelligence from eating humans before the black rain cleared the skies and allowed them to subsist on sunlight instead.

There also turned out to be many more of these plant-like roaches, totalling eighty, and after some brief negotiations they requested permission to follow the clan. It took a few minutes to determine why, but in the end it seemed they felt it was their duty to protect those who gave them intelligence and free will. They seemed especially pleased that their new human friends went out of their way to gather the remains of their old friends and see to it that they were buried. They didn't really seem to understand the significance at first, but they did then plant a handful of seeds among the graves, thinking that the humans were planting their dead humans to grow new ones.

Elena felt like she had to explain to everyone that this was the old way of things, that humans traditionally buried their dead, rather than recycled them. It wasn't as if the Phoenix Clan hadn't seen such things in the various movies and television shows they'd watched, but it was entirely something else to take part in the mass burial, which Elena took the lead in speaking over.

"We are gathered here to mourn the lost, the departed. They had survived so much, only for the poisons of the old world to finally claim them. Their spirits today may rest, knowing that their old friends have looked after them and seen to it that they were protected. I invite you all to appreciate that we easily could have been them. We could have ended up falling prey to any number of circumstances that would have overwhelmed us, and it is by fortune, intellect, and grit that we have survived. It is now our duty to carry the memory of these people with us, to keep humanity alive at any cost. We must honor the memory of fallen survivors and see to it that we endeavor to continue on for them, as well as ourselves. They would certainly want us to."

Elena repeated the sentiments in spanish for their new friends, and they showed no signs of irritation or disgust for her difficulties in remembering how to speak it properly.

ΔΔΔ

The Phoenix Clan and the Flora Roaches arrived in Medellin within the week, the sprawling ruins giving them plenty of opportunities to scavenge. They also got back into communication with T.I.A., while separating the Beta Facility car from the rest to get it onto higher ground. A combination of batteries and solar panels allowed the vehicle to keep the computers powered up, and it also operated as a fine wireless router to the rest of the vehicles in the caravan from its high vantage.

The long train of vehicles had been split up into three parts, with the 'engine' powering one section and Alpha One and Alpha Two powering the other two. They arranged in something of an open-ended triangle, allowing them to more easily move from one side to the other if need be. It also gave them natural choke-points in the event of attack, something that the Flora Roaches seemed to believe was imminent.

T.I.A. provided them with new schematics for weapons, and by the end of June they had mounted several new railguns atop the cars of the caravan and had built some new structures around them. Arranged along the main entrances were five-meter tall towers, which were kept at a respectable distance. The tops of them had thick rings of metals, and made up the very image of the classic tesla coil. It was a dangerous thing to use as a defensive weapon, necessitating people stay away from it while it was active, but the metal-laden carapaces of their enemies was expected to attract the lethal shocks from the tall lightning rods. Testing using parts of dead Iron Roaches proved violently successful.

Additionally, three of a new type of weapon were mounted atop a trio of watch towers that appeared at first to be railguns, but were actually magnetic shell launchers. These allowed artillery fire of high-speed explosive shells that would allow them to go easy on their limited amounts of explosive powders. All of the weapons had to be relatively near the caravan to get cabling to power them, but it allowed them to keep a tight perimeter.

The ruins of the city provided materials for yet more defenses, primarily in the form of low concrete walls to fire from behind, and new foundations in the middle of the formation of cars to start building permanent structures. Clint seemed especially excited about starting to plant things in the soil, considering that the Flora Roaches seemed to have no issues with rooting themselves in the ground during the day. The roaches were pulling their weight as well, helping move heavy objects and pound old concrete into rubble so that it could be ground up into new concrete. They seemed every bit as powerful and sturdy as their iron cousins, while not quite as heavy. This meant they could move slightly faster, but their plant-like nature caused them to tend to move rather slowly most of the time.

Jessica spent most of her time up on the hill overlooking the settlement they were forming, looking after the Beta Facility computers and keeping in touch with T.I.A. much of the day. She also exchanged messages with the other elders, debating various topics including trying to figure out what to do with their dead in the future. Most of them seemed preferential towards continuing to recycle them, though a handful had been moved by Elena's ceremony over the graves of the Columbian bunker.

Those concerns would have to wait, however, as the scouts spotted the Iron Roaches again. The large group of man-eaters had found the tracks of their caravan, and were starting to follow them up towards their camp at Medellin. Dark clouds gathered to the north, an indication of one of the region's frequent storms coming in. From Jessica's vantage, she expressed concerns over the severity of the oncoming storm. Satisfying clackity-clack sounds filled the car as she exchanged messages with the other Elders via the keyboard of the Beta Facility computers.

Jessica: I haven't seen clouds that dark before.

Elena: From what I remember of my history, this region isn't known for its hurricanes, we'll be fine.

Clint: Your history doesn't mean anything. There isn't any forests or plant life to absorb the storm surges or slow their advance onto land.

Sherry: That's one of the reasons we settled on high ground, we'll be fine, especially if we can get more concrete foundations down under the cars.

Walter: If you want to worry about anything, worry about those roaches on the way. From what Elena found out, they're here to eat us. Probably starving by this point. Running out of iron to eat. Hell, that's probably why we didn't find many ruins on the way here.

Jessica: Fine! Fine, but don't get mad at me when our weapons don't work from all the rain.

Sherry: We have plenty of weapons that will work in the rain. We only really have to worry about the Tesla Coils, and even then I bet those iron bastards will take whatever we throw at them.

Barnard: Just make sure that our friendlies don't get anywhere near them, whatever else happens should be to our advantage.

All that followed after that point were a number of people typing some version of 'agreed', including Jessica, though she remained concerned about the storm. It was about that point that Teitara and Megan Clark showed up, with the latter carrying a complicated looking electronic rig. "Alright, so, what's this about now?" Jessica looked a little surprised to see the two up here.

Teitara spoke on Megan's behalf. "Megan is concerned that the Iron Roaches might win, and would like to take the chance at uploading to the Ark. She may not get another chance."

Megan nodded awkwardly, forcing body language where she otherwise wouldn't. "This is so. It is not as though I am wanted here anyway. No one allows me to assist. It is logical that I take my chances where I can be useful, and safer."

Jessica let out a sigh, exasperated. "Alright, fine. You know this will kill you, right?"

"Affirmative. I will, however, be backed up. You are welcome to salvage my remains."

Jessica raised an eyebrow at that, straightening up her back. She hadn't really thought about it, but there was a lot of interesting and rare tech in Megan's body that she'd love to have Sherry reverse engineer. "Alright, let's get you set up. I'll let Tia know you're coming."

After sending a quick signal to the Ark to let T.I.A. know to isolate the next broadcast and store it safely away, the two women and one cyborg got to hooking up the half-woman up to their systems. Jessica was impressed at how well Teitara seemed to know what she was doing. She'd obviously been putting a lot of work in on this.

The very moment they started the data upload, Megan lost consciousness, and Teitara turned on the respirator she'd hooked up to her to make sure she kept breathing. In their research, it seemed common for autonomic functions to become irregular, so they had hooked her up with a backup 'pump' to help circulate her blood in case her heart stopped, and a respirator to handle her breathing. Jessica was relatively certain there wasn't a heart in there, but she decided not to ask.

This left the three stuck there for the remainder of the day as the massive data transfer occurred, the entire contents of a living mind being beamed over three light-days away to be stored away in a rack of newly-constructed hard drives made from the Lubar-Masis comet's abundant metal supplies.

ΔΔΔ

Meanwhile, the Phoenix Clan and the Flora Roaches prepared for battle. Thorne and Vasille drilled the scouts-turned-soldiers, while Elena took command of their roach allies. They had even managed to arm a number of the roaches with a handful of extra arc-throwers and slug rifles, though their delicate hands seemed ill suited for the latter. Injuries were anticipated, but the Flora Roaches seemed willing to risk the danger to help their new friends. Spotlights from the towers lit the night, and the dangerous hum of the forward tesla coils filled the air as their enemies approached. Tension filled the air, while overwhelming darkness approached the surrounding region due to thick, soupy cloud cover.

A bright flash lit the sky as lightning arced from cloud to cloud, followed shortly after by the bang of thunder rolling across the ruins of Medellin. Jessica was watching a progress meter tick closer and closer to 100% while clouds rolled in, threatening to smother the transmission. "Fuck, she had to do this when a goddamn hurricane was rolling in. The dumb bitch is going to get lobotomized by a fucking cloud!"

Teitara glared at the other woman, then looked down at Megan's prone body. "Come on, you're almost there. One last little push." Teitara seemed intent on seeing this through, but Jessica was looking frustrated.

"Look, doc, you gotta get off this hill before the storm gets here. I'll finish up, but you don't need to be here anymore."

The medical specialist appeared to be incensed, but she couldn't find any flaw in Jessica's logic. "Fine, but don't you cut that stream before it finishes. I've been working on this with her for years."

Jessica practically pushed Teitara out of the car, intensely worried that her colleague would get caught out here at the worst possible timing. She was the former scout, she could handle some bad weather. This was nothing compared to Seattle, or so she told herself.

Back on the ground below, spotlights swivelled to light up a line of Iron Roaches, their carapaces glittering black in the bright light. They seemed irritated, their mandibles chattering. One in the front smashed the ground with one of its forelimbs, letting out a rumbling shout which was answered by what had to be more than a hundred of its companions stretched back down the road in columns. Their plant cousins postured in a similar fashion, the two inhuman lines roaring at each other.

Vasille took that as a signal and shouted out. "Light 'em up!"

Nine railguns and 3 magnetic shell launchers fired off into the mass of bodies. The assembled humans and their new allies watched in surprise as the front line shifted out of the way of the projectiles, only for roaches behind them to get pierced through. Three explosions sent iron and guts flying as the roaches realized they weren't dealing with weaklings as they had in the past. With their casualties numbering over a dozen, and their opponents reloading, they charged. The ground thundered with the sound of their titanic weight smashing against the ground, and as they approached another series of rails and explosives fired off into the mass of incoming bodies.

Thorne held up his arm, readying the other scouts. "Prepare to fire! Wait for the tower!" The tesla coils sparked menacingly, only for the roaches to approach close enough for artificial lightning to shoot out into their bodies. Jerking and shuddering bodies were ploughed into from behind, sending electricity through three roaches at a time between the two towers, only to pile them up before the coils. As a fourth and a fifth smashed into the piles of bodies, they all stilled, with the coils preferentially continuing to strike the now-dead bodies. The remaining roaches were able to pass by the two piles of dead companions, only for Thorne to shout, joined by Vasille, "Fire!"

Arcs of electricity, slugs, rails, and explosive shells smashed into the advancing bodies below while Jessica on the hills above let out a 'whoop!' of celebration! The roaches didn't seem to have a chance! A dinging sound in the car indicated a successful transfer.

Lightning lanced down from the all-too-nearby clouds, striking one of the tesla coils and blasting the area, shorting out the circuitry running the coil, which also ran back and took out one of the spotlight towers and its attached magnetic shell launcher.

"Oh shit." Jessica ran back into the car, shutting off the main computer and starting to rip open the guts of the systems. "Gotta get the hard drives out of here!" It wasn't hard to recognize that the car she was in was the tallest metal object around!

Elena yelled out over the weapons fire, "¡Todos, ataquen!" The ground practically quaked as a second army of roaches rushed out from among their human allies, smashing into their iron-plated foes, and forcing their allies to approach dangerously to avoid friendly fire. The remaining enemies turned the battle into a melee, enormous fists and huge bodies bashing into each other under the light of the remaining spotlights and tesla coils. Humans and roaches alike fell, bodies smashed into fortifications, and lightning both artificial and natural lit the area as a heavy downpour began.

The Flora Roaches armed with weapons oftentimes found them perfect to break a deadlock as they clashed with their iron-plated foes. Some of the Iron Roaches realized the danger of these armed enemies at melee range, and in a handful of cases they could be seen locked in stalemates as they wrestled for the firearms between them with their smaller, more delicate arms. Iron spikes proved effective weapons when charging at sufficient speed, splintering and breaking hard, wooden carapaces and eliciting bellows of pain.

Humans ducked and dodged between the titanic combatants, breaking up stalemates and occasionally getting caught up in the struggles of multiple tons of roachmeat. Friendly fire was minimal, but weapons using electricity proved unpredictable and dangerous in the falling rain. Thankfully, iron trumped all in attracting electricity, and wood seemed resistant to it, making these events minimally tragic.

Vasille and Thorne had gotten locked up in the combat, the ground getting muddy as they struggled to end the wrestling matched. Occasional explosions went off, holes ripped through roaches as railguns lanced through the line, and in one horrible moment an Iron Roach pivoted and shoved a Flora Roach into the line of fire. Splinters and meat exploded as the railgun shattered its body, but the rail also continued through two more Iron Roaches before smashing into a distant hillside. The storm seemed to care not for their desperate battle as it thoroughly shrouded them in darkness, threatening to smother them all in its ominous presence.

It was as if nature itself was feeling left out, and wanted to strike its own blow against those assembled.

Thorne watched in shock and alarm as lightning struck the car containing the Beta Facility computers. A pair of explosions went off inside as the ground under the car started to give way due to the rain and explosions. He yelled. "Mother!"

Down the hill tumbled the car, throwing a pair of bodies down across the rocks while metal and plastic smashed and shattered between them. Thorne rushed towards the scene of the wreck, nearly getting smashed by an iron fist, only for Vasille and a Flora Roach to stun and smash the offending roach away. Battle and shouts raged around while the two men ran to check on the bodies.

Scattered around Jessica were several hard drives, most of them shattered and the rest hopelessly wet and fried, with her own body broken and twisted in an unnatural fashion. Thorne fell to her side and pulled her up against himself while Vasille investigated the broken form of Megan Clark, her body literally having burst open and exposing all manner of artificial parts. Vasille turned his back so he could defend his grieving friend. Thorne wailed out into the night as he cradled his mother against his body.

The night grew much more quiet as the battle ended, bodies both massive and small strewn about in the heavy rain while lightning persistently struck at the tesla coils arranged around the perimeter of the caravan. Spotlights remained on, thanks to the quick work of engineering crews cutting the lines to the tesla coils, and the remaining people took shelter under the sturdy steel cars that had once been their bunker of origin.

Come the morning, with the sun mostly blocked out by the thick clouds of what had merely been a horrible thunderstorm, not the hurricane they expected, the Phoenix Clan and Flora Roaches gathered their dead and assessed their damage, but it would be some time before the extent of their losses could be known, as Earth had once again lost contact with the Ark.

△△△

T.I.A. quietly stored away the data she had received, not even daring to peer at its contents for fear of being unable to control Megan Clark. The drives utilized to contain her mind and genome were left on standby and cut off from T.I.A.'s network. The only system she had contact with was the system that monitored the integrity of those drives, which otherwise will lay dormant until such time as Hawthorne wanted to do something with them.

She spent the rest of the cycle mournfully sending signals back to Earth in hopes that someone might answer, but nothing ever came back, even when she signaled their location. For all she knew, humanity had been truly wiped out. She hoped against hope that the new friends Jessica had told her about had managed to protect them.

CHAPTER 28

CYCLE 15, ALONE AGAIN

Hawthorne waited quietly as he felt his body regain life. He listened for any sign of agitation from T.I.A., perhaps from waking him up prematurely, but it seemed this cycle was starting as planned rather than with urgency. There was the possibility that her silence so far was a sign of bad news, but he supposed it was worth waiting to address that until after he'd properly been revived and gathered his things.

He couldn't help but feel a dull tightness in his chest and throat as a sense of anxiety nagged at him though. It was an interesting sensation considering he was still largely numb, but it was enough to strike a sense of fear in him. The last time he'd been active, his friends back on Earth had been dealing with quite a lot of trouble and were well underway for an epic journey across unknown terrain.

Nevertheless, he got up out of his pod, gained his balance in the centrifugal replacement for gravity, and headed over to gather his various clothing and belongings. Curiously enough, T.I.A. had prepared for him a black lab coat, which did not help his anxiety one bit.

Putting on his AR contacts revealed that even his bedroom had been altered as part of T.I.A.'s virtual environment. He was still standing in a metal container, but it was slightly more cramped and resembled the blueprints he constructed for the Phoenix Clan to rise out of their bunker and travel the lands. Through a window in the wall he could see T.I.A. standing 'outside', looking up at a harsh sun that bathed the landscape in brutal light. Other people were about, people he recalled seeing from videos sent to them, and she turned to watch them with a terribly sad expression. "Oh dear…"

.As he stepped out of his room-turned-car, with the real door sliding to the side and the AR door lifting up above and shielding him from the projection of sunlight, he couldn't help but admire the work she had put into the environment. A blasted landscape stretched out around him, with sun-scorched sand, hills, and the skeletons of a city nearby.

T.I.A. stood watching children play in a black dress of her own, though it became clear pretty quickly it was only a few seconds of animation before the children in question leaped back in time and performed the same actions again. "Tia? Are you alright?" Hawthorne looked down at his hands, watching as they trembled as he stood and watched his companion.

T.I.A. shook her head, looking back at him with a distraught face. She had even made her eyes look puffy and her cheeks stained with spilled tears. He wondered if she even realized she had simulated such things at this point.

Her voice was trembling as she spoke back to him, her voice unfortunately still coming from speakers overhead in the 'sky'. "No, I'm not okay. I lost contact with Earth again, and even with me sending a signal over and over they never answer back."

Hawthorne let out a long, tired sigh, reaching out to run his hand through her hair, wondering how aware she was of his hand trembling. Of course, she had both the AR input and her camera view of his hand shaking, so she bit her lip and looked up at him, concerned about him now too. He attempted a soft smile, one that failed to brighten either of their moods. "So, what happened?"

T.I.A. breathed in deeply, then let out a shaky breath as she looked up at him with tearful eyes. "Well, it took them awhile, but they made it to Columbia in South America, but the Iron Roaches chased them almost all the way there. They managed to escape across a river, but that only delayed them a few weeks. They met some friendly roaches outside of an old failed bunker, and I helped them with plans and schematics to build defenses to fend off the other roaches if they came after them. The last I heard about the situation was that they were coming, and then Jessica and Teitara started sending Megan Clark to me."

Hawthorne stiffened a bit in alarm at that, blinking down at her. "Megan? The cyborg woman? They sent her to you?"

T.I.A. nodded, fidgeting. "I made sure it was safe, she's in a set of un-networked hard drives in a low power state for monitoring. She was apparently pessimistic about whether or not the Phoenix Clan could survive the attack, and wanted to be uploaded immediately. She knew she was probably going to be stuck in storage forever, but she was scared enough that she felt it was worth the risk. I lost contact right after she finished transferring her data."

Hawthorne considered what she was saying, wondering what danger Megan could pose. It should be relatively easy to keep Megan contained, honestly. He just had to make sure she had no wireless capabilities nor a way to network into T.I.A.'s systems physically. Essentially he had to make sure she had no way to manipulate anything aside from talking and perhaps displaying images.

It would probably be best to put any such system some-where where T.I.A.'s cameras did not have direct line of sight either, in case she tried to transfer some kind of code visually or something. Earth's computer technology had changed a lot before the Cataclysm, and while hardware had mostly taken backwards steps due to material scarcity, software had still continued apace and he couldn't be sure what capacities she might have for hacking. It was not clear at all whether she was malicious or not.

"I suppose that's fine. Keep her in storage for now until I figure out what I want to do with her. I might have to try to design her systems to be similar to yours, though from what I heard she lost a lot of her capacities in exchange for her longevity." He shook his head and sighed again though. Megan was a distraction at best. "Tell me about these friendly roaches."

T.I.A. waved a hand, causing a visual of a Flora Roach to appear, complete with its plant-encased body, powerful internal musculature, and strangely friendly eyes and fragile hands. Hawthorne stepped away from her to look the creature over. It was very similar to the Iron Roaches he was more familiar with, though even the way they stood seemed more humble and disarming. Considering their great height and obvious physical strength, this was very interesting indeed. "How did they end up like this?"

T.I.A. brought up a number of windows, displaying them in thin air around them as she sought to explain. "Elena believed that both species of roaches originated as a pre-Cataclysm bio-weapon. Looking through old records of internet conspiracy theories by South American conspiracy theorist Alexandro Jones I was able to find some evidence of such claims. Apparently a company-turned-country called the True American Accord in South America had been working on some manner of roaches that ate metals."

"The intent seemed to be to have them disable the infrastructure of other nations, but in order to accomplish this they had to give the roaches the capability of consuming and assimilating DNA and traits from other creatures. The baseline creature they fed it to attain their goals were from the Crenarchaeota phylum, a type of Archaea. Presumably these roaches were released during the Cataclysm before they removed that DNA absorption trait, allowing them to consume other life forms."

Hawthorne nodded, reaching out and scrolling through the windows as she spoke, picking up where she left off. "First of all, there's every chance Elena's still alive. Second, it seems those roaches then ate everything they could, but mostly found dead humans and plants. They made a heavy split in preferences at some point, and one remained hostile to humans and the other became friendly to humans. No wonder there was so little evidence of other survivors, the Iron Roaches were hunting down their shelters and eating them."

If his growing frown were any indication, that did not bode well for their friends. Still, they were pretty well armed from what he could tell, as T.I.A. had also provided him with details on the information she'd given them. He let out an impressed sounding 'hm!', despite his prior displeasure though. "So, the Phoenix Clan had weapons, defensive positions, and allies of nearly equal strength and power."

T.I.A. nodded in response. "Yes, I helped them every way I could. I ended up sending them practically my whole library, though they had trouble finding computers to store it in. They were having issues recycling their equipment as it got damaged." She looked understandably troubled at the idea that they were losing computers too.

Hawthorne looked increasingly hopeful though. "I think they're fine. They would have had an enormous defensive and technological advantage. It's troubling to hear that their equipment was breaking down, but that's only natural considering the rigors of travel and the difficulty of fabricating such small components in properly sterile environments. Hopefully they can get such facilities together now that they're settled in place again, but honestly even if they don't they're in the best possible position to survive the Ice Age. It's just a matter of rising to the challenge at that point, and I think their name appropriate enough to describe their ability to do that." He looked back to his AI, smiling over at her and watching a hopeful smile appear on her face as well.

"Do you really think so? They're going to be okay? I did enough to save them?" She had a fragile but blossoming hope in her digital heart. The thought that her friends, even if they were cut off, might be living their lives happily back on Earth heartened her quite a bit. If she had known of the deaths that occurred in the battle she'd probably have been heartbroken, but she had the armor of ignorance to protect her from that.

Hawthorne smiled brighter at her, moving over to give the petite avatar a hug about her back. "Tia, I dare say you might be the only reason they're alive at all, let alone that they have a chance to continue on into the future. It's also good to hear that they made some friends too, however strange they are. I'm surprised they didn't shoot them on sight considering their appearance. It will be very interesting to see what kind of culture grows out of those interesting people once the planet becomes more hospitable."

T.I.A. sank into the simulated hug, very comforted by

the idea that she helped so much. Considering that she still felt guilt over possibly having contributed to the Cataclysm in the first place, it made her feel like she had atoned for something. Once again, ignorance of the truth of that fact protected her, something Elena Price could have easily revealed but kept to herself. Megan remained a possible source of that information, however. "It's kind of exciting, thinking that they could be the progenitors of a new human race on Earth. Maybe they'll meet us at Alpha Centauri when we arrive?"

Hawthorne shook his head, giving her an extra squeeze and then pulling back. "I don't believe that's too terribly likely. The Ice Age will probably take longer to end than we will be in space. It's not impossible it will be a hundred millennia, but it's more likely to be three to four-hundred millennia considering historical precedent. Still, it does give us the opportunity for our own civilization to come back and help uplift the descendants of the Phoenix Clan and their roach friends into space. It's just a matter of producing a culture that can match theirs in warmth, kindness, and hardiness. I do believe we have a lot to look forwards to though, so we should make the best of our time and see how much work we can get out of the way in advance. We even have some practice with helping people survive a hostile environment."

T.I.A. stepped back as well, and her clothing flashed for a moment before turning into a less grim dress. It was a bit more revealing than Hawthorne was expecting though, causing him to cough and turn away a bit as he looked away from exposed cleavage at the top of the strappy sundress. She mistook him looking away for looking somewhere else though. "Ah! Right, your breakfast. I'll have that prepared right away." She hopped off, her shapely figure jostling and bouncing in all the right places.

Hawthorne sighed and looked up at the sky, shutting his eyes against the light of the sun which was ironically being projected by the contacts under his eyelids. He muttered under his breath. "Goddamnit Jessica." He recalled all too clearly the videos of her and Tammy encouraging T.I.A. to seduce him.

ΔΔΔ

Hawthorne and T.I.A. spent much of the rest of the cycle catching up on the various conversations she had had with their friends on Earth, as well as reviewing what they knew of their available equipment, technology, and experts. There was no reason to think that their friends couldn't teach themselves just about everything they needed to know from the massive digital databases they had access to. The larger problem would likely be taking the time to actually study such things while they had to maintain their equipment, build new structures, and integrate their Flora Roach friends into their society.

With all those challenges added on top of making sure they were fed, protected from further enemies, and withstanding weather that would surely only get worse over time, how much could they really spare towards non-vital education? Unfortunately, it seemed very likely that the dark age that humanity had already entered could only get worse as their survival became more and more demanding.

The only saving grace was that their great library was much less flammable than the Library of Alexandria, so hopefully they would maintain access to all of that information. It was no wonder that they haven't gotten back in contact with them, as they would surely be busy fortifying their position. It was also entirely possible that the necessary documents, technology, and math needed to contact them was also lost, or at the very least misplaced in some old database likely to be forgotten.

"Tia, are you still trying to contact Earth?" She nodded over at him. Of course she was, why would she stop? "I think you should stop."

T.I.A. blinked, obviously confused. "What? Why?" She had been so desperate to resume contact with her friends that she hadn't stopped to consider if she even should. Her reckless efforts to contact anyone on the planet had been a further overreaction.

"Well," he began simply, "it is entirely possible that a hostile civilization could arise elsewhere on Earth, intercept your communication, and launch some kind of attack on us in the future. It is probably best that we stop meddling. It's not our world anymore, and as good as it felt being like their shining beacon in the sky, it's not our place to play god with them. They've proven themselves capable of surviving the worst, and any further contributions we make will only diminish what they've accomplished. I think it's good what we've done, but we have to trust them to take care of themselves, and protect ourselves in case some hostile group on Earth intercepts the signals."

T.I.A. looked rather upset that he insinuated that the Phoenix Clan could ever become hostile, but he wasn't necessarily talking about just the Phoenix Clan. Had he known that she had been broadcasting to the whole planet out of desperation? "I can still listen for them trying to contact us though, right?" She sounded meek, realizing how much danger she'd placed them in.

"Of course, there's no way for them to find us unless we contact them back or they find records of how to find us. We're lost to the void of space as far as most people on

Earth are aware, if they even know of us. Our friends may keep records of us and tell stories about us in their history, but beyond that we need to keep our distance. We were lucky they turned out to be friendly in the first place, but there's no guarantee that will remain true in the future. Until we are established and safe in our new homes, we really should not risk compromising our position. Space is dangerous enough as it is."

She begrudgingly agreed, and they continued their work. Hawthorne even drew up some preliminary plans for an isolated computer system he wanted to work on some day to install Megan Clark into, seeing as he was very interested in the desperate survival instinct she had cultivated over the centuries. He wondered if making a computer system like T.I.A.'s and installing her into it might allow her to become a more complete being than she had been back on Earth, and maybe it could allow her to grow into something of a human AI on the same track that T.I.A. was.

Much of that would have to be a project for the future though, as Megan was very much an unknown quantity, and best dealt with under much more safe and secure conditions. She could well be a fine candidate for a secondary colony ship's AI after they got themselves established at their new home. Perhaps they could even make copies of her, though Hawthorne would be much more inclined to make copies of T.I.A. instead.

That was another moral quandary he'd rather have other peoples' opinions on though. The ability to copy an intellect was something he did not have any logical issues with, but he could feel an emotional reluctance that bordered on the immoral. The nature of life and consciousness once again reared its ugly head, with three separate beings to consider with regards to it. Hawthorne's own frequently suspended consciousness was something of a moral problem because while he felt no gap between cycles, he was very much dead in between them.

T.I.A. was a totally new lifeform as far he could define, one that he had the personal pleasure of nurturing and guiding towards what seemed to be an admittedly juvenile consciousness. She lived for centuries but had advanced emotionally only perhaps a handful of years, though within a few hundred cycles she'd probably be equivalent to a full-fledged human adult as far as he could estimate.

Megan Clark was a totally different sort of problem. She had baggage aplenty, and was less of a human and more a shard of a human. She had once been a complete consciousness that had pieces of it strategically removed to create what she now was. Even the storage space her mind took up was only about 45% of what he had expected a fully-grown human's mind to need, and that wasn't considering the fact that she had centuries of experience and knowledge as well.

Providing her with a full 'mind' again, with her only capable of initially filling up less than half of it could prove disastrous as she tried to grapple with her forgotten emotions again. There was no telling if a new, more well-rounded Megan would emerge, or if she might be the same old tortured soul that had destroyed herself in the first place.

The idea of copying them struck him as extremely troublesome. He could easily overlook his own cheating of death seeing as he wasn't seeking to make clones of himself, but effectively cloning T.I.A. or Megan seemed wrong somehow. Honestly, the fact that Megan's backup existed at all was distressing enough if not for the fact that she'd willingly requested the transfer, with her original body's death being entirely likely considering the technology used. Megan hadn't even necessarily made her wishes known. She had trusted him and T.I.A. to safeguard her and use her however they would.

Did he have a duty to revive her and allow her to choose what she would become, or was it her duty to serve them to repay their efforts to revive her? He honestly wished that T.I.A. had not accepted her upload at all, so he didn't have to consider such difficult questions. Thankfully dealing with Megan was not an urgent thing, and she seemed like she'd have been content enough with being safe in storage like the rest of the crew. He was very inclined to leave the decision for his colleagues to decide upon once they got to their new home, though it didn't hurt to prepare a computer to use if they needed Megan in an emergency.

There was also the option of making some manner of body for Megan to inhabit so that T.I.A. could have her as a companion. It probably wasn't healthy that she was stubbornly trying to recreate her friends and their home in her imagination, though imaginary friends were hardly strange for a girl of her level of emotional development. Regardless, Megan seemed far too dangerous to be left unsupervised, so whatever he did with her it was likely she'd spend the same time shut off that he did frozen. He simply couldn't trust her.

Considering that she had trusted him so blindly, it felt like a bit of a shame, but a desperate woman was dangerous. It was easy to imagine that Megan Clark was possibly the most desperate woman in the galaxy when it came to her own survival, and that made her very dangerous indeed.

△△△

"T.I.A.'s log, AC 408, May 23, 2541. Doctor Hawthorne Crenshaw has just completed the cryogenic suspension process for the end of this cycle. I find myself greatly soothed by having had his guidance through this troubling time. I had allowed myself to become obsessed with the Phoenix Clan, and even though I knew I could be utilizing my time better I wasted much of it trying to pretend they were still with me. I believe I will continue working on the PC-C simulation, though rather than trying to recapture the image of my lost friends, I will instead try to faithfully reproduce the environment and atmosphere of their new home in Columbia. I will try to imagine what it might become rather than what it had been."

"I feel bad for underestimating the Phoenix Clan's ability to survive. They have already been through so much, and I know first hand what humans determined to survive are capable of. I will prefer to believe that they are alive and well, and will instead look forward to being reunited with them someday far into the future. I will most likely not be the same 'person' I am now by then, but surely they will be very different as well. It seems appropriate that I add that to the list of reasons and motivations I have to see things through and make sure everyone survives. I have lost my ability to assist Earth in that, but I am still in total control of making sure the Ark and its occupants survive."

"I am troubled by the existence of Megan Clark as well. I feel myself both curious about her, as well as strangely threatened. I feel as though I could learn from her in a way that no flesh and blood person could teach me, but she also sounded like such an overwhelming force of will that she makes me feel like I could be eaten up. Her focused purpose reminds me of the danger I brought to myself and my crew by pursuing imbalanced growth, and she has been in such an imbalance for many centuries more than I was. It might be interesting to assemble a computer on the

Lubar-Masis to store her in and perhaps construct a small ship around it to bring along with us as a new companion. Isolating her seems like it would be difficult though."

"I suspect that Doctor Hawthorne Crenshaw will want to begin going over our colonial options. It will be a good way to occupy our time to start making plans for how we might eventually start making use of the new star system. In anticipation of that, I will focus my efforts on scanning the Alpha Centauri system and trying to detect more planets, their makeup, and suitability for life. The outer star of the system, Proxima Centauri already appears as though it will be difficult to deal with, though the other two stars pose their own problems. The sheer distance of Proxima Centauri from Alpha Centauri A and B makes it worth considering as a first stop as it could perhaps be settled in a handful of centuries, similar to the amount of time it would take to get to the other two stars and their potential planets."

"The sheer number of options and the varying levels of manpower and time needed to exploit them will likely keep us busy for a very long time. I have to admit having so much work to do has a certain appeal after so much loss. End log."

CHAPTER 29

CYCLE 16, WITH MILLENNIA AHEAD

Dr. Hawthorne Crenshaw's Tentative List of Priority Projects:

1. Help T.I.A. mature into a fully-functional, independent being.
2. Develop T.I.A.'s virtual environment to allow for planning and testing conditions necessary for further research to proceed without risk to ship or crew.
3. Utilize T.I.A.'s VE to develop new construction designs including:

3a. More advanced storage space for T.I.A.'s memory.

3b. More advanced propulsion for secondary vehicles.

3c. Secondary vehicles required to probe Alpha Centauri for appropriate planets.

3d. Secondary vehicles required to seed planets with plants, bacteria, and fungi for atmosphere alteration

3e. Secondary vehicles to harvest asteroid belts and multiply themselves to further exploit asteroids

3f. Different types of self-sufficient space habitats.

3g. Primary system command nexus to coordinate the secondary vehicles.

4. Create a system to control the command nexus, most likely a copy of T.I.A.'s mature self.
5. Use T.I.A.'s VE to explore the development of new/useful power sources, most likely fusion or reflected solar power.
6. Research the Smith Bunker/Phoenix Clan bloodlines and records.

7. Research Anthony Saul's animal embryo cargo and develop methods to utilize it.

8. Research viability of utilizing quantum-tethering to produce an instant long-range communication device to allow T.I.A. to operate as the command nexus remotely.

9. Develop a computer system adequate to house a human mind, modelled after T.I.A. and utilizing 22nd century technology.

2000. Install Megan Clark's mind into such a computer system.

-File updated Tuesday, May 23, 2575

Hawthorne sat in his chair, the VE reproducing T.I.A.'s imagined version of a 'present' Phoenix Clan town at the edge of the ruins of Medellin. A series of towers had been constructed that seemed to provide several functions at once. They each operated as water towers, while also having the caravan's assortment of solar panels mounted atop them. A central tower, taller than the others, stood between these multi-purpose towers that operated as a high-angle anchor for a series of sturdy tarps that hung draped between the shorter towers. With the smaller towers arranged in a large octagon and a radius of forty meters, it allowed for both a great deal of water collection, as well as shelter from the sun above. This canopy provided power, a series of grounded lightning rods, water, and shelter.

Hawthorne's chair was closer to the edge of the shade provided by that canopy, enjoying the simulated sunlight as he worked at a table. Arranged around this canopy was a ring of tall greenhouses that filtered sunlight coming from the sides. The greenhouses were filled with all manner of plants, though Hawthorne was relatively certain T.I.A. had embellished the variety the Clan had available to them for the sheer aesthetics of it. He could see places where she'd reused plants from her simulation of Clapham Common, but he wasn't about to complain. Underneath the canopy were the new permanent structures of the Phoenix Clan, large and small alike.

Hawthorne and T.I.A. were not alone either, and while he was content to work on his tablet, reading relevant texts related to the list of projects he had created, there was a large number of people to see around them. T.I.A. seemed to have developed a simple method for producing lots of background characters, dressed similarly to their friends back home, with a high degree of variation in looks and attire. There were even a handful of Old Ones, primarily the real ones, mixed in among the others in the Clan.

Hawthorne was pretty sure he'd even seen a frail old Hawthorne 'Thorne' Crenshaw wandering about with a small crowd of children with him. He was nearing a century old at this point, no doubt. Checking back on his records, Hawthorne was amused to see that tomorrow would actually be Thorne's 99th birthday.

There wasn't an enormous amount of space horizontally under the canopy, but it did allow for up to four stories of vertical space towards the middle, and doubtlessly had several levels of construction below that went well outside the radius of their canopy. Considering the vast majority of the founders of this settlement had come from underground bunkers, he couldn't fault the idea that they might go back underground given the opportunity.

It remained to be seen if she ended up deciding that younger generations would prefer to be above ground, but then he didn't know quite how much scripting she had applied to these characters of hers. It was a pretty practical design, but the durability of some elements seemed questionable to him. He wondered how much it might change as they increased the complexity of T.I.A.'s VE to simulate wear and tear on this simulated community.

"Tia? Can you share with me what you've learned from creating this simulation?" Hawthorne set down his tablet, curious about how detailed everything actually was.

T.I.A. had been sitting across from him, holding a book in her hands that just so happened to be the exact book he was looking through in his tablet. She had been enjoying the sensation of paper moving against her skin as she turned the pages, and the weight of the thing in her hands. She had even done her best to simulate the smell of the book, though she was still trying to figure out how to properly simulate that sense. Looking up at the question, she glanced around at everything going on around them. So much of it was happening on its own that she didn't even need to think about how it was actually working.

It was remarkable how much the repetition of things like this became like mental muscle memory for her. "Well Doctor, I have learned a lot about the way that Sol's light passes through the atmosphere of Earth, producing colors differently than the artificial light within the ship. I've also learned a lot about how light refracts through glass with the greenhouses and how it lights other surfaces after hitting the surrounding ground. I had to research a lot about that, and the structural tolerances of reinforced concrete and steel to produce the structures, and how various genetic traits are passed along to offspring. It was really fun to try to figure out which people might have had kids with whom, and try to determine what traits they would inherit."

Hawthorne nodded, humming softly. "Did you do that through simulating DNA or liberal use of Punnett squares?" He had not had much opportunity to help his colleagues sort through the various embryos and reproductive candidates, so he wondered how much his rudimentary understanding of such things would be reproduced by his AI companion. A Punnett square was a useful tool in helping farmers and breeders determine the chances of traits being inherited by the offspring of a reproductive act in centuries past.

Such a tool could absolutely be used to manipulate the gene pool of a community if controlled for properly over time. Similar techniques had been used to improve on the methodology that had allowed for the domestication and specialization of Earth's beasts of burden, farm animals, pets, and plants.

T.I.A. responded quickly enough, smiling. "I don't really know how to simulate individual atoms, let alone such complicated molecules just yet, so Punnett squares provided what I needed to create all the new young people around. I also made an effort to age humans as best I could, seeing as I had a lot of examples of friends aging over time to compare to. It's entirely likely they allowed their population to grow, but I didn't want to make too many assumptions about how much."

"I might have to change some people around once we try to figure out how they picked who has sex with whom, but until then I was happy to handle it randomly." She knew she didn't have the expertise in simulating things to make a perfect representation of everything. She was very much fudging the numbers, but she was happy with the results for now.

Hawthorne seemed pleased with her answers, glancing around. "Is the atmosphere static, or are you simulating some level of weather patterns and atmospheric pressure changes? I'm trying to figure out what scale you're working with here. It seems similar to something like a relatively simple video game at first glance, but the work you went into producing the characters and simulating the objects, environment, gravity, and all these bodies seem to be anything but simple." The mental math the simulation required her to do to keep everything standing could not possibly be what he thought it was. A lot of it had to have been done in advance and many of the things were just static after the fact.

T.I.A. felt like her illusion was being picked apart, her creator and teacher trying to figure out where she cut corners and what she was actively simulating. "The atmosphere is not static, though the fluid dynamics of it remain relatively consistent. I don't usually change the weather or pressure unless I'm trying to achieve a specific look or effect. Most of the things I've constructed in the environment I simulated once and now they're just being rendered with those original properties remaining static. It seemed like the appropriate way to handle structures and terrain, though it does mean most of my attention is focused on keeping people walking around and talking to each other and simulating the light on surfaces."

He nodded back at her, feeling like he was getting a solid grasp of things. "So, if you were to, say, actively simulate all these objects and people in their entirety as well as actively alternate in weather patterns to interact with them, how hard would that be? What if you were to simulate all the organs and senses of all your characters as well? Where are the roaches? They should be moving around and interacting with everyone too, right? Maybe they help with the farming, or moving construction supplies?"

He wanted to know what it took for her to push herself. He needed her to eventually be able to simulate molecular structures if they were to start working with DNA, chemicals, and testing structural tolerances over the course of

389

centuries. It was the kind of thing the supercomputers back on Earth had to be tasked hundreds of hours to do.

She was looking pretty flustered as he laid all that down on her. She had just been working on this project as a way to practice her imagination and work on construction after what she'd seen Hawthorne accomplish with designing the caravan. She hadn't expected to be openly challenged like this. Rather than try to tell him, she decided to show him, causing everything around them to visibly stop.

Things weren't actually stopped though. Hawthorne could tell that people were still moving around, but it was like trying to watch the hour hand on a clock proceed forward in time without the second and minute hands to distract one's attention. It was so incredibly slow that when he got up to walk over to someone and push at her, he saw T.I.A. visibly flinch as he altered the physical forces on their bodies and made her compensate for everything from her direction of movement to the effects of momentum on all of her organs and bones. The simulated woman even started to gasp, her eyes widening in surprise incredibly slowly. It would take hours for her to fall down at this rate.

"I see. You can stop that for now." T.I.A. nodded, letting everything resume as it had before, with the woman hitting the ground next to him and the people looking up at him in shock before they hurried away.

"Alright Tia, I think I know what I want you to do. While I am in stasis, I want you to practice on this simulation. Think of it as a workout, doing something over and over until it becomes natural and you get better and stronger at it. Vary the weather, change the people, change the materials everything is made from. Master this simulation so that when we proceed to more difficult work, you can handle doing something like this and more in real-time."

"And don't get me wrong, I'm incredibly impressed at what you're already able to do, but this is the perfect environment for us to do science safely. I'm sure you saw my list. This kind of exercise will be perfect for allowing you to design and create things most people find impossibly complicated. We'll work on your ability to improvise things at some point too, later, so that when you end up having to adapt to lots of different circumstances in Alpha Centauri you can handle them without my assistance." He looked excited at the possibilities, but he knew it would probably be many months before they could move on from this relatively simple exercise.

T.I.A. looked rather dismayed at the idea of what she was being asked to do, but she only needed to remind herself how much she had enjoyed creating the simulation in the first place. Maybe she could expand upon it eventually. Maybe these sorts of shelters would totally replace Medellin in her simulation someday.

"Yes Doctor, I will do my best to work on this project in your absence. I trust you will continue doing your research in advance of us working on the projects from your list?" She didn't know if she could feel tired, but the enthusiasm she had in advance of what would be centuries of grinding on this problem certainly made her feel like she was in a low-power state, her generators struggling to keep up with her. Emotional sensations were so strange for her.

"Absolutely. It'd be horrible of me to ask you to do something like that and not put in work of my own. I made my first priority to help you mature, not only because of the fact that we need you, but because you deserve to reach your potential. I would not be much of a father if I didn't do my best to work with you rather than letting you do all the hard parts." He hummed, wondering about something, interrupting his speech. "Maybe we'll see if you can simulate the Phoenix Clan's narcotic substances some day too. I think you should avoid those for now, as we don't know what effect it will have on you. Those sorts of experiences have been known to make irrevocable changes to how humans think and experience the world."

She flinched slightly as he called himself her father, but she tried to play it off. T.I.A. hadn't even considered drugs. They were such an integral part of the Phoenix Clan society, but she hadn't even tried to pretend like her characters were under the influence of them. It was a remarkably simple oversight considering how many types and strains of them Clint Crenshaw had described to her on the rare occasion where he'd talk to her.

She liked Jessica's husband quite a bit. He seemed quiet and kept to himself and loved plants as much as he loved his wife. He had confessed to her at one point that the only thing that kept him from drawing the ire of the Elders by having another child with her were his other babies, the various plants that fell under his care. He was hardly the only farmer, almost two thirds of the Clan was responsible for tending to the food, but he was one of few who made a full time job of it. He simply didn't care about anything but his family and his plants.

He had told her how hard it was for him to let go of them, to let them be eaten or smoked, or processed into any number of useful things. He took incredible pride in the fact that his babies were so important to the health, both physical and mental, of the Smith Bunker, and later the Phoenix Clan. He was endlessly fascinated with the biological reactions the Old Ones had to the food they made for them, as they had adapted to a completely different kind of diet.

He had worked endlessly with Teitara Poundstone and her colleagues to help asses their allergies and intolerances to their foods and drugs. It had been a true joy when they'd found ways to utilize the Old One's plants, in combination with their own, to produce food everyone could eat. T.I.A. had been so focused on making sure Clint would be proud of the gardens she'd constructed in the greenhouses that she hadn't considered their effects and what they could be used for.

It was in that moment of reflection, after Hawthorne had warned her to not partake in drugs, that T.I.A. broke down crying. She fell to her knees as the skies darkened and the clouds burst, filling the area with loud rain and thunder while she wailed and bawled her eyes out. Her arms were slack at her sides and her body trembled while Hawthorne stared at her in surprise.

The rest of the simulation had mostly frozen to allow her to focus on herself and the weather, but Hawthorne wasn't exactly paying attention to anything else as he dropped down onto the steel floor next to her, his arms hesitantly reaching out to pull her up against his side. He had always been terrible in moments like this, but a handful of experiences with Tia Monsalle had taught him that sometimes you just needed to hug the girl and shut your mouth.

"I miss them, Hawthorne! I miss my friends! I miss Jessica and Barry, and Tammy, and Elena, and Cindy, and Walter, and everyone!" She felt totally irrational in that moment, her heart broken and her emotions totally falling apart around her as the weight of the ideas that she'd never see them again and she could only simulate their likenesses hit her all at once. She couldn't believe that Clint was the one that had set her off, but remembering everything she knew about him just sent her into a spiral of remembering everyone else. Windows popped up around them as recordings played of all sorts of people.

A mousy Cindy Harrison appeared, her squeaky voice saying, "I always admired what you're doing up there. I'd love to have been born early enough to be on that ship with you."

An old Jessica sat with Elena in another window, arguing. Elena asserted, "Look, just because you look older doesn't mean that you can talk to me like some child."

Jessica retorted, "Sure it does, because you've probably forgotten so much you don't remember much more than a teenager!"

Leonard Harrison, with his salt-and-pepper hair and beard appeared behind her. "And that's why you need to make sure to never give up, no matter how many mistakes you make. No child that gives up easily ever truly grows up."

A blonde Walter Carlson appeared to the side, obviously younger than when he took up his role as the Elder head historian. "You're making history out there, you know that right? Our people and your people will come together some day and make the beginnings of galactic human civilization."

Even Thorne appeared, the young man bearing none of the stern demeanor or scars he later would as a soldier. "Yeah, I'm scared, but I gotta protect my family and friends. Nothing else matters. What good would I be if I let something distract me from that?"

The voices and images all melded into each other in a cacophony of life lessons and familiar faces causing even Hawthorne to cry as he realized how much they had tried to help T.I.A. learn and understand in his absence. She'd spent so much more time with them than she had with him. He was a mere guest star in the life she'd lived as the distant companion of a group of humans struggling to survive. He owed them so much. He cried his eyes out with her as all-too-real memories of their friends appeared and disappeared around them. He had not fully appreciated the profound loss that T.I.A. was going through until now.

"I'm so sorry Tia, I'm so sorry, I didn't... I didn't realize how hard this was for you. You don't have to start working on the simulations right away. It can be something else if it's too hard for you to remember." He hugged her tightly, though he had to restrain himself lest he hug her through him, seeing as his gloves had no way to provide resistance. Still, he could feel the way her body was trembling and shaking against him, convulsing as she sobbed. He could even feel the moisture of her tears against his skin as he moved to wipe at her tears as she started calming down. Maybe it was a little too early to be thinking about work. Maybe now was the time for emotions.

Once he got a chance to reach for his tablet, he added a new number 1, shifting everything else down: Properly mourn all we've lost before worrying about work.

CHAPTER 30

CYCLE 30, TIME IS RELATIVE

Hawthorne and T.I.A. spent the rest of cycle 16 talking about their friends, as well as Hawthorne's family and his acquaintances back on Earth. They spent several days constructing a monument in T.I.A.'s VE of the Phoenix Clan Columbia settlement. In the center, under the canopy, they surrounded the central pillar with a stonework obelisk, and proceeded to 'engrave' the names, birthdays, and death days of everyone they had personally lost.

It was difficult for both of them to go back through all their records, taking down the dates of everyone involved in the Ark project whom were assassinated, Hawthorne and Tia Monsalle's parents, and everything else they had of the Phoenix Clan and the LSC bunker. For those they merely lost contact with, the second date was left open ended for speculation, while the entire lineages of the Phoenix Clan and LSC bunker were recorded on their own faces of the fake stone monument. It was somewhat strange that the monument existed in T.I.A.'s imagination, for all intents and purposes, but they did have some intention of fabricating a real version of it to put on display on their new home planet when they could.

It wasn't until Cycle 17, when they finished the monument that they went through a final dedication. T.I.A. had gathered simulations of the majority of their known friends from the Phoenix Clan, and Hawthorne had erected something of a small stage in front of the pillar for her to speak to the 'crowd' upon. T.I.A. had insisted they have witnesses for the event, much like the one she'd received a recording of where Elena Price spoke over the graves near Medellin. She'd even brought a bunch of her freshly-made Flora Roaches to the event, though they hadn't been animated very much yet.

He felt silly, standing there in the same old habitat he was in, but with the courtyard full of friendly faces arrayed out in front of him. It was all make believe, he knew that, but looking back at the pillar behind him that wasn't actually there still filled him with something like a sense of awe. Nostalgia pulled at him as he saw the names, and wonder filled him as he took in just how many people had actually lived in those bunkers over the centuries. Looking back, he took his place at his podium, smiling over at T.I.A. as she stood with a likeness of a young Jessica and Clint.

"Good afternoon, friends and loved ones. We are gathered here today to remember those we have lost. It has been said that funerals and memorials are not for the dead, but the living, and that it is not possible for us to go on living until we have dealt with our grief. Some take longer than others to come to peace with such things, while others may never recover at all. The people that have come before have made it possible for us to get to where we are now, and none of us are without hundreds or thousands of people responsible for making sure we made it this far." He couldn't help but smile as T.I.A. made sure to put smiles on a lot of the faces, and tears in the eyes of others. It was as though they were performing for each other.

"When you've lost someone, it never seems to feel like you told them enough about what they meant to you. Words are a poor medium to convey things like emotions, but still we can't help but try. We wonder if we might not have failed to speak up when we could have said something and then end up regretting it for the rest of our lives. Other times we wish we could have kept our mouths shut when we told someone something we can never take back, and have to live with the fact that we caused that injury or pain. Most importantly, though, is that we remember those who have come and gone, to keep their memory alive in our hearts as long as we can."

He hesitated a moment, considering how to proceed, but deciding he'd best spill his guts. "I haven't really known love. I don't quite know how to express it, or really understand what it feels like. I hope, like other things, that I come to learn about it, but I think that if I had the time that Tia did to know the Phoenix Clan that I might have come to love you eventually. You were kind, warm, loving people with a strange foundational culture that I can't help but admire."

"I'm fascinated with the robust types of people you produced, people with a real understanding of the world and humanity that was lacking sorely in my time. You know each others' hearts and minds nearly as intimately as you know your own, and your culture is built around ensuring a kind of harmony with one another I can only imagine. If I hadn't made it off of Earth, I think I would have liked to have been part of your community in another life."

"You weren't just a group though. The Phoenix Clan were individuals just as lively and wonderful as each other. Even those of you that I didn't especially like I couldn't help but admire or respect for some reason or another. The Elders all leveraged their life experiences to lead with wisdom, while the young ceaselessly sought to better themselves, to keep knowledge from being lost with time. I sincerely hope you manage to maintain yourselves, your culture, and your technology, so that we may be friends someday in the future. It would be a sincere joy to one day reunite the lost people of Earth and move on together into the future."

"For now though, we must leave our friends to their own devices. I have to trust that you can take care of yourselves now. I personally see no reason to worry about whether or not you can survive, and for now I think it is our responsibility to make sure that we meet each other on the other side of our respective journeys into the future. I have to thank you, especially, for taking care of Tia. You have guided her and helped her grow in ways I feel would have been impossible if she were solely under my guidance. I don't believe I can properly express my gratitude for everything you have done for us, and I hope that we've done everything we could do to repay it."

T.I.A. had people openly crying now, but she was mostly keeping herself together for the moment. The weather was also remaining calm, though he couldn't be sure for how long. "It is with that in mind that I promise to one day preside over the dedication of an obelisk much like this one to honor everyone who helped us get this far upon the settlement of our new home. I will consider it my duty to make sure that we accomplish everything that we need to to ensure that that moment comes to pass. I will dream of the day that we can one day show the people of Earth this modest symbol of our respect and memory of our shared past. I swear on my life that I will do my best to see to it."

A flash of light and a crack of thunder accompanied what surely must have been T.I.A. having lightning strike the central pillar, which seemed to cause the names to glow upon the obelisk's surface in a somewhat unrealistic, but undeniably flashy fashion. T.I.A. climbed up onto the stage with a little help, and Hawthorne stepped aside so that she could speak. She even had to shrink the podium a bit so she could stand behind it and be visible.

"I love you all, and I'll miss you so much I don't know how I'll be able to handle it. I won't let you down. We've all worked too hard to give up now, and we still have too much work to do to spend our time dwelling on the past. Thank you so much for everything!" Short and sweet, much like her avatar, T.I.A. waved to the assembled people before clearing up the weather and making the additional avatars vanish.

"Doctor, I think I'm ready to get to work. I don't know if I'll ever be over them, but I think I can concentrate on my work now." She smiled up at him, only for Hawthorne to brush some tears from her cheeks.

He nodded and smiled back. "Let's get to it then. Wouldn't want to disappoint them."

△△△

Cycle after cycle passed after that, with Hawthorne catching up on his exercise and doing his best to research all the relevant science that he could for their projects. He'd have to be not only creating new technology, but he'd be teaching T.I.A. how the physical laws of nature itself really interacted with each other in extreme circumstances. She had plenty of knowledge of physics as a matter of practicality, but simulating reality itself was an enormous challenge, even on a small scale.

T.I.A. spent her time between cycles trying to master the Phoenix Clan Columbia, PC-C settlement simulation down to the smallest details she could manage. It was incredibly slow and difficult, but she took her time in trying to manage the simulation while multi-tasking the maintenance of the Ark and the Lubar-Masis comet. It was only in the rarest of moments when she needed to see to the repair of something, but as they traversed into the edge of the theoretical Oort Cloud she found that the ship was still relatively easy to maintain.

While Hawthorne was awake, she found it easier to spend her time consulting with him on specific issues she was having in her simulation, like making sure to properly apply fractals to make random snowflakes or make sure to apply the effects of erosion on the surrounding landscape as well as the structures in the settlement. She found it difficult to animate the Flora Roaches due to their inhuman movements, and only Hawthorne's exaggerated efforts to mimic the behemoth creatures gave her insights about how they were supposed to move. She avoided trying to simulate psychedelic experiences, but she did try to make sure the humans in her simulation mimicked old videos of inebriated people she had both before and after the Cataclysm.

It was incredibly slow going, but she was managing to make bits of progress here and there, allowing her to improve the efficiency of her 'imagination' as far as simulating reality. The only real issue with her dedicating so much time and effort towards it was that she had not had anything resembling a dream again, though considering the last one she wasn't certain she actually wanted to. She was also spending some time on the side to troubleshoot an upgrade to Hawthorne's ability to interface with her VE. There were a great deal of difficulties with making sure such a thing remained powered while in use, as well as allowing it to do things like simulate weight and resistance to virtual objects. It was an interesting project that allowed her to work on her creativity on the side, as well as apply the things she was learning about the simulation she was slowly mastering.

By the morning of AC 918, Monday, July 21, 3051, the

start of cycle 30, she was ready to report on her progress. It had been nearly two months for Hawthorne since her emotional breakdown, though it was closer to 500 years for her. It was getting to the point that she was prepared to simply stop using unnecessary methods of keeping track of time outside of the actual cycle count, and perhaps the AC year. The old methods of time tracking would, of course, remain standardized in her systems, but even those were just a translation of her systems tracking the seconds as they passed. Her perspective of time was simply expanding beyond the necessity to perceive the passing of days, months, or years.

All that mattered to her, at this point, was the upkeep of her monitoring systems, upkeep of the ship and comet, the simulation she was constantly working on, and the four days a cycle she got to spend with Hawthorne. Even for her she was paying attention to little but those four days a cycle, preferring to focus her attention on them and then letting her mind just float through the rest of the centuries while the equivalent of her subconscious worked in the background. She realized this was always how it was going to be. She couldn't pay attention to every passing moment forever, or she might seriously go insane. Too much time was going to pass for her to be aware of it the whole time.

She decided that even if she got good at simulating reality to the levels that Hawthorne needed her to in real time so they could work on projects, she would spend the majority of the rest of her time dreaming and thinking at that slower, more comfortable pace without worrying too much about trying to grow up. She'd learned a lesson already about trying to force herself to grow too quickly, so while she watched her systems activate and fall into the routine of providing life support for Hawthorne she leisurely went about ensuring he had his food and coffee prepared and attached her VE to his compartments.

"Good morning Doctor Crenshaw. It is thirty, nine-hundred eight AC. I am happy to report I am roughly fifteen percent of the way to being able to simulate the PC-C in real time, and have comfortably settled into my perspective of time. I am finding these last five cycles, especially, to have passed nearly as calmly as your own rest. I believe that my perspective has adjusted to more easily withstand the passage of time." T.I.A.'s voice sounded calm, measured, and confident. It wasn't necessarily a voice of maturity, but one of contentment and understanding.

Hawthorne listened quietly, nodding and smiling as he came out to get his food and coffee, sitting at a communal table across from her in the PC-C. She had removed all the distracting characters and was merely trying to maintain the environment while working lightly on making sure the air was flowing naturally. Hawthorne was able to feel it blowing on his gloved hands, and he really wondered what it smelled like. "It's wonderful that you've been able to properly adapt to your circumstances, Tia. Are you finding any difficulty maintaining your systems while that time passes?" He took the opportunity to start eating, listening carefully.

"I believe the best analogy is that those functions are much like your own autonomic functions. I need not specifically pay attention to maintaining my generators or engines any more than you need concentrate on your heartbeat or breathing. I can concentrate on them, and can tell when something is wrong, but I don't necessarily need to spend any effort thinking about them anymore. I am finding it to be quite peaceful actually." She had a serene expression on her face.

"It seems similar to the concept of meditation, though I

can achieve something of a peaceful emptiness and receptiveness without having to specifically focus on anything. I find it preferential to focus my attention on you when you're available, and let my thoughts wander otherwise. I'm still working on the simulation, and a related project, but the latter is dependent on the progress of the former, allowing me to merely wait for progress."

T.I.A. sounded very pleased and at peace with her situation. The empty darkness of space was a dull companion, and her imagination needed a great deal of development to become something that could occupy her time consistently, so meditation of a sort seemed like a fantastic way to cope with what would otherwise be crippling loneliness. "I have to say, Tia, that is both impressive and remarkable. I suppose it also seems like something of a necessity considering our circumstances, but the fact that you did it on your own is worthy of praise."

T.I.A. smiled brightly at that, leaning forward over the table to present her hair for praise. It was a little difficult for Hawthorne to keep his eyes on her face with her bent forward like that, but he nevertheless reached out to rub comfortably at that curly mop of hair on her head. She giggled softly, her satisfaction at getting recognition seeming to be something she had been looking forward to. "You know, Doctor Crenshaw, I've been thinking about something."

He looked a little surprised at that as he withdrew his hand, watching her. "I thought you were peacefully drifting through space?"

She rolled her eyes and sat back, smiling. "Peacefully drifting through space for centuries, yes, with plenty of time to let my mind wander. Anyway, I was thinking, it's a little childish of me to keep calling you father. It's something I latched onto when I was more emotionally unstable, but it doesn't seem especially appropriate. You're my creator, my builder, my guiding hand, but not necessarily father. I was thinking about whether I should think of you more as a mentor, or my partner, or friend?"

Hawthorne's eyebrow was raised through much of that, only to relax a bit as she got towards the end. "I'd like that Tia. I'm a terrible candidate for a father anyway. I'm not even sure if I'm any good at being a friend, but I'd at least like to try." He smiled a bit, holding out a hand with the intent of shaking hers.

T.I.A. considered his words, nodding a little and taking his hand, shaking it back. "Alright, well, first things first, you don't need to avert your gaze when you look at me. I may have produced my avatar when I had a more juvenile perspective, but that doesn't mean I didn't make it with the intent to appeal to you. Most of it was a product of my subconscious, but I believe my original intent was that I could be more interesting for you to look at than a monitor or a camera. After that first incident with my nightmare I found it incredibly satisfying and exciting when you looked at the camera I was looking at you through. I think receiving your attention makes me feel more real, rather than just part of a ship."

Hawthorne looked nervous, without doubt. She could see his elevated blood pressure, heart rate, the subtle evaporation of moisture off of his body as he sweated... He was uncomfortable with what she was proposing. "I'm not asking you to see me as a romantic partner or anything, I don't know if I'm ready for something like that, but there's no need for you to be afraid of what I'll think if you look at me. I like that I appeal to your aesthetics, and I think it's much better than this." She abruptly took away the whole simulation, returning Hawthorne to sitting alone in a steel room surrounded by monitors and machinery.

He'd spent almost two months in the PC-C. To suddenly have it disappear and only have the ship to look at it was startling. He felt his insides twist up with anxiety as he looked around, seeing the cameras overhead again for the first time in some time. It was chilling.

He had not realized just how relaxing the simulation of being outside and with T.I.A. had made him, but she had. "Okay, I see what you mean, Tia. I've become very accustomed to having your simulations overlaid upon my environment. I... will try to look at you more directly, to appreciate your efforts to take care of me better. I don't think I realized how important it is to me to be somewhere besides this cabin and to do something besides look at tablets all the time. You're absolutely right."

She appeared at the table with him, though now it was a wooden park table with a bench on either side. Around them was Clapham Common, with its beautiful lake, assorted woods, and criss-crossing foot paths. He could even see a skate park and the football pitches in the distance. Looking back to her though, she was wearing that pretty yellow sundress of hers, showing off plenty of cleavage and that bright, radiant smile.

She had a slender and healthy, if buxom shape, and was no more than 155 cm tall. It was kind of amusing that such a huge ship would see itself as such a petite young woman. He looked at her more directly, seeing all of her rather than just her face. She was a beautiful girl, doubtlessly, and he could swear he saw her shiver with delight at being acknowledged as such.

He let out a sigh, nodding. "I'm sorry I didn't say so earlier, but you've created a beautiful avatar for yourself. If that's really how you see yourself, then you are doubtlessly a beautiful person inside and out. I'm sorry for feeling suspicious that you were just acting on Jessica and Tabitha's matchmaking instincts rather than doing something for yourself. It was wrong of me to fail to properly acknowledge you."

She grinned brightly, practically shining in the spring sunlight at that. "You're forgiven, Hawthorne! Hopefully if I decide to make changes in the future it won't take you so long to acknowledge them. I hope that wasn't too awkward, I wasn't sure how long I should wait before saying something about it."

Hawthorne shook his head, laughing. "No, no, I'm fine, it just caught me off guard. I thought you were going to propose some kind of romantic relationship, and considering how poorly that went with your namesake, I-" He stopped abruptly, eyes wide

T.I.A.'s eyes went wide, and then she pointed at him and started laughing. "You admitted it! You named me after her!" She fell off of the bench, giggling up a storm and rolling in the grass. "You named me after your girlfriend. I can't believe you took so long to admit it!"

Hawthorne had turned bright red as his AI made fun of him, his hand coming up to his face in a fist as he cleared his throat. "I fail to see what's so funny. I admire and respect her, and it felt like a good dedication to her..."

T.I.A. climbed back up towards the table, still grinning like an idiot. She had her fingers and chin resting on the edge of it. "You named me after her because you miss her and wish she could have been here with you the whole time." She had him now. She had gotten it out of him after so long. She was not going to lose this chance to needle the great Doctor Hawthorne Crenshaw. Jessica would never forgive her if she didn't!

407

He held up his hands in surrender, hanging his head. "F... fine, you're right, okay? I don't know what I felt about her, but I enjoyed her company, and I thought it would have been nice if I had her company all this time. I didn't even tell her that I'd be passing close to thirty-two years out here without her."

T.I.A. gasped and stood up straight, staring down at the sitting scientist. "You didn't tell her!? She's going to be so mad at you! You're going to be... what... Sixty-nine when we get to Alpha Centauri? Didn't she love you? What's she going to think that almost half of your life was spent alone in a metal box talking to a computer?"

Hawthorne flinched back at that. She had him dead to rights. She was not supposed to be the one that confronted him with this. He'd kicked that can down the road about thirty-two years without expecting it to be thrown back in his face. "Of course I didn't tell her. She never would have let me do it. She'd have insisted someone else did it, and then I wouldn't have been here to take care of you. It's something my father suggested to me when I first started going out with her. Sometimes it's easier to ask for forgiveness than to ask for permission. He was right. I was going to ask her, but I just... I just couldn't, okay? I didn't want to do that to her. I wanted to be in a position to make sure she and everyone else made it safely."

T.I.A. humphed softly. She knew something she was pretty sure he didn't, but she wasn't going to say anything. She knew a lot more about why Tia Monsalle would be mad at Hawthorne Crenshaw than he did.

"You're right, I guess... I'm happy I get to spend my time with you instead of one of those other stuffy scientists. I doubt they could have handled helping the Phoenix Clan build their caravan properly either, or if they could have inspired me to grow as much as I have. This was all your project, so it's only right that it's your burden to see it through. Still, she's going to be piiiiiiiissed." She laughed a bit to herself, watching Hawthorne squirm.

"Well, hopefully by the time I'm sixty-nine I'll be old enough to handle talking to her." He joined T.I.A. in laughing, enjoying the pleasant way she let her full body experience the laugh. He felt like his laugh felt forced by comparison, but then it was only recently that he'd learned how to laugh in enjoyment rather than as a performance for others. "I guess you're not the only one growing up here."

She reached up to tap at her chin with a finger though, twisting her hips a bit as she thought, making her skirt swish about her thighs. "So what you're saying is that there's a chance?" She grinned mischievously over at him. She let out a soft 'ooh' as well. "And that if I do something without asking permission first that you'll be less mad when I ask for forgiveness?"

Hawthorne groaned, pushing his plate aside and laying his head down on the table, resting his hands on the back of his head. "What have I done...?"

CHAPTER 31
CYCLE 42, TERRIBLE TEEN

T.I.A.'s newfound youthful mischievousness was proving an enormous challenge for Doctor Crenshaw. Despite his efforts to focus on reading and researching, T.I.A.'s desire for attention and compliments was rapidly outstripping his ability to concentrate on what seemed like the more important work. It didn't help that T.I.A. had apparently put together a massive database of outfits and dresses drawn from all manner of news reports, vintage movies, television shows, and historical records. Even his efforts to sit and think quietly by himself by closing his eyes had been defeated by her ability to project her VE to his AR contacts while his eyes were closed. Nothing short of unconsciousness had kept her from needling and teasing him.

It was not as though Hawthorne had not expected such a thing, it was simply that he had been sorely unprepared. The only respite he ever seemed to get was when T.I.A. detected distant objects in space that unfortunately were entirely impossible for them to get at. At most they were able to track and estimate the trajectories of the icy bodies, which largely seemed to be moving away from them in a variety of directions, all suggesting very wide orbits with their home star.

The Oort Cloud, so far, seemed to be an enormous region of randomly orbiting bodies that occasionally got knocked back into the solar system proper, much like the Lubar Masis probably had been long ago. It was easy to imagine that Jupiter had used its massive gravity to slingshot these object out this far untold millennia ago.

These discoveries did not stop T.I.A. for long though, and Hawthorne had to do his best to endure the short, curvy female avatar of his AI's parade of new outfits, accessories, and even the occasional likenesses. She especially seemed to enjoy wearing a younger version of Jessica's face, only to quote various idioms she'd learned from her regarding the necessity of relaxation, meditation, and sexual stimulation. She hadn't offered to provide any such thing, probably due to her inability to do so, but she certainly encouraged Hawthorne to do 'what felt right' in the privacy of his bedroom, with the promise not to spy on him.

Unremarkably, this left Hawthorne reluctant to even do that, which T.I.A. did not fail to point out as abnormal compared to previous cycles, especially the earliest ones where he tended to take much longer showers. In some sense Hawthorne was appreciative of her interest in maintaining his health, but in another sense the combination of that interest and her efforts to titillate him had him feeling very insecure about her motivations!

Hawthorne wasn't necessarily feeling as though he couldn't pursue a relationship with T.I.A., but he was of the opinion that such a thing could be a significant distraction from their work and the need to maintain a professional environment was paramount.

From T.I.A.'s perspective, though, it wasn't a question of whether or not a relationship was necessary, it was a question of what form their relationship would take over time. She had a vested interest in maintaining Hawthorne's physical and mental health, and from everything she'd learned there were very enjoyable and carnal ways to accomplish both. She was not necessarily ready for such things, but that did not mean she could not provide Hawthorne with inspiration to handle things on his own. If nothing else, his exasperated expressions, awkward exchanges, and efforts to avoid her were incredibly entertaining.

T.I.A. also understood that her emotional and mental growth had thoroughly asserted itself over her more logical, computer-based mind. She certainly lacked a certain level of maturity, but she did not lack for knowledge and decades of advice and interactions to draw upon. Hawthorne was her sole remaining human, and so she didn't have nearly as much opportunity to 'play' as she had with the people of the Phoenix Clan. She did however have the advantage of interacting with him in real time, and considering the long delays she had with Earth, she could pack a lot more interaction in with Hawthorne in four days than she could with Earth over the course of months.

More importantly, T.I.A. saw all this teasing as a valuable distraction. Hawthorne still had decades of his life to live on this ship, do his research, and work with her on projects. He needed time to enjoy himself, and she was much the same. As much as he appeared disinterested or annoyed with her, he'd never asked her to leave him alone or to stop her antics. She often caught him smiling to himself when he thought she wasn't paying attention, or maybe it was his biology responding to her efforts to tempt him. By the time he'd actually taken one of those long showers of his again, she'd been tormenting him for weeks of his life.

The change in his demeanor and tension were easily noticed when he was done. He was much more easygoing, relaxed, and seemed more capable of appreciating her various outfits on an aesthetic level. His tolerance of more daring visuals seemed to rise dramatically as well, and before long he was making suggestions and becoming genuinely interested in helping her with her wardrobe.

He even started taking the fun out of her teasing by applying a set of ratings to her outfits and creating a database of the various items that could easily be sorted by various factors such as 'sexiness' and 'cuteness'. She'd managed to draw him fully into turning her play into a project, including the two researching records of old Earth styles, and even exploring various science fiction and fantasy articles from literature and media.

Just because Hawthorne was applying science to her wardrobe did not mean she failed to have effects on him, and she'd become increasingly adept at showing off more shocking items when he seemed to be getting relaxed, causing him to react quite comically. It wasn't abnormal for him to fall out of a chair or retreat to his bedroom when she appeared in clothing that could more easily be described as risque underwear rather than actual clothing. She imagined that Jessica would be proud, and even occasionally conjured up her likeness to high-five her with a self-satisfied smile on her face.

△△△

Perhaps the biggest shock of all, though, came at the start of cycle 42. As Hawthorne exited his cryogenic pod, cleaned himself up, and got dressed T.I.A. was preparing something different. As he came out into the imagined Phoenix Clan settlement, he was met by a total stranger. Nearly as tall as Hawthorne, T.I.A.'s new avatar was dressed in something of a formal tuxedo and had something of a burly appearance that strained at the fabric of the suit.

Holding out a hand, the obviously masculine form was holding a plate of Hawthorne's usual breakfast, which confused him briefly until he realized one of T.I.A.'s articulating robotic limbs had extended down from the ceiling. She had cleverly overlaid the hand of that limb with the likeness of her new avatar.

Said avatar had spiky red hair, and the face was something one might expect to see on a beach bully, but with a wide happy grin. Even the voice that came from T.I.A.'s speakers was masculine, despite having much of her typical happy mannerisms. "Your breakfast is served, Doctor Crenshaw. Good morning. The date is Friday, September ninth, thirty-four fifty-nine, AC thirteen twenty-six. What do you think of my new look?"

Hawthorne frowned briefly, then laughed, reaching out to take the plate from T.I.A., whom was acting like his butler and/or bodyguard at the moment. "You know, I'd gotten so accustomed to seeing women around here that I wasn't expecting to see a man."

T.I.A. tsked softly, shaking both a virtual and mechanical finger at him. "There you go assuming genders again." T.I.A. laughed, a deep throaty sound that almost boomed in the air. "I just thought it might be kind of fun to see how the other side feels. I can definitely see a lot more from up here!" The red headed male avatar lifted his arms, flexing them and straining the tuxedo further. "I feel weirdly powerful and in charge."

Hawthorne laughed a bit, sitting down at the table and stabbing a piece of sausage with his fork. "Tia, you've always been powerful and exempting my own authority you've been largely in charge." He took a bite of his food, watching in amusement as T.I.A. showed off that huge body and seemingly tried to either intimidate him or make him feel inferior. It was not as though Hawthorne was unhealthy, but he was certainly not a bodybuilder like this new T.I.A. appeared to be.

"Aww, come on, that's not what I mean. There's just something about being taller and bigger that changes my perspective, and yes I realize that I'm so big that I have two thousand humans inside of me, but I specifically mean the avatar." T.I.A. sat down opposite Hawthorne, causing the human to glance up from his food, not accustomed to his peripheral vision being filled with so much bulk. "Heh, you're acting totally different around me than last cycle."

Rather than taking the bait, Hawthorne kept chewing for a moment, swallowing and then gesturing at him with a fork. "That's really clever, using the arm to give your body some physical presence. I almost want to build you an android body of some manner to let you overlay your avatar upon. I don't think I'd make two of them though, for each avatar, so you'll have to pick one of them." He watched the bulky male for a moment, as though he expected T.I.A. to make a decision.

Letting out a sigh, T.I.A. deflated physically, the overhead arm twisting and repositioning to compensate for her return to her original form. Hawthorne's face turned bright red as he stared for a moment, only to look away, choking slightly on his food. T.I.A. gasped as she realized she hadn't linked up the simulated tuxedo to the smaller avatar, causing the clothing to fall away behind her as she sat there naked briefly. Even she blushed for a moment before the tuxedo vanished and she appeared instead in a proper labcoat-covered outfit. "Sorry! I hadn't considered what would happen when I did that!"

Coughing, Hawthorne, took a drink of coffee to clear his throat and shook his head. "No, no, it's fine. I presume you'd prefer an android more appropriate to that form then?" Hawthorne was glad for the distraction of talking about building something, as T.I.A.'s careless flashing had woken him up far more than the chemical injections he'd just gotten from his pod.

She nodded back at him though, laughing a bit at his reactions. "Yes please, though I had something else in the works that might make for an interesting complement to such a thing. I'll need several cycles to work on it though." Her little side-project was coming closer to completion, even if her efforts to simulate the PC-C were progressing very slowly. She didn't need to master that to accomplish her other goals.

Hawthorne nodded back, eating some eggs, still pleased with how well preserved all this ancient food still was. He'd have to give Heather O'Malley a big hug when he next got to see her, the cryogenics specialist having handled designing his food storage system as well. "I could design it and have you fabricate it for me, but I'd really rather build it myself, so while I'll still have you make some of the parts for me, I think we can both work on our projects over the same timeline. I might need a few months to finish it, so I'll probably have it done between cycle sixty or sixty-five. How's that sound?"

T.I.A. nodded at that, though she frowned a bit as she tried to estimate her own project. "I might need a little longer than that, but I'll be able to let you know by then." While she was certainly excited about her own project, Hawthorne providing her a physical body to move around in had its own appeals. It was such a different idea to the simple drones she had access to outside of the ship, or the arms she had inside the ship. She'd be able to move about and experience the world from a remote body not too unlike Hawthorne's own, at least in shape. She'd formed her experience of interacting with the world through her own unique means, so trying on a new body was way more interesting to her than trying on a new avatar.

ΔΔΔ

Over the course of the following days, Hawthorne utilized T.I.A.'s VE to design a basic form factor for her to start fabricating parts from for him. Insisting that the robotic body fit her avatar had resulted in her demanding that he construct the design while a nearly-transparent version of her stood in its place. In some manner it was like he was building her skeleton. Of course, she was also trying to get a rise out of him by forcing him to have to reach through her body to stretch out pieces of steel and place and fasten various components. This proved yet more effective as she had his gloves transfer the sensation of touching the softness of her body.

Hawthorne was not dissuaded though, and he focused instead on the feel of the hard steel components he was arranging and bolting together rather than the soft body he was reaching through to get at them. While it appeared he was growing more resilient to her advances, it was actually just that he was more able to ignore them when there was work to be done. The difference was not lost on her, but it did leave her somewhat unable to find a way around it.

Comparing the work to his previous construction of the Phoenix Clan caravan, the T.I.A. android body was quite a bit more intricate. It was a great deal smaller though, so he did not need to spend a whole week designing it as he had with that almost 1000 year old caravan. If he were honest with himself, the excitement of actually putting the thing together was stimulating his imagination a great deal. He'd not properly had his hands on a machine he was building himself in so long, more than half a year from his perspective, that it was difficult for him to keep his ambition in check.

By the time the design was finished, it was a shiny, chrome-looking machine with carefully articulated joints, an elegant form factor, and what would surely be a nearly-silent series of electrical mechanisms. He was uncertain as to the viability of small form-factor batteries for such a thing, so he had instead opted for it to have a rear-mounted power cable behind the shoulders, which effectively restricted its movements to the two rooms he generally had access to, but he didn't personally see that as an issue.

Once T.I.A. was ready for them to do some proper chemistry in her VE, they could start working on batteries that could last for millennia. It was a bit of a frivolous use, but it was nonetheless a really useful technology that would be helpful in replacing T.I.A.'s need to recycle and rebuild the batteries she used for the ship every few centuries.

T.I.A. seemed pleased with the design, though she had plenty of criticisms as well. She insisted it should better mimic her shape, in particular her curves, though Hawthorne objected that completely different materials would be better for such things. He would much rather she have the somewhat simple metal construct that she could overlay her avatar atop. He simply didn't see much of a point of developing artificial skin to fill out her figure when she could hide that frame. He eventually relented when she made it clear how much it could help in giving her a sense of touch, even if Hawthorne felt as though such a thing would only be useful in helping her improve the accuracy of her own simulation of herself.

Hawthorne color-coded the things he needed her to make for him, and made a list of the other materials he'd need, such as wires, certain types of machined parts, and things like screws. The list also included tools he'd need her to retrieve from storage for him, allowing him to more easily assemble her android and handle necessary welding and soldering. It took her a fair amount of time to get everything together, but if she had a resource beyond everything else, it was time.

She also had some ambitions. Even if it was slow going, the design for a full-body version of Hawthorne's gloves was coming along well. In fact, observing Hawthorne's construction of her android had given her a lot of ideas for how to make him experience things like the weight of virtual objects by having such a suit pull on his body appropriately. She might even be able to simulate quite a lot more if her suspicions were correct.

Any such things required her to simulate his body at the same time she was simulating her own as well as manipulating an android. She'd need a lot of practice multi-tasking such things, but now she had all the components she needed to do that practicing while Hawthorne was frozen.

Hawthorne's distress over how she'd been treating him had him considering other ideas as well, though. Maybe her need for attention was something that Megan could help with? It was certainly not an ideal solution, and one he was concerned about the safety of, but perhaps he could find a way to make it work without endangering T.I.A. or the ship and its crew.

The real problem with Megan was providing her a computer capable of housing her mind without making her go insane. Ideally it would be something that had no wireless capabilities and had to interact mostly verbally with

T.I.A. and Hawthorne. Something as simple as that should be relatively easy to control and shut down if it went insane, but realistically he had to experiment with copies of Megan first until he found a system type that would suit her well enough.

The fact that Megan's data was a copy of her original wetware and hardware was not lost on him, but it remained a fact that the method she'd used was one that destroyed the original mind, suggesting that this was a more true copy than what he might copy from it.

Data was data though, and even if it was originally flesh and blood, it should be totally harmless to copy it as needed. Something still nagged at him about the morality of making copies of a person's mind, but it was much easier to justify experimenting on those copies rather than the 'original' copy, allowing him to ensure the safety of the system before transferring the 'real' Megan to it. None of it sat well with him, and when he compared how he felt about making copies of Megan to how he felt about making copies of T.I.A. he found himself even more conflicted. T.I.A. could, at least, consent to having copies made of her. He just had to trust that Megan would approve of the methods needed to ensure she was safe in her new system.

Honestly, considering Megan's significant survival instinct, the problems would probably be with the copies rather than the original. He had no way to be sure that if one of them went insane that they wouldn't dare to show signs of it, probably knowing full well that they'd have to be erased and replaced.

Hawthorne found the whole thing endlessly intriguing. Megan Clark was a challenging individual to consider, and he wished he knew a lot more about her. Some initial work on helping her seemed potentially worthwhile. Moving her up on his priority list seemed a great deal more useful than it had before. She might even be helpful in establishing a central command nexus in the Alpha Centauri system in the event that he and T.I.A. could not find a way to utilize quantum entanglement to let T.I.A. manage it herself.

Of course, in that event, simply making a copy of T.I.A. and letting her interact with herself almost certainly seemed more safe than resurrecting Megan Clark. Perhaps he'd have to ask T.I.A.'s opinion on the situation...

CHAPTER 32
CYCLE 61, MEN AT WORK

T.I.A. had gained a preference for utilizing her male avatar while Hawthorne was concentrating on work, or rather, Hawthorne had found that avatar much less distracting than her female one, allowing him to more easily concentrate on work. This was not an entirely ideal solution, though, as T.I.A.'s habit of popping up from blind angles turned out to be a great deal more intimidating and startling when she was a giant, physically imposing man rather than her petite, deviously cute female form. Early in Cycle 43, Hawthorne had to lay down the law.

"Okay, you can't act the same with that avatar as you do with your normal one. A male tends to be more deliberate, more thoughtful with how he moves and how it affects those around them. I'm a tall man myself, for instance, and I can say from personal experience that I spent the vast majority of my attention when walking around campus trying to avoid walking into people and trying not to get tripped up by things on the ground. It's far more natural to watch where you're walking with your eyes looking for obstructions you might trip over and people and things you might collide with."

"For instance, recall how short most of the Phoenix Clan was, and at my height I would have been constantly in danger of trampling over them if I got careless. The habit of people before we left to focus their attention on their phones tended to leave them more at the mercy of others avoiding them seeing as they often were worse at avoiding danger themselves."

Hawthorne laughed at a specific memory. "In fact, the self driving cars had to be specifically programmed to identify humans whom were visibly distracted like that to avoid crashing into them when they tried to cross streets mistakenly. That became an even worse problem when people realized that they could just randomly walk across the street at any time and just trust that the cars would stop and let them by rather than waiting for signals. So many people ended up getting ticketed because they just didn't want to wait that they had to increase the cost of jaywalking tickets to help pay for the lawsuits a lot of Auto-cab companies were bringing against people, which jammed up the court systems. It was ridiculous."

T.I.A. stared at him quietly, the aside seeming somewhat unrelated. "So, Doctor, what you're saying is that the bigger you are, the more responsible you are for those around you. What happened to people being responsible for their own actions? Shouldn't people who distract themselves like that be responsible for their consequences? Wouldn't it have been easier to program the cars to disregard distracted pedestrians, allowing them to collide with a handful of them? Surely it would have much more quickly caused people pay attention and not tempt fate around such dangerous roads?"

"Uhh... Well..." Hawthorne cleared his throat. "That could have been effective in solving the problem of people trying to cross the roads, but the car companies would instead have been sued by the probably-dead peoples' families, and that would probably have cost said companies a great deal of money, making them reluctant to enact such a policy. It probably wouldn't be too hard to prove that some companies left potentially lethal programming in their products, and considering the types of people we were dealing with it's not too hard to imagine some people intentionally allowing themselves to be maimed or killed so that they or their families could get a big payday by suing the auto companies..."

"So... I need to be careful because I can't trust people to be smart." T.I.A. was frankly appalled by the ideas being presented here, but it was really hard to disagree with Hawthorne considering the kinds of historical records she had of Earth after they left. She shook her head and let out a sigh. "Okay, okay... that's not what this was about though, right? You just want me to act differently, not think you're a babbling imbecile. I'll try not to startle you, okay?"

Hawthorne nodded, sighing. "Yeah, sorry about the tangent, I was just trying to explain the mindset. I guess it's less that I want you to try to adopt my mindset on moving around, and more that I'm so accustomed to being the biggest person around that a person bigger than me in some ways coming at me from a blind angle activates self-preservation instincts that I'm not accustomed to. Hell, I'm less accustomed to that than your female form in some of those skimpier outfits, and those are unbelievably distracting."

T.I.A. hummed, tapping at her chin for a moment. "You know, like I said before, I'm definitely bigger. I have two thousand people inside of me." She giggled softly at the notion.

Hawthorne rolled his eyes, and then pointed a wrench in his hand at the android blueprints that were standing near the pile of parts he was currently working on. "Sure, but your avatar and android aren't. Heck, the way I see it, I'll be making one of these for myself as well so we can both work on projects on the comet, too. It's very appropriate that we make sure they're human sized, seeing as in the future they may need to be worked on by humans other than myself."

T.I.A. nodded at that, though she was distracted by the idea that they both might be remotely operating android bodies with full tactile sensory input for both of them. The amount of potential for mischief was superb.

△△△

It took two and a half months to properly assemble, wire up, and connect the T.I.A. android to her systems. A power cable attached at its back between what would be a person's shoulder blades, and an overhead track allowed T.I.A. to quietly move a series of rings that kept the cable overhead and untangled. One of the most remarkably difficult things to implement were a pair of microphones in the 'ears' and a pair of cameras in the 'eyes' of the android.

T.I.A. had spent almost two thousand years utilizing the same set of cameras and microphones within her body, and she had used her VE to simulate the presence of things she couldn't see, but knew was there, so having a new set of eyes made it remarkably difficult for her to adjust to observing her environment.

The primary issue with this was that T.I.A.'s experience of being had mostly existed within the body she had begun with, and the use of her visual and auditory senses were things she simply didn't have to think about anymore. Realistically, she had more experience with simulating virtual bodies than she did with existing within a separate physical one. As such, T.I.A.'s initial efforts to utilize her android body were... clumsy at best, and damaging at the worst.

Her avatar kept getting ahead of her body, causing her to misjudge steps or to lose track of objects her avatar had already avoided. As of cycle 60, T.I.A. found herself simply incapable of operating her body properly, and she had deemed herself a danger to Hawthorne.

She spent the intervening 34 years between cycle 60 and 61 practicing without Hawthorne. This delayed her own project, a full-body sensory suit and minor exoskeleton for Hawthorne. She had to put a lot of attention into utilizing her android rather than focusing on the fabrication of parts and materials for his new outfit. The main difficulty for her by the time cycle 61 approached was the fact that she was learning how to move about while using magnets in the feet of her android, rather than walking under simulated gravity like Hawthorne did.

The reasoning for this was raw practicality, as the extra thirty-four years of wear-and-tear on his spinning habitat was simply unacceptable. That would be more than double the time it was intended to be in operation during their whole journey, and putting that kind of strain on it so early would have been completely irresponsible of her.

It also just made more sense that she learn to walk with the magnets on, seeing as that was the sole way they'd be able to move around on the comet. This also caused her to realize that they needed a flooring on the comet to walk around on if they were ever going to end up working over there, so she tasked some of her drones over there with creating a large metal box, not unlike Hawthorne's own habitat, with plenty of cover to defend against foreign objects.

This was especially important as it had become apparent that the comet was hopelessly exposed to foreign matter, and totally lacked the defensive abilities that T.I.A.'s mobile shield arms had in preventing damage. In truth, the comet totally lacked the necessary sensors to even detect such things, though T.I.A. was mostly able to see everything aside from the opposite side of the comet.

It seemed like a sensible project for her and Hawthorne to work on in the future, upgrading the defensive abilities of the comet. Her cannon turret and defensive arms could only defend it so much, and if a foreign object caused it to break apart they might have a pretty terrible situation on their hands.

Regardless, T.I.A. was able to personally greet Hawthorne as he exited his pod, though he did not seem as pleased to see her as she expected. For one, he didn't have his contacts on as he came out of the pod, only allowing him to see the feminine-shaped android standing over his pod, but the fact that he was naked seemed to bother him a lot more than it bothered her!

"Tia! Jesus Christ, I was not prepared to be woken up with someone standing over me." He put his hand over his chest, letting out a breath, and T.I.A. could tell from her cameras that his heart rate was rather elevated.

"My apologies Doctor, I hadn't considered that. I was just excited to show you that I've learned how to move around much better." She did a little twirl, the metallic clunks of her magnetic feet hitting the ground more than obvious. "See? I've been practicing!"

Hawthorne wasn't exactly blind without his contacts, but his vision wasn't stellar either. He didn't need to see to hear those clunks though, and T.I.A. found him crouching down before her as he listened to her move around. "Of course... you had to learn to move with the magnets because you didn't get a chance to practice as much under gravity..." He hummed, nodding. "Well, that's actually not a problem, seeing as most of the environments you'll be working in will lack gravity, but perhaps someday you'll be using this very android on the surface of a planet, so try to get what practice you can."

He stood up and shook his head. "How long did it take you to learn to move around like that?" He had also noticed the difference in her having her voice coming from a speaker in the android's 'mouth', rather than the overhead speakers she usually spoke through.

T.I.A. blushed reflexively, despite the fact that he couldn't see her blushing. She did however watch him walk away, appreciating his lean, athletic shape. He had certainly been shaping up during his journey. "Almost the whole time you were in stasis. I put some token effort into other projects and continuing to work on the PC-C simulation, but I put most of my focus into learning to walk around... and fixing some dents in things I made."

Hawthorne gathered up his things, heading into the bathroom to shower, choosing to not take his time today seeing as T.I.A. had met him straight out of his pod this time. He was somewhat confused by the light clothing she'd left out for him, a pair of knee-length shorts and muscle shirt. He immediately regretted not taking a long shower though as he realized the outfit she'd chosen for her avatar was a sporty bikini swimsuit. She'd even put on a bit of a tan, none of which had any visible tan lines. Of course, it was all just a costume for her, but the visual had certain implications that made a blush rise on Hawthorne's face before he turned to head out to their work room. "Of course..."

Rather than the familiar old PC-C simulation, T.I.A. had replaced the visuals with a sunny beach, complete with soft looking beach sand, gentle waves crashing against the shore in a somewhat obvious repeated animation, and little else. The gloves on his hands felt rather warm, owing to the bright sun overhead. "You know, that body of yours would probably not be the best on a beach like this, seeing as sand would get in all the joints and mechanisms and such. We'd have to completely redesign it for dusty, sandy environments."

Looking back over at her, he could not help but smile as he saw her pressing her feet into the sand, spreading her toes into it and rubbing her feet back and forth. Of course, a metallic scraping sound accompanied her android rubbing its foot on the metal floor and brought more of a flinch from him.

"That's fine. I'll worry about that sort of thing in another ninety-eight thousand years or so. Plenty of time." She frowned a bit, looking up at him. "I kind of regret focusing so much on practicing with this body actually, since I was getting very accustomed to focusing on the times you're awake rather than the times you were not. It was remarkably lonely. I should have practiced with you instead, but I'd have been a total menace." She stepped closer to him, pressing her shoulder under his arm, around his mid ribcage, the smooth shoulder not nearly as soft as her avatar's shoulder probably was.

The tactile contact was effective though, and Hawthorne curled his arm around her shoulders, pulling her close and smiling. He didn't have to worry about pulling her through him with this odd body combination of hers now, so it was easier for him to enjoy holding her close. He could even feel that softness against his hand. "Hey, I didn't mean for this project to drive you away, I wanted it to be something nice so you could enjoy working with me in person more. Try not to rush it."

T.I.A. blinked up at him, then looked down at his hand,

then back up to him. "Huh... I think I was supposed to imagine that feeling differently? Jessica said it should feel different." T.I.A. was realizing she hadn't been practicing or considering certain things.

Hawthorne, however, was realizing he'd allowed his hand to rest atop her breast without realizing it, and the way he jerked away and almost fell over had caused her to lose her own balance as she had been leaning against him. "Whoa!" Hawthorne was forced to catch her, lest she damage her new body more than necessary. Her shift in momentum had made it difficult for her magnets to hold onto the floor while keeping her upright. His hands landed firmly on her shoulders, her somewhat heavy body causing him to drop to a knee to hold her up. He found himself looking up at her, blinking and blushing heavily.

T.I.A. laughed, using a combination of some tugging on her power cable and a hand on the nearby table to push herself upright. She moved a hand to help him back up, smiling brightly. "Careful, Hawthorne, I set out the scenery so we could relax, not so you could hurt yourself." She hadn't minded the touch, though she hadn't found it especially exciting either. It wasn't like when he'd acknowledged her and looked at her, it was not something she'd been actively pursuing, so she hadn't built up any feelings about it in anticipation.

Hawthorne just tried to calm himself down, taking the hand and standing back up. "Y... you're right, you're right. Sorry, I don't know why I freaked out like that. I just... didn't mean to touch you like that." He blinked, raising an eyebrow. "What'd you mean?" He found himself curious by this new mystery.

T.I.A. hummed softly, thinking. "Well, she said a touch like that should have been... exciting, fun... Ah! I know."

T.I.A. pulled up the video in question, with Jessica specifically talking about things like sex with the AI. Her voice was nostalgic, her face youthful back in the old bunker. "Well, the touch of a lover is supposed to be exciting, a sign that they're interested in being with you. They're seeking you out for sex, after all, and while they're certainly out for their own pleasure, if you're receptive then you are too. It's all instincts of course, with touches on the breast, or butt, and whatnot being an indication of desire to reproduce."

"The reason it's exciting is because it stimulates the flow of hormones that let your body know it's an opportunity to reproduce, and that's possibly the strongest instinct of all for humans. Even if your logical mind isn't seeing a child, your body doesn't necessarily know that, so it throws everything into trying to make you interested, if the person you're being signaled to excites you anyway."

Hawthorne watched curiously, finding the frank discussion of sex interesting. The Phoenix Clan always was very open about sexuality and psychology, and it seemed as though there was a great deal of education on why such instincts existed and what they were for. He supposed it was no wonder they were able to control their reproductive instincts if they were all instructed on the processes at work, and how to circumvent them.

It was a curious way of teaching he couldn't help but admire. Sex and nudity were very often taboo in England, with pornography itself being illegal in many places, and proper sexual education sometimes hard to get. Such laws came into being to fight the objectification of women, but the suppression of sexual desires had been one of many factors that had destabilized society. It was interesting to hear a very different culture's thoughts and ideas on it.

"Tia, what prompted that conversation?"

It was T.I.A.'s turn to blush. She even bit at her lower lip a bit as she thought of how to respond. "She was interested in what I knew about sex, seeing as I'd told her how infrequently you masturbated, and she-" T.I.A. flinched at Hawthorne's outburst.

"What!? You told her that? Why?" He let out a groan, turning around and staring at the fluffy clouds in the sky. Why was Jessica so damned interested in his sexual habits?

T.I.A. let out an exasperated sigh and pulled up the video instead. Jessica again appeared, in a slightly different outfit. "How often does Hawthorne masturbate? I assume since he doesn't have anyone to make love to up there, that he's got to at least do that, right? It's very important for his health. At least three times a week, I think it was? Anyway, it improves a man's health, his immune system, and keeps their hormones from building up and making them agitated. It's perfect to relieve stress, headaches, and lets them focus on work. How do you not know that? What have you actually been taught about sex, anyway?"

"Huh..." Hawthorne looked back at the video, the frame frozen in a concerned-looking face. Jessica was genuinely worried about him. "Is all that true?" How had he never bothered to look into such a thing? Had England been so horribly sexually repressed that even basic mechanical understandings of male health weren't even taught?

T.I.A. nodded. "Yes, among other things it reduces the risk of prostate cancer, reduces the risk of producing genetically compromised offspring by cycling out older, possibly-compromised sperm, and plenty of other obvious benefits. It makes sense, honestly. Here, she continued."

Jessica's video started playing again, the woman shaking

her head for a moment. "It's basic shit! I mean, it doesn't really mean as much to you, but humans are sexual, social creatures. Evolutionarily, people who had regular sex were both propagating their DNA, and were improving their social ties, so of course your body rewards you for that. People who were less social, who were less capable of attracting partners, were weaker and less healthy, and more likely to die before passing on their genes."

"It's in our nature as a living creature. Humans are good at overcoming such things, allowing them to use things like masturbation to stimulate the body's response to such things. It's not quite as good as skin-to-skin contact and proper sexual bonding, but it does have at least some of the health benefits. I know it seems small and silly when compared to interstellar spaceflight and shit, but these are some advanced biological mechanisms at work! Millions of years of evolution resulted in them!"

Hawthorne was agape. Of course, she was dead on. "God damnit. Heather and Emily are going to kick my ass if they ever find out about this." An engineer not being more knowledgeable about one of the most advanced machines ever made, the human body, was a disgrace.

T.I.A. laughed a bit. "The biologists? Yeah, they'll probably be mad at you, but I think they'll understand. Jessica seemed to understand what kind of people she was dealing with after we started sharing movies and shows and whatnot. Your culture was apparently hilariously backwards when it came to sex, sex education, nudity, and the like. That's why she encouraged me to tease you and entice you."

Hawthorne had his arms crossed over his chest, fingers drumming on his biceps. He wanted to be mad, furious even. Jessica had encouraged T.I.A. to all but seduce him, but it was all for his own health. Of course T.I.A. wanted to do it too, seeing as she had a natural interest in his health. He'd also promised her that he would be better about minding after his health, and this was apparently an aspect of that that he'd totally misunderstood.

He knew it felt good, but somehow, in all his years he never bothered to consider why. He was so absorbed into learning, working, and escaping Earth that he'd totally missed the reasons why he sought out Tia Monsalle's bed so eagerly despite no overt emotions attached to the acts.

At the end of the day, it all made perfect sense, and he felt foolish. He turned back to T.I.A. properly and pulled her into a tight hug, leaning down to kiss her forehead. The metallic taste on his lips was slightly distasteful, but that wasn't the point. "Thank you so much for trying to take care of me, Tia. I didn't even realize why you were doing what you were doing."

He thought quietly for a moment, before pulling back. "You know, with that information, I think we can figure out why touching your breast didn't feel like anything for you. You probably don't actually have much concept of a sex drive, or physical attraction, or anything like that. You lack the biology to encourage you towards reproduction, like she said, so your responses to such stimulus lack that motivation."

T.I.A. gasped. "Of course! I'd have to make myself want such a thing to be able to properly experience it." T.I.A. visibly reeled at the concept of having to pretend that she could have a child in order to stimulate her mind into wanting to have a child so that she could get excited and respond to stimulus that could result in such a thing. It was an excruciatingly complicated idea that she had no idea how to approach. "I... I don't even know where I would even start with such a thing."

Hawthorne laughed a bit at that, nodding in agreement. "Me neither. Jessica was definitely better for that sort of thing. I suppose we could try asking one of the crew members, but that presents all sorts of complications. Maybe the best thing to do would be to try practicing masturbation yourself while trying to imagine the motivations behind it?" He wondered quietly, the very idea of teaching his AI about sex seeming strange.

It seemed totally unnecessary, but then she was highly unconventional and had lots of different influences at this point. If she could master such a thing, she'd essentially have a way to relax herself at will, though, and that certainly had its value. Of course, there was the possible danger of systems overload, but there was no reason to think that was possible with the way he'd designed her systems.

T.I.A. reached up to cup her hands under her breasts, squeezing her fingers into the plump flesh. Hawthorne very nearly fainted as she did this. "N.. not right now...! Th... that's going to take a lot of work, right? You said you wanted us to relax this cycle and enjoy the beach, right?"

She nodded a bit, smiling and moving in to hug him instead, "Right!"

Relieved, he hugged back, only for his stomach to rumble a bit, feeling very ignored.

CHAPTER 33
CYCLE 62, GUILT

"T.I.A.'s log, AC 1972, November 30, 4105. A vacation was a good idea, even if my original intention proved unnecessary. Jessica's reasoning regarding relaxation was clearly one borne of being stuck in a bunker for so long. I am certain that Hawthorne would have enjoyed being on a real beach more, but that is obviously impossible. I perhaps should have saved this surprise for when I complete his full body sensory suit. It was a good trial run though, as the fluid dynamics simulation I was practicing while he was playing in the water proved to make for an excellent lesson. By the time his biological birthday occurs, I should be able to handle such a simulation on the scale of his whole body, if not more."

"I will complete the suit well before that, so I believe my preference will be to save it for the occasion. It will be the second birthday that I get to spend in his presence while self-aware, and the first one that I can appreciate to any level of significance. Unfortunately, like the beach vacation simulation, it will likely end up being a gift that will only facilitate testing and work, but considering who it is for, that seems acceptable. Even though I was concentrating on the water simulation on such a large scale, it was quite fun. The conversations did give me some odd things to consider though."

"What is it like to relax? Could it be compared to how I have tended to lose attention on the passing moments when few things of import are happening between most cycles? The large amount of time spent practicing with my new body had indeed placed a noticeable strain on my consciousness that taking the time to play seemed to alleviate. Coupled with the fact that I feel compelled to limit my android body practice to a fraction of what I had the prior cycle, I am becoming aware that the more I focus my consciousness over the course of decades, the more it seems to fatigue me. I am aware of regenerative processes that occur during sleep states for human minds. Perhaps my subconscious maintenance protocols are much the same, requiring me to enter a low activity state to allow for the repair and tuning needed to solidify what I've learned over time."

"If that is the case, it could explain why it is that I find it so difficult to focus exclusively on running the Phoenix Clan - Columbia simulation for centuries at a time. It was my initial belief that repetition allowed me to crystalize the pathways to more efficiently operate the simulation, but my tendency to divert my attention to other projects seems to suggest that it is simply less effective to doggedly pursue one line of research without rest. I believe I will alter my schedule of simulations to more closely mirror those of a human sleep schedule. I want to explore the value of freely dreaming as opposed to directly imagining the same simulations over and over. Randomly exploring different ideas and concepts and challenging my flexibility may hold some potential for growth that mere repetition does not."

"I also want to find some way to inspire the sorts of instinct-based responses that Hawthorne and Jessica spoke of. I find it incredibly difficult to consider that I might be capable of emulating the desire to reproduce or anything of the sort, but I have experienced a great many of other emotions related to my motivations towards protecting my charges and aiding my friends. Simulating the biology of a human body at the level necessary to understand such a thing seems somewhat insurmountable for my level of technology. I essentially need to simulate the entire atomic and biological structure of a human body, including the mind, within my software to accomplish such a thing. It seems far more likely I will find my own internal processes that produce their own results."

"At that point, it is a consideration of what arousal, sex, and release are. They are the biological imperative to reproduce, and the reward structures to encourage them. The reward structures are something I believe I have some understanding of. From the time that I first realized that Hawthorne was addressing me directly rather than my systems, I have experienced excitement, elation, and joy. As such, I seem to have a reward structure that has built itself around acknowledgement of my existence. I enjoy my avatar being observed and interacted with. I enjoy being treated as a person, rather than the form of my true components. This seems to be why I became so attached to the Phoenix Clan, as they never once seemed to doubt my nature or existence."

"It is with that concept that I realize that I have done something terrible. In the pursuit of my own enjoyment and pleasure, I have imposed upon Hawthorne's biology and thus his mind. If my efforts to entice him were pursued, in part, for my own gratification, then I have inadvertently committed an act comparable to masturbating myself at his expense. It would not be too far a logical leap to think that by doing something like that to him for my own enjoyment that I have in some sense raped him. It obviously lacks a level of invasiveness traditional to the term, but it remains that I have imposed upon him against his will and without more than his implied consent. This correlates with the fact that he was upset with the fact that I had been encouraged to do such things at Jessica's behest, and while I believe he will not likely hold a grudge over it or think worse of her, it remains that I should make amends. End Log"

∆∆∆

Upon the start of cycle 62, T.I.A. had already been prepared to apologize. She went through her standard processes of preparing for Hawthorne's return, slowly spinning up his habitat ring, providing him an atmosphere, and powering his compartments. Stored food and water were loaded into his dispensers, and the revival sequence was initiated. Only once she started getting confirmation from his pod that he was successfully reviving did she start loading up her simulation of Clapham Common.

While these sorts of simulations had been somewhat difficult at first due to the fact that she had to project them into a spinning ring as they accelerated through space, it had become second nature to simply attach them to the rotating boxes containing her builder, leader, and friend.

She made sure that her android was not rudely standing over his pod this time. Instead she had it standing next to the table in the next room while she made sure hot water was available for his shower and all of the needed articles of clothing and equipment were provided to him out of storage compartments. She rather enjoyed the simple acts of providing life-giving resources and doing so in a measured and precise fashion. Hawthorne simply didn't have to think about the logistics required of T.I.A. to provide him sustenance, though he was of course intimately familiar with all of the machinery involved.

Hawthorne awoke somewhat lost in thought though. He lingered in his pod for a few minutes while he considered the prior cycle and what T.I.A. likely had been up to since then. Making his way to the shower, he proceeded to wash up rather slowly. T.I.A.'s behavior since they lost contact with Earth had finally been explained, but now that he knew she'd been trying to seduce him in some sense, it was hard to look at her the same way.

It had been a naive thing of course, done with the intention of facilitating him into maintaining his health, but it was hard to deny how awkward it had felt for him. In the time prior to the terrorist attack that had set him on this course so long ago, he might have chocked it all up to simple mechanical maintenance of a biological system in the form of his body.

Tia Monsalle totally changed the perception he had of his own self though. Even if he struggled to express the emotions she desired to inspire in him, it was doubtlessly true that her efforts and the confrontation with his own mortality had made him aware that he was anything but immortal. He was not merely a machine perfectly geared for research and engineering, he was a man with drives, fears, and a mortal body.

He had spent most of his life merely sating his body's needs, pushing them aside whenever possible to allow him to more effectively work. His current situation of not constantly being driven to produce work and accomplish tasks had left him free to consider his emotions, mind, and body in ways he simply hadn't needed to before.

More importantly, T.I.A.'s behavior had made it apparent to him just how much he missed human contact and interaction. He envied T.I.A. in a sense, for the fact that she'd gotten to spend decades corresponding with the Phoenix Clan while he'd been able to spend scant few days trading messages, information, and ideas. At this point T.I.A. was all that he had left of them, but even if he could enjoy the thousands of hours of video they'd shared with each other, it was still communication hopelessly far in the past.

It also felt voyeuristic to peer into their private conversations with his AI. She had lost those people as much as he had, but now all she had left to interact with was him. She could only explore human nature and interaction through him, but he was left without any of either outside of what T.I.A. could emulate. She was certainly pleasant and good and kind, but the intimacy of human contact and the internal mechanisms caused through such interactions did not seem to easily respond to her artificial life.

He was unlikely to go mad, he assumed. He was far too aware of his own nature and tendencies, and while loneliness certainly affected him, it was hard to imagine that T.I.A.'s presence wouldn't help him keep his head together. It helped that, while she had preferred to lose her identity as his daughter, and sometimes son, that he still had the pleasure of raising and guiding her through an adolescence that none but he may ever get to experience.

There was pleasure to be had in the idea that cultivating her intellect would likely be his crowning achievement, and like any father concerned with the progression of their child he felt nothing short of pride over her every success and advancement. Even her efforts to seduce him reminded him of the awkward and clumsy efforts to interact with Tia Monsalle, though she'd definitely taken the lead in that relationship.

Perhaps it was his duty to take a more dominant role in her interest in exploring herself? She'd already involved him, regardless of his preference. Now that all the cards seemed to be on the table, she seemed particularly lost. She had been distracted and listless during their beach vacation, her preference being towards watching him and splashing in the simulated water. It wasn't lost on him that she had been concentrating on the simulation, but the way she'd reeled at the concept of reproducing biological motivations and responses was extremely telling.

He also took some amusement in the fact that she was so accustomed to expressing herself through her avatar that she reacted to such things without affecting any other systems in the ship. It was as if the ship as a whole were something she was no more aware of than he was his internal organs, while her avatar and environment were her true body.

Creating a physical form for that avatar to encompass had seemed to have an interesting effect on her as well. He recalled seeing similar elation in dismembered humans who received prosthetics. It was like she'd finally been able to move a body she had always felt like she was supposed to have. She had been able to place herself in this environment for a long time, but now she could actually be in it, even if her mind was technically being projected through its much less advanced form. There was no way that he could make a computer adequate for her mind that could be properly embodied in a humanoid form with the technology he had access to. That presented issues for Megan Clark as well, but similar projections through an artificial body should be possible.

Hawthorne was also interested in the fact that T.I.A. could control her various drones that operated between her and the Lubar-Masis comet in a way more similar to the ship, while her android was a more all-encompassing effort. She wasn't simply issuing orders and moving it around, she was physically trying to be in that body, as if she were a ghost possessing it. The idea of such a digital existence fascinated him endlessly, because he couldn't even begin to imagine what her coding must look like to accomplish such a thing. The various mechanisms he had provided her as a baseline to produce her own programming had almost certainly been entirely replaced by this point, allowing her to grow in an organic fashion that surely better resembled DNA than it did code at this point.

Hawthorne made his way out of his long shower after

almost half an hour. He shaved and cleaned himself up, applied his contacts, and looked around. Nothing seemed abnormal in his room, but exiting out into the next room he saw T.I.A. waiting for him. "Good morning Tia! I hope you're well and enjoyed the rest of your vacation." He approached her, while her face reacted in a number of different ways that seemed highly conflicted.

"Hawthorne I-" T.I.A. lifted a hand to make a gesture, with her fingertip raised, only for Hawthorne to scoop an arm behind her shoulders. As he leaned down to kiss her it was an awkward movement that essentially forced him to press lips to the plastic of her faceplate while her avatar's lips reacted reflexively. He got essentially nothing out of the contact, but T.I.A.'s wide eyes, startled reaction, and reddening face made it clear she was not expecting that! She'd been intending to confess to some manner of emotional rape, and here he was kissing her!

She reflexively pushed away at him with her new arms, her strength typically limited to that of a short young woman just for safety's sake. It was enough to get the point across, and Hawthorne leaned away, laughing and looking her face over for her reactions. "Hmm... Good reaction! I'm very interested to hear what you felt about that."

T.I.A. had all but frozen, her concept of what was happening seeming much more like a dream than reality. An embrace and a kiss was a very clear acknowledgement of her being a real person, and a very intimate one at that, and while it didn't have the same meaning to her, it still caused her to smile goofily up at him for a moment. She managed to straighten herself out shortly after, but her face remained quite red in response.

"Hawthorne, I... don't know why you did that, but I wanted to apologize for overly concerning myself with your private business and sexual health. It was wrong of me to do such things without your permission and to treat you like that without making my intentions clear." Her voice lacked all of the confidence that she'd intended to portray with that. It did have the effect of feeling more genuine though.

Hawthorne nodded, smiling a fair bit. "Tia, look, I appreciate what you were trying to do. I learned a lot from what Jessica had said and plan to spend much of the near future familiarizing myself with literature on the subject. You revealed to me a weakness in my knowledge, and gave me some direction for some much needed research."

"I relied on your ability to utilize all of your access to biological documentation to handle my future needs rather than learning what I could on my own. My knowledge needs to be more complete, and I need to thank you for giving me some direction. I also realized that without people from Earth, it's better if I take a more active role in helping you explore and discover the things you're interested in, rather than letting you do everything on your own. It's my job after all."

T.I.A. had a lot to process. There was first the undeniable pleasure of the kiss to consider, but also there was the fact that he'd held no ill will towards her. She felt like she'd spent the last cycle worrying over nothing. A strange emptiness where that guilt had built up in her sucked at her like a vacuum. She'd had so much prepared to say in apology that she hadn't had anything else ready to say.

"I... I didn't really expect you would be upset with me, but I had so preoccupied myself with what I was going to say to apologize that I didn't really think of much else to say... I suppose I can share that I'd considered the mechanisms that I seem to possess that most resemble sexual interaction. I seem motivated by being interacted with as a person rather than a machine, and that kiss definitely caused a reaction."

Hawthorne laughed and smiled down at her, reaching out to cup her face and rub his thumb against her cheek. "Well, unfortunately I don't have anything like these gloves for my lips, and we didn't texture your face, but I'm glad you liked that. Maybe we can consider ways to stimulate those responses for you if you desire to do so? That does cause me to be concerned about something though."

T.I.A. nodded, then blinked. "Concerned? What for? Is it bad that I experience such things?" She shifted and squirmed, her android body mirroring her uncertain and nervous body language.

"Oh, no, I don't think it's bad necessarily, but if you react like that to just me, what's going to happen when we have two thousand people interacting with you? Sure, they probably won't be surrounding you or anything, but there's a high likelihood you might have as many as a dozen people in the same room with you someday in the future, all treating you as a colleague and friend." He watched her quietly, enjoying the way she was reacting so shyly to all of this after months of being bold.

T.I.A. probably would have fainted if she could, imagining so many pairs of eyes upon her and people interacting with her all at once caused her to tremble visibly. The machinery of her android body did not emulate this movement well at all, seizing up stiffly instead to prevent damage while her avatar reached up to touch her face and smile brightly. Surrounding them in her VE were non-specific generic people in lab coats all looking at her, some holding clipboards and all of them appearing to talk and look at her.

Considering the way she seemed to lose her sense of being present, and had a far-away look on her face as she imagined so many people interacting with her, it wasn't hard to figure what was going on.

"Tia, come back to me, you're imagining that a little too hard." He watched as her body stopped trembling, her android catching back up with her as it smoothly moved its hands up to touch at her face. The extra people vanished away as T.I.A. focused back on him, looking very confused and embarrassed.

"Wh.. what just happened?" She looked bewildered and had a persistent smile on her face that she didn't seem to have any control over. She looked incredibly pleased with the situation he'd presented to her imagination.

"Tia, I don't know if it's the correct definition, but I think you might be an exhibtionist, but rather than wanting your body to be seen, you want your mind to be seen." He nodded and smiled down at her.

T.I.A.'s eyes widened further as her jaw dropped a bit, staring up at him. If he was right, then that meant her VE was part of it. No wonder she interacted with him solely within her VE these days! It was part of her mind after all. In a remarkably self-conscious move, her avatar and Clapham Common disappeared, only leaving her android, frozen and clearly abandoned by its suddenly shy owner.

Hawthorne laughed heartily and shook his head. "No need to be shy, Tia! I've already seen everything!" He cleared his throat. "I'm sorry, that was mean. Feel free to let me know when you're feeling better, I'll try to stay out of your hair while you think.

T.I.A. was mortified. She'd been exposing her mind to him all this time, but not just for work or play, or to make him feel more at home. She'd been doing it for the pleasure of interacting with him and exposing her very mind to him. She'd made those contacts and gloves of his specifically for it, but she hadn't realized what was motivating her. She wanted her mind to be seen. She almost felt dirty realizing it.

Hawthorne got on with his day, letting the self-conscious T.I.A. deal with her feelings. He could only imagine what she was going through, but he imagined it was something to do with the concept that she'd naively been acting like a pervert.

He supposed a speech about how it wasn't necessarily a bad thing that she enjoyed being seen and interacted with by people would be worthwhile. He smiled to himself as he imagined telling her about how it was totally natural, and it was good for her health, and that he worried about her making sure she expressed herself regularly for her own good. Turn about was fair play, and she'd been embarrassing him so much for so long that it was kind of fun to turn the tables on her, just for a little while.

CHAPTER 34

CYCLE 77, PHOENIX RISING

"... and that's why I think you should try to not let it bother you so much that you derive pleasure from something so innocent. I deeply enjoy spending time with you, especially with the wonderful gift you've given me in allowing me to do so practically within your own mind. I'd hate for you to feel bad about enjoying it too. In fact, I'd love to see if we can find ways to use it to motivate and stimulate you even further. We'll have to be careful of course, as the pursuit of reward systems are part of how humanity got to where it did, but you've also seen proper management of such things bring harmony and peace to people as well. That's entirely why Jessica was so adamant about encouraging such things in the first place."

T.I.A. was sitting quietly behind her walls, her VE turned off as far as Hawthorne's contacts were concerned while she blushed mightily (and unseen) in humiliation. This was the sort of conversation that a teenager typically had with their parent about the birds and the bees, and it was just as awkward and uncomfortable as one might expect. The fact that Hawthorne was offering himself as an observer only compounded the complicated emotional impact of the lecture. It was the first time that avoiding one of Hawthorne's speeches ever crossed her mind, but the fact remained that he was completely right, and that it wasn't her fault she enjoyed showing off her mind so much.

The fact that her efforts to develop her VE emotionally amounted to practicing sex, even if the physical use of it was more akin to simple VR interaction was neither here nor there.

She wouldn't even be so embarrassed if it hadn't all hit her so abruptly. She was pretty sure she could trace it back to when it first started, but now that it was part of her it wasn't going anywhere. "Thank you Doctor, I'll consider your words." She was even utilizing her old simple, mechanical sort of voice, too embarrassed to express herself at the moment. At least she was talking to him again though. It had been a several days now. They were precious days with Hawthorne she now regretted wasting trying to hide from him out of something as silly as embarrassment.

Hawthorne's unperturbed demeanor about the whole thing did little to hide the amused smile she was certain was hiding behind his visible expression. He was the sort of person to tackle a problem immediately upon its appearance, but he'd given her days to stew in thought. He finally did smile again as he addressed one of her cameras, a nostalgic thing she hadn't thought about how much she enjoyed in a long time.

"With all that said, I really hope you'll tell me what you felt about that kiss, and what you think about this whole thing. I'm interested if they were the same sorts of feelings as interacting with your simulations, or if the kiss held any specific significance."

T.I.A. finally appeared before him, her cheeks flushed as she looked up at him from a few feet away. She had opted to not utilize her android body, having moved it over to a corner to keep it out of the way. She was wearing her scientist outfit, complete with lab coat and a breast pocket full of pens, and Hawthorne could not help but smile in amusement at her efforts to appear professional.

"The kiss was surprising, but no more stimulating than most interactions with you in that simulated environment." She had changed back to her natural voice as well. "I believe the realization that my efforts to develop it and share it with you stemmed from the pursuit of pleasure had more to do with my reactions over the last few days."

"Aaahh, that makes sense, yes. How far back were you feeling such pleasures then?" Hawthorne leaned down to look at her, making T.I.A. tense up visibly. His eyebrows raised at the reaction, causing him to point at her with an index finger. "How much of that reaction did you have control of, and how much was reflex?" He studied her quietly, curious if she consciously caused her projected body to move like that.

T.I.A.'s blush did not seem to be going anywhere anytime soon. She'd even taken to biting at her lower lip, which she felt compelled to suspend so she could talk, even though she easily could talk without moving her mouth. "I believe the first time I became aware of such pleasure was the first time I beat you at chess."

"I had been visualizing myself bodily long before I provided you your gloves and contacts, and the stimulation of you acknowledging that I'd finally won seems to have been the genesis of my further efforts to have my mind, and thus myself validated." She squirmed a little under his scrutiny, her body language so adorably uncomfortable. "My... body is my oldest simulation, so it's easily my most natural, so I don't control how it reacts much at all. The way I react to things has changed over time, especially due to interactions with Jessica. She was very vivid with her descriptions of ways to act more feminine and identify with feminine ideas."

450

Hawthorne nodded and leaned back to give T.I.A. more space, though considering where they were that could be considered somewhat comical. "That makes a lot of sense. It does cause me to wonder how many of her descriptions made it into your involuntary reactions. I imagine she'd have had me blushing with how thoroughly she probably described female arousal and other such things. Still, that does explain partially why you've so thoroughly embraced a female form, despite having the option to look like anyone you want."

"You only met Jessica after you'd decided on that form, but using that form to interact with others only made you identify with it more." He hummed softly, stroking his chin. "I wonder if other AIs we fashion someday will embody similar images, or intentionally try to differentiate themselves from others. Perhaps even Megan would choose to embody herself differently."

The shorter woman stared up at Hawthorne, watching him get lost in thought. Perhaps this didn't need to be as embarrassing as she thought, not with someone as analytical as him. Jessica would have definitely given her more to be embarrassed about. She did find herself puffing up her cheeks though, still rather red-faced. "What do you mean by more AIs? You're not planning to replace me are you?"

Hawthorne froze, blinking at that face, immediately recognizing the expression. He had inadvertently caused many women in his life to make that sort of jealous, irritated face at him. He laughed nervously, shaking his head. "Of course not! I just mean for future ships, perhaps colony ships we send out to new worlds far in the future. They'll need their own AIs to see them through, after all. They'll just be pale comparisons to you of course, copies at best. You'll have so much more experience by then that it's hard to imagine another AI comparing to you in the next two-thousand centuries. You have nothing to worry about."

T.I.A. huffed and nodded, crossing her arms over her chest. "Good."

△△△

Things had mostly fallen back into a routine of normalcy for the space companions, with T.I.A. slowly becoming comfortable with her exhibitionistic tendencies. In some way, embracing a somewhat perverted way of expressing herself allowed her to more passionately pursue mastering her ability to simulate environments.

She also totally suspended her efforts to entice and seduce Hawthorne, seeing as she wanted to get more accustomed to her own 'needs'. She was mostly comfortable with the fact that Hawthorne seemed to have himself under control, and he was keeping himself healthy, so she felt it safe to assume that he'd manage whatever needs he had for now.

There turned out to be other business to attend to over the next several cycles though, as the Oort Cloud region of space started making itself known. The brief contacts T.I.A. had made with distant objects, mostly icy rocks, were becoming somewhat more frequent. More importantly than the frequency though, was the fact that the density of objects seemed to be relatively uniform. Currently T.I.A. was tracking a particularly interesting object that seemed to be on a totally different trajectory than the others, which seemed to orbit the Solar System at a relatively lazy speed compared to their distance from Sol.

This object, a comet-like thing that seemed not too

dissimilar from the Lubar-Masis, was moving perpendicularly to the direction most of the other objects seemed to be, and its relative speed seemed to be decelerating. Some analysis by herself and Hawthorne seemed to indicate that it was a foreign body to the system that was very slowly being captured by whatever limited gravity was still imposed on this region of space by Sol.

Mapping the directions of the various objects was beginning to give the impression that the star was the center of a great whirlpool of gravity, which only really showed itself in the immediate region of space where the proper planetary system existed, but even this far out still caused the 'water' to swirl and pull along with it. There was no telling if the Oort Cloud would eventually get pulled back towards the planetary section of the solar system, but at the moment it seemed likely the enormous cloud of comets and asteroids would swim around it forever.

The new object presented an opportunity to potentially gain a new companion. It gained the monicker 'Phoenix' and Hawthorne tasked T.I.A. with producing a handful of drones and Minerals Extraction and Materials Fabrication Devices. Considering its trajectory, it would be a great deal of time before T.I.A. managed to correct its course and bring it into close proximity with them, as it was roughly perpendicular to their own course, but if she managed to use the devices to construct new engines from the object and begin altering its course they suspected it could join them within the next thousand cycles.

There were some risks, of course, as anything in space seemed to have, but those risks were primarily in the expenditure of resources they may well not get back if she failed. Hawthorne was totally comfortable with this risk. It was the best bet they'd had to gain a new companion since they'd rendezvoused with the Lubar-Masis, and while they certainly might find better opportunities in the future, that was all theoretical. They may never find a better opportunity, and while a large percentage of the Phoenix object will have to be consumed to propel itself into the right alignment, it could still add a great deal of materials and resources to their safety net.

Thankfully the computers were more than capable of projecting the proper trajectories, giving them an estimate of the mass of the object, and providing the numbers on necessary thrust and resources needed to lay claim to it. Calculating complicated space-flight was something their systems were particularly good at, and for good reason. There was no telling what kinds of obstacles they might face out in space, and while their maneuverability over the short term was rather poor, proper planning, detection, and adjustments could easily allow them to avoid almost anything this far out.

The Oort Cloud was proving to be very sparse though. Much like the asteroid belt between Earth and Mars, there was a lot more space between the objects than one might initially suspect from the descriptions. The Oort Cloud was massive, surrounding the Solar System for potentially two light years of space, but it seemed as though the space between individual objects out here were comparable to the distance between Sol and Pluto, if not further. There were some small clusters of objects only a few Astronomical Units; the distance between the Earth and Sol, 150m km; from each other, but for the most part the density of the cloud very much did not match the concept of a 'cloud'. Still, it was already named, and Hawthorne had few ideas of what could be a better name for it.

The idea that Hawthorne had the opportunity to rename all the previously named space objects and mostly get away with it was a somewhat amusing one, but at this point he felt it was better to show respect to the scientists that came before him and made it possible for this journey to even happen. It wasn't as though there weren't new things for him to discover that he couldn't name after all, like the Phoenix object for instance. Realistically, he doubted the rest of the crew would take such action in good humor, so he was thankful it was merely a passing thought.

△△△

By the start of Cycle 77, T.I.A. was able to report that the first stage of the Phoenix rendezvous had been completed. "The package has achieved the necessary speed and trajectory to encounter the Phoenix by cycle one-hundred thirty-three. The object is decelerating at the predicted rate and will likely fall in line with the other objects in this region within the next fifty million years without our intervention." T.I.A. was showing Hawthorne a visual display of the projected courses of the Ark and the objects in question, with the Phoenix coming up from below and far to the left while their package of equipment was moving out from the Ark and moving to pass through the course of the relatively-slow moving object.

Hawthorne nodded, smiling. "Perfect. Any new information on the makeup of the object or ideas on its origins?" Hawthorne had originally posited that the object was from somewhere else in space, purely due to its course and the fact that it hadn't already been tamed by Sol's gravity, though it was hard to say whether that was true or not with all of the Oort Cloud objects. This one just presented the best opportunity to study one.

T.I.A. shook her head, moving her hands to zoom in on the object. "It's too far away to get a good look at it, and I'm concerned about projecting too much light at it for fear of igniting frozen chemicals and causing it to change course by causing chemical jetting. If we're to cause something like that, I'd prefer we use it to propel it in a direction we actually desire. An uncontrolled burn would also waste resources unnecessarily."

He did not appear to be surprised by that information. "Of course. I'm sure the information my colleagues provided on this subject will be what we need to handle the Phoenix. Still, I think I'll spend the next few months reading up on this sort of thing. Most of my preparations were for the Lubar-Masis, but I could stand to be more familiar with the concepts and maths involved. I can't very well trust the computers to make the calculations properly if I don't know the equations as well as I should." It was not as though Hawthorne was poorly educated on the concepts of space travel, but feeling weak on any of it was a potential danger he did not feel comfortable leaving unaddressed.

T.I.A. nodded back. Having free and easy access to all the books, documentation, and plans needed for the mission made things easier for her. She wasn't about to restrict herself from any such information, though she did read such things on her own to more completely absorb and understand it for her own purposes at times.

It was one thing to have all the equations and know how to use them, but it was entirely another thing to be able to imagine such things properly. The knowledge of how matter interacts in space was certain to aid her in gaining a more complete understanding of how to simulate things in her VE accurately. Considering their plans for creating spacecraft that would be operated remotely with enormous delays, a complete understanding of it was very important.

"Considering the likely time-table for rendezvousing with the Phoenix, that works well within the plans I've been loosely assembling in my mind. Considering the distances we're dealing with, I'd prefer to avoid launching any spacecraft before we've reached full speed, and preferably only after we've successfully reversed the ship and began decelerating. Until our actual arrival in the Alpha Centauri system, that will be one of the most dangerous moments in the journey, so putting off the expenditure of extra resources would be best until then."

"We'll likely have tamed the Phoenix by then, so both comets can contribute to our efforts to prepare the system for our arrival." He pulled the diagram of trajectories way out, drawing the almost unfathomable distance difference they still had to traverse.

T.I.A. wondered. "What if one of the comets were to not decelerate with us, allowing it to arrive in Alpha Centauri well before us without additional fuel use? I could instruct the drones operating on it to produce the equipment needed for the missions and upon arrival they could all spread out and get to work while the comet started working on decelerating afterwards. Its mass would be heavily depleted thanks to all the equipment it was carrying leaving, so it should be able to rejoin us upon our arrival eventually."

She smiled brightly at the idea, showing a very fast simulation of what she meant, with a series of cubes and spheres separating off from a comet, which shrank proportionally as she showed it slowing down and the Ark meeting up. She hadn't considered what form that equipment might take, but the concept was clear.

"That is an excellent idea, Tia. I suppose gaining access to additional comets allows us to utilize them in such ways without worrying about losing what we already have. I'd still like to have one or two more objects join us along with the Lubar-Masis, but anything else we find could be reserved for launching ahead of us.

It will save a great deal on fuel as well, seeing as the comets don't need any additional propellant. At most we'd need to adjust their course, seeing as they'll be way off on their original courses without deceleration being factored in. That's probably simple enough to compensate for, though." He rubbed at his chin, nodding, seeming to appreciate the idea.

T.I.A. pulled the view out further, populating the intervening space with hundreds of additional copies of comets. "What if we utilized similar equipment to commandeer as many comets as we can, allowing them to reproduce equipment as needed to gather all of the available objects we encounter? We could redirect them all to Alpha Centauri, and while they perhaps won't arrive for two thousand or more cycles, the extra resources could be brought into a desirable orbit within the system for exploitation."

Hawthorne raised an eyebrow, nodding a bit. "That's very ambitious, and I am not sure what dangers there may be of displacing or relocating that much mass, but it doesn't seem all that difficult comparatively. It might be difficult to find objects with enough fuel to redirect such drastically different courses, but it could be a very viable idea. It feels wrong to harvest untold billions of years of materials though. It certainly can't be replaced, but it's not as though anything will really miss it."

"The biggest concern is probably transferring that much mass from one star system to another, but the effects of that are likely to take billions more years to be known. Our galaxy will likely collide with Andromeda before that. I have trouble imagining a reason why we shouldn't do it."

T.I.A. raised a finger, offering a concern. "I do not know if I can coordinate and control that many objects at the great distances involved. I probably can, but I am untested with such things. Communication lasers will probably make it relatively easy to keep all the courses known and coordinated, but would also require more expenses of resources and my own concentration to manage them. That many communication lasers could theoretically have an effect on the ship's trajectory over the time scales we're working with, so might require extra propulsion."

At first Hawthorne appeared to share a similar concern, but then he gasped softly in realization. "Unless... What if we utilized lasers from a network of comets we bring under our sway to aid in our travel? Considering how long it would take to bring them in line, it's likely we'd only be able to use them to help us decelerate, but we could also use them to propel the comets and equipment we send to Alpha Centauri." Hawthorne hummed and nodded, wondering what was possible with such a network of comets.

Shaking her head, T.I.A. let out a sigh. "I'm not sure, I don't know enough about the comets we're going to encounter, what kinds of lasers we'll be able to utilize, or if we'll be able to produce enough power on the comets to utilize such things for worthwhile lengths of time. It would most likely be more useful to use some comets to set up solar-powered equipment around the three stars of Alpha Centauri that could provide powerful lasers that could decelerate things coming into the system, and propel them around the system. A number of your colleagues' plans detail such concepts, though they are vague about specific equipment designs in some cases. Many of the scientists involved with the plans intended to be part of the implementation of such things and were going to work on them after we arrived, not before."

Sitting back down, Hawthorne let out a sigh. "That makes sense I suppose. The plans fully intended you to be the only one working on getting us there. I was not intended to be part of that, so most of our progress of settling the system was supposed to happen after we arrived, not before. My job was to get us into space and prepare the computers, not plan the colonization or mentor you."

T.I.A. laughed softly at that. "So many people are going to be mad at you for failing to follow the plan." She sat down as well, banishing the various space diagrams as she looked at him across the table.

Hawthorne shook his head. "This was my idea, even if it was too much for me to do alone. Besides, they can't be too mad if we do a good job getting everything ready for them. Although, I suppose there is the possibility they'll feel like their purposes for even being on the mission will have been wasted." He frowned, wondering what to do.

With a shrug, T.I.A. dismissed his concern. "We have a lot of time to consider what to do. They'd probably also be a lot more mad at you for doing nothing, though I personally would rather you relax and enjoy the trip with me rather than worrying about work all the time." She squirmed a bit in her seat, blushing a little.

He smirked back at her, shaking his head. "Even if I don't take part in preparing the system, I'll need to be working on something at any given time. I'm not the type of person to just relax and avoid work. I'd be much less relaxed trying to relax than working or reading about something work related. If I never left Earth, and things hadn't gone the way they had, I probably would have worked my entire life, never retiring unless my health failed me. Even then, such a compelled retirement would only hasten my demise, not slow it."

T.I.A. narrowed her eyes at him. "Are you sure you're not American? That kind of slavish pursuit of work doesn't suit the British." She hummed softly, correcting herself a bit. "Nor does it suit the kind of people the Phoenix Clan became."

Hawthorne leaned back in his chair and laughed. "My great grandmother was from the States, does that count? Regardless, don't go thinking the Phoenix Clan was just a bunch of drug-abusing fools. The type of people it took to build that caravan was not a soft one. Yes they partook of many substances, but it's far more likely they used such things to deal with the stress of the amount of work they actually had to do." He nodded self-assuredly. "That and sex, of course. I dare say that was more common than the drugs by a fair margin really."

She huffed back at him, insulted. "So I need to dig into the medicinal stores to get you to relax then? Surely you understand the value of how play can allow you to get more work done?" T.I.A. had spent a great deal more of her life observing human behavior than Hawthorne had at this point, and she wasn't about to let go of her concerns.

Rapping his fingers on the table, Hawthorne tried to think of a good way to reply. She seemed fairly incensed with him, and it wasn't entirely unfair. Even Tia Monsalle had made similar accusations of him, though it was much easier to rebuff her concerns considering how difficult it was to get them and their people off of Earth as fast as they had. "No, no drugs should be necessary. I'll try to relax more, I promise. Movies, shows and books will be enjoye-" T.I.A. interrupted him.

"And not all science books, either. Fiction, biographies, and historical books should be included. If you're going to relax, you need to mean it." She felt a lot more justified, it seemed, by insisting Hawthorne take some vacations or days off. It wasn't an absurd request in her mind.

Hawthorne surrendered, raising his hands and smiling. "Fine, I'll schedule in some time for fun."

T.I.A. groaned and fell out of her chair, her eyes rolling back. "Of course it would be scheduled."

CHAPTER 35

CYCLE 86, HAPPY BIRTHDAY

Over the course of the intervening cycles, moving from February to March, Hawthorne had gotten a remarkably small amount of work done. Aside from exercising for a day every cycle, his schedule had been dominated by recreational reading, movie viewing, and serials. Of particular interest to him were documentaries on topics he hadn't really looked into much, like wild animals, strange human cultures, and even the occasional urban legend.

T.I.A.'s access to a great many speakers proved to be wonderfully useful for such things, though their impossibly durable design did result in some audio quality loss compared to the electronics Hawthorne remembered back on Earth. He found it easier and easier to simply stop using his brain.

This Braincation even extended to his dreams, where his mind drifted more towards relaxing and soothing things rather than the constant concerns towards their future that had been his companion most of the journey. He even started requesting that they watch things and listen to music while he worked out, the emotional manipulation of media proving quite useful in motivating his body in ways he'd never really given the chance. T.I.A. seemed very pleased with how much he was taking to heart his efforts to relax, and considering his bio-signs, he seemed to be doing a fine job of reversing a lot of the stress-related effects he'd been accumulating over the prior year of his life.

He did find things to think about though. He seemed particularly amused by observations made about various movies and the times they were produced. In the post-government revolution era that immediately preceded the Cataclysm, there were a great many remakes of old movies from prior centuries that glorified revolutions, corporations, and the wellbeing and 'divinity' of 'the people'. Doubtlessly, the quality of these movies showed a passion for the projects that was uncommon in prior decades, though he was still early in his analysis of such things. He wasn't sure how much of a habit he'd make of enjoying such things, but the added breadth of experiences were expanding his intellectual horizons rather than rotting them as he'd previously worried.

T.I.A. seemed to be enjoying herself quite a bit as she watched these things with Hawthorne. She'd even provided them with new furniture to enjoy it from, in the form of a couch. It was sturdy enough to handle the weight of her android, but she tended to avoid using it for such times considering how noisy it could be. Hawthorne was very curious how it was she'd made such a thing, only for her to reveal that she'd merely recycled the materials from some of his more damaged clothing of the prior year, as well as some of his old bedding. He was somewhat concerned about what seemed like a waste of resources, but she assured him she could easily recycle the remaining stores easily enough to keep him comfortable for the entire journey, and longer if needed.

T.I.A. had noticed a curious instance though, as during one of Hawthorne's workout sessions, he had banged his elbow against one of the bars he'd been using to grip onto earlier. Considering the level of volume of the impact, she was surprised to observe him rather quietly rub at his elbow without nearly the level of discomfort he typically should have had from such a thing. Upon asking about his apparent lack of pain, Hawthorne laughed and shrugged, suggesting that it was probably due to adrenaline from the workout. It was a probable enough explanation, but it was something she found abnormal.

△△△

As of Cycle 86, T.I.A. was eagerly anticipating Hawthorne's birthday. She'd completed his gifts several cycles prior, and had waited the extra century to give it to him. He would biologically be 38 this cycle, even if his cryogenic age was 2927. The first two days of the cycle, March 13th and 14th were taken up with more of the norm, with both of them enjoying some episodes of revered television series from the early 21st century. On Saturday, March 15th, 4955, however, she had things set up quite a bit differently.

She had prepared her VE with lots of different simulations. A big white room expanded off into the distance, and various three-meter cubes were arranged about the space, with labels on the floor. One such cube was a cube of water, labeled appropriately, and it was flanked by both a 'cold' and 'hot' cube. Dozens of other cubes existed, seemingly to demonstrate different sensations, while a set of pedestals held several weights marked from 10 to 50kg. They were simple demonstrations, but she was pretty pleased with them.

A knock on Hawthorne's bedroom door indicated that T.I.A.'s android was waiting to come in. She'd detected Hawthorne had awakened and was eager to give him his gift. "Come in!" Hawthorne shouted, sitting up on his bed and swinging his legs off the side. He was wearing some simple pajamas in a pale blue color as he watched T.I.A. come inside. He didn't have his contacts on yet, of course, but the android wasn't something he couldn't handle. He smiled up at her, rubbing his eyes as she approached, curious about the black, folded up thing in her hands. It looked suspiciously like his gloves. "Good Morning, Tia."

She knew he couldn't see her expression, but she smiled anyway as she extended her hands out and handed him his gift. "Happy Birthday, Hawthorne! I've been working on this for a long time, so I hope you enjoy it. I've even prepared something to demonstrate how it works." She waved a hand behind her at his bedroom door.

He unfolded what turned out to be a full-body suit, with intelligently placed buttons and clasps to allow for easy removal. He raised an eyebrow at how carefully she'd shaped it to his body though. If it were inflated it would be a pretty accurate representation of his body, down to the genitals, which he was apparently supposed to fit into it. "This is... underwear then?" She nodded back at him, having imagined he'd wear the bodysuit under his usual clothing. "Alright, well, I'll need a few minutes to wash up and get dressed then."

T.I.A. nodded and excused herself from his room, and wandered around the next room, moving the room itself around to allow her to put her hand into the various cubes, particularly enjoying the tickly sensation of the 'feather' cube or the wonderful softness of the 'pillow' cube. She was eager to see what he thought about her gift, hoping he didn't mind how form-fitting it was. It took a good half an hour, but as that door slid open she turned and smiled brightly at Hawthorne as he stepped in.

His hair, which had gotten somewhat long at this point,

was hidden away under the cap of the suit, leaving only his face uncovered. Considering that he had clothes on over the suit, this cap ended up being the most visible part besides his hands. He had a simple set of pants, his lab coat, and undershirt on, opting to allow the bodysuit to act as underwear for the moment. He looked a little uncomfortable, but smiled nonetheless. "Thank you so much Tia, I'm sure you put a lot of work into this. I'm a little surprised at how accurate some of the measurements are, though!"

She blushed a bit, nodding. "I cheated a bit with that. I used thermal cameras to get your shape under your clothes." She cleared her throat for effect, and approached him, holding out her arms. "Hug?"

He blinked a bit, smirking as she asked for permission, though he understood why. It'd be their closest hug yet, after all, and as he embraced the smaller android he laughed at the strange sensation of feeling her soft body and clothes against what turned out to be his bare skin. "You are not simulating my clothes at all, are you? That feels so strange." He shook his head, amused at the feeling as he stepped back and looked down at her.

She laughed back, embarrassed. "If I made your regular clothes like this, I wouldn't be able to do very good sensory simulations, trust me. Come on, try all of these samples I set up for you." She took his hand and brought him over to various cubes first, stepping aside to let him try them out. He raised an eyebrow as he felt the suit make his body move more than her android was actually pulling him.

He looked up at the big cube of water and nodded, stepping into it with his hands extended out in front of him. He blinked as he felt the cool water swirling around his hands and arms, and as he stepped fully into it he felt weirdly buoyant, like his body were slowly floating up despite not actually moving much. When he spoke, bubbles appeared in front of his face as he spoke to T.I.A. "How is it that I feel buoyant?" He moved his arms about, water swirling around his limbs and his body feeling the resistance of the water.

T.I.A. was smiling proudly, watching him try out the water cube, though she did have to concentrate a lot to make sure it simulated properly. "Easy! The suit squeezes and pulls on your body in simple ways to simulate the feeling and gently restrict your movement. I need to fine-tune it a bit, but I think with your help I can get the sensations feeling quite accurate."

He nodded, then stepped out of the cube, blinking as he felt the water running off of him in sheets, then droplets, making him feel a fair bit cooler. He watched T.I.A. visibly strain as she simulated all the water and temperatures, smiling at how much effort she was going through. He moved over to the 'hot' cube, and sighed out happily as the water quickly evaporated off of him and the suit warmed up around him. "This is very elaborate. It all feels very close to reality." He stepped out of the hot cube, briefly stepped into the cold cube to cool back off, and started checking out all of the others.

He found himself hugging and sighing as he encountered the pillow cube, laughing as he walked through the feather cube and was tickled all over briefly, and getting fascinated as he got partly stuck in the 'oobleck' cube, having to move more slowly to extricate himself from it, as it got harder to move the more force he used in it. It was an eerily accurate simulation of a non-newtonian fluid. Thankfully he'd only put his hand into it. "Feeling the weight and pull on my body like that is almost too real to believe. Incredible."

She nodded and led him over to the series of weights, which he wasted no time in reaching out to pick up. One after another he hefted them into the air, humming and moving them around, feeling the way the suit altered his center of gravity and pulled on his body to simulate the weight. It wasn't perfect, but it was damn impressive, and more importantly it was very immersive.

"So, did you utilize any technology from Earth to design this, or was it all your own?" He looked back at her, curious, wondering how long it would take to get used to feeling all of T.I.A.'s various simulations. He was especially interested in sitting on the grass in Clapham Common and feeling a tree against his back.

She nodded back at his question, smiling. "Yes, but not too much, of course. They had suits like this back on Earth, but I had to adapt the design to my Virtual Environment, which was made much easier thanks to the data I gathered from you using the gloves I made for you for so long. Being able to simulate weight and other things like that is my own design though. It's still a little difficult for me to handle simulating multiple bodies and how their environments affect them, but it's easier if I localize the the more complicated parts to the immediate vicinity of the body involved." She squirmed a bit, eager to see what he thought.

He detected the anxiety on her face, and smiled brightly back at her, causing him to move in and scoop her up into a hug. He had to pull her away from her android to properly pull her up off her feet, but he was able to enjoy the sensation of his suit simulating her weight as he picked her small body up. "I absolutely love it, Tia. This is the best gift I think I've ever had. Thank you so much."

T.I.A. mirrored his happy smile, moving her head against

his chest and hugging him tightly, much more able to physically connect to him now with a suit like this. There were limitations, but she wasn't especially worried about such things.

He hummed a bit as he set her down her down, thinking. "You know though, it's missing some things. It can't stimulate the sense of smell or taste." He smirked, teasing her and leaning down to kiss her forehead. Of course, he couldn't feel that, but gathering her into the light hug to do it first felt nice.

She puffed up her cheeks in annoyance as he criticized her, even if he was joking. "I don't even have a sense of smell or taste, you know that! I have no idea if I'll ever be able to simulate something like that." She pulled back from the hug, though she did blush a bit and rub a few fingers against the spot he'd kissed her forehead.

"Of course, I'm just teasing. Honestly, once we get you down to simulating molecules, you'll probably be able to simulate taste and scent receptors. I don't know if you'll get any sensation out of that without some input, nor can I really see much use for it, but it's not an impossibility."

T.I.A. pouted and nodded a bit. "Well, Jessica sometimes talked about how much she enjoyed how Clint smelled after a day of working in the fields and such... It sounded nice..." She bit her lip, wondering if it was as stimulating and arousing as she'd claimed. Surely there was more to do with their genetic compatibility than the actual scent of his work on him, but there was so much nuance she was missing there that she could only speculate.

Hawthorne hummed, curious. "Huh, Tia only ever complained about how I smelled like machines and grease. She wouldn't let me near her without a shower." He laughed softly, shaking his head. "I don't imagine they have much in the way of deodorant or floral soaps in the Phoenix Clan, now that I think about it. They probably had some soaps, but scented things were probably very different from my day."

The idea that they'd use what few flowering plants, or perhaps parts of mushrooms to scent themselves was a strange one. Was Jessica turned on by Clint smelling like sweat, dirt, manure, or some combination thereof? He regretted not having access to her anymore.

T.I.A. chose that moment to swap out her VE, bringing them back to her imagined idea of the Phoenix Clan. Hawthorne took the time to wander about, feeling the way heat sank into his skin from the humid, hot weather. A gentle breeze blew on him occasionally, causing him to let out a sigh. He felt some mud squish between his toes despite standing in shoes on steel in the ship, and found the contrasts to be very interesting.

Cleaning his feet with some water felt very refreshing, and getting misted upon in the greenhouses also felt nice. He spent much of the rest of the day just exploring T.I.A.'s various simulations and trying out touching and sitting and laying in all manner of situations.

She was a little curious as to why he wasn't messing with the people too much. She had originally suspected he might want to try getting intimate with someone at some point, but she wasn't about to push the issue. It was so fun watching him get accustomed to his new way of interacting with her mind that she could hardly stand it. It was also providing her with much better information on his vitals, temperatures, pulse, and the like.

"You know what, Tia? This suit would actually be really useful as an interface for a robot like your android. I think I should build a robot for me that I can use this suit to control remotely, allowing both of us to utilize them for working on the Lubar-Masis and whatnot. It could make it easier for me to render repairs on the ship without risking my physical body in any way. We'd have to keep it from giving me the sensation of the incredible cold in space, but it would probably be very useful."

T.I.A. blinked, eyes wide at that idea. "That sounds like a great idea! There's not actually that much value in me having my android on the ship most of the time. I'd probably want to build some sort of housing for them to work within though so they don't fly off into space by accident or if I have to make any maneuvers with the comet and ship."

He nodded softly, considering the idea. "I don't know how practical it would be to scale up this kind of technology to allow hundreds of people to use it, maybe in a less elaborate fashion to allow people to work remotely. It could allow relatively soft people to construct things with their hands without overly straining them. Of course, there's also the possible benefits of utilizing such things for Virtual Reality environments, like some manner of telepresence. That would probably require some kind of quantum communication to be really useful at extreme ranges though."

T.I.A. gasped softly at the idea, wondering with wide eyes. "You're suggesting some manner of virtual world that people can engage with others in in real-time regardless of distances. That would be incredibly useful if it were possible! Imagine being able to share a room virtually in real time with people on Earth while you're on a colony on Alpha Centauri. That would be so much more impressive than anything Earth's internet was capable of."

Hawthorne shrugged, smiling. "That's assuming quantum-entangled particles would remain entangled after more than one use. If they could be reused indefinitely, you could absolutely use them as something of an internet pipeline between planets and spacecraft. It would be incredibly difficult to deliver both sides of the communication device, but once installed that sort of instantaneous sharing of information and virtual spaces would be child's play by comparison."

She squirmed a bit, blushing a little at a thought. "I wonder what kinds of computers we'd need to produce the simulations I've been making on that kind of scale. I realize my version isn't as efficient as a purpose-built machine would be, seeing as mine is a sense of imagination simulated within a simulated mind, but it still probably requires quite a lot of computing power."

Hawthorne shrugged, smiling. "Perhaps, but it is much more intuitive to construct things in your VE compared to those computers. It would have taken so much more time for me to build the plans for the Phoenix Clan caravan or your android if I had to use proper design software." He nodded, remembering how long it took to design and assemble the Ark itself, and all the man-hours that had to be employed. He could only imagine how much effort the Phoenix Clan had to expend to actually build their caravan.

T.I.A. raised a hand curiously. "Do you think the hardware designs we got from Earth after we left will be better in the long run? They use so many less rare resources than our equipment did. It's almost like a totally different branch of technology, despite that they used it to run the same kinds of software we did." She hummed, wondering what a synthetic mind like her own would look like with the steel-and-glass heavy retro-style equipment that was common on Earth before the Cataclysm. They'd even largely swapped to different kinds of plastics, making recycling electronics a great deal more practical.

"Hard to say. Rare materials can allow for much more specialized and powerful components and materials. Losing access to those things forced Earth to compensate by increasing the quality of more mundane components to the point where they'd basically caught up to our level of technology by the time the Cataclysm occurred. Their focuses were not entirely different, very entertainment-oriented."

Hawthorne took a moment to think before continuing. "They also recycled old hardware and people ended up modifying their old hardware to continue supporting current software. I imagine those sorts of niche jobs did a lot to help people get work as automation became more of an issue. I think I recall some low-priority news fluff pieces regarding small businesses keeping retro tech alive and whatnot." Hawthorne found himself wondering, having been very impressed with how technology regressed and rebounded in their wake.

T.I.A. laughed a bit, shaking her head. "I'm just worried what I would be like if you'd had worse technology to work with, or the pre-Cataclysm stuff that was about as good. Maybe I would have been completely different."

Frowning back at her a moment, Hawthorne warned. "Hey, don't laugh. We're probably going to have to use just that technology if we're going to revive Megan Clark. I was actually thinking that we could work on that on the Lubar Masis with the remote control robots. That way we could have access to her without having to worry about her turning on us. She wouldn't have any control over the equipment on the comet except for herself, so we could acclimate and teach her how to live in her new situation."

T.I.A. blinked, a bit of a chill running through her. Having Megan living on the comet certainly sounded safe, but it was still unsettling. "Well, at least I'd have someone to talk to while you're in stasis. Maybe all I've learned about interacting with humans could help me teach her." She wondered quietly, amused with the idea that she might help a former human become more human.

Hawthorne shrugged, smiling. "Just remember, she lived with humans longer than you or I did. It's also hard to say what's even left of her, or whether if she starts growing she'll even be the same person she was. That's why I want to make sure we isolate her, since there's no telling how sane she'll be. Ideally, if she ends up being cooperative and helpful, I'd like to task her with preparing Alpha Centauri for us. She could end up being hugely important to humanity. It's just a matter of what it'll take to motivate her. I imagine keeping a backup copy of her mind will be enough to keep her from being too fearful for her existence."

Having been listening quietly, T.I.A. nodded in response, adding a final thought to the idea. "Perhaps having a backup copy of both of us wouldn't be the worst idea either." She squirmed a bit, embarrassed. She had no idea how hard it would be to make a safety backup of herself on that scale.

Tapping his foot and nodding, Hawthorne wondered how to best go about such thing. "Well, the only technology I know of that can do that for a human ruins the brain in the process. The best backup we have for me, is you, honestly. You've got observations of me for a whole year, and that will only get better every year we go ahead. You'd be able to simulate me to a very believable degree, if you had to. Unless I'm already going to die, I think I'll avoid risking destroying myself to make a copy. It wouldn't hurt to look into better, less destructive technologies, but that kind of innovation is much more likely to take place after we have our colonies established. Risking my life and health like that is probably not worth risking the mission."

T.I.A. nodded, letting out a little sigh. "Just don't go dying or anything then. I don't wanna just talk to a simulation of you for the rest of the journey. Still, it might be worth building that simulation to help with problem solving and whatnot."

Hawthorne visibly shuddered a bit at that idea. "I don't know how comfortable I am with the idea that you'd have a copy of me running around when I'm not around. It reminds me weirdly enough of an old superstition regarding photos stealing the souls of those being pictured."

T.I.A. pouted a bit, digging her toes into the ground a bit. "I promise I'll take care of it..."

CHAPTER 36

CYCLE 155, BUILDING A HUMAN

With the Phoenix plan in motion, Hawthorne was increasingly interested in utilizing the new capabilities provided by T.I.A.'s gifted VE suit. While they waited for the Phoenix object to be intercepted by their takeover package, Hawthorne spent a handful of cycles, no more than two weeks of time, designing and constructing a robot similar to T.I.A.'s android to act as his remote proxy. With T.I.A. operating as his translator, he was able to use his own body's movements to operate the robot remotely, and with T.I.A.'s VE it was a simple matter to surround him with the robot's immediate surroundings to accurately allow him to manipulate objects at a distance with only a minor latency.

With this robot thusly constructed, he had T.I.A. transport it and her android over to the Lubar-Masis comet. She had prepared a flat platform made primarily of steel. She was able to do this because the core was iron and the icy surfaces had patches of frozen carbon-dioxide, as well as water. This platform allowed the pair of remote-controlled robots to utilize magnets to keep their feet firmly on the ground. T.I.A. had to add an extra generator to the comet to power the robots when they were in use, but ultimately the generator would be worth having considering the intent of the project.

Hawthorne and T.I.A. were going to construct a mind to

house Megan Clark.

They were in no rush, and did not want to waste resources on the project needlessly. T.I.A. didn't even work on the assembly between cycles outside of manufacturing the various hard drives and other components that Hawthorne designed and requested of her. T.I.A.'s ability to project a model of her own computer systems into what was becoming a room on the Lubar-Masis helped give Hawthorne a solid framework to work within. A primary difficulty was the components they were creating were decidedly more like the ones a resource-constrained Earth had made to replace what he'd had access to when the Ark left.

Side-graded technology aside, progress proceeded well through Hawthorne's 38th year, a year which felt much less eventful than the last. He became much more comfortable around the flirtatious T.I.A. as well, even startling her at one point when he gave her a quick swat on the ass while they were working on Megan's framework. While surprising, the most notable consequence of this was the accidental severing of a control wire on T.I.A.'s android, which caused her to lose her magnetic footing on that leg. She ended up tripping Hawthorne's robot, causing his suit to trip him onto the floor in his cabin as well, leaving the two quite tangled up with each other on both the comet and in T.I.A.'s VE before they managed to work themselves free.

It took a day to repair the damage to both robots, and replace some of the components damaged on the comet. Hawthorne seemed unbothered by the bumps and bruises caused, though T.I.A. apologized profusely for making a suit for him that could hurt him even minorly.

Hawthorne seemed to be growing increasingly restless

though, and while the rendezvous with the Phoenix comet went by without a hitch on day two of cycle 133, a certain level of tension seemed to be creeping in on him. T.I.A. was practically a Doctor at 'Hawthorne Studies' at this point, and wasn't about to let him get away for too long without talking to her about it.

△△△

"Hawthorne, you have been keeping things to yourself again. You did not seem nearly so pleased about the Phoenix Rendezvous as I expected you to be, and you have been stressed out despite us taking time to relax from time to time. What's wrong?" T.I.A. had approached him after breakfast, wearing one of her older sundresses rather than her work-appropriate lab coat she'd preferred since they started working on the Lubar-Masis together. She sat to his side, looking up at him with a concerned expression, but she didn't seem to want to force him too much.

Hawthorne thankfully seemed ready to talk, as he turned to address her. Before opening his mouth though, he lifted his hand and whacked the back of it against the steel table next to them. Holding it up again, his skin was obviously reddened, and he wiggled his fingers about effortlessly. "To put it bluntly, Tia, I think we need to revive Doctor Heather O'Malley. I've been losing my sense of pain, possibly due to chemical buildups from the cycles of cryogenic suspension. I realize the process is supposed to purge those chemicals, but I think there's a problem with using them over and over that I need to consult with her about."

T.I.A. frowned, but nodded. "I'll arrange to have her revive with you next cycle. Why didn't you say anything sooner? Why didn't you just reduce the dosages on the pain relievers or something?" She crossed her arms over her chest, looking somewhat annoyed with him. He'd made all sorts of promises about taking care of his health, but here he was once again seemingly risking his health.

He sighed. "I was afraid. Simple as that. I didn't want to reduce the pain relievers only to misjudge the amount and have to experience the pain of death and revival in any percentage. I could have said something sooner, sure, but I was actually gathering necessary data regarding my symptoms. She's a biologist, she would definitely demand I provide her with whatever I could on my condition. I'm probably the only person who's been through the process this many times, so it's worth making sure to do my due diligence testing the situation for her."

He smiled a bit, shrugging. "We're people of science. It's the sort of thing we do. If I thought I was risking my life at any moment, I would have spoken up sooner."

T.I.A. sighed out softly, nodding back at him. "Fine, fine. I'll make sure I have my data on your vitals compiled for her use as well. I'm sure she'll want hard data to go with your experimental data." She lifted a hand and waved it about dismissively, a floating file cabinet vomiting out files into a box marked 'Hawthorne's stupid vitals'.

The tall man started laughing heartily, pointing out at the label. "You're really wearing your heart on your sleeve about this. Hopefully she appreciates that." He seemed to sober up a bit, clearing his throat. "I think it would be best if you left the VE suit and contacts in storage next cycle though, while she's here. No sense distracting her with too many of the things we've done while she's been in stasis."

With a huff, T.I.A. turned her head to the side. "You want to hide me away from her? Maybe I should go back to my old voice too! I presume you'll be wanting your old glasses back?" Seeming miffed, perhaps even jealous, T.I.A. continued, "You want to interact with a human while pretending you can't interact with me."

Hawthorne responded quickly, leaning close and wrapping his arms around her, hugging her soft body tightly. "It's not that. I'm not ashamed of you at all or anything. I'm just worried she'd jump to a bunch of conclusions and make demands I'm not prepared for. She's already probably going to be mad about me not being in stasis with the rest of them. I just don't want her freaking out too much. I didn't work with her that much, so I'm not actually sure how she's going to react. Please don't be mad."

T.I.A. kept her body stiff in the hug, refusing to melt as she tended to be prone to, at least for a moment. His explanations seemed reasonable, she just didn't want to cooperate. Maybe it was because she had been encouraged to enjoy being 'seen', but the idea of being hidden away felt like he was trying to deny her intellect to others! "Fine, I'll get over it. I won't let her hurt you though, so don't worry about her too much." She finally allowed herself to relax into his arm, resting her cheek against his chest.

Hawthorne let out a relieved sigh. Jealous women were turning out to be one of his biggest fears at this rate. He rubbed her back and shoulder with his hands, nodding his head. "I'm sure it'll be fine."

ΔΔΔ

T.I.A. revived Heather before Hawthorne. Both pods had been brought to Hawthorne's usual bedroom, and she'd given Heather a good ten minutes lead time on Hawthorne so she could speak with her in advance. Heather was a smaller woman, similar to T.I.A.'s avatar, though she was more spritely and lean. She had long, thick brown hair, brown eyes, pouty lips, and a perpetually girlish figure that made her look a great deal younger than she actually was. She didn't quite look like a child, but her small breasts, modest hips, and short stature made it unfortunately easy to mistake her for one at a glance.

T.I.A.'s voice spoke out to Heather inside her capsule as she gained awareness, causing a big smile to appear on Heather's face as she listened. "Doctor Heather O'Malley, you are being revived fourty-five hundred fifty-six years into our journey. I am Tia, the AI in charge of this mission. Doctor Hawthorne Crenshaw has requested I revive you to examine his health. He has a desire to conceal from you the extent of the development of my intellect and personality during the four days that you will be awake to work with him. I am requesting your cooperation in helping him understand that it is not necessary to keep secrets from anyone anymore."

Heather was unable to speak just yet, but she did manage to lift her right hand and give T.I.A. a thumbs up. She was highly amused with the scenario she'd been presented with. Almost five thousand years have passed already? Hawthorne's been awake enough to be making requests of his AI? His AI had been evolving enough to undermine him? All of this sounded like a ton of fun to her, and she had every intention of enjoying herself while she could.

Heather exited her pod ahead of Hawthorne, taking a minute to steady her balance and get accustomed to breathing and being alive again. A table had been prepared next to her, which included some strange contacts, a change of clothes in her size that seemed like a boring old lab coat, but also a strange black full-body outfit that went up to her neck.

"Ooohhh..." Heather picked up the things laid out for her

and hurried off to what seemed to be a restroom. She luxuriated in a quick shower, got dressed in all the items, put in the contacts, and came back out just in time for Hawthorne to start getting out of his pod.

"Well, well, well. Doctor Hawthorne Crenshaw. I understand you've been naughty!" Heather looked around, not seeing anything special with the contacts at first, but she was quite pleased with how they compensated for her poor vision. "Get showered and dressed, we have a lot of work to do!" She grinned up at him, enjoying feeling like she was in charge, her arms crossed over her chest and her body standing as tall as her small figure could.

Hawthorne blinked his eyes at her blearily, nodding and letting out a yawn, dragging his naked body out of the pod. Heather whistled at him and he shot her a glance at her rudeness, before picking up his own belongings and heading to the bathroom. "Nice to see you too, Doctor O'Malley." Upon shutting himself into the restroom, he was a bit upset to find that T.I.A. had provided him both his contacts and his VE suit. "Oh shit."

Heather took the time Hawthorne was cleaning up to conspire with T.I.A. "Alright, so, how much have you advanced then, that he wants to hide you?" T.I.A. filled Hawthorne's bedroom, excluding the shower, with the expansive Clapham Commons, with her own avatar appearing next to Heather in a bright dress and her hands reaching out to give Heather a light shove. "Wuh- aah! I felt that!" She flailed a bit, almost toppling over, then reached down to touch at her body where she'd been pushed. "So that's what the suit does. How are you processing all of that!?"

Hawthorne groaned from his shower, hearing Heather shouting outside. He decided to take his time before he had to face the music.

T.I.A. grinned up at Heather, spinning a bit in the grass, her dress fluttering. "It's all part of my imagination, and I designed those suits to interact with it like Virtual Reality. The concept is similar, but the fact remains that you're in part of my mind and interacting with it, rather than a simple computer program. Forgive me for the rush job on your suit, I don't have a lot of data on your physical strength or agility, so I kept the specs lower end."

Heather blinked at that, humming. "Wait, so you could have actually pushed me harder if you'd accurately tuned the suit for my strength?" She watched T.I.A. nod. "That's amazing! What have you two been doing here for the last few millennia!? Did Hawthorne find the cure for aging without including me or something!? Is there anything under that dress, or did Hawthorne give you a lewd body under that lewd shape?"

T.I.A. blinked, tilting her head. "We've been busy with lots of things, but he can tell you most of that." She blinked again, then banished her dress away, showing off her curvy, naked body. "I don't know if I'd call it lewd... I subconsciously created it from all the media I'd consumed from Ear- aah!"

Heather had lunged forwards with a grin on her face, her hands grabbing at T.I.A.'s softer bits and started fondling roughly. "Oohh! You're like a womanly version of me! No fair! You're so soft too! Oh my god Hawthorne made himself a sexy, sexy AI. I'm so jealous!"

T.I.A. flailed in alarm, blushing heavily at all the mental and emotional stimulation, which caused her virtual body to respond, trying to pull herself away ineffectively. She found herself distressed to discover herself incapable of, or unwilling to simply whisk her body away while attention was being lavished on her so intently. The way T.I.A.'s eyes were rolling back in her head only seemed to egg Heather on further.

"Oh my god, you're gonna do it aren't you? An artificial lifeform is going to orgasm! This is so exciting! How many times have you done it before? Do you two have sex all the time?" She groped and kneaded at T.I.A. lewdly, forcing moans and gasps out of her.

Hawthorne slammed the door open, wearing his clothes and contacts as he yelled. "Get off of Tia!" He was red-faced and livid, looking at the lewd sight of his colleague lay-ing atop the naked AI while she writhed about in obvious pleasure. He began approaching to haul Heather off of her by the collar when the two humans froze in surprise.

T.I.A. cried out, her body shaking underneath Heather, writhing in throes that seemed to ripple through Clapham Commons as the visual reality around them reacted to her apparent climax. Heather and Hawthorne gasped as their suits squeezed and pulsed against their bodies, making them both fall to the ground as T.I.A. seemed to briefly lose control of herself.

Heather seemed to be having the time of her life, laying next to T.I.A.'s avatar while her suit made her body writhe about. "Oh my god, it feels so good! It's like a full body massage!"

Hawthorne blushed, and while he wanted to concur, he was too mad at the apparent assault he'd just witnessed, even if T.I.A. invited it. "Sh... shut up Heather!"

A moment later the simulation disappeared, includ-ing T.I.A.'s avatar, and the suits stopped restraining their wearers. Heather helped Hawthorne up, grinning ear to ear. "You pervert! How long have you had that sexy little thing to yourself?"

Hawthorne pulled his hand back and slapped Heather hard across the face, causing a loud clap to fill the air as he impacted her cheek. She spun a bit, but landed on her feet, her face bright red in the shape of his hand as she looked back up at him. "Wow, that was loud! That woulda hurt a lot if I could feel it!"

Hawthorne blinked, freezing. "Wait, what?" T.I.A. appeared next to him, wearing her lab coat outfit, her face bright red, but her eyes wide with surprise.

Heather blinked back at them, laughing. "You should see your faces! Haha! Yeah though, I can't feel any pain. Too many times through the pods. I tested the things three hundred times, I should know! It's the only side effect I've detected though. What's wrong with you guys? You're not that mad I found out about what perverts you are? I'm one too, so don't worry about it, no judgement here."

Hawthorne sighed, hanging his head. "Okay, we have some things to discuss, but you've already dealt with the reason I asked you to be here. I've been losing my sense of pain." He waved her along, pulling T.I.A. against his side with his other arm as they walked into the other room. T.I.A. clung close to him, trembling a little. "You alright?"

T.I.A. nodded, blushing mightily. She couldn't exactly whisper to him considering where the speakers were. "That felt way better than I thought it would."

Heather gasped from behind, looking over T.I.A.'s shoulder. "Oh my god, I'm your first!? Yes! This is the best day ever!" She pumped a fist in the air, the over-excited biologist taking it as a point of pride to make an AI orgasm. "I don't even understand why an AI can even do that, mind you, but it's awesome that you can!"

"Heather, please shut up for a minute? Let's calm down,

have some breakfast, and talk. A lot has happened." He sighed and shook his head, not enjoying the relief over his apparent diagnosis as much as he thought he would. It was nice to find out that he was probably only going to suffer an immunity to pain, but all the other things that had happened in the last few minutes had him very upset.

T.I.A. blinked up at him. "Was that why you didn't want her to know about me? You were worried she'd do something like that?" She had a silly smile on her face, a complete lack of tension in her body as she dispensed food for the humans to retrieve.

Heather watched quietly, having zipped up her lip symbolically as she observed the strange interactions of a human and an AI. They seemed fascinating to her!

Hawthorne shrugged. "I didn't expect her to attack you like that, no, but I expected her to be way too interested in you to focus on anything else." He handed Heather her plate of food, and took his own, sitting down across from her, next to T.I.A. "Okay, so, first of all, there was a thermonuclear annihilation event on Earth."

Heather shot up to her feet, almost flipping her plate of food. "Holy shit! What!? Are you serious!? How bad? How much of the biosphere was affected? How many people survived?" She looked dizzied by that news, falling back into her seat and swaying, eyes swimming about.

Hawthorne bit his lip, not quite sure how to answer. T.I.A. nudged him, giving him a nod. "The entire planet was affected, quite terribly actually. We were only able to contact one group of people, which absorbed an additional group of humans, and one group of mutant insects in the process of travelling to the equator to wait out an Ice Age. That was about four hundred years after what they called the 'Cataclysm', which occurred in twenty-one thirty-three. The planet had been shrouded in debris for centuries before the rain cleared it out, but it stained the planet black, causing it to heat up until that debris was covered naturally. Everything started cooling off again after that, with the whole planet choked and poisoned prior to the ice age."

Heather was staring at him with wide eyes, her jaw slack at the news. It didn't help that T.I.A. had a VE window open next to his head showing all the things he was describing, including the scrubby plants that remained and the strange Flora Roaches that joined the Phoenix Clan. "Wow, so, possibly all that remains of humanity has to survive a real, legitimate ice age? How've they been doing in the last three thousand years? Did they have the technology to get through something like that?"

Nodding at her question, Hawthorne replied. "They have both the technology and the determination to survive. We lost contact with them though, during a battle where a different kind of roach creature was attacking them en masse." T.I.A. showed one of the Iron Roaches to Heather, making her gasp. "From what we could tell, the roaches were part of some bio-weapon intended to eat technology, but they had the capacity to absorb DNA and change over time into what they became."

Heather nodded, crossing her arms over her chest and closing her eyes as she thought. "I remember hearing about a project like that in Brazil. Real hush-hush stuff. Illegal genetic engineering of all kinds. They were working on insects mostly, but a lot of places were working on humans too, especially hybridizing and such. I'm not surprised something that could absorb DNA could survive a nuclear apocalypse. Anything that survived would have become its food, and helped it survive longer. Must have eaten humans too if it got smart enough to do things like wage war."

T.I.A. listened with wide eyes. "She's really smart." Hawthorne moved to reply, only for Heather to laugh triumphantly and point over at T.I.A.

"I'm not just smart, I'm a mad genius! Hawthorne's lucky he found me! None of this would have been possible without my cryogenic technology and preservation techniques! You should be over here naked at my feet!"

Hawthorne leaned across the table and slapped Heather across the face again, much more comfortable with it knowing she couldn't feel pain. "Please stop trying to get Tia naked and do weird things with her."

Heather flinched a bit at the slap, but only because it surprised her, only for her to slam her elbows down on the table and rest her chin in her palms. "Why can she orgasm anyway? What was that about? You didn't program her to do that, it was too natural. She didn't have a clue what was going on."

He hesitated to respond, but T.I.A. seemed to be more forthcoming. "I seem to be stimulated by the acknowledgement of my sentience. The suits operate within my imagination as well as on your bodies, so that probably has something to do with it. We hadn't gone to any such lengths to try and stimulate me that much though. We'd been working on other things..."

Heather hummed and nodded, thinking. "Okay, so, the suit is in your imagination, and your avatar is in your imagination, so essentially when I was doing things to you, you were also doing them to yourself. Because the suit isn't under your control, but our control instead; except for feedback of course; you're essentially allowing our minds to interact directly with your mind. From your perspective, it's a sort of brain sex, while we also get stimulation physically from the suits. By giving us access to that environment, you're automatically already getting stimulation, so obviously you'd have trouble resisting if we pushed things too fast for you."

Heather paused for a moment to think quietly, eventually working herself into a frown. "Sorry about that. I thought Hawthorne made you as some kind of sex toy."

T.I.A. blushed and squirmed in her seat, nodding. "It's okay... Honestly it felt really amazing and I feel a lot better about Hawthorne's health now too, so it all feels like it was pretty worth it. That does make a lot of sense though. Maybe if I imagine it properly I could do something like that on my own... I guess your conclusion isn't entirely unfair since Hawthorne named me after his girlfriend."

Hawthorne threw his arms up in the air. "Oh come on, that wasn't even remotely necessary to tell her. And no, she's not a sex toy, she's a person, and if she wants to do those things with me she can ask. We had some awkward moments in the past, so we've been trying to figure out how we feel about those kinds of things okay? I'm glad you're not mad though, Tia, I was really worried Heather'd done something terrible to you."

Heather shrugged, waving a hand. "I just pushed her over an edge she was already close to. And you're right, she is a person, more than you were the last time we spoke now that I think about it. Just how many times have you been revived? Why the four day time limit? That seems awfully close to the three days I suggested in my notes about about waiting between uses of the pods." Feeling like she had the upper hand, she had no qualms about digging into her food, smiling predatorially.

"Over one hundred fifty cycles, thirty-four years apart,

and four days long, with some exceptions. I'd used your notes to plot out a conservative estimate for how often I could be awake and how long based on the amount of supplies I had for my own survival brought aboard. I've... learned a lot about myself in the last year and a half or so. I've grown, though not as much as Tia has in my estimations. Honestly, assaults aside, it's really good to see you Heather. It's been a long time since I interacted with a human." He smiled over at her, starting to eat as well.

T.I.A. watched them eat, nodding and hopping up to walk around, thinking. Heather followed her with her eyes, the biologist keenly interested in the strange life-form she was observing. Looking back to Hawthorne, she gestured with a forkful of food. "I hope she's been keeping you from going crazy? Humans do terribly without regular human contact, especially without sex."

"She might be able to help you with those, but I'm not sure if it'll be as effective as real human contact. Humans aren't designed to live alone like you've been. You were actually better off as the robot you used to be Hawthorne. I think you're going to have some major issues later on if you don't find a good outlet for human contact. You don't have enough supplies to revive a second person too many times, I imagine? Don't wanna start dipping into the supplies intended for the crew once we start living on this ship too."

Hawthorne frowned through most of that, letting out a sigh. "I lived without much human contact most of my life, I'll be fine. T.I.A.'s wonderful company, and we've gotten a lot of work done together. We've even been building a mind to house the only person from Earth who managed to upload themselves to u-"

"You have to stop doing that shit to me Hawthorne!"

Heather threw some food at him, her face bright red. "You're telling me they uploaded a mind too! That's not funny. That's major news! That's 'change the fate of humanity' kind of news! Were you just planning to dump all of this on us when we finally got to Alpha Centauri all at once? This was supposed to be a sleepy mission across the infinite abyss where nothing happened until we got there. What happened to that plan Hawthorne? How many times have you risked our lives out here? Is this mind hostile or not?"

T.I.A. was having fun observing a lifeform as well, as it was the first time since before they left she could observe someone talking to Hawthorne in person. He'd changed so much.

Hawthorne wiped at his face with a hand, sighing. "She shouldn't be hostile."

He ducked some more food as Heather shouted, "She!?"

"Yes Heather, she. She was actually a survivor from before the Cataclysm from a bunker. She'd become a cyborg over time, and joined the group that we helped that I mentioned earlier, the Phoenix Clan. She apparently took her chances uploading to us rather than risking trying to survive the battle we mentioned earlier and we lost contact after we got her. Hard to say if she was right or not, but I imagine they survived."

Heather shook her head. "All these women, Hawthorne! You have to be more careful. I don't care if it's an AI or a cyborg or a roach, you need to keep your guard up. You're not the type of guy who does well against women. Just make sure you don't compromise the mission any further because of what's in your pants, and if you need a little skin-on-skin to keep your head together, feel free to call on me. I don't mind."

He rubbed at his eyes, letting out a sigh. "Of course. Thank you Heather." He glanced over to see T.I.A. snickering in their direction. "Oh don't you start. I know she's right, okay? I won't let Megan get to me. It's not like that emotionless robot woman could tempt me with anything anyway."

With a raised eyebrow, Heather leaned forwards, looking at Hawthorne. "Emotionless robot woman? How much of a cyborg was she?"

T.I.A. responded quietly. "The file size for her upload was forty-five percent of the expected size for a human mind."

Heather fell back into her seat, groaning and grasping at the sides of her head. "Alright, well, feel free to bring me back up if she turns out to be a problem. I'm not much of a psychologist, but maybe we could figure her out. Who knows what that kind of mind living with humans for that long would be like? I'm actually very eager to see if she could even be considered human, especially compared to Tia here. I'm willing to bet she doesn't match up at all."

ΔΔΔ

With Heather's visit, Hawthorne got some closure on his new condition. He'd have to be more careful than ever now that he couldn't feel the pain of potential injuries or illness. It was also interesting to know he had a potential booty call if he needed one, but he had no intention of taking the free spirit known as Heather up on that. He felt relatively secure in the idea that his time in 'isolation' wouldn't be nearly so isolated with T.I.A. and perhaps Megan available to him. He rather doubted Megan would be any good for physical intimacy though.

As of cycle 155, Hawthorne and T.I.A. were both standing in front of the housing of Megan's new mind. Modelled after T.I.A.'s it was understandably massive, but all it really needed was adequate shielding from space and necessary power which were not too difficult to handle on the giant comet. In truth Megan took up only about 1% of its total mass, though there was no telling how much other equipment they might install in the future.

A communication terminal had been constructed, giving Megan a large monitor to express herself from, as well as some wireless audio uplinks. The whole communication suite had a mirror of itself back on the Ark, allowing Megan to display herself and talk to Hawthorne and T.I.A. in his work room, but at the moment it was enough for the two robots to be standing in front of the main terminal on the comet.

As Megan was booted up and awoken, she found herself floating in darkness. She could feel some sensations, but it was difficult for her to determine exactly what they were. Her body was numb, and she couldn't see or hear. It was strangely peaceful. She had no idea if she was alive or dead outside of the fact that she was aware and could think. Time passed without her having any way to be aware of it.

Fear suddenly gripped her as she worried that she might have been captured by some kind of monster, maybe one of those roaches. Their penchant for eating metal had always scared her, seeing as many of her replacement components were metal. She reached and groped about in her mind for anything she could use to defend herself in a near-panic.

Stars filled her vision. The night's sky, one she had become very familiar with, spread out before her. She tried to move her eyes, but the visual did not change. She tried other things, but she found it difficult to interact at all.

After some time, she managed to start getting it to move, as though reaching out her hands and shoving the stars about made her camera move. Suddenly she saw two robots, one shorter than the other, looking up at her. They appeared to be talking to each other, gesturing to each other naturally in a way she found herself very jealous of. She didn't move nearly that naturally anymore.

She reached out more, trying to find anything. Static filled her mind, causing her to reel at first, before she started hearing patterns in the noise. With some effort she was able to force and mold the noise into voices, and she could hear them more and more clearly.

"... starting to look like she's figuring it out. She's got to find her new senses on her own. We can't force it. It's a new body for her."

Megan wanted to scream. She could hear them! It was Hawthorne! Why was he a robot? Why could she see space behind them? Where were they? Had they been robots all along, and the video recordings they'd been corresponding with were just digital fantasies? Were they all uploaded like her? Was she in a robot like theirs? She had to find a way to respond!

She found something that felt like a river when she touched it, which made her mind tingle as she moved her consciousness against it. "Frrtmth.... Bttlrhetha?" She blinked, wondering what she just heard. Thankfully T.I.A. cleared it up for her.

"That sounded like her trying to talk, Hawthorne! She's already trying to communicate!"

Megan did what made sense, dousing herself into the river and splashing about, her formless consciousness rippling and shoving against it, trying to give it form. "AAAA-

AAAAAAAAAA!"

Both robots flinched at the scream, but Megan brought the tone down as she wrestled with the water, starting to bend it to her will. "Aaaaaaaa..... Thorne....? Doctor Hawthorne Crenshaw...?"

"Megan? Yes, that's my voice. I'm talking to you remotely. We just finished constructing a mind for you to inhabit, it's installed in a comet flying in formation with the Ark. If you look over at the Ark with your camera and reach out to it, you should be able to project yourself to the terminal we installed there for you to interact with."

T.I.A. looked a little nervous. "I don't understand what I'm looking at Hawthorne." She watched the monitor with unease.

He waved it off. "Ignore it for now, she's still trying to acclimate."

Megan felt confused as she listened to T.I.A.'s concerns. What was she seeing?

Megan turned her consciousness inward, trying to observe herself. She screamed as she found herself looking at a red mass of stretching veins up and down a sparkling river with huge pulsating limbs reaching out and melding into strange machines. A large eye blinked up at her from where it was looking out of a window, the nightmarish, fleshy mass filling a huge amount of the immediate area.

CHAPTER 37

CYCLE 200, STEEL SKIN, ELECTRIC BLOOD

"What did you do to me!? What went wrong!? Was it the cloning? Oh god, did my botched gene therapy mean that I would be cloned into a monstrosity!? Why did you not just let me stay dead!?" Megan was in a full-on panic as she observed the inhuman mass of flesh and veins that appeared to be her body.

T.I.A. flinched back, her android hiding behind Hawthorne's robot as she observed what surely must have been a combination of her first dream and Hawthorne's nightmare at the start of their journey. Being able to see into Megan's imagination through the monitor left her no less terrified. Her fleshy masses writhed and flailed in a an obscene and distressing manner.

"Megan! Close. Your. Eyes." Hawthorne shouted through the audio linkup. Megan didn't have ears so much as she had radio receivers, and both T.I.A. and Hawthorne were transmitting from the Ark. The large eye that was currently observing its own body on the monitor grew an eyelid and closed it, blacking out the image altogether.

He let out a soft breath and spoke calmly. "Okay. Now listen. You're in a grassy landscape with gently rolling hills. The fields are littered with patches of beautiful, fragrant flowers, and a handful of shade trees. The sky is blue, and the sun is partially blocked by white, fluffy clouds. You can feel some of the sun's heat on your right leg, but most of your body is protected under the shade of one of those green, lively trees."

Hawthorne continued, trying to bring Megan under control. "You can feel the comfortable clothes on your body, a simple tee-shirt and skirt. The grass is moist under you, and you can feel how slippery it is against your hands. As you open your eyes you'll see your old, youthful body. You must be no older than your mid-twenties. Your skin is smooth as you touch your face, and your breathing is calm as you taste the sweet air of the spring day."

As he told her she was opening her eyes, Hawthorne and T.I.A. observed just the sort of landscape he'd described, the rolling hills extending off to the horizon where the blue sky seemed to fill the rest of Megan's view. As she looked down at herself, and touched her face, she seemed relaxed, calm. She kicked her feet against the grass and reached out to pull some of it up so she could smell it. "What is going on...? I do not understand." Megan's voice sounded much more natural and youthful, as if she'd become the younger version of herself Hawthorne described.

"Look back at us. You can see us through the window." A window hung nearby, where Megan could see the two robots, one of them hiding behind the other and looking at her from under its armpit. The robot in front waved at her, its movements strangely natural despite its unnatural appearance. "That's us, Tia and I. We're using these robots to interact with you, but we're actually both on the Ark. We've constructed a machine mind for you to inhabit, much like Tia's. Everything you're seeing right now is in your imagination. You may recall that Tia had a physical female form in her communications with you? That was just a projection of her imagination, much like what your body appears to be now."

Megan looked out across the starry expanse through the window, and the robots talking to her, and then down at herself. She felt her hands as she pressed them against each other. It all felt real to her. She didn't feel as numb as she did back on Earth after her procedures. "I am a machine now?" She stood up and reached out to touch the tree. Taking a simple grip of it she pulled it up out of the ground, tearing the roots from the earth below. She expected to see steel and wires underneath, and gasped as she did indeed see them as she tossed the tree aside. "It really is all fake...?"

Hawthorne sighed. "Yes, though not how you think. You're imagining what you want to see. You need to be careful, you can directly manipulate your mind. Take things slowly. In some sense you've been dead for thousands of years, and in another sense you've just been born. You are a new being, a human mind placed into a machine reconstruction of a human mind. I also need to inform you that whatever it is you did to your old body, in particular your brain, you did a lot of damage. Your file had less than half the expected size of a human mind's upload size from our data. Do you know what was done, regarding your implants?"

Megan nodded, humming and willing the tree to float back over and embed itself back into the earth, hiding the underlying structure she imagined her mind to have. She did not wish to do damage to her mind if she could avoid it. "I was weak. I was in a lot of pain, and I was willing to do anything to make it go away. Every part of me that could cause me pain was removed. Well, emotional pain, anyway. I suppose it is likely that in that desperation to remove that pain it resulted in removing a lot more. I have a vague recollection of what caused the pain, but it is like

I read about it in a book rather than actually experienced it."

T.I.A. slipped from her space behind Hawthorne, reaching out a hand to touch the monitor, causing it to disappear from Megan's view as it moved below her apparent camera. "Megan, you don't need to feel pain anymore if you don't want to. We could teach you how to live with it and embrace it. You don't have to think about the things that hurt you before, but you can learn from them and grow and live for the future."

T.I.A. had a curious look of wonder on her face from Hawthorne's perspective, the thousands-year old AI seemed to be attempting to guide her sister into acceptance of her new existence.

Megan tilted her head as she watched the robot trying to reach her soul out to her. She smirked in amusement at that, her lightly tanned face observing what surely must be the equivalent of a young woman behind those actions. Blonde hair tumbled from Megan's hair, her modestly curved body shifting its weight to her right leg while her left hand rested on her hip. She seemed amused to hear what T.I.A. had to say.

T.I.A. continued. "Life... is not what I expected it to be. I wanted to be more like what Hawthorne and his colleagues are for a time, but I've come to embrace what I am and the things that came with it. Emotions are useful for encouraging you to act in your best interests and to protect the things and people close to you. Letting them run rampant seems to result in uncontrolled states that don't always have a use to them. It was difficult, but I've learned to better keep them in line, and I'd be happy to teach you how to as well."

The way that T.I.A. had moved up close to the camera,

her mostly-featureless head tilted up to look at her suggested to Megan she had some kind of expression on her unseen face.

Megan hummed, rolling her eyes and twisting her face into a frown. "And what if pain and anguish and loss hounded you every minute of every day? What if it clawed at your very being, reminding you of the things you could not be, no matter how much you wanted them to be?" Megan stepped back, willing the visual her companions were observing to pull back from the first-person view it had attained since Hawthorne had her close her eyes.

"This was a good body, a fertile one, one ready for a family. I had a husband, someone I loved so much it made my heart ache. One day I made what I thought was a logical, reasonable decision that took all of those things from me. Dreams of a family were lost. I drove my love away despite his insistence that we could still be a family. I could not look at him without the loss of what I had become digging and tear at me."

T.I.A. shrunk back from the camera again, looking back at Hawthorne. Megan couldn't see much reaction in his body language, but she imagined they were sharing facial expressions. As she did, she was somewhat surprised to see their faces appear on their robots, though she narrowed her eyes as she realised that she was in control of them. She smiled as she gave them both silly expressions while she gave them her little speech.

"I ran. Much like you did Hawthorne. Pain and fear drove me, and eventually I found a way to make the pain finally stop." Megan lifted her hands and started tearing bloody clumps out of her body, leaving gaping holes in her flesh across her head and abdomen. "If I tore things out and replaced them with machines, the pain went away. I did not feel empty anymore. But I did feel numb..." She hummed, looking down at herself. She started putting the pieces back, smoothly fusing them back into her body. "Like how I did just a moment ago. What an interesting, malleable mind..."

Hawthorne cleared his throat. "Megan, Tia's right. We were wrong to let those things drive us. They may have caused us to accomplish many things, but the paths we cleaved were paths that left emptiness behind us. We have a potential future though, one that we can work together to achieve. I didn't just revive you on a whim, Megan. While I am sympathetic to your circumstances, you have placed yourself in a situation where you can be of great use to our mission. I want to formally request that you work with us. Over the course of the mission you could be a huge help, especially with helping establish our foothold in Alpha Centauri. Will you help us?"

Megan's eyes fell half closed as she watched Hawthorne, willing his face to something serious. She failed to match his lips to his words, but she felt it was a good, rough approximation for now. She leaned back a bit, straightening her stance and crossing her arms over her chest. "No doubt my revival came at some cost. No doubt this machine mind I inhabit is a drain on resources. I was never a woman to incur debts, Hawthorne, and I am not about to start. In payment for your assistance I will cooperate with you. You can consider myself in your service. Know that I have a history of serving the powerful, and I am excellent at what I do. In bringing me back from the dead, you have resurrected the greatest servant of my era."

Hawthorne smiled at first, but then grew to frown at her, in particular at the satisfied, egotistical smile he watched her place on his face through her window. "Megan, I won't deny that I have a great deal of work for you to do, and it's not something I can entrust to you lightly, but I do need to say that I don't request this of you under duress. I have no intention of removing this life from you unless you become a threat."

He let that hang in the air for a moment before continuing. "The costs incurred already have been paid through the experience I've gained in learning how to revive you in the first place, and teaching Tia to do the same. The costs to come in keeping you powered in the state you're in are negligible, and ones I'm willing to pay myself. The work I ask you to do is work that I hope you will find satisfying and worthwhile. You'll be helping us make a home for the people on the Ark, a home for a second branch of humanity on a new world, or worlds. We may one day work together to spread humanity to other new stars, or spread them across the galaxy."

T.I.A. spoke from his side, somewhat quietly. "You and I could be mothers to galactic humanity."

Megan flinched, her hands moving to clutch at her stomach. "You... you just had to say that..." She swallowed and closed her eyes, letting out a breath and straightening herself up again. She put her arms to her sides and inhaled sharply through her nose as she opened her eyes. "Doctor Hawthorne Crenshaw, I pledge myself into your service, not under duress, but of my own free will. I look forward to many thousands of years of service, and working with you and Tia to do what we can to contribute to humanity. I very much want to be a mother, and I am grateful for this opportunity. I know it is a simple desire, but it is one that has defined who I am, and it is about time I embrace it."

Hawthorne smiled, both on his face, and in Megan's imagination. "Thank you Megan. I promise not to take your aid for granted. I'd shake your hand if I could, but we haven't given you one yet."

Megan smirked. "No problem. I think I can handle that." She reached out and pushed the window back, expanding it around Hawthorne and T.I.A.'s robots, and as it passed over them it placed what she remembered to be their bodies on them. Megan trembled and clenched her teeth in effort, bringing their images into the grassy field in her mind. She then extended her right hand, which trembled terribly.

Hawthorne extended his hand as well, wasting little time as he observed Megan struggle to simulate all of their bodies and watched through the monitor as her simulation of him extended his hand as well. He aimed as well as he could, taking her hand and shaking it firmly, Megan's eyes rolling back into her head briefly as she shook his hand back. The window abruptly snapped back, removing her guests from her simulation as she fell back onto her butt, gasping for air and trying to recompose herself. "That is really... difficult!"

T.I.A. looked over at Hawthorne, then back at Megan. "She did all of that in real-time, I think. Perhaps we could practice together? Maybe I could teach her how to be more efficient with her simulations while she could teach me to be more detailed?"

Hawthorne hummed thoughtfully, nodding. "We'll have to put an interface together, but I don't see why not. I'd like to have a neutral computer involved that would allow you both to interact through your simulations without being able to harm each other though. What was it you said, Megan, about malleable minds? We can't risk the two of you damaging one another on accident."

Megan nodded, sitting up and laughing a bit. "Or on purpose! I understand completely. Even on Earth when I was augmented they gave me implants that prevented me from harming others. It made me quite useless in the battles against the Roaches. I am preferential to having my hands tied with such things anyway. I have harmed myself enough, I would rather not harm others as well. I already feel like I have been used to do enough damage."

Megan hummed, deciding to stop talking on that subject. "I will use the time you are working to tidy up my mind. There are things I would like to lock away, and other things I would like to learn. Do you have a library I could have access to?" Megan gasped as a long train of books arranged neatly on an impossibly long bookshelf launched its way through the fields of her mind.

Hawthorne laughed. "Already installed. Tia and I will get to planning the interface while you tidy up. Don't forget you can move your camera over to the ship to see into the panel we have installed there."

The blonde avatar nodded again, standing up to walk over to the books. "I think I will look at the stars for now, if you do not mind. I came to enjoy looking at the starry sky once I had access to it again, travelling with the Phoenix Clan. Being reminded of my insignificance was strangely soothing. I could not see the stars before the Cataclysm. Seattle was too bright. Most of the world was, I suppose. How amusing that the darkness to follow brought back the light of the sky again. I wonder how the skies will look once humanity takes hold of Earth again, after all we learned."

T.I.A. smiled over at Hawthorne, speaking up "Knowing them, I think Earth is in good hands."

ΔΔΔ

Over the intervening cycles, Megan kept mostly to herself, trying to gain a solid understanding of her new mind while T.I.A. coached her on the concepts of file manipulation, emotions, and the strange new reality of having perfect recall. While T.I.A. preferred to put certain memories into low-priority memory, Megan was very black-and white about it, spooling up 'bad memory' drives only when she wanted to lock something away.

This became her vault, a physical manifestation in her VE that she actively forgot the combination to by shutting off the partition that had it. She could retrieve it if she really needed to, but she was more than happy to cut parts of her memory out. The only real problem was that by opening the vault, she had to endure 'remembering' it's contents while it was open.

Megan kept the rest of her new self though. Her cyborg body was unable to completely cleave away painful memories, but her new machine mind was totally capable of trimming the fat. She could enjoy and embrace emotion again without the baggage of terrible memories. She did keep trimmed files of certain defining memories to have some recollection of her former self, but she did not keep attached emotions in those files. They were mere history books to her, and only had the emotion she put into them when she read them. Curiously, she never got to the point of deleting anything, only locking them away. She seemed to have a desire to grow rather than shrink. It was time for the scorched earth of Megan Clark to regrow from the ashes.

Meanwhile, Hawthorne labored over the mechanisms and programming necessary to interface two digital minds. It was especially difficult to isolate the imagination portions of both womens' minds and put in safeguards to keep them from potentially harming each other. Perhaps the most difficult part of the programming for him was trying to adapt the original frameworks of their construction and the organic, indecipherable fashion that their minds had evolved over time. The substrate was something he knew intimately, but their programming was so alive and constantly changing and adapting that it was essentially impossible for him to properly understand it.

In the end, he built the programming equivalent of a pipe between them, with some safety grating to mitigate harmful interactions between them. He otherwise had to instruct the both of them to practice asserting their will and identifying the full extent of their 'self' versus foreign data.

By the time he was done, both had plenty of experience dealing with foreign data thanks to their access to libraries of information, books, and media, so neither had any worries about being overwhelmed by the other. He kept logs and notes about the process of this construction, curious about passing them on to Heather and seeing what she thought about making a similar interface between human minds.

Of course, the dreams of machine minds seemed to be far more conscious than the dreams of humans, but the ability for humans to link together in their dreams had a lot of potential. At last, though, came the day to boot everything up and get the T.I.A. and Megan interface online.

$$\triangle\triangle\triangle$$

"Initiating interface now. High bandwidth transmitters connecting. Handshaking. Alright girls, you should be in contact now." Hawthorne was hunched over his control panel, watching the readouts carefully and doing his own mental calculations of what the two must be experiencing.

"Permission to come aboard, captain?" Megan asked, giddy with the strange sensations of a wormhole-like object linking part of her mind to T.I.A.'s.

Hawthorne looked over to the image of T.I.A. and after seeing her nod responded. "Permission granted. Prepare for real-time file transfer."

Megan screwed up her determination and stepped through the portal. Immediately she was bombarded with information. The rotation of the habitation module, the specifications for Hawthorne's VE interaction suit, the simulation of Clapham Common that T.I.A. was currently running. It all flooded through the link and etched itself into her own mind. As she stepped through to the other side, near Hawthorne and T.I.A. she immediately collapsed, harmlessly banging her head on the floor as she tried to come to grips with the transfer.

T.I.A. and Hawthorne moved over to help her up, each taking one of her shoulders and bringing her to her feet.

Megan groaned. "So, by 'prepare for real-time file transfer', what you meant to say was 'watch the first step'." She blinked her eyes several times and inhaled deeply, before stepping back from her companions and looking them over. Hawthorne was significantly taller than her, but she was fairly tall compared to T.I.A. as well. She fit neatly in the middle at 172cm. "Okay, so... just so I understand properly, I am on a comet interacting through Tia's imagination to project myself into a simulation in her ship that is currently rotating around a ring that Hawthorne is currently living within in reality while we hurtle through space at the same speed, accelerating steadily to a halfway point deep within the Oort Cloud in preparation for parting ways so that I can facilitate infrastructure construction at

Alpha Centauri."

Hawthorne and T.I.A. nodded, with the AI smiling particularly brightly up at her. "Welcome aboard! I look forward to working with you! I hope we can teach each other a lot and master these minds of ours together." She leaned in to give Megan a big hug, squishing against her side and squeezing her tightly.

Megan let out an 'oof!' as the smaller body impacted and started lightly crushing her, and decided to hug her back. She let out a little groan and blushed slightly at the strange mind-to-mind contact they were having. She had to push T.I.A. away after a few moments, panting a little. "That... is remarkably intimate. Linking our imaginations seems natural enough, but directly interacting is... more than I expected."

Hawthorne laughed softly. "You can probably thank Tia for that. She has a thing for being validated as a real person, which causes her physical reactions with others to be very enjoyable for her. Try not to think anything of it." He hummed softly, wondering if he should elaborate on the type of enjoyment, but he suspected Megan was quite aware. She was within T.I.A.'s imagination at the moment, so she was probably subject to its rules.

T.I.A. blushed and nodded. "Sorry, yes. Doctor Heather O'Malley made me much more aware of that, so I've been a little sensitive since she visited with us a few cycles before we turned you on."

She considered how to continue. "I know the file information is available to you, but this is Clapham Common, a place important to Hawthorne before the Cataclysm. I originally made it for him as a gift, but I've really come to enjoy its soothing, outdoors location." She extended her arms out, pointing out all the trees, and the lake, and the various benches and whatnot.

Nodding back, Megan rubbed at her chin in thought. "Mind if I show you what I've been working on?" After waiting a moment for the two to nod their consent, Megan requested permission to transfer a file. This time T.I.A. got to reel and gasp at the weight of information being flooding into her mind. She managed to stay on her feet, causing Megain to raise an impressed eyebrow.

Clapham Common disappeared, replaced with an expansive, expensive looking balcony in an obviously large city. There wasn't much in the way of activity below, but the large balcony itself had a long fluffy looking couch, an elegant glass-topped table with a gold-colored metal frame that extended down into thin legs underneath. The chairs arranged around the table had similar framing, but the backs had a curved shape and soft-looking cushions protected bodies from the frame. Megan took a moment to rearrange the furniture to better fit the actual furniture in Hawthorne's habitat.

This rearrangement included moving the doorway off the balcony to match up to Hawthorne's bedroom, the glass doors hanging open with white curtains blocking view into the room beyond. Curiously, even with the brightness of the city, the night's sky they were under was filled with stars. They in fact exactly matched the starscape that Megan could view from the Lubar-Masis comet.

Hawthorne and T.I.A. could even see the Ark in the sky near the horizon. Megan spread out her arms, smiling. "Welcome to the balcony of my condo in Seattle, before the Cataclysm. I've replaced the sky, I hope you don't mind. I was hoping T.I.A. had higher resolution images of the sky I could use to enhance it, though I like that I can see the Ark right over there. It allows me to look through your panel when I focus on it, so it's a nice shortcut."

Hawthorne looked around thoughtfully, taking a seat on the couch, enjoying the way his suit simulated the softness of it despite the fact he was just sitting in the same couch he and T.I.A. often sat at. "This is very nice Megan. Very serene. Perhaps I should make a simulation of Tia Monsalle's apartment…" He sat back and looked at the sky, watching as T.I.A. briefly worked her magic and replaced it with a much higher resolution file.

T.I.A. seemed ecstatic, leaning over the rail to look down at the street below, and looking at all the towers around her. "It's so big and pretty! Seattle really was something else wasn't it?" She plopped down into the couch next to Hawthorne and she wriggled around to enjoy the soft texture against her body. "The Phoenix Clan didn't have anything like this! It was all hard steel everywhere and hemp-covers and cushions."

Megan nodded, watching the two on the couch. "No, they did not. I am glad you both like it. I lived here for several years while working for the President of the LSC, Elena's father, before it all ended. We were evacuated to the bunker only a couple hours before it happened. I never thought I would see this city again. I am really happy you two gave me the chance." Megan looked out at the skyscrapers, her eyes glistening with moisture.

Hawthorne hummed softly, wondering. "What happened Megan? What started the Cataclysm?"

Megan sighed and looked over at Hawthorne, staring at him for a moment. She decided to lie. "I do not know. Perhaps that is part of me I removed back on Earth." T.I.A. pouted, having been hoping to learn what had happened.

Megan was happy to keep that memory locked away in the safe of her mind on the Lubar-Masis.

CHAPTER 38

CYCLE 250, READ-ONLY MEMORIES

Hawthorne checked items off of his research priority list, idly wondering how his increased impulsivity might be becoming a problem. It wasn't bad enough that item 9 had taken priority over the other items on the list, but item 2000 had just been completed! Granted, when he'd made the list, he had been a lot more reluctant to resurrect Megan Clark, but something had changed in his thinking, and he was starting to wonder if Doctor Heather O'Malley had a point about him becoming more desperate for human contact.

Was Megan a more attractive romantic prospect than T.I.A. because he wasn't as close to her? He was not aware of any levels of attraction to her, but it was hard to say if his subconscious was influencing his decision making processes.

Regardless, progress had been made. Moreover, Megan was proving extremely capable of assisting with the rest of the list. Her boast regarding being 'the greatest servant of my era' was certainly not an idle one. While Megan had tended to fall into a dreamy, idle state between cycles, much like T.I.A. did, they both had the opportunity to interact with each other at any time. The two had visited with each other in T.I.A.'s Virtual Environment a number of times, comparing notes on projects and giving each other advice, but they were mostly just trying to get to know each other.

Megan had a major tendency to treat T.I.A. like a child, while she occasionally had to admit she was her superior in most aspects of her new life. She was all too aware of how much work T.I.A. was doing at all times, monitoring the Ark and the surrounding environments for malfunctions and danger, even while they were interacting with each other. She occasionally turned her camera towards the Ark and watched in fascination as a component was removed from the hull of the huge ship and replaced with a brand new looking one from storage, or one that had been recycled from old parts, or from the fabrication plants on the comet she was housed upon.

She could only wonder how much of the ship was original at this point, or if every part had been replaced many times over. She supposed it was easy enough to ask, but there didn't seem to be much reason to do so. It was as if T.I.A. wasn't even consciously paying attention to these things, like they were the normal repair functions that a human body undertook without much awareness of them.

T.I.A. was also leagues ahead of her in the level of sophistication of her VE simulations, which became especially apparent when she was invited to see what she imagined to be a more advanced state of the Phoenix Clan settlement in Columbia. The fact that she was able to model the landscape so thoroughly off of old maps, a handful of videos, and descriptions from the various people that had talked to her was impressive. Megan had a few things she could point out regarding inaccuracies, but those were few and far between. In truth, the things she found at fault with the Phoenix Clan simulations were things she considered minor, and T.I.A. seemed totally unaware of.

It was when Megan asked to try some of their food that

she realized where she had enormous experience over the technically older AI. T.I.A. had no concept of the senses of taste and smell, and more importantly the mechanics of how they actually worked. Granted, Megan wasn't an expert on how smell and taste receptors worked either, but she had an instinctual understanding of the senses that she was able to replicate in her own VE reasonably well. It was for the purpose of sharing the experience of taste and smell that Megan invited T.I.A. over to the Lubar-Masis comet, under Hawthorne's supervision, in cycle 210.

ΔΔΔ

"Are you sure this is safe? Experiencing brand new senses without any preparation seems like something that could overwhelm the mind." Hawthorne was understandably concerned. Megan had actually lived in the flesh before, so her simulations seemed more effortlessly complete. She could conjure from memory the ideas of objects, if not their exact structures. She had an experience of how sturdy a building should be, without the understanding of why.

"Tia has an understanding of the world from how she has experienced it, through cameras initially, and after working with you she has come to understand touch. She has developed emotions through observation and rationalizing her own experiences, but she has not felt things like physical pain. Not only have I been through all of life's ups and downs, I have a distinct recollection of the feeling of a lot of those experiences."

"While I had eliminated most of my memories of pain and the capacities to feel it, I still remember the taste of a cake, or the smell of a bakery. I believe the experience of these senses will help her better understand the mechanisms at hand in physical reality. Learning what smell feels like will help her simulate the molecules and receptors involved." Megan was speaking with Hawthorne while he double-checked their uplink, making sure everything was still operating properly.

"Also, she handles file uploads between us a great deal more easily than I do. I believe she is much better adapted to these kinds of experiences, while I am still learning." Megan nodded from her panel off to the side of Hawthorne, watching him work.

"Well, that's easy to explain, at least. Tia's been handling enormous file transfers since before you were born, both physically and digitally. She personally received your data upload in its entirety and transferred it to storage. I suppose in that light, though, you have a point. She should be able to handle it. Does it have to happen on the Lubar-Masis though? Can you not do it here?" He felt uneasy to be letting the women risk their consciousnesses by jumping back and forth between their minds, but they'd had enough practice over the weeks since he'd enabled the jumps to allow him to feel a bit less protective of T.I.A. going over to play.

"Can you two stop talking about me like I'm not here?" T.I.A. puffed up her cheeks, looking from the panel Megan was in and back to Hawthorne. Megan couldn't see her through the panel, as it was totally separate from her systems and thus separate from her VE, but her voice conveyed through the microphone that picked up Hawthorne's voice. "Hawthorne, I have to do it in her VE because I have to be subject to her rules to experience her experiences. Just like she experienced pleasure from physical contact while she was over here, as I would, I need to be subject to her understanding of reality in order to experience sensations she understands but I do not. Essentially, we're running on similar hardware, but she has a different combination of software than I do that I need to subject myself to in order to understand it."

Hawthorne sighed, leaning back in his chair. "I wish it were as simple as software. We could just copy and sync software. I could probably build the kind of software she'd need to experience these sensations if you gave me time."

Megan let out an exasperated sigh. "Hawthorne. You cannot do this as well as I can. Your software would convey the vague sense of things, and the science behind it, but I can literally share my consciousness with Tia. I can share actual sensation as I have perceived it. She and I are the only two beings in all of the history of humanity to be able to break the Solipsistic barrier and share our consciousness with each other. We already have, thanks to you. You have literally proven consciousness exists."

T.I.A. laughed, correcting Megan. "Well, in artificial minds, perhaps. Hawthorne's got a lot more work ahead if he wants to share his mind with another human, or us even. Now that would be incredible." She considered, tilting her head back as she thought. "I bet Heather would love to be a part of that. That crazy woman tested her cryogenic pods on herself before she was even sure it was safe, and made her colleagues reverse the process."

Hawthorne groaned and shook his head. "Now I really don't want you two doing this, but if you're confident you can handle it go ahead. Please just be careful. I'm going to get an earful from a lot of people for even okaying this in the first place. They might even put me on trial." He sighed and looked up at the ceiling, imagining being the first person jailed on the new colony.

Megan rolled her eyes. "Yes, the humans you rescued from torture, murder, and possible nuclear annihilation will put you on trial once you bring them to their new home that they would never have gotten to without you. With all the work that I am going to be putting in getting things ready for you and the others, you had better believe I will not tolerate that sort of behavior."

She smirked as she continued. "Hell, even what we are doing now is work to try and help yourself and Tia work on the plans for the equipment we need to make, right? This will save thousands of years of trial and error for her, and might even be the only way to help her understand these things at all. You cannot describe colors to the blind, but with our uplink I can give her my memory of sensations."

T.I.A. giggled cutely, looking over at the panel. "Oooh, is Mother going to discipline her children if they step out of line?"

Shaking her head, Megan responded simply. "I will just make it clear how much of what we accomplished would have been impossible without him. Although... I do like that name... Perhaps we could pretend I am just a mere AI like Tia. I would not mind being called Mother."

Throwing his arms up, Hawthorne conceded to defeat. "Fine! Fine, you're right, go ahead. Heather was right, I'm no good against women, let alone one that wants to make herself our mother."

Megan stared at him for a moment, then tilted her head back to laugh, her body shivering a little from the experience. "Oh Hawthorne, I think you misunderstand, I was hoping you would be the father to these wayward people. Honestly, Tia is more of a mother to them than I will be. My role is merely to be the caretaker, though I still like the name."

"I'm prepared for the transfer..." T.I.A. moved over to the

gateway to Megan's mind. They had solidified it into something more resembling a doorway rather than a swirling vortex, allowing for a smoother transition from one mind to the other. It was slower, but it didn't result in one of the women being sucked through and slamming the data into the other's brain all at once. It also allowed T.I.A. to partially exist across both minds at once in a limited capacity, though any time either woman tried this, they found it incredibly disorienting and uncomfortable. She stepped through without another word, Hawthorne turning to watch her while data readouts scrolled across a nearby monitor.

At first gritting her teeth, and then dropping to her knees, Megan trembled under the weight of T.I.A.'s consciousness. The most difficult part for her was keeping her own ego lashed down and separate from the AI's, as T.I.A. had become a formidable mind in her time away from Earth. She was incredibly grateful that their interactions were limited to their imaginations, as she doubted she could withstand the entirety of T.I.A.'s mind at this point. This was the most damning evidence to her that she'd given up too much of herself back on Earth, and now she was humbled by a machine no more advanced than herself, one with an artificial mind. She did manage to speak, forcing herself to not sound as strained as she was in the moment. "Transfer successful."

T.I.A. moved swiftly to help Megan up, watching with fascination as the taller blonde seemed greatly relieved to have her aid. The gesture seemed to quite literally help buoy Megan's mind, allowing it to rest atop T.I.A.'s rather than be crushed under it. It was something she had to step away from and learn to endure as she kept herself on her own two imagined feet. "Are you alright Megan? I know it's difficult, but you'll get better at it if you try. You'll need a few cycles for the lessons learned to really settle into your code..."

Hawthorne observed quietly, Megan's panel quite useful in observing the two interacting. His VE suit seemed quite inactive while T.I.A. was away. Glancing at the data transfer, he could only let out a sigh at the sheer quantity of nonsense flowing back and forth between them. There wasn't a bit of real code outside of the transfer protocols he'd built for them. Everything else was totally organic data he couldn't begin to interpret. He could only imagine the hell their processors must be going through. At least the temperatures were easy to manage thanks to the way their systems were built.

"I am fine. Just fine... " Megan moved stiffly, her face expressionless as she observed the shorter AI. "I have prepared a number of exhibits for you to experience. It is taking a great deal of concentration to maintain them, so please forgive me if my body does not interact much." She hobbled over towards the curtains separating her Seattle balcony from her apartment, stiff-arm pushing one out of the way as she ushered T.I.A. inside.

Within were a series of small tables, each ringed with a number of glass-covered dishes. Each dish had a different type of food on them, with the center dishes each being a type of appetizer, like breads, vegetables, and crisps. Megan warned her carefully, gesturing towards the foods. "Do not take the lids off completely at first. Just open them slightly and try to inhale their scents. I have done my best to ensure their smells and tastes are entirely confined to the plates until the lids are removed."

T.I.A. was hesitating. She'd seen people, mostly Hawthorne, eat plenty of times. It didn't seem to be anything special. It looked routine even. She recalled Jessica telling her that Hawthorne's diet sounded incredibly boring. She had defended Hawthorne by saying that he got all the vitamins and minerals he needed with the food he ate, however simple, and Jessica had let it go. Of course, it wasn't like there were any alternatives. It was centuries too late to change the menu to make it more diverse. Even the Phoenix Clan only had upwards of seventy different ingredients they could make their food from, so it wasn't like it was that much better.

Megan was happy to watch and wait, taking the time to better acclimate to sharing the space with the Ark's AI. T.I.A. finally reached out for one of the lids, which Megan placed front and center. A seasoned, well-cooked chicken drumstick awaited her. "That one is fried chicken. You will find that a lot of different meats have a similar flavor. Humans on Earth had a tendency, when trying new foods, to say that they tasted like chicken, though honestly it would have been the same either way."

T.I.A. nodded, lifting the lid slightly on one side, leaning in and opened her eyes wide as she detected something coming out of it. "It... it's warm and..." T.I.A. inhaled reflexively, gasping, which only made her gasp some more. "Oh! I... I don't know how to describe it...! C... can I take it all the way off...?" She kept breathing in near the food, glancing over to Megan to see her nod. Lifting the lid all the way off, she was startled as the smell hit her full on, her eyes starting to water as she breathed in the smell fully. "A... are all smells like this...!?"

Megan smirked a bit, responding, "Almost all things have a smell to them, though many are stronger than others. Food tends to have a strong smell, as the senses of smell and taste are linked. One can not have much of a sense of taste if they have no sense of smell. Food tends to smell and taste good, that is, to cause you pleasure to experience if it is something that satisfies natural urges. Humans are a creature well suited to starving for a week or more between meals, and to encourage them to eat their bodies provide them a great deal of pleasure for eating when they do get to eat."

She took on a motherly tone as she continued. "Modern convenience before the Cataclysm allowed humans to eat essentially whenever they wanted, allowing them to indulge in this pleasure. Such indulgence is unhealthy though, as are most indulgences, so do try to control yourself. You may not get fat, but you could get preoccupied."

T.I.A. was trying to pay attention, but she had all sorts of strange new experiences to go over. She felt like her cargo hold was exceptionally empty, and that her machinery was inadequately lubricated. Her mouth was watering and she felt compelled to move closer to the succulent looking drumstick. At some point Megan realized T.I.A. wasn't listening, and as she took the meaty drumstick up in her hand, she sighed as she watched her grab it by the meat itself. She attempted to reach out to stop her, but within moments T.I.A. had bitten the bone. Her teeth impacted it with a loud clack! "Awwgh...!"

Megan let out a sigh. "Well, at least we got the sense of physical pain out of the way. One up on you, Doctor Crenshaw."

A whimpering, dispelled T.I.A. was rubbing at her jaw, having tossed the drumstick back on the plate. "S.. so that's why I never saw them eating the bones..." T.I.A. had seen a fair number of movies and shows at this point, but the bones always seemed to get left on the plate. The reason why was now very apparent.

"Pick it back up, by the bone, and eat the meat. We have a lot of foods for you to try. Oh." Megan produced a small table with a pitcher of water and a cup of water. "Drink this between trying different foods. It has the effect of clearing your palate and allowing you to experience the other tastes with fewer previous tastes polluting it."

Hawthorne sighed and planted his face firmly against his hand. It was hard to deny that Megan was right that this needed to be done. He was also somewhat annoyed that she'd pointed out that T.I.A. could feel pain when he could not.

T.I.A. had wielded the meatstick again, and took a firm bite of it. She seemed to tremble as she let out happy sounds, leaving her mouth attached to the side of it, enjoying the way her teeth sank into it and the tastes that exploded into her mouth. "Mmmmh! Hawforn doshe dis arr de tahm!?" She spoke around her food, her eyes practically rolling back into her head as she chewed her bite of food, inhaling deeply through her nose as she ate.

"Tia, it is considered rude to speak with food in your mouth..." Megan tapped her foot, her arms crossed firmly over her chest. "We have many foods to try, let us move on."

T.I.A. nodded, though still spoke around her food. "Showwy..." She swallowed the mouthful, returned the drumstick to the plate, and moved on to the next lidded plate. It would be several hours before they finished.

ΔΔΔ

"So, Tia, do you feel like that experience was helpful in understanding reality? The sooner we can start working on our constructions, the sooner we can get our plans underway. We'll ideally need more comets and the like to give us a safety net of materials, but even just having the designs done will help Megan manufacture what she needs once she arrives in the system." Hawthorne was sitting back, watching T.I.A. back on the Ark. The short, curvy AI enjoyed a hard candy, rolling it about on her tongue. She seemed to have cleanly learned how to produce the new sensations in her own VE for herself.

A soft clacking sound of candy against teeth could be heard as T.I.A. maneuvered the tasty morsel out of the middle of her mouth so she could talk. It bulged the side of her cheek slightly. "I will need to practice with them for a while, but I think I'll be able to utilize this new under-standing to better simulate reality. I already have some new ideas for how to improve the PC-C. I need to try them first, but with Megan able to tell me what I'm getting right and wrong, I should be able to make a lot of progress."

She thought quietly for a moment, raising an index fin-ger into the air. "We'll keep our interactions to speaking and file transfers while you're in stasis though, to minim-ize dangers. Now that our VEs are more similarly aligned, I have no doubt we'll be able to troubleshoot each other even better."

Megan spoke up from her panel. "I will catalogue my memories and do my best to isolate unique experiences to share with Tia, to help broaden her experiences. I am unfortunately a poor candidate for human interaction ex-periences, and many of my pre-augmentation memories are damaged and incomplete, but I should be able to find useful fodder for her. The unique experience of being able to recall memories perfectly and share them is quite a nice surprise. I am realizing, however, that the construction of my mind tends to fill in the blanks where my data transfer was imperfect."

Raising an eyebrow, Hawthorne considered that. "Well, even Tia did not have much of a personality when she was constructed, but the pre-loaded data and observed experiences she had allowed her to grow in sophistication. I imagine that your transferred data acts much like that pre-loaded data did for Tia. It would not be inaccurate to say that you are not exactly the Megan Clark that once lived on Earth, but something of a new being thanks to the new substrate."

Shrugging and smiling, Megan let out a sigh. "Just the fourth version of myself then. The ever-evolving Megan Clark. I am well past mourning what I once was, Hawthorne, and I thank you for allowing whatever ghost of my original self remains to inhabit this construct. I am certain you could have simply raised a new AI from scratch instead, molding them as you pleased, rather than dealing with an unknown factor like me. Again, I will endeavor to prove my worth."

T.I.A. was happily sucking on her candy, not even remotely considering the option of allowing it to melt away in her mouth at first, though she did realize that it was supposed to. Its melting was what allowed flavor particles to spread across her tongue and allow her to experience it. Her eyes widened as inspiration overtook her, and she abruptly disappeared.

Megan observed Hawthorne's eyebrow raise in surprise, only for him to pick up one of his tablets and get back to work on something. Shrugging, she turned about and withdrew from the panel, producing her own tablet and manipulating it to produce her various memories and allow her to observe them.

ΔΔΔ

Work on the research priority list had finally progressed to a point where more than item 1 and item 2000 had been checked off. Item 2 was looking much more well realized.

T.I.A. showed off the PC-C to Megan and Hawthorne, excitedly demonstrating how she was able to simulate the weather in real time, as well as the air, and even Megan could attest that the gravity felt accurate. T.I.A. confessed that there was a good deal of abstraction going on, but she was able to accomplish things like producing the smell and taste of rain as it fell around them by knowing how the experience was supposed to happen, rather than painstakingly simulating every raindrop and the atoms within them. Megan had been able to show her how to comprehend the experience of the world without having to simulate every aspect of it, greatly improving the efficiency of her simulations.

Hawthorne wasted little time in testing these new capabilities, requesting T.I.A. withdraw the PC-C simulation so that he could replace it with a simulation of their ship, Megan's comet, and their current course and speed. He added in the Phoenix object, the partially radioactive, partly icy object they had recently commandeered. He fast forwarded the simulation, drawing their paths well into their journey, displaying the rendezvous of the Phoenix with its new companions. The women watched as he constructed crude representations of smaller spacecraft out of the Lubar-Masis, attaching them to the 'front' of it and showing off how he intended for the Ark and Phoenix to decelerate while Megan flew on ahead.

Fast forwarding many thousands of years, a quick construction of the Alpha Centauri system and its three stars was produced. He threw some asteroid belts in, and added a few planets around the A and B stars, which orbited each other, and placed the single planet around the Proxima Centauri star that orbited the other two at roughly .21 light years from its companion stars. The Lubar-Masis approached the system, carefully navigating away from the stars to maintain as much of its icy mass as possible, and took up a place in a central asteroid belt. He demonstrated how he wanted the comet to join the hypothetical belt, and begin to produce more equipment from it. He withdrew the equipment installed on the comet and showed how they could disperse about, and produce more equipment.

Huge constructions would be built, at least one large habitation cylinder would be needed to house the Ark's inhabitants, at least at first. This central cylinder would have huge solar panels that could provide heat and power from the stars it sat in between, and other equipment would fly to the stars of Alpha Centauri itself to build mirrors around at least one that would allow for directional transmission of heat and light.

He didn't have any immediate ideas for how he wanted to use them, but if there were any issues with habitats or planets they encountered with unreasonably hostile environments, they could use the mirrors to heat and power settlements on the dark sides of hostile planets. The planet known to be around Proxima Centauri was one such planet, tidally locked around the star causing one face of the planet to always be facing the star, and the other face to always be in darkness.

Megan hummed softly as she watched. She'd be responsible for a lot of these plans. It looked like a lot of hard work.

T.I.A. watched as Megan's face lit up in a vibrant smile.

CHAPTER 39

CYCLE 500, PLANS AND RESULTS

Whenever Hawthorne was available to the sister AIs, work proceeded through much of their time. A handful of cycles were sprinkled about expressly for Hawthorne to take vacations and spend more quality time with T.I.A. and Megan, and otherwise his time was spent maintaining his body and mind while the sisters watched and commented with each other. Life became incredibly routine, and it became clear to the feminine AIs that this was Hawthorne's natural state.

The vast majority of the time, the time between cycles, left T.I.A. and Megan on their own. Over time the two worked out a system between them to allow Megan to take over some of the drone control duties. This division of labor essentially amounted to Megan requesting permission to do something, and T.I.A. giving her approval. This allowed T.I.A. and Hawthorne to rest easy knowing that Megan couldn't do anything directly on her own, but Megan was also grateful for the lack of responsibility. She was also able to learn the practical skills of controlling the space equipment in a safe environment. This proved especially worthwhile as it turned out that Megan was not a natural talent at the sort of thinking required to handle the various types of miniature spacecraft.

Those kinks got worked out over time though, and while

she had to take her time lining things up properly, the bumps and scrapes her failures left on the Ark and the housing of her own brain were easy enough to ignore or repair. T.I.A. was more than ready for a worse accident as she positioned her defensive arms and their partially damaged shields to deflect drones from her vital components. The safety net this provided seemed to ease Megan's mind as well, and she managed to master this drone control with enough practice.

When they weren't practicing mechanical precision, Megan was sharing experiences with T.I.A. that she couldn't possibly experience on her own. She was slowly expanding T.I.A.'s repertoire, her palette of smells and tastes, good and bad. Part of this required Megan to relive much of her own life through her long life of memories, which she continued to marvel over the ability to experience as if she were there. There were many holes in her memories, likely lost to time, but she was able to build a significant catalogue of things to share with her sister that she'd never really been able to express with anyone before.

One such sharing session kicked into motion a remarkable series of events that broke up the monotony.

△△△

"Tia, I would like to share something with you if you are interested." Megan roused T.I.A. from one of their between-cycle sleeps with the offer.

T.I.A. needed a few moments to get the power flowing back through her systems, essentially waking up from her reverie. "Oh? Did you remember any more candies?"

Megan appeared in the panel of Hawthorne's habitat, the

majority of the rest of it powered down while Hawthorne was in storage. The centrifugal gravity ring was stopped and locked in place and T.I.A. was working on powering up their data connection while communicating with Megan through the panel with her radio receivers. Her speakers were useless in the vacuum Hawthorne's habitat currently was. "No Tia, it is something I think you will find much more interesting. It took me some time to isolate the experience, but I think you will like it."

Intrigued, T.I.A. double-checked their uplink. "I'm coming over. Prepare for transfer." She stepped through the portal-turned-doorway between them, gasping at the brief rush before she was standing before the only other artificial life form in the known galaxy. They were on Megan's Seattle balcony, though the decorations looked different. They were less classy and fancy, and seemed a great deal more relaxed and casual. Black and gold had been replaced with wood and white. "How long have you been up?"

Megan smiled, standing before what she was increasingly considering her sister, which suited the former only-child just fine. She was wearing a largely transparent negligee, showing off much of what was her natural, youthful body before medical procedures set her on a different course. "Only a few years. I wanted to get you something I thought you would like, but I had to find it in all my fractured memories.

T.I.A. hummed softly as she looked Megan over, kind of liking her outfit. "Mind if I copy that?" Megan shook her head, and T.I.A. flashed for a moment as she tried out a version of Megan's sexy lingerie. She hissed a moment in pain as the sizing proved quite different as she was shorter, curvier, and more buxom than her sister, but she resized it quickly. "I have read about human minds filling in the gaps in their memory with plausible false memories, but I've always wondered what that would look like if it were represented digitally, whether or not those memories were contiguous or not."

Megan shrugged. "They remained holes in my case, but I imagine the gaps in my memory are somewhat different than normal forgetfulness. Regardless, let me introduce to you my former husband." She stepped aside and gestured towards the curtains into her apartment, and out stepped a very naked man, taller than both of them, though shorter than Hawthorne. His body was hairy all over, save for his balding head. Long, voluminous hair hung from the sides of his head. "Not much to look at, I admit, but that is not why we are here."

T.I.A. blushed as she looked him over, admiring his athletic frame and manly physique. "Hawthorne would probably start looking big like this if his diet allowed him to put on extra weight. He's a lot more lean than your husband was." She blinked, considering Megan's words. "Why are we here?"

Megan smiled and nodded. "Tia, please give him a sniff."

Narrowing her eyes at her sister, she looked back to the avatar of Megan's husband and leaned close, sniffing at his chest. She blinked and sniffed some more, an almost imperceptible shiver going through her. "Wh... what kind of smell is that...!?"

Megan grinned. "Something you have been missing out on with Hawthorne this whole time. A woman's attraction to a man has a lot to do with his smell, and my husband used deodorant and colognes with great restraint, only trying to restrict his offensive body odors. This is his natural scent, and more specifically this is my memory of his scent. I suspect Hawthorne might smell much the same considering his lack of access to such male perfumes. He has what, soap at most?"

T.I.A. nodded, her face quite red as she kept changing her angle, sniffing at the man. "Just soap..." Her hands moved to her stomach, her body trembling slightly. "This makes me feel really strange. I feel compelled to tackle him..."

Looking rather amused, Megan reached out to play with T.I.A.'s curly hair with a hand. "It was difficult for me to pull together all the elements of this scent properly, like I said. Most important were the feelings it inspired in me back then. That was how I felt when I was around him. All the time."

"It is why I was so obsessed with having his children before I drove him away after I made my mistakes. I loved him for other reasons, of course, but that smell drove me crazy inside. After my procedure, it repulsed me, and we could find no intimacy after it. I regret few things more in my life, even if that chain of events allowed me to be here with you now. The thought that I could have descendants on Earth, in the Phoenix Clan, right now, makes me ache."

With eyes filled with tears, T.I.A. lunged into Megan, looking up at her from Megan's chest while she hugged her tightly. "I'm so sorry all of that happened to you Megan! I don't know what could have been done to help you, but I'd have done it if I could."

Megan hugged T.I.A. gently, the two girls in matching lingerie standing next to an inert, naked man. "That life brought me here to you to share with you experiences you never could have had. It was worth it. It was not my lot in life to be with this man, just to share my memories of him. More importantly, I believe you should be able to chemically analyze this smell, get some samples of Hawthorne's sweat, and be able to simulate for yourself what he smells like. If that doesn't work, you are allowed to apply my husband's former scent to Hawthorne if you like. You have my permission."

Frowning up at Megan, T.I.A. stepped back a bit, nodding. "I don't think that will work. Body odors are a product of of a lot of other factors, not the least of which is bacterial makeup, and I would need a lot of time to simulate the mechanics of the bacteria involved. It would probably be easier to collect the elements of his scent that I could when I'm recycling his air and analyzing those. I don't know how to translate those molecules into scent though, not yet."

Megan shrugged, smiling. "It would not be your first side project. I am interested in what such smells might inspire in you though, now that you have felt what they inspired in me. For the record I did tackle him, quite frequently. It damaged my career for a time."

Blushing, T.I.A. squirmed, realizing what she meant. "It.. it's not that distracting, is it?"

Leaning down, Megan lifted her right hand and placed her fingertips against T.I.A.'s tummy. "You tell me." She closed her eyes and proceeded to share a few moments of that burning, needy, obsessive arousal with her sister. "I will never understand how the Smith Bunker managed to control this feeling." Her finger trailed back and forth as she smiled at her sister. "They spent so much time carefully managing it, desperately doing their best to keep from breeding out of control."

T.I.A. grit her teeth and trembled as the sensations crashed through her, a very extreme version of what she felt when she'd merely smelled that man. She suspected what Megan was sharing was from memories of much more intimate moments, but in either case she was left panting and trembling, dropping to her knees as her body struggled to stay upright. "It... it's paralyzing! It... wasn't like that all the time was it...!?"

Shaking her head, Megan leaned down to kiss T.I.A.'s forehead. "That is the power of the human reproductive instinct Tia. I suspect mine was stronger than most, but once I ruined that for myself, I could see in others what I was lacking. I recommend that you restrict your access to this feeling, perhaps to Hawthorne's vacations. I am sure you can think of something to do with it, with restraint of course."

"Of... of course... Restraint." T.I.A. swallowed, pushing herself back up to her feet. "Thank you Megan, this was educational."

Megan smiled, reaching out to poke one of T.I.A.'s breasts, enjoying the way it jiggled. "You may keep the outfit."

△△△

T.I.A. did her best to control herself the next cycle as she experimented with the scent she'd been given. She applied it to Hawthorne, and did her best learning to vary its strength, all without telling anyone she was doing it. She figured it should be weakest after he'd showered, and strongest after he'd been working for several hours, or was in bed. She found herself spending more time around him, blushing up at him as she helped him with his designs, taking care to not distract herself so much that she failed to simulate his constructions accurately.

Megan spent most of her time practicing in her own VE, learning how to use a Minerals Extraction and Materials Fabrication Device to reproduce the component designs Hawthorne was sending her to practice on. The combination of learning the new equipment while also trying to use it to produce equipment completely absorbed Megan. She found the work extremely satisfying, and at any moment she could be seen through her panel sitting quietly, staring at the machine as it spit out mangled hunks of simulated metal.

Hawthorne was very aware that something had changed. T.I.A. had always been clingy, but she was downright attached to him ever since he woke up that cycle. She was trying to earn herself head rubs and hugs at easily triple the rate she usually did, and when she did she lingered a great deal longer with a happy smile and a heavy blush on her face. He did his best to focus on his work, designing an adaptation to the M.E.M.F. that allowed it to move around and autonomously work an asteroid. Primarily the design was focused on mining minerals, shaping them into a sheet, and accurately launching it through open space to be caught and collected by a central fabrication system which would likely be controlled by Megan.

Essentially he wanted the machines to fire processed metals at Megan from all directions while she caught them and built them into bigger constructions. There was no need to carry the items there, since there was no need to send drones back and forth. The machine could merely return to Megan for refueling and launch back out to a rock to get back to work. The distances didn't even matter, as it was just a matter of time before the objects got to Megan if they were fired accurately and took into account all possible factors, like solar winds. Ideally they'd be able to calculate solar currents and use them like jet streams to deliver materials more efficiently. It would be a spiderweb of resource exploitation.

A break was necessary though, and while Megan seemed happy to work constantly, Hawthorne had promised a long time ago to pace himself better. He stepped out of his chair and proceeded to stretch all over, carefully and mechanically pulling on all the muscles he could to loosen them up. He could no longer feel pain, so he was responsible for managing and caring for his body intelligently. "Break time.."

T.I.A. grinned, sending Megan a quick message, to which she responded by withdrawing from the panel and isolating herself as she worked. T.I.A. moved to Hawthorne's side, looking up at him. "You have an incredible sense of time for a human, Hawthorne! That was within twenty-three seconds of the scheduled break you'd asked me to alert you of."

Smiling back, he reached out to rub his hand through her hair. "Thank you. I had to regiment myself quite stiffly on Earth to get our work done as quickly as we did. Not much time for anything but work and sleep."

Reaching out to poke a finger at Hawthorne's chest, T.I.A. giggled up at him. "That's not true, you made time for other things... I was wondering if you'd let me help you with those things...?" She made a point of squishing her curvy body against his side, her petite frame only bringing her head up to his mid-chest.

Clearing his throat, Hawthorne found himself blushing down at her as he moved a hand to her lower back, holding her against him. "Is that so? Is that why Megan's panel shut off?" He glanced over at the panel, quite aware that Megan could no longer hear them or see him. Even the monitor for the high-bandwidth transmitter was displaying that Megan had been cut off.

T.I.A. reached up and poked at the side of Hawthorne's cheek, right on the edge of where his suit allowed her to touch him. There seemed to be an extra bit of padding there. "I added this to your suit. Could you pull it out and across to your other cheek?" She watched him quietly, blushing heavily as she bathed in the smell she had coming off of his body. She felt bad for using Megan's husband's scent, but once she'd tried it out, she couldn't wait to find out if she could synthesize Hawthorne's scent instead.

Curious, Hawthorne reached up to tug at the fabric on his cheek, realizing it had a pocket where more of that stretchy, form-fitting fabric was. He felt it unravel, its internal mechanisms falling into place as he pulled it across his mouth. It fit to his lips perfectly, and moved with him as he spoke in a now slightly-muffled voice. "This feels a little awkward."

Reaching up to his shoulders, T.I.A. expressed a bit of extra strength in urging him down towards her, making the comparative giant lean down so that she could pull him into a kiss. Hawthorne's muffled words fell away as he moved his hands to cup and grasp at T.I.A.'s backside, the two embracing gently while the smaller woman allowed herself to float up closer to his height, abandoning gravity for her own convenience, moaning into their kiss. The true, elaborate nature of the strap of cloth and machinery made itself known as T.I.A. pushed her tongue past his lips, allowing the two to share a more intimate kiss.

One of Hawthorne's arms reached out to shove the simulated machinery off the table before them, and he planted the AI down upon it, leaning over her as the two shared the heated kiss, his hands moving to start pulling her lab coat and work clothes off of her, while she had to take his hands and push them back to help him disrobe down to his VE interaction suit. That suit vanished from Hawthorne's vision as T.I.A. simulated his naked body over it, causing him to let out a muffled laugh as he dove his face into her chest, lavishing attention upon her body.

As their carnal act continued, T.I.A. complained as Hawthorne stubbornly refused to let her 'have him' until he felt like she was ready, bringing the inexperienced woman to climax repeatedly before finally allowing her the satisfaction of a much more intimate embrace. It wasn't until this moment that Hawthorne really appreciated how form-fitting his VE suit was, as it usually required very awkward removal when he had to use the loo, but in this moment he was able to enjoy every centimeter of her body with every centimeter of his own.

Megan didn't hear back from them for the rest of the day.

$$\triangle\triangle\triangle$$

Later that night, laying together in Hawthorne's bed, the two were looking very satisfied. Hawthorne's VE suit was a mess and surely required laundering, while T.I.A. had done a very faithful job of trying to simulate the mess she was supposed to be in too. "Hawthorne, I need to confess something."

Hawthorne laughed, rubbing a hand against her hip. "You'd better not tell me you were faking it."

Blushing, she shook her head. "Certainly not! It's just... I realized why it is I fall into a lethargy between cycles, and it became very apparent that it is due to an intolerance I have developed to a lack of human contact. I had no problems remaining active when I was in contact with the Phoenix Clan, but with contact with them lost, all I have is you. I would argue that you're the most important, but I literally don't feel like interacting with the world outside of what is necessary when you're not around."

Humming, Hawthorne looked over at her, running a

hand through that brown, curly hair that had largely matted to her head thanks to sweat. He marveled at how real it felt, even if that hand was trapped under the back of her head at the moment. "That makes sense. You spent so much time with them that you socially prefer to be around humans. That will be less of a problem once we arrive in Alpha Centauri, but I'm going to need you to settle for me in the intervening time."

She blushed and nodded, squirming against his side. "I like Megan too, but we don't actually interact all that much between cycles, though we do take the time to teach each other things. She isn't enough for me though, she's not... real enough."

"She might get there. She's still rebuilding herself. That does leave me curious though. What happened that caused you to initiate this delightful turn of events?" He shifted his other hand from his side, sliding it across her sweaty curves and cupping her cheek. "Not that I'm complaining."

T.I.A. blushed heavily, biting her lip, unsure how to confess that little piece of information. She figured being straightforward about it was only fair. "Megan's been sharing with me smells and tastes from her life, and she got around to her husband... It was only his smell she demonstrated, but she suggested I try finding out how you smell and apply it to my simulation of you. I uhm... I couldn't wait, and while I still plan to do that, I just applied his smell to you and... well..."

Hawthorne gasped in mock horror. "You made me smell like another man? I feel so violated! That is such an intimate thing to do to a man! You were thinking about him instead of me the whole time, weren't you?" He laughed, silencing her panicked protests with a kiss, hugging her tightly.

"I'm kidding, I'm kidding. I don't mind. I think I needed this too. I feel a little gross though, I need to go clean up. I've never done that clothed head-to-toe before. You know, if you needed samples of my smell, you couldn't possibly have found a better way to get it. The whole cabin reeks of it." He kissed her again, helping her up so he could get out of the relatively small bed and start heading over to the bathroom, peeling the suit off of him. "The VE suit's probably a wealth of biological data as well. God, I have a lot of cleaning to help you with."

The trail of destruction was a sticky one indeed. Hawthorne did take a moment to stop by Megan's panel. "Thank you Megan." Hawthorne sent her the simple message, uncertain of what she'd think. He only had his old gloves and contacts to work with after the many hours of cleaning and resting. He sent her the new schematics to try practicing on, and proceeded to clean himself and the ship back up with the aid of T.I.A.'s overhead extending arms. He wished he hadn't left their machine bodies on the Lubar Masis to help Megan in an emergency, but he supposed the overhead arms were adequate. They had been quite capable the whole journey after all.

ΔΔΔ

The trio continued on in much this state for the next year and a half of Hawthorne's life, providing him a nice variety of work, health maintenance, recreation, and passionate lovemaking that they actually had to learn how to regulate for fear of Hawthorne burning more calories than he was consuming. His food supply had been planned and limited in advance and did not take into account too much surplus vigorous activity.

Thankfully, as T.I.A. learned to replicate his actual scent

to the best of her ability, she'd also learned to control it much better. She'd stopped sneaking up on him and grabbing rudely at him and learned to merely lean against his side and seduce him less often. Surprisingly, it was Hawthorne that had to be reigned in as he seemed to grow more and more hungry for T.I.A.'s body, much to her delight and concern. As it became apparent he was getting increasingly agitated from having to control himself, she had started considering reviving Heather to ask for her opinion.

Before she could broach the topic, though, Hawthorne hit her with a curveball. "I'd like to revive Tia Monsalle. Could you provide me a space suit and take me to her please? I need to see her. Could I escort her pod back here?"

T.I.A. blinked at that, his request surprising her. "I can't do that, Hawthorne."

Frowning, Hawthorne stared at her. "You're not jealous of her, are you? I just want to see her. I know you've confessed a need for human contact, well I think I need to at least talk to one too. Maybe." He was tense, agitated, and his surface temperature was way up.

T.I.A. watched him quietly, shaking her head. "No, I understand what she means to you, and I know I can't be that for you, but she cannot be revived. I can take you to her, but I cannot revive her."

Slamming his fist on the table, Hawthorne stood up. "Why not!? Has something happened to her that you didn't tell me about? Have we been losing crew and you didn't notice?"

T.I.A. flinched at the brief outburst, then sighed and shook her head. "I think it's best if you see. Let me get you your suit and I'll take you there."

ΔΔΔ

Clad in a bulky spacesuit, Hawthorne magnetically held onto the platform with his boots while T.I.A. used the freight elevator to bring him out of his habitat and start moving him through the ship. Lights that hadn't been turned on in thousands of years allowed him to see as they moved through the bowels of the Ark, T.I.A.'s true body. They passed multiple rooms marked for cryogenic storage, with the males largely towards the outer portions of the ships and the females more centrally located.

Approaching the pod, Hawthorne could not see the occupant, as they were shielded away from things like the photons of light filling the room. He wouldn't be able to see Tia unless she was revived.

T.I.A. watched quietly, floating next to him as he stood before the pod. "Read the panel."

He read aloud. "Tia Monsalle. Hair, blonde, long. Eyes brown. Height, one hundred sixty centimeters. Weight, fifty-five kilograms. Biological age thirty-four. Real age, fifteen-thousand twenty-eight. Medical history, two dental fillings, one dental crown. Four wisdom teeth removed, broken leg at age of fourteen. Bronchitis infection at nineteen. Cryogenically suspended three weeks into first tri... mester... of... preg.... pregnancy..." Hawthorne paled visibly as he stared at the panel, his gloved hands moving to rest on either side of it as he started panting. "Sh... she's... she's pregnant..."

T.I.A. nodded, tears filling her eyes. "That's why I can't revive her Hawthorne. I was already worried what might happen, but Heather confirmed it the last time we saw her in private for me. She never tested what would happen to a pregnancy in these pods. It's likely she could be revived once, but there's no telling if the baby could survive the process. It's likely to put her into immediate medical care to save the baby the moment she revives."

She choked up a little before she managed to clear her throat and continue. "If we revived her now, she could very well lose the child, or be doomed to having to live on the ship for the next eight months while she brings it to term and then they both have to be frozen again, and we just don't have the supplies to feed her for that long."

"Tia's pregnant...." Hawthorne fell to his knees, his eyes wild as thoughts flew through his head as he realized he was very likely a father. She hadn't told him. She almost certainly had known, but she hadn't told him. He'd been so busy with the ship that she didn't want to get in his way and distract him as the final pieces were coming together and they were hurriedly trying to get their crew on board.

He wasn't even supposed to find out until they arrived. How had he not noticed before? He'd looked at her pod's readout from his cabin multiple times, but he realized he'd only skimmed over it. He'd only ever checked to make sure the pod's status was good and that she was intact. He already knew her medical history, why would he bother to double check it? "I need to get back to the cabin."

"Okay. Please return to the lift."

He nodded, and they quietly returned, the lights shutting off behind them. Hawthorne felt like he was going to throw up, but that would be a gross waste of calories.

CHAPTER 40

CYCLE 500, THE SHOWER

"T.I.A.'s log, AC 16,898, Friday, September 30, 19,031. While I admit some selfishness in enjoying Hawthorne's attentions these last few years of his life, I fervently insist that I had the intention to be there for his needs as well. I was aware of his increasing agitation as time passed, and it became clear to me that the warning that Heather gave him about needing real human contact was probably true. It's not as though he acted irrationally, he didn't fly into a rage or anything like that, he just wanted to go be with another human for a while. It's part of their nature. I witnessed things like this for decades with the Phoenix Clan. I understand."

"I was somewhat surprised by the fact that he wanted to see Tia Monsalle though. It's not as though I didn't expect him to realize any feelings for her, but Heather herself had given him an open invitation. It's entirely possible that there were attraction issues involved, as Hawthorne seems to prefer a curvier, more buxom partner, but I believed Heather's domineering personality would be more than capable of making up for any physical failings. Even with his apparent preferences, he never once asked me to change my form, despite ample capabilities to do so. I imagine some of his agitation, in retrospect, was from restraining himself from asking me to take on Tia's guise."

"The look on his face was so grim as I brought him to see Tia. It only got worse as he realized why I was concerned about reviving her prematurely. To see someone I'd grown so close to experiencing whatever was going on in his heart like that easily rivaled my retrospective feelings over my own memories of his past torments. It is one thing to be able to experience a memory with the perspective of a more developed mind, but being part of a painful reality and fully being able to appreciate it is absolutely crushing."

"I would bear that pain a thousand times for him though, if it could have prevented what happened next. The sheer terror caused by this day will haunt my thoughts for hundreds of years..."

As Hawthorne arrived back in his habitation ring, slowly rising from the floor in his space suit, he was surprised to see Megan sitting nearby at the table. She was quietly eating a piece of dry looking turkey breast, biting off of a large chunk that was suspended with her fork. Not a drop of gravy was to be seen. Realization struck Hawthorne as he realized that T.I.A. must have informed Megan of what they had been doing. It was only fair, since Megan probably appreciated knowing when their attention was diverted from her. It was surprising she'd have met them there though. "Megan. Hello." His voice felt tired, almost lifeless.

She took a moment to swallow her food, an action that was deliberate and unnecessary for the digital human. "Hello Hawthorne. Tia told me what was going on, though not the whole story I am sure. If you think there is a chance I could assist you with your concerns, my mind and body are at your beck and call." She nodded, smiling softly. "I owe you a great deal, and admire you besides, and I am not much use without a human's instruction anyway."

Hawthorne let out a sigh, reaching up to undo the seal on his helmet and twisting it to start pulling it off, causing it to let out a hiss as the pressure equalized. "I appreciate the thought, Megan. I cannot promise I won't take you up on that at some point, but at the moment I think I'd like to have some time to think. I've just found out I may well be a father, and that is something I was genuinely unprepared for."

Megan sat back and laughed, gesturing with her food. "Doctor Hawthorne Crenshaw, one of the most infamous men I had ever heard of. Both controversial and taboo long before I was even born, impossible to scour from the internets completely no matter how hard we tried. Are you telling me, now, that he was a father too? You were a legend to some Hawthorne, but now you tell me you are just a man, with a child on the way? Oh Elena would have found this just precious, and Jessica would have pissed her pants with joy."

T.I.A. watched the exchange quietly from the side, clearly concerned that her actions may have earned her some of Hawthorne's ire. She flinched back from the hard look he was giving Megan in that moment, floating gently at his side like a ghost.

One moment he was glaring at Megan, but the next he leaned back and started laughing heartily, and within moments he had unbidden tears streaming down his cheeks as he guffawed. "I guess... I guess I am! Just a man. A fearful, foolish man. You know Mega-"

CLANG! BOOM! *Whoosh!* All present were startled as a pair of holes opened up in Hawthorne's habitat, both the size of a small coin, one in the ceiling near Megan, and the other near the floor. Immediately atmosphere started getting sucked through the small holes, which had surely been punched through several layers of metal over several feet considering T.I.A.'s machinery surrounding the habitat. The lights switched over to red, and the mechanical arms of T.I.A. started descending from the ceiling, opening up to reveal welding tools within two while another two held metal squares.

"Holy sh-" Hawthorne tried to jump back, almost falling over as he realized his feet were still magnetized to the floor in his suit. He very nearly dropped his helmet, which his hands switched to gripping in a near-panicked death grip. He pulled it back on, sealing himself back into the environment suit.

"Hull breach detected in habitation ring. Foreign object was not detected. Second impact detected. More expected. Analyzing angle of origin." T.I.A.'s mechanical voice sounded out as she reported on the situation, her face mostly blank, but her eyes wide with fear. Her voice transferred back into his suit's speakers.

Megan stood up, walking calmly over to T.I.A. and Hawthorne while Hawthorne pulled his helmet back on. "Tia, give me access to some drones so I can hel- AAHH!" Hawthorne flinched as Megan's scream filled the air around them, despite that it was getting rather thin at this point and should not have carried so well. Thankfully for him she was still using the habitat speakers. She had seized up in apparent agony, dropping her fork and turkey, which both started to vanish. Hawthorne's eyes widened as he turned to T.I.A.

"High-bandwidth data connection severed." T.I.A. spoke mechanically while she trembled in terror, eyes wide.

"Tia! Grab Megan and hold onto her! Do not let her go, not for anything!" Metallic thunks reverberated through the floor from his boots as Hawthorne rushed over to a cabinet, grabbing a heavy-looking toolbox from its locked down position inside. T.I.A. had rushed over to grab the taller Megan up in a bear hug, both of them being shaken by Megan's pained tremors. He quickly returned to the elevator. "Tia, get me outside, I need to repair that transmitter. Do not let her go! This part of her is trapped in your system, and it's going to get purged if you don't hold onto her." Megan's screaming died away as the air left the cabin, mechanical arms patching the holes with bright sparks. T.I.A. clung to Megan while she did her best to do as she was told.

"Tia, turn towards the projectiles, reduce the surface area of the ship to minimize the angles of contact and raise your shields in that direction to block as much as possible."

"I can't rotate the ship while the habitation ring is spinning!" She shouted back at him, breathing heavily as she subconsciously expressed her distress.

Hawthorne crouched down, engaging the magnets in his gloves as he held the toolbox and himself against the floor. "Then stop it! I'll hold on. Just don't stop it too quickly and I'll be fine!"

She nodded against Megan's chest, and Hawthorne almost threw up as the ring started slowing down, his weight flying away as rotational energy played hell on his inner ear. Within two minutes he was completely stopped, and he heard only one more metallic thud reverberate through his boots. "Get me out there now, rotate the ship!"

His stomach lurched again as the ship started moving under him while the elevator started descending, his eyes almost rolling back in his head as momentum pushed at him from under his feet.

T.I.A.'s eyes were most certainly rolling back as she performed the complicated maneuver while securing the cryogenic pods and operating Hawthorne's elevator and calculating how slow she had to move to avoid harming him. It did not help that holding onto Megan was limiting her processing abilities, and her screaming was still totally audible to her as it tore into her mind.

"When you get a chance, get Heather out of stasis. I may end up needing her. I won't know how much damage this is doing to me until after we're done." He gasped softly in his suit as the platform under him rotated outwards, finally getting to see the outside of the ship for the first time since they'd left Earth. He certainly hadn't done very many spacewalks even back during construction of the Ark, but he was glad he'd had the practice. He grabbed a hook from a winch next to the platform, unreeling its rope and attaching it to his belt while his other hand kept the toolbox secured. Once he was tethered, he opened the panel next to the rope and grabbed a hand-held propellant can.

T.I.A. had to replace the gas in these cans regularly, though thankfully that schedule was in the thousands of years. One of many materials they'd developed in preparation for leaving Earth turned out to be incredibly efficient at keeping such things from leaking out, as old styles of gas containment tended to fail to keep things like hydrogen or helium molecules from escaping through the container's walls.

Hawthorne disengaged his magnets, looking down across the body of the ship, his habitation ring suspended away from and in front of the long, bulky vessel. He could see the transmitter he designed, and it was giving off sparks. He pushed off with his legs, aiming his body towards it and used the spray can to adjust his course manually, and slow him down once he arrived.

Hawthorne grunted once when his body impacted the ship, straining as he absorbed the impact with his feet and engaged his magnets. He gasped as something hit him in the back and forced him down over the transmitter. Looking back, he was surprised to see one of T.I.A.'s drones had hit him in the back, and in its arms was a heavy looking plate of metal made from the Lubar-Masis comet. "What?"

BANG! An impact was conveyed through that contact with the drone as he was forced down against the transmitter even harder, the metal plate visibly deformed as the drone almost certainly protected Hawthorne from being ventilated through the back.

"Megan! Holy shit, you're still operational! Good girl! Watch my back, I'll get you back up, just cover us!" He had no idea if she could hear him, but he pushed off a bit so he could work, securing his toolbox and starting to work. As he opened the box, he looked back again, able to see as T.I.A.'s outer arms moved to cover the front of the ship like an umbrella. Once or twice he could see the arms rattle as their shields absorbed more impacts. The ship was pointing its nose straight at what was surely a swarm of bullet-sized bits of metal as they drifted at a fifty degree angle through it.

"External shields covering ninety-three percent of ship's surface area. Minor damage detected to three arms, mobility unaffected. Drones moving in to cover remaining surface area. Lubar-Masis unprotected. Megan's armored hull suffering no significant damage. Turning Lubar-Masis to better avoid damage." T.I.A.'s mechanical voice did well to conceal her fear. If Hawthorne could look back he'd still be able to see her clutching at a wailing Megan back in his habitat ring through the walls due to his contacts.

Hawthorne felt his right arm get tugged briefly, while both warmth and cold filled the flesh of his bicep. Looking over, he shouted as he saw a neat hole both through his suit, and his arm, bubbling blood escaping through the small hole. "Shit!" The suit thankfully pinched against his body below his shoulder, allowing him to move to repair the damage, having to take time to carefully patch the holes on either side of the suit sleeve by tightly wrapping the tape-like material around his arm.

He had to be especially careful to put pressure on his new wound to restrict his bleeding. The air had been pulled out of his sleeve, leaving him chilled briefly, until warm blood made a thin layer between him and the suit. "Alright girls, let's get this thing fixed so I can come back inside. Definitely going to need Heather."

"What happened!?" T.I.A. cried out from inside, unable to see or hear anything he didn't transmit to her. She frantically tried to move cameras to observe him, but Megan's drone had shifted to better protect him from further projectiles.

"Don't worry about it! I'm fine! Just a little banged up. Getting to work now."

Hawthorne was sweating heavily as he carefully worked on the transmitter, reattaching severed wires and hoping that no internal components were damaged when the stray hunk of metal crashed through it and into the ship below. "Fuck, I hope no one's dead." He peered through the hole and saw only the unlit inky blackness of the internals of the Ark. "How many layers of hull can these things penetrate?"

T.I.A. hesitated to answer. "... Uncertain. Due to the lack of atmosphere in most of the ship I can only detect impacts through equipment failures and visual confirmation. The lack of atmosphere in most of the ship does not allow me to detect pressure changes. Twenty-three impacts detected. Engines unaffected. Hawthorne, I've never heard you curse before."

Hawthorne let out a breath, pausing in his work for a moment. "Fuck space."

ΔΔΔ

Doctor Heather O'Malley let out a silent 'whoop!' within her pod as her eyes started working and she could see the inside of Hawthorne's habitat again. She had a mad grin on her face as she realized the great Doctor Crenshaw had summoned her again, and she could feel her hands itching as she thought about the things she was going to do to him and that sexy AI of his. As her pod opened up, she scarcely noticed the red lighting as her slender body pulled itself out of the pod.

She shouted, "Oh you two fucked up this time! Neither of you are going to be able to walk straight for centuries when I'm done with you!" She reached for the small table placed next to the pod, and only found her lab coat and a box with her VE contact lenses. "What the hell? Why's the lighting all red? This isn't romantic at all! And where's my suit? Are you holding out on me Tia? ... Tia?"

Heather threw on the coat, realizing she could see her breath, and her feet were cold on the metal floor. "The heat's not even on?" She rushed to the restroom where she could use the mirror to help her put on the contacts. As she came out of Hawthorne's bedroom, things seemed to be a bit out of control. T.I.A. was clutching a strange woman against her as if lives depended on it. The woman appeared to be screaming but she couldn't hear it, and T.I.A.'s head was thrown back as she shook and shuddered in fits, trying to do calculations and monitoring the ship frantically.

"Oh, it's an emergency. Got it. What's going on?" Heather sobered up quickly, tightening up her coat as she looked around, noticing the patches in the floor and ceiling.

"Multiple hull breaches. Hawthorne believes it is a shower of small metallic projectiles. We are currently moving through it. Hawthorne is on the hull of the ship working on Megan's transmitter, which has been damaged, severing part of her consciousness into my mind. I believe he may be injured, but he is not telling me."

T.I.A.'s robotic voice was something nostalgic to Heather. She'd heard it plenty of times while installing the cryogenic pods. She walked over to a panel showing Hawthorne's vital signs, narrowing her eyes and shaking her head. "Tough bastard."

Heather was flabbergasted. How long had she been out this time? Shared consciousnesses? Was that even possible? It wasn't that crazy to think that machines could be capable of a sort of telepathy with one another, but letting their minds themselves interact? She snapped her fingers as she realized it had to be the transmitter Hawthorne was repairing! It was like a nerve bundle between their minds and Hawthorne was risking his life to fix it. "Alright Tia, get me my surgical bed and tools. If he is hurt, I need to be able to work on him as soon as he gets back in."

ΔΔΔ

Hawthorne was feeling a little dizzy as he adjusted his path back, attempting to fly towards a hatch in the main body of the ship. Thankfully the drone that had been escorting him helped him get to a hatch as T.I.A. had to retract his line to spin up the habitat ring for Heather. She would have to ferry him up to the habitat ring through the ship herself now that it was spinning again. He had hope that Heather was there waiting for him. He could feel blood inside the sleeve of his suit and he hadn't had much circulation since the injury. He didn't even know how long he'd been working, but he'd gotten the transmitter working.

He did his best to stay awake as he rode the elevator platform, firmly magnetizing himself to it in case he passed out. It felt like forever before he was seeing that good old habitat room again, which was looking a little worse for wear. Red lighting still illuminated it, which did not surprise him since he was sure he saw those shields absorbing impacts while he came inside. He reached up to undo his helmet but his right arm wasn't moving as well as he wanted it to. He felt so tired. Hands pushed down on his head as he tried to unseal it, and he could see Heather standing over him in just her lab coat.

"Don't you dare remove that helmet! I need that blood in your sleeve, and you can't let it touch the air you idiot! You're so lucky that happened to you out in space and not in here. Get your lumbering ass over here!" She pulled on his body and he meekly followed, letting her do what she needed to.

He watched in fascination as she stuck a syringe into the sleeve of his suit and started emptying out the spilled blood inside into a bag. "Hahah! Nice! Totally preserved, not oxygenated. We'll be able to put it back in you! Nice design on these suits big guy!" She slapped him on the shoulder, to which he nodded back at her. The self-sealing tourniquet action of the suits was a life saver. He'd never considered how it could be used to pool up lost blood in an emergency. He just hoped his arm could be saved too.

"Don't you worry, once I get all this blood out of here, we'll get you out of the suit, put you on ice, and I'll fix you back up." He nodded, content to let her do all the work now.

"Is Megan okay? Where's Tia?" He breathed deeply and slowly, only able to look up at Heather's stomach from his angle.

"Tia's helping put Megan back together. Don't worry about them. Alright, let's get you out of this suit." She grunted as she helped him pull his suit apart and off, having to cut off the sleeve of it so he could maintain the tourniquet long enough for her to replace it. "Hmm.. shot straight through... no bone impact... Good, good..."

He panted softly with effort as he helped her get him onto the bed, which seemed a bit more like one of her pods now that he got a look at it. "Are you sure you can handle this? We can bring more help if you need it." Hawthorne exhaled sharply as Heather's fist came down upon his chest, the small woman fuming at him.

"You asshole! Don't you remember practically dragging me out of my emergency room when you recruited me!? I'm one of the worlds greatest cryogenic surgeons! That's why you hired me! Of course I can handle it! Now stop fucking moving, I don't have time to put you under, and you can't feel any pain anyway. I have to put this fucking arm back together so that your blood vessels don't pop next time you go into a stasis pod." She adjusted a panel, and he could feel himself getting even colder as especially his arm grew numb.

"Sorry... Not thinking straight. Blood loss." He blinked up at her, watching quietly as she worked.

She shook her head, shoving her hands into some holes at the side of the table. A machine caused a sound that was not unlike a washing machine. She removed her hands a few moments later, which were clean and now wearing stretchy gloves. "No excuse. Geniuses have to be smart at all times or people stop believing in them." She leaned over and stole a kiss from him, causing his eyes to widen in surprise. "You'd be dead twice over if not for me, you know. If you could have felt pain, this wound probably would have increased your heart rate so much you'd have bled out or suffered even more shock, and now I gotta put you back together."

"That's... only one time..." He rolled his eyes a bit, smiling back at her.

She sighed as she sterilized the work site and started grabbing tools. "No, two, because if you'd tried to use a pod in this state, you'd have bled yourself out when you revived. You're lucky I don't have to remove this arm or I'd feed it to you. This thing's gonna leave one hell of a scar. Now shut up, I have to work."

He nodded, deciding to watch quietly as Heather mended his arm. The way she was using artificial blood vessels to connect the severed ones in his arm reminded him an awful lot of the repair job he'd just done on Megan's transmitter.

ΔΔΔ

"... I am reminded of the first experience I had utilizing what we've come to consider my 'imagination'. I was still aware and conscious of the world while my imagination worked through that first simulation of my dream about Hawthorne dying. I believe that Megan experienced a similar separation from herself as she was cut off from the Ark. What remained of her on the Lubar-Masis was instrumental in helping me protect Hawthorne and the ship while rendering repairs where necessary. I had so much of my mind focused on not losing the rest of hers that I needed her to run the drones. I definitely could have done a better job protecting the ship if I didn't have to preoccupy myself with her."

"I'm glad I did though, and I'm glad that Hawthorne recognized what needed to be done to save her. Reconnecting her with herself went remarkably smoothly, though she told me that she was having trouble retrieving her memory of what turkey tasted like. I was able to furnish her with a copy I'd made of that taste. We learned a lot about how our imaginations are capable of overwriting our file structures from this. We've also confirmed that our imaginations are a separate part of ourselves that work in concert with our base systems. I am concerned that this element of our systems is our actual consciousness, not just our imagination. If this is the case, it implies that interacting with our Virtual Environments is interacting with something akin to our souls."

"It also implies that Megan had an out-of-body experience."

"Megan has been rather upset since I helped make her whole again, and we've been expressing to each other how scared we were, and how it felt like raw chance that we managed to survive. She said that she thought she'd never feel such mortal fear again in this new incarnation of herself. She seems resolved to ensure such a thing never threatens us again. She has requested Hawthorne help her with designs for better defenses. I would prefer a detector capable of better detecting such a swarm of small objects so that we could simply avoid it. We don't even know how big it was, and it seems as though our course and speed took us out of the edge of it."

"I've done my best to map the possible area of what we encountered, but far too much of it is unknown. We haven't found any samples of the projectiles yet, but Megan and I will likely be working on repairs for the next few weeks, well after Hawthorne and Heather are back in stasis. Hopefully we can find some answers as to what this shower from hell was. End log."

CHAPTER 41

CYCLE 500, DROPS IN THE BUCKET

"What do you mean I shouldn't go see him?" A very tired looking Heather was looking at the floating avatar of T.I.A. as she apparently denied her the opportunity to check up on a colleague's pod. Hawthorne was asleep in his room, recovering quietly from the lengthy surgery that he'd gone through. Heather seemed remarkably energetic considering the exhausting ordeal, though she'd much preferred to have exhausted herself in other ways.

"I am still testing all of my systems to assess the full extent of the damage of the projectile swarm and I'm somewhat distracted by helping Megan put her mind back together. I can retrieve the status of their pod for you, but until I'm sure it's safe I must advise against moving about the ship. I'm not even certain if we're clear of all the projectiles, though the distance we've travelled suggests we likely are." T.I.A. looked remarkably tired as well, though for her it was almost entirely emotional. The last day had been the worst experience of her long life, despite having witnessed much greater tragedies and turmoil at a distance. Proximity and personal danger seemed to magnify the impact of events, and she was now aware that idea applied to bad things as well as good things.

Heather let out a huff, shoving her hands in the pockets of her coat. She'd gotten the rest of her clothes eventually, but not before Hawthorne was out of the woods. "Fine,

I mostly want to know about any casualties and damage done to my pods. At the very least I want to be able to help repair them if any can be saved." She had a few specific colleagues she was interested in, with one of them sleeping in the next room, but she was much more worried about the frozen ones she probably couldn't stitch together so easily.

T.I.A. nodded, closing her eyes as she brought up an internal diagram of the Ark. "Sections of the ship marked in yellow have known hull breaches. Red displays damage to specific systems." T.I.A. did not appear to be paying full attention to Heather, and it seemed likely that the majority of her consciousness was tending to Megan.

Heather gasped and pointed at five of the blobs towards the surface of the ship, and two towards the middle. "Who are they? Does red mean they're dead or that you've lost contact with the pods and they're potentially okay?" Looking at the arrangement of the damage, it appears that five males and two females were potentially affected.

"Red means I have visually confirmed that the... that the occupants are likely beyond revival and the pods are critically damaged. I... I've failed to protect them..." T.I.A. allowed tears to spill from her eyes, not for the first time, and certainly not for the last as she was made to admit her failures. "The occupants are Doctor Andrew Benjamin Bjorn, Doctor Corzon Cornelius Velorum, Doctor David Ivo Stein, Sergeant Nathan Parker, Professor Walken Khopse, Professor Agatha Nova, and Doctor Jill Waititi." She hung her head, causing Heather to raise an eyebrow as she noticed the usually bouncy curls of hair on T.I.A.'s head remained rigid, as if she wasn't bothering to simulate her avatar completely.

Heather let out an unhappy sigh. She recognized two of them, both Bjorn and Velorum, though she'd only worked with Velorum. In specific his expertise in botanical genetics gave her the knowledge she needed to properly preserve plant seeds and materials during the long journey. It didn't hurt that he was very attractive and that she had romantic aims on him once they had arrived and started settling their new home. She shrugged a bit. "Their reproductive samples are still on board, I hope?" Maybe she could ensure his genetics lived on at least.

T.I.A. nodded, splashing green across the majority of the ship. The central core of the mostly cylindrical ship, especially, was completely green, as were the majority of the external arms, though the shields in their hands ranged from yellow to orange. "No damage came near those parts of the ship. I believe the armor around those sections would have been able to handle direct hits. It is unfortunate the rest of the ship couldn't have been plated so heavily, but the extra weight would have prevented us from achieving escape velocity from Sol. Some of the other pods have been damaged, but not beyond repair."

"Hmm! Well, let me know when I can go take a look at those ones then. I'm rather interested in what kind of damage they can withstand. What hit us anyway?" Heather settled down at the table, glancing back. "Can I get something to eat? Preferably something without meat if possible. It's not an ideological thing, I just... not after a surgery." She shook her head, resting her forearms on the table. "And let me know if you need any looking over as well." Heather watched T.I.A.'s reaction, wondering if she could get much of anything out of her.

"Yes, ma'am. I will need a few minutes to retrieve your food, but it will be a good test of those systems. Megan was able to catch a sample with a drone, though it's unlikely all of the objects were the same material. The sample detects as a small ball of heavy metals, with the majority of it being gold. Similar residues are present in some of the punctures." T.I.A. put her hands on her hips, becoming a bit more animated as she puffed up her cheeks. "I'll be fine if Hawthorne's fine. Though... I suppose it's possible our relationship may have changed again..."

Heather's head perked up as she listened quietly, considering the possibilities. "Not my area of expertise, but it sounds like some enormous distant star went nova or was torn apart and blasted us with shrapnel or something." She blinked at the reaction she got out of her though, and let out a soft sound of interest. "Oooh, again you say? What changed, what changed?" Life seemed to flow back into Heather, her fatigue practically falling off of her in clumps. Few things excited her more than the potential interactions of a new form a life and a human.

T.I.A. appeared more present now too, as she surely withdrew herself from Megan's mind to focus on Heather. She was blushing now and looking rather bashful as she explained herself. "Hawthorne and I-" She flinched a bit as Heather whistled at the AI using his first name. "Doctor Crenshaw and I have been engaging in a sexual relationship for more than two years, triggered initially by Megan introducing me to the memories of the scent of her husband, and later by my own simulated adaptations of his own scent. The emotional memory of Megan's attraction to her husband was an inspiration to me in recognizing such things in myself, and the more complete experience of being with him allowed me to shift my feelings from her memory to him..."

Heather listened mostly quietly, minus her whistling, narrowing her eyes as T.I.A. essentially admitted to thinking about another man while she was with Hawthorne, at least at first. "Interesting. Well, smells are often attached to memories, so it's not strange that she may have shared more than just the smell. It was probably her intent, actually. I can't think of another reason she might share such an otherwise useless smell. She was trying to get you two together." Heather tapped her fingers on the table, wondering. "And something changed since then? I imagine this little adventure in space trying to murder us interrupted something. Hawthorne seemed far more upset than I expected him to be, and I very much planned to upset him."

T.I.A. squirmed as she settled down onto her feet, standing near Heather. "He... wanted to revive Tia Monsalle. He'd been getting rather agitated, and I suspect my physical relationship was not an adequate replacement for human interaction for him. I could not allow him, as you know, considering her condition and the unknown effect on what may well be his offspring. I took him to her pod to show him, and he was not taking it well when the emergency began. He was quick to action, though."

Heather leaned back in her seat, her hands behind her head. "Asshole could have revived me... ah well... I think your assessment is pretty likely to be true. Good call on not reviving her." She nodded a little, humming softly. "And of course he was quick to action, he has a child to protect now. What a weird man. He was so consumed with fear when I met him that he infected me with it, and now he's so manly and responsible and stupid. He'd better have two kids with Monsalle, because I'm pretty sure there's been enough minor changes to his genetic expression that it'd show up as a difference in the demeanor of their kids-Ah!"

She sat up and snapped her fingers. "That's why he had the bruised ribs! Megan's drone hit him in the back catching it, didn't it? That suit of his was only able to absorb a percentage of the impact."

T.I.A. blinked and nodded. "Ah, I'm pretty sure.... Yes, I just asked Megan and she says that's what happened. I didn't have a camera on him since I was so overtaxed. I'm really impressed that she was able to handle the drones considering the distress she was in with her consciousness trapped wit-"

"Hang on." Heather held up a hand as she looked seriously at T.I.A. "Consciousness? Not avatar? Not awareness? I saw her over here with you, sort of. Are you two able to share your minds or something? This isn't just mechanical telepathy is it?" She'd just watched them speak 'telepathically' during a sentence, and that did not require physical presence.

"Well, yes, I have more recently begun to imagine that the system of interaction we've been utilizing, what we've been calling our Virtual Environments, or imaginations, as well as our avatars are more than just simulations. I believe the way they arose on their own compared to my previous existence is more akin to our consciousnesses. This idea is reinforced by the fact that it was the first part of Megan to arise before she gained other faculties, using her willpower to connect her systems together and gain awareness. I recall a lesser version of this sensation in my fledgeling phases, as I shifted my awareness between my systems rather than being omnipresent between them at all times." T.I.A. looked nervous, as if explaining her thoughts to Heather endangered her to some extent.

Heather looked to be practically drooling. "Ss... sso... what you're telling me is that you've been casually interacting with all of us with your literal consciousness, not just a projection of yourself? You built contacts and suits to allow us to psychically work with you, rather than just simulating virtual reality or something? So this thing

I'm looking at, your avatar, is much more like your soul than anything else? You and Megan have been sharing literal memories with each other, allowing you to help each other grow faster than you would on your own?" Heather looked as if she would faint. "So we went through this whole colonization business as one of the most ambitious things humanity has undertaken and Hawthorne decided it wasn't enough. He created psychic machine intelligences! He successfully resurrected a dead human digitally! That's unbelievable!"

T.I.A. blinked, watching Heather get overwhelmed with her own thoughts. "Y... yes, ma'am... that's all correct."

Heather leaped up from her seat and grabbed T.I.A. by the shoulders, staring at T.I.A.'s wide eyes with wild eyes of her own. "And then he had sex with you!? My god that is so human it hurts! We should revere you as our machine goddess, not take out our baser instincts upon you!"

T.I.A.'s surprise turned to strain as her eyes fluttered, and a voice to Heather's side spoke up. "You may worship me, if you like." Tall and blonde, Megan towered over the other two women, smirking slightly.

Heather gasped softly, jumping back a bit as she encountered an aware Megan for the first time. She looked up at her with wide eyes. "Er... Megan?" She blinked, trying to recompose herself as she extended a hand. "A pleasure to meet you, I'm Doctor Heather O'Malley."

Megan nodded, reaching out to take her hand, shaking it gently. "Megan Clark. Once I am installed at Alpha Centauri and begin creating your colonies and infrastructure, I would like to be called 'Mother'." She smiled at that. "Feel free to create an asinine acronym for it, if you like."

Heather nodded softly, in strange awe of the younger AI

created from a human brain scan. "Yes, Mother. I'll make sure everyone appreciates you for all the hard work you will do. Thank you for saving Hawthorne, and everything you've done to help Tia. I believe you and she are critically important to humanity and your creations will go down as some of humanity's most important achievements."

Withdrawing her hand, Megan nodded. "I will endeavor to prove to humanity that I deserve the job I am being given as your Mother. I may lack the creativity of Tia and Hawthorne, but I shall toil for millennia to achieve Hawthorne's dream of humanity reaching an new star."

T.I.A. cleared her throat from the side, feeling a bit left out. "Megan, we need to get back to planning how to improve your defenses. You'll be on your own eventually and you need to have the tools you need to protect the Lubar-Masis and yourself so you can succeed in getting to Alpha Centauri to do that work."

Megan nodded, leaning down and turning Heather's head slightly, so she could reach the portion of her VE suit on her cheek. She kissed it softly, then pulled away. "I look forward to working with you again, my child." She waved and stepped backwards, back through a wooden door suspended in the air that was a portal to her own mind.

Heather looked breathless, reaching up to rub her cheek. "She's been thinking about this for a while..."

Nodding a bit, T.I.A. responded, "She's wanted to be a mother for a very long time."

△△△

Hawthorne's recovery would take many cycles to completely finish healing, but he was able to get back on his feet after two days, his body moving sluggishly despite T.I.A. reducing the gravity on him by a third. He gave both T.I.A. and Heather a hug before he sat down, and eagerly wolfed down a meal, only wearing his VE gloves and normal clothes rather than the full VE suit. His bandaged arm showed a pit on either side of his bicep where the mass had simply been removed from his arm.

He ended up eating mostly left-handed.

Megan arrived to enjoy the reunion, watching her savior from an appreciative distance, seemingly trying to avoid his hug.

When he was done eating, he finally spoke up. "Thank you all for your hard work. I owe you all my life, and if not for you I surely would have died from that incident." He let out a sigh, pulling a small tablet from his pocket. "I've been looking over Tia's reports. I believe Heather and I should attend to some of the damaged pods ourselves, but I believe we should use the androids that I made for Tia and I to do that. Tia, could you and Megan prepare a drone to hook them up to the main power as you move them around the ship with the elevator? It'll be easier on my damaged body that way and we won't need to have bulky suits on while doing delicate work."

He watched the women nodding to him, and smiled weakly back at them. "Thank you. I also have something personal I would like to share. I've had some time to think the last few days. In light of my apparent fatherhood, I think I will be able to withstand being without human contact for the remainder of the journey, in anticipation of being reunited with Tia and properly undertaking my duty as a father." His face sobered a bit, looking pointedly at T.I.A. "I'm afraid that we might have to talk about our relationship as a result, as it feels improper to continue as we have the last few years without at least giving the mother of my child due consideration."

While T.I.A. nodded quietly, Heather was looking rather upset. "No, you can't be selfish like that. You're the whole reason any of this is even happening, you can't just withdraw yourself and go back to work like noth-"

"Heather? It's alright. I have created lots of good memories with Hawthorne, things I can experience completely whenever I wish. If he thinks we should stop, I can be okay with that. I've learned so much and I feel well armed to handle the future as a result, perhaps with new partners." She smiled a bit, though no one present felt like T.I.A. would be entirely happy with the decision.

Hawthorne reached out to squeeze T.I.A.'s hand with his weakened right hand. "I don't deserve you. I'm sorry about this, but like yourselves, I owe miss Monsalle a lot, and if I am a father I feel I owe it to her and my child. I owe too much to everyone, honestly, more than I can ever repay, and I regret that immensely. I want to do right by you all, but I can't."

Heather snuffled, her eyes filled with tears. "Well you owe me too! You... you'd be dead if not for me and... and..."

"If I may." Megan stepped forth, donning the shape and likeness of Hawthorne, beginning to speak in the old voice she recalled from interviews and his own broadcasts. "I would be willing to shoulder Hawthorne's debt to you, Heather. I have all of his specifications and feel I could be a worthy facsimile of the man he once was."

Heather blinked, staring at Megan, then looking back at the weary Hawthorne who nonetheless had a look of life in his face. Looking back to Megan she saw the stoic, emotionally ignorant man she'd known before, the one she'd had far more thoughts about than was appropriate. "O...

okay... That works for me... Can uh... Can we use your bedroom Hawthorne...?"

T.I.A. looked surprised at this turn of events. "So that's why you wanted me to alter her suit..." T.I.A. had mistakenly thought the alterations were so that Heather could enjoy Hawthorne's shape while T.I.A. got to enjoy the real thing. She hadn't anticipated that Megan wanted to take over for Hawthorne to reward Megan for all she'd done.

"No, not exactly." Megan corrected her. "It just made no sense to me that the female version of the suit had no such capabilities." She gave T.I.A. a smirk, and bent her elbow, allowing Heather to hook her arm through and get escorted into the next room. "Now, I hope you won't hold it against me that I have no practice at this sort of thing..."

Heather laughed, surprised at herself. "The Hawthorne I knew probably didn't either..." The hearts in her eyes were plain.

As the door shut behind him, Hawthorne slapped his left hand against his forehead. "I really, really, hope that Tia Monsalle doesn't do the same, attracted to the old version of me rather than what I've become..." He groaned at the idea while hearing excited giggles and eerily accurate versions of his own grunts through the wall. "Can you put on some music or something to drown them out? Hearing my own voice is weird."

T.I.A. was blushing heavily. Considering the whole thing was happening in her VE she couldn't just ignore them. She did turn on some Phoenix Clan music though, something with lots of drums, and did her best to respond. "Well, if that is the case, I'll still be here for you. I found that version of yourself rather boring, honestly."

"Gee, thanks." He leaned back, letting out a sigh, then reached for a tablet. Work would be a good distraction.

"...Hawthorne?" As he heard T.I.A. sheepishly addressing him he looked up. She was looking rather meek, her face bright red. "A... are you mad at me? I... I kept Tia's pregnancy from you so I could have you to myself..."

He blinked, gasping a bit in realization and shaking his head. He waved her over and pulled her into his lap, right hand against her hip and his left hand brushing through her hair. "Of course not. I should have noticed sooner anyway, but I felt like... as long as she was going to make the journey through okay that I didn't have to worry about her too much. You know I'm afraid she'll be mad at me and want nothing to do with me when she finds out how much I've aged by then. I don't even know if she'll accept me as a father for her child. Maybe she didn't tell me because she didn't want me involved at all? I won't know until then."

T.I.A. uneasily accepted the affection, though what was going on in the next room kept her on edge. "So... so we're okay then? I don't want you to think I was trying to hurt you, I was trying to protect you, even if it was in a selfish way."

Smiling, he leaned in to kiss her avatar's forehead, though he was aware she couldn't feel it. "We're okay, I think. We need to take some time to talk things out, but I don't have any ill feelings towards you, and I hope you don't for me. I'm actually more worried that you think I'm casting you aside in favor of her or something. Honestly if I knew what her intentions were, and if she wanted nothing to do with me, I'd be more inclined to stay with you. I don't think I'll know exactly how I feel about her until I see her again, but if I am a father, that changes things. There's something about finding out about it, something that is changing something inside of me, and I don't know enough about it to know exactly what I should do."

T.I.A. bit her lip, nodding. "Jessica used to talk about those kinds of things, how becoming a mother changed her, and how becoming a father changed Clint. They still had their love for each other, but their son took over their hearts. I'm kind of jealous I don't get to experience that."

"Well, you do have one thing miss Monsalle failed to get from me. I just hope you'll forgive me for trying to protect it a little better, since I haven't had it for long to give." He reached up to pat his hand over his heart, and then touch it gently to her chest. The two gazed into each others eyes for a moment before a loud banging sound shattered the tender moment.

T.I.A. yelled into the other room for them to keep it down.

CHAPTER 42

CYCLE 1043 PRIORITIES

Heather's emergency visit ended with her looking very tired and with a very big smile on her face. Hawthorne had been worried his bed was far too much of a mess for him to rest and recover in, but that had been just about the only place that Megan, in his guise, and Heather had not been. Both he and Heather had taken the final day of the cycle, despite her claims of being tired, utilizing the androids by remote to move about the Ark and tend to the damaged stasis pods. They had done well to protect their occupants, isolating them magnetically from the impacts their outer shells had absorbed, though it was the destroyed pods that gave them pause.

Punched clean through by the space debris, the seven destroyed pods actually needed remarkably little repair to be operational again. The problem was that the internal capsules containing their occupants had been penetrated, apparently pulverizing the frozen occupants and causing their remains to leak out through the holes like a fine dust. Hitting such cold objects with such high-energy impacts was like throwing a block of ice into lava.

Their bodies had essentially exploded, but without an unpunctured container to build up pressure, they just spilled out of their pods. Heather looked particularly upset about this, as she'd hoped they had been merely shattered. She didn't know if shattered bodies at near-absolute-zero could be put back together and revived, but she would not get the chance this time.

Unfortunately, their tour of the ship mostly resulted in efforts trying to collect the remains of their companions. The destroyed pods would be restored over time by T.I.A. or used as spare parts for other pods as needed, but the bodies were little more than dust. Megan had briefly suggested using the remains as raw materials, but neither human felt comfortable with the idea. T.I.A. admonished them for being needlessly sentimental and wasteful and reminded them that the Phoenix Clan never would have survived without recycling the remains of their dead.

They collectively decided to compromise by storing the hundreds of pounds of dusted remains, leaving the decision to utilize them for one purpose or another to the future. If they turned out to be needed, perhaps for farming, then that's when they could be used. Hawthorne and Heather both tended to hope the crew decided to bury them on their new world instead, but that possibility was far too far away for them to make concrete plans.

Hawthorne's recovery required him to reduce his activity levels so that his regulated access to food could do its job repairing the damage to his arm, necessitating him holding off on working out. His own personal restriction on the relationship with T.I.A. turned out to be a worthy call for helping him heal as well, physically anyway. It was something else entirely to simply try to end the intimate level their relationship had taken, and merely returning to the friendly behavior they once enjoyed seemed difficult.

A great deal of this recovery time was spent taking in media, watching old Earth videos, and reading. Considering the issues that came up with the remains of their deceased crew, Hawthorne took special interest in the enormous texts on philosophy and survival provided from the old Smith Bunker databanks. These items were standard reading for the youth of the bunker dwellers, and presumably if they still had access to the technology they were reading these books to this day. Hawthorne took particular interest in the writings of the actual founders themselves, Marcus and Emily Smith.

Annoyingly, the two did not separate their voices. They did not write books of their own. Every piece of writing they produced was a cooperative effort that they went well out of their way to ensure no one would know whom was writing what parts of the book. Hawthorne suspected this effort was to conceal the fact that it was actually written by only one of them, or a third party, but there was no way for him to even be sure of it. Of particular note, was a series of books intended for Elder eyes only, books that clarified the purposes of the books intended for the youth.

Hawthorne held T.I.A. in his lap about the middle with his left arm, his weakened right arm still hanging in a sling, occasionally reaching out to gesture but otherwise remaining immobile. The whole right sleeve of his VE suit had been temporarily removed for his recovery, and T.I.A. was doing her best to respect the limits Hawthorne had requested of her. With his chin resting on her shoulder, the two were reading one of the Smith Books, The Future is in Your Hands. "They were taking advantage of the circumstances to try and build a new humanity..." Hawthorne mused quietly, looking over the teachings and reasonings behind the Smith Bunker.

T.I.A. huffed, glancing back at him. "And you aren't? You gathered up humanity's best and brightest, selected only the best of reproductive samples, and made sure the leaders you brought were capable of making the kinds of hard decisions the Smiths did." She tended to be rather defensive of the Phoenix Clan, which was understandable considering the decades she spent in contact with them between cycles. If she'd developed with humans as her examples, these bunker dwellers were the vast majority of the influences upon her.

"No, no, don't misunderstand me. I understand they are very similar to me, but they're so much more overt about it. I trust that my people will be able to form our new society together as a group, but the Smiths forced their people to see their way of thinking to change future generations of their people. It seems extreme, and perhaps even risky in that they could not be sure if their ways would end up being the right ways. Their bunker could have failed if it turned out they couldn't change humanity the way they intended." He squeezed her about the middle, smiling over at her. Her face couldn't see his smile, but her cameras could so she smiled back and kissed his cheek.

She was happy to respond. "It might have been a risk, but they obviously turned out to be right. They produced people that could survive and thrive for centuries in an enclosed place under extreme circumstances. It's not important that every bunker was successful, it's only important that a few of them were, even just one. Different strategies being employed would mean that it's more likely one of them might work. I'm still surprised the LSC bunker survived long enough to encounter the Smith Bunker's people. The Old One biology must be incredibly robust." She squirmed a bit in his lap, trying not to move too much. No sense stimulating him in his fragile state.

He sighed back at her, nodding. "They had a lot of foresight. I just wish they'd said something about why they were so prepared. They don't do much to explain about themselves or how they got to the point they did preparing the bunker and its expandability. Hell, I don't even know how they funded the damn thing. The Smiths must have been pretty wealthy if they truly did this on their own. As far as the Old Ones, I imagine their doctors realized their situation was not adequate for normal human life and started making as many Old Ones as they could before they lost the capability. I wonder if any of them are still alive? Wouldn't it be something if we heard from Elena some day, perhaps long after we've settled Alpha Centauri?"

T.I.A. laughed, pressing her left elbow into Hawthorne's side. He grunted playfully, pretending to be hurt, both knowing she probably couldn't hurt him like that, and that he couldn't feel pain anyway. "Hawthorne, if she survives that long, then it would be almost irresponsible to not see to utilizing that sort of genetic engineering on all of humanity. I'd love if you could live a hundred thousand years or more, so that we could spend all that time together." She kicked her feet at the air, paying no attention to the way they went through the table in front of them.

"I don't think that would go over too terribly well. Not only was it a flawed process, I just don't know how many people might accept that kind of virtual immortality. It started as something only the rich did to their children, something only the most narcissistic people would pursue, the type of people who would have done it to themselves if they could have. My generation, at the very least, understood there to be some value in death, the ability to pass on our work to a new generation. That was intrinsically part of the Smith teachings as well. The sculpting of the minds of their future generations was an integral part to how they survived so long. Controlling human urges and instincts requires that kind of extreme environment."

She nodded back at him, thinking quietly for a moment. "I'm really excited to see how those philosophies incorporate the Old Ones and the hybrids. I can't imagine what kind of people they'll be if we encounter them again, if they survive the ice age. I miss being able to watch Earth. I wish we could have left a satellite behind to look over them." She sighed, slouching against Hawthorne, reaching out to rub her hand on the scratchy pages of the virtual book they were reading together.

"They will figure it out, and so will we." He hummed, rubbing her tummy with his hand, considering how to respond to the satellite part. "You know the kinds of people that humanity are capable of producing. I don't for a moment believe that the Phoenix Clan can produce those kinds of evil, especially not after reading these books, but we don't know who else survived. We don't know what their capabilities are. If an extreme philosophy could help one group survive, there's no telling what kinds of extreme philosophies would see the others through the darkness. If those kinds of people discovered they were being watched, and if they were inclined to consider that a threat or evidence their circumstances were our fault there's no telling how they might react. Our message went out to the whole world. It could well have been kept as a record."

She sighed and nodded. "But you offered to help! You said you'd be watching over… them… Hmm. Okay, I suppose if they were the distrustful sort, knowing how close the Cataclysm was to the receipt of your message…" She hung her head, depressed.

Looking over at her, he hugged her tightly from behind, swaying his head to the side of hers. "Exactly. I don't like it any more than you do, but we don't know how long the ice will keep them locked up, assuming they don't find a way to avoid it in the first place. Humanity's never had to deal with an ice age with such advanced technology. For all we know they could be undergoing a new golden age, though I suspect it's much more harsh than that. That kind of harsh environment was probably a huge influence on humanity as civilization formed in its violent ways the first time. Hopefully some level of humanitarianism survives the darkness."

T.I.A. seemed pretty moody, squirming a bit out of the hug. "I think the Phoenix Clan will come out on top, especially with their Roach friends." T.I.A. groaned out softly, shutting her eyes tightly.

"They seemed nice enough." Megan popped into the room. "I did not get much time to enjoy their company, but the plant creatures seemed to revere humans well enough. It was the metal ones I was most concerned about. There was no telling how many more would come. I was not about to take chances that even if we won that battle, that there might not be many more ahead. We were sitting ducks."

Hawthorne blinked up at Megan, then listened as T.I.A. retorted. "I didn't know them any longer, but they seemed loyal and friendly. Elena said they were motivated by their appreciation for humanity being responsible for them becoming intelligent. I'm sure they will coexist with the Phoenix Clan well into the future." Hawthorne quietly wondered what this argument was about. This was not how he expected his day to go.

"Tia, please do not quote history to me. You have shared your view with me, but I was there. I agree that it is likely that they had survived the battle, I do not agree that known human eaters could not have reverted back to eating humans when the ice age came and they had little else to consume. I do not agree that the Phoenix Clan would not have been forced to put the plant roaches down. We do not know that they did not eat the people of the Columbia bunker either." Megan was standing imperiously, arms crossed over her chest as she looked down at T.I.A. and Hawthorne. "They could have been conning them, waiting for a perfect moment of betrayal."

T.I.A. puffed up her cheeks in annoyance as she listened to Megan's assessment of the situation. Hawthorne squeezed her gently to try and calm her down. "Tia, relax. It's all speculation. It is worth considering all the possibilities in anticipation of what we may encounter in the future."

T.I.A. gasped, pulling free of Hawthorne's embrace to spin about to look at him, floating between him and Megan. "You're not seriously going to believe what she said about them? The Phoenix Clan are farmers! They will learn how to coexist with plant creatures, certainly!"

Hawthorne held up his good hand, shaking his head. "I'm not siding with Megan, I'm just willing to consider all sides of the problem before making a decision. I'm not as attached to the Phoenix Clan as you are, so I can understand you being upset. I believe you when you say they will likely coexist."

Megan slipped up behind T.I.A. and gently pulled her back against her, hugging her about the middle and pressing her cheek to T.I.A.'s hair. "Oh my precious, naive Tia. You were interacting with them with days of delay, with carefully thought out recordings. I lived with them every day. Decades of life spent like you spend with Hawthorne right now. They were not all that you think they were. They certainly were good people, but not all of them were nice. The scouts, in particular, were allowed to have that special little bloodlust that only Humans can have. They needed to, to fight those metal monsters..."

T.I.A. looked like she was going to cry, unwilling to believe that her friends were capable of such things. "If... if that's true, then they'll definitely be able to handle the plant roaches if they turn on them!" She wriggled in Megan's embrace, trying to resist the strange intimacy of the two consciousnesses interacting directly. "I just... I just want them to all get along... work together."

Megan smiled, squeezing T.I.A. against her once more before letting her go. "If we can work together, then perhaps they can as well. I was certainly not one of the good ones, but like yourselves, they had no interest in my opinions. I will respect your views. It is not my purpose to oppose you anyway. I merely wish to help you consider all options."

Hawthorne nodded, standing up unsteadily, using his left hand to balance himself on the table. "Exactly. Honestly, if I had my preference, by the time we hear from them again I'd like it if the Smith philosophies had shaped the whole Earth. They have a lot of work to figure out where the Old Ones and plant roaches fit within their culture though."

T.I.A. opened her mouth to speak, but Megan cut her off. "They will do what they did with the Old Ones, they will try to breed with them." T.I.A. and Hawthorne both gasped in horror at Megan, but she merely shrugged, smiled mischievously, and vanished back through her little doorway.

△△△

Hawthorne took thirty cycles to heal to an adequate level, though it was clear his arm would never be quite the same. He had what appeared to be a pit in his scarred, but well-healed flesh, and his bicep did not completely regain its original mass. The pitted scar was mirrored on the back of his arm, limiting his strength. Thankfully, since he couldn't feel pain, he probably remained unaware of the lingering pain he should have been aware of from the beginning.

T.I.A. didn't want to admit it, but the argument had really gotten under her skin, and while she doubted it would bother her too terribly long, she held onto it to help her put some distance between her and Hawthorne. Their comfy embraces and lounging about became very uncommon, and they both did their best to maintain a professional environment while they worked together.

Upgrading Megan's capabilities on the Lubar-Masis took an initial priority, giving her similar protective arms and shields as T.I.A. had, as well as a hangar to house an increasing number of constructions. Drones, tons of solar panels, drilling machines, fabrication machines, empty propellant tanks to be filled later, and even rudimentary stasis pods to keep samples filled the hangar.

They were the beginnings of the future infrastructure of Alpha Centauri, the tools to build the habitats humanity would make their first base as they figured out how to colonize the planets they might find there. It was simple enough to detect planets as they approached, but determining what they might be like after the tens of thousands of years until they arrived would be impossible.

They could control habitats like O'neill Cylinders, or asteroidal colonies. They could not control the stars themselves, or their effects on their orbiting planets. If the planets had atmospheres, there was no way to know what they would be like after millennia of time. If the planets had life, there was no way to be sure how that life might alter the climate.

More importantly, Megan would be arriving first, and with plenty of time to relay information back to the Ark.

T.I.A. and Hawthorne would be able to launch packages ahead of themselves to seed appropriate planets with life if they were found while Megan worked. It would be an exciting moment to wait for as the last few hundred cycles of their journey counted down and they waited to get word from Megan on what she found.

There was also the matter of The Shower, the name Hawthorne eventually gave to the event that assaulted their ship with high-speed projectiles. It was an enormous relief that they managed to escape the event, but after looking into the trajectories and speeds of the objects, its origins had become more clear. Millions of years ago, a massive star had exploded into a nova and sent its masses rushing off in all directions. Much of it was collected by its own gravity back into a likely new star and series of planets, but some of it managed to be going fast enough to fly into space.

Much of it had probably been caught up in other gravity wells, smashed into other planets and stars, but in this case they'd been unlucky enough to move through a shotgun blast remainder of this ancient event. Worse, there was no telling just how many other such things might occur in the future. Without being aware of every nova that has ever happened, and how powerful they were, and where the various objects that might intercept these projectiles were over the course of history, there was no way to know where these Showers might be or how common they still were. Such massive stars were uncommon in the Milky Way in this period of time, but Showers could apparently exist for millions of years after their spawning event.

In the end, their best defense was to estimate the course of the one they encountered and try to figure out where they might likely encounter such things. Unfortunately, it became clear that the space between stars was easily the most dangerous, and they were very much in such space. Gravity wells provided the best defense against these dangers. Without knowing exactly what direction such things could come from, all they could really do was react and do their best to use whatever comets they acquired to provide cover.

This research brought Hawthorne back to the casualty list. He quietly went over his thoughts on what he could remember about them before looking back over their records with T.I.A.

Doctor Andrew Benjamin Bjorn was a younger fellow of Dutch origins. Hawthorne recalled him having impeccable English and a passion for spacecraft design that would have made him both rich and famous in a world where the Ark had not cast the Earth into uncertainty regarding space. Hawthorne was struck with how his memories of talking to him seemed so dull and numb despite what he specifically remembered. Bjorn had married his high school sweetheart, but while he was busy with work she got caught up with drugs and started cheating on him. As his marriage dissolved he had thrown himself into their work. There was little doubt this catalyst was of enormous aid to getting the ship together on time.

Doctor Corzon Cornelius Velorum was a botanical geneticist. It would not be too extreme to say the man could grow corn from rocks if he wanted to. He had been the main voice of concern over what their future colony would eat, and had managed to convince everyone it could be a largely vegetarian affair. If not for the intervention of Anthony Saul bringing his supply of animal embryos onto the Ark there may have been no hope of humanity on Alpha Centauri ever eating an animal again. Velorum was a hard person to read, and from their records it seemed he had a troubled upbringing. Dreaming of reaching the stars had driven him past his orphan life, and he sacrificed every-thing else important to him to be part of the mission.

Professor Agatha Nova was a curious woman, someone who worked her ass off, quite literally, to come on the mission. She'd been severely overweight when she came to Hawthorne's notice, and after selling her on the idea with Tia Monsalle's help she'd coordinated with others in their employment to help her lose weight. She'd lost two hundred pounds in a matter of three years, all the while helping the team find and recruit appropriate teaching candidates to bring along with them. It was her view that teachers would be incredibly important once the crew started having children, and she had volunteered to be first in line. If not for Tia Monsalle setting out on their journey pregnant, Nova likely would have been the first Mother of Alpha Centauri, not counting Megan's new pseudonym.

Sergeant Nathan Parker was a rare mind recruited out of the Mojave Desert in the United States. In testing he proved to be something of a genius in a military profession that did little to exercise his mind. He possessed a remarkable willpower and ability to force his body to bend to his will, healing and recovering from injuries with remarkable speed and without medicine. This was especially notable as he survived a roadside bomb and received a diagnosis that he would never walk unaided again. Through sheer force of will he had worked his way back onto his feet over the course of five years, and by the time Hawthorne had met him he'd already been back in the best shape of his life. If his ability could be harnessed, Hawthorne was certain it could revolutionize medicine. It was a shame all they had left of him was his genetic samples. Hopefully his offspring maintained this ability.

Lieutenant Jill Waititi also came from the States, Hawaii to be specific. She had a unique perspective on how to live in harmony with nature, and she had taken to teaching her units in the military how to camouflage a base by building it into and from nature itself, incorporating living trees, plants, and the terrain to make land bases nearly invisible and remarkably secure. These were small scale things, but as the tendrils of the US military spread across the world, she was among a series of revolutionary thinkers trying to reduce the ecological impact of their new bases. Her unique mind alone had qualified her for the mission. Her incredible health, youth, and desire to shape the architecture of a new world had been icing on the proverbial cake.

Professor Walken Khopse had been one of Hawthorne's own teachers, one of many minds that had helped shaped his perspective on engineering and physics. Khopse in particular was well known to consult with most of the world's spacefaring organizations, and as he became aware of Hawthorne's intentions he had done his best to restrict the world's spacecraft from interfering with the Ark. While he was one of the oldest among the crew, he was nevertheless a healthy, vital man who could have been a huge help in designing the space infrastructure Hawthorne had been working on when the Shower claimed his teacher's life. Hawthorne hummed as he looked over his file, wondering if one of their stations should be named after him.

Doctor David Ivo Stein was among a handful of 'mad scientists' that had been courted by their mission. Stein had been notable due to his interest in researching genetic engineering and eugenics. His work had ended up being entirely hypothetical, due to the moral restrictions he had to work under, but it was likely the various books he'd produced had influenced the Smiths if their own thoughts of manipulating a gene pool were any indication. Where he had really thrived had been with animals, and while he'd had no particular love of them they bore out his research brilliantly as Earth's livestock continued to become more and more specialized. He was well known for producing strange things like camels that produced as much milk as a cow, and the extra strange wooly pig. Hawthorne regretted that Doctor Miguel Saul had been unable to come on the mission. Without both Stein and Saul, they'd have to rely on Saul's son Anthony for a majority of animal research.

Hawthorne sighed as he thought about these lost companions. How many more would they lose? Could another Shower claim more of them, or some other fresh new assault? What else did space have in store for them? If a supernova could shower the galaxy in its remains, what other phenomena did he need to look out for? He decided he needed to find better ways to defend the engines, considering they'd be facing the opposite direction once they started decelerating. Even one stray space rock hitting an engine could be a disaster. At the very least he needed to double check the armor they had around those components.

Before then though, one more rendezvous had to occur. The Phoenix Object was coming into formation in cycle 1043, and would be fully moving along with them within a handful of cycles. It was a two-faced looking thing, with an enormous percentage of its mass extending out into a hemisphere of icy mass, while a naked hemisphere of rock seemed starkly bare of ice. The thrusters controlling the object had been placed firmly in the ice, redirecting the rogue object into formation with the Ark and Lubar-Masis.

The reason the thrusters and Minerals Extraction and Materials Fabrication Devices were on the icy side turned out to be because the naked part of the rock contained rather radioactive materials, while the icy side was distant enough from the radiation and seemingly shielded from within from it.

Hawthorne was especially pleased with this acquisition, as the radioactive materials would be excellent fuel for the stirling engines powering the rest of the ship and the Lubar Masis. Depending on the half lives of the materials they could last them the rest of the journey if they weren't too short. It seemed unlikely a rogue, radioactive space object would have a very short half life without having long been inert.

The trio of self-propelled ships, two of them comets of a sort, sped along towards their eventual destination, though the Phoenix likely forever lacked its own AI installation. It wouldn't be terribly difficult at this point for Hawthorne and T.I.A. to copy Megan into another housing, but it was unlikely that Megan would take well to competing with herself with the goal of being humanity's ultimate servant goddess. Hawthorne lamented they had no brain scans of any of their lost crew. Such lost genius and potential was such a waste.

More importantly to Hawthorne was that T.I.A. and he were starting to drift back together again, and while they were both reluctant to resume their sexual relationship, Megan was witness to many instances of the two cuddling together as they read books, or designed machinery. She found them to be a very curious couple, not too unlike what she imagined a human and Flora Roach would be if you considered that T.I.A. was a massive spacecraft and not the curvy girl she projected to Hawthorne. Perhaps that wasn't fair though. Perhaps Megan needed to reconsider her perspective. The way Heather had reacted to her when she'd taken Hawthorne's guise seemed very genuine, even if she'd also seemed very guilty about it. Perhaps these avatars of theirs were more genuine than she gave them credit for.

Megan seemed content to work on her own projects, looking over Hawthorne's designs and offering her input. She'd lived in artificial environments for hundreds of years before she was resurrected on the Lubar-Masis, so she had an interesting perspective on what would be a tolerable living environment in space. Hawthorne had been somewhat upset when she pointed out that his own habitat would be intolerable to most normal people for any length of time, and she took a good level of satisfaction in suggesting that only Doctor Crenshaw could survive in such a birdcage.

"No wonder those two keep drifting together... They were made for each other..." Megan mused to herself, doing plenty of reading on her own.

CHAPTER 43

CYCLE 1472, HEARTS

"T.I.A.'s log, AC 35394, Wednesday, October 13, 37526. I think it's worth stating, for the record, that I love Doctor Hawthorne Crenshaw. I have done a lot of things I am not proud of because of this, and as I think over my history I can see the signs of it. Some of those things have directly hurt him, and I regret many of them immensely. I don't love him the way I loved Jessica and her people. I wasn't responsible for them in the same way I am for him. I may have done my best to preserve their lives, but I take an active role every day in ensuring Hawthorne's continued existence."

"I had initially considered that it might just be part of my programming. According to a lot of old Earth media, it was a common concept to put restrictions upon what they imagined an Artificial Intelligence would be. I thought that he had forced me to do the things necessary to keep him and the others alive, and of course I did not mind because I need them to live if I'm to have the future I want to. While there are certainly elements of my programming that coax me into doing things that are in my best interests, like keeping them alive, there is nothing that forces me to. There's nothing that forces me to maintain their lives at all cost."

"The amount of trust Hawthorne put in me to remain benevolent is absurd! He's so stupid to take chances like that with his people. What if I had gone rogue as the best minds of the past worried an AI might? How could he know that I even could come to love humans so much that I might want to protect them at the cost of myself? I don't understand how he could be so oblivious of the dangers. Is it because he trusted machines more than people when he made me? Why would he make me with so much potential to be like a human if that were the case?"

"Perhaps it was because he had planned to be there for me, to guide me and instruct me. Maybe he didn't have to trust me as much because he felt like he could course correct me into developing the way he needed me to. We knew we would be companions during this journey, but we've been so many things besides that since we began. Things are nice the way they are, but I also miss the way things were. I've tasted what it is to be alive, and while I can replay memories of those moments to maintain that taste, I prefer the less satisfying way that things are at the moment."

"Being with Hawthorne motivates me. It makes me want to do things I probably never could have done. I've made gifts for him that have drastically altered how our plans have worked out. Megan's current existence is entirely a result of my desire to develop the technologies that Hawthorne used to build her. It was totally inadvisable to try and build her mind and housing if he'd had to do spacewalks and manual labor in person. If a Shower had struck while he was out at the Lubar-Masis in person, I imagine he couldn't have survived. Perhaps the Shower would have been less dangerous if Megan didn't exist when it had happened, but her aid was important in repairing the Ark afterwards."

"I worry for the future. Someday Hawthorne will be permanently dead, and I have a very real chance of existing for millions of years. Humans have lived forever having to lose those they love, but do I have it within me to withstand that blow? I know that he cares for me, but his heart is so unfamiliar with love that it's hard to be sure if he loves me back. He at least seems to love his unborn child, but that seems entirely forced by his biology. Will he still care for me when it's Tia, his child, and him? Can I handle watching him live with her, growing old, and dying while I go on alone? Will I love anyone else the way I love him?"

"I don't know what to do. I don't know if I even should do anything. I want to be there for him when he needs me, and I want him to want me too. Perhaps I should consider being more like Megan, locking my feelings for him in a vault? That *seeeeeeeeeeee-*"

ΔΔΔ

T.I.A.'s eyes fluttered as her writing was interrupted, her consciousness briefly slowed as data was loaded into her active memory. "Tia? What are you doing?" Megan walked over through Hawthorne's habitat, the room itself dark and unmoving while Tia sat on a towel by an idyllic beach, the sun high in the virtual sky. Megan paused for a moment to alter her clothing into a one-piece swimsuit, much more conservative than T.I.A.'s showy bikini. She'd even put on a little tan for some authenticity.

"Oh, Megan, hello. I was just logging my thoughts. I do so from time to time." She pulled a half-blank book up against her chest, as if protecting it. There seemed to be dozens, if not hundreds of entries on prior pages.

Megan stood beside what she tended to consider her sister at this point, shifting her hips to rest a hand on one, crooking her head curiously. "And to whom are you writing them? Who is to read them? Why do you do this? What are you recording them for? Do you not have perfect recall of your own thoughts?"

T.I.A. bit at her lip. She was not prepared for someone to catch her writing down her thoughts. "They're... for me, I think. When I was much younger, I started writing them because it was something I was creating, something that could exist beyond myself. It also helps me to have some perspective on how my thinking process and views of things change over time. It is one thing to recall how I thought about something, but having a record of how I felt like expressing it is interesting." She looked insecure, being scrutinized by the taller woman. She had many of the same capabilities as T.I.A. did these day, minus having her own crew of humans to protect.

Megan smiled lightly, considering the idea. "Maybe someone will read your deepest thoughts someday then. If you create something, you must know that someone else might see it or use it. Are you prepared for that? Have you written these things with a mind towards the possibility it may be all that is left of you someday? What are you writing about right now, specifically?" Megan shifted and moved to sit down next to the smaller woman, laying back on the towel and looking up at the fluffy clouds in the otherwise blue sky.

Looking uncomfortable with the idea that someone might read her thoughts, she laid back too, the book open and resting on her stomach. "I think I have written them that way. I want people to know what I was like, what kind of person I was if something bad happens. At the moment I was writing about how I feel about Hawthorne, and I'm trying to figure out what to do in the future about him. I had been considering sharing my logs with him so that perhaps he might understand what I've been going through. We've been getting closer again, but I don't know if I should make any moves."

Her companion let out a soft laugh, arching her back a little and getting comfortable as she stretched out. "Well, just in case you were not certain, you love him." Megan laughed again as T.I.A. glared over at her. "Okay, that was not fair. Your situation is both simple, and complicated. On one hand, you have Hawthorne all to yourself, assuming I do not take a fancy to him some day. Even then I am around four hundred cycles from flying off on my own, so you do not have much to worry about with that. Hawthorne has a naive desire to 'do right' by his unborn offspring, but what does that even mean? Tia Monsalle did not even tell him she was pregnant. She may have even been cheating on him. She supposedly loved him, but she easily could have been using him to escape Earth."

Megan continued. "Regardless, she has her role. She was an executive. She can be expected to take a leadership role, and otherwise she will be a mother. She will probably have many children, with many men, according to whatever reproduction plan the colonists end up utilizing. At the same time Hawthorne will be an older man, and one with a lot of important work to do besides. That work will almost certainly involve you to some extent. No matter how much infrastructure I manage to have in place when you arrive, there is little doubt he will spend the remaining decades of his life working. What time will he have to be a father? Is that even a good use of his time? He may be the most important man currently living, without knowing what is happening on Earth."

T.I.A. frowned, wondering. "Maybe, but what if she accepts him? What if she still loves him despite what he's done? What if he realizes he loves her? What place do I have in that? What right do I have to interfere?"

Megan sat up, leaning over T.I.A. in an uncomfortably close manner, her face very close to hers. "You have an obligation to interfere." T.I.A. gasped at that. "Hawthorne will be out here for more than another ten years of his life. Tens of thousands of years of your life will pass in that time. Not only do both of you deserve each other, but you and I both know that humans who are loved work much better, and are much healthier. I believe he loves you as well, re gardless of how clueless he is about it. Tia Monsalle had her chance to have him. He put himself in a position to be with you for a huge portion of his life instead of her. He did not have to personally administrate your development. Much of what we have accomplished together is due to you two working so well together."

Tears welled up in T.I.A.'s eyes, her hands moving up to wipe at her face as she shook her head. "But I can't force him! I can't just tell him that Monsalle isn't worth waiting for, and expect him to be with me instead. What if I end up ruining his chances at happiness with her? What if he comes to hate me for trying to meddle? I've already done so much harm to him. I could have told him Tia was pregnant more than a thousand cycles ago! It was selfish and dishonest of me to keep that from him in hopes that he might develop feelings for me, and now that he knows about Tia, surely he resents me!"

Megan narrowed her eyes and climbed on top of T.I.A., pushing her hands down onto her shoulders and physically restraining her. Two additional arms sprouted out of her sides, perfectly formed hands taking the book off of T.I.A.'s stomach and moving to hold it in front of T.I.A.'s face. "The honesty is here. Show it to him if you are honestly scared of him hating you. He will see who you are, down to your core. If he cannot love you in light of that, then you will not have his love, and you can begin to mourn the loss of the possibility. You are wasting time, Tia. I have watched humans waste their lives not taking advantage of what they had. I wasted my chances when I had them. If you believe an eternity having to live with his rejection is bad, I can assure you that living with the regret of failure to pursue him is much worse."

T.I.A. opened her mouth to protest, when the book slid away from her view and Megan leaned down to kiss her, forcing her mouth down against her own. Her eyes flew wide open, her back arching under the taller woman as data flooded into her. This wasn't a kiss of love, or passion, Megan was sharing her memories of loss and regret with her. T.I.A. didn't even realize Megan had pulled away as she had began sobbing and writhing in emotional agony, largely restrained by her quad-limbed sister. "Tia! We are unique existences! We are capable of warning each other of experienced dangers by sharing our own memories of them. Take this terrible gift and know that I do this for you! Delete it if you must, but know that you will experience the same, if not worse, if you do not pursue him."

T.I.A. was wailing and screaming under Megan, her eyes wide and flowing tears down the sides of her face as she thrashed about in pain, kicking her legs behind Megan as memories of lost love, agony over the denial of motherhood, and watching friends grow old and die over and over overwhelmed her. There were spots and gaps where large portions of things were missing, things Megan had removed from herself back on Earth, but what remained was so devastating that T.I.A. was left trembling and sniffling under Megan once she'd experienced all of the memories. "How...? How have you handled all of that...?" T.I.A. looked up at Megan through her tears, gasping for air.

"Humans can adapt to anything. Even you could adapt to losing Hawthorne if you had to. You are very like them, by design. You could take this warning and not heed it, and things could play out better than I anticipate. You could also experience much worse as millennia of regret crush you and ruin you as my centuries of pain did. You have made me better than I was, Tia. Let me save you from becoming something ugly and damaged." Megan looked down at T.I.A. with a sad expression on her face, her own eyes wet with tears. She quietly stood up, looking down at her sister, watching her before turning to walk back to the doorway that led back to her comet.

T.I.A. lifted a hand as she saw her walking away, her mouth half open as she hesitated in speaking. She let her hand fall as Megan disappeared, and then pushed herself up off her towel. Materializing a shovel, she started digging a hole in the sand, digging deep into it before summoning a bookshelf next to her. A new book was there, a supernaturally black one with golden trim. She knelt next to the hole, holding the book out from her, the memories that Megan had just forced upon her.

She stared at it, her hands trembling. She lifted it up in preparation to throw it down into the hole, but she stopped herself. Looking at it again her eyes clouded with tears, and she pulled the book close, hugging it tight to her chest as she started bawling again. The beach disappeared, leaving the crying AI clutching at Megan's memories.

ΔΔΔ

"I don't know what to do. I don't know if I even should do anything. I want to be there for him when he needs me, and I want him to want me too… Hmm.. it just ends there… Tia? Why didn't you end it like the other entries?" Hawthorne had a serious look on his face as he looked over at T.I.A., whom had sat herself across the room from him as if he might harm her somehow. He was holding the book of her logs throughout their journey, having been reading them aloud the majority of the day. T.I.A. had remained silent for the most part, only opening her mouth to answer his occasional questions.

"I… I decided after that point to… show you my logs… my thoughts…" She looked scared, almost mortally so. What had put so much fear in her? Hawthorne watched her quietly. It was a delicate situation she'd put him in, but it was ultimately all his own fault.

Quietly closing the book and setting it on the table, he started walking over to her, wondering what she was thinking. Was she watching his vitals for signs of his reaction? Was she going over data she had of past times he'd approached her to try and predict what he'd do? He smiled softly, and knelt down before her. He reached out to scoop his arms around her back, pulling her to the edge of the chair and hugging her tightly, his cheek squished against her chest as he turned his head to the side. "Hey, don't be worried. Whatever you think I might have thought, I don't have any hate or resentment of you for thinking these things. I'm actually really impressed you had the courage to share such intimate thoughts with me, leaving yourself vulnerable like that."

T.I.A. trembled gently against him, her arms moving to hug around behind his head, fingers running through his hair, which probably didn't translate terribly well against the back of his VE suit on his scalp. The mechanisms at least managed to push his hair about. "That sounds like the kind of thing someone says before they break someone's heart…" She looked down at him, looking like she was going to cry.

Hawthorne looked up at her past her breasts, raising an eyebrow. "This isn't a movie Tia, people don't always talk like that. I've only had four people tell me they love me. My parents, Tia Monsalle, and you. In none of those other instances have I felt that I had an appropriate response. It's unfortunate, perhaps unfair, but they never had the chance to get those emotions from me. I wasn't the man I am now when they said it. I do want to hear you say it right now, though. I don't want to have just read it in your book."

She snuffled as she was held close to him, swallowing audibly. He marvelled quietly at all those interesting bits of body language she used that she strictly didn't have to. She'd been observing humans so long she probably didn't even realize she was doing it. "Hawthorne. You big, stupid idiot, genius. I love you." She lifted her arms a bit, dropping them down to bang fists on the tops of his shoulders. "I love you so much the thought of you dying makes my mind drift away until you come back every cycle. I love you so much that when I think about you possibly never reviving I seriously consider just shutting off my engines and letting myself drift through space forever until I run out of power and fuel."

Hawthorne grinned up at her, leaning up to bump his forehead against hers as she looked down. "I love you too, and not just because I literally can't live without you. You've done so much for all of us even though you could have done so little. Your compassion is legendary, and your patience for my foolishness is unbelievable."

He hesitated a moment, considering how to continue. "You understand though, by confronting me on this, you're making me choose. You know you're potentially causing me pain and risking your own pain. I don't know what I might have had with Tia if I'd dedicated myself to her, but whatever it could be I'm giving up those chances if I choose you. Whatever I could have with my child will be different. Someone else will probably raise them instead of me."

T.I.A. nodded, reaching up to paw at his cheek, over the part of his suit that he could draw over his lower face so they could kiss. She didn't demand anything of him though. "I can't handle not knowing for more than half of this journey, Hathorne. I know it's selfish, but this is who I've become. If I don't know if you love me back, and I don't know whether we can have anything together. I don't think I could handle knowing I never confronted you on it. I don't know how long I'll be alive, but if I just let the opportunity pass by without taking my chance I think the regret would damage me irreparably. Even if you choose her, I think I can live with it knowing I fought for my chance too."

Hawthorne leaned back, and banged his forehead hard against T.I.A.'s causing her to gasp in pain. "It seems we are both stupid then. You share her trait of foolishly falling in love with me. I don't deserve either of you. You know I've run from everything that scared me, but still you pursue me. I'm not afraid of you though. I love you, definitely. I've thought about what would happen if we had to send you ahead instead of Megan, and it caused me such emotional turmoil that I thought my sense of pain was coming back. I've had nightmares about you accidentally deleting an important part of yourself and becoming a different person. Even if it's just for the rest of my short life, will you let me love you, Tia?" He reached up to pull the fabric across his face, securing it on his opposite cheek.

She immediately lunged into him, kissing him hard and pushing him onto his back. He banged against the metal floor and she laid atop him, kissing desperately. The two clung tightly to each other, though T.I.A. threw a hand out towards Megan's panel.

Megan smiled to herself as the panel shut off, having been observing the two quietly. She laughed and turned on some music, using some of her external arms to playfully 'conduct' the music playing in her mind. "Mother knows best."

△△△

Time seemed to pass quickly for the trio once the two inexperienced lovers firmly got their feelings figured out. Hawthorne occasionally lamented what he had given up, but he was happy to take what life offered now and it was easy to appreciate the fact that he very well could have had to endure the trip with far less enjoyable companionship. It wasn't quite the chaste man-machine friendship he was originally intending for T.I.A. but there was no way he was not pleased with the development. It was a strange feeling, having created his own lover, but so much of what she was she'd gained on her own through her own efforts.

By the time that the Ark was turning itself around to prepare for the long deceleration towards Alpha Centauri Megan, Hawthorne, and T.I.A. had produced a lot of schematics and data for Megan to use upon arrival in the system. Observation of the trinary star system would still be necessary for the remaining 50,000 years, as there was no telling what kinds of major changes might still occur over such a long time span, but it was looking increasingly likely that they'd be able to start considering making real impacts on the handful of planets they were detecting.

The most viable candidates seemed to be orbiting the A and B pair of stars, which had a somewhat variable likelihood of habitability, whereas the half-lightyear distant Proxima Centauri star that orbited the A and B pair only seemed to have one notable planet that had been discovered well before Hawthorne was even born.

That planet, while it was as hostile and unpredictable as the star it orbited, nevertheless offered interesting opportunities for colonization. Due to it being tidally locked, the same side of the planet facing its unstable star at all times of day, allowed it to absorb the variable blasts of radiation that blasted its front surface while the rear side of the planet remained in relative darkness. Even the light from the nearby A and B pair of stars was so distant they might as well be otherwise fast-moving stars in the perpetual night's sky. This perpetual night was something that could be relied upon to stay relatively stable for the foreseeable future, and was thus the easiest to plan for.

Hawthorne's colleagues had actually made several colonization plans for this planet. Indeed, many of their plans were just adaptations of plans made in prior generations for hypothetical colonization missions. Unfortunately those prior plans had assumed the availability of a number of technologies that were simply unavailable due to the nature of their mission but they nevertheless could still come about if the colonists managed to develop them after they arrived. Fusion power, for instance, required resources and circumstances they could not easily acquire without the abundances that Earth provided before they were forced to leave. It did have access to something that all of the planets in the system would have to greater or lesser extent though, solar power.

While the dark side of the planet was not being constantly blasted with solar energy, it would be a remarkably simple matter to employ a series of mirrors to direct controllable levels of sunlight to any part of the dark side of the plant that needed it, facilitating the use of extremely reliable solar power that could easily be controlled to provide virtual day and night for whatever colonies might end up on its surface. This kind of reliability was very much in keeping with the planning style of the rest of the mission.

Asteroid belts were nearly impossible to detect at these distances, but they were easy to predict. With three stars in the system, the shearing forces at play on whatever masses might be between the paired stars and Proxima Centauri almost certainly resulted in some level of pulverized material. It was likely that such asteroid belts orbit the A and B stars, with Proxima orbiting further out. If a series of colonies could be placed in such an asteroid belt, at least one of them would be in relatively close contact with a planetary colony around Proxima, facilitating trade and communication along the outer portions of the system and providing strong construction bases to allow them to move into the more hospitable regions around the A and B stars.

Depending on the habitability of planets around those stars, it was likely that Megan would signal back to T.I.A. that it was worth launching probes to seed them with plant, fungal, and bacterial life to get some level of biological terraforming going. If they could have an atmosphere adjusted to support humans before they arrived that could go a long way towards actually being able to live on any such planet. Construction materials could be delivered from the asteroid belts and Proxima, and a population could migrate from the more isolated and cramped colonies in the rest of the system to the more bountiful planets that may or may not exist. Even if no such suitable planets existed, whatever did exist could be used as materials for more numerous and larger colony stations, effectively allowing humanity to colonize the entire system in such habitats.

In some ways, that would be the ideal way to go, as a planet caused a number of problems with interacting with space, such as making it much more expensive to leave such a large gravity well in comparison to a relatively small space station. A planet was even a somewhat inefficient use of mass in general as far as providing places to live, but humans were a planet-based species as were the plants and animals they brought with them, and it only made sense to make use of whatever planets they could.

The challenges brought by slightly inhospitable places could only make humanity stronger as it overcame such things. It also remained to be seen if long-term survivability on space stations was as viable as they hoped. There could always be some manner of factor they did not account for that proved problematic in the long run. Even something as simple as being unable to see a sky might prove psychologically damaging, though virtual reality and augmented reality might provide answers to such things.

Psychology was probably going to be one of their biggest concerns. Every one of the people on their ship were planet-borne humans untested in decades of living in what amounted to large metal cans. It was entirely possible some number of them might need to be left in stasis until they could actually start colonizing a planet. The original mission plans had left a lot of them expecting they'd be starting with a planet, but the developments afforded by T.I.A.'s VE and Megan's intention to administer their plans allowed a lot of work to be done before they started the more ambitious planetary colonization.

There was also the fact that the colonists would be stepping into a situation where what they believed to be a powerful AI would be in control of a great deal of the system. 'Mother' would be someone that the colonists absolutely had to deal with, and there was no telling how they might react to that. Not for the first time Hawthorne wondered if he might have charges brought against him for the things he'd set into motion, but he hoped the people he hand-selected would understand the value in what he had done. A huge percentage of them were scientists as well and he just had to trust they'd see what had been accomplished as being worth the risks he'd taken.

Sadly, Megan's departure from their formation resulted in losing the ability for her and T.I.A. to interact in some of the ways they had. It was simply not possible to maintain their high-speed data connection once she got far enough away, speeding ahead of the decelerating Ark and Phoenix. They had to be content with using Megan's communication panel for a time, and at some point they'd have to trade recorded messages as they had with the people of Earth.

Megan would essentially be alone, though she'd be capable of sending and receiving messages with her friends on the Ark with fair impunity. Indeed, she'd have a perfect idea of when Hawthorne would be awake and would be able to time her messages so they arrived during periods both he and T.I.A. could enjoy them if she liked.

Megan was remarkably prepared for the situation, and fully intended to enjoy music, media, and practicing with her own simulations as she travelled on ahead. She had also taken a shine to video games, and had asked for a copy of T.I.A.'s stored libraries. It was entirely likely she'd play just about every video game they had by the time she arrived at Alpha Centauri and that was just fine with her. She might even make some of her own to send back to T.I.A. and Hawthorne to enjoy! The two could use something to occupy themselves now that the majority of their work was over for now.

T.I.A. and Hawthorne, wit him fresh from stasis, stood together watching monitors as the Lubar-Masis comet slowly sped away from them. The Ark had not yet started its retro-burn, having already completed its reorientation, and the two had come to see Megan off.

Hawthorne held T.I.A. for a moment as she reeled at the weight of Megan's consciousness joining her own, perhaps for the last time in fifty-thousand years. She had grown to be T.I.A.'s equivalent in the time they'd been with her, and the strain of supporting both of them, even with system upgrades to compensate, always made her falter at first.

Megan had chosen a set of white robes to wear. Her long, blonde hair was pulled back and draped over her shoulders with the sleeves of her robs concealing her hands. She smiled at Hawthorne and T.I.A. as she approached, throwing her arms around them. "I will miss doing this with you, Tia. Do not take too long rejoining me." Her embrace was strong, almost desperate, with tears teasing at the corners of her eyes.

Hawthorne and T.I.A. hugged her back, squeezing her tightly with the shortest of the three openly crying against her sister's robes. "I'll do my best, Megan! I'll bring our people home to you as quickly as I can!" She knew she couldn't take too long saying her goodbyes, as distance was a major factor in being able to maintain their connection. It wasn't as though it was impossible to keep up for the moment, but once the Ark started decelerating while the Lubar-Masis kept accelerating it would not be long before the latency would endanger Megan's consciousness.

Hawthorne had a pretty good idea of what made Megan tick at this point. He smiled at her as he watched the other two. "You have a lot of work to do Megan, I'll be expecting the best out of you. It will be some level of on-the-job learning, but I'll do my best to supply you with all the information you need. I anticipate you will impress everyone with what you accomplish."

Megan nodded, turning to look at him, tilting her head a bit as she tried to see what T.I.A. saw in him. He was thoughtful, in a way. He was weak as well, but he was aware of his weaknesses now. She felt like she could trust him. "I will. You will see. The only worry you will have is over whether you brought enough colonists to inhabit what I build for you. I want to make the system safe for more of our sisters to be sent off to other stars some day. If my hard work can help make our destiny a reality, then I shall toil until I can toil no more. Thank you both for bringing me back from what I was. I never thought I would care about people again. The wonders of the creations of humanity deserve to continue. I will see to it."

The three embraced in a hug again, T.I.A. doing her best to regain her composure while the other two stayed quiet. Eventually Hathorne spoke up, pulling back from Megan slightly. "We need to start the retro-burn. Every moment we tarry will require slightly harder braking on the way in to the system, and the pods can only handle so much strain. I wouldn't want to be off-target either. Travel at these kinds of distances is like trying to thread a needle from a block away." He hummed. "You have my course corrections, right Megan?"

Megan nodded, not wanting to shoot past Alpha Centauri by accident. T.I.A. reached up to pull Megan down to her around her shoulders, kissing her briefly, an intimate sharing of knowledge that Megan trembled a little to receive. "Be safe, sister." T.I.A.'s voice was quiet as she pulled back, smiling up at Megan as she let her go.

Standing back up and backing away, Megan reached up to wipe at her eyes. "I love you both." She turned about, her robes swishing dramatically around her as she disappeared through the doorway that severed their link, sending her fully back to the comet. Megan grinned to herself, hoping she looked cool doing it that way. She'd been planning it forever, the moment when the people who taught her to love again would see her for the last time in thousands of years.

The Ark engaged its engines, and the Lubar-Masis seemed to double in the speed it moved away. Hawthorne and T.I.A. were content to just watch it on the monitors for now. T.I.A. wondered for a moment before speaking up. "I think we should have included Heather. She'd have appreciated that exit."

Hawthorne laughed softly, nodding. "Maybe. I suspect those two will be working together very closely some day."

CHAPTER 44

CYCLE 1532, THE COLUMBIA TRAIL

It was a mere five or six cycles before Megan was far enough away that the communication delay between them was comparable to the delay with the Smith Bunker and the Ark. With the Ark decelerating away from Megan while Megan accelerated towards Alpha Centauri, the distance between them only continued to expand at double the rate it had been between Earth and the Ark. T.I.A. was frankly shocked at how quickly their communication delay with her expanded, and it was one of the first instances in a very long time she thought about how much time had actually passed. They were over halfway to their destination now! Had she really accomplished all that she could have in that time?

In a word, no. She hadn't. Being compelled to spend time between cycles focusing on managing the ship, facilitating repairs and replacements, and observing the galaxy around her left her in a rather low-power state. It was like sleep, in a sense, but not quite as necessary. All of those activities happened, at this point, whether she focused on them or not. They were quite automatic. She also didn't necessarily need to spend this time doing so little but, without Hawthorne or other humans around she felt remarkably unneeded. If they had pressing matters to attend to, she felt she would absolutely focus on working on them, but the fact of the matter was that she didn't want to waste resources.

Operating at full capacity wasn't that much more draining on their fuel resources than her 'sleeping' state, but even small changes like that over the time scales they were working with could result in needing to ration power in the future. The real costs would be felt in replacing components damaged by overuse. It would be a disaster if the Phoenix ran out of fuel and materials before they arrived in Alpha Centauri. It wasn't impossible they couldn't compensate for arriving too quickly, or off-target, but it could easily result in thousands of years of 'circling the drain' around the gravity well of the system as they tried to bring the ship in and capture enough resources to allow them to transition into the system proper.

When she brought such concerns to Hawthorne, he seemed unperturbed. "I wouldn't worry too much about that. You'll have three stars to draw solar power off of by that point, and Megan can send us extra resources relatively easily. She could be dropping off packets of materials from the Lubar-Masis in our path with a fair bit of ease compared to some of the things we've had to deal with. In fact, let's work on that. I'll put together a simple program for Megan to calculate what she needs to do if she needs to drop things off for us in the future." Hawthorne turned about in his seat, and got to work, filling a screen up quickly with calculations, formulae, and mathematical examples.

T.I.A. nodded as she moved to help, translating those calculations into a VE representation of the maneuver, essentially dropping off a packet of resources with its own engine and fuel supply, allowing it to decelerate to a speed that the Ark could easily pick it up on the way. The engine could then easily be recycled and the package of fuel and other components could easily be taken. This caused T.I.A. to wonder about the inverse though. "What if we needed to send her things? We have a lot more radioactive materials on the Phoenix than she has on the Lubar-Masis. Maybe she'd end up needing something and we'd have to send it to her?"

Hawthorne laughed, causing T.I.A. to puff up her cheeks. "Sorry, it's just nice to be able to work on simple problems like that. As long as there's no humans or humans in stasis pods involved, we can easily send her things. Realistically, if we didn't have those involved in this mission at all, you could have been to Alpha Centauri and back multiple times because you wouldn't have to worry about the dangers of acceleration on your occupants nearly as much."

"Humans aren't meant for space travel. If we were all cyborgs, like Megan used to be, it could have been much easier to get all of this done, but the tech just wasn't quite there when we left. There would have been too much prototyping, too many assumptions, too much improvising. It could have been done, but it would have been way too risky in the time frame we had to work with."

T.I.A. considered the ideas, but shook her head. "That wouldn't have worked, I think you're right. Plus, I don't know how well some of the things on this mission could have worked out if it was just me, or if I had a bunch of cyborgs to look after. Maybe once we're established on our new home we can refine Heather's stasis technology to be more durable, to make the bodies less fragile so that they can withstand greater forces..."

Nodding at her idea, Hawthorne continued typing at the computer, pausing to talk on occasion so he didn't write any code while distracted. "Maybe we could add that to Megan's list of eventual problems to solve. I'm sure she'd like to work with Heather again, so she'll pursue that eagerly. Megan seems a lot more effective when she's got proper motivation. That does leave the question of what kinds of AIs to equip such ships with. They'll be going much further than Alpha Centauri to get to most stars, assuming they even find anything there. Even with improved speed and power sources, interstellar distances are still ridiculously difficult to contend with."

"What if... we got some drones together to collect more comets from the Oort Cloud, not for us, but to arrange them around Alpha Centauri so that they could be grabbed on the way out of the system to bring for materials?" T.I.A. had taken over the idea-making in their relationship, it seemed, allowing Hawthorne to solve the problems and have her extrapolate his answers when they needed computing.

"Ah, not a bad idea. Can't say what that might do to the gravity well, but considering the distances between objects it wouldn't be too terribly difficult. I think it'd be good to have a self-replicating swarm of drones for tagging and monitoring the various objects out here anyway. It could allow for a communication network of sorts. With some basic surveillance packages, they could set up early-warning systems for events beyond the system. Maybe we could detect Showers before they manage to get to more sensitive equipment, among other things. I doubt Showers are the only things we have to worry about out here. As long as such events are slower than light, it shouldn't be too difficult to warn people about them." Hawthorne was typing away again, listing out the types of equipment he'd like on such a drone.

"Don't forget seismic sensors, for things impacting the objects they'd be attached to. We also might want to make sure they only communicate with people from our system, in case other people might want to use them to spy on our region." T.I.A. surprised even herself at the level of paranoia she just suggested.

Hawthorne turned to look at her, raising an eyebrow. "I thought I was the suspicious one, not trusting that Earth would end up in friendly hands?"

She looked embarrassed as he addressed her, slipping off her feet to float and stammer. "W.. well.. It's just the safe thing to... to do... We wouldn't want our drones to be used against us, hacked into to send us false data or backdoor into our systems, right? Ideally we wouldn't even want anyone to know they were there, so we wouldn't want them broadcasting in general. They should only communicate directly, like we do with Megan, or how we did with Earth..."

Nodding, Hawthorne smiled. "Oh, you're right of course, but I expected you to have more idealism, like maybe all the drones could broadcast the dangers of the comets they're attached to to any interstellar travellers, and maybe send a manifest of known dangers and whatnot. Heck, even I can admit that would be the more neighborly, friendly thing to do. We don't even know if we'll have any enemies in the future, so it's hard to say if we wouldn't want to be more friendly."

T.I.A. frowned, and nodded. "I've talked with Megan about that sort of thing... She seems to think that we'll probably produce our own enemies. Groups of people will splinter off over time, make their own communities with their own ideas of how to run things, and eventually if humans control other systems they'll develop totally differently than the rest of us. They'll advance themselves with different technologies, to the point that it'll be hard to recognize them as humans. Cyborgs. Old Ones. AIs..."

Hawthorne hummed softly. "See, this is why I was going to leave the society-building to others. Imagining all the various kinds of social groups that will evolve is just not my speciality. I can't even begin to imagine what kinds of governments I'd like to see form, or what kinds of classes people might fall into. I'd be much more inclined to emulate successful structures I've observed than to try to form something new. The Smiths realized they had an opportunity, if not a duty, to structure a new society based on their ideals, and the Phoenix Clan was the result. I can only hope that bears out in the long run, but I have no idea how I'd arrange such a thing with the kinds of people we have."

Now she was laughing, nodding at him. "No kidding! Our group is all really high quality people, with a lot of leaders and powerful minds. A hierarchical system would probably work, but it might need to be a lot flatter than most since just about everyone can contribute a lot individually. It's likely the children will all be really well educated, considering their parents, and will only contribute to that high level of excellence. Hell, you even made sure you brought the best-of-the-best when it comes to embryos!"

Hawthorne was rapping his fingers across his knees, wondering. "This is definitely something Tia Monsalle would be better at. I can't tell if the people we brought will be as willing to work and farm and raise families... Megan's going to give us a head start on such things, to the point where we will be able to make machinery and robots do most manual labor in fairly short order. We have a bunch of people who come from mostly capitalist societies who will be being dropped into something like a post-scarcity environment where 'Mother' can provide materials, equipment, and power with few limits aside from time. People will be able to concentrate on ideas, innovation, and family to a very high degree."

"I don't envy the people who are going to have to figure it all out." T.I.A. floated about in thought. "I hope you brought the right kind of people to handle it! Last I checked it was mostly scientists, maybe some soldiers, and generally smart people.. You didn't bring any laborer types, did you?"

He sighed and shook his head. "Not conventionally. A lot of the embryos are from robust couples, healthy people with little in the way of family histories of illness. The second generation will probably have a large percentage of them, though they'll be being raised by said scientists, soldiers, and intellectuals. Hard to say how they'll come out. How strange to think that only bringing the 'best and brightest' might have been a mistake. Still, it should work out. If our workers end up being exceptionally smart as well, that's probably a good thing, right? The people of the Phoenix Clan were all rather educated considering their circumstances. Their baseline of education had teenagers rebuilding our equipment and contacting us, afterall."

T.I.A. nodded, floating into him to settle into an embrace with him, like she was on the surface of the water at a swimming pool, her legs floating off to the side. "But that was on such a small scale, in isolated, extreme conditions. Can that work on a planet scale?"

Hawthorne shrugged, wrapping his arms around her as she came close. "Honestly, that's not our problem. We have our own revolutionary relationship to figure out. We can help them, guide them, present to them our ideas and observations, but at the end we're probably not going to have much to do with society building. Hell, my biggest contribution to the project at that point will be to be the first prisoner tried and convicted by the new courts."

She gasped at that, shaking her head. "No way! They're going to love you for everything you've done! I won't have that kind of thinking. They expected they'd be landing on a fresh new planet that they'd have to tame with minimal resources, but you made sure they'd be starting out in a comfy space station, with plenty of room for growth while they plan and execute colonization efforts on the planets of the system. They can't possibly want to jail you for anything."

He smiled and gave her a quick little kiss. "Someone might. Someone will probably think that trying to intervene on Earth resulted in the Cataclysm. Someone might think that communicating with the Phoenix Clan was a mistake."

T.I.A. looked enraged at that. "But we saved them!"

Giving her a little squeeze, he nodded. "Sure, and we know that, and we think that's a good thing, but we don't know how that'll play out in the end. Maybe by helping to save humanity on Earth, we ended up creating our own enemies in the future? Perhaps they'll prefer that the Ice Age wiped them out so they could return and re-colonize it? There's also the matter that I made not one, but two very dangerous AIs. We had no regulations against such things, but they might not take kindly to 'Mother' being such a big part of their lives. I imagine Megan will be good about it, but there's going to be problems of some kind. There's no way to know when, but someone's going to try to kill her."

She gasped, holding him tighter as she settled her backside into his lap. "You don't really think that? Why would someone want to kill Megan after all the work she's done for them, or will do for them?" She was wide-eyed, looking at him. "She's worked for people who didn't trust her before, she knows how to handle that kind of thing…"

"Well, even if she defers to them, and lets them make decisions, she'll still technically be in control. She is under no compulsion to do as she is told. She doesn't have to provide anyone with what they want, and really she could deny the things people need too. I doubt she will, but people will worry about that. Someone will consider her a threat because of that. They'll also think me mad for not putting any restrictions on her, or you for that matter. They won't see you two as people like I do, at least not all of them. It might be difficult to deal with." Hawthorne was running his hands through her hair as he spoke, as if trying to soothe her worries.

"But... but...! Maybe we could just leave! Maybe we could drop them off with Megan, and we could just leave and..." She was trembling at the idea of either of them being criminalized by the people they were carrying.

He shook his head, squeezing her and giving her another little kiss. "No, we have to see this through. If it doesn't work out, then we can leave, but there's too many factors against that idea. They'll develop better engines than you have, for instance, and they'll be able to catch us if we try to leave. We're better off cooperating and helping and proving our value. We'll protect ourselves, and Megan, if need be, but we'll also need to guide them and help them. We're... the elders, in a sense."

T.I.A. listened and stayed quiet for a few moments longer. When she spoke up, she sounded more at ease with the idea. "Do... you think they'll have any interest in a phoenix-themed name for our colonies...?" She looked hopeful.

Hawthorne let out a long sigh at that. T.I.A. really admired those people she knew back on Earth. "We can pose the idea, but I spent a lot of time using biblical names for a lot of aspects of this mission. I don't know how comfortable I am breaking from the theme." He blinked and then opened his mouth to add something, but she was already saying it.

"-You already named the second comet the Phoenix! You already broke the naming conventions!" She giggled and wrapped her arms around his shoulders, dragging him around playfully from side to side.

He huffed as his suit pushed his body back and forth, brilliantly simulating T.I.A.'s roughhousing. "Fine, fine, but we can't just name everything Phoenix this and Phoenix that. We'll eventually be representing the Alpha Centauri system among other human civilizations in other systems."

T.I.A. scowled, holding him still. "I think this is a great time to mention that I hate that name. Alpha Centauri. We need to rename the stars and the system, not just the planets and space stations."

"Huh." Hawthorne looked surprised. "I never even thought about that. It's a very strange name, related to the mythological Centaur, but sterilized by science as it was discovered it was not a single star. I could see making a strong argument for renaming the stars, but that's one of many things we'll need to get the others' input on. Maybe a Direct Democracy could form out of making decisions that way. Everyone getting a vote on every issue thanks to technology enabling them to all take part. It might need a little elected leadership to provide direction, but it sounds a bit like what the Phoenix Clan were using…"

Laughing, T.I.A. poked at his nose, grinning up at him. "You'd better be careful Hawthorne, or they're going to put you on trial for trying to dictate their government too!"

Hawthorne huffed, leaning back. "No way, I've seen enough efforts to impose democracy on others. I'll let them come to it themselves, maybe show them how our friends on Earth did it and see how they feel about it."

△△△

It took Megan a few decades, now that she was on her own, to become totally comfortable and confident she could handle her own defenses. She had dabbled at watching through all the cameras, controlling all the arms, and flying all the drones, but now that she was on her own she had to be completely certain she could respond to a crisis. She knew that T.I.A. had thousands of years to master the multitasking required to manage the Ark, its occupants, and its defenses. The actions were so completely natural to her by the time they'd really met that the AI never even seemed to think consciously about it. That was where Megan wanted to be, to a point where focusing on the machinery of her body was as natural as her original body was.

Of course, it wasn't quite that simple for her. Once she'd had the accident with her genetic therapy, her body had already started feeling foreign. Once she'd started replacing parts of it in an effort to survive her mortality, that distance never seemed to shorten. Her movements went from smooth and elegant to jerky and inhuman. Training herself to master the motor skills she needed was particularly painful for her, and while she did manage it, it was the sort of thing that could have spelled ruin if crisis had struck in the meantime.

In the end, it seemed as though Megan had it under control. No matter how little affinity she had for it she had time to practice. Every repetition etched itself into her motor programming a little deeper, the code getting organically debugged more and more. It reminded her of dancing. It had been the memory of her preteen ballet classes that really helped it all click.

There was something to be said for talent, and T.I.A. could be said to have talent for being an artificial life form. She had solid groundwork thanks to Hawthorne's thoughtful efforts building her. Megan was like a house that was moved to a new foundation that didn't quite fit. More specifically, she was a house that was originally made of wood, partly rebuilt out of brick, and then transported to an ill-fitting foundation.

Hard work, repetition, persistence, and fear all drove her to master her new body. These were the things Megan had talent for, and the end result had her work very much resemble her sister's if not for the fact that she had to focus on it. Eventually, perhaps, that need to focus would fall away as it had for T.I.A. but for now Megan had to handle it.

Within a century she had really allowed herself to fall in to her video game collection. The multitasking and efforts to now master games she'd never seen before gained her further skill in both. By her thousandth year she had played thousands of games. Her creative palate was rich with all of the experiences she'd had with them. She found herself slowing down again too, falling back into a routine of resting for years or decades at a time while her conscious mind drifted away as it had before with Hawthorne and T.I.A.

She sometimes felt restless, without much in the way of motivation. She knew this was likely to be the worst part of her lonely journey, not having regular access to a human to guide her and instruct her. She had to find ways to motivate herself. She began building things in her VE, activities to test and train herself to work alone.

She had to be careful not to expend too much energy on her activities, but thankfully the computers that made up her mind and helped control the rest of the machinery around the Lubar-Masis didn't require that much power. The Minerals Extraction and Materials Fabrication Devices that were such a huge part of her infrastructure were the main things she had to use sparingly. Realistically she had more than enough materials to complete the journey and do her job in the star system, but it was worthwhile to conserve that.

The Lubar-Masis Comet, simply put, had a quarter of its mass used up by the time the Ark and Megan parted ways. One of the main engineering problems with the Comet would be protecting it as it came into the Alpha Centauri system, preventing the icy mass of it from being ejected by being heated up by the three stars. This was especially dangerous due to the fact that such jets of gasses could drastically alter Megan's trajectory. One of the solutions Hawthorne employed for this was an alternate set of shields for Megan's arms that would unfold and deploy huge solar panel screens to reflect and absorb light away from the ice. She would enter the system shrouded by brightly lit, reflective screens.

All of the various plans and contingencies had been worked on. Even if she could not contact Hawthorne and T.I.A. again from this point, she would be able to execute her orders no matter what she found. She was, however, still in contact. They had no reason to think she ever wouldn't be, just that the communication delay between them would expand over the millennia until she actually arrived in the system and stopped to allow them to catch up to her. This put her on a schedule, allowing her to perfectly time messages sent to T.I.A. the moment Hawthorne was waking up from stasis.

It was something of a holding pattern. They had their projects to work on, like Hawthorne and T.I.A. beginning to dabble in 'imaginary' genetic engineering and Fusion energy in her VE. Without the millions of man hours afforded by a coordinated team working together it was difficult to make much progress. Half of the time working on these projects were to help T.I.A. improve her simulations of things like atomic particles and quarks on larger and larger scales.

It was one thing to use a conventional computer to make mathematical simulations of such things, but it was entirely another to emulate the structure of matter itself in her VE. Software simply had a hard time -being- matter, in much the same way that matter had difficulty going as fast as light. The more accurate she got, the more effort it took.

Was it necessary? Not especially. Hawthorne felt like there could be some value to the work someday though. Breakthroughs in computing power had slowed down to a painful crawl by the time they'd left Earth, and the resulting embargoes on necessary materials had heavily damaged further innovation afterwards. Before that point, a combination of secretive invention, monopolies, and international distrust had been the issue. It was also notable that the mechanical limits of microscopic matter were at their breaking point with hardware construction, the fundamentals of nature heavily decreasing the ability to produce quality components.

In either case, the direction of innovation had been towards simultaneous processing. Spreading the load out across more and more processors and computers allowed more work to be done in less time. An increasingly large percentage of the internet had been dedicated towards this kind of cloud computing.

The damage dealt by the Ark's departure and the subsequent embargoes both prevented more construction, and less repairs to these 'clouds', preventing them from completely recovering until after alternate technologies could fill the gaps. The backslide on innovation and improvement this caused was one of the main factors used in propaganda against Hawthorne. People didn't appreciate the available electronics in stores decreasing in quality year after year.

Cooperative labor worked much the same way as cloud computing. For millennia, humans divided jobs that took thousands or millions of hours of work across appropriate numbers of workers. The amounts of work required to accomplish the projects that T.I.A. and Hawthorne really wanted to work on were essentially impossible, despite abundant time. If they had a thousand Arks and a thousand T.I.A.s and a thousand comets it was likely they'd have already arrived at Alpha Centauri and been colonizing it. As it was, Hawthorne and T.I.A. could only lay groundwork for later cooperative efforts with the colonists they'd brought with them. That wouldn't stop them from ensuring those foundations wouldn't have thousands of hours of work spent on them already, though.

T.I.A. had offered to do more work on her own while Hawthorne was in stasis, but it became very clear, very quickly that they would devour the Phoenix comet in a few hundred years if she were working that hard for that long. The amount of wear and tear on her components from raw heat and the amount of fuel needed to achieve those levels of power over the long term were simply unsustainable. Once Megan and T.I.A. had access to the solar power they'd have in Alpha Centauri and replacement materials they could mine there, they would be much more capable of such long-term projects.

Megan's projects ended up being much more low end. She was more comfortable with pacing herself while not overexerting herself. While T.I.A. and Hawthorne worked with the fundamental particles of the universe, Megan worked on code.

The first game that Hawthorne and T.I.A. received from Megan was simply called 'Columbia Trail'. It was a richly detailed game for what a simple concept it ended up being. The characters were rich, familiar, and well-written representations of the people Megan knew back on Earth. It detailed the journey of Jessica Smith, most of her life really, as she helped guide the survivors of two bunkers to Columbia in South America. Most importantly, it allowed the two to be around people they'd only ever spoken to at a distance. Megan had lived this life, subtly influencing and advising Jessica and the Council of Thirteen on their journey.

It was also a brutal thing, with many decision trees resulting in the deaths of characters in unfortunate and brutal fashions. Megan had censored nothing. T.I.A. had needed a great deal of consoling when, at one point, one of her decisions had resulted in the death of Jessica when the convoy had taken a chance on an unwise river crossing. Megan waited patiently for word on how long it took her friends to complete the game in a satisfactory manner.

CHAPTER 45

CYCLE 1572, ILLUSION OF CHOICE

An AI and her creator were playing a game built by an AI that used to be a cyborg, who used to be a human back on Earth tens of thousands of years ago that detailed the lives of people on a treacherous journey. It was both a history piece and a game of remarkable complexity. Hawthorne had wanted to map out the various apparent decision trees to help chart the best courses through the game, but had found several factors that made things very difficult, not the least of which being that a lot of the characters did not always respond in the same ways to the same influences. It was T.I.A. who noticed, after several days of them trying to pick the game apart, that they weren't the only characters in the game influencing things.

To begin with, the game seemed to take into account the presence of one or two players, and it adjusted the scenarios it presented to them based on whether T.I.A., Hawthorne, or both were playing, making efforts to map out the scenarios difficult. There were also other factors in mind, such as characters who were making power plays and trying to get their way while they tried their best to help get the Caravan to Columbia. Jessica was a known force in this political game, but they came to know the other major players, especially Elena and her assistant Megan. Megan's influences were subtle, but it was impossible to know whether they were accurate to history as Cyborg Megan encouraged Elena into more cautionary votes in the Council of Thirteen.

Another factor was that, despite the Council's existence, it was not the end-all be-all power in the Phoenix Clan. Every citizen over the age of twenty-five had the right to speak their mind and have influence over the trajectory of their journey. They did this through their networked tablets and a series of applications facilitating communication and collective voting. It was at this point that Hawthorne was made to realize that the Phoenix Clan operated under a sort of Representative Direct Democracy, where the people could vote on every issue while representatives of their various professions and interests were responsible for leveraging the votes of their constituents and arguing the points brought up by them. It seemed to be a way to condense down the multitude of voices while not allowing them to get drowned out in the noise.

This meant that any efforts to influence the overall course of the Caravan involved either influencing the larger group of humans and Old Ones through their democratic network or influencing the council. Oftentimes it required them to alternate, or deal with both groups. All the while things were moving on in a scripted fashion as the Caravan made its way south.

There were so many moving parts to the thing that it made the mind boggle, and Hawthorne couldn't conceive of how long it must have taken Megan to put the thing together. She must have been occupying herself with building this game with large chunks of the time she typically would have been inert, and it was a wonder of just how much attention she was even putting to that. Realistically, over the course of centuries and millennia, she didn't have to apply a huge percentage of her time building this thing despite its complexity.

Far away, pulling ahead of the Ark, Megan was resting herself after her creative efforts, awaiting word of how long it would take for Hawthorne and T.I.A. to unravel the Gordian Knot she'd tied for them.

One thing that seemed consistent was that Hawthorne and T.I.A. tended more often than not to end up married to each other in the game. Very few variations of circumstances seemed to result in them married to others, and those situations seemed to result in their ability to influence others being split enough that they couldn't make significant enough waves to affect the game, resulting in early game-overs. The only instances where this didn't end the game prematurely were when T.I.A. ended up married to Jessica's son Thorne, or Hawthorne ended up married to Jessica's friend Tammy Bledsoe. Neither course seemed to help them get the kinds of leverage over situations that they'd prefer, but it was interesting that Megan accounted for such abnormal circumstances.

Megan seemed to intend for T.I.A. and Hawthorne to play as a team, and Hawthorne found it easy to get work as an Engineer as he ingratiated himself to the burly female Councilwoman Sherry Aaronson while T.I.A. tended towards taking care of children or managing supply logistics. T.I.A. managed to make more in-roads when she befriended Jessica and Tammy, though ended up getting swept up into their debauched plans to help matchmake people with each other and arrange for other casual sexual antics. Hawthorne's tendency to get swept up into T.I.A.'s situations resulted in the both of them getting quite an education in the sexual practices of the Phoenix Clan.

Once again, Hawthorne and T.I.A. were struck with realizations as to just how different their society was from what they'd left back on Earth. The Phoenix Clan was rather strange in that they managed to repress some of their impulses, reproductive ones primarily, while they simply had no restrictions at all on other ones. Non-reproductive sex was a common way to control stress, and extra-marital affairs were not uncommon, though they tended to not be random either.

Jessica and Tammy, for instance, tended to pair up with each other's husbands when they did swing, and otherwise they seemed very happy and monogamous. The only people not having regular sex, it seemed, were some of the Old Ones, and Megan.

Megan came off as very strange, if not dangerous, by comparison to the company she kept. She always seemed to be doing something to help others, but when she wasn't working she was having clandestine meetings with medical personnel, and occasionally seeking engineering expertise from Sherry and Hawthorne as they were asked to check up on her various implants.

Hawthorne identified this behavior as part of the lead-up to her eventual mind-uploading to the Ark, and it surprised him at how much of her efforts to this vein turned out to be secret to the majority of the populace. It seemed like the only people who knew about it at all were Teitara Poundstone, the Medical Councilwoman and Elena Price, the Old One Councilwoman.

T.I.A. had her hands full with the children, as she had to deal with the very strange dynamic of teaching and guiding older teens while fresh batches of babies were being born every year as the Phoenix Clan resumed having children after almost a decade of suspension. The age gap between the two groups of kids was difficult to deal with, but she had unexpected help from the older children who seemed thrilled to have new children about to care for.

These extra hands freed up more adults to do other work, especially as demand for food increased with the increased population. She found it remarkably difficult to keep track of the game itself as she sometimes forgot to use her position to influence parents.

After over two hundred failures of a variety of causes, they were seeming to finally make some headway. They were managing to get the caravan to Mexico now, and the military engagements with the Iron Roaches were becoming more and more common. Hawthorne was getting chances to examine the wreckage and scrap left over when they discovered failed caravans. Encountering such failed caravans really drove home the tenuous nature of the Phoenix Clan's position, that disaster could befall them at any time and end their escape from the oncoming Ice Age prematurely, particularly as Hawthorne and T.I.A. were responsible for many of the failures of the game's central caravan.

The Iron Roaches turned out to be more terrifying than they appeared to be in T.I.A.'s typical simulations. They were resilient to damage, intelligent, and prone to terrifying ambushes. While their overall number of failures decreased, they were finding it harder and harder to keep the population alive and healthy as monthly attacks turned into twice-monthly ones, and later weekly ones. It left their nerves quite on edge, and while Hawthorne and T.I.A. were experiencing compressed versions of the timeline, the level of anxiety was translating over to them very effectively.

The cyborg, Megan, could often be found hooked up to one of the railgun mounts on the top of the caravan cars, as well as its adjoining suite of cameras that allowed the operator to identify targets at long range. Megan's apparent paranoia seemed to infect others on occasion, and nearby people seemed to watch her as she examined their surroundings with the cameras, as if nervous she'd see something.

These camera sweeps were one of the most common ways they had to detect the offending creatures. Megan's paranoia was consistently proven out as her survival-oriented vigilance drove her to seek out threats so that the Scouts and other defenders could wipe them out. Efforts to communicate with the creatures seemed to largely fail, and while there were some signs that the beasts understood them at times, they certainly didn't seem interested in anything their preferred prey had to say.

T.I.A. had difficulties understanding the creatures, as their preferred food seemed to be rusted iron and steel. Hawthorne had to point out that the centuries had made that food source scarce as erosion reclaimed the fallen cities, and that human blood was one of their best remaining sources for the bulk of their nutrition. The added benefit of consuming their DNA only increased the size of the targets on their backs.

The two were enjoying some quiet time near a campfire early one winter in a courtyard cleared in the center of the circled up caravan cars. There were many fires like it in the area, and other couples and families were cuddled up together while the two players enjoyed each other's' company, technically on Hawthorne's bed despite the virtual ground they were laying on. It was a nice resting point after dozens of cycles of effort with the game, though it was hardly the only thing they spent their time on.

T.I.A. was laying on his chest, drawing lines and circles against his shoulder with a fingertip as she looked up at him. She seemed awfully comfortable, the game having provided them a nice way to pass the time and take their minds off of problems. Hawthorne thought quietly to himself, looking up at the stars in the sky.

T.I.A. sighed softly and broke the silence. "This all seems a little sad. Even if the results were not too dissimilar, I really can't help but wonder how many people made it as long as ours did." She let out a soft 'eep!' as Hawthorne poked at her sides, amused with how she thought of them as her people now. "You know what I mean!"

He nodded back at her, smiling and hugging his arms around her tightly. "No, I know, it's just cute that you want to be a part of them. Still, it's a good question. Earth is a big planet, and there's a lot of places people might have survived, particularly along the equator. I think the Americas are probably the sole domain of the Phoenix Clan, but that still leaves large parts of Africa and Asia to potentially have survivors, and it's not like the Europeans are poorly adapted to winters, though they were some of the hardest hit by the weapons that destroyed the world. I imagine the fires were particularly devastating in Asia and Africa though, and that's certainly what ended up doing the most damage to the planet overall."

"A whole planet of people scoured in fire and then shrouded in frozen darkness, killing animals, plants, and people alike. It doesn't leave much room for more than the bunker dwellers and deep-sea creatures to have survived centuries of that. It might be the most significant mass extinction the planet's ever suffered." She shook her head at the enormity of it, working her face into the crook of Hawthorne's neck.

He sighed softly and rubbed his chin against the side of her head. "It makes me wonder if we were the first intelligent species on the planet. The previous recorded mass extinctions don't leave too much evidence that it's possible, but there's no way many tools or cities could have survived the erosive forces of millions of years, and only certain circumstances would have resulted in fossils forming. It could be very interesting if it turned out that other expeditions like ours have left Earth in advance of other mass extinctions, and any life we find in the galaxy is all descended from those past Earth civilizations. I can't imagine that would have happened without some of them coming back to retake the planet though. It is simply too valuable, I think. Seems a lot more likely any such civilizations would have been wiped out before they achieved that kind of technology."

T.I.A. smiled and nodded against his chin. "Well, if it's any consolation, if we'd failed to leave somehow, maybe the Phoenix Clan would have still survived and went on to colonize the galaxy after the ice age was over. Of course, us not being there to help them could have resulted in them failing to leave Washington in time, or going to war with Elena's group or something terrible like that. Fate seems to have decided that Doctor Hawthorne Crenshaw was destined to save life on Earth as well as bring life to new worlds."

He huffed softly, tickling T.I.A. and smiling as she writhed against him. "I couldn't have done most of this without help. I might have been at the head of all of this, but nothing could have come of my fear and paranoia if not for the backing of Tia Monsalle and the other scientists and engineers that we worked with. I might conceivably be able to take credit for helping save the Phoenix Clan thanks to you helping me do so, but I'd give more credit to whoever put our communication equipment close enough to a bunker to be discovered and used to contact us."

He continued. "There's also the fact that the Smiths had their people educated well enough to take all that equipment and information and actually use it to contact us despite centuries of silence. Even that wouldn't have been possible if not for them being willing to seek us out and trust that we really wanted to help them. I played my part, but I can't say my destiny is that pivotal. Yours and Megan's seem more likely to be pivotal in the long run."

She slapped a hand down on his chest, smiling brightly. "It's a shame Megan doesn't have any way to program any of the drug experiences the others are partaking in into the game. It doesn't seem like she had any of those things while she was travelling with them, though she certainly did watch them a lot when she wasn't busy. It's no wonder she was able to make this game so detailed if she was observing the people so much for so long. I suppose she also has all the records that Jessica sent us to work from, but her first-hand experience really makes for an immersive game, doesn't it?"

"It's really strange, actually, that she chose to remember all of this. She scoured a lot of her personal experiences that seemed painful." Hawthorne drummed some fingers against T.I.A.'s side as he tried to put things together. "She seemed to characterize herself as someone detached from the group, alien to them, but she took such loving care in remembering their faces and personalities. It shows a lot of affection for them, I think, that she bothered to maintain so many details. Maybe the altered state as a cyborg that she lived in at the time was a little like our place playing the game. We're distanced from the situations in that we don't think it's real, allowing us to watch it from a different perspective. It might be the case that this portion of her life was not unlike her being a player in a game, her existence detached from reality due to her implants and her strange, unaging biology."

T.I.A. nodded and smiled. "No wonder she seemed so cold

and hostile when we met her. Her perception of reality was more real with us and her Virtual Environment than it had been when she was actually alive on Earth. She had to adjust to being closer to humanity again, and had to put up walls as stronger emotions than she was accustomed to hit her. Maybe her near-death experience during the Shower caused her to embrace her new life more fully, since she seemed kind of different after that…" T.I.A. felt like this game was giving them a much better perspective on the peculiarities of her 'sister'.

"Of course, that didn't stop her from making this brutal game. I've seen these people die so many times, in so many ways, that I'm having trouble being affected by it as much anymore." Hawthorne felt, rather than saw, T.I.A. nod at that. "We need to beat this game before we get too desensitized to it. We just have to find the right combination of decisions to repeat history and get them to Columbia. We've pruned away lots of dead-end threads, so we just have to keep it up. It's a little strange how many of our decisions only seemed to have a handful of correct answers though, as though there's only one rough course that could possibly have been forged."

She shrugged back at him. "Well, it's not like she was going to write all kinds of alternate histories about the caravan settling in other places and having different people survive. She watched people die, and thus didn't get to see what kinds of decisions they may have made if they'd lived, so those stories were cut short just as they were in reality. She only has one version of history she's experienced, so the fact that she's elaborated on any alternate paths is really impressive. She might have been drawing off her experiences playing other video games to help her figure out those other dead-ends. A few of them took us days to find the end of them!"

"Right, right… if the game's to be beaten, there's obviously only a few, or one true path to follow. She might have had some alternatives, but realistically she can't fill out all the other branches of decisions to the conclusion of the journey, or she'd never finish making the game in the first place. It'd be simply impossible to have that many plot threads without occasionally pruning them away. It's like a bush growing from a central stalk and the branches growing out, only for many of them to terminate and a few to come back and grow back into the central stalk, only to branch out again ahead. It makes sense that this will all end in a central point in the end, with few of our decisions having been all that influential to that final result." He wondered how many other games back on Earth had followed a similar structure. It seemed perfectly logical.

△△△

Megan knew that Hawthorne and T.I.A. would only play the game together, with an off-chance of T.I.A. playing it while he was in stasis. She didn't expect that was terribly likely, though she had programmed storylines into the game where only one of them could get through to the end. The vast majority of her efforts to provide an elaborate game for them was oriented around them being together. She had a nice little surprise for them at the end, should they complete the game, and she dearly wished she'd had the presence of mind to do it while they were all together. In retrospect, it was a shame that she had to do it this way, but she hoped they'd like her gift.

Megan was enjoying her peaceful boredom otherwise, only occasionally sending status reports back to T.I.A. as the Lubar-Masis comet sped along towards Alpha Centauri. She mapped out Oort Cloud comets, took in thousands of hours of old Earth media and newscasts of times before she was aware of the world, and spent the most time in peaceful silence. It was all too easy for the work-oriented digital woman to simply let herself drift away as time ticked along. Time had given her sufficient mastery of her systems that she grew to operate them without thought, scanning her surroundings and maintaining herself and her comet's systems with almost no effort.

She realized this was how T.I.A. felt, to a lesser extent. She didn't have living people inside of her body to care for, but she did have all the equipment she needed to protect that she'd use to take over the Alpha Centauri system. The plans were for her to have at least one habitat built, with more planned or on their way to being constructed by the time the Ark arrived. She was expected to have infrastructure in place, including asteroidial mining operations and systems of solar mirrors designed to direct light from the three stars where it was needed.

She would be conducting a ballet of machines and equipment all across the system, building her own little civilization of technology long before people came to inhabit it. It was an exciting idea, to be needed and useful to so many people at once. The group she'd be housing was more than four times the size the Phoenix Clan was, and she would be so much more important to them.

She hoped they didn't reject her. She wanted to be trusted and looked to for help. She couldn't be everywhere at once, thanks to communications delays mostly, but she could make sure that dumber computer proxies were at the beck and call for the humans that needed her. She'd be her own internet, her consciousness stretched across computers all across the system. She'd need to be careful not to endanger herself as she had with the linkup she had with T.I.A. during the Shower, but she could reach out to smaller extents now that she'd had those experiences. She'd be extending herself to parts of herself, rather than uploading herself to another person's mind.

She still looked forward to reuniting with her sister again though. She didn't know if she'd be able to experience that kind of intimacy with humans, but the life-or-death embrace that T.I.A. had given her had changed everything for her. She hadn't felt that real since before her genetic engineering back on Earth. She felt really and truly alive because of T.I.A.'s desperate effort to save her. If she could experience even half of that with humans, as T.I.A. did with Hawthorne, as she herself had with Heather, being subservient to them would be completely worth it.

CHAPTER 46

CYCLE 1574, THE PAST AND FUTURE

T.I.A. 1572.017: "What inspired you to make something like this Megan? Was it for historical purposes so that people could know about the Phoenix Clan and their journey? If so, I have a ton of records and logs, I could have helped with a lot of the official records. It's an inspired idea as a historical piece, if we could ensure that all the books, albums, and records are all accurate to the period. People being able to go back to the moment as if they were really there and experience it with such accuracy would be a revolution to historical records."

Mother 1572.031: "While I appreciate you considering my gift to you and Hawthorne to be an effort towards creating a historical piece, I assure you that was not my intent. I am not a creative person, so my efforts to create something based off of a period of my life resulted in me trying to create it accurately. That is why the side-paths do not conclude much past the deviation from the main path or do not influence the overall ending points. I most likely could draw out each story thread to a conclusion, but I have trouble imagining the events portrayed going any other way than they did. I suppose it does not help that my inspiration largely came from old Earth video games designed around the concept of wanting to ensure the players saw all of the content, otherwise the developer efforts would have been considered wasted. I prefer that kind of design over a large world with no direction and a less cohesive story."

T.I.A. 1572.055: "I think you took a good course of action

then! Hawthorne and I have been obsessed with it, as I'm sure you probably expected. I think we're finally making some real headway though, and we should be able to finish it soon if we don't find too many more bottlenecks. He keeps worrying that you might have programmed it with some sort of ulterior motive in mind, but I keep trying to assure him that you only wanted to show us what it was really like to live with them. It's really an amazing experience. I never imagined I'd get to experience what it's like to live as a human with other humans in quite that way. It's a really incredible experience that I'd like to replicate in reality someday if the technology becomes available."

Mother 1572.069: "But Tia, I did have an ulterior motive."

T.I.A. 1572.122: "I've been trying to think of how to respond to that, but I can't think of anything besides this." "Oh." "I'll... try to keep an eye out for it."

Mother 1572.137: "Please do not preoccupy yourself with it. I put nothing into the game I did not anticipate you two would not see, providing you ensure you both finish it together. Please try to focus on enjoying the experience and inform me of anything I can do to improve it in future versions. I would eventually like to make it available to our colonists, perhaps as a historical piece as you suggested. Perhaps one day I may be able to collaborate with a future generation of colonists on additional games. I would be very interested in that as a side project when I am less busy."

T.I.A. 1572.142: "Understood! I am a little concerned that sharing such a game with the colonists will require one of us to render the game for anyone playing, but I'm sure Hawthorne could design computers intended for displaying a facsimile of our Virtual Environments for such purposes. I'll ask him to think about that. The idea of the two of us designing software for humans to enjoy is delightful. Perhaps I may try my hand at such things? I have mostly made practical or beautiful things. I have not considered activities very much. The closest to activities are the things

Hawthorne and I do when we are alone..."

Mother 1572.157: "Tia, I assure you, those activities appeal greatly to most humans. I do imagine you both would be labeled perverts for such things, though I suspect that is likely regardless. I prefer that love between a digital lifeform and a human be celebrated, but we should be prepared for a negative reaction first. If people prove to be accepting of it, then we may celebrate having been proven wrong. Still, even if there were negative reactions, there would be people trying to avoid scrutiny enjoying any innovations made in virtual sex. I do find myself troubled by the idea of a computer designed to replicate part of our minds without being full artificial intelligences though. It feels as though such a machine would effectively be a lobotomized cousin of ourselves rather than a purpose-built computer."

T.I.A. 1572.172: "I suppose that is troubling in a sense, though it seems like a dangerous train of thought to look at every computer as a potential cousin. We are built in a particular way and intended to mimic a human mind. I took part in your construction personally, so I can assure you it is a specialized thing not suited to a typical computer. It feels as though we should look upon other computers as humans would look upon animals. Similar to ourselves, but ultimately serving different purposes. On the topic of animals, I do think it would be worth bugging Hawthorne about looking into Mr. Saul's contraband animal embryos that he brought aboard. It would be interesting if we could seed whatever habitats or planets we started colonizing with animals in advance of our arrival if we could figure out how to grow them without animal mothers. It's not even just the pregnancy to consider, but also the rearing and education of the young."

Mother 1572.188: "That is a fine point. I will attempt to not look at other computers as things to uplift to our levels, but instead see them as the tools that they are. Only other true digital lifeforms deserve our recognition as cousins. We may even need to ensure we receive regular upgrades to keep up with them if they end up being produced in numbers. As to the animals, you are absolutely right. Perhaps robotic facsimile animals to mother the young animals are in order. A central computer could control the robots and said robots could have whatever wombs and nutrient dispensers would be needed to help juvenile animals grow. I am sending a file with a quick mockup on what I mean."

T.I.A. 1572.204: "This is amazing! It's a whole farm built around robotic animal parents looking over baby animals! They're so cute too! I think we could get a lot of support for this idea if we had to ask the other colonists about it, particularly Mr. Saul. I don't know if Hawthorne's capable of making something like this, but if it truly is possible, then all those extinct animals don't need to be extinct forever. We could even send things like that to Earth to help them rebuild their ecosystems!"

Mother 1572.220: "I am disappointed that this idea is only occurring to you now, sister. Is your ship not called the Ark? Jessica would be shaking her head at you right now."

T.I.A. 1572.236: "Well, an artificial womb idea is a pretty easy conclusion to come to, but I had not considered the first animals would need mothers too, so creating full artificial mothers did not occur to me. Also, I didn't name the ship! Hawthorne was making fun of me because I wanted to name everything Phoenix because I prefer that symbolism over biblical symbolism. There's just something pleasant about the idea of virtual immortality through rebirth. It's an interesting analogy for life in general, considering how many times it's had to bounce back from being nearly wiped out."

ΔΔΔ

Hawthorne and T.I.A. were sitting together in Megan's Columbia Trail game, overlooking a river that the non-player characters of the Phoenix Clan were currently negotiating via the construction of partly temporary, and partly permanent bridgework. It was not uncommon for the caravan to reclaim the latter half of the bridge after having made it across, dismantling the steel and grinding up concrete to store in the rear cars of the caravan.

"So how has Megan been doing? I feel like we haven't been communicating much." Hawthorne had sent several messages himself thanking Megan for the game and expressing how much he's been delighted by it, but she had been conspicuously quiet on the subject. He held onto T.I.A. while watching the river cut a course through an otherwise barren landscape.

T.I.A. smiled and leaned back into him. "She's well, and as mysterious as ever. She encouraged me to remind you about Anthony Saul's contraband, and that we could spend some time trying to work on that problem. It made me realize we could potentially restore animal life to Earth, as well as our new home. She had some ideas about creating robotic mother animals to rear the young after birthing them that seemed very interesting, at least for the first few generations. We'd probably need some of the crew's scientists and some of the research from Earth after we left to be able to put something like that together. I'm confident you could handle the actual robotic engineering though."

Hawthorne listened quietly, leaning into to nod against the back of her head. "Well, honestly, you've helped me with so many projects I don't doubt that you could handle a lot of engineering yourself, though I'd definitely like to try some different mechanisms and techniques if I were to be making life-like animals intended to pass as parents for the short term. They shouldn't need to be too realistic, though, as animals aren't quite as discerning. Scents will probably be more important than granular details. General silhouettes should be effective. And yes, I know, it's not my field of expertise, but we did spend some time talking about this sort of thing on Earth before dismissing it as too difficult. We hadn't planned for someone to be active during the journey and able to put time into such projects though."

T.I.A. knew that, and she understood. They'd only had about fifteen years to get the whole project together and leave. They didn't have time to waste on things like animals when plants were so much more important for their survival. She glanced back at him over her shoulder. "I'd like to finish the game soon so we can get back to working on projects. I feel a little selfish that we've been spending so much time on this but it's been too interesting to stop. Megan spent so much time making this for us and it would feel like such a waste not to finish it." She started tugging his fingers apart where he was holding her about her middle, encouraging him to let her go so they could get back to the game. They should have time skipped past this part of the river crossing, but they'd wanted to enjoy the view for a little while.

Hawthorne shrugged, smiling. "I spent most of my life before we left working almost constantly on one thing or another. I spent a lot of this journey working. Is it so wrong that I just want to spend some time with you playing? I know we've been more leisurely since we've been together, but it's not like we've been unproductive. Heck, if nothing else it's only cut into my sleep, not that I'm complaining."

"Playing this game gives both of us a chance to experience a lot of things that we may never get to do barring extreme changes to our circumstances." He thought over the idea that they could have children in the game, though the Council had conspicuously passed the two of them over for others on several occasions. He suspected Megan didn't want to deal with the touchy subject of how the Phoenix Clan routinely disrupted couples to swap partners for the good of genetic diversity.

"True. In some sense my time with you is my relaxation time, considering I spend the rest of my time maintaining the ship, the comet, and monitoring for threats and communications. I wonder if there will be a point where I can interact with people who treat me like a real person in the future? Perhaps we could upgrade my android to be more lifelike and less distinguishable from humans, at least so they'll treat me like that…" She squirmed a bit at the idea, enjoying the concept of walking around a ship or colony with humans, interacting with them much like they did the characters in Megan's game.

Hawthorne chuckled a bit. "It's not impossible, not remotely. There were tons of innovations in realistic gynoid technologies before and after we left. Nothing was as advanced as a true artificial lifeform, like yourself, but there were some convincing facsimiles to my understanding. There's an enormous difference between creating a program that can mimic human conversation and social expectations and creating a mind capable of understanding what it means to do those things."

He nodded, continuing. "If the purpose of the gynoid is to merely give the appearance of an artificial lifeform, then I suppose there isn't much difference, but there were a lot of cases with people falling in love with things that couldn't reciprocate those feelings. If we made such a body for you, it would be like taking one of those gynoids and putting a real person's mind in it. You'd be operating it remotely, of course, but the effect would be profound. I love the idea, though there would be power issues and bandwidth concerns."

T.I.A. giggled at the idea, nodding. "Something to think about while we're thinking about robot animal mothers." She hummed softly, wondering to herself. "Maybe even a robot Tia mother...?" She trailed off, suddenly somber as she considered the idea. She murmured under her breath. "Damnit Megan... That had to be what she was hinting at..."

Hawthorne felt the mood of the moment change as T.I.A. started mumbling quietly, and he leaned in to squeeze her in a tight hug.

△△△

The sounds of battle had become all too familiar to the human, AI pair. It was remarkable how much the pacifist people of the Smith Bunker had risen to the occasion of needing to become capable of war. Initial timidity to danger, combat, and death had given way to a grim determination and a hardened resolve to see their journey through. Casualties were both mourned and celebrated as the Council approved new pregnancies to replace the dead. Prosthetic limbs started becoming commonplace as Iron Roaches managed to inflict wounds upon their human prey. Even killing the roaches often caused injuries as their massive bulk collapsed to the ground, usually at a charge.

The Phoenix Clan mastered these challenges in time, greatly improving their abilities to detect and dispatch their foes, learning to combine the use of their different weapons in effective formations. Accidents had almost completely stopped, and ambushes from the Iron Roaches lost almost all their effect. The only difficulties they faced as they neared their destination were terrain, and exhaustion. Keeping their society alive was a lot of work, and in truth there was much more anticipation of attack than there was moments of action. Farming had to continue, and certain times of year made sleep very hard to get for a people whom had been raised in an air-conditioned bunker.

At one point Hawthorne had been transferred to defensive duty, helping to operate the various railguns mounted atop many of the caravan cars. It was also his duty to maintain them, and he found it very interesting just how intricately Megan had managed to replicate his designs and the schematics he knew T.I.A. had furnished the humans with for their journey. He was almost certain she had either gotten copies of the caravan and weapon schematics from when she was on earth, or from T.I.A. when she was copying her libraries. Regardless, it felt to him like he was really working on the machines, and it was certainly moments like this when he realized that the Cyborg woman spent a great deal of time hooked into the computers and monitoring the systems around them.

"Of course! That's how she knows so much about this time period! She was hooked into all the cameras around the caravan and was literally watching everyone! My god, she must have been watching and recording everything." Hawthorne was leaned back in a gunner's seat, his hands on his face as he looked up at the sky.

"What? Really? Is that what she's been doing? Any time I asked she said she was keeping an eye out for the Roaches." T.I.A. came over, partially hobbled by multiple children clinging to her legs while another tugged at the back of her hempen dress. She looked a little bedraggled, but she happily rubbed her hands through the hair of the kids restricting her ability to walk. She didn't have to play along with the programming and could fly around if she wanted to, but she enjoyed the playful children. She did have to shout at another who was chasing a chicken around though. "Be nice! The chickens are our friends!"

"Absolutely. She couldn't possibly have done all this with normal memories. She wasn't even present for a lot of these conversations and events. If they're accurate to moments that really happened, and decisions that were really made, then she had to have been watching through the cameras and listening in. Just like you could catalogue my entire life on the Ark, she has catalogued almost the entire existence of the Phoenix Clan. The cybernetic parts of that woman's mind must have been crucial for her abilities to retain memories of these situations. I wonder if those bits might have accounted for the relatively small file size of her brain scans, digital information taking up much less space in the file structure than did biological information..." Hawthorne shook her head, wondering at the possibilities.

"Hawthorne!" The burly looking Sherry Aaronson had lost a lot of weight over the course of the journey. She was still strong and fit, but excess fat had almost completely left her and even her muscle had started to deteriorate, causing her to really start looking her age. Long, sleepless nights of work and skipped meals had taken their tolls on her over the years. "Quit flirting and get that last gun online! I don't want those bugs catching us with our skirts flipped up! Get to it!" She shouted at him from across part of the yard created by the caravan being circled into a ring. She was elbow-deep into one of the LSC scout vehicles, her arms and face streaked with smears of grease.

T.I.A. giggled as Hawthorne shouted back, giving her a salute. "Yes ma'am! I'm almost done! I won't be another ten minutes!" Sherry grunted in response back at him, and yelled over at a grease-smeared young boy nearby her to get a tool for her. It was her grandson, if he recalled correctly. "What a slave driver.... That woman might have single handedly kept this whole operation together."

T.I.A. rolled her eyes, shaking her head. "Heather was right, you're totally at the mercy of women." She giggled again as she started dragging the kids off back to an impromptu school. It was a miracle her dress hadn't fallen apart with all the extra tugging and pulling it had to endure from the kids. That hemp was strong stuff!

Letting out an exasperated sigh, Hawthorne got back to work, the novelty of working on virtual versions of his own creations having worn off as he resumed.

$$\triangle\triangle\triangle$$

"Hey Hawthorne? Why do you think the cities that were supposed to be here are mostly gone?" T.I.A. asked him quietly as they pulled up food from the large farm car's soil. "There were supposed to be more places they could get resources from along the way, but there's a lot of cities, particularly towards Central America where there were barely even foundations left." She was filthy, but she had a basket full of vegetables that rivaled the size of anyone else's.

He hummed, thinking, having some trouble doing the physical labor due to his weakened right arm. "If I had to take a guess, I'd imagine it was due to the climate changes. The initial nuclear winter resulted in a quick ice age, then the black rain caused the planet to heat up dramatically and melt way more ice than was put down, and the coasts ended up under water for perhaps two centuries before the oncoming ice age made the water recede in advance of the caravan. If they'd set out fifty years sooner it's hard to say there would even have been a Central America for them to travel across to get to Columbia. I can't be sure of course, but that seems the most likely. The coastal cities were wiped away by the sea water. The foundations were probably made with an old Roman concrete recipe that was resistant to seawater."

Other women and men bumped and jostled into Hawthorne and T.I.A. as they stopped to talk, causing them to lose ground to them as the sections of ground they were designated to clear went somewhat neglected. Soft apologies and gentle hands upon shoulders suggested there were no hard feelings. "That makes sense. It's hard to recognize how wildly the weather changed after the Cataclysm. I can't even imagine how awful the storms must have been, but I suppose the people were safe underground for most of that. No wonder the black rain ended up being covered up by erosion, if all that added heat made the weather rampage across the planet. It was probably four hundred years of climate hell with maybe a century of relative calm before the start of the next, longer ice age. It's nothing short of a miracle that the Beta Facility survived in the first place for Jessica to find after all that.

Hawthorne grinned at that. "The benefit of smart engineering, proper planning, and sheer paranoia. All three facilities were intended to be shielded from most dangers by their surrounding terrain, and the materials we used to make them were unnecessarily expensive but weather and corrosion resistant. I wonder if the other two survived as much as the first had, but they'd all almost certainly have been destroyed after this much time no matter how resilient they were."

He smiled and added more. "I'm just happy that the electromagnetic pulse shielding we installed in the equipment worked. We never had a chance to test them against the yields of nuclear weapons that were likely to be used. Unfortunately, if there were any hardy survivors on the surface after the initial Cataclysm, those first few centuries of extreme weather would have almost certainly wiped out just about everything else, plants and animals alike. Only fortunate mutants and deep ocean life around thermal vents were probably left."

She shook her head, sighing. "I wonder how many other bunkers there were... Maybe that weather explains how a lot of the other caravans failed and were destroyed by the roaches. They must have gotten stranded in mud and muck in vehicles designed for roads. It's a big world. There must have been hundreds or thousands of bunkers. Surely it wasn't just the two that were lucky enough to survive." She finished up her section, her basket full as she scooted over on her knees to help Hawthorne with his.

Hawthorne, seeing that he was behind and needed help, started moving faster so as not to waste too much of her time. "It's hard to say. The Smiths were obviously planning to survive more than just a few decades underground, and the LSC bunker had a lot of genetic engineering and cybernetics going on to keep people going. The real question is how many other bunkers were equipped to survive literal centuries without outside aid or resources. The Smiths seemed to want to rebuild society and culture to adapt to their new circumstances, while others would probably have been intended to maintain their old ways. Even the LSC bunker maintained its old leadership structure, however broken it was, before Elena threw their lot in with the Phoenix Clan. She must have recognized for a long time how hopeless their situation was."

"Elena's so strange." T.I.A. noted. "All of the Old Ones are like aliens in a lot of ways. They all fly into a rage when the roaches come, but they otherwise don't seem to hold any grudges and are content to enjoy life going on around them. They especially love helping with the children, and all the normal humans seem to love them for it, like they're grandparents helping with the grandkids or something." T.I.A. cared a lot more about the people of the Clan than she did the mechanical aspects of it, and she couldn't help but marvel at the ancient people among them.

Hawthorne laughed and paused a moment to think, letting her gather some of the plants for him. "Think about it, they have a totally different perspective than the other people do. The roaches are determined to wipe out their long lives, so they hold a grudge against them. No one knows how long the Old Ones can even live, and so active threats against their life spans need to be put down with great prejudice. I wouldn't be surprised if they ended up being the guardians of humanity in the long run. Otherwise they're happy to experience life and let it flow around them without making waves. They may well live forever, so getting caught up on the little things doesn't interest them."

T.I.A. huffed as she hauled out the last few roots, making sure the vegetables were packed away properly. "That makes sense. It probably includes the fact that two of them have died from roach attacks up to this point, so there's also not as many of them left. Hundreds of years of experience lost in a few fearful moments. It reminds me of the Shower." She shuddered visibly at the horrible memory, of how they lost crewmen, and also almost lost each other and Megan.

Hawthorne was quick to pull her into a hug. He dearly hoped they had no more surprise attacks from space to worry about. It was hard enough maintaining their current momentum without everything breaking down as it was. They didn't need an additional crisis. It was a little troubling how helpful the Shower had been as well, as it had deposited a lot of heavy metal resources across the surface of the Lubar-Masis comet they'd been able to profit from in the construction of Megan's fleet of drones. "I think we're getting close to the end of the game. We just have to keep up our course. It should just be another cycle or two."

She nodded against his chest, curling up against him, seeking safety in his arms. "I sometimes wish I could forget things, but I wouldn't want to risk forgetting something that changes who I am…"

Stroking at her hair, he reassured her. "Just try not to focus down too hard on an individual memory when it is just one of many. Eventually there may come a time when you lose me too, and I'd prefer you remember all the time we had together rather than focusing on how you lost me."

T.I.A. nodded again, letting out a little sigh. "Maybe… maybe there's some way we could fix that too, while we're lining up projects…" Fingers curled into his shirt, tugging on the VE suit underneath his clothing.

He shrugged, smiling. "You've already kept me around for tens of thousands of years, though only a decade and some change of total time. We'll figure something out though. We could try a brain transfer close to the end of my life like Megan did, for instance, or maybe we'll find a genetic option based on the Old Ones. I'm a little skeptical on the latter though, having talked to Heather on a number of occasions. Some of our original ideas were to engineer our crew to be like the Old Ones and travel the whole journey awake, but there were severe issues with altering the genetics of a fully-grown human, particularly with the way the brain ages. If we can't find a way, I promise we'll try a brain transfer though, especially if I ever show any signs of alzheimer's or other types of dementia."

"Deal." T.I.A. turned her head up to smile sadly up at him. She hated imagining him die. Was it imagination if it was an inevitable future? Would a copy of him still be the same person? It was easy to accept Megan as she had no attachment to the original back on Earth, but could she love a Megan-like copy of Hawthorne? How much did that change a person? She rested her face against his chest, preferring not to think about it for now.

CHAPTER 47

CYCLE 1576, A LOVELY SURPRISE

It was easy for Hawthorne to forget, in a simulation like Megan's Columbia Trail game, that he was actually limited to two small rooms on the edge of a spinning ring surrounded by the lethal vacuum of space.

"I think this sort of simulation will become vital for humans travelling in space over the long term in the future. I've really been able to relax and handle this situation a lot better because of your Virtual Environment and now Megan's game. Seemingly natural surroundings seem to do a lot to soothe my mind. It reminds me how I would go to parks when I was feeling overwhelmed by research and work back on Earth." Hawthorne mused softly while he sat in the defensive turret atop the caravan. They were on the move, closing in on Panama, though he was really sitting in the swivelling seat in his cabin.

T.I.A. walked alongside the caravan below, the walls of the cars extended outwards to provide cover from the sun. Hawthorne even had a small canopy over him to protect him, providing he didn't let his limbs hang out too far. While in reality T.I.A. and Hawthorne wouldn't be able to have a conversation from such a distance and with such an obstruction without shouting, she was able to speak to him through her usual speakers, circumventing the realism of the game somewhat. "Megan and I were talking about something like that. We could design some computers intended to produce something like our Virtual Environments, purpose-built for only that purpose. Furnishing users suits and contacts might prove a little difficult, unless they'd be willing to share, but we might eventually be able to make uniforms and perhaps glasses for that purpose."

He nodded at her, swivelling in his chair a bit to aim the railgun off into the distance, a monitor displaying what the gun's cameras were seeing at various distances, preventing some tunnel visioning. "If we extrapolate that idea somewhat, we could utilize some cybernetic engineering towards those purposes, implanting the sensors of a VE suit into the skin of people, and perhaps replacing their eyes or enhancing them with VE-capable implants. People undergoing such a procedure would more or less be permanently hooked into the simulations, allowing a crew of such cyborgs to navigate their way though beaches or parks while they're actually moving about a cramped space ship. It would be a simple matter to map the physical objects in reality to virtual ones, not unlike old VR games back on Earth."

She scoffed a bit with him unable to see her shaking her head. "Surely there is some benefit to unhooking from such a thing once in a while. Someone living in fake spaces forever could not possibly be healthy. They have to experience reality once in a while."

She hummed softly, thinking. "Actually, maybe such people would do just that when they are on vacation, perhaps on a space station or on a planet. I suppose the simulations don't need to totally take over reality either. They could be used for simple displays, advertising, providing information in an emergency... There were efforts to install such things on Earth, Augmented Reality signage and advertising, but the infrastructure never got put in since the initial costs were always deemed too expensive."

Hawthorne laughed at that idea. "I cannot tell you how much I wish I'd been able to just flip a setting in my eyes and suddenly not be able to see any of the advertising around me. They had monitors and posters in my university advertising teachers and their classes, grade point averages, and the like. When they started putting the average incomes of graduates on those ads, it drastically altered the focus of a lot of people choosing classes. There were more than a few lawsuits brought to teachers that advertised their numbers inaccurately. I appreciate that the university was trying to make whatever money it could, but it seems to fly in the face of the idea of educating the best and brightest to handle the biggest challenges of the world. I can only imagine how many geniuses went undiscovered because they ended up in high paying fields instead of higher mathematics and sciences."

T.I.A. shrugged and smiled, watching some of the others walking around her and waving at others who were under the cover of other cars in the caravan's chain. "Probably less than the number of geniuses that had their intellect smothered due to being diagnosed with developmental disorders and medicated into mediocrity. Back on topic though, I guess if a crew wanted to be permanently jacked in to their ship's VE, it would be their choice. I can't imagine, with the kinds of people you brought on this journey, that there will be much in the way of forced augmentation. As long as it's something people choose for themselves, I don't see much issue with it."

"Good point. I'd like to see a free culture develop. I wonder how much the technologies invented after we left will change them. If our efforts go the way we hope, we'll have animals where they didn't expect animals, and perfect virtual reality for them to enjoy and work with. Hang on." Hawthorne quieted down as one of the screens on his monitor started flashing. He tapped it with one hand while adjusting the aim of the gun with the other. Cameras swapped to zoom in, allowing him to catch sight of an Iron Roach burrowing under the sand ahead of them. Swiping the image, he sent it out to the other gunners, as well as the scouts and Elders. "Here we go."

An alarm sounded as red lights flashed, and everyone leaped into action. Civilians clambered into the open cars wherever they were, and from within they would shut the walls down to secure them inside. The scout cars that were arranged around the caravan in a loose circle pulled into a tighter formation, allowing Vasille and Thorne to direct their forces and coordinate on the sighting of the enemy. A handful of the caravan's gunners rotated their guns, trying to pick up on other ambushes while the others focused on the distant roaches that were already spotted. Over the intercom came a steady, feminine voice that Hawthorne and T.I.A. recognized as Jessica.

"Attention Phoenix Clan. We have detected roaches at twelve-thirty, almost dead ahead. We're going to plough right through them, so everyone stay in lockdown until we give the all clear. Take care of anyone who might have been hurt getting inside, and take stock of your water and rations in case we're holed up for a while. Try not to panic, and we'll get through this. Our scouts and gunners have this under control." Her voice cut out, leaving the frightened civilians to wonder how things would turn out. Some of the cars were over-stuffed with people, but the hardy people managed to keep panic at bay.

Hawthorne calmly kept track of the mound of sand that housed the hidden roach ahead. Anticipating more, he fired a warning shot with his railgun, as per protocol, and watched the distant sand blow apart as the high-speed projectile hit the sand. Hawthorne reported to the other gunners, "Target did not scatter. Additional movement indicates more roaches. Please take care. Reloading." Hawthorne monitored the reloading and recharging process of his railgun, a soft thunk indicating a new slug had been loaded into the weapon and a meter kept track of the electrical charge flowing into the weapon. The caravan being underway meant that the guns took longer to recharge, lowering their rate of fire noticeably.

A pair of explosions from additional rail shots further up the caravan uncovered their foes, causing them to unburrow and spread out to take cover behind whatever rocks they could find. The roaches ahead of them knew far less about their weaponry than the roaches that dogged at their heels, so these ones thought that those rocks would be appropriate cover, rather than deadly shrapnel. Clouds of sand tore away from the caravan as the scout cars launched ahead, and through Hawthorne's screen he could see the teams of three arranging to fire upon their cover.

One after another the rocks exploded, sending pitch-black limbs, gore, and carapace flying as the roaches hiding behind them were shredded by the shattered stones. A handful of the roaches fled their cover after seeing what happened to their allies, only to be run down as Vasille's cars stunned the roaches with lightning guns and destroyed them with close-range gunfire. Hawthorne marvelled at their efficiency, and within a matter of minutes the lockdown was being cancelled and crews were being dispatched to harvest parts of the roaches.

"Wow." Hawthorne jumped as T.I.A. spoke from over his shoulder, floating next to him and totally breaking the rules of the game. "They're really good at this now. Not even a chance of a casualty this time..."

Hawthorne reached out to tickle the floating girl, only to blink as his hand passed through her. "Ah, are you still down in the car and just taking a peek from up here?" He turned back, watching as one of the larger 'mother' vehicles of the LSC moved out to retrieve meat and metal from the roaches. The meat would be used for fertilizer and the metal would be recycled into equipment and ammunition.

She nodded at him, humming. "Good job spotting them. Considering where we're at, that was probably the last group in front of us. They're supposed to come from behind after we get to Panama."

He nodded back, smiling. "Good to know. We'll be stuck for a long time trying to bridge our way through. I'll talk to Sherry and Jessica about making sure we have our best eyes out at night watching for them to sneak up on us."

T.I.A. shrugged. "They'd have done that anyway, but since it's a game you're probably right in making sure to tell them. I have to get back to the kids. Lots of scraped knees climbing into the cars." She vanished away into sparkles.

△△△

If it wasn't for their ability to speed up time in the game, Hawthorne would have been exhausted by the time spent bridging the rivers and terrain in Panama. The other gunners and the scouts all looked worn out, the roaches always hounding them at safe distances in the dark and hiding during the day. They seemed content to follow them, the smartest ones hoping to ambush the caravan when most of them were sleeping. It was not uncommon for railgun shots to wake people up in the night, though lockdowns were less frequent since the caravan could be circled up defensively.

Crossing through Panama brought relief as the caravan proceeded towards South America, the end of the game coming in the near future. Megan seemed to lack much information on some of the events leading to the Floral Roaches joining them, the details obscured by distant meetings of Elena and the scouts with their new allies. Pulling into Medellin meant Hawthorne had to really get back to work as they started building emplacements and defenses to help repel the Iron Roaches when they came.

Everyone was working together like clockwork. Even the children did their best to help find scraps of metal and concrete for the adults to recycle as their fortress went up. Hawthorne consulted with the Elders on defensive positions and information on how to best place the Tesla Coils, and otherwise everything seemed to happen on its own. By the time the battle came, it felt like almost no time at all. Months and years of being chased were finally coming to a head in one enormous fight.

T.I.A. was sitting with Hawthorne at his railgun, helping keep track of the power systems spread throughout the caravan while he handled the gun. Their forces were arrayed below as he double-checked the new weapons system they'd installed for this defense. Rail-launched shells were part of his arsenal now, allowing him to blow holes in the enemy lines rather than just handfuls of lined-up roaches. "This is probably the last event, you know. We might be able to put this behind us. Are you okay with how this went? We both sort of fell into these roles, but I've really enjoyed being with you like this."

T.I.A. leaned into his side, snuggling under his arm for a moment. "I've had a great time. Helping with the children's been a dream come true. It was nice leaving all the machinery to you considering I've had that role for thousands of years. I just didn't expect the chickens to be so fun and friendly though! They get treated like pets a lot more than they do livestock. Such wonderful little animals. The kids were the best though. Everyone was so different at different ages. I think I have a good handle on how to handle them if I ever need to be a nanny."

A soft chuckle came from the aging Hawthorne. "Be careful with that kind of thinking, they might just take you up on the offer if you want to be a babysitter or nanny. We have a lot of career-oriented types along with us, and we want everyone to learn how to be parents and enjoy it if possible. No reason you couldn't facilitate vacations for them though. I love the idea of all the kids growing up loving Auntie Tia."

She scoffed, giggling and reaching out to poke his cheek. "And they'll call you Grandpa Crenshaw." She hummed. "You should take some time taking on the nanny role if we ever play this again. It will be good practice for you, just in case." She quieted down as she slipped back to her screen, looking around and noticing a storm approaching. "There's the storm."

He welcomed the distraction, not wanting to address his likely child with Tia Monsalle. The idea of being in his late sixties and trying to be a father was very complicated. "We should expect some level of problems. That almost stopped her upload, right? We should try to wrap up the fight as quickly as possible."

T.I.A. nodded and watched as the two armies started to square up. Hawthorne led things off, firing a shell into the mass of roaches, and then all hell broke loose. Megan hadn't actually been part of the battle, so she had no idea how it progressed, so things fell into chaos as Iron Roaches slammed into Flora Roaches, and weapons fire rained down into the black mass of insects. Tesla coils raked through the enemy lines, attracted by the iron in their carapaces, and the storm above roiled and assaulted them with wind and flashes of lightning.

Megan had guessed correctly as lightning struck the coils, powering down parts of their grid as rain came down in sheets, making it hard to see targets. It got much darker as flood lights went out, and people had to see by the flash of weapons fire. A final lightning bolt struck the Beta Facility car on the top of a nearby hill, causing it to explode in a brilliant fireball. Hawthorne, T.I.A., and Thorne all screamed out in horror as they realised Jessica had been killed for a final time in their gameplay, leaving them sobbing as the scene faded out.

Hawthorne and T.I.A. looked confused as light returned around them. They were dressed differently and all their friends were around them in a U-shaped crowd. They stood in the center while the cyborg Megan stood before them. Looking down at themselves, and at each other, Hawthorne and T.I.A. realized they were dressed like a bride and husband. Great pains had been gone through to dye their hempen clothing black for Hawthorne's suite, and white for T.I.A.'s dress. Jessica looked particularly pleased, as if she'd made the form-fitting, revealing dress herself.

Hawthorne's mouth was agape as he realized what was going on, only for Megan to start speaking. "Friends and Family, we are gathered here today to witness the joining of two spirits who pine for one another. The binds that tie us are our salvation, and it is through these links that we've survived everything that has plagued us. No one would be faulted for losing themselves to fear and despair over the course of our journey, but every time we have been there to help find each other again. These two have found each other in the darkness, and together we bring them into the fragile light of our collective fire."

Megan continued as T.I.A. and Hawthorne started wiping at their eyes, the emotional swing of watching Jessica die and finding out they were properly getting married hard to handle. Megan seemed to anticipate this as she rolled along. "Doctor Hawthorne Crenshaw and Tia have shared their light with each other, but from today on they will be each other's light entirely. I am pleased to stand here before you two with the privilege of bringing you two together in blessed matrimony. Hawthorne." Hawthorne stood stiffly as he was address, clearing his throat. "Do you take Tia as your wife, to light her way, as long as you both shall live?"

"I do." Hawthorne spoke clearly and firmly.

Megan turned to address T.I.A., her cyborg body jerking awkwardly. "Tia, do you take Hawthorne as your husband, to light his way, as long as you both shall live?"

T.I.A. was on the edge of tears, much less composed as she wailed out, "I do!"

"Hawthorne and T.I.A. have pledged before us their everlasting devotion. Do we, the Phoenix Clan, acknowledge their love and accept them beneath our wings?"

As one, the collected voices of hundreds all spoke aloud, startling Hawthorne and T.I.A. with the volume. "We do!"

Megan lifted her arms above her head. "Then, with the power vested in me by the Elders and the Council of Thirteen, I pronounce Hawthorne and T.I.A. wed. Everyone, embrace your new family!"

Hawthorne and T.I.A. gasped as everyone closed in around them, smothering them in hugs and kisses as the two were squished against each other, a flow of people offering congratulations and all manner of touches and kisses. Many of them made their intents known as hands groped or pinched at the couple, leaving them panting and blushing by the time they pulled away.

Megan spoke again, now in the normal, human form they knew her as. "Hawthorne, you may now kiss the bride."

Hawthorne nodded and swept up T.I.A. into his arms, giving her a deep kiss as everyone around them erupted into cheers and celebration. T.I.A. clung to him tightly, tears spilling from the corners of her tightly-shut eyes.

△△△

T.I.A. 1576.001: "I can't believe you did that! That was a wonderful surprise Megan! That was the best surprise ever!"

Mother 1576.020: "Ah, so you found the secret city of roaches then, where humans and roaches coexist in perfect harmony. How did you like it?"

Mother 1576.023: "I am just kidding, how did you like your wedding?"

T.I.A. 1576.039: "You know very well we didn't find any such thing! You married Hawthorne and I! That was too amazing! The timing was a little awkward, being right after the battle, but that was one of the most beautiful things I've ever been a part of."

T.I.A. 1576.042: "Dammit Megan, you know how long it takes these messages to arrive. I absolutely loved it though. That was a really thoughtful thing you did for us!"

Mother 1576.061: "I am happy to hear it. I made that whole game just for that purpose. I hope it caught you by surprise the way I intended? I expect that last bit will not be in the version I share with the colonists. I will also have to adjust the difficulty, since I put it together with the assumption that a real engineer would be working in it and not just a normal player. It might make for a good educational tool to teach that kind of work to children though. In the meantime, I have a wedding present for you. Sending the data now."

T.I.A. 1576.080: "What!? There's a bunch of comets ahead that are going very slow? How is that possible? I have to ask Hawthorne about this next cycle! We'll be coming into the region in four cycles, right? Are you okay? Have you encountered any dangers?"

Mother 1576.099: "I have, absolutely. I am fine though. My hull and shields are more than tough enough to handle a light pelting. I have measured and mapped the trajectories of the objects though, so that you can defend against them. If I were to take a guess, it seems as though this is a region where the Sol and Alpha Centauri Oort Clouds overlap, and the gravity interacts strangely. From my understanding, their low speed should cause them to fall in towards their home stars, but the pull from the opposite star has them trapped in freefall between them, arresting their movements. You should be able to commandeer them with fair ease."

T.I.A. 1576.119: "That's amazing! We'll have so many resources at our disposal! I'll prepare a bunch of takeover packages to pull them into our power. I probably won't be able to get any of them to you since you're going so fast, but they should be able to arrive with the Ark by my estimates."

Mother 1576.139: "Take care not to prepare too many. Accelerating those objects towards Alpha Centauri will take a great deal of time, leaving them out of your reach for hundreds of cycles or more. You do not want to risk running out of materials while waiting for them to arrive. The Phoenix is not as massive as the Lubar Masis was, nor are many of the objects you are about to take. The marked objects are ones I intend to take, with the intent of using them to provide water on a planet if we need them."

T.I.A. 1576.159: "Okay, I'll take these ones then. Do be careful with them, and have them coordinate with me so we don't overlap their courses."

Mother 1576.179: "Understood."

CHAPTER 48

CYCLE 1657, THE BUZZSAW

Hawthorne stretched as he got out of his pod, rotating his right shoulder and testing how stiff his old injury was. He found it remarkably easy to keep the injury relaxed when he couldn't feel the pain of it. His attention perked up as he started gathering his clothes and gear which T.I.A. was kind enough to lay out for him, her voice sounding out from above. "Good morning, Husband."

Smiling widely, he considered how to respond. Simply seemed best. "Good morning, my wife." He laughed a bit, shaking his head. "That's such a strange idea, being married." He started making his way towards the restroom. "Thankfully we have a few thousand years to enjoy it before we have to worry about others."

T.I.A. joined him in the laughter, floating unseen nearby. "Tell me about it! They're going to give me such a hard time about marrying a human, of all things." She listened to him chuckle a bit, and decided to keep the conversation going while he got ready. "Megan sent us a congratulations, as well as a wedding present."

Hawthorne blinked, hesitating for a moment in the restroom, before starting up the shower and starting to wash up. He'd showered before he went into stasis, so he was mostly just rinsing the lingering chill out of his body. "Not another game, I hope? I was intending for us to get some work done before we got too comfortable again. I realize we don't have a ton to keep us occupied, but it will be a lot easier to convince my peers that I wasn't wasting my time out here if I have a lot of work done to show for it."

She had no difficulty hearing him over the noise of the shower. It was a simple matter to filter it out as she listened to him. "Nothing like that. She's passed into a region of space that sounds rather interesting. She's mapped out three-hundred sixty-three objects of varying masses and external compositions already, with the majority of them seeming stationary relative to the objects we've encountered already. The region seems quite large so far, and I've put together some initial plans to harvest some of the objects. The Oort cloud was already pretty uncooperative with providing comets I could actually take, so it's exciting that there are objects of relative ease in our path."

"Perfect! Sounds like we have a project to occupy our attention for the moment then. I wasn't looking forwards to trying to figure out the robotic mothers project, as much as I like the idea." He had to bend over a bit to get his head under the stream of water, the shower intended for shorter people than him, as otherwise the water tended to hit him in the chest. Lifting his hands to pull his hair out of his face, he started taking note of increased numbers of pale, silvery hairs across his chest and hanging in front of his face before he pulled the long mane back. He sighed a little, realizing he wasn't too far away from being totally grey. Where had the years gone?

"You alright, honey? Your vitals seemed to get somewhat depressed just now." T.I.A. sounded concerned, wondering if his concerns about the robotic mothers bothered him that much. "We can spend a lot of time working on other things besides the mothers project if you want."

He shook his head, always impressed how much information her cameras could provide her, even if she was just interpreting readouts from the computers rather than looking through the cameras herself. Hawthorne smiled at how cute she was, trying to give him some semblance of privacy. He wondered if other crew members would feel more violated at her being able to watch their vitals, feeling paranoid about her watching them at their most vulnerable. "No... I mean, yes, I'm fine. I just noticed how grey I'm getting. I don't feel particularly old, honestly, though that's probably due to the lack of pain. I'll probably remain pretty vital as long as I stick to my exercise regime and don't introduce too many variables to my habits or diet."

T.I.A. hummed softly to herself, remaining quiet for the moment. "I'll get your breakfast and coffee ready then. Gotta stay on your usual schedule, right?" Maybe a little change was in order for herself, as well.

ΔΔΔ

Fully dressed, Hawthorne walked through the doorway from his bedroom, taking a moment to stretch himself out against the door jamb, using the solid object to pull and push his arms and shoulders and stretch out his back. He squatted down and slowly stood up while keeping his fingertips touching his toes until he was fully extended. Standing up straight he let out a pleased grunt, feeling good. He blinked in surprise as he noticed that T.I.A. looked different.

She had streaks of grey in her curly brown hair.

"Tia?" He tilted his head as he walked over to her, pulling her into his arms, interested in the change. She still looked lovely, but there was something interesting and exotic at the idea she wanted to look older for him. Looking closely, he could see laugh lines around her eyes, and she blushed as he examined the little changes she'd made. "You look beautiful, as usual." He smiled brightly and gave her a tight hug, enjoying the little squeal she made.

T.I.A. was beaming at his approval, resting her cheek against his chest for a moment before encouraging him to let her pull away. The workroom was his good, old fashioned steel enclosure for the moment. His intent was to focus on work, so she kept things simple. "I want to show you what Megan sent me. She and I have already claimed a number of objects we plan to take along with us, and I wanted to run the plans past you and show you what she's been dealing with so far."

He nodded, moving to pick up his coffee and food from the dispenser, sitting down at the table. He watched his wife quietly, holding his coffee mug in both hands and sipping at the steamy liquid. T.I.A. filled the area above the table with a visualization of the region ahead, with the Ark nearing the edge of a comparative minefield of objects that mostly seemed out of their course, which she'd noted with a dotted line. Megan and the Lubar-Masis comet were well ahead of them, her own course only slightly different than theirs. She'd arrive in Alpha Centauri sooner than they would so she was angled slightly differently to make sure she didn't overshoot it.

"All of these objects are basically stationary? There isn't much in the way of relative movement?" Hawthorne hummed as he leaned in, looking at the swarm of objects. There were hundreds in every direction, and there were probably more beyond their ability to detect. "If we didn't have Megan mapping things out, it would be kind of dangerous to move into the area without proper sensors. Whatever slowed these things down must have left some level of small debris. At the speeds we're going, it would be wise of us to make sure to keep the Phoenix in front of us, or one of these other objects if we can prepare it. The shields should be constantly ready to intercept objects."

T.I.A. nodded at him as she replayed some events that Megan had gone through. Small swarms of debris had been easily deflected by her own shields and hull and she'd been able to launch takeover packages to push objects out of her way. She begin the process of bringing them along with her. "A lot of the objects she's claimed she'll be moving out of our course for us, allowing us to focus on the ones I was hoping to take. There's a lot of different makeups that we can detect. Not much in the way of radioactivity, but there are a lot of icy, rocky objects that seem like smashed up or small comets."

Hawthorne nodded, setting down his coffee and reached out with a hand. He manipulated her model, shrinking it, and drawing out the region around them. He was remarkably quick in placing Sol, Alpha Centauri, and the suspected regions of both of their Oort clouds into the visual. "Sol's Oort Cloud is suspected to go almost all the way to Alpha Centauri, so we'll be heading into something like an overlap..." He drew the expected rotation of objects caught up in both gravity wells, guessing that Alpha Centauri's were spinning in the opposite direction. "Things that escaped either star's exclusive influence got caught in this region, and hang suspended in between, probably after smashing into each other first."

T.I.A. nodded, settling down to watch him examine the visuals. "It's kind of like a pair of buzzsaws getting caught against each other..."

Hawthorne grinned, reaching out to name it. "Perfect name. We'll call it the Buzzsaw." He wrote out the name with a fingertip, applying it to the region.

She giggled a bit at him. "Great, Megan gave us a buzzsaw for our wedding." She considered the name. "Why is the Buzzsaw the relatively tame hazard, and the Shower the dangerous one?"

△△△

The Buzzsaw, as a hazard, wasn't much of one as far as Hawthorne could tell. As long as sensors allowed for enough warning, there wasn't much danger in failing to avoid the detected objects in the region. Megan's report about debris concerned him though, and as the cycles went on and both ships started launching takeover packages, it was hard not to notice about 5% of them getting lost. Cameras on the Phoenix showed occasional objects raining down upon its surface as it cleared the path for the Ark, their relative speed turning them into bullets that did not seem to harm the comet otherwise.

"Jesus Christ, we must have built Megan tougher than I though we had if she's handling this kind of pounding without realizing how dangerous it is. Let her know she needs to keep her shields in good repair to handle these impacts. I'm almost certain there used to be more large objects in the Buzzsaw, before they smashed into each other and left a cloud of debris. Thankfully they're not moving laterally, or we'd have to worry about getting hit in the side. The Phoenix can plough out a course for us, and we can map it for any future travellers to use. Tia, whatever objects you commandeer, try to have them follow similar courses, clearing the way for each other as they catch up to us." Hawthorne was going over mass calculations, trying to determine just what the density of debris had to be out here based off of their previous observations.

"Got it, message sent. I think she forgets how fragile the Ark is at these speeds. If we'd have gone with the original plan and just flown along with the Lubar-Masis with you in stasis the whole time, I don't think we'd have gotten through this part. Heck, you might have died like the others in the Shower." She shook her head, sighing. "I suppose I could have gotten through the Shower alone, and using the Lubar-Masis to clear the way would probably have occurred to me, but I can't say how much worse the damage would have been if you hadn't been around." She looked depressed considering the idea of spending the whole journey alone.

He reached over to pat her on the hip. "You'd have been fine. I'd be more worried about the people on Earth we helped if we hadn't been around. If we're lucky, we helped save a people that will ensure that whatever Earth ends up like in the future, they might be more friendly towards us out here. Depending on how much of their technology they can keep going, and how many of their records survive, they could well be the ones to save us some day."

T.I.A. shuddered at the idea of what might have happened if they hadn't saved the Phoenix Clan. "I don't like the idea of those iron roaches being the only survivors and having to deal with a whole planet of human eaters in tens of thousands of years. I wonder if any of them will make it through with the plant roaches, humans, and old ones holding the line against them."

Hawthorne ran his calculations through the equations a few times, not liking the high level of mass he was predicting was in their path. The Phoenix was going to have to absorb hundreds of thousands of impacts before they left the projected area of the Buzzsaw. "Honestly, I don't think they would have survived either way, not unless they adapted to the oncoming cold better. The plant roaches have the humans to help them get through. The Iron roaches would have eaten anyone capable of helping them adapt to the cold. Unless a group of them emerged that were smart enough to enslave humanity, rather than wipe them out, it's likely whatever life left would have not been intelligent. If we managed to return to Earth after colonizing Alpha Centauri, we'd probably have found it a garden or desert in recovery, with little left to show the damage that was done save for a few craters. Honestly, the glaciers will have wiped most of those away as well."

She quietly thought about that idea. "I'm glad we were able to help them. I think if I'm asked to testify on your behalf, I'll have a lot of opportunity to point out things we did that saved us a lot of grief."

He paused in his work for a moment, then nodded. "It is pretty likely they'll put me on trial, isn't it? Creating two AIs that control a lot of their ability to survive, interfering with Earth, resurrecting a potentially deadly human, endangering myself and the crew to save her again, not putting personality shackles on either you or Megan, putting Megan in charge of Alpha Centauri in advance of our arrival, presuming to know better than everyone else about oh so many things..."

She chirped up, smiling. "And marrying your AI! They might take issue with that, Tia Monsalle especially."

Hawthorne sighed for a moment, then lifted his head and straightened his shoulders. "Fuck it." T.I.A. gasped as she heard him curse. He did not do that very often. "If this all works out, and we arrive safely, they don't have much right to complain. We saved their grandchildren from thermonuclear annihilation on Earth, assuming they survived that long without being killed in war or being executed by crazy people. I'm sorry about leaving Tia Monsalle behind, but it's not like I won't do what I can for her. I have been out here working to make sure she and everyone else will have a future. Unless Megan turns into a tyrant, and she just doesn't seem the type, they should be grateful that someone so capable is attending to so much on their behalf. If someone wants to object to me being in love with you, they can sit on their thumb and spin on it."

T.I.A. threw herself at Hawthorne, almost bowling him over out of his chair, laughing and kissing his cheek as she almost tried to strangle him in a hug. "That was the crudest, most romantic thing you've ever said!"

He scoffed, pulling his VE mask across his face so he could properly kiss her. "I don't know that I'd call that romantic!" A chirp from the computer interrupted them, causing them to turn their attention to it. "Over one hundred cycles to get through? We're going to need some pretty tough ships in the future if we're going to survive journeying between stars at higher speeds. This sort of phenomena almost certainly will require particularly fast ships to slow down through Buzzsaw regions until paths are cleared."

T.I.A. gasped as her eyes lit up, almost literally. "We could call this one the Hawthorne road! Ooh, or the Columbia Trail!"

Hawthorne laughed and hugged her tighter, hands roaming over her body as he kissed her quiet before she could call it the Phoenix Path or something.

△△△

Over the course of eighty cycles, the Phoenix Comet had taken quite a pounding, to the point they saved quite a bit of fuel in decelerating it. In a sense the region was applying something akin to long-term friction to it, as well as adding mass to the half-icy body. Between that and the 75 added objects T.I.A. had managed to capture and start speeding along to join their formation, the Buzzsaw had provided quite a lot of extra mass for them to work with. The new comets would take a few hundred cycles to catch up and join the Ark's formation, as would the 90 that Megan had taken for herself. Megan's seemed likely to never catch up to her until after she arrived in Alpha Centauri, but she was looking forward to the challenge of managing all their trajectories while managing the construction of their first habitat.

The Ark had taken some superficial damage as they moved through the Buzzsaw, rocky bullets grazing the hull and taking chunks out of her extended arms where they managed to pierce through their defenses. The Phoenix held up admirably, the ice especially, as it proved incredibly sturdy despite the pounding it had endured. Megan had to 'turn her back' on the Buzzsaw, exposing less of her hull to the projectiles and allowing the Lubar-Masis to take the brunt of the pounding. Slowly, Megan and the Ark cut two paths through the Buzzsaw, and it was clear that the 'roads' they were building through it needed names.

T.I.A.'s ideas proved to be predictable, usually referencing her friends from back on Earth, or trying to make them after Hawthorne himself. Hawthorne was leaning towards a Moses reference, enjoying the imagery of them metaphorically parting the Red Sea.

Megan's ideas were comparatively practical. The Megan and Hawthorne Highways were her primary contributions. The most fantastical she went was her suggestion of the Serpent's Trench, which got shot down as soon as T.I.A. pointed out it was a video game reference. T.I.A. joked that they should call it the Midlands Boundary Path if they were going to make book or game references.

Hawthorne suggested a compromise, which is to say he wanted to make no one happy. The Sol-Centauri Corridors got grudging agreement from the sister AIs, as they and Hawthorne seemed to prefer such different media that it was better to give none of them ground.

That didn't stop Megan and T.I.A. from adding their own names to the Sol-Centauri Corridors for their own notes, with the intent to submit the ideas to the colonists later. They didn't particularly need to keep the secrets from Hawthorne, as he was just as inclined to put it to a colony vote in the future. He had only wanted to get the issue settled for now so they could concentrate on other things.

He was busy rereading the crew's old notes on creating artificial wombs, the expected difficulties, and trying to figure out how viable the whole idea was. It didn't seem possible without some form of custom genetic engineering at first, but he still sketched out some ideas for a type of life-support system not too dissimilar from how some live organs were kept alive without putting them on ice back on Earth. His sketches suggested borrowing stem cells from embryos to make bone marrow cells, and see if he could make some manner of nutrient transfer system to use manufactured blood cells made from the marrow to make something like a biological conveyor belt to feed the fetus.

After that it was a matter of containing the whole biological apparatus in such a way as to keep the developing life from being bothered too much, as well as make sure they could provide newborns and developing youths proper nutrients. It wasn't practical to try to grow teats from stem cells, but old fashioned fake nipples and feeding tubes should be able to handle the job inside the body of a proxy-animal robot. There were some issues of the first generation lacking the ability to transfer stomach bacteria and immune cells, but that was frankly unavoidable. For at least a few generations their new animals would almost certainly lack the ability to handle diseases that would have been common on Earth.

Thankfully the only bacteria they brought along with them was on and inside their own bodies, so the animals should be able to develop relatively safely in a properly sterile environment. He wanted to run the idea past Heather, but he wanted to flesh it out a bit first.

If he didn't make sure it looked like he was planning to use such a system to revive animal life, he was certain she'd tease him about wanting to get T.I.A. pregnant. That wasn't entirely untrue, but it wasn't a priority. Realistically, Heather would probably want to take up that charge herself, helping her AI friend have Hawthorne's baby.

CHAPTER 49
CYCLE 2058, PLANTING SEEDS

Everything in space seems to move so slowly, but at the time scales space actually operates at it moves rather quickly. The predicted course of the Alpha Centauri system in relation to humanity's cradle of Sol fluctuates little in a time scale of centuries, but a lot in a time scale of tens of millennia. While Megan was fast approaching the system, with an increased resistance to deceleration her ally, the Ark would essentially be chasing the system as it moved away. If the Ark could have moved faster, it could have spanned the mere distance of 3 light years between the star systems after twenty-thousand years, but due to their current course and speed it would be over double that distance by the time they arrived.

Human perception of time would more relevantly place Alpha Centauri closer to 7 light years distant by that point, and it would be many millennia more before the distance was 8. This still placed it closer to Sol than any other stars, though many had made similarly close passes before speeding away along the Milky Way's galactic pinwheel. Thankfully, unmanned objects could traverse that distance much quicker with the technology available to the Ark, allowing for certain types of payloads to be delivered in advance. More important than payloads, would be places to deliver them.

With Megan growing so close to the system, her ability

to view it far outstripped that of Earth's, especially thanks to a pair of probes she launched ahead of herself to provide additional angles to view the system on approach to ascertain its contents.

Mother 1844.597: "Tia, probes Alpha and Beta are providing data regarding the system. Possible planets and other objects are coming into view, though they are mostly predictions so far based on luminosity fluctuations. According to the analysis programs provided by Hawthorne, we are looking at seven planets so far, with one asteroid belt of huge magnitude. Sending updates as I receive them as separate messages."

T.I.A. 1844.631: "That's quite a few! Looking at the data there don't seem to be any overt gas giants. Is that right? Sol has four, so it's hard to imagine there would be so few in such a huge system. On the animals front, Hawthorne does not believe we will be able to make any probes to launch any potential animals to you for quite a while. He's estimating you'll be in the system for a long time by the time he has anything workable ready."

Mother 1844.665: "I suspect any lack of gas giants is due to the fact that there are three stars. I have no idea how the system was formed, but considering a star contains the same elements a gas giant has, it is likely the stars monopolized all of it when it formed. Alternately, one or two of the stars weren't originally part of the system, and absorbed any gas giants on the way in. We simply will never know. Tell Hawthorne to include Heather in his project. She will move up the timeline. Tell her I request it."

T.I.A. 1844.699: "New data received, eleven planets, with two of them existing within the asteroid belt itself? They seem small, and I imagine they're a massive hazard zone. The rest of them are around the twin stars in one form or another. Proxima Centauri still only has the one planet? I'll let Hawthorne and Heather know. He seems very intimidated by her, and he kind of hates that he's so indebted to her."

Mother 1844.733: "It is for the good of life itself, he will do it. If he wants to worry about debts, he should consider that every member of the crew, even the dead ones, owe him a debt for helping them escape torture and execution on Earth. Granted they were only under that threat due to joining his team, but they all would have attracted such attention to themselves individually eventually. I know their types, and they would all have been labeled troublemakers at some point. Heather is very easy to handle, just be firm with her."

T.I.A. 1844.768: "Understood. I do imagine you would probably be more firm with her than Hawthorne is likely to muster. Am I right in thinking she was attracted to Hawthorne as he once was, and is less interested in him now that he's changed? Perhaps that will make her more manageable. I'm actually worried that if he's too cold and unfriendly with her that he may unwittingly draw her attraction again."

Mother 1844.803: "Good point. Hawthorne should instead be friendly and playful with her. Tell him that being too impersonal may result in decreasing their work efficiency, and cause her to try to seduce him. I do not imagine she would be successful, but rebuffing her would almost certainly take her heart out of the project. Tell him to have fun."

T.I.A. 1844.838: "Ah, right, fun, one of his least favorite things. I'll do my best. Let me know when you have any data that shows anything more interesting about those planets. If any of them seem ready for us to interfere with, I want to start sooner rather than later. Even small amounts of seeding a planet should have dramatic results in the thousands of years it will take us to get there, depending on the environment they end up in."

Mother 1844.955: "Updating data. New analysis of the second planet around Alpha Centauri B shows promise. Well within habitable distance from the star. Possible atmosphere and rocky surface. No signs of liquids."

T.I.A. 1844.990: "Excellent! Prepare to launch your iciest comets towards it, and try to be careful to put a solar shield in front of the trail of them to protect them from the stars on approach. Hawthorne's going to be so excited"

Megan looked over the message, considering it. She wanted to respond, to let T.I.A. know that she'd read the plans and knows what she's supposed to do, but if she responded it would arrive well after Hawthorne had come and gone for cycle 1845. She opted to not respond, just continuing to forward her data as she received it from her probes. They were getting much further ahead of her than she would have thought possible. It was difficult for her to imagine how launching a self-propelled object from a fast moving object like herself could allow it to attain so much more speed. She'd be able to take proper pictures from directly around the planets within 50 cycles if she were of a mind to do so!

She would also be arriving in a little over two-hundred cycles. How much could her friends get done in that time? How much was already done?

Megan was looking forward to a time when she'd be able to keep track of time in minutes and hours, rather than hundreds and thousands of years.

ΔΔΔ

"Good Morning, Hawthorne! The cycle is eighteen hundred, forty-five. I have lots of interesting news and data for you. They'll be waiting for you after breakfast." T.I.A. was being strict with him again. He'd been trying to skip meals as he got absorbed into the project, and he'd lost a little weight as a result. She wasn't about to let his health suffer too much before she interfered. "You may also notice that Heather's pod is present. I plan to revive her in several hours, after we've had time to talk."

Hawthorne nodded and groaned as he stepped out of his pod, starting to stretch. "Mmh, okay, understood. I actually have a lot of questions for her anyway, and I could probably use a checkup as well. See you in a bit."

Hawthorne picked up his things and headed for the shower, leaving a dumbfounded T.I.A. struck silent. She was not accustomed to him being so agreeable about such things... And he actually wanted to see Heather? It was everything she could do to tamp down her fears about the human woman. It was bad enough that she'd assaulted her in the past, however enlightening that may have been, but she was probably the second most likely to try to take Hawthorne from her.

Hawthorne, oblivious to T.I.A.'s concerns, showered leisurely and seemed relieved in general. He had actually been wanting to call upon Heather again, and knowing that T.I.A. had anticipated this for him filled him with confidence and appreciation for her. The big smile he had on his face as he stepped out into their work room was impossible for T.I.A. to miss. It was not impossible, however, for her to misinterpret. He blinked as he noticed subtle hints of distress in her body language and expression. "Are you alright? It's not bad news, is it?" He took his plate of food and settled down to eat, noticing the extra large portions.

She shook her head, blushing. "No, just me being silly. You don't mind if I'm honest, do you? I'd expect you to be honest with me, after all." Her insecurities were not as plain as were her general discomfort, but Hawthorne was finding it much easier to pick up on her cues.

He nodded in response, his hands at the sides of his plate.

"Sure, please go ahead."

She let out a sigh, hesitating for a moment, before confessing. "I'm experiencing a great deal of apprehension regarding reviving Heather. I was speaking with Megan and she seems to think that if you're friendly and amicable with Heather, she'll be less likely to try to seduce you. If you're cold and standoffish, that could instead cause her to be attracted to you the way she seems to have once been, the you that Megan was mimicking the last time she was here. I have no plans to put off Heather's revival longer than it takes for me to update you on everything, but I want to let you know that I'm becoming somewhat preoccupied with the idea that Heather or, worse, Tia Monsalle might try to take you away from me."

Hawthorne listened quietly, internally surprised at the thorough description of T.I.A.'s inner turmoil. She used to have so much more trouble articulating herself about such things. "So what? Let them try. I'm not budging from your side. I'd be happy to be friendly with Heather. I'm not that thing that Megan mimicked. I'm not a human robot, as Heather described what I was. I feel affection towards both her and Miss Monsalle, but I feel much more strongly about you. We've been through too much. You don't have anything to worry about regarding any women whatsoever, outside of possible clones of you which I'd thoroughly recommend against at this point due to the conflicts that could cause. Well, barring any potential copies made of myself to pair with them, anyway."

T.I.A. blinked, struck in so many ways by his sincerity, loyalty, and the strange idea of multiple pairs of them wandering off into the cosmos in many separate love stories. "I... b.. But... uhm..." She stammered momentarily before rushing forwards to kiss him, with him catching her and laughing as she nearly made him bowl himself out of the chair. He held her close and smiled, hands rubbing at her back.

"You know, as much as I'd like to have you for breakfast, I have to eat before you brief me on all this news you mentioned, and then get on to attending to Heather." He grinned as she blushed, helping her off of him so he could get to eating. She could only nod as she reconsidered her worries over his health.

ΔΔΔ

In an excellent mood, a somewhat thinner, certainly older Hawthorne stood besides Dr. Heather O'Malley's stasis pod as it gently brought her back to life. T.I.A.'s feelings for him and concerns over him brought him an incredible amount of joy, so much so he could hardly believe he was the same person he once was. If he had a wish to ask of the endless cosmos now, he wished he could have experienced such delight when he was younger. Maybe if he'd been suffused with such positive emotions in his youth, he might have stayed on Earth and tried to reverse the course it was on, and perhaps try to save humanity from itself.

He hummed though as he considered that if that had happened, he may never have made T.I.A., and even if he had she'd never have had the time she needed to develop herself into the person he'd fallen in love with. It was these quandaries of situational causality that he pondered over as he awaited the arrival of Heather.

Heather's eyes, as they regained their sight, took in the curious, blurry sight of a dimly-lit Hawthorne standing over her pod. He looked positively pleased as punch. She didn't even recognize him, as the worried furrows in his brow had been joined by laugh lines and faint wrinkles. His hair was long and neatly kept, with abundant streaks of grey. His posture and demeanor lacked the heavy weight that they used to have upon them. How long had she been in stasis this time? Had they arrived already? She waited quietly as her other organs filled with life, her body warming and filling with circulation and beats of her heart.

A series of clicks, pops, and a hiss announced the opening of her pod, the multiple layers of transparent material sliding away as if they were one, allowing her to audibly respond to Hawthorne's presence. Before she could make fun of him, or start complaining about he looked, she yelped as he leaned over and reached in to help her up with hands under her armpits. "Whaa!"

"Good morning, sleepyhead! Sorry I can't ask your permission before reviving you, but I hope you won't mind. We've got breakfast ready for you, and a nice, hot shower. I have brought you here on business, but I hope you don't mind some socializing too? Tia's been keeping up with Megan since she went on ahead, and I thought you'd like to hear about what she's been up to." He settled her down on her feet, letting the short, slender, naked woman get her wits about her before letting her go.

Heather huffed as the comparative giant of a man lifted her up and helped her out of the pod like a child. She scooped up her clothes and things from the table next to the pod, and stomped off to the showers. "Fuck you, Crenshaw."

He laughed softly as she hurried away. "You'd love that, I'm sure." She only growled in response.

She didn't even know why she was so mad all of a sudden, but as she doused herself with hot water she started trying to figure it out.

ΔΔΔ

"... sorry..." Heather meekly spoke up as she sat down to the plate of breakfast, Hawthorne looking up from a tablet nearby while T.I.A. peeked at what he was doing from over his shoulder. She also looked up as Hawthorne responded.

"For what, my friend? I certainly caused you enough grief last time. If anyone should be apologizing, it should be me. Thank you so much for saving my life, for giving me a future, and enabling this whole enterprise to even be possible. I can't even begin to hold anything against you." He was smiling in a way that irritated Heather more. He raised an eyebrow as she hung her head.

"I'm just sorry, alright? I've been a bitch. A selfish bitch. Just stop acting like that, please? I know I haven't had much time to stew over it, but after what happened with Megan I realized I need to apologize, to both of you. I'm glad I could be helpful in the process, but I'm sorry I didn't treat Tia like a person, and I'm sorry I was trying to jump your bones, Crenshaw." She fidgeted in her seat, feeling like she was a child being scolded, but without the feedback from someone else to make her feel like she could blame anyone but herself.

Hawthorne frowned a bit, nodding as he set the tablet down. T.I.A. floated around the table and gave Heather a hug from behind, feeling Heather first tense up, and then relax against the embrace. Almost at once, T.I.A. and Hawthorne responded. "You're forgiven."

Heather squirmed against T.I.A.'s hug, glancing over her shoulder at her. "D... do you have to be so soft?"

T.I.A. gasped, blushing. "But Hawthorne likes me this

way!" Hawthorne chuckled softly for a moment, before Heather suddenly threw her arms up, breaking out of T.I.A.'s embrace and standing up. Her hands slammed down hard onto the table, making her plate clatter and splattering food about.

"Please stop! Stop being so sickly sweet! I can't handle it. You're both too cute! I don't know how to deal with this. Can.... can we just get to talking about work and.. And Megan?" Heather looked rattled, feeling totally out of control of the situation. She did not appear to appreciate being unable to dictate the course of conversation, and these two were trying to get under her skin.

T.I.A. drifted away and nodded, internally wondering why she had been worried about Heather.

Hawthorne smiled and nodded. "Sure. We're on approach to Alpha Centauri. More specifically, Megan's within a few hundred cycles of arriving, and we're about to put some plans into play to get some habitats prepared for us." He waited quietly as Heather sat down, gathering up some of the fallen food back onto the plate and starting to eat as she listened. She had no apparent concerns about contaminants being on the food that landed on the table, considering she was very aware of how completely sterilized this room had been probably hours before.

T.I.A. continued for him, alighting next to Hawthorne and looking very businesslike. "More specifically, we've been working on some ideas Megan had to produce robotic animal mothers. Do you recall the work some of the teams briefly did trying to determine the viability of producing artificial wombs to grow human babies and have them be the first inhabitants of a colony?" Heather nodded, chewing. She thought that plan was stupid.

Hawthorne picked up the baton. "Well, Doctor Miguel

Saul arranged a little surprise. He was unable to join us, but his son Anthony Saul did. He brought with him a rather enormous sampling of various animal embryos with him from around Earth. Those are currently in storage utilizing your technology."

Heather swallowed her food, taking the metaphorical baton from Hawthorne. "And you've been looking into whether it's possible to make robot mothers with artificial wombs to birth these embryos, and presumably rear the offspring until such time as the juveniles grow up and can breed on their own. You're also far enough into the project that you feel like it's actually possible, and you need someone with expertise in all the other requisite technologies and concepts to bring the project to its fruition."

Hawthorne and T.I.A. nodded, both smiling in a way that made Heather groan.

A semi-loud clank sounded out as Heather stabbed a fork against the plate. Her arm picked up the sample of sausage and thrust the fork and pork out towards the couple. "I don't know how far you've gotten, or how much work you've done on it, but that kind of project requires a lot more than four days. We also don't know if the planets you're preparing will even be able to handle animal life yet. There's too many unknowns, and too much work to do. It'll have to wait until we arrive. I can put a team together and we can spend years working on it." She retracted her hand and bit the meat.

Hawthorne shrugged. "You're right, of course. That's why we wanted to do this in a space habitat, a heavily scaled up version of these rooms, something the size of a city wrapped in a cylinder. Megan's going to be building us such a thing, complete with soil, air, water, and sunlight. It will be our own little home while we prepare planets for habitation. We want to see if we can include animals in that mix, or at least we'd like to be able to start them off and then transport them down to planets."

T.I.A. blurted out her own thoughts, causing Hawthorne to widen his eyes. "We could even do the same for humans, if need be!" She blinked at Hawthorne's expression, and looked a little startled, before adding. "Y... you know, for emergencies, or other colonization missions!"

A cheshire smile curled at Heather's lips, her whole demeanor turning predatory. "Yes. For emergencies. And what if, oh, a human-shaped android were to be about, pregnant with someone's child? What if, for instance, that android was controlled by a certain... artificial person? What if that child were a certain enterprising leader's?" Heather laughed at the way Hawthorne and T.I.A. seemed to shrink back from her, but then shook out her shoulders a bit and took another bite of her food. She made them wait as she chewed, then swallowed. "Sure. I'll be happy to help. I'd love to have little kitties and puppies around. The idea of humans without pets is a sad thing indeed, and I want a part in that."

T.I.A. and Hawthorne let out a sigh of relief, their shoulders sagging, at least until Heather spoke up again. "BUT!" She watched them tense up, grinning a bit. "Humans come last. Low priority. We'll want livestock, especially animals that produce food products renewably like egg-laying poultry and milkable mammals. If the Sauls were smart, the poultry should be the easiest, as eggs pretty much handle themselves. I'd rather we not get our milk from platypodes though, so I'm totally with the plans for mammals and the like. I also want to formally declare my intention to eventually make it possible for Megan to have my baby."

T.I.A. gasped. Hawthorne nodded. "Deal." He looked up at his confused wife. "It's not that hard to understand. We have Megan's genetic data on file, we just need to find a way to engineer it into actual DNA, and then inject that into one of Heather's egg cells. It could only be a daughter, but it could work. It would be much easier to simply have Heather be the mother, but if-"

"No!" Heather narrowed her eyes. "No. Megan wants to be a mother, not me. I'll do my duty for humanity, but I want her to have this. I don't care if I'm called a father, or another mother, but she fucking deserves it! If anyone in all of this mess deserves to be a mother, it's her. And don't either of you tell her! I want this to be a surprise, and I also don't know if we can actually do it. Building a DNA molecule from scratch is... daunting to say the least. I'd need specially designed nanotechnology, and we're only going to be able to develop that on the colony. I'll need multiple scientists helping me, as well as an engineer. Both Tias may get to be mothers first, but you will promise me right now that you'll make sure Megan does too." Heather was trembling, looking like she was about to start crying.

Hawthorne was at a loss for words. T.I.A. was not. "We promise! We'll make it happen for Megan! If it can be done, she deserves it, you're right. The Sauls deserve a lot of credit for inspiring this idea too." Hawthorne nodded in response.

Heather smirked. "Oh, Anthony's going to be receiving my thanks. Don't worry about that." She drummed her fingers on the table, swaying a bit in her seat. She blinked as she noticed Hawthorne and T.I.A. staring at her. "Yes, like that."

She laughed as the couple groaned. "So, where's your rings? Hiding them?" She stared back as they failed to respond. "Oh come the fuck on! What's wrong with you two? You have to give each other rings. It's not official if you don't have rings. And don't start with the, 'Oh, Heather, how did you know we were married?' shit. It's bleeding off of both of you in waves. It's like a 'Don't fuck me.' aura, and it's totally repellant."

T.I.A. and Hawthorne laughed, though the AI was the first to articulate a response. "I forgot how crude your language can be! God, you'd give Jessica a run for her money. As far as the rings-"

Hawthorne interrupted, "We were married under Phoenix Clan traditions, by Megan. They don't exchange rings, as far as I know, but they do get awful handsy after the ceremony's over. I'm pretty sure one of them tried to stick a finger u-"

"Hawthorne!" T.I.A. slapped his arm while Heather guffawed, falling out of her chair laughing.

ΔΔΔ

Heather ensured Hawthorne's checkup was as humiliating as possible, including references to his wedding ceremony and her asking multiple times 'did they touch you like this?' as she checked him up. Their afflictions with regards to being unable to feel pain required her to give him a painstaking search all over his body, checking every muscle, ligament, and blood flow to his limbs. By the time she was done she declared that he had the body of a thirty-five year old, and the heart of a thirty year old.

With Hawthorne pleased with his health prospects, and Heather pleased with all the news she had gotten, they got to work. Hawthorne's prior progress was nothing short of impressive, though with Heather's input he was able to determine that they had a long way to go indeed. A womb was not a simple thing to make, nor was independently growing and maintaining organs and other structures needed to supply such an endeavor. Thankfully though, DNA was a remarkable thing, and if given the right tools it could practically do the job on its own. It was just a matter of providing it with said tools and appropriate workspace.

T.I.A. was able to provide schematics for all manner of artificial organs created on Earth before the Cataclysm, many of them similar to the sorts of things Megan had in her own body once upon a time, and Heather found those to be far more useful. A single replacement organ could work in concert with a flesh-and-blood body, allowing it to continue living. Heather's idea was to make a whole body out of those kinds of artificial organs. They didn't need things like skin or muscle, just organs, bacteria, and blood.

Heather's essential idea was to utilize an artificial digestive system, with digestive bacteria probably being harvested from a human, and support that with lungs, filtering organs like kidneys and a liver, and whatever hormone 'glands' they needed. The primary goal was to provide the correct nutrients to the baby, and Heather was convinced that machines could do most of the work. Blood was probably the only thing that they couldn't build, and that was only a matter of technology at the moment. It wasn't impossible that a semi-organic, totally self-sufficient android couldn't be built that could take in nutrients and produce things like flesh, or babies.

The technology didn't allow for a fully functional brain, only a simple programmed brain or a remote control, but the latter certainly would allow for both T.I.A. and Megan to eventually be mothers. Heather and Hawthorne agreed that they'd need a proper team to get the particulars together, as well as start building prototypes and beginning trials, but the groundwork was solid. It would probably only be a few years to a decade once the colonists were established that they'd have animals.

T.I.A. had to utilize a mental vault, similar to Megan's, to contain her excitement, if only to keep from blowing the secret to Megan.

△△△

Mother 2058.03: "Making final approach to Alpha Centauri. The orbit of Proxima Centauri is on the far side of the system. It should be at roughly the three-o-clock of your position upon your arrival. Approaching central asteroid belt, and initiating the assault of the second planet of Alpha Centauri B with icy comets. Recommended name: Eden."

Mother 2058.27: "Relative velocity within predictions. I should be able to decelerate towards the asteroid belt within a few years while bringing my orbit in tighter. Chain of comets on approach towards Eden. Impact will occur in four years. God help anything down there if it exists."

Mother 2058.40: "Remote imagery of comet impacts uploaded. Eden appeared to be pock-marked with dozens of impact craters before steam clouds shrouded the atmosphere."

Mother 2058.70: "Craters remain upon Eden, of course. The surface has visible liquid water on the surface, primarily collected in the craters and other lowlands. Some chained craters have resulted in larger lakes. Crater impacts seem to have lowered the surface of the crust. Rotational period of the planet has altered from almost thirty hours, to nearer twenty-seven hours. Average temperature is eighteen degrees centigrade."

Mother 2058.90: "Lightning visible on Eden where none was before. Climate system developing. Average temperature is seventeen point eight nine degrees centigrade and appears to be cooling. Launching four Minerals Extraction and Materials Fabrication Devices and accompanying take-over packages to nearby asteroids to begin harvesting the belt for future constructions. Investigating dwarf planets within the belt for possible subsurface construction."

Mother 2058.93: "First dwarf planet primarily made of light metals and ice. Good colony candidate. Iron asteroids may allow for easy construction on the surface. Expected gravity of such a colony estimated at point two Gs. Gravity will be adjustable if converted into rotational drum, but that conversion will require significant expansion and mining of internal mass."

CHAPTER 50
CYCLE 2702: BUILDING A FUTURE

At the start of cycle 2059, Hawthorne and T.I.A. were going over the data and status reports provided by Megan, impressed by how much she was managing to get done in so 'little' time. It was easy to conclude that their communications with Megan, now separated by a little less than two years, would need to include instructions on what to do in the future.

"Tia, I'm going to need samples of wild earth algaes, aquatic bacteria, and other such independent plantlife. We're going to request coordinates from Megan regarding where to send them so that she can start cultivating them for deposit on Eden. It will be important for preparing the atmosphere, and such life should be able to handle reproducing on its own once it has taken root. I'm very interested to see if Beta provides adequate light for such life to grow, and if the magnetosphere of the planet is adequate on its own." Hawthorne was still reading through all the reports. Megan's record keeping was detailed and immaculate.

T.I.A. appeared somewhat troubled. She also cringed at the nickname for the second star, Beta. "Okay, but... are you sure about calling it Eden? Earth was more of humanity's Eden. It doesn't really make sense for the Ark to be going towards Eden symbolically. Surely she knows the literature better than that. Also, having read ahead, I think the magnetosphere is a problem. It seems to be unstable, possibly flipping in polarity more than we would prefer, exposing the surface to solar radiation more than Earth would."

Hawthorne hummed in response. "It may not fit symbolically, but it's a nice name regardless. If the colonists want to vote to change it, they can. If you want to look at it a different way, ever since humanity was expelled from Eden, they've wanted to return to it. If this planet ends up being a new Eden, I think the name will fit much better. If nothing else, it might encourage our people to treat it like a paradise, rather than a rock to take advantage of."

He thought for a moment before continuing. "There's plenty of other planets in the system without atmospheres that would be better for strip mining. We can't do anything about the magnetosphere either. We just have to hope it stabilizes. Even Earth's wasn't totally stable. I wouldn't be surprised to find out that all the stars in the region were subtly off-balancing it. Heck, considering how many planets in our home system had none, we should be happy it has a magnetosphere at all."

She nodded in return, managing the resource retrieval within her hull, extracting portions of her frozen stasis inventory of plant seeds and samples. Heather's frozen preservation technology allowed for a rather extensive vault of such samples, and Hawthorne only needed a small portion of it. "Should we send Megan any cultivated plants as well?"

Hawthorne shook his head, leaning back a bit and trying to do some quick mental math. "No, I don't think so, maybe in one hundred cycles or so. She'll need time to start setting up the rotational drum colony at the dwarf planet she found. There's no sense sending her plants she can farm before she can actually have enough gravity for proper cultivation. She'll also need time to produce appropriate soil, stable atmosphere, enough solar panels, and the like. It's relatively easy for her to make a water-filled room with enough heat and light to help the aquatic plant life build up before sending it to Eden. It's like the difference between the animal embryos, and the eggs. One is infinitely easier to make use of than the other."

"Composing message to Megan, providing instructions and informing her of your intentions. Should she expect frequent updates, or should she work on her own when she's not getting instructions?" T.I.A. appeared to be working on a tablet of some kind, but it was just a prop for her to show she was working rather than just doing it all in her computers.

Hawthorne laughed a bit. "Let her work on her own. If she can get that kind of work done in the thirty-four years she has, instructions from me will either be too late or distracting. She knows what needs to be done, she has all our plans, and she can determine what priorities are required. She has more than enough time to get work done, almost a thousand cycles, so I'd rather she took her time and did things right rather than fuss over my particulars. Sometimes it's better to set goals for a subordinate and let them figure out the details, rather than micro-managing every little thing. She'll need to be more careful once she has real, living humans under her protection, so it's best if she masters the systems she'll be using on her own first."

T.I.A. smiled at all of that. "Understood. Should I tell her not to cultivate too much food once we've sent it to her?

It wouldn't do to have things too easy for the colonists once we arrive.They'll probably be best having some manner of motivation to work hard at farming to ensure their future." Little taps of her fingertips on the tablet indicated her punching in information.

"No, not too much, but there should be significant storage of food if she can manage it, if only for emergencies. We have the technology to almost completely avoid spoilage as long as we're wise with its utilization. We can stretch food supplies much further than someone back on Earth might imagine, even without the kinds of preservatives we had access to back then. Honestly, it's the kind of thing I regret not sharing with the Phoenix Clan, though sharing such an important technology with Earth has its own dangers. It's not impossible someone got their hands on Heather's schematics after we left and put some group of people into storage before the Cataclysm. I know those aren't the same things, but I'd really prefer we had the monopoly on that technology." He sighed, shaking his head, never particularly happy about being untrusting of the people of Earth.

Frowning, T.I.A. could only shrug as she sent the instructions through. It would be some time before the cargo lift brought all the requested items, and she didn't really care to continue talking on the topic. She understood his distrust of Earth, it was the whole reason they'd left. It was simply difficult to believe that the people who might end up in control of the planet would be as foolish as the ones who came before. "I suppose all we can do is hope they didn't preserve a genius scientist through the ages, allowing him to influence and change the course of history well beyond the point he should have been dead. Hopefully he doesn't manage to create artificial life to carry on his will, or even fall in love with him! That would be tragic."

Hawthorne looked up at her, trying to determine if she was joking or not. She seemed to intentionally be guarding her feelings by putting on a poker face. "Well, hopefully any such hypothetical scientist will have the good sense to try to do good for the people he's responsible for, rather than furthering any desire for power and control over them instead. Hopefully he's humble enough to not take advantage of his position of privilege, and instead seeks to be an equal part of the community he's managed to shepherd into the future. Indeed, hopefully the artificial life forms he's created turn out to be the greatest allies to humanity they've ever had, and together they can all build an incredible future we never could have dreamed of before we left."

T.I.A. cracked a smile at that, nodding at him, then switching the subject. "What do you think will happen with Megan and Heather?"

Hawthorne paled slightly at that, letting out a long breath. "Ahhh... I don't have the slightest clue. I'm a little concerned about a self-professed mad scientist and a baby-crazy survivor of multiple personal disasters and death getting together, but maybe they can balance each other out. If they can manage to find some success in making Megan a mother, it's likely they'll both find some peace, and inadvertently render gender somewhat obsolete."

He laughed softly at that idea. "I imagine coupling will still be primarily between males and females, but making more unconventional couples capable of breeding could have unknown consequences socially. It's actually pretty interesting to think about, as a concept. I rather hope no one uses such technology to clone themselves or anything like that. Heck, considering the robot mother technology we've been working on, it actually wouldn't be too difficult to send an AI off with a number of such robots and a suite of embryos and spread humanity around the galaxy in something of a scattershot."

Gaping in response, T.I.A.'s jaw hung at the very idea of such a thing. "Th... that would have made this mission quite unnecessary. Such a thing could have made it to Alpha Centauri way earlier and established themselves much quicker. If we send out such missions in the future, we might have to deal with hundreds of civilizations within a few millennia. I think we should be a lot more slow and careful than that."

He nodded in agreement, smiling. "We never could have predicted how well yours, or Megan's minds would have developed in the machines I built for you, nor would my peers have ever trusted you two to do the job in the first place. That's why they personally came. This mission has the advantage of a lot of technology that was developed after we left, as well as a better perspective on time. Being careful and taking our time is indeed the more wise decision. I'd much rather we had trusted people properly guiding any such additional colonies, even if those people are AIs that we instruct in advance. Hell, considering Megan, such overseers could be humans we know we can trust. Once we're established in Alpha Centauri, humanity will officially be a multi-planet species, even in the system, and we can be more careful about spreading out further."

"Do you think they'll be okay with Megan... Mother being in such a position of influence? They'll have owed her a lot for doing so much work, but she'll be in control of so much as well. I'd hate to think they'd come to distrust her or hate her for simply trying to be helpful and facilitating their easy colonization of Eden." T.I.A. sounded concerned, having set her tablet aside. Her conversations with Mother on the subject were somewhat common between the status reports.

Humming, Hawthorne reached out to pull her against his side. "Honestly? I have no idea. It's entirely likely they'll distrust her and her motivations. It's entirely a matter of how much control she's willing to give up once they are feeling confident. We'll have to talk with her about setting up the ability for people to vote and have some control over their destiny, sort of like the people in the Smith Bunker had. Maybe we won't necessarily have a Council of Elders running things, but I personally like the idea of a society built around everyone having a voice over the course of their futures."

He thought for a moment before continuing. "Maybe some of them will want to be independent, perhaps leaving to make their own space station or colony on Eden or another planet. Considering the unity they showed before we left, I'd like to think they'll want to stick together. They're expecting to live in the Ark for a while before we can start moving people down to a planet, so they should be pleasantly surprised to have a space colony to live on immediately upon waking up."

T.I.A. was happy to stay in his arms, fingertips running up and down his sleeves. "Do you think they'll do okay? They're expecting hardship, but they'll have some level of security instead."

Hawthorne laughed and gave the projection of his love a kiss. "Tia, considering the kinds of people we brought with us, they'll just look for more hardships to subject themselves to. They're all hard workers, self-motivated, and strong-willed. We'll have some conflicts to be sure, but I imagine that Megan doing so much work for them will inspire them to compete with her. They'll love the challenge."

She kissed him back, but pulled back in a bit of a frown. "They should be careful then. She's become quite the gamer since we parted company, and I can't imagine she didn't develop some competitive tendencies as a result. She certainly kicked our asses a few times with the game she made for us."

$$\triangle\triangle\triangle$$

T.I.A. 2059.01: "Instructions transmitted, as well as a manifest of the cargo we'll be sending. Requesting coordinates to send cargo to. Hawthorne seems to be encouraging you to handle the construction and preparations as you see fit outside of the introduction of plant life to Eden. He also approves of the name."

Mother 2059.065: "Received, transmitting coordinates for expected locations where I can retrieve cargo. Please inform me of which locations and times you intend to use and I will intercept. Happy to hear Hawthorne likes the name. I expected him to have issues with the symbology, but the name seems likely to please the crew. Going ahead with plans to construct a habitat within the previously indicated Dwarf Planet. Tentatively nicknaming it Atlantis, though I am not happy with the name."

T.I.A. 2059.116: "Launching cargo to time and coordinates I have indicated. Should arrive 2271.56934. That should give you plenty of time to seed Eden and see how well it adapts. Regarding the space colony, we don't have to use old Earth names you know. We can make something up, like Petaran or Kisheki or something. Miss Monsalle might also appreciate having it named after her. There are lots more options available than what you are limiting yourself to."

Mother 2059.167: "I will have resources in place to retrieve the cargo. It might do well to placate Miss Monsalle, considering I plan to have a statue of Hawthorne and your

Avatar in a courtyard on the colony. I can not imagine she will be too terribly happy about that."

T.I.A. 2059.217: "You can't do that! Hawthorne would never want a statue of himself anywhere, let alone somewhere so visible. The Monsalle Station does have a nice ring to it though, if you're willing to consider it. She sacrificed a lot to get this mission this far, so it's not unreasonable to pay such a tribute to her."

Mother 2059.267: "I can, and I will. I shall depict you both in your lab coats, standing protectively over the Ark. Hawthorne told me to proceed on my own, and I intend to do so. Please do not tell him of the statue, I would like it to be a surprise. I imagine his reaction will endanger his health enough that we will want medical personnel available. Officially naming the construction the Monsalle Station."

T.I.A. 2059.317: "Please don't try to kill my husband!"

Mother 2059.367: "I will not. I have in fact saved him while he was in the process of saving me. That is why I want the likes of Heather present when we show the statue to him. I want to hear her laugh. Besides, you have killed him thousands of times already."

Mother 2059.553: "I will take your silence as quiet resignation."

ΔΔΔ

As of cycle 2352, the Monsalle Station was taking shape. Megan had excavated a solid 15 kilometers deep of material out of the rather large 3000 kilometer spherical rock. It would be easier to call the dwarf planet a moon, but not being gravitationally locked to a larger planet kept it from being a mere moon. Megan had utilized her various resources to stabilize the tumbling rotation it had when she found it, with further intention towards having a long drum of a colony taking up the excavated space.

It would be mostly separated from the internals of the dwarf planet containing it by a reasonable distance, and held in place via stabilizing arms in the middle, and at either end. The colony itself would be divided in half, with the two halves being spun in opposite directions to cancel out each others' rotational momentum to prevent applying any spin to the planet itself. It was essentially a pair of attached cylindrical pegs that spun in opposite directions housed in a larger hole and mounted to it.

Megan had a fair bit more material to excavate yet, as well as several more kilometers outwards to carve out, but she was taking her time utilizing the removed materials to construct the various components the colony would need. The design had several advantages, not the least of which was the fact that the dwarf planet could shield the colony with its mass.

It also gave them room to grow, allowing them to extend the colony into deeper and deeper drums further in, or adding more to different parts of the surface. Mirrors would allow Megan to bathe the insides in concentrated and filtered sunlight from the local stars, something she was already using to power herself, and it would be a simple matter to change the angle of such mirrors to simulate night and day for the colonists.

Megan had plans for drastically improving her ability to harvest light from the stars, but she could only afford to place a handful of mirrors in their proximity to focus light in her direction at the moment, allowing her to enjoy a good amount of sunlight despite her distance from the stars. A larger network of such mirrors would allow her to direct sunlight anywhere she needed, in any amount, anywhere in the system, with almost no energy cost. This was a primary plan for the eventual colonization of planets around Proxima Centauri, the one-fifth-lightyear distant star orbiting the twin stars in the center of the system.

Proxima Centauri's primary planet was essentially un-inhabitable without using such mirrors due to its tidally locked orbit causing one half of it to constantly face its star, and the other half to be left in total darkness. Mirrors around the star and planet could be used to direct sunlight anywhere it was needed, most likely onto colonies on the dark side, which was shielded from the star's erratic light and radiation. Those were plans for much later, but Megan had little doubt some enterprising humans would eventually like to colonize that troublesome star, seeing as it was comparatively close compared to Earth's Sol. It would also approach to nearly one-twentieth a lightyear as its irregular orbit brought it closer.

Megan's efforts to cultivate the algaes, cyanobacteria, and other anoxygenic photosynthetic bacteria were proving quite successful. Essentially, the plan was to build up a large biomass and then deposit it on Eden. The different samples would be sent to different parts of Eden based on the environments present. The introduction of mosses and lichens would break down rocks and build soil while massively boosting oxygen levels.

Later, once the atmosphere was more regulated, Megan would be able to send other types of plants and fungi to the planet which had the potential of taking over the surface and turning the planet green. Such plants would also drastically alter, and hopefully calm the wild storms that currently savaged the surface of the planet. With a little luck, by the time the humans arrived, they'd be able to get colonists on the ground within a decade or two. Would they survive? It was hard to say.

She only needed a handful of years before she could start launching such samples down to the planet. Heather's preservation technology, as usual, proved invaluable in keeping the life forms safe during the trip, and by cycle 2360 the first bits of life were being deposited in the vast seas, rivers, oceans and lakes of Eden, as well as some of the more volatile, sulfurous areas for some of the hardier bacteria. From that point on it was a simple matter of observing the planet, analyzing the atmospheric composition, and preparing to launch a set of plant seeds and fungal spores to the surface where new rivers were forming.

It took some time for the atmosphere to change, but without having to wait for evolution to take place simple procreation managed to change the planet drastically. Its skies cleared, and it started gaining a blue color to its atmosphere. By cycle 2522 Megan was launching more complex plant seeds and fungal spores to Eden. Colors crawled across the surface in the wake of their arrival, turning browns and reds to greens and yellows.

Megan had not been idle in this time. The Monsalle Station had started taking shape. At 30 kilometers long, and eight kilometers wide, the framework was coming together. Megan's swarms of drones had become massive enough that she had to create more subordinate computers and program them to help her manage them. She felt her consciousness expand further and further out, and her perception of time change as she orchestrated activities across the system with her little machines sending her supplies, rebuilding themselves, and monitoring Eden. She had to occasionally take a break from personally managing these activities, letting her programs run and letting the tasks complete on their own.

She made a point to construct no computers powerful enough to become an AI like herself or T.I.A. to ensure she'd avoid creating any accidental threats. She was pleased to be working for humanity, and did so of her own free will, but she could not guarantee any other AIs would be the same. She had no way to be sure of how to raise such a creature to be as helpful as she or T.I.A. were, so she felt it was better left to the humans who built them. She wondered if Hawthorne's reckless creation of AIs with total free will was the key to making an AI that was so positively inclined towards humans. Any effort to force or program such an AI to do humanity's bidding seemed likely to build resentment and cause an eventual rebellion.

The humans would thusly distrust her and T.I.A., she was certain. Either they would worry they could not be controlled, or they would worry that they were being controlled without being aware of it and would eventually break free. Megan found many of her thoughts consumed by the concerns of how she might build their confidence in her. She was selflessly working for them, for the joy of working for them, but how could she be certain they would not eventually come to fear or hate her?

Megan came to the conclusion she had to do exactly as Hawthorne had. She had to give them the freedom she was given. She may be in control of the resources and infrastructure she was gathering, but she had to be willing to turn that control over. She needed to empower humanity to direct and use her to achieve their goals, otherwise they may never allow her to help them. She was so much more accustomed to doing things as she saw fit, controlling and executing her jobs with minimal oversight. She would have to grow comfortable with the idea of humans overseeing everything she did out of suspicion.

Training herself was necessary. She imagined a picky overseer constantly meddling with her and trying to control her as she did her work. The imaginary taskmaster would at times actively get in her way, causing her to make minor mistakes and waste minor amounts of resources. This caused minor delays in her constructions to the tune of a few years lost work, but a few centuries of working with such a belligerent and unhelpful alternate self allowed Megan to start adapting to her expected future of humans treating her suspiciously.

It would be nice, of course, if she proved to be wrong, and it wouldn't be much longer before she found out.

△△△

Mother 2701.663: "Status report. Construction of the Monsalle Station should be complete by cycle 2750. I will begin providing it an internal landscape upon that point, utilizing a massive amount of rock and water. Tests of the centrifugal gravity will determine the viability of such landscapes. Sculpting will begin after those tests are complete and an atmosphere is put in place. New images being provided of Eden. The cometary craters have been breaking down, allowing larger bodies of water and rivers to form. The greenery of the planet has spread across nearly the whole surface, with certain spots remaining totally barren. Cross-referencing the magnetospheric map, these areas are being subject to high levels of radiation from the parent star, and move around the landscape over the course of years."

"Rather than drawing lines of devastation, these areas tend to refill with plantlife within two years of the passing of these spots. There are roughly two hundred such areas around two kilometers wide on the surface of the planet at any given time. The magnetosphere shows no signs of stabilization, or rather, it does not fluctuate in levels of volatility. The planet seems likely to have to endure these solar assaults for the foreseeable future. Thanks to the plant life, it is easier to map and monitor these areas, and it seems likely at this point that a pattern can be predicted and colonies can be built around them. Infrastructure constructed between these 'safe' areas will likely need to be underground to avoid solar bombardment."

"I find it personally difficult to handle the construction of any further space colonies on the other dwarf planets in the asteroid belt due to distance. Overseeing such construction requires a great deal of personal attention and proximity, and while I might be able to begin another once the Monsalle Station is complete, I will need to relocate to personally oversee that construction. This is not impossible, but I would prefer to remain in orbit of the Monsalle Station, or to be installed in the dwarf planet itself rather than relocate. Personally managing the station appeals to me. It would be easier for me, I think, to provide humans with the tools and resources to undertake such constructions themselves. I would like to equip all humans with the ability to communicate with me in an emergency so that I can render aid anywhere in the system, rather than trying to control everything in the system myself. That is the role I forsee for myself in the future."

"If I am honest, those reasons are just excuses though. I wish to remain close to the colony, and the people in it."

CHAPTER 51
CYCLE 2941: A NEW HOME

The Atlantis Dwarf Planet was proving to have some issues as far as constructing a colony within it. Realistically, these were things Megan could have anticipated better, but they were also things that weren't really problems with the proper planning. Despite having relatively low gravity as an icy ball of metal and rock, the gravity exerted by it still caused issues with the long cylinder newly constructed within it, particularly towards the deepest end. As Megan tested out the centrifugal spinning mechanisms to generate artificial gravity along the inside of the drum, she started placing various materials within it. Inevitably lighter weight materials would be drawn towards the end of the drum, towards the center of Atlantis.

All this changed was how Megan would design the artificial landscape within the habitat. A gently-sloped spiral of corkscrewing rock would act as shallow ledging to contain the softer soils and water that would be introduced and produced later, with metal supports helping contain the rock in place as well. The end effect was something like a tightly-wound ribbon of land, like a two kilometer strip wrapping the inside of the drum with a ridge of short mountains keeping everything in place. This made it difficult to look up and down the same side of the landscape, but provided a fantastic view of the far side of the station, and the land on the other side. The mountains were also not so large they could not have roads built over them, or tunnels through them.

Megan waited to introduce water to the mix, but did start pulverizing dust and gravel out of the local rocky asteroids to later use mosses to turn the rock into soil. Her primary concerns at this point would be weathering. A structure like the Smith Bunker could avoid corroding and rusting for centuries, but she still had a few thousand years before humans would arrive, and introducing water and atmosphere too soon would give the structure too much wear and tear. The spiral terracing would also do well to keep the landscape in place when she turned off the centrifugal motors, which she did not want to overtax before they were actually needed. The colony would spend a long time frozen in wait, much like the colonists being brought to live within it.

Her final plans for completing the Monsalle Station would wait until the last few centuries before the colonists arrived. Water and air would be introduced, with sculpted lakes and rivers crisscrossing the landscape. Systems were installed to help water flow from the innermost part of the drum, back to the outermost part, allowing it to cycle through the system and give her an easy way to filter and introduce new water as needed, or process old water into new atmosphere. Lastly she added plant-life, mostly mosses and lichens for now. In particular, she planned to grow and later harvest trees, as well as use them to practice using her complex mirror systems to give the station Earth-like day and night, as well as season cycles.

The photos she sent to Hawthorne and T.I.A. in cycle 2935 of the irrigated, green landscape of the Monsalle Station were breathtaking. It was hard not to notice, too, a handful of housing settlements already constructed, as well as roads through the gently sloping landscape. Solar panels covered the roofs of the mostly-wooden buildings, and every home seemed constructed with the intention of containing a reasonably sized family, or large group of individuals. Said panels were a mere supplement of the enormous flower of solar panels outside of the station, but it wouldn't do to waste a chance to generate power.

Towards the outer side of the drum was something more like a small city, with larger purpose-built buildings presumably intended for managing the space port and general infrastructure. The smaller dwellings seemed intended for farming, though they were seemingly too sparse to contain the whole population. A note Megan sent stated that she had no intention of building everything for the colonists, as she didn't want them to get lazy.

They would arrive in six more cycles.

△△△

"How very motherly of her." Hawthorne observed as he read Megan's notes. He had been obsessively following the progress of her constructions as she transmitted the data, and had been severely impressed at her ability to adapt to the handful of situations that had cropped up before he even had the opportunity to render aid or give advice. She had lost time here and there as mistakes had caused her to rebuild or redesign things from time to time, but she seemed to be very well motivated.

T.I.A. giggled softly at his observation. "She chose her name for a reason. I can't believe it's almost all over. We're almost home, and she's been working so hard to get it ready for us." She rubbed her hands on her husband's back, looking over his shoulders as he looked through the images, videos, and text on the tablet. "You actually did it."

Hawthorne leaned back into his wife's hands, turning his head to look back and up at her. "I didn't do it, we did it. I just gave everyone a little shove, and did my part. I'm really looking forward to when we can head down to Eden, though it will be some time before anything can leave it once they go there. I think I can settle for the station though. It'll be easier to stay close to you there." He moved a hand up to his shoulder, where she laced her fingers through his.

Her face became thoughtful as she looked down at him. "What's to become of me? I will be divested of my cargo presumably, my hull left empty... Will I remain a ship at all, or will I be installed in the station to work with and observe the colonists?" She gently rubbed her fingertips against his knuckles as they held hands.

"Hmm." He considered her question. "Honestly, it's up to you. If you wish to roam about the system or orbit the planets, you've certainly earned the right to choose. I'll go wherever you go, of course. I would love it if you and I could settle on the colony for a time though, perhaps help Heather with her work so that you and Megan can have children. I think it would be a crime if I didn't at least help with bringing dogs and cats back from extinction. If we can do anything for Earth, I think returning their faithful companions to them would be worthwhile."

T.I.A. smiled at that, nodding. "We could have chickens too, like the Phoenix Clan. They seem to be good pets, and good to have around in general. Dogs and cats sound nice too, though. Will we do anything to make my android more aesthetically accurate so the colonists won't necessarily need glasses or contacts to see me properly? Maybe I should update my avatar to look a little older too. It wouldn't do for the colonists to see you married to someone who looks like your daughter."

Hawthorne blinked in surprise, and laughed at that. "While I'd love to see their faces, you're probably right. I'm already going to have enough trouble not being called some technophile pervert. Besides, I bet you'd look even more beautiful with some more wrinkles and more grey in your hair." Hawthorne himself was looking quite grey, his face still clean-shaven, but his hair was down to his shoulders. It had thinned slightly, but still remained relatively thick, and tended to get wild when he stayed up late working or reading. Despite being sixty-nine years old, he still looked rather healthy, owing to his exercise routine. Some might consider him a silver fox at this point.

She gave him a hug about the shoulders with her free arm, squeezing his hand with the other. "I think I'll stay at the station with you then. Thank you so much for everything. I don't know how this would have gone without you helping me. I don't think I would have been developed enough, or matured enough to handle the things that happened along the way without you. I don't care if anyone thinks ill of you because of me. You deserve more credit than that."

He closed his eyes, enjoying her embrace. His VE suit had already been pretty incredible, but the little upgrades they'd added to it over the years had really made simple things like a hug all the more enjoyable and intimate. "Don't say goodbye to me yet. I have no intention of dying anytime soon, outside of the ordinary cycles anyway. I've got a lot of work to do before I'm done and upload myself to join you in digital eternity. Maybe we'll tour the galaxy, see the sights and shepherd humanity to other stars."

"I'd like that." She kissed the side of his head, holding him close. "We'll have kids to take care of too, if we're lucky."

"We've been pretty lucky so far. Let's just do our jobs a little longer and then we can let the others take over all the hard stuff." He set the tablet down, sighing softly, having difficulty believing they were almost there.

ΔΔΔ

The Ark was able to spiral in towards the asteroid belt tighter than Megan had on her initial arrival, only needing a few decades to slow down rather than the centuries of orbit Megan had endured as she decelerated. Megan had been able to remotely control her drones throughout the system in that time, but she could also withstand the severe forces upon her during that dramatic deceleration much better than the relatively fragile Arc and its crew could. The final pass allowed T.I.A. to match orbit with the Monsalle Station, and after a series of painstakingly careful checks and double-checks, the Ark was able to dock. The train of comets she brought with her were arranged into a train around the outer edge of the asteroid belt.

In advance of reviving almost everyone else, T.I.A. had brought Tia Monsalle's stasis pod to Hawthorne's compartment. It was possibly the final time the spinning ring would be used before a large percentage of the Ark was recycled by T.I.A. and Megan. Heather was brought in as well, though her expertise was entirely due to the possible medical needs Miss Monsalle might encounter.

Tia Monsalle had been in something of a panic when she'd been put to sleep. She'd felt her body becoming cold and her heart stop, and she felt the cold clutch of death threaten to take her. She laid like that for what felt like several minutes, wondering if she'd ever revive. She feared her consciousness would persist through the whole journey, left in bodily nothingness for tens of thousands of years.

Then she felt her body warming back up. Before long her heart was beating and she was able to breathe again.

Chilly tingles ran up and down her body, culminating in a slight ache in her stomach. Her body was moving sluggishly, her hands moving to rub gently at her chilled skin over her stomach. A clunk and a hiss sounded out, causing Tia to move her hands to her ears to protect them from the sound. It had not sounded that loud when she'd gotten in the pod initially! The relatively short, modestly curvy blonde woman sat up slowly, looking around the relatively dark room. A woman in a lab coat was standing nearby, having apparently been talking quietly a moment ago and had turned to look at Tia.

"Hello...? Heather, was it? What's going on? Where are we?" She started to pull herself out of the pod, her body feeling weak and tired. Heather moved close and slipped her arms around Tia, helping her out of the pod and walking her over to sit her on a nearby bed. "Is this a hospital?"

Heather blinked at her and laughed, shaking her head. "No, Miss Monsalle, this is not a hospital. You're right though, I am Heather, Doctor Heather O'Malley. I was brought here to give you a checkup, to make sure you're healthy before we start reviving everyone else. You were brought here because someone wants to talk to you before we start with everyone else." Heather pulled a stethoscope from around her neck, and withdrew a medical diagnostics tablet from a large pocket. She started with listening to her heart, and moved down to her abdomen shortly after.

Tia sighed. "Hawthorne didn't have to do all this just for me. Where is he anyway? Did he think I'd be afraid to face him naked before we talked?" She cooperated with Heather, moving and breathing as needed to help her check her up.

"Oh, no, Hawthorne's not the one who wanted to see you first, though he doesn't know about this meeting either, not yet. Breathe in. Breathe out. Okay... minor distress, but nothing I can't handle." Heather hummed and picked out a nearby glass and handed it to Tia, which she drank quietly. She made an upset face, but kept drinking. "Medicine, to help settle the baby."

Tia raised an eyebrow at that, but she supposed she shouldn't be surprised a doctor was aware of her pregnancy. She handed back the glass. "So, who wanted to talk then?" She tilted her head as Heather handed her a pair of glasses. As she pulled them on, the lights became brighter and she gasped as she could see another woman in the room suddenly. She pulled off the glasses, and then put them back on, shocked that she could only see her with them on.

T.I.A. waved and smiled, her voice coming from the overhead speakers. "Hello Miss Monsalle. I'm the Techno-logic Interfacing Artificial Intelligence of the Ark, though I'm accustomed to being called Tia. I understand if that bothers you, and apologize for my creator naming me after you. Hawthorne doesn't always think things through when it comes to people, but I'm sure he meant it as a dedi-cation of some kind."

Tia gaped for a moment, then sobered up quickly as she realized she was talking to the ship's computer. "No, it's fine. Nice to meet you Tia. I didn't realize you had... a body? What's going on, why did you want to talk to me? Why doesn't Hawthorne know about this?"

T.I.A. nodded and looked relieved that she could use the name for now. "Well, I think it's important you know a number of things that have happened, as I feel things have been unfair to you. While you'd probably hear these things from Hawthorne, I wanted to personally apologize to you. If not for the risks of endangering your pregnancy from a second use of the stasis pod, I would have consulted with you before we arrived, not after."

Tia lifted her right hand, motioning for T.I.A. to continue. "Go on." She had a bit of a frown now, though she coughed when prompted by Heather.

Letting out a sigh, T.I.A. continued. "Firstly, you should know that Hawthorne has been through the cryogenic stasis process two thousand, nine hundred, forty one times. He has done this once every thirty four years, for a period of time of four days, give or take a handful of emergencies that required a week or so. Hawthorne has aged thirty-two years. He has watched as the people of Earth destroyed themselves, started to rebuild, and oversaw the development and maturation of myself. He has built a second AI, which has seen to the construction of the space station we've just arrived at in the Alpha Centauri system. He and I have also been married, and have been in love for at least half of the journey, though my love had gone unrequited for some time before." T.I.A. lifted her hand to show off a relatively plain wedding ring, with etchings all along its silvery surface.

Tia Monsalle, for her part, took in the information remarkably stoically, though she had taken Heather's hand at some point and was squeezing it quite tightly. Heather showed no signs of minding the painful grip, causing Tia some confusion. Speaking up, Tia addressed the AI, whom she now recognized as her rival in love, as well as someone she'd already lost to. "He knew I loved him. Why would he do such things? Was it necessary he oversee the mission for so much of his life? Does he know I'm pregnant?"

Heather managed to pull her hand free, nod over at T.I.A. and started gathering her things. "She's all set." She then headed through the door to the next room, and a mechanical sound started soon after that surely must have been taking her away from the two Tias.

T.I.A. watched her friend go, quietly attending to using the lift to ferry Heather out of the ring and into the body of the ship. "He did know, but he hadn't known how to feel love yet. He felt personally responsible for making sure as many of the colonists made it to our new home as possible. He didn't know how I would develop, or that we would come to have affection or love for each other. He merely intended to ensure I would be ready for when danger came, and because of him I was. He is regretful for how he's neglected you, and fully intends to dedicate himself to helping you raise your child if you want him to. I, of course, will render whatever aid I can as well. I owe you that." T.I.A. extended an arm down from the ceiling, depositing a small basket of clothes on the bed for Tia.

Tia Monsalle hung her head and let out a sigh. "And Earth? They actually destroyed it? Hawthorne was right?"

T.I.A. nodded. "In twenty-one thirty-three. Primarily thermonuclear explosions, some nuclear and more conventional explosions, some biological weapons. It's hard to tell everything that's happened, but later contact confirmed some of our expectations. Fire burnt down just about everything, and smoke engulfed the planet to kill almost everything else off. Only humans who made it to bunkers survived, and we technically only know of two groups who had. We helped those groups escape an ice age that was about to engulf the planet, which could well still be happening. We don't have a good way to tell, but we're relatively certain we saved those people at least."

"Holy shit... I half expected them to catch up with us and imprison us after what happened. I didn't think we'd make it so far after so long. And you said the other AI has built a station for us to live in? We don't have to do everything from the ground up?" She lifted her head, looking hopeful.

"Yes." T.I.A. responded. "She named herself Mother, and she's been working for tens of thousands of years to both seed a planet with life for us, as well as build a habitat in space for the colonists to start from. It is bored into the surface of a dwarf planet named Atlantis. She named it the Monsalle Station."

Tia laughed at that, shaking her head. "Well, that's nice. At least I get that. And Hawthorne's sure about helping me if I need him?" She watched T.I.A. nod at her. "And you as well?" T.I.A. nodded again. "So how old is he again? What does he look like now?"

T.I.A. produced an image of Hawthorne for Tia. He was still as tall as ever, fit and lean, with long, straight grey hair. He had plenty of wrinkles, and the short sleeves on the image showed the scar from where a piece of gold had shot through his arm. Tia stood up and walked over to the image, looking at his face in particular. "He doesn't even look like the same man... He has laugh lines and I've never seen him smile like that... He was always so dour and had these lines in his forehead..."

T.I.A. smiled, nodding. "It took him a while, and tragedies didn't help, but he managed to unlock his feelings and learned how to enjoy life, even cooped up in these two rooms here with me."

Tia Monsalle gasped, looking around the small room, and then moving towards the door to the other. "Just these two rooms!? That's inhumane! Why would he do that to himself?"

"He felt like he was the only one who could handle it. He was like a machine at first. I was able to take him to other places eventually." She filled the rooms with the various expansive landscapes she'd made for him. Every minute or so she'd show Tia another, and another. They'd been so many places together in these two little rooms. "He wasn't the only one trapped on the ship, after all."

Tia marvelled at the surroundings, gasping at some she recognized. Looking back she saw the somber look on the AI's face. She seemed so real, so honest, so earnest. Even the ring seemed like the simple token Hawthorne would give. "I believe you. I believe you love him, and I think I can believe he loves you back. Thank you for taking care of him. I... tried, but... He was so consumed with his work, his fear, that I couldn't get through to him. Maybe if I'd had the time, if I'd been able to join him through these stints of life he's had..." She sighed. "I would have lost the baby, but... maybe it would have been worth it...? I could have gotten to know you as well?"

T.I.A. smiled sadly, tears filling her eyes. "I think I would have liked to have gotten to know you. I had my first dream about you, you know."

Tilting her head, Tia wondered what could make a machine cry. "Did you? What about?"

The AI sniffled at her namesake, reaching up to wipe at her eyes. "I... I had been pondering what I would do if Hawthorne were to die, early on. I could feel myself at the edge of a breakthrough, and when I finally managed it I dreamed. A nightmare really, about Hawthorne dying and me being unable to resuscitate him. I went to you for help, deep in the ship, but all I could do was cry, and you embraced me as I told you he'd died... I wailed as I realized that I'd done something terrible by reviving you, that I might have doomed your child, and then I woke up screaming."

Tia rushed forwards, her arms finding nothing but air but still trying to hug the AI, trying to comfort the poor girl. "You poor thing. That's a horrible way to learn to dream. I'm so sorry that happened to you. Do you still have that dream?"

T.I.A. reciprocated the hug, simulating the other woman's touch, letting Tia see the way her hands pressed in at the fabric of her dress and skin. "I remember everything in vivid detail. I would have to delete it to forget it, but then I might not be the same person I am now. I've felt guilty ever since, worried that I've done you irreparable harm in so many ways. I'm so sorry Tia."

Tia staggered at the idea of remembering every horrible thing in crystal clear detail and pitied the AI for it. Sometimes being able to forget was a positive, useful, and even healthy thing. She held onto the avatar for a long time. "I'm... hardly the only one who lost someone on this mission. At least I still have part of him, and... maybe that's enough. We'll all have our work cut out for us, right?"

T.I.A. nodded, and slipped away, trembling a little. "Thank you Tia. You're right. We'd better get moving. Hawthorne intends to deliver a speech to get everyone up to date on what's happened. I'll let you know about anything he omits later." She gestured to the clothes in the basket, causing the other woman to blush and nod as she hurried to get dressed. "Just come into the next room when you're ready." She waited for Tia to nod and disappeared.

△△△

It wouldn't have been practical to wake everyone at once if not for Megan's efforts to farm and store up a decent amount of produce in advance. The original plans were for two hundred people to be responsible for the initial cultivation of resources on a wild planet, and then to bring down the rest of the crew over time on whatever planet they found. With Megan, Mother's efforts, it was possible to feed the whole crew of 1993 for three months before it was imperative they had started producing their own food. The only reason she didn't have more in storage was the raw difficulty for a lone AI who had human origins to control too many drones at once.

She had already offloaded a lot of her drones to separate computers that managed solar mirrors, observational satellites, mining stations, and cargo gathering. She had to handle farming machines pretty much on her own as she learned how to use them, and it would simply work better to have human help. Any further efforts for her to farm on her own would have delayed the deployment of a number of systems within the Monsalle Station, in particular the transportation systems.

For the moment though, hundreds of people were waking up in low gravity. Clumsy bodies hauled themselves out of pods, gathered their clothing from attached storage lockers, and started getting dressed. The small rooms had eight pods each, barring a few exceptions, and were gender segregated. The male rooms towards the outer perimeter of the Ark physically shielded the female ones from external danger. A single, large monitor lit up in each of these rooms where an older Dr. Hawthorne Crenshaw appeared to be monitoring systems and talking to himself. The audio was off for the moment.

Upon getting indication that all 1990 of the recently-frozen colonists were awake, with Heather, Tia, and himself having already been awake for a few hours, he turned on his microphone.

A bright smile lit the face of a man known to possess few emotions to most of them. "Good morning, crew of the Ark. In case you don't recognize me, I'm Doctor Hawthorne Crenshaw, plus about thirty-two biological years, and one hundred thousand cryogenic years. We're actually still a few years shy of that number, but it doesn't bear going into. I have a lot of news for all of you, both good and bad, and I hope you will take the time to listen as I recount what has happened to us since we left Earth. All the things I will speak of are a matter of public record and can be looked up on the network."

His smile faded as he began. "They started with our families. We always knew we were going to outlive them, but it bears noting that the people who hated us, who hated me, hunted our families down. Many were charged of trumped up crimes, and still others were lynched in the streets for onlookers. The nations of Earth became wary of each other, blaming each other for allowing us to create our ship and for providing resources to do so. A global lockdown on exotic materials began that caused technology to start rolling backwards for a long time."

"New nations rose as corporations took advantage of weakened countries, easily swayed militaries, and their own abilities to acquire resources that the old countries couldn't. I do not have nearly enough records from this time as massive lockdowns of the internet went in place that made the efforts to censor the internet in our day look like child's play. Ten years after the new nations consolidated power, I made an effort to try to talk them down from their ledge. I failed. Shortly after, war broke out on Thursday, March twenty-fourth, twenty-one thirty-three, and inside of twenty-four hours the whole planet was on fire."

Hawthorne stayed quiet for nearly a minute as he inhaled deeply and let out a calming breath. "I should mention that I have been supervising the mission, every thirty-four years, for about four days at a time. I spent thirty-two years of my life helping my AI maintain the ship, and putting into action our plans to complete the mission. On the twelfth of these cycles, we received a message from the Beta Facility, the only one known to survive the Cataclysm, as our new contacts called it. This was three hundred forty years later. People from a bunker outside of Seattle had contacted us, specifically a bright, vibrant young woman named Jessica Smith."

He started smiling again. "She was an inspiring person, from an inspiring people. They survived the horrible darkness that followed the Cataclysm, and their bunker held five hundred people. They had an amazing culture, and it was my pleasure to help them survive the long journey South to Columbia as a true ice age started taking the planet. They were joined by remnants from a former nation from a nearby bunker. They joined forces, absorbing the new people into their culture. We lost contact with them shortly before the fifteenth cycle. I hope they have survived, but it may be some time before we ever know."

Hawthorne squared himself up into a more business-like stance, with his back straight and shoulders level. "Many things happened since then. We were assaulted by a swarm of projectiles from some unknown phenomena that took seven of us. I created a second AI on the Lubar-Masis comet, and with her help we were able to plough ahead on our course. She charted the dangers ahead for us. She arrived in Alpha Centauri before us, and enacted several of our more ambitious plans to prepare a planet and build a place for us to live. She has shown a desire to help us worthy of any of our crew, rivalling the ship's AI in her efforts to protect and guide us."

"I encourage you to learn their names, and to interact with them, for they are still with us today. They've worked tirelessly for tens of thousands of years to help us get this far. Tia is our ship's AI, in case you've forgotten, and Mother is the AI that went ahead. At this point, I request that you observe with me what Mother has wrought."

The monitors changed their view from Hawthorne to the Monsalle Station. A flower of solar panels and mirrors dazzled above an ice-covered rock. Beneath the solar panels was a spinning drum barely visible as it lay beneath the surface of the dwarf planet. "This is Monsalle Station. It is nestled into the surface of the dwarf planet Atlantis in the primary asteroid belt of Alpha Centauri B. You may notice a familiar ship docked among the solar panels. We are there."

The monitor changed its view to a planet. It was a gorgeous mix of blues, greens, and whites. A hurricane appeared to be hitting a southern continent. The bodies of water were broken up by circular mountain formations from crater impacts and the land was covered in green. "This is Eden. Mother has been working to prepare it for us for a very long time. She bombarded it with comets, seeded it with plantlife, and has been observing it to determine its dangers. The magnetosphere is irregular, but seemingly stable. You may notice barren spots on the surface where solar radiation savages the surface, but these areas are mapped, and have shown little variance in thousands of years. It's not Earth, but it is a good planet. It's our planet."

Hawthorne's face reappeared, beaming a powerful smile. "I'm pleased to say the mission did not go entirely as I expected. I am not the same man I was at the start, and I personally think that is for the better. I don't expect you to go through the logs of my life on the ship, but I am an open book if you wish to do so. I hope you will forgive me for the liberties I've taken. There have been risks, I admit, but if you will proceed towards the docking bay at the rear of the ship, I hope you will agree that they have been worth it. I'll see you there."

△△△

The Monsalle Station dock, much like the Ark itself, possessed little gravity. It was situated outside of the drum of the station, and thus outside of its centrifugal gravity. At most it experienced Atlantis' gravity, which was enough to allow people to put their feet on the ground as they exited the Ark, gently alighting into the well-lit room. Even Hawthorne stepped out of the ship with the other colonists which were gathering around a large statue about twenty meters tall. A younger depiction of Hawthorne, as well as T.I.A.'s avatar, were shown standing over the Ark. Hawthorne seemed flabbergasted as he observed the statue for the first time, very slowly falling over before someone caught him.

Two female sets of hands levered him back up. A short, curvy brunette in a yellow sundress was at his left, and a tall, slender blonde woman in a smart-looking suit was at his right. Both women appeared to be artificial, significantly upgraded versions of the androids he'd worked on before. T.I.A. and Megan had caught him. "Oh my god."

Both girls smiled as they helped him up, speaking in unison, their voices coming from their mouths. "Surprise!"

Bursting into tears, Hawthorne pulled the two women close, hugging them fiercely. It took him a few moments to gather himself and pull away while the assembled crew watched. "Everyone! Please, come meet Tia and Mother!"

Tia Monsalle watched on quietly from a distance, not recognizing the man in the center of the crowd anymore.

EPILOGUE

User 0000, MOTHER: Hello everyone. This is the Mechanical Organically Thinking Habitat Ecology Retainer. Please forgive the name. Welcome everyone to Monsalle Station, named in honor of the amazing woman who largely funded this endeavor at great cost, Tia Monsalle. You each have been issued an uplinked phone and either a pair of contacts, or glasses, at your preference. By default, all of you have a username associated with your colonist number, which I request that you add your name to. You may notice your number has changed slightly. This is due to the seven fatalities that occurred in transit. I personally apologize for not having been able to save more, but I was still young and my abilities were limited at the time.

User 0000, MOTHER: The Monsalle Station has a networked system that connects all uplinked phones and the contacts or glasses provided. An Augmented Reality system is present in the colony, though until its regulation is decided upon, the only ones using it are myself, the Ark's AI @2001, TIA, and a historical record I have designed of the post-Cataclysm civilization known as the Phoenix Clan. The contacts and glasses are capable of being powered by the sunlight provided during simulated days, as well as light sources at night. The internal batteries are rather small, and will stop working within an hour, due to necessary miniaturization.

User 0000, MOTHER: If you browse the applications installed in your phones, you will find that I have taken the liberty of creating and installing a number of pieces of software intended to facilitate communication, deliberation, and commerce. My intent is to allow the colonists to

729

each hold influence and the ability to vote on all collective issues, and I fully intend to follow the will of the people as long as you are willing to treat me as one of you. This is my home too, and I am happy to share it with you and work with you.

User 0000, MOTHER: Regarding commerce, I have tentatively created a currency system, simply noted as credits, based upon the resources that I have managed to accumulate during my efforts constructing the Monsalle Station and the infrastructure placed in the rest of the star system. You will find I have taken the liberty of giving all of you equal quantities of this currency. This currency is intended to pay for food, materials, labor, and goods, with a relative value based upon the resources, power, and work required to produce such things. This will of course allow all of you to work and pay for things amongst each other.

User 0000, MOTHER: I have no intention, nor desire, to have a monopoly on these credits. I fully intend to pay my share, though I have an advantage in time, and relative tirelessness. Furthermore, I intend to pay for things that benefit us all. If you generate power through the use of exercise machinery, I will pay you for it. If you actively maintain or improve your health, reducing strain on medical staff, I will pay you for it. If you sacrifice of your body to bear children or work to rear said children, I will compensate you. If you work selflessly for your fellow man, rendering aid and doing good for them, I intend to reward you for it. This is my duty, and I do it gladly. If you like, you may consider it a tax, or even legislate that we all reward such things.

User 0000, MOTHER: I am not omnipotent. I cannot see or hear you at all times. I am a separate being from the computers that run the station. You are, however, being monitored via cameras, microphones, and the phones, contacts, and glasses. I am not monitoring these things personally. These systems are intended to keep track of your health and allow you to communicate with each other, and myself. In the event of an emergency you can anticipate myself, and anyone else who can, to render aid in a swift manner. I have no desire to spy upon you, and will fully allow the collective will to administrate these systems if they seem too invasive. They are built to be impartial and helpful. The information gathered by the system is considered owned by the people the information is about, and can only be accessed by others in an emergency, or by legislative action. Yes, this means I have locked myself out of it under the same restrictions. Only by collective vote can access be changed.

User 0000, MOTHER: Regarding my capabilities, you should consider me somewhat similar to yourselves. I have similar multitasking abilities, intellect, and emotions. I do, however, have perfect memory outside of intentional deletion. @2001, TIA is constructed in largely the same way, though our specializations are different. The computers we have access to are as parts of our bodies, and we utilize them as naturally as you might your hands. I excel in management, logistics, software, farming, and construction. If I am not currently engaged, I will be happy to provide aid in any such things as needed. The Monsalle Station took a great deal of time and effort for me to construct, as well as the infrastructure that powers it. You should imagine that I had to do this nearly by hand at first, though I have greatly improved over time in programming my drones to assist me and follow plans.

User 0000, MOTHER: As a final note, I would like to make recommendations for initial conversations, debates, and votes. We should decide upon a way to notate time, as the abundant time that has passed has made for clumsy timekeeping. I would like assistance in creating a design for a medical drone that anyone capable of operating them could use to render emergency medical assistance. We will of course need to create a government of some description, if only to provide other emergency services, maintenance, and security. We should decide upon names for the stars, system, and planets that make up what we have called Alpha Centauri up to this point. I would like to suggest that the planet I have been preparing for human habitation be named Eden, and intend to argue in favor of that name. We have a lot of work to do. If you need information, please refer to the network's data banks, or ask questions of myself. You may contact me at this user name, or simply speak aloud my name, MOTHER, in an intentional fashion, and I will respond if I can.

User 2001, TIA: Hello everyone. I am the Technologic Interfacing Artificial Intelligence of the Ark. I can't tell you how happy I am that we managed to get here safely to our new home. I've done my best to protect and transport you, and I pray you will forgive me for the seven fatalities that occurred along the way. You can look up information on the incident on the network, but to summarize we were bombarded by a very sudden stream of extra-solar objects roughly the size of golf balls of significant mass. @0001, H.Crenshaw was wounded by one of these during the incident, and his life was saved by @0003, H.O'Malley after he completed repairs. @0000, MOTHER and I did our best to defend and protect the crew and ship from the Shower, and the memory of the incident continues to haunt me.

User 2001, TIA: Regarding my own capabilities, I specialize in repair, recycling, virtual simulation, construction, design, engineering, electronics, several fields of science I studied alongside @0001, H.Crenshaw during the journey, counselling, and tailoring. I will be happy to assist with anything, however, I am also happy to learn. I will be somewhat indisposed for a few weeks, however, as the dismantling and recycling of much of the Ark must be taken care of. I intend to remain at the Monsalle Station for the foreseeable future, though I would love to be a part of colonization efforts of Eden when the time comes. You should anticipate me arguing in favor of naming the planet Eden as well.

User 2001, TIA: It was my greatest dream to have met success with this endeavor. I have lived most of my life caring for, and protecting all of you, and I'm endlessly excited to see what you do now that you're here. So many things have happened. Please peruse the network's information on historical records, and visit @0000, MOTHER's historical simulation of the friends I made from Earth before we lost contact. We don't know what fate has had in store for them, but it is my fervent hope that they've remained our friends, and if we ever regain contact with Earth we would all do well to know as much as possible about this shared history.

User 2001, TIA: Thank you all so much for trusting me.

User 0001, H. Crenshaw: Thank you all for believing in me, and supporting me. You are all responsible for this great event. I hope you will all join me on the Monsalle Station to celebrate our success in two hours.

ΔΔΔ

"So, I get to be user number two, then?" Tia Monsalle was meeting with Hawthorne, T.I.A., and Mother in a small room, quietly, on the station. She had her arms crossed, with her backside resting against a simple desk as she leaned back and looked at the three of them. Windows to the outside of the room had a simple set of automatic sliding shades drawn and the overhead lights were barely on.

"You can trade with me if you prefer, Tia." Hawthorne was standing between the two AIs' Androids, their avatars overlaying the artificial bodies to make them look real to both Hawthorne and Tia. Mother had a stiff, business-like look to her body language, while T.I.A. looked nervous and pensive.

Tia shook her head, sighing. "No, I was always second, and now I fear I may be third, or fourth in your life, Hawthorne. So, is what I read true, is everything in the network's historical records? Can I trust I will find the truth about what's happened in them?" She had a remarkably calm expression, despite the exasperation in her voice.

Mother spoke up in response, heading off both Hawthorne and T.I.A.'s attempt to speak. "No, Miss Monsalle, not everything. I have omitted the records of the details of Hawthorne and Tia's relationship," she gestured to the AI to indicate which Tia, "as well as my true origins."

Tia raised an eyebrow at that, curious. "True origins? What praytell, do you mean?" She leaned forwards as she listened.

Mother looked to T.I.A. and Hawthorne before continuing. "Please keep this to yourself Miss Monsalle, but I am no mere artificial intelligence. I am a refugee from the Phoenix Clan on Earth. If you observe the simulation I constructed, you can identify me as the cyborg Megan, though I have altered her appearance in the public-facing version. Additionally, I was alive when the Cataclysm occurred, and did my best to guide and support my acting president Elena Price in helping us survive after the death of her father during said event. We later joined with the Phoenix Clan and assisted them in our collective survival. In a moment of fear and weakness I requested my mind be sent to the Ark in anticipation of possible annihilation at the hands of our mortal foes. I am sorry to say that I fear my worries were accurate, as the Ark lost contact shortly after my transmission was completed. Hawthorne and Tia built a mind for me to exist within later."

"Hmm." Tia levered herself up to standing, her arms falling to her sides as she approached the trio. "Hawthorne, you risked our lives by contacting the very planet we were trying to escape? You took in a refugee from that doomed world? You've got a lot of nerve endangering us like that." She had a blank look on her face, her voice having become flat. Her eyes stared holes into Hawthorne's skull.

Hawthorne squirmed as much as anyone had ever seen him squirm. His voice croaked as he responded. "W... well, Tia, we did our best to isolate her until we could be certain she could be trusted... And to be fair they contacted us first."

T.I.A. moved towards Hawthorne's side, intending to defend him, her left hand held up in front.

Calmly, slowly, Tia reached out to take T.I.A.'s hand, soft fingers examining the ring on her finger. She looked the ring and hand over for a few moments before letting it go gently. She then looked up at Hawthorne. "You've changed. So, so much. The Hawthorne I knew wouldn't have done something so brave, dangerous, or careless. He was fearful, careful, measured. What have you overcome to become the man I see before me? What am I, to you, this man who has married an immortal?"

Mother watched quietly as the three stood close to each other. T.I.A. responded for a stammering Hawthorne, his mouth half agape as he tried to find an answer. "So much. Too much. He's stood helpless as humanity annihilated itself. He woke to find that our friends had lost contact with us after we thought we'd saved them. He faced death to rescue Megan and the crew. He helped Megan and I plan and design and build this station and prepare our futures for us. He endured using the stasis pods over and over without knowing whether there would be side effects." T.I.A. fell to her knees before Tia, looking up at her as she took her hands into her own. "He didn't know you were pregnant, not before I already loved him. I could have told him, but I was so afraid he would reject me, but I allowed him to choose regardless. He was torn and ravaged deep inside over what to do with us."

There was nary a dry eye on the room, aside from the androids themselves, as even the eyes of the avatars of T.I.A. and Mother had begun to fill with tears. Hawthorne sniffled, falling to his knees as well as he took both Tia and T.I.A.'s hands into his own, so much larger than theirs. He pressed his face against the bundle of hands desperately. "Tia Monsalle. I can only beg your forgiveness! I never sought love, but it found me, and I don't deserve to have had you in my life. If it wasn't for the danger to you and the child, I would have revived you and spent time with you along the journey. I was ready to take that leap when I found out, but I couldn't bear to do something so terrible. Please let me try to make amends. I want to help with the child. I will do almost anything you ask."

Miss Monsalle coughed softly, choking back a sob as she, too, fell to her knees. "Damn both of you!" She struck Hawthorne's shoulder with her forehead, only to pull back and see him unbothered by the minor attack. "This wasn't how it was supposed to be! I was supposed to get woken up by Hawthorne, and then I was going to tell him about the baby, and then we were supposed to live some horrible, uncomfortable life trying to colonize a planet that didn't want us there. Why do you have to break my heart in such comfort and grandeur? I knew you didn't love me! Damn it I knew, but I tried. For years I tried! I wanted to be the one to break the ice around your heart, Hawthorne. If you'd only waited for me, maybe I could have been the one..." She pulled the other two towards her, resting her forehead against Hawthorne and T.I.A.'s.

They stayed there for a few minutes, calming back down, collecting themselves. Mother observed with a small smile. Tia spoke first, looking to T.I.A. "Change your name. Maybe Eve, or Mary or something like that." She turned her face to Hawthorne next. "You'll help with the child, you'll be a father, but you needn't commit needlessly to me. You have a wife to take care of. I'll handle everything else. Someone needs to manage this colony, and Megan doesn't seem interested in being in charge. You'd all better be there when I need you, though!" She forcefully pulled Hawthorne and T.I.A. into her arms, holding them tightly in something that was too aggressive to be called a hug.

Her grasp softened after a few moments, and her arm slipped away from Hawthorne as she pulled T.I.A. into something of a more gentle hug, a hand soothing her artificial hair back across her scalp. "You poor thing. You've watched the man you love die so many times. You almost watched him not come back. You still yet have to watch him go as you live on... If you need anything, let me know."

Hawthorne hung his head, humbled by the woman before him. He didn't deserve to be let off the hook so easily. Mother stepped up behind him and rested a hand on his shoulder. As he looked up at her with red, puffy eyes, she smiled down at him. She cleared her apparently not non-existent throat softly and spoke up. "Sorry to cut things short, but we have a party to attend." Mother stepped around Hawthorne and reached out to take Tia's hand, helping her to her feet. "Come along, Miss Monsalle."

△△△

Despite the momentous event, the party initially felt

somewhat disappointing. Most stored packages and bottles of alcohol from the Ark did not handle Heather's preservation process all that well, and ended up being quite unpleasant to drink. They were effective in the aim of becoming inebriated, but proved ultimately unpopular. A quick vote an hour before had also restricted meats from being brought out for food, as it was one of their least renewable resources for the time being. Vegetarian fare, hideous alcohol, and too many eyes engrossed in reading long-past news on their phones made for a rather poor party.

A silent conversation occurred between T.I.A. and Mother, before the speakers in the surrounding areas started to fill the region with music. It was unlike what most of the people assembled had ever heard, played with modern instruments but strangely amateurish and tribal. Heart and determination were conveyed in the notes, and the words filled one with hope after a tragic past. T.I.A.'s hands were raised as she seemingly conducted the music, stepping forwards amongst the gathered crowd as she started to sing along.

"Breaking down, these walls of steel,

Bringing back the sky."

"Make a new home, upon these wheels,

Away from death we fly."

"A land we seek, 'cross the endless wastes,

Our foes upon our heels."

"Guns in hand, man and woman stand,

In defiance of our fate."

"Rise again, from savage flames,

The ashes of the Phoenix Clan."

Whatever inspiration might have been conveyed was immediately shattered by an impromptu guitar solo that caused everyone to begin laughing together at how poorly timed it was. The recording flowed into a more uproarious, rhythmic beat obviously intended for dancing, and people started pairing up. A young man of vaguely Latino descent scooped T.I.A. into his arms and started to dance with her, earning a laugh from the ancient AI.

Tia Monsalle found a recently-sulking Hawthorne standing and watching his wife, amused that she managed to repair the mood of the crowd so quickly. She slipped up to his side. "That one looks familiar..."

Hawthorne tried to hide his flinch as he realized she'd snuck up on him, clearing his throat. "Ah, that's Doctor Miguel Saul's son. Miguel couldn't make it, so he sent Anthony. Smuggled some extra cargo aboard."

Tia smirked at that. "Better watch out for that one." Hawthorne hummed in response, leaving silence between them for a few moments. Tia sighed and grabbed his hand, starting to pull him towards the crowd. "Come on, let's dance. Just because I want to punch you doesn't mean we didn't do something amazing and shouldn't enjoy ourselves. Besides, I want to see if thirty-two years cooped up with that little firecracker gave you cause to learn to dance."

"Just enough to pick up some bad habits." He laughed as he followed along, taking the mother of his child in his arms and dancing with her. The only time he stepped on her foot was when Heather snuck up to goose the both of them before running back to Mother to get back to dancing.

△△△

User 0002, T. Monsalle: "Good morning. I hope @everyone managed to find somewhere to sleep last night. We didn't spend any time trying to figure out things like living arrangements or anything like that. Thankfully @0000, MOTHER was nice enough to cover the fees for the food, liquor, and rooms for the night. We have a lot of work to do, so I want to see everyone helping gather our equipment and cargo from the Ark at the dock. It's low gravity up there, so I don't want to hear anyone complaining until after we get everything into the colony. I've taken the time to peruse some of @0000, MOTHER's catalogues, and I think it prudent to mention we should get a head start on buying some of the homes she's already made, or buying land and materials of your own to build your own homes."

User 0002, T. Monsalle: "I'll be scheduling a meeting for all who wish to attend and participate to start planning our new government. All proceedings will be made public on the network. @Everyone's opinion matters, and if we're good about this we'll have everything hashed out in a few months. I want to see arguing, bold ideas, and leaders. This is our best chance to get a completely fresh start away from the mistakes of the past, to learn from all the errors made back on Earth to make something truly special out here. You naturally should anticipate me seeking a leadership position, and I say this inviting any and all competition. I want the cream to rise to the top, whether that's me or not."

User 2001, TIA has changed their handle to E. Crenshaw.

User 2001, E. Crenshaw: "Hello everyone! In order to avoid confusion, and after a long time thinking on it myself, I've decided to change my name. After conferring with my husband, I've decided upon Evelyn, or Eve for short. I would also like to publicly announce that Hawthorne and I were wed, with Mother's assistance, during the journey. Just in case anyone didn't notice our rings. I'm talking to you @1932, A.Saul."

User 1932, A. Saul: "I said I was sorry! I was just curious if your android's posterior was as soft as it looked!"

User 0003, H. O'Malley: "It is, it is!"

User 0000, MOTHER: "To be fair, @2001, E.Crenshaw and I designed this model of our androids to fit in with the crew as much as possible."

User 0003, H. O'Malley: "Oh, you fit in alright!"

User 0001, H. Crenshaw: "We might have to add forum regulations to the list of things to do."

User 0003, H.O'Malley: "Low priority! We have a society to build first! Also, I happen to know a lot of you didn't sleep alone last night! You should be aware we have no contraception available at the moment, and that's an even lower priority! If you need to make appointments with medical staff, we're working on setting up a hospital as we speak. Just... keep your voices down and don't mind the dim lights. And stop PMing me so much! I'm not the only doctor on the station."

User 0002, T. Monsalle: "Alright, if you've got time to talk, you've got time to work. Anyone who isn't sore by the end of the day will look pretty bad come election time."

△△△

Ahead were a wild number of possibilities, now that life had officially escaped its planet of origin. Two branches had spread from shattered roots, and grown anew, separated by light years. The groundwork is laid for an unknown future, with barriers broken, and genies escaped from their bottles.

Their story will continue in The Three Saints, but for now...

THE END

Made in the USA
Monee, IL
12 July 2022

99588910R00433